Praise for *Forever Amber*

"Every ounce sizzles."

—*Time*

"Winsor is a born storyteller."

—*New York Times*

"The first *real* historical romance. This is the book that started it all."

—Bertrice Small, author of *Adora*

"The bawdiest novel I have read in years. . . . It teems with action, color, zest, and gusto. . . . The conversation of its tremendous gallery of characters is stridently alive, vibrant with the color of Charles II's reign."

—*Saturday Review of Literature*

"A fluid and robust tale of the courts and prisons, the extravagances and the squalors of Restoration England. The smell of London is there, its fopperies and its licentiousness. History moves in full panoply, but only as a part of the story of Amber St. Clare, as conniving and pretty a vixen as ever flaunted her sex in the pages of a novel."

—*Springfield Republican*

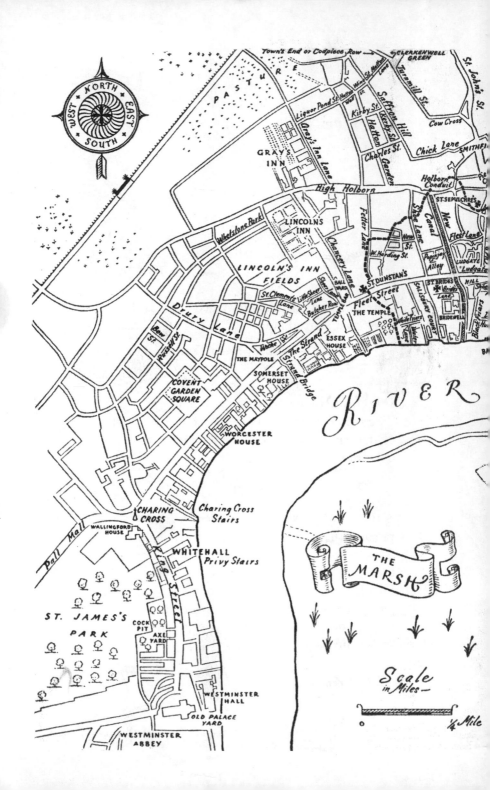

LONDON under Charles II

The dotted line encloses the district destroyed in the Great Fire

GEORGE ANNAND

Based on the endpaper map in "Samuel Pepys" by Arthur Bryant.
By permission of the Cambridge University Press.

FOREVER

Amber

KATHLEEN
WINSOR

CHICAGO
REVIEW
PRESS

Library of Congress Cataloging-in-Publication Data

Winsor, Kathleen.
    Forever Amber / Kathleen Winsor.
        p. cm.
    ISBN 1-55652-404-8
        1. Great Britain—History—Charles II, 1660–1685—Fiction. 2. Great
    Britain—Kings and Rulers—Mistresses—Fiction. 3. Women—England—
    London—History—Fiction. I. Title.

    PS3545.I7575 F6 2000
    813´.52—dc21

                                                                    99-051817

To Lieutenant Robert John Herwig, U.S.M.C.R.

This edition of *Forever Amber* is an unabridged republication of
the first edition published in New York in 1944, with a new
foreword by Barbara Taylor Bradford.
It is published by arrangement with the author.

Published by Chicago Review Press, Incorporated
814 North Franklin Street
Chicago, Illinois 60610
ISBN-13: 978-1-55652-404-2
ISBN-10: 1-55652-404-8
10 9 8

FOREWORD

WHEN *Forever Amber* was first published in 1944 it created a sensation and catapulted its author to instant fame. The novel sold 100,000 copies in its first week, and Kathleen Winsor became a household name. Considered bawdy and immoral, the book was banned in Boston, and the Hays office pronounced that it was too impure for the movies in its present state. But in the end it sold over two million copies in hardcover, and it did become a movie starring Linda Darnell and Cornel Wilde.

I first read *Forever Amber* when I was a teenager. I remember that I could not put it down. In fact, I read it so quickly that I immediately reread it to be certain I hadn't missed anything important. At the time, all of my girlfriends had their noses buried in it. Like me, they found it compulsive and compelling reading. I became a fan of the author's and read all her other novels as they were published over the years, from *Star Money* to *Calais*. But *Forever Amber* has remained a particular favorite.

When I was asked to write a foreword to this new edition, I picked up the novel again and once more discovered it was a genuine page-turner; it had lost nothing over the years. Time had not dimmed it, nor had the changing fashions in fiction diminished it. The book remains a smashing read, as compelling now as it was all those years ago.

What struck me most forcibly was the enormous amount of research the author had done—impeccable research that cannot be bettered, in my opinion, and certainly worthy of a historian.

Intrigued by the depth and enormity of the research, I inquired as to how the author had gone about it. I discovered that when Kathleen Winsor was married (in 1938) to her first husband, Robert Herwig, she became fascinated by the books he was then reading for his college theme on Charles II. She began to read them as well, and went on reading books about this period for the next five years. After that, she wrote the novel.

Forever Amber is set during the English Restoration, after Charles II returned to London from exile in Europe and the monarchy was restored. Every detail of life in that period—food, fashions, architecture, interior design, and politics—is covered in the fictional tale of Amber St. Clare. Winsor skillfully dissects the manners and mores of that age in every echelon of society, from peasants to princes of the blood. We see the pomp, ceremony, and magnificence of the court and how it coexisted with poverty, sickness, cruelty, and despair. We get more than a glimpse of such court beauties as Barbara Villiers, Countess of Castlemaine, the King's mistress; we meet Samuel Pepys, the diarist; Sir Peter Lely, the great portraitist; and Nell Gwynne, the orange seller and actress who became another mistress of the sexually driven king. The author pinpoints the excesses of the court—adultery, rape, rampant love affairs, illegitimate children, and abortions—and we recognize the everyday sensuality, greed, duplicity, and treachery of the era; in essence, we witness life as it was lived by rich and poor alike. We suffer through the Great Plague, during which we see Amber at her best, full of heart and compassion. And in consequence we are caught up in her life, and we root for her.

Kathleen Winsor managed to make the Restoration Period vivid and real, and her fictional characters spring readily to life on the page. She also created a marvelous sense of time and place and atmosphere, and it is this that sets the tone of the novel.

Amber, beautiful and sexy, may well be immoral, but the court of Charles II is worse: bawdy, brutal, cruel, licentious, and wicked. On the other hand, when it comes to intimate sex scenes between Amber and her many and varied lovers, a great deal is left to the imagination of the reader. As perhaps it should be.

In a curious way, I think those critics of long ago were really reviewing the Restoration Period itself, and not the story Kathleen Winsor wrote. However, the book does indeed have an overwhelming sense of sexuality, which comes from both the writing and the many characters the author invented, most especially Amber. Born illegitimate, of aristocratic but unwed parents, she is brought up by a farmer and his wife as their niece. At the age of 16 she is captivated by a dashing cavalier passing through her village, and she goes off to London with him. She never looks back. Her adventurous life, her many loves, and her rising fortunes make for compelling reading.

I once described fiction as a monumental lie that has to have the absolute ring of truth if it is to succeed. And that ring of truth invariably comes from research, which in turn gives a novel its authenticity. It is this kind of authenticity plus good storytelling that made *Forever Amber* a bestseller 56 years ago.

Now it has become a classic, and that is as it should be.

BARBARA TAYLOR BRADFORD
March 2000

"But, good God! What an age is this, and what a world is this! that a man cannot live without playing the knave and dissimulation."

SAMUEL PEPYS

1644

PROLOGUE

THE SMALL ROOM was warm and moist. Furious blasts of thunder made the window-panes rattle and lightning seemed to streak through the room itself. No one had dared say what each was thinking—that this storm, violent even for mid-March, must be an evil omen.

As was customary for a lying-in chamber, the room had been largely cleared of its furniture. Now there remained only the bed with its tall head and footboards and linen side curtains, half a dozen low stools, and the midwife's birth-stool, which had arm rests and a slanting back and cut-out seat. Beside the fireplace was a table with a pewter water-basin on it, brown cord and a knife, bottles and ointment-jars, and a pile of soft white cloths. Near the head of the bed was a very old hooded cradle, still empty.

The village women, all perfectly silent, stood close about the bed, watching what was happening there with tense, anxious faces. Sympathetic anguish, pity, apprehension, were the expressions they showed as their eyes shifted from the tiny red baby lying beside the woman who had just given it birth to the sweating midwife bending down and working with her hands beneath the spread blankets. One of the women, pregnant herself, leant over the child, her eyes frightened and troubled—and then all at once the baby gasped, gave a sneeze, and opening its mouth began to yell. The women sighed, relieved.

"Sarah—" the midwife said softly.

The pregnant woman looked up. They exchanged some words in low murmuring voices and then—as the midwife went to the fireplace and sat down to bathe the child from a basinful of warm red wine—the other slid her hands beneath the blankets and with firm gentle movements began to knead the mother's

3

abdomen. There was a look of strained anxiety on her face that amounted almost to horror, but it vanished swiftly as the woman on the bed slowly opened her eyes and looked at her.

Her face was drawn and haggard, with the strange new gauntness of prolonged suffering, and her eyes lay sunk in dark sockets. Only her light blonde hair, flung in a rumpled mass about her head, seemed still alive. As she spoke her voice, too, was thin and flat, scarcely above a whisper.

"Sarah—Sarah, is that my baby crying?"

Sarah did not stop working but nodded her head, forcing a quick bright smile. "Yes, Judith. That's your baby—your daughter." The baby's angry-sounding squalls filled the room.

"My—daughter?" Even exhausted as she was, her disappointment was unmistakable. "A girl—" she said again, in a resentful tired little whisper. "But I wanted a boy. John would have wanted a boy." Tears filled her eyes and ran from the corners, streaking across her temples; her head turned away, wearily, as if to escape the sound of the baby's cries.

But she was too exhausted to care very much. A kind of dreamy relaxation was beginning to steal over her. It was something almost pleasant and as it took hold of her more and more insistently, dragging at her mind and body, she surrendered herself willingly, for it seemed to offer release from the agony of the past two days. She could feel the quick light beating of her heart. Now she was being sucked down into a whirlpool, then swirled up and up at an ever-increasing speed, and as she spun she seemed lifted out of herself and out of the room—swept along in time and space . . .

Of course John won't care if it's a girl. He'll love her just as much—and there will be boys later—boys, and more girls, too. For now the first baby had been born it would be easier next time. That was what her mother had often said, and her mother had had nine children.

She saw John's face, the shock of surprise when she told him that he was a father, and then the sudden breaking of happiness and pride. His smile was broad and his white teeth glistened in his tanned face and his eyes looked down at her with adoration,

4

just as they had looked the last time she had seen him. It was always his eyes she remembered best, for they were amber-coloured, like a glass of ale with the sun coming through it, and about the black centers were flecks of green and brown. They were strangely compelling eyes, as though all his being had come to focus in them.

Throughout her pregnancy she had hoped that this baby would have eyes like John's, hoped with such passionate intensity she never doubted her wish would come true.

From the time she had been a very little girl Judith had known that one day she was to marry John Mainwaring, who would, when his father died, succeed to the earldom of Rosswood. Her own family was a very old one in England—their name had been de Marisco when they had first arrived with the Norman Conqueror, but during the centuries it had changed to Marsh. The Mainwarings, on the other hand, had sprung to their greatest power in the last century, sharing the spoils from the break-up of the Catholic Church. Their lands adjoined and there had been friendship between them for three generations—nothing could be more natural than that the eldest Mainwaring son should marry the eldest Marsh daughter.

John was eight years older than she and for many years he paid her scant attention, though he took it for granted that eventually they would marry; the betrothal papers had been signed while he was yet a child and Judith no more than a baby. All during the years that they were growing up she saw him frequently, for he came often to Rose Lawn to ride and shoot and fence with her four older brothers—but he was no more interested in her than in his own sisters and merely tolerated, with good-natured indifference, her awe-struck admiration. He went away to school—first to Oxford, then to the Inner Temple for a year or so, and finally off to Europe for his Tour. When he returned he found her a young lady, sixteen years old and beautiful, and he fell in love. Since Judith had always been in love with him and the families were so well agreed, there seemed no reason to wait. The wedding was planned for August: the August that war began.

Judith's father, Lord William Marsh, immediately declared

for the King, but the Earl of Rosswood—like many others—spent some weeks of indecision before joining the Parliamentarians. Judith had heard the two of them arguing, time and again, for the past year or more, and though they had often grown so angry that they began to shout and brandish their fists, at the end they had always agreed to drink a glass of wine and talk about something else. She never guessed that the quarrels might change her life.

The Earl of Rosswood had said a hundred times that he could stand Charles I's absolutism, but not Laud's church policy— while Lord Marsh was convinced that should the crucial moment come his friend would gather his wits and go with the King. When Rosswood did not he was shocked and furious, incredulous at first and then filled with bitterness and hate. Judith had not actually realized that England was at civil war until her mother coolly told her that she must think no more of John Mainwaring—the wedding would never take place.

Stunned, Judith nodded her head in agreement—but she did not really believe it. The war would be over in three months, her father said so, and when it was they would make up the quarrel again and all be friends. The war would be merely a brief unpleasant interval in their lives—it would change nothing of importance, undo no serious plans, destroy no old familiar customs. It would not really affect her or anyone she knew.

But when John came to tell her goodbye before he left for the army, Lord William rode out to meet him in a threatening rage and ordered him off the grounds. Judith cried for hours when she heard about it, for now he was gone away to war with never so much as a kiss between them.

A few days later Lord William and her four brothers went to join the King and with them went most of the able-bodied men on the estate and from the village. The war began to seem real to her now and she hated it, resented the intrusion into her life which had been so secure, so gracious and happy.

As Lord William had predicted, success ran with the Royalists. His Majesty's nephew, gigantic, handsome Prince Rupert, won victory after victory, until almost all England but the south-

6

east corner was in the King's hands. But the rebels did not give up, and the months began to drag on.

Judith was busy, for there was a great deal to do now that the men were gone. She had no time to practice her dancing or singing, to embroider or to play the spinet. But no matter how much work she did she continued to think of John Mainwaring, wondering when he would come back to her, still planning for a future untouched by civil war. Her mother, who guessed easily enough at the reason for Judith's thoughtful quietness, impatiently ordered her to put him out of her mind. She hinted that she and Lord William were planning another and more suitable marriage, to a man whose loyalty was unquestioned.

But Judith did not want or intend to forget John. She could no more have considered marrying another man than she could have accepted some strange new God thrust suddenly upon her.

When John had been gone five months he managed to send her a note, telling her that he was well and that he loved her. "We'll be married, Judith, when the war's over—no matter what our parents have to say." And he added that as soon as he could he would come, somehow, to see her again.

It was mid-June before he was able to keep his promise. Then, making up some story to tell her mother, she rode out to meet him by the little stream which ran between the two properties. It was the first time in all the years they had known each other that they had been perfectly alone, free, and unwatched; and though Judith had felt apprehensive and nervously embarrassed—now she was off her horse and into his arms without hesitation or misgiving. Never before had she felt so sure of herself, so right and content.

"I haven't long, Judith," he said swiftly, kissing her. "I shouldn't be here at all— But I had to see you! Here—let me look at you. Oh, how pretty you are—prettier even than I remembered!"

She clung to him desperately, thinking that she could never let him go again. "Oh, John! John, darling—how I've missed you!"

"It's *wonderful* to hear you say that! I've been afraid— But it doesn't matter, does it—that our parents are quarreling? We love each other just the same—"

"Just the same?" she cried, her throat choking with tears of happiness and dread. "Oh, John! We love each other more! I never knew how much I loved you till you were gone and I was afraid that— Oh, this terrible, terrible war! I hate it! When will it end, John? Will it end soon?" She looked up at him like a little girl begging a favour, and her blue eyes were large and wistful and frightened.

"Soon, Judith?"

His face darkened and for several moments he was quiet while she watched him anxiously, fear creeping through her.

"*Won't* it be soon, John?"

He slipped one arm about her waist and they started to walk, slowly, toward the river. The sky was blue with great puffs of fleecy clouds, as though a shower had just cleared; the air was full of moisture and the smell of damp earth. Along the banks grew delicate alder and willow trees and white dogwood was in bloom.

"I don't think it will be over soon, Judith," he said finally. "It may last a great while longer—perhaps for years."

Judith stopped, and looked up at him incredulously. At seventeen, six months was an age, one year eternity. She could not and would not face the prospect of years going by in this way, separated.

"For years, John!" she cried. "But it can't! What will we do? We'll be old before we even begin to live! John—" Suddenly she grabbed him by the forearms. "Take me with you! We can be married now. Oh, I don't care how I have to live—" she said quickly as she saw him begin to interrupt. "Other women go with the camp, I know they do, and I can go too! I'm not afraid of anything—I can—"

"Judith, darling—" His voice was pleading, his eyes tender and full of anguish. "We can't get married now. I wouldn't do that to you for anything in the world. Of course there are women following the camp—but not women like you, Judith. No, darling—there's nothing for us to do but wait— It'll end some day— It can't go on forever—"

8

Suddenly everything that had happened this past year seemed real to her and sharp and with permanent meaning. He was going away, soon, this very day—and when would she see him again? Perhaps not for years—perhaps never— Suppose he was killed— She checked herself swiftly at that, not daring even to admit the possibility. There was no use pretending any longer. The War *was* real. It *was* going to affect their lives. It had already changed everything she had ever hoped for or believed in—it could still take away her future, deny her the simplest wants and needs—

"But, John!" she cried now, bitter and protesting. "What will happen to us then? What will you do if the King wins? And what will become of me if Parliament wins? Oh, John, I'm scared! How is it going to end?"

John turned his head, his jaw setting. "God, Judith, I don't know. What do people do with their lives when a war ends? We'll work it out someway, I suppose."

Suddenly Judith covered her face with her hands and began to cry, all the loneliness that was past and still to come flooding up within her, bursting out of her control. And John took her into his arms again, trying to soothe and comfort her.

"Don't cry, Judith darling. I'll come back to you. Someday we'll have our home and our family. Someday we'll have each other—"

"Someday, John!" Her arms caught at him desperately, her face was frightened and her eyes reckless. "Someday! But what if someday never comes!"

An hour later he was gone and Judith rode back to the house, happy and at peace, content as never before in her life. For now—no matter what happened, no matter who won or lost the war—they were sure of each other. Sometimes they might have to be apart, but they could never be really separated again. Life seemed simpler to her, and more complete.

At first the thought of seeing her mother again, of looking her squarely in the face, confused and frightened her. She felt as she had when she was a little girl and Lady Anne had always known —even without seeing her at it—whether she had been into mischief. But after the first few uncomfortable days were safely past

9

Judith let herself settle into the luxury of remembering. Every smile, every kiss and touch, each phrase of love, she brought forth again and again like precious keepsakes, to solace her empty hours, comfort her doubts, banish the dark enclosing fears.

Only a month later news came of a great Royalist victory at Roundway Down and Lord William wrote his wife to expect peace at any time. Judith's hopes soared with wild optimism, heedless of Lady Anne's stern warning that neither John Mainwaring nor any member of his family would ever set foot on Rose Lawn again. If only the war would end, no matter *how* it ended, they would work out their problems someway. John had said so.

And then she realized that she was pregnant.

For some time she had been noticing strange symptoms, and though she believed at first that it was only some slight indisposition, finally she knew. The shock sent her to bed for several days. She could not eat and grew pale and thinner, and whenever her mother was in the room she lay watching her with sick apprehension, dreading each glance, each sentence, sure that she saw suspicion in her eyes and heard contempt in her voice. She did not dare think what would happen if they should ever find out. For her father's temper and prejudices were so violent he would surely seek John out and try to kill him. Somehow, before it became noticeable, she must get away—go to John, no matter where he was. She could not give birth to an illegitimate child; it would be a stain upon the honour of her family which nothing could ever erase.

Lord William came back in September, jubilant with tales of Royalist success. "They won't be able to hold against us another month," he insisted. And Judith, who had had not a word from John, listened to her father eagerly—hoping to hear at least the mention of his name, some hint that he was alive and unhurt. But if Lord William knew anything about him he did not speak of it before Judith, and her mother was equally uncommunicative. Both of them pretended to be unaware that John Mainwaring existed or had ever existed.

Then she was told that they had selected a husband for her.

He was Edmund Mortimer, Earl of Radclyffe. Judith had met him a year and a half before, when he had paid a visit to Rose Lawn. He was thirty-five years old, not long widowed, and the father of a baby son. She remembered little except that she had not liked him. He was no more than five feet six or seven inches tall, with delicate bones and head too large for his narrow shoulders and thin body. His features were aristocratic, narrow-nosed and tight-lipped, and though his eyes were hard and cold they reflected a trained, austere intelligence. These were not qualities to recommend him to a girl of seventeen whose heart was full of a handsome, virile, gallant young man. And something about the Earl, she did not know what, repelled her. She would not have wanted him for a husband even if she had never seen John Mainwaring.

"I don't want to get married," she said, half surprised at her own audacity.

Her father stared at her, his eyes beginning to glitter dangerously, but just as he opened his mouth to speak Lady Anne told her to leave the room, adding that she would talk to her later. Judith's sulky stubbornness angered and surprised her parents. Nevertheless they went briskly ahead with plans for the wedding, and did not consult her again, for they were convinced that the sooner she was married and began to get John Mainwaring out of her head the better it would be for everyone concerned.

Her wedding-gown, made a year and a half ago for her marriage to John, was taken out of its trunk, brushed and pressed and hung up in her room. It was heavy white satin, embroidered all over with seed pearls. The deep collar and cuffs were cream-coloured lace, and the slit skirt draped up in back over a petticoat of luminous, crusty silver-cloth. Hand-made in France, it was a beautiful and very expensive gown, and at first she had loved it. Now she could not even bring herself to try it on, and passionately told her nurse that she would as soon be fitted for her own shroud.

Sometime later the Earl arrived and Judith, though she had been warned repeatedly to show him all respect and affection, refused to do either. She avoided him whenever she could, spoke to him coldly, and cried in her own room for hours without end. The fourth month of her pregnancy had passed and she was in constant terror of being discovered, though her full skirts would certainly give no hint for several weeks longer. Worry and anxiety had made her thin; she jumped nervously at the slightest unexpected sound and was quiet and moody and easily irritated.

What's going to happen to me? she would think wildly as she stood by the windows, hoping, praying to see John or some messenger sent by him come riding up over the hill to save her. But no one came. Since June she had not heard from him. She did not even know whether he was alive or dead.

Her relief was intense, if guilty, when—less than a fortnight before the day set for the wedding—news arrived that the Parliamentarians had attacked a great house twenty miles to the southeast, and the Earl rode off with her father.

Rose Lawn lay on the boundary which separated Royalist territory from that held by Parliament, and news of an attack so near had ominous significance. The house had been kept in readiness for any possible emergency since the beginning of the war and now, following her husband's instructions, Lady Anne began to make preparations for a siege. It was not unusual for a few women and old men to stave off an attacking force for weeks or months, and no one who knew Lady Anne could doubt that if Rose Lawn were to be besieged she would hold it until every last child and dog was dead of starvation.

The following night there was a sudden alarm from the watch. The women began to scream with terror, thinking that the moment had come; children bawled and dogs barked; somewhere a musket went off. Judith leaped from the bed, flung on a dressing-gown, and rushed out to find her mother. She discovered her downstairs in conversation with a farmer, and as she appeared Lady Anne turned and handed her a sealed letter. Judith gave a little gasp and her face turned white, but even under her mother's cold and accusing eyes she could not mask the passionate gratitude and relief she felt. It must be from John. While she tore open the seal and began to read, Lady Anne dismissed the farmer.

"In a few days we will attack Rose Lawn. I cannot prevent the attack but I can carry you and her Ladyship to a place of safety. Bring nothing with you that will make travelling difficult and wait at the mouth of the river beneath the house as soon as it is dark tomorrow night. I won't be able to see you, but I have a servant I can trust and I have made arrangements for you to be cared for until I can come to you."

Judith raised her eyes to her mother's and then slowly, as if by compulsion, she handed her the letter. Lady Anne gave it a quick glance, crossed the room and threw it into the fire. She turned back to face her daughter.

"Well?" she said at last.

Impulsively Judith ran toward her. "Oh, madame, we've got to go! If we stay here we may be killed! He'll take us where we'll both be safe!"

"I do not intend to leave my home at such a time as this. And certainly I will not accept the protection of an enemy." Her eyes watched Judith coldly. She looked proud, indestructible, and a little cruel. "Make your own choice, Judith, but make it carefully. For if you do I shall tell your father that you were captured. We will never see you again."

Judith had a moment of intense longing to tell her mother what had happened. If only she could explain it to her somehow, could make her understand how truly they loved each other— how impossible it was to stifle that love merely because England was at war— But looking into Lady Anne's eyes she knew that her mother would never understand, that she would only despise and condemn her. The decision was hers to make, and there could be no explanation once she had made it.

With only one extra gown and her few jewels, she left Rose Lawn. All that night she and the servant travelled and by mid-morning of the following day had come to a farmhouse in Essex which was well within the borders of Parliamentary domination. There she was introduced to Sarah and Matthew Goodegroome as Judith St. Clare, wife of John St. Clare, who had left her home because of a quarrel between her family and her husband's. Sarah knew that she was a lady of quality but did not know her rank; and Judith, according to John's instructions, told her nothing more. When the War was over and John came for her they would explain everything. Meanwhile Sarah introduced her to the village women as her own sister, come to live with her because the armies were fighting about her husband's farm.

There was something sure and free and vibrantly contented about Sarah Goodegroome that gave Judith a sense of security and brought back her optimism. They became close friends, and Judith was happier than she had been for a long while.

Whenever he could, John sent her a message, always saying that he would join her as soon as possible. Once he mentioned, briefly, that Rose Lawn still held. But her home, her parents, the Earl of Radclyffe, seemed almost unreal to her now. Her life was absorbed in the farmhouse, in her new friends and the little village of Marygreen, in her thoughts and dreams of John—and most of all in the tiny creature her body carried. Now that her worries and apprehensions were over, now that she was thought to be—and almost thought herself—as respectable a married woman as any of them, she grew happier and prettier by the day. Pregnancy became her well. But she was eager for the day when she would bear John his first son; never once did it occur to her that the child might be a girl.

She was beginning to move restlessly, conscious of painful cramps in the muscles of her arms and legs. She could see only dimly now, as if she had her eyes opened under water. And though she could not tell how much time had gone by, Sarah was still working, kneading her belly with capable strong fingers, her face strained and wet.

I must tell her to stop, thought Judith drowsily. She looks so tired.

She heard the baby squalling and remembered again that it was a girl. I've never even thought of a name for her. What shall I call her? Judith—or Anne—or perhaps it should be Sarah—

And then she said softly, "Sarah—I think I'll name her Amber —for the colour of her father's eyes—"

She became aware of the other women nearby, of a bustle and stir in the room, and now one of them leaned down to lay a

14

warm cloth across her forehead, at the same time removing another which had grown cool. Blankets had been piled on her, but still her face was cold and wet and she could feel moisture on her fingers. Her ears were ringing and the feeling of dizziness came again, swooping down and whirling her up and away until she saw nothing but a hazy, blur, heard only a confused murmurous babble.

And then as she moved slightly, trying to ease the cramps that knotted again and again in her legs, Sarah suddenly put her face in her hands and began to sob. Without an instant's hesitation another woman bent and began to work, firmly kneading and massaging.

"Sarah— Please, Sarah—" whispered Judith, full of pity for her.

Very slowly and with great effort she drew her hand from where it lay at her side under the blankets and raised it toward her. As she did so she saw that the palm and fingers were smeared with wet blood. For a moment she stared at it dreamily, without comprehension, and then all at once she understood why she had had such a strange sense of comfort, as though she lay in a warm bath. Her eyes widened with horror and she gave a sharp cry of pleading and protest.

"Sarah!"

Sarah dropped to her knees, her face contorted with grief.

"Sarah! Sarah, help me! I don't want to die!"

The other women were sobbing wildly but Sarah, gaining control of herself again, forced a smile. "It's nothing, Judith. You mustn't be frightened. A little blood is nothing—" But the next moment her features twisted with unbearable anguish and she was crying, unable to control herself any longer.

For several seconds Judith stared at her bowed head and shaking shoulders, full of wild, angry, helpless resentment, terrified. I *can't* be dying! she thought. I can't! I don't want to die! I want to live!

She tried to speak to Sarah again, to beg for help—to demand it—Sarah! Sarah—don't let me die— But she heard no words, she could not even tell if her lips formed them.

And then slowly she began to drift, floating back into some

warm pleasant world where there was no fear of death, where she and John would meet again. She could see nothing at all now, and she let her eyes close—the ringing in her ears had shut out every other sound. She was no longer struggling; she drifted willingly, suffused with so intolerable a tiredness that she welcomed this promise of relief. And then all at once she could hear again, loud and clear, the sound of her daughter's cries. They were repeated over and over, but grew steadily fainter, fading away, until at last she heard them no more.

1660

PART I

CHAPTER ONE

MARYGREEN DID NOT change in sixteen years. It had changed little enough in the past two hundred.

The church of St. Catherine stood at the northern end of the road, like a benevolent godfather, and from it the houses ran down either side—half-timbered cottages, with overhanging upper stories, and thatched with heather or with straw that had been golden when new, then had turned slowly to a rich brown, and now was emerald green with moss and lichen. Tiny dormer windows looked out, wreathed with honeysuckle and ivy. Thick untrimmed hedges fenced the houses off from the road and there were small wooden gates, some of them spanned by arches of climbing roses. Above the hedges could be seen the confusion of blooming flowers, delphinium and lilacs, both purple and white, hollyhocks that reached almost to the eaves, an apple or plum or cherry tree in full blossom.

At the far end from the church was the green, where on festive occasions the young men played football and held wrestling matches and all the village danced.

There was an inn built of soft red brick and showing the aged silver-grey oaken timbers of its frame; a great sign painted with a crude golden lion swung out over the street on an elaborate wrought-iron arm. Nearby was the blacksmith's cottage with his adjoining shop and the homes and places of business of the apothecary, the carpenter, and another tradesman or two. The rest of the cottages were occupied by husbandmen who divided their time between working on their own small holdings and on the large neighbouring farms. For there was no manor or squire's estate near Marygreen, and the economic existence of the village depended upon the well-to-do yeomen farmers.

The day was quiet and warm, the sky blue with long streaks of white clouds, which seemed to have been put there by a paintbrush drawn across wet water-colour; the air was full of spring moisture and a rich loamy smell of damp earth. Chickens and geese and tiny sparrows had taken possession of the road. A little girl stood before one of the gates, holding a pet rabbit in her arms.

There were few people in sight, for it was late afternoon and each person had his own work to do, so that the only idlers were dogs, a playful kitten or two, and children too young to have learned a useful task. A woman with a basket on her arm walked along the street, pausing for a few moments to talk to another housewife, who threw open an upstairs casement window and leaned out, surrounded as though in a frame with wandering clematis and morning glories. Grouped about the village cross, which had somehow escaped Cromwell's soldiers, were eight or ten young girls—cottagers' daughters who were sent every day to watch their parents' cattle on the common and make sure that no single goat, cow, or sheep should stray or be stolen.

Some of the younger ones were playing "How many miles to Babylon?"—but the three oldest girls talked among themselves, full of indignation and bad humour. With hands on their hips they glared across the common to where two young men, thumbs hooked awkwardly in their breeches, shifting their weight from one foot to another, stood deep in conversation with someone who apparently upset their not too well established poise. But their combined bulk hid whoever it was from view.

"That Amber St. Clare!" muttered the eldest girl with a furious toss of her long blonde hair. "If ever there's a man about, you may be sure *she'll* come along! I think she can smell 'em out!"

"She should 've been married and bedded a year ago—that's what my mother says!"

The third girl smiled slyly and said in a knowing sing-song: "Well, maybe she an't married yet, but she's already been—"

"Hush!" interrupted the first, nodding toward the younger children.

"Just the same," she insisted, though she had lowered her voice to a hiss, "my brother says Bob Starling told him he had his way with her on Mothering Sunday!"

But Lisbeth, who had started the conversation, gave a contemptuous snap of her fingers. "Uds Lud, Gartrude! Jack Clarke said the same thing six months ago—and she's no bigger now than she was then."

Gartrude had an answer. "And d'ye want to know why, Lisbeth Morton? B'cause she can spit three times in a frog's mouth, that's why. Maggie Littlejohn seen her do it!"

"Pooh! My mother says *nobody* can spit three times in a frog's mouth!"

But the argument was cut short. For suddenly a sound of galloping hoofs echoed through the quiet little valley and a body of men on horseback rounded the turn of the road above St. Catherine's and came rushing headlong up the narrow street toward them. One of the six-year-olds gave a scream of terror and ran to hide behind Lisbeth's skirts.

"It's Old Noll! Come back from the Devil to get us!" Even dead, Oliver Cromwell had not lost his salutary effect on disobedient youngsters.

The men reined in their horses, bringing them to a prancing nervous halt not more than ten yards from where the girls stood in a close group, their earlier fright and apprehension giving way now to frank admiring interest. There were perhaps fourteen men in all but more than half of them were either servingmen or guides, for they wore plain clothes and kept at a discreet distance from the others. The half-dozen in the lead were obviously gentlemen.

They wore their hair in the shoulder-length cut of the Cavaliers, and their dress was magnificent. Their suits were black velvet, dark red velvet, green satin, with broad white linen collars and white linen shirts. On their heads were wide-brimmed hats with swirling plumes, and long riding capes hung from their shoulders. Their high leather boots were silver-spurred and each man wore a sword at his hip. They had evidently been riding hard for some considerable distance for their clothes were dusty and their faces streaked with dirt and sweat, but in the girls' eyes they had an almost terrifying grandeur.

Now one of the men took off his hat and spoke to Lisbeth, presumably because she was the prettiest. "My services, madame," he said, his voice and eyes lazily good-humoured, and as he looked her over slowly from head to foot Lisbeth blushed crimson and found it difficult to breathe. "We're looking for a place to eat. Have you a good tavern in these parts?"

Lisbeth stared at him, temporarily speechless, while he continued to smile down at her, his hands resting easily on the saddle before him. His suit was black velvet with a short doublet and wide knee-length breeches, finished with golden braid. He had dark hair and green-grey eyes and a narrow black mustache lined his upper lip. His good looks were spectacular—but they were not the most important thing about him. For his face had an uncompromising ruthlessness and strength which marked him, in spite of his obvious aristocracy, as an adventurer and gambler, a man free from bonds and ties.

Lisbeth swallowed and made a little curtsy. "Ye mun like the Three Cups in Heathstone, m'lord." She was afraid to recommend her own poor little village to these splendid strangers.

"Where's Heathstone from here?"

"Heathstone be damned!" protested one of the men. "What's wrong with your own ordinary? I'll fall off this jade if I go another mile without food!" He was a handsome blonde red-faced young man and in spite of his scowl he was obviously happy and good-natured. As he spoke the others laughed and one of them leaned over to clap him on the shoulder.

"By God, we're a set of rascals! Almsbury hasn't had a mouthful since he ate that side of mutton this morning!"

They laughed again at this for apparently Almsbury's appetite was a well-established joke among them. The girls giggled too, more at ease now, and the six-year-old who had mistaken them for Puritan ghosts came out boldly from behind Lisbeth's skirts and edged a step or two nearer. At that instant something happened to create an abrupt change in the relationship between the men and girls.

"There's nothing wrong with our inn, your Lordship!" cried a low-pitched feminine voice, and the girl who had been talking to the two young farmers came running across the green toward them. The girls had stiffened like wary cats but the men looked about with surprise and sudden interest. "The hostess there brews the finest ale in Essex!"

She made a quick little curtsy to Almsbury and then her eyes turned to meet those of the man who had spoken first and who was now watching her with a new expression on his face, speculative, admiring, alert. While the others watched, it seemed that time stopped for a moment and then, reluctantly, went on again.

Amber St. Clare raised her arm and pointed back down the street to the great sign with its weather-beaten gilt lion shimmering faintly as the falling sun struck it. "Next the blacksmith's shop, m'lord."

Her honey-coloured hair fell in heavy waves below her shoulders and as she stared up at him her eyes, clear, speckled amber, seemed to tilt at the corners; her brows were black and swept up in arcs, and she had thick black lashes. There was about her a kind of warm luxuriance, something immediately suggestive to the men of pleasurable fulfillment—something for which she was not responsible but of which she was acutely conscious. It was that, more than her beauty, which the other girls resented.

She was dressed, very much as they were, in a rust wool skirt tucked up over a green petticoat, a white blouse and yellow apron and tight-laced black stomacher; her ankles were bare and she wore a pair of neat black shoes. And yet she was no more like them than a field flower is like a cultivated one or a sparrow is like a golden pheasant.

Almsbury leaned forward, crossing his arms on his saddle bow. "What in the name of Jesus," he said slowly, "are *you* doing out here in God's forgotten country?"

The girl looked at him, dragging her eyes away from the other man, and now she smiled, showing teeth that were white and even and beautifully shaped. "I live here, m'lord."

"The deuce you do! Then how the devil did you get here? What are you? Some nobleman's bastard put out to suck with a cottager's wife and forgotten these fifteen years?" It was no uncommon occurrence, but she looked suddenly angry, her brows drawing in an indignant scowl.

"I am *not,* sir! I'm as much my father's child as you are—or more!"

The men, including Almsbury, laughed heartily at this and he gave her a grin. "No offense, sweetheart. Lord, I only meant you haven't the look of a farmer's daughter."

She smiled at him quickly then, as though in apology for her show of temper, but her eyes went back immediately to the other man. He was still watching her with a look that warmed all her body and brought a swift-rising sense of excitement. The men were wheeling their horses around and as his turned, its forelegs lifted high, he smiled and nodded his head. Almsbury thanked her and lifted his hat and then they rode off, clattering back up the street to the inn. For a moment longer the girls stood silently, watching them dismount and go through the doorway while the inn-keeper's young sons came to take care of their horses.

When they were out of sight Lisbeth suddenly stuck out her tongue and gave Amber a shove. "There!" she cried triumphantly, and made a sound like a bleating female goat. "Much good it did you, Mrs. Minx!"

Swiftly Amber returned the shove, almost knocking the girl off balance, crying, "Mind your knitting, chatterbox!"

For a moment they stood and glared at each other, but finally Lisbeth turned and went off across the green, where the other girls were rounding up their charges, running and shouting, racing with one another, eager to get home to their evening suppers. The sun had set, leaving the sky bright red along the horizon but turning to delicate blue above. Here and there a star had come out; the air was full of the magic of twilight.

Her heart still beating heavily, Amber crossed back to where she had left her basket lying in the grass. The two young farmers had gone, and now she picked it up again and continued on her way, walking toward the inn.

She had never seen anyone like him before in her life. The clothes he wore, the sound of his voice, the expression in his eyes, all made her feel that she had had a momentary glimpse into another world—and she longed passionately to see it again, if only for a brief while. Everything else, her own world of Marygreen and Uncle Matt's farm, all the young men she knew, now seemed to her intolerably dull, even contemptible.

From her conversations with the village cobbler she knew that they must be noblemen, but what they were doing here, in Marygreen, she could not imagine. For the Cavaliers these past several years had retired into what obscurity they could find or had gone abroad in the wake of the King's son, now Charles II, who lived in exile.

The cobbler, who had fought in the Civil Wars on his Majesty's side, had told her a great many tales of things he had seen and stories he had heard. He had told her of seeing Charles I at Oxford, of being almost close enough to have touched him, of the gay and beautiful Royalist ladies, the gallant men—it was a life full of colour and spirit and high romance. But she had seen nothing of it, for it disappeared while she was yet a child, disappeared forever the morning his Majesty was beheaded in the yard of his own Palace. It was something of that atmosphere which the dark-haired stranger had brought with him—not the others, for she had scarcely noticed them—but it was something more as well, something intensely personal. It seemed as though, all at once, she was fully and completely alive.

Arriving at the inn she did not go in by the front entrance but, instead, walked around to the back where a little boy sat in the doorway, playing with his fox-eared puppy, and she patted him on the head as she went by. In the kitchen Mrs. Poterell was rushing about in a frenzy of preparation, excited and distraught. On the chopping-block lay a piece of raw beef into which one of the daughters was stuffing a moist mixture of bread-crumbs and onions and herbs. A little girl was cranking up water from the well that stood far in one corner of the kitchen. And the turnspit-dog in his cage above the fireplace gave an angry yowl as another boy applied a hot coal to his hind feet to make him move faster and turn the roasting-joint so it would brown evenly on all sides.

Amber managed to catch the attention of Mrs. Poterell, who

was careening from one side of the room to the other, her apron full of eggs. "Here's a Dutch gingerbread Aunt Sarah sent you, Mrs. Poterell!" It was not true, for Sarah had sent the delicacy to the blacksmith's wife, but Amber thought this the better cause.

"Oh, thank God, sweetheart! Oh, I never was in such a taking! Six gentlemen in my house at once! Oh, Lord! What shall I do!" But even as she talked she had begun breaking the eggs into a great bowl.

At that moment fifteen-year-old Meg emerged from the trapdoor which led down into the cellar, her arms full of dusty green bottles, and Amber rushed to her.

"Here, Meg! Let me help you!"

She took five of them from her and started for the other room, pushing the door open with her knee, but she kept her eyes down as she entered, and concentrated all her attention on the bottles. The men were standing about the room, cloaks off though they still wore their hats, and as she appeared Almsbury caught sight of her and came forward, smiling.

"Here—sweetheart. Let me help you with those. So they play that old game out here too?"

"What old game, m'lord?"

He took three of the bottles from her and she set the other two on the table, looking up then to smile at him. But instantly her eyes sought out the other man where he stood next the windows with two companions, throwing dice on a table-top. His back was half turned and he did not glance around but tossed down a coin as one of the others snapped his fingers at a lucky throw. Surprised and disappointed, for she had expected him to see her immediately—even to be looking for her—she turned again to Almsbury.

"Why, it's the oldest game in the world," he was saying. "Keeping a pretty bar-maid to lure in the customers till they've spent their last shilling—I'll warrant you've lured many a farmer's son to his ruin." He was grinning at her and now he picked up a bottle, jerked out the cork and put it to his lips. Amber gave him another smile, arch and flirtatious, wishing that the other man would look over and see her.

"Oh, I'm not the bar-maid here, sir. I brought Mrs. Poterell a cake and helped Meg to carry in the bottles."

Almsbury had taken several swallows, draining half the bottle at once. "Ah, by God!" he declared appreciatively. "Well, then, who are you? What's your name?"

"Amber St. Clare, sir."

"Amber! No farmer's wife ever thought of a name like that."

She laughed, her eyes stealing swiftly across the room and back again, but he was still intent on the dice. "That's what my Uncle Matt says. He says my name should be Mary or Anne, or Elizabeth."

Almsbury took several more deep swallows and wiped his mouth with the back of his hand. "Your uncle's a man of no imagination." And then, as she glanced toward the table again, he threw back his head and laughed. "So that's what you want, is it? Well, come along—" And taking hold of her wrist he started across the room.

"Carlton," he said, when they had come up to the group, "here's a wench who has a mind to lay with you."

He turned then, gave Almsbury a glance that suggested some joke between them, and smiled at Amber. She was staring up at him with her eyes big and shining, and had not even heard the remark. She was no more than five-feet three, a height convenient for making even a moderate-sized man feel impressive, but he towered over her by at least a foot.

She caught only a part of Almsbury's introduction. "—a man for whom I have the highest regard even though the bastard does steal every pretty wench I set my eyes on—Bruce, Lord Carlton." She managed a curtsy and he bowed to her, sweeping off his hat with as much gallantry as though she were a princess royal. "We're all of us," he continued, "come back with the King."

"With the King! Is the King come back!"

"He's coming—very soon," said Carlton.

At this astonishing news Amber forgot her nervous embarrassment. For though the Goodegroomes had once been Parliamentarian in sympathy, they had gradually, as had most of the country, begun to long for monarchy and the old ways of life.

Since the King's murder his people had grown to love him as they had never done during his lifetime, and that love had been transferred to his heir.

"Gemini!" she breathed. For it was too great an event to realize all at once—and under such distracting conditions.

Lord Carlton took up one of the bottles which Meg had set on the table, wiped the dust from its neck with the palm of his hand, and pulling out the cork began to drink. Amber continued to stare at him, her self-consciousness now almost drowned in awe and admiration.

"We're on our way to London," he told her. "But one of our horses needs shoeing. What about your inn? Is it a good place to stay the night? The landlord won't rob us—there aren't any bed-bugs or lice?" He watched her face as he talked, and for some reason she did not understand there was a look of amusement in his eyes.

"Rob you?" she cried indignantly. "Mr. Poterell never robbed anybody! This is a mighty fine inn," she declared with stanch loyalty. "The one in Heathstone is *nothing* to it!"

Both men were grinning now. "Well," said Almsbury, "let the landlord steal our shoes and the lice be thick as March crows in a fallow field, still it's an English inn and by God a good one!" With that he made her a solemn bow, "Your servant, madame," and went off to find another bottle of sack, leaving them alone.

Amber felt her bones and muscles turn to water. She stood and looked at him, cursing herself for her tongue-tied stupor. Why was it that she—who usually had a pert remark on her tongue for any man no matter what his age or condition—could think of nothing at all to say now? Now, when she longed with frantic desperation to impress him, to make him feel the same violent excitement and admiration that she did. At last she said the only thing she could think of:

"Tomorrow's the Heathstone May Fair."

"It is?"

His eyes went down to her breasts which were full and pointed, upward tilting; she was one of those women who reach complete physical maturity at an early age, and there had long since ceased to be anything of adolescence about her.

Amber felt the blood begin to rise in her neck and face. "It's the finest fair in all Essex," she assured him quickly. "The farmers go ten and twenty miles to it."

His eyes came back to meet hers and he smiled, lifting one eyebrow in apparent wonder at this gigantic local festival, then drank down the rest of his wine. She could smell the faint pungent odour of it as he breathed and she could smell too the heavy masculine sweat on his clothes and the scent of leather from his boots. The combination gave her a sense of dizziness, almost of intoxication, and a powerful longing swept through her. Almsbury's impertinent remark had been no very great exaggeration.

Now he glanced out the window. "It's growing dark. You should be getting home," and he walked to the door, opening it for her.

The evening had settled swiftly and many stars had come out; the high-pitched moon was thin and transparent. A cool little breeze had sprung up. Out there they stood alone, surrounded by the talking and laughter from the inn, the quiet country sounds of crickets and a distant frog, the whir of tiny gnats. She turned and looked up at him, her face white and glistening as a moonflower.

"Can't *you* come to the Fair, my lord?" She was afraid that she would never see him again, and the idea was intolerable to her.

"Perhaps," he said. "If there's time."

"Oh, please! It's on the main road—you'll pass that way! You *will* stop, won't you?" Her voice and eyes pleaded with him, wistful, compelling.

"How fair you are," he said softly, and now for the first time his expression was wholly serious.

For a moment they stood looking at each other, and then Amber swayed involuntarily toward him, her eyes shut. His hands closed about her waist, drawing her to him, and she felt the powerful muscles in his legs. Her head fell back. Her mouth

29

parted to receive his kiss. It was several moments before he released her, but when he did it seemed too soon—she felt almost cheated. Opening her eyes again she saw him looking at her with faint surprise, though whether at himself or her she did not know. The world seemed to have exploded. She was as stunned as though she had been given a heavy blow, and all the strength had gone out of her.

"You must go now, my dear," he said finally. "Your family will be troubled to have you out so late."

Quick impulsive words sprang to her lips. I don't care if they are! I don't care if I never go home again! I don't care about anything but you— Oh, let me stay here and go away with you tomorrow—

But something kept her from saying them. Perhaps the image —somewhere not too far back in her mind—of Aunt Sarah's troubled, cautioning frown, Uncle Matt's stern, lean, reproving face. It would never do to be so bold, for he would only hate her then. Aunt Sarah had often said men did not like a pert woman.

"I don't live far," she said. "Just down this road and over the fields a quarter-mile or so." She was hoping that he would offer to walk the distance with her but he did not, and though she waited a few seconds, at last she dropped him a curtsy. "I'll look for you tomorrow, m'lord."

"I may come. Good-night."

He made her a bow, sweeping off his hat again, and then with a smile and a glance that took her in from head to foot he turned and went inside. Amber stood there a moment like a bewildered child; then suddenly she whirled about and started off at a run and though she stopped once to look back he was gone.

She ran on then—up the narrow road and past the church, quickening her pace as she went by the graveyard where her mother lay buried, and soon she turned right down a tree-lined lane leading over the fields toward the Goodegroome farm. Ordinarily she would have been a little scared to be out alone when it was almost dark, but ghosts and witches and goblins held no terror for her now. Her mind was too full of other things.

30

She had never seen anyone like him before and had not realized that such a man could exist. He was every handsome, gallant gentleman the cobbler had ever described, and he was what her dreams had embroidered upon those descriptions. Bob Starling and Jack Clarke! A pair of dolts!

She wondered if he was thinking of her now, and felt sure that he must be. No man could kiss a woman like *that* and forget her the next moment! The kiss, if nothing else, she thought, would bring him to the Fair tomorrow—draw him there perhaps in spite of himself. She complimented herself that she understood men and their natures very well.

The night air was cool, as though it had blown over ice, and the meadows were thick with purple clover and white evening campion. Amber approached the farmhouse from the back. She crossed the creek on a bridge which was nothing but a couple of boards with a hand-rail, passed the plot where the cabbages and other vegetables grew, and made her way between the numerous outbuildings—barns and stables and cow-sheds— all of them white-washed, their roofs covered with moss and yellow stone-crop. Then, skirting the edge of the duckpond, she entered the courtyard.

The house was two-storied, the oak frame ornately carved, and the soft red brick walls were spread with vines. Each chimney was muffled in ivy, and an arched lattice overgrown with honeysuckle framed the kitchen-door, above which had been nailed a horseshoe for protection against witches. In the brick-paved courtyard, over against the walls, grew Sarah's flowers, low clusters of white and purple violets, hollyhocks reaching up to the eaves, a thick clump of fragrant lavender to put between the sheets. Several fruit trees were in bloom, scenting the air with a light sweetness. A low wooden bench had two thatch-roofed beehives on it; attached to the wall beside the door was a tiny bird-house, lost in the pink roses; and a saucy green-eyed kitten sat on the door-sill cleaning its paws.

The house had beauty and peace and the suggestion of an active useful life. It was more than a hundred years old and five generations had lived in it, leaving behind them a comfortable aura of prosperity—not of wealth but of solid ease and plenty, of good food and warmth and comfort. It was a house to love.

As Amber went in she stooped and took the kitten up into her arms, caressing its smooth soft fur with her fingers, hearing it purr with a low, contented little rumble. Supper was over and only Sarah and fifteen-year-old Agnes remained in the kitchen—Sarah just drawing hot loaves of bread from the oven sunk into the wall beside the fireplace, Agnes mending a rush-light.

Agnes was talking, her voice petulant and resentful: "—and it's no wonder they talk about her! I vow and swear, Mother, I'm ashamed she's my cousin—"

Amber heard her but did not care just then. Agnes had said the same thing often enough before. She came into the room with a joyful little cry and ran to fling one arm about her aunt. "Aunt Sarah!" Sarah's head turned and she smiled, but there was a look of searching worry in her eyes. "The inn's full of noblemen! His Majesty's coming home!"

The troubled expression was gone. "Are you sure, child!"

"Aye," said Amber proudly. "They told me so!" She was full of the importance of her news and the wonderful thing that had just happened to her. She thought anyone must be able to tell by looking at her how greatly she had changed since leaving home two hours before.

Agnes looked frankly suspicious—and contemptuous—but Sarah turned and rushed out of the house toward the barns, where most of the men had gone to finish their evening tasks. Amber ran after her. And the moment the news was told, by both women at once, a general shout of rejoicing went up. Men came running out of the barns and cow-sheds, women rushed from their little cottages (there were several on the farm), and even the dogs barked with a loud gay sound as if they, too, would join in the hilarity.

Long live his Majesty, King Charles II!

At market the week before Matthew had heard rumours of a Restoration. They had been floating through the country since early March, carried by travellers, by itinerant pedlars, by all those who had commerce with the great world to the south. Tumbledown Dick, the Protector's son, had been thrown out of his office. General Monk had marched from Scotland, occupied London, and summoned a free Parliament. Civil war seemed on the verge of breaking out again between civilians and the great mobilized armies. These events had left in their wake a trail of weariness and hope—weariness with the interminable troubles of the past twenty years, hope that a restored monarchy might bring them peace again, and security. They yearned for the old familiar ways. And now, if the Cavaliers were returning, it *must* mean that King Charles was coming home—a Golden Age of prosperity, happiness, and peace was about to begin.

When at last the excitement had begun to die down and everyone went back to his work, Amber started for the house. They would get up early tomorrow morning to leave for the Fair and she wanted to sleep long enough to look and feel her best. But as she was going by the dairy on her way into the kitchen she heard her name spoken softly, insistently, and she stopped. There was Tom Andrews standing in the shadows, reaching out a hand to catch her wrist as she went by.

Tom was a young man of twenty-two who worked for her Uncle, and he was very much in love with Amber who liked him for that reason—though she knew that he was by no means a match for her. For she was aware that her mother had left her a dowry which would enable her to marry the richest farmer in the countryside. But she found a certain luxury in Tom's adoration and had encouraged him in it.

Now, with a quick glance around to make certain that neither Aunt Sarah nor Uncle Matt would see her, she went inside. The little room was cool, sweet and fresh, and perfectly dark. Tom caught hold of her roughly, one arm about her waist, his hand immediately sliding down into her blouse as he sought for her lips. Obviously this was not new to either of them, and for a moment Amber submitted, letting him kiss and fondle her, and then all at once she broke away, pushing violently at him.

33

"Marry come up, Tom Andrews! Who gives you leave to be so bold with me!"

She was thinking that it was incredible the kiss of an ordinary man should be so different from that of a lord, but Tom was hurt and bewildered and his hands reached out for her again.

"What's the matter, Amber? What've I done? What's got into you?"

Angrily she wrenched her hand free and ran out. For she now felt herself above such trifling with men of Tom Andrews' station and was only eager to get upstairs and into bed where she could lie and think of Lord Carlton and dream of tomorrow.

The kitchen was deserted except for Sarah, sweeping the flag-stoned floor one last time before going to bed. There were three or four rushlights burning, a circle of tiny moths darting about each tenuous reaching flame, and only the bell-like song of the crickets invaded the evening stillness. Matt came in, scowling, and without a word went to the barrel of ale which stood in a far cool corner of the room, poured himself a pewter mugful and drank it off. He was a middle-sized serious man who worked hard and made a good living and loved his family. And he was conscientious and God-fearing, with strong beliefs as to what was right and what was wrong, what was good and what was bad.

Sarah gave him a glance. "What is it, Matt? Is the foal worse?"

"No, she'll live, I think. It's that girl."

His face was sour and now he went to stand before the great fireplace which was surrounded on all sides with blackened pots and pans, gleaming copper, pewter polished till it looked like silver. Bacon and hams, in great nets, hung from the overhead beams, and there were several thick tied-up bunches of dry herbs.

"Who?" asked Sarah. "Amber?"

"Who else? Not an hour since I saw her come out of the dairy and a minute later Tom Andrews followed her, looking like a

34

whipped pup. She's got the boy half out of his noddle—he's all but useless to me. And what was she doing, pray, down at the inn with a pack of gentlemen?" His voice rose angrily.

Sarah went to stand the broom just outside the door and then closed it, throwing the bolt. "Hush, Matt! Some of the men are still in the parlour. I don't think she was doing anything she shouldn't have. She was just passing by and saw them—it's natural she should stop."

"And come home alone in the dark? Did it take her an hour to hear that the King's to return? I tell you, Sarah, she's got to get married! I won't have her disgracing my family! D'ye hear me?"

"Yes, Matt, I hear you." Sarah went to the cradle beside the fireplace where the baby had begun to stir and whimper, took him out and put him to her breast, then she went to sit down on the settle. She gave a weary little sigh. "Only she don't want to get married."

"Oh!" said Matt sarcastically. "So she don't want to get married! I suppose Jack Clarke or Bob Starling's not good enough for 'er—two of the finest young fellows in Essex."

Sarah smiled gently, her voice soft and tired. "After all, Matt, she is a lady."

"Lady! She's a strumpet! For four years now she's caused me nothing but trouble, and by the Lord Harry I'm fed up to the teeth! Her mother may have been a lady but she's a—"

"Matt! Don't speak so of Judith's child. Oh, I know, Matt. It troubles me too. I try to warn her—but I don't know what heed she pays me. Agnes told me tonight— Oh, well, I don't think it means anything. She's pretty and the girls are jealous and I suppose they make up tales."

"I'm not so sure it's just tale-telling, Sarah! You've always got a mind to think the best of folks—but they don't always deserve it. Bob Starling asked me for her again today, and I tell you if she an't married soon not even Tom Andrews 'll have her, dowry or no!"

"But suppose her father comes, and finds her married to a farmer. Oh, Matt, sometimes I think we're not doing the right thing—not telling her who she is—"

35

"What else *can* we do, Sarah? Her mother's dead. Her father's dead, too, or we'd have heard some word of him—and we've never found trace of the other St. Clares. I tell you, Sarah, she's got no choice but to marry a farmer and for her to know she's of the quality—" He made a gesture with his hands. "God forbid! The fellow who gets her 's got my pity as 'tis. Why make it any the worse for 'im? Now, don't give me any more excuses, Sarah. It's Jack Clarke or Bob Starling, one or t'other, and the sooner the better—"

CHAPTER TWO

IN their painted blue and red wagons, on foot and on horseback, every farmer and cottager within a twenty-mile radius converged upon Heathstone. With him he brought his wife and children, the corn and wheat and livestock he had to sell and the linens or woollens woven by the women during long winter evenings. But he came to buy also. Shoes and pewter-plates and implements for the farm, as well as many things he did not need but which it would please him to have: toys for the children, ribbons for his daughters' hair, pictures for the house, a beaver hat for himself.

Booths were set up on the green about the old Saxon cross, making lanes which swarmed with people in their holiday dress—full breeches and neck-ruffs and long-sleeved gowns—all many years out of the style but nevertheless kept carefully in wardrobes from one great occasion to the next. Drums beat and fiddles played. The owners of the booths bawled out their wares in voices which were already growing hoarse. Curious crowds stood and stared, each face contorted with sympathy, to watch a sweating man have his rotten tooth pulled, while the dentist loudly proclaimed that the extraction was absolutely painless. There was a fire-eater and a stilt-walker, trained fleas and a contortionist, jugglers and performing apes, and a Punch and Judy show. Over one great tent flew a flag to announce that a play was in progress—but the Puritan influence remained strong enough so that the audience inside was a thin one.

Amber, standing between Bob Starling and Jack Clarke, frowned and tapped her foot as her eyes ran swiftly and impatiently over the crowd.

Where is he!

She had been there since seven o'clock, it was now after nine, and still she had seen no sign of Lord Carlton or his friends. Her stomach churned with nervousness, her hands were wet and her mouth dry. Oh, but sure, if he was coming at all he'd be here by now. He's gone. He's forgot all about me and gone on—

Jack Clarke, a tall blunt-faced young man, gave her a nudge. "Look, Amber. How d'ye like this?"

"What? Oh. Oh, yes, it's mighty fine."

She turned her head and searched the gleefully yelling group about the jack-pudding who stood on a stand, covered from head to foot with a mess of custard which had been thrown at him, so many farthings a custard.

Oh, why doesn't he come!

"Amber—how d'ye like this ribbon—"

She gave them each a quick smile in turn, trying to drag her mind away from him, but she could not. He had been in her thoughts and heart every waking moment, and if she did not see him again today she knew she would never be able to survive the disappointment. No greater crisis had ever confronted her, and she thought she had met many.

She had dressed with extraordinary care and was sure that she had never looked prettier.

Her skirt, which did not quite reach her ankles, was made of bright green linsey-woolsey, caught up high in back to show a red-and-white-striped petticoat. She had pulled the laces of her black stomacher as tight as possible to display her little waist; and after leaving Sarah she had opened her white blouse down to the valley of her breasts. Wreathing the crown of her head was a garland of white daisies, their stems twisted together, and in one hand she carried a broad-brimmed straw bongrace.

Now, must all that trouble go to waste on a pair of dolts who stood hovering over her, jingling the coins in their pockets and glaring at each other?

"I think I like this—" She spoke absently, indicating a red satin ribbon which lay in the pile on the counter and then, frowning again, she turned her head—and saw him.

"Oh!"

For an instant she stood unmoving, and then suddenly she picked up her skirts and rushed off, leaving them to stare after her, bewildered and astonished. Lord Carlton, with Almsbury and one other young man, had just entered the fair grounds and were standing while an old vegetable woman knelt to wipe their boots according to the ancient custom. Amber got there out of breath but smiling and made them a curtsy to which they all replied by removing their hats and bowing gravely.

"Damn me, sweetheart!" cried Almsbury enthusiastically. "But you're as pretty a little baggage as I've seen in the devil's own time!"

"God-a-mercy, m'lord," she said, thanking him. But her eyes went back instantly to Lord Carlton whom she found watching her with a look that made her arms and back begin to tingle. "I was afraid—I was afraid you were gone."

He smiled. "The blacksmith had gone off to the Fair and we had to hammer out the shoe ourselves." He glanced around. "Well—what do you think we should see first?"

In his eyes and the expression about his mouth was a kind of lazy amusement. It embarrassed her, made her feel helpless and tongue-tied and awkward, and a little angry too. For how was she to impress him if she could not think of anything to say, if he saw her turning first white and then red, if she stood and stared at him like a silly pea-goose?

The old woman had finished now and as each of the men gave her a coin to "pay his footing" she went on her way. But she looked back over her shoulder at Amber who was beginning to feel conspicuous, for everyone was watching the Cavaliers and, no doubt, wondering what business a country-girl might have with them. She would have been delighted by the attention but that she was afraid some of her relatives might see her—and she knew what that would mean. They must get away somehow, to a safer quieter place.

"I know what I want to see first," said Almsbury. "It's that booth down here where they're selling sack. We'll meet you at the crossroads below the town, Bruce, when the sun gets here—" He pointed high overhead and then, with another bow, he and the other man left them.

She hesitated a moment, waiting for him to suggest what she wanted to do, but when he did not she turned and started toward the pillory and wooden stocks and the tent where the play was going on. The crowds were still thick, but it was away from the center of the fair grounds. He walked along beside her and for several minutes they said nothing. Amber was glad that it was too noisy to talk without shouting—and she hoped that he would think that was what kept her quiet.

She had a miserable sense of inadequacy, a fear that whatever she said or did would seem foolish to him. Last night, lying in bed, she had seen herself very gay and easy, casting her spell over him as she had over Tom Andrews and Bob Starling and many, many others. But now she was once more aware of some great distance between them and she could not find her way across it. Every sense and emotion had heightened to an almost painful intensity and there was an unnatural brilliance about everything she saw.

To cover her embarrassed confusion Amber looked with the greatest interest at each booth they passed. Finally, as they came to one where a young woman had a great deal of sparkling jewellery for sale, Lord Carlton glanced down at her.

"Do you see anything there you'd like to have?"

Amber gave him a quick look of delighted surprise. All of it looked wonderful to her, but of course it must be very expensive. She had never worn any such ornaments, though her ears had been pierced because Sarah said that when she married she was to have a pair of earrings which had belonged to her mother. Now, of course, if she came home wearing something like that Uncle Matt would be furious and Aunt Sarah would begin to talk to her again about getting married—but the lure of the jewels and the prospect of a gift from his Lordship was more than she could resist.

She answered without hesitation. "I'd like to have some earrings, m'lord."

Already the young woman behind the counter, seeing them pause, had set up a noisy babble and was picking up necklaces and combs and bracelets for her inspection. Now, as Amber mentioned earrings she snatched up a pair from which dangled pieces of crudely cut glass, both coloured and clear.

"Look at these, sweetheart! Fine enough for the ears of a countess, I do vow! Lean over, dear, and I'll try 'em on you. A little closer— There. Why! will you look at that, your Lordship! I vow and swear they make her quite another person, a lady of quality, let me perish! Here, my dear, look at yourself in this glass— Oh, I vow I've never seen such a change come over *anyone* as those jewels make in you, madame—"

She rattled on at a furious rate, holding up a mirror to let Amber see for herself the phenomenal improvement. And Amber leaned forward, tossing her hair back from her face so that her ears would show, her eyes shining with pleasure. They made her feel very grand, and also a little wicked. She gave Lord Carlton a sideways smile to see what he thought about it, longing to have them but afraid of making him think something bad about her if she seemed too eager. He grinned at her, then turned to the other woman.

"How much?"

"Twenty shillings, my lord."

He took a couple of gold coins from his pocket and tossed them onto the counter. "I'm sure they're worth every farthing of it."

He and Amber started on, Amber delighted with her gift and positive that it was all real gold, diamonds, and rubies. "I'll keep 'em always, your Lordship! I vow I'll never wear another jewel!"

"I'm glad they please you, my dear. And now what are we to do? Would you care to see the play?"

With a nod of his head he indicated the tent which they

were approaching. Amber, who had always wanted to see one—
for they had been forbidden ever since she could remember—
cast a quick wistful glance toward it. But now she hesitated,
partly for fear of meeting someone inside whom she knew—
perhaps even more because she wanted to be alone with him,
away from everyone else.

"Oh—well—to tell you truly, sir. I don't think my Uncle Matt
would want me to go—"

And as she stood there beside him, wishing that he would
make the decision for her, she saw—not ten yards away—Agnes
and Lisbeth Morton and Gartrude Shakerly. All three of them
were staring at her with their mouths wide open—amazed, indignant, shocked, furious with jealousy. Amber's eyes met her
cousin's for one instant, she gave an involuntary gasp of horror, and then swiftly looked the other way and tried to pretend
she had not seen them. Nervously her fingers began to pick
at the brim of her bongrace.

"Uds Lud, your Lordship!" she muttered in an excited undertone. "There's my cousin! She's sure to run and tell my
aunt! Let's go over this way—"

She did not see the smile on Carlton's face for already she
had started off, making her way through the crowd, and without glancing around at the three girls he followed her. Amber
looked back just once to make sure that Agnes was not at their
heels and then she gave him the brightest smile she could
muster. But she was scared now. Agnes would rush to find Sarah
or Matt, and after that she would be sought out by some member of the family and summoned back to safety. They must
get away, out of sight—for she was determined to have this hour
or two, whatever discomfort it caused her later.

Now she said hastily: "Here's the churchyard—let's go in and
make a wish at the well."

He stopped then and she stopped too, looking up at him with
a kind of apprehensive defiance. "My dear," he said, "I think
you're only going to get yourself into trouble. Evidently your
uncle's a very moral gentleman and I'm sure he wouldn't care
to have his niece in the company of a Cavalier. Perhaps you're
too young to know it, but the Puritans and the Cavaliers don't

trust each other—particularly where it concerns female relatives."

There was the same lazy sound in his voice, the same look of mild amusement on his face that had so strangely affected her the night before. For she was able to sense that this idle indifference but thinly concealed a temper at once relentless, fierce, and perhaps a little cruel. Without being able to recognize her own desires she was vaguely conscious of wanting to break through that veneer of urbanity, to experience herself something of the stormy power which was there just under the surface, not dormant but carefully leashed.

She answered him recklessly, for she was beginning to feel more sure of herself. "I don't care about my uncle— My aunt always believes me— Leave me alone for that, your Lordship. *Please,* sir, I want to make a wish."

He shrugged his shoulders and they started on, crossed the road and went through the ivy-grown lych-gate to where two small wells stood three feet or so apart. Amber dropped to her knees between them, plunging one hand in each until the cold water covered her wrists, and then closing her eyes she made a silent wish.

I wish for him to fall in love with me.

For a moment she remained still, concentrating intensely, and then lifting each cupped hand she drank the water. He reached out one hand and raised her to her feet.

"I suppose you've wished for all the world," he said. "How long before you'll get it?"

"In a year—if I believe it—but never, if I don't."

"But of course you do?"

"All my other wishes came true. Don't you want to wish too?"

"A year isn't long enough for most of my wishes."

"Not long enough? Gemini! I'd thought a year must be long enough for anything!"

"When you're seventeen, it is."

She began looking around her then, partly because she could no longer meet the steady stare of his green-grey eyes, but also because she was searching for some place where they might go.

The churchyard was too public. Other people were likely to wander that way at any time, and every man or woman or child seemed a threat to her happiness. She felt that they were all in league to call her away, to make her leave him and go back to the dry sterile protection of her uncle and aunt.

At the side of the church was a garden and beyond it the meadow which separated Heathstone from Bluebell Wood. Why, that was the place of course! In the wood it was cool and dark and there were many little nooks where no one would ever see them—she knew several, remembered from the Fairs of the past three or four years. Now she started off that way, hoping that he would think they had merely chanced upon it.

They went through the garden, climbed the stile, and set out across the meadow.

The grass there was sown thickly with buttercups and field daisies and wild yellow irises. Underfoot the ground was spongy with contained water and their feet sank a little at every step. Farther ahead near the river was an orange wash of colour where the marigolds grew, and as they came closer they could see the tall green reeds standing in the water. On the banks were pussywillow trees and across the stream at the edge of the forest was a cluster of aspen, their leaves glistening like sequins in the sun.

"I'd almost forgotten," he said, "how beautiful England is in the spring."

"How long since you left it?"

"Almost sixteen years. My mother and I went abroad after my father was killed at Marston Moor."

"Sixteen years abroad!" she cried incredulously. "Lud, how'd you shift?"

He looked down at her, smiling with a kind of tenderness. "It wasn't what any of us would have chosen, but the choice wasn't ours. And for my part I've got no complaint to make."

"You didn't like it over there?" she demanded, shocked and almost indignant at this blasphemy.

Now they were crossing the swift-flowing river on a narrow shaky footbridge built of logs; below them the fish darted and dragon-flies zoomed low over the water and among the lilypads that grew in a quiet pool. On the other side they entered the forest and took a wandering faint little path which led among the trees and ferns and flowering wild hyacinth. It was cool in there and still, fragrant with the smell of flowers and rotting leaves.

"I suppose it's petty treason for an Englishman to admit he likes another country. But I liked several of them—Italy and France and Spain. But America most of all."

"America! Why, that's across the ocean!" That was, in fact, all she knew about America.

"A long way across," he admitted.

"Was the King there?"

"No. I sailed once on a privateering expedition with his Majesty's cousin, Prince Rupert, and another time on a merchant-fleet."

She was entranced. To have seen such faraway places—to have even sailed across the ocean! It was incredible as a fairy-tale. Heathstone was as far from home as she had ever been, and that just twice a year, for the spring and autumn fairs. While the only person in her acquaintance who had been to London, twenty-five miles south-east of Marygreen, was the cobbler.

"What a fine thing it must be to see the great world!" She heaved a sigh. "Have you been to London, too?"

"Just twice since I've been old enough to remember. I was there ten years ago and then again a couple of months after Cromwell died. But I didn't stay long either time."

They had stopped now and he gave a glance up at the sky, through the trees, as though to see how much time was left. Amber, watching him, was suddenly struck with panic. Now he was going—out again into that great world with its bustle and noise and excitement—and she must stay here. She had a terrible new feeling of loneliness, as if she stood in some solitary corner at a party where she was the only stranger. Those places he had seen, she would never see; those fine things he had done, she would never do. But worst of all she would never see him again.

"It's not time to go yet!"

"No. I have a while longer."

44

Amber dropped onto her knees in the grass, her mouth pouting, eyes rebellious—and after a moment he sat down facing her. For several seconds she continued staring sulkily, mulling over her dismal future, and then swiftly her eyes went to his. He was watching her, steadily, carefully. She stared back at him, her heart pounding, and there began to steal over her a slow weakness and languor, so consuming that even her eyes felt heavy. Every part of her was tormented with longing for him. And yet she was half-scared, uncertain, and reticent, filled with a sense of dread almost greater than her desire.

At last his arm reached out, went around her waist, and drew her slowly toward him; Amber, tipping her head to meet his mouth, slid both her arms about him.

The restraint he had shown thus far now vanished swiftly, giving way to a passion that was savage, violent, ruthlessly selfish. Amber, inexperienced but not innocent, returned his kisses eagerly. Spurred by the caressing of his mouth and hands, her desire mounted apace with his, and though at first she had heard, somewhere far back in her mind, Sarah calling out to her, warning her, the sound and the image grew fainter, dissolved, and was gone.

But when he forced her back onto the earth she gave a quick movement of protest and a little cry—this was as far as her knowledge went. Something mysterious, almost terrible, must lie beyond. Her hands pushed at his chest and she gave a frightened little sob, twisting her face away from his. Her fear now was irrational, intense, almost hysterical.

"No!" she cried. "Let me go!"

She saw his face above her, and his eyes had become pure glittering green. Amber, crying, half-mad with passion and terror, suddenly let herself relax.

With slow reluctance Amber became again conscious of the surrounding world, and of both of them as separate individuals. She drew a deep luxurious sigh, her eyes still closed—she felt that she could not have moved so much as a finger.

After a long while he drew away from her and sat up, forearms resting on his knees, a long blade of grass between his teeth, staring ahead. His tanned face was wet with sweat and he mopped across it with the black-velvet sleeve of his doublet. Amber lay perfectly still beside him, eyes closed and one arm flung over her forehead. She was warm and drowsy, marvellously content, and glad with every fibre of her being that it had happened.

It seemed that until this moment she had been only half alive.

Aware of his eyes on her she turned her head slightly and gave him a lazy smile. She wanted to say that she loved him but did not quite dare, even now. She wished he would say that he loved her, but he only bent and kissed her, very gently.

"I'm sorry," he said softly. "I didn't expect to find you a virgin."

"I'm glad I was."

Was that all he was going to say? She waited, watching him, beginning to feel uncertain and a little afraid. He looked again as he had when she first saw him—she could never tell now by his expression or manner how close they had been. She was surprised and hurt, for what had happened should have changed him as much as it had her. Nothing should ever be the same again, for either of them.

At last he got up, squinting overhead at the sun. "They'll be waiting for me. We want to get into London before nightfall." He reached down a hand to help her and she jumped up quickly, shaking out her hair, smoothing her blouse, touching her earrings to make sure she had not lost them.

"Lud, we mustn't be late!"

Knocking at the dust on his hat, he gave her a glance of quick astonishment, then set it back on his head. He scowled, as though he had got more than he had bargained for.

At his look, Amber's smile and excitement went suddenly dead. "Don't you *want* me to go?" She was almost ready to cry.

"My dear, your aunt and uncle would never approve."

"What do I care! I want to go with *you!* I hate Marygreen! I never want to see it again! Oh, please, your Lordship. *Let* me go with you." Marygreen and her life there had suddenly become intolerable. He had crystallized all the restlessness, the thirst and longing for a broader, brighter life which had been

46

working within her, half ·unrealized, ever since she had first talked to the cobbler many years ago.

"London's no place for an unmarried girl without money or acquaintance," he said in a matter-of-fact tone, which even Amber knew meant that he did not care to be troubled with her. And then he added, perhaps because he was sorry to hurt her, "I won't be there long. And what would you do when I go? It wouldn't be easy to come back here—I know well enough what an English village thinks of such escapades. And in London there aren't many means of livelihood open to a woman. No, my dear, I think you'd better stay here."

All of a sudden, to his surprise as well as her own, she burst into tears. "I won't stay here! I *won't!* I can't stay here now! How d'ye think I'm to explain to my Uncle Matt where I've been these two hours—when a hundred people I know saw us leave the fair grounds!"

A look of annoyance crossed his face, but she did not see it. "I told you that would happen," he reminded her. "But even if he's angry it'll be better for you to go back and—"

She interrupted him. "I'm not going back! I won't live here any more, d'ye hear? And if you won't take me with you— then I'll go alone!" She stopped suddenly and stood looking up at him, angry and defiant, but pleading, too. "Oh, please— your Lordship. Take me along."

They stood and stared at each other, but at last his scowl faded away and he smiled. "Very well, you little minx, I'll take you. But I won't marry you when we get there—and don't forget, whatever happens, that I told you so."

She heard only the first part of what he said, for the last seemed of no immediate importance. "Oh, your Lordship! *Can* I go! I won't be any trouble to you, I swear it!"

"I don't know about that," he said slowly. "I think you'll be aplenty."

It was mid-afternoon when they rode into London over Whitechapel Road, passing the many small villages which hung on the edge of the city and which despite their nearness to the capital differed in no external aspect from Heathstone or Marygreen. In the open fields cattle grazed, wrenching lazily at the grass, and cottagers' wives had spread their wash to dry on the bushes. As they rode along they were recognized for returning Royalists and were cheered wildly. Little boys ran along beside them and tried to touch their boots, women leant from their windows, men stopped in the streets to take off their hats and shout.

"Welcome home!"

"Long live the King!"

"A health to his Majesty!"

The walled City was a pot-pourri of the centuries, old and ugly, stinking and full of rottenness, but full of colour too and picturesqueness and a decayed sort of beauty. On all sides it was surrounded with a wreath of laystalls, piled refuse carted that far and left, overgrown with stinking-orage. The streets were narrow, some of them paved with cobblestones but most of them not, and down the center or along the sides ran open sewage kennels. Posts strung out at intervals served to separate the carriage-way from the narrow space left to pedestrians. And across the streets leaned the houses, each story overhanging the one beneath so as to shut out light and air almost completely from the tightest of the alleys.

Church-spires dominated the skyline, for there were more than a hundred within the walls and the sound of their bells was the ceaseless passionately beautiful music of London. Creaking signs swung overhead painted with golden lambs, blue boars, red lions, and there were a number of bright new ones bearing the Stuart coat-of-arms or the profile of a swarthy black-haired man with a crown on his head. In the country it had been sunny and almost warm but here the fog hung heavily, thickened with the smoke from the fires of the soap-boilers and lime-burners, and there was a penetrating chill in the air.

The streets were crowded: Vendors strolled along crying their wares in an age-old sing-song which was not intended to be understood, and a housewife could make almost all necessary purchases at her own doorstep. Porters carried staggering loads on their backs and swore loudly at whoever interrupted their progress. Apprentices hung in the shop doorways bawling their recommendations, not hesitating to grab a customer by the sleeve and urge him inside.

There were ballad-singers and beggars and cripples, satin-suited young fops and ladies of quality in black-velvet masks, sober merchants and ragged waifs, an occasional liveried footman going ahead to make way for the sedan-chair of some baronet or countess. Most of the traffic was on foot but some travelled in hackney-coaches which plied for public hire, in chairs, or on horseback, but when the traffic snarled, as it often did, these were liable to be stalled for many minutes at a time.

It took no sharp eye to see at a glance that the Londoner was a different breed from the country Englishman. He was arrogant with the knowledge of his power, for he was the kingdom and he knew it. He was noisy and quarrelsome, ready to start a murderous battle over which man got the walk nearest the wall. He had supported Parliament eighteen years before but now he prepared joyously for the return of his legitimate sovereign, drinking his health in the streets, swearing that he had always loved the Stuarts. He hated a Frenchman for his speech and his manners, his dress and his religion, and would pelt him with refuse or blow the froth from a mug of ale into his face before proposing a toast to his damnation. But he hated a Dutchman or any other foreigner almost as fiercely, for to him London was the world, and a man worth less for living out of it.

London—stinking dirty noisy brawling colourful—was the heart of England, and its citizens ruled the nation.

Amber felt that she had come home and she fell in love with it, as she had with Lord Carlton, at first sight. The intense violent energy and aliveness found a response in her strongest and deepest emotions. This city was a challenge, a provocation, daring everything—promising even more. She felt instinctively, as a good Londoner should, that now she had seen all there was to see. No other place on earth could stand in comparison.

The group of horsemen parted company at Bishopsgate, each going his separate way, and Bruce and Amber went on alone with two of the serving-men. They rode down Gracious Street and, at the sign of the Royal Saracen, turned and went through a great archway into the courtyard of the inn. The building en-

49

closed it on every side and galleries ran all the way around each of the four stories. Bruce helped her to dismount and they went in. The host was nowhere about and after a few moments Bruce asked her to wait while he went out to find him.

Amber watched him go, her eyes shining with pride and admiration and the almost breathless excitement she felt. I'm in London! It can't be true but it is. I *am* in London! It seemed incredible that her life could have changed so swiftly and so irrevocably in less than twenty-four hours. For she was determined that no matter what happened she would never return to Marygreen. Never as long as she lived.

Wearing Bruce's cloak she moved nearer to the fire, reaching out her hands to its warmth, and as she did so she became conscious that there were three or four men sitting over against the diamond-paned casement, drinking their ale and watching her. She had a quick sense of pleased surprise, for these men were Londoners, and she turned her head a little to give them a view of her profile with its delicate slightly tilted nose, full lips, and small round chin.

At that moment Bruce came back, looking down and grinning at the little man who walked beside him and who reached scarcely to his shoulder. Evidently he was the host, and he seemed to be in a state of great excitement.

"By God, your Lordship!" he was shouting. "But I swear I thought you were dead! They were here not a half-hour after you'd gone, those Roundhead rogues, and they tore my house apart to find you! And when they didn't they were in such a rage they carried me into the courtyard and flung me into the coalhole!" He made a noise and spat onto the floor. "Bah! Plague take 'em! I hope to see 'em all strung up like hams on Tyburn Hill!"

Bruce laughed. "I don't doubt you'll get your wish." By now they had come to where Amber was standing and the host gave a start, for he had not realized she was there; then he made her a jerky little bow. "Mrs. St. Clare," said Bruce, "may I introduce our host, Mr. Gumble?" She was relieved that he called her "Mrs." St. Clare, for only very little girls and professed whores were called Miss.

Amber nodded her head and smiled, feeling that she had now advanced too far in the world to curtsy to an innkeeper. But she did have an uncomfortable moment of wondering if the look he gave her meant that he disapproved of his Lordship travelling with a woman who was not his wife. Bruce, however, seemed as casual as if she were his sister, and Mr. Gumble immediately took up the conversation where he had been interrupted:

"It's mighty lucky you're not a day later, my lord. I vow and swear my house has never been so crowded—all England's come to London to welcome his Majesty home! By the end of the week there won't be a room to let between here and Temple Bar!"

"How is it you haven't set a crown on your Saracen to pass him for the King? Half the signs we've seen are King's Heads ·or King's Arms."

"Ho! They are, at that! And have you heard what they're saying now? If the King's Head is empty—the King's Arms are full!" He shouted with laughter at that, Bruce grinned, and even the men across the room gave out noisy guffaws. But Amber did not know enough of his Majesty's reputation to quite understand the·jest.

The little man took out his handkerchief and mopped at his perspiring brow. "Ah, well, we'll be mighty glad to have him home, I warrant you. 'Sdeath, your Lordship! You'd never think what we've been through here! No cards, no dice, no plays. No drinking, no dancing. My God! They even wanted to make fornication a capital crime!"

Bruce laughed. "I'm glad I stayed abroad."

But again Amber missed the point because she did not know what "fornication" meant. Still, she smiled appreciatively and tried to look as though such witticisms were a commonplace to her.

"Well, enough of this. Your Lordship must be hungry, and perhaps tired. I have the Flower de Luce still vacant—"

"Good! It brought me luck last time— Perhaps it will again."

They started up the stairs and as they went they heard the

men below begin to sing, their voices roaring out in jovial good humour, off key and untuned:

"The King he loves a bottle, my boys,
The King he loves a bowl!
 He will fill a bumping glass
 To every buxom lass
And make cuckolds of us all, my boys.
And make cuckolds of us all!"

At the top of the staircase Mr. Gumble unlocked a door and stepped back to let them go in. The room was of good size and, in Amber's opinion, very magnificent, for she had never seen anything like it before.

The walls were panelled oak, dark and rich, and the chimney piece was also oak, elaborately carved with patterns of fruit and flowers. The floor was bare and all the furniture was in the heavy florid style belonging to the early years of the century, though the chairs and stools had been covered with thick cushions of sage-green or ruby-coloured velvet, worn just enough to have acquired a look of mellowness.

In the bed-chamber was an immense four-poster bed hung with red velvet curtains which could be pulled at night to enclose the occupants in privacy and suffocation. Two wardrobes stood against the wall for clothing. There were several stools and a couple of chairs, a small table with a mirror hung above it, and a writing-table. One side of the room was filled with long windows and had doors opening onto the gallery, from which a flight of stairs led down to the courtyard.

Amber stared about her, momentarily speechless, while Bruce said, "It looks like home. We'll take our supper up here— Send whatever you think is best."

After several assurances that he would furnish anything at all which either of them might require, Mr. Gumble left—and Amber burst suddenly out of her spell. Flinging off the cloak she ran to look out the parlour windows, down two stories into the street. A group of boys had built a fire there and were roasting skewered chunks of meat in derision of the Rump Parliament; the voices of the men still singing downstairs filtered up faintly through the solid walls.

"Oh! London! London!" she cried passionately. "I love you!"

Bruce smiled, tossing off his hat, and coming up behind her he slid one arm about her waist. "You fall in love easily." And then, as she turned about quickly to look up at him he added, "London eats up pretty girls, you know."

"Not me!" she assured him triumphantly. "I'm not afraid!"

CHAPTER THREE

AND now at last, when it had seemed that nothing would ever change, he was coming home to England and to his people. Charles Stuart was Charles Lackland no longer.

Eleven years before, a little band of Puritan extremists had beheaded his father—and the groan that had gone up from the watching thousands echoed across Europe. It was a crime that would forever lie heavily upon English hearts. Exiled in France, the dead King's eldest son first knew that his efforts to save his father had failed when his chaplain knelt and addressed him as "your Majesty." He turned and went into his bedroom to mourn alone. He found himself a king with no kingdom, a ruler with no subjects.

And in England the mighty heel of Cromwell came down on the necks of the English people. It was now a crime to be a member of the aristocracy, and to have been loyal to the late King was an offense often punishable by confiscation of lands and money. Those who could followed Charles II abroad, hoping to return someday in a happier time. A gloomy piety settled over the land, discouraging much that was essentially English: the merry good humour, the boisterous delight in sports and feasts and holidays, the robust enjoyment of drinking and dancing and gambling and love-making.

May-poles were chopped down, theatres closed. Discreet women left off their gaily coloured satin and velvet gowns, put away their masks and fans and curls and false hair, covered in the low necklines of their dresses and no longer dared touch their lips with rouge or stick on a black patch for fear of falling under the suspicion of having Royalist sympathies. Even the furniture grew more sober.

For eleven years Cromwell ruled the land. But England found at last that he was mortal.

When news of his illness began to get abroad an anxious crowd of soldiers and citizens gathered at the gates of the Palace. The country was in terror, remembering the chaotic years of the Civil Wars when bands of roving soldiers had pillaged through all the length and breadth of England, plundering the farms, breaking into and robbing houses, driving off the sheep and cattle, killing those who dared to resist. They did not want Cromwell to live, but they were afraid to have him die.

As night closed in, a great storm rose, gathering fury until the houses rocked on their foundations, trees were uprooted, and turrets and steeples crashed to the ground. Such a storm could have for them only one meaning. The Devil was coming to claim the soul of Oliver Cromwell. And Cromwell himself cried out in terror: "It's a fearful thing to fall into the hands of the living God!"

The storm swept all of Europe, raging through the night and on into the next day, and when Cromwell died at three o'clock in the afternoon it was still desolating the island. His body was immediately embalmed and buried with haste. But his followers clothed a waxen image of him in robes-of-state and set it up in Somerset House, as though he had been a king. In derision the people flung refuse at his funeral escutcheon.

But there was no one to take his place, and almost two years of semi-anarchy followed. His son, whom the Protector had designated to succeed him, had none of his father's ability, and at last the military autocrats got rid of him—much to his own relief. Immediately skirmishes began between the cavalry and the infantry, between veterans and new recruits, and another civil war between the army and the people seemed inevitable. Despair flooded the land. To go through with it all again—when nothing had been gained the first time. They began to think of a restored monarchy with longing, as their only salvation.

54

General Monk, who had served Charles I but who had finally gone into service for Cromwell when the King was dead, marched from Scotland and occupied the capital with his troops. Monk, though a soldier, believed that the military must be subordinate to the civil power, and it was his hope to liberate the country from its slavery to the army. He waited cautiously to determine the temper of the country and then at last, convinced that the royalist fervour which swept through all classes was an irresistible tide, he declared for Charles Stuart. A free Parliament was summoned, the King wrote them a letter from Breda declaring his good intentions, and England was to be, once more, a monarchy—as she preferred.

London was packed to overflowing with Royalists and their wives and families, and if a man existed in all the city who did not wholeheartedly long for his Majesty's return he was silent, or hidden. And the gradual return to laughter and pleasure which had been apparent since the end of the wars took a sudden violent spurt. Restraint was thrown off. A sober garment, a pious look were regarded as sure signs of a Puritan sympathy and were shunned by whoever would show his loyalty to the King. The world did a somersault and everything which had been vice was now, all at once, virtue.

But it was not merely a wish to appear loyal, a temporary exuberance at the returning monarchy, the joyousness of sudden relief from oppression. It was something which struck deeper, and which would be more permanent. The long years of war had broken families, undermined old social traditions, destroyed the barriers of convention. A new social pattern was in the making—a pattern brilliant but also gaudy, gay but also wanton, elegant but also vulgar.

On the 29th of May, 1660—his thirtieth birthday—Charles II rode into London.

It was for him the end of fifteen years of exile, of trailing over Europe from one country to another, unwanted anywhere because his presence was embarrassing to politicians trying to do business with his father's murderer. It was the end of poverty, of going always threadbare, of having to wheedle another day's food from some distrustful innkeeper. It was the end of the fruit-less efforts to regain his kingdom which had occupied him incessantly for over ten years. Above all it was the end of humiliation and scorn, of being ridiculed and slighted by men who were his inferiors in rank and in everything else. It was at long last the end of being a man without a country and a king without a crown.

The day was clear and bright, brilliantly sunlit, perfectly cloudless, and people told one another that the weather was a good omen. From London Bridge to Whitehall, along his line of march, every street and balcony and window and rooftop was packed. And though the procession was not expected until after noon, by eight in the morning there was not a foot of space to be found. Trainbands to the number of 12,000 men lined the streets—they had fought against Charles I but were now detailed to keep the crowds in order for his son's return.

The signs were draped with May flowers; great arches of hawthorn spanned every street; and green oak boughs had been nailed over the fronts of many buildings. Garlands looped from window to window were decorated with ribbons and silver spoons, brightly polished, gleaming in the sun. From the homes of the well-to-do floated tapestries and gold and scarlet and green banners—flags whipped out gallantly on even the humblest rooftop. The fountains ran with wine and bells pealed incessantly from every church steeple in the city. At last the deep ponderous booming of cannon announced that the procession had reached London Bridge.

It began to wind slowly through the narrow streets, the horses' hoofs clopping rhythmically on the pavement, trumpets and clarinets shrilling, kettledrums rolling with a sound as of thunder echoing across the hills. The whole procession glittered and sparkled—fabulously, almost unbelievably splendid. It passed in a stream that seemed to have no end: troops of men in scarlet-and-silver cloaks, black velvet and gold, silver and green, with swords flashing, banners flying, the horses prancing and snorting, lifting their hoofs daintily and with pride. Hour after hour it went on until the eyes of the onlookers grew dazzled and began to ache, their throats were raw from shouting, and their ears roared with the incessant clamour.

The hundreds of loyal Cavaliers, men who had fought for the first Charles, who had sold their goods and their lands to help him and who had followed his son abroad, rode almost at the end. They were, without exception, handsomely dressed and mounted—though all this finery had been got on credit. After them came the Lord Mayor, carrying his naked sword of office. On one side of him was General Monk, a short stout ugly little man, who nevertheless sat his horse with dignity and commanded respect from soldiers and civilians alike. Next to the King he was perhaps the most popular man in England that day. And on the Lord Mayor's other side rode George Villiers, second Duke of Buckingham.

The Duke, a big, handsome, flagrantly virile man, with hair blonde as a god's, smiled and nodded to the women in the balconies who flung him kisses and tossed flowers in his path. His rank was second only to that of the princes of the blood, and his private fortune was the greatest in England. For he had contrived to marry the daughter of the Parliamentarian general to whom his vast lands had been given, and so had saved himself. Many knew that for his numerous treacheries he was in disfavor amounting almost to disgrace, but the Duke looked as well pleased with himself as though he had personally engineered the Restoration.

Following them came several pages, many trumpeters whose banners bore the royal coat-of-arms, and drummers shining with sweat as they beat out a mighty roar. At their heels rode Charles II, hereditary King of England, Ireland, and France, Monarch of Great Britain, Defender of the Faith. A frenzy of adoration, hysterical and almost religious, swept through the people as he passed, and surged along before him. They fell to their knees, reaching out their hands toward him, sobbing, crying his name again and again.

"God bless your Majesty!"

"Long live the King!"

Charles rode slowly, smiling, raising one hand to them in greeting.

He was tall, more than six feet, with a look of robust good health and animal strength. His physique was magnificent and never showed to better advantage than on horseback. The product of many nationalities, he looked far more a Bourbon or a Medici than he did a Stuart. His skin was swarthy, his eyes black, and he had an abundance of black shining hair that fell heavily to his shoulders and rolled over on the ends into great natural rings; when he smiled his teeth gleamed white beneath a narrow moustache. His features were harsh and strongly marked, scared by disillusion and cynicism, and yet in spite of that he had a glowing charm that went out to each of them, warming their hearts.

They loved him on the instant.

On either side of him rode his two younger brothers. James, Duke of York, was likewise tall, likewise athletic, but his hair was blonde and his eyes blue, and more than any of the other children had he resembled his dead father. He was a handsome man, three years younger than the King, with thick well-defined dark eyebrows, a slight cleft in his chin and a stubborn mouth. But it was his misfortune that he did not have his brother's instantly winning manner. And from the first they held in reserve their estimation cf him, critical of a certain coolness and hauteur they discovered in his expression which offended them. Henry, Duke of Gloucester, was only twenty, a happy vivacious young man who looked as though he was in love with all the world and did not doubt that in return it loved him.

It was late that night when at last the King begged off from further ceremonies and went to his own apartments in Whitehall Palace, thoroughly exhausted but happy. He entered his bedchamber still wearing his magnificent robes and carrying on one arm a little black-and-tan spaniel with a plume-like tail, long ears, and the petulant face of a cross old lady. Between his feet scampered half-a-dozen dogs, yapping shrilly—but at a sudden raucous screech they skidded to a startled halt and looked up. There was a green parrot, teetering in a ring hung from the ceiling, eyeing the dogs and squawking angrily.

"Damn the dogs! Here they come again!"

Recognizing an old enemy the spaniels quickly recovered their courage and ran to stand in a pack beneath him, jumping and barking while the bird bawled down his curses. Charles and all the gentlemen who followed him laughed to see them, but finally the King gave a tired wave of his hand and the menagerie was removed to another room.

One of the courtiers thrust his fingers into his ears and shook his head vigorously. "Jesus! I swear I'll never be able to hear again! If there's a man left in London who can use his voice tomorrow—he's a traitor and deserves to be hanged."

Charles smiled. "To tell you the truth, gentlemen, I think I can blame only myself for having stayed so long abroad. I haven't met a man these past four days who hasn't told me he's always desired my return."

The others laughed. For now that they were home again, lords of creation once more and not unwanted paupers edged from one country to another, they found it easy to laugh. The years gone by had begun already to take on a kind of patina, and now they knew the story had a happy ending they could see that, after all, it had been a romantic adventure.

Charles, who was being helped out of his clothes, turned to one of the men and spoke to him in a low voice. "Did she come, Progers?"

"She's waiting belowstairs, Sire."

"Good."

Edward Progers was his Majesty's Page of the Backstairs. He handled private money transactions, secret correspondence, and served in an ex-officio capacity as the King's pimp. It was a position of no mean prestige, and of considerable activity.

At last they trooped out and left him alone, giving them a lazy wave of his arm as he stood there in riding-boots, knee-length breeches, and a full-sleeved white linen shirt. Progers went also, by another door, and Charles strolled over to stand by the open windows, snapping his fingers impatiently while he waited. The night air was cool and fresh, and just below ran the river, where several small barges floated at anchor, their lanterns pricking the water like so many fireflies. The Palace lay round the bend of the Thames, but the innumerable bonfires back in the city had cast a glow against the sky and he could see the flashing yellow trails of rockets as they shot up and then dropped hissing into the water. The booming of cannon came again and again, and faintly the sound of bells still ringing.

For several moments he stood at the windows, staring out, but the expression on his face was moody and almost sad. He looked like a tired, bitter, and disappointed man, far more than like a king returned in triumph to his people. And then, at the sound of a door opening behind him, he spun swiftly on his heel, and his face lighted with pleasure and admiration.

"Barbara!"

"Your Majesty!"

She bent her head, curtsying low, as Progers backed discreetly out of the room.

She was some inches smaller than he but still tall enough to be imposing. Her figure was magnificent, with swelling breasts and small waist, suggesting lovely hips and legs concealed by the full satin skirts of her gown. She wore a violet velvet cloak, the hood lined in black fox, and she carried a great black-fox muff with a spray of amethysts pinned to it. Her hair was dark red, her skin clear and white, and the reflection from her cloak changed her blue eyes to purple. She was strikingly, almost aggressively beautiful, creating an immediate impression of passion and a wild, lusty untamableness.

Instantly Charles crossed and took her into his arms, kissing her mouth, and when at last he released her she tossed aside her muff and dropped off her cloak, aware of his eyes upon her. She stretched out her hands and he took both of them in his.

"Oh! it was wonderful! How they love you!"

He smiled and gave a slight shrug. "How they'd have loved anyone who offered them release from the army."

She disengaged herself and walked a little from him toward the windows, consciously flirtatious. "Do you remember, Sire," she asked him softly, "when you said you'd love me till kingdom come?"

He smiled. "I thought it would be forever."

He came to stand behind her, his hands going to her breasts, and his head bent so that his mouth touched the nape of her neck. His voice was husky, deep, and there was a swift demanding impatience on his face. Barbara's hands had tight hold on the window ledge and her throat arched back, but she stared straight ahead, out into the night.

"Won't it be forever?"

"Of course it will, Barbara. And I'll be here forever too. Come what may, there's one thing I know—I'll never set out on my travels again." Suddenly he put one arm under her knees and swung her up off the floor, holding her easily.

"Where does the Monsieur think you are?" "The Monsieur" was their name for her husband.

She put her lips to his smooth-shaven cheek. "I told him I was going to stay the night with my aunt—but I think he guesses I'm here." An expression of contempt crossed her face. "Roger's a fool!"

CHAPTER FOUR

AMBER sat looking at herself in the mirror that hung above the dressing-table.

She was wearing a low-cut, lace-and-ribbon-trimmed smock made of sheer white linen, with belled, elbow-length sleeves and a long, full skirt. Laced over it was a busk—a short, tight little boned corset which forced her breasts high and squeezed two inches from the twenty-two her waist normally measured. With it on she had some difficulty both in breathing and in bending over, but it gave her such a luxurious sense of fashionableness that she would gladly have suffered twice the discomfort. Her skirt was pulled up over her knees so that she could see her crossed legs and the black silk stockings that covered them; there were lacy garters tied in bows just below her knees, and she wore high-heeled black-satin pumps.

Behind her hovered a dapper little man, Monsieur Baudelaire, newly arrived from Paris and having at his fingers' ends all the very latest tricks to make an Englishwoman's head look like a

Parisienne's. He had been working over her for almost an hour, prattling in a half-French and half-English jargon about "heart-breakers" and "kiss-curls" and "favourites." Most of the time she did not understand what he said, but she had watched with breathless fascination the nimble manipulations of his combs and oils and brushes and pins.

Now, at last, he had her hair looking glossy as taffy-coloured satin, parted in the center and lying sleekly over the crown of her head in a pattern of shadowy waves. Fat shining curls hung to her shoulders, propped out a little by invisible combs to make them look even thicker. In back he had pulled all the hair up from her neck and braided and twisted it into a high scroll, securing it there with several gold-headed bodkins. It was the style, he told her, affected by all the great ladies and it quite transformed her features, giving her a piquant air at once provocative and alluring. Like a cook decorating his master-piece he now fastened one pert black-satin bow at each temple and then stood back, clasping his hands, tipping his head to one side like a curious little bird.

"Ah, madame!" he cried, seeing not madame at all but only her hair and his own handiwork. "Oh, madame! C'est mag-nifique! C'est une triomphe! C'est la plus belle—" Words fail-ing him, he rolled his eyes and spread his hands.

Amber quite agreed. "Gemini!" She turned her head from side to side, holding up a hand mirror so as to see both back and front. "Bruce won't know me!"

It had taken six weeks to get a gown made, for every good tailor and dressmaker in London had more orders than it was possible to fill. But Madame Darnier had promised to have her dress finished that afternoon and his Lordship had told her that he would take her wherever she wanted to go. She had been counting the days eagerly, for so far she had had little amuse-ment but hanging out the windows to watch the crowds in the streets and running down to make purchases from every vendor who passed. Lord Carlton was gone a great deal of the time—where, she did not know—and though he had bought a coach which was usually at her disposal she was ashamed to go out in her country clothes.

Now, everything would be different.

When she was alone she had occasional pangs of homesickness, thinking of Sarah, whom she had really loved, of the numerous young men who had run at her beck and call, of what a great person she had been in the village where everything she did was noticed and commented upon. But more often she thought of that bygone life with scornful contempt.

What would I be doing now? she would ask herself.

Helping Sarah in the still-room, spinning, dipping rush-lights, cooking, setting out for the market or going to church. It seemed incredible that such dull occupations could once have engaged her from the time she got up, very early, until she went to bed, also very early.

Now she lay as long as she liked in the mornings, snuggled deep into a feather mattress, dreaming, lost in luxurious reverie. And her thoughts had just one theme: Lord Carlton. She was violently in love, completely dazzled, dejected when he was gone and wildly happy when they were together. And yet she knew very little about him and most of that little she had learned from Almsbury, who had come twice when Bruce was away.

She found out that Almsbury was not his name, as she had thought, but his title, the whole of which was John Randolph, Earl of Almsbury. He had told her that they had passed through Marygreen because they had landed at Ipswich and gone north from there a few miles to Carlton Hall where Bruce had got a boxful of jewels which his mother had not dared take when they fled the country—the territory having been at that time in Parliamentary hands and overrun with soldiers. Marygreen and Heathstone lay on the main road from there to London.

It seemed to her a miracle wrought by God Himself that she had chanced to be standing near the green at the moment they had come along. For Sarah had first told Agnes to take the gingerbread, but Amber had coaxed until she let her go instead— she was always eager to get away from the farm and out into the wider world of Marygreen. Agnes had been furious but Amber had sailed off, humming to herself and keeping a quick eye for whatever or whoever might be about. And then she had loitered so long with Tom Andrews coming across the meadow that another quarter-hour and she would never have seen them at all. By such thoughts she convinced herself that they had been fated since birth to meet on the Marygreen common, the fifth day of May, 1660.

He told her that Bruce was twenty-nine, that both his parents were dead and that he had one younger sister who had married a French count and lived now in Paris. She was very much interested in what he had done during the sixteen years he had been away from England, and Almsbury told her something of that also.

In 1647 both of them had served as officers in the French army, volunteer service being an expected part of every gentleman's training. Two years later Bruce had sailed with Prince Rupert's privateers, preying on the shipping of Parliament. There had followed·another interval in the French army and then a buccaneering expedition to the West Indies and the Guinea Coast with Rupert. Almsbury himself had no taste for life at sea and preferred to remain with the Court, which had led a wandering hand-to-mouth existence in taverns and lodging-houses over half of Europe. With Bruce's return they had travelled together around the Continent, living by their wits; which meant, for the most part, by the proceeds from their gambling. And two years ago they had been in the Spanish army, fighting France and England. Both of them, he said, were the heirs of their own right hands.

It was the pattern of life which had been generally followed by the exiled nobility, with the difference that Carlton was more restless than most and grew quickly bored with the diversions of a court. To Amber it sounded the most lively and fascinating existence on earth and she always intended to ask Bruce to tell her more of what he had done.

To help her while away the days he had employed a French instructor, a dancing-master, a man to teach her to play the guitar, and another to teach her to sing: each one came twice a week. She practised industriously, for she wanted very much to seem a fine lady and thought that these accomplishments would make her more alluring to him. She had yet to hear Lord Carlton say that he loved her, and she would have learned to eat fire or walk a tightrope if she had thought it could call forth the magic words. Now she was counting heavily upon the effect her new clothes and coiffure might have on his heart.

Just then there was a knock at the outer door and Amber leaped up to answer it. But before she had got far a buxom, middle-aged woman came hurrying into the room, her taffeta skirts whistling, out of breath and excited.

She was Madame Darnier, another Parisian come to London to take advantage of the rabid francophilia which raged there among the aristocracy. Her black hair was streaked with grey and her cheeks were bright pink, a great chou of green satin ribbon was pinned atop her head just behind a frontlet of false curls, and her stiff shiny black gown was cut to a precarious depth. But still she contrived, as a Frenchwoman should, to look elegant rather than absurd. In her wake scooted a young girl, plainly dressed, bearing in her arms a great gilded wooden box.

"Quick!" cried Amber, clasping her hands and giving an excited little jump. "Let me see it!"

Madame Darnier, chattering French, motioned at the girl to lay the box on a table, off which she grandly swept Amber's green wool skirt and striped cotton petticoat. And then, with a magnificent flourish, she flung up the lid and at one swoop snatched out her creation, holding it at arm's length for them to see. Both Amber and the hairdresser gasped, falling back a step or two, while the other girl beamed with pride, sharing Madame Darnier's triumph.

"Ohhh—" breathed Amber, and then, *"Oh!"* She had never seen anything so lovely in her life.

It was made of black and honey-coloured satin with a tight, pointed bodice, deep round neckline, full sleeves to the elbows, and a sweeping gathered skirt, over which was a second skirt of exquisite black lace. The cloak was honey-coloured velvet lined in black satin and the attached hood had a black fox border. There was a lace fan, long perfumed beige gloves, a great fox muff, and one of the black velvet vizard-masks which every fine lady wore when going abroad. In fact, all the trappings of high fashion.

"Oh, let me put it on!"

Madame Darnier was horrified. "Mais, non, madame! First we must paint the face!"

"Mais, oui! First we must paint the face!" echoed Monsieur Baudelaire.

They went back to the table, all four of them, and there Madame Darnier untied a great red-velvet kerchief and spread out its contents: bottles and jars and small China pots, a rabbit's foot, an eyebrow brush, tiny booklets of red Spanish paper, pencils, beauty patches. Amber gave a surprised little shriek when the first eyebrow was pulled out, but after that she sat patiently, in a condition of ecstatic delight at the change she saw coming over herself. Arguing, chattering, shrieking among themselves, in half an hour they had made her into a creature of polish and sparkle and artifice—a worldly woman, at least in appearance.

And then at last she was ready to put on her gown, a major enterprise, for there must not be one wrinkle made in it, not a hair displaced, not a smear of lip-pomade or a smudge of powder. It took all three of them to accomplish that, with Madame Darnier scolding and clucking, screaming alternately at the girl and at Monsieur Baudelaire. But at last they had it settled upon her, Madame pulling the neckline down so that all of her shoulders and most of her breasts showed, and finally she put the fan into her hand and ordered her to walk slowly across the room and turn and face them.

"Mon Dieu!" she said then, with complacent satisfaction. "If you don't outdo Madame Palmer herself!"

"Who's Madame Palmer?" Amber wanted to know, looking down to examine herself.

"His Majesty's mistress." Madame Darnier rustled across the room to adjust a fold, twisting one sleeve a quarter of an inch, smoothing a tiny wrinkle from the bodice. "For today, at least," she muttered, frowning, absorbed in what she was doing. "Next week—" She shrugged. "Perhaps someone else."

Amber was pleased by the compliment—but now that she was finally ready she wished he would come. Outside she felt new and crisp as tissue-paper, but her stomach was fluttering with nervousness and her hands were moist. Maybe he won't like me this way! She was beginning to feel scared and almost sick. Oh! *why* doesn't he come!

And then she heard the door open and his voice called her name. "May I come in?"

"Oh!" Amber's hand flew to her mouth. "He's here! Quick!"

She began shooing them out and the three rushed everywhere at once, gathering up boxes and bottles and combs, flocking out the door of the bedroom just as he reached it. Bowing and curtsying as they went, they could not resist looking back gleefully over their shoulders to see what he would do. Amber stood in the middle of the room, lips parted, not even breathing, her eyes glistening with expectation. He walked through the doorway smiling and then suddenly stopped, surprise on his face, at the threshold.

"Holy Jesus!" he said softly. "How lovely you are!"

Amber relaxed. "Oh—*do* you like me this way?"

He came toward her and took the fingers of one hand to turn her slowly about, while she looked back at him over her shoulder—unwilling to miss the slightest expression of pleasure on his face. "You're all the dreams of fair women a man ever had." At last he picked up her cloak. "Now— Where shall we go?"

She knew exactly and was eager to set out. "I want to see a play!"

He grinned. "A play it is—but we'll have to hurry. It's almost four now."

It was after four-thirty when they arrived at the old Red Bull Playhouse in upper St. John Street, and the performance had been under way for more than an hour. The theatre was hot and stuffy, almost humid, and it smelt strongly of sweat and unwashed bodies and powerful perfumes. There was a bustle and stir over the house which never ceased, and dozens of heads turned curiously as they went to their seats in the fore of one of the boxes. Even the actors took time out to give them a glance.

Amber was completely intoxicated, trying to see everything at once, thrilled by the whole noisy, bad-smelling, ill-bred but strangely exciting conglomeration. She felt that the triumph

67

was peculiarly her own—and did not realize they would have stared at any other pretty woman arriving late. Any diversion was a welcome one, for neither players nor audience seemed seriously interested in the performance.

All the bottom floor of the house was called the pit and its benches were crowded with about three hundred young men who buzzed eternally among themselves. A few women were seated there also, most of them rather well-dressed but boldly over-painted, and when Amber asked Bruce in a loud whisper who they were he replied that they were prostitutes. There had been no prostitutes in Marygreen and if there had they would have been set up in the stocks and pelted with refuse by every right-thinking farmer and housewife. And so she was amazed to see that here the young men used them with apparent respect, talked to them openly, and even occasionally kissed or embraced one of them. Nor did the ladies themselves seem in any wise self-conscious or remorseful. They laughed and chattered loudly, looked happy and quite at their ease.

Ranged against the apron-shaped stage, which extended out into the pit, stood half-a-dozen girls with baskets over their arms, bawling out their wares—oranges and lemons and sweetmeats—which they sold at exorbitant prices.

Above the pit, but down close to the stage, was a balcony divided into boxes, and there sat the ladies of quality, gorgeously gowned and jewelled, with their husbands or lovers. Above that was another balcony filled with women and rowdies. And in one still higher were the apprentices who beat time to the music with their cudgels, gave a loud hum by way of disapproval and, when really indignant, sounded their cat-calls—loud whistles that filled the theatre.

Essentially the audience was aristocratic—the harlots and 'prentices being almost the only outsiders—and the ladies and gentlemen came to see and to be seen, to gossip and to flirt. The play was a secondary consideration.

Amber found nothing to disappoint her. It was all she had expected, and more.

Taut with excitement and happiness, she sat very straight beside Bruce, her eyes round and sparkling and travelling from one side of the theatre to the other. So *this* was the great world!

Yet she could not but be poignantly aware of her new gown, her elaborate coiffure, the scent of her perfume, and the unfamiliar but pleasurable feeling of cosmetics on her skin, the silken caress of her fur muff beneath her fingers, the voluptuous display of her breasts.

And then, as she looked around at the boxes near them, she encountered the eyes of two women who were leaning slightly forward, watching her—and the expression on their faces was a sudden rude shock.

They were both handsome, richly dressed, sparkling with jewels, and they had an indefinable hauteur and confidence which she already associated with quality. Bruce had bowed and spoken to them when they came in—as he had spoken to several other men and women nearby and had acknowledged waves of greeting from gentlemen in the pit. But now, as her eyes met theirs, they gave her a sweeping contemptuous glance, exchanged smiles with each other; one woman murmured something behind her fan—and with a concerted lift of the eyebrows they both looked away.

For an instant Amber continued to stare at them, surprised and hurt, almost sick with humiliation, and then she looked down at her fan and bit her lower lip to force back the sudden impulse of tears. Oh! she thought in passionate mortification, they think I'm a harlot! They despise me! All at once the glory was gone from her outing into the gay world and she wished she had never come, had never exposed herself to their scorn and disdain.

When Bruce, who had evidently seen the exchange of glances, gave her hand a warm reassuring pressure her spirits lifted a little and she flung him a look of gratitude. But though she returned her eyes to the stage then and tried to take an interest in what was going on she found it impossible. She only wished that the play would end so that she might get back to the comforting seclusion of their apartment. How ashamed Sarah would be, how furious Uncle Matt, to see to what a condition she had come!

At last the epilogue had been spoken and the audience began to rise. Bruce turned to her with a smile, putting her cloak over her shoulders. "Well, how did you like it?"

"I—I liked it." She did not look him in the eyes and dared not glance about for fear of confronting the two women again, or some other sneering face.

Below in the pit several of the men were clustering about the orange-girls, kissing them, handling them familiarly, while others indulged in horseplay among themselves, clapping one another on the back and pulling off hats. The actor who had impersonated Juliet, still in his long blond wig and a gown with padded chest, came out and stood talking to some of the beaus. Others were climbing up onto the stage and going back behind the scenes. Overhead they could hear tramping feet making for the exits, and the ladies and gentlemen about them were pausing in small groups—the women kissing one another and squealing while the men smiled with smug tolerance. But all the while Amber stood with a troubled frown on her face, her eyes fixed on Bruce's cravat, wishing they would all get out.

"Shall we go, my dear?" He offered her his arm.

Outside the theatre they made their way through the loiterers to his coach where it stood in line with several others, all jamming the streets until foot-traffic was almost at a standstill. Everyone was pushing to get through and vendors and porters were swearing angrily. All of a sudden a beggar thrust himself before them, making weird undistinguishable sounds, his mouth open, and he put his face up to Amber's to show her where his tongue bled from having been cut out. Sickened with pity and a little frightened she drew closer to Bruce, holding his arm.

Bruce tossed the man a coin. "Here. Out of the way."

"Oh—that poor man! Did you see him? Why did they do that to him?"

They had reached the coach and he handed her in. "There was nothing wrong with him. It's a trick they have of rolling their tongues out of sight and poking them with a stick until they bleed."

"But why doesn't he work instead of doing that?"

"He does work. Don't think begging's the easiest profession in the world."

She sat down while he turned to talk to two young men who

had called his name, and she saw them both looking at her from over his shoulder, frank appraisal in their eyes. For one bold instant Amber returned their stares, lifting her brows and slanting the corners of her eyes—and then suddenly she blushed and looked the other way. Oh, Lord! they were most likely thinking the same thing about her that the women had! But still she could not resist sneaking them another slow cautious glance—and her eyes met once more the full stare of the handsomer one. Swiftly she glanced away. And yet—there was no doubt it did not seem so insulting, coming from a man.

Bruce finally turned back, spoke to the driver and got in, sitting down beside her as the coach gave a jog and started to move. He took one of her hands in his. "You've set the town by its ears. That was my Lord Buckhurst and he says you're far more beautiful than Barbara Palmer."

"You mean the King's mistress?"

"Yes. How the devil do you manage to get all the current gossip?" He looked down at her, amused as though she were a pretty doll or a plaything.

"The dressmaker told me about her. Bruce—who were those two ladies? The ones in the next box that waved to you?"

"Wives of friends of mine. Why?"

She looked down at her fan, frowning, counting the sticks. "Did you see how they looked at me? Like this—" She pulled her face into a sudden grimace, a perfect though somewhat exaggerated and malicious imitation of the stares they had given her. "They think I'm a harlot—I know they do!"

Bruce gave her a look of surprise and then, to her astonishment, threw back his head and laughed.

"Well!" she cried, offended. "What the devil is there to laugh at, pray?"

She was beginning already to pick up some of his expressions, words and phrases Matt Goodegroome would never have allowed even his sons to use. It seemed to Amber that all fine persons swore and that it was a mark of good breeding.

"I'm sorry, Amber. I wasn't laughing at you. But to tell you the truth I think they glared at you for another reason—jealousy, no doubt. Certainly neither of them has any reason to have an ill opinion of another woman's character. Between 'em I think they've laid with most of the men who went to France."

"But you said they're married!"

"So they are. If they weren't they might have been more discreet."

She was relieved, but at the same time a quick suspicion entered her mind. Could *he* have been one of those men? But she promptly decided that if he had been he would never have mentioned the matter at all—and she thrust that thought aside. She began to feel happy again, and eager for the next adventure.

"Where are we going now?"

"I thought you might like to have supper at a tavern."

Back in the City they stopped in New Street before a building which bore the sign of a great golden eagle. When she stepped down Amber lifted her skirts high to show her black lace garters, just as she had seen several ladies do outside the theatre. Then, as they were about to go in the door, they heard a loud shout in a familiar masculine voice.

"Hey! Carlton!"

Curiously they looked around. It was Almsbury, riding by in a hackney jammed with several other men, and as the coach pulled up he jumped out, waved his companions goodbye and came toward them at a run. He blinked his eyes twice as he saw Amber and then swept off his hat in a deep bow.

"Holy Christ, sweetheart! Damn me if you aren't as beautiful as a Venetian whore!"

The delighted smile froze on Amber's face.

Well! So that was what *he* thought of her too! Her eyebrows drew together in a furious scowl, but at a glance from Bruce the Earl hastened to repair his breach. He shrugged his shoulders and made a comical face.

"Well—after all, you know, Venetian prostitutes are the prettiest women in Europe. But then, I suppose if you—"

He paused, watching her with an ingratiating grin and Amber slowly raised her eyes to his again. She could not resist his friendliness and all of a sudden she smiled. He took her arm. "Lord, sweetheart, you know I wouldn't offend you for anything on earth." The three of them went inside and, at Bruce's request, were shown upstairs to a private room.

After the men had ordered, the waiter brought them a small barrelful of oysters and they began cracking them open, eating them raw with a sprinkle of salt and a few drops of lemon juice, scattering the shells on the table and floor. Almsbury predicted that oysters would become the staple food at Court and when Amber looked puzzled Bruce told her what he meant. She laughed heartily, thinking it a very good joke.

By the time they had finished the oysters the rest of the meal appeared: a roast duck stuffed with oysters and onions, fried artichoke bottoms, and a rich cheesecake baked in a crust. After that there was Burgundy for the two men, white Rhenish for Amber, fruit, and some nuts to crack. For a long while they sat at the table talking, all of them warm and well-fed and content, and Amber quite forgot her earlier chagrin.

The wine was stronger than the ale to which she was accustomed and after a couple of glasses she became quiet and drowsy, and sat with her eyes half closed listening to the men talk. A sense of lightness pervaded her, as though her head had become detached and floated somewhere far above her. She watched Bruce admiringly, every expression that crossed his face, every gesture of his hands. And when he would turn to smile at her or, as he did once or twice, lean over to brush his lips across her cheek, her happiness soared dizzily.

At last she whispered in his ear and, when he answered, got up and crossed the room to a small closet. While she was in there she heard a knock at the outer door, another voice speaking, and then the sound of the door closing again.

When she came out, Almsbury was sitting at the table alone, pouring himself another glassful of wine. He glanced around over his shoulder. "He's been called out on business but he'll be back in a moment. Come here where I can look at you."

Ten minutes or more dragged slowly by with Amber watching the door, looking up with swift eager expectancy at each slight sound, nervous and unhappy. It seemed as though he had been gone an hour when the waiter came in. He bowed to Almsbury.

73

"Sir, his Lordship regrets that he has been called away on a matter of important business, and asks that you do him the kindness of carrying madame to her lodging."

Almsbury, who had been watching Amber while the man delivered his message, nodded his head. And now Amber looked at him with her face white, her eyes as hurt as if she had been struck.

"Business," she repeated softly. "Where can he go on business at this hour?"

Almsbury shrugged his shoulders. "I don't know, sweetheart. Here, have another drink."

But though Amber took the wine-glass he proffered she merely sat and held it. For a month and a half she had looked forward to this night—and now he must go off somewhere on business. Every time she asked him where he had been or where he was going it was always the same answer—"business." But why tonight? Why this one night for which she had planned so long and from which she had hoped so much? She felt tired and discouraged and hung listlessly in her chair, scarcely speaking, so that after a few minutes Almsbury got up and suggested that they go.

During the ride back she did not trouble herself to make conversation with the Earl, but when they reached the Royal Saracen she asked him if he would care to come upstairs, half hoping that he would refuse. But he accepted readily and, while she went on ahead to take off her gown, stopped in the tap-room for a couple of bottles of sack. Coming out of the bedroom in a pair of clopping mules and a gold satin dressing-gown—another recent acquirement—she found him stretched comfortably on a cushion-piled settle before the fire. He gave a wave of his arm, signalling her to come to him and, when she sat down beside him, took hold of one of her hands, looked at it reflectively for a moment and then touched it to his lips. Frowning, Amber stared off into space, scarcely conscious of him.

"Where d'you think he went?" she asked at last.

Almsbury shrugged, tilted the bottle again.

"What the devil is this 'business' he's always about? Do *you* know what it is?"

74

"Every Royalist in England has business nowadays. One wants his property back. Another wants a sinecure that'll pay a thousand a year for helping the King on and off with his drawers. The galleries are full of 'em—country squires and old soldiers and doting mamas who've heard the King has an eye for pretty women. They all want something—including me. I want Almsbury House back again and my lands in Herefordshire. His Majesty couldn't please all of us if he were King Midas and high Jupiter rolled into one."

"What does Bruce want? Carlton Hall?"

"No, I don't think so. It was sold, not confiscated, and I don't believe they'll give back property that was sold." He finished the bottle and leaned over to pick up another one.

The Earl could drink more with less effect to himself than any man she had ever seen, and Bruce had told her that it was because he had lived so long in taverns that his blood had turned to alcohol. She still was not sure whether he had meant it as a joke or the solemn truth.

"I don't see what he can want," she said. "As rich as *he* is."

"Rich?" Almsbury seemed surprised.

"Well—isn't he?"

Amber knew very little about money for she had never had in her possession more than a few shillings at a time and could scarcely tell the value of one coin from another. But it seemed to her that Lord Carlton must have fabulous wealth to own a coach-and-four, to wear the clothes he did, to buy such wonderful things for her.

"By no means. His family sold everything they had to help the King and what they didn't sell was taken from them in the decimations. That jewellery he found at Carlton Hall was just about everything that was left. No—he's not rich. In fact, he's damned near as poor as I am."

"But what about the coach—and my clothes—"

"Oh. Well—he has that much. A man who knows what he's about can sit down for a few hours at cards or dice and come away several hundred pounds to the good."

"Cheating?" She was rather shocked, almost inclined to think that Almsbury was lying.

But he smiled. "Well, perhaps he plays a little upon advantage. But then, we all do. Of course some of us are clever at it and some not so clever—Bruce can slur and knap with any man in Europe. He made his living for most of fifteen years with a pair of dice and a pack of cards—and he lived a damned sight better than most of us did. In fact, the other night I saw him win twenty-five hundred in four hours at the Groom Porter's Lodge."

"Is that what all this business is he goes upon—gambling?"

"Partly. He needs money."

"Then why doesn't he ask the King for it—since everyone else does?"

"My dear, you don't know Bruce."

At that moment she heard a coach come banging down the street and left him to rush to the window—but to her disappointment it continued on by and rounded the next corner. She stayed there, looking out into the darkness, for there were no street lights of any sort but only the pale gleam from the new moon and the stars. The streets were deserted, not a person was in sight. London citizens stayed home at night unless they had a very good reason to go abroad, and then they took with them an escort of linkboys or footmen.

In the distance she saw the glow of the bellman's lantern and could hear his monotonous refrain: "Past ten o'clock of a fine warm summer's night and all's well. Past ten o'clock—"

Completely absorbed in her worries about Bruce, she had forgotten that Almsbury was there at all. But now she felt his arms go around her, one hand sliding into her dressing-gown, and with the other he turned her about and kissed her on the mouth. Astonished, she gave a little gasp and then suddenly shoved him away, slapping him resoundingly across the face.

"Marry come up, sir!" she cried. "A fine friend you are! When his Lordship hears about this he'll run you through!"

He stared at her for an instant in surprise, and then threw back his head and laughed. "Run me through! Jesus, sweetheart, but you've a droll wit! Come, now—surely you don't think Bruce would give a damn if I borrowed his whore for a night?"

Amber's eyes blazed in violent anger. Then in a fury she kicked out at his shins, beginning to pound his chest with her clenched fists. "I'm *not* a whore, you damned dog! Get out of here— Get out of here or I'll tear you to pieces!"

"Hey!" He grabbed her wrists, giving her a shake. "Stop it, you little vixen! What are you trying to do? I'm sorry. I apologize. I didn't—"

"Get out, you varlet!" she yelled.

"I'm going. I'm going— Hold your bawling."

Picking up his hat, which she had knocked off, he crossed to the door. There, with his hand on the knob, he turned to face her. She was still glaring at him, fists planted on her hips, but tears glistened in her eyes and it was all she could do to keep from crying. His flippancy vanished.

"Just one thing, sweetheart, before I go. Contrary to what your Aunt Sarah may have told you—a man's not insulting you when he invites you to bed. And if you'd be honest you'd admit yourself you're flattered that I did. For if there's one thing a woman will never forgive a man—it's not wanting to lie with her. Now I'll trouble you no more. Good-night." He made her a bow and opened the door.

Amber stood and looked at him like a little girl getting a lesson in etiquette from her grown-up uncle. She was beginning to find that her suit of country morals was as much out of fashion here in London as her cotton petticoat and green woolen skirt had been. Now she held out her hand in an impulsive but still uncertain gesture, and took two or three steps toward him.

"My lord—don't go. I'm sorry— Only—"

"Only you're in love with Bruce."

"Yes."

"And so you think you shouldn't lie with another man. Well, my dear, perhaps someday you'll discover that it doesn't make so very much difference after all. And if you do— Your servant, madame." He made her another bow.

She stood and looked at him, not knowing what to do next. For though she had to admit to herself that she really was, in a sense, flattered by his proposal, she could not agree with him that fidelity to the man you loved was of no importance. It seemed incredible she could ever so much as think of lying with another man. She never would, not as long as she lived.

And then there came again the sound of a coach rattling over the cobblestones; she whirled around and ran once more to the window. The coach came careening down the street, rocking from side to side, the driver hauled on the reins and it stopped just beneath. Nimbly as a monkey the footman got down from his perch and ran to open the door, and after a moment Lord Carlton got out, turning then to speak to someone inside. Another footman held a flaring torch which lighted one side of his Lordship's face and threw stark shadows up the street and upon the walls of the houses.

Amber was about to lean out and call a greeting when, to her horror, a woman thrust her head from the coach-window and she caught a glimpse of a beautiful white face, laughing, and a tumbling mass of red hair. Bruce's head bent above her and she heard their voices murmuring. After a moment he stepped back, bowing and removing his hat, the footman closed the door and the coach rolled away. He turned and disappeared through the arch below.

Amber stood clutching at the sill, almost sick enough to faint. And then, by a great physical effort, she straightened again and turned slowly about. The colour had washed out of her face and her heart was beating violently. For several moments she stood and stared before her—not even seeing Almsbury who was watching her with a kind of compassionate sympathy on his face. She let her eyes close and one hand went up slowly to her forehead.

At that moment the door opened and Bruce came in.

CHAPTER FIVE

HE paused as if in surprise, glancing from one of them to the other, but before he had had time to say a word Amber burst into tears and ran into the bedroom, slamming the door behind her and flinging herself onto the bed.

The sobs wrenched and tore at her and she gave herself up to them with complete abandon. This was the most miserable moment in all her life and she had no wish to be brave and restrained. Suffering in silence was not her way. And, when he did not come in immediately, running after her as she had expected, she grew increasingly hysterical—until finally she began to retch.

But finally she heard the door open and then the sound of his footsteps crossing the floor. Her sobs became louder than ever. Oh! she thought vehemently, I wish I'd die! Right now! Then he'd be sorry!

The room began to glow as he lighted a couple of candles. She heard him toss his cloak and hat aside and unbuckle his sword, but still he said nothing. At last she lifted her head from her arms and looked at him; her face was streaked and her eyes red and swollen.

"Well!" she cried, challenging him.

"Good evening."

"Is *that* all you have to say?"

"What else should I say?"

"You might at least tell me where you've been—and who you've been with!"

He was untying his cravat now, and taking off his doublet. "Don't you think that that's my business?"

She gasped, as hurt as if he had struck her. She had given herself to him so wholeheartedly, with not a single reservation, that she had made herself believe he had done the same. Now she realized all at once that he had not. His life had not changed, his habits had not changed, she had scarcely touched him at all.

"Oh," she said softly, and looked away.

For a moment he stood watching her, and then he came suddenly and sat down on the bed. "I'm sorry, Amber, I didn't mean to be rude. And I'm sorry I had to leave you—spoil your evening that you've been counting on for so long. But it really was business that called me away—"

She looked at him skeptically, the tears brimming over her

eyes again and falling in drops onto her satin gown. "Business indeed! What kind of business does a man do with a woman!"

He smiled, his eyes tender and yet amused. She always had the feeling, and it made her uncomfortable, that he did not quite take her seriously.

"More than you might imagine, darling, and I'll tell you why: The King can't possibly satisfy or repay everyone who was loyal to him—he's got to make a choice from among a thousand claims, one as good as another. I don't think his Majesty could ever be persuaded by a woman—or anyone else—to do something he didn't want to, but when it comes to choosing between several things he'd like to do—why then the right woman can be very useful in helping him to make up his mind. Just now there's no one who can do more to persuade the King than a young woman named Barbara Palmer—who's been kind enough to use her influence in my behalf—"

Barbara Palmer!

So that was the woman she had seen!

She had a sudden horrified sense of defeat, for certainly the woman who could charm a king must have some almost unearthly allure. Her confidence plunged, beaten and overwhelmed by her own superstitious belief that a King and everything which surrounded him was more than half divine. Her head dropped into her hands.

"Oh, Amber, my dear—please. It's not as serious as that. She happened to be driving by and saw my coach and sent up to ask if I was there. I'd have been a damned fool to refuse. She's helped me get what I wanted more than anything on earth—"

"What? Your lands?"

"No. Those were sold. I won't get them back again unless I can buy out the present owner, and I don't think I will. She helped me persuade the King and his brother to go into a privateering venture with me; they both contributed several thousand pounds. I got my letter-of-marque yesterday."

"What's that?"

"It's a letter from the King authorizing the bearer to seize the vessels and cargo of other nations. In this case I can take Spanish ships sailing off the Americas—"

Her fear and jealousy of Barbara Palmer vanished.

"You're not going to sea?"

"Yes, Amber, I am. I've bought two ships of my own, and with the money I'll get from the King and York I can buy three more. As soon as they're provisioned and the men are signed we'll sail."

"Oh, Bruce, you can't go away! You can't!"

A flicker of impatience crossed his face. "I told you that day in Heathstone I wouldn't stay long. It'll be two months yet, or perhaps a little longer, but as soon as I can, I'm going."

"But *why?* Why don't you get a—a—I forget what Almsbury called 'em—where you get money for helping his Majesty put on his drawers?"

He laughed, though her face was passionately serious. "As it happens I don't want a what-d'you-call-'em. I need money, but I'll get it my own way. Crawling on my belly for the rest of my days isn't the way I want to do it."

"Then take me with you! Oh, please, Bruce! I won't be any trouble—let me go along, please!"

"I can't, Amber. Life on ship-board is hard enough for a man—the food's rotten, it's cold and it's uncomfortable, and there's no getting off when you get tired of it. And if you think you wouldn't cause any trouble—" He smiled, running his eyes over her significantly. "No, my dear—it's no use talking about it."

"But what about me? What'll I do when you go? Oh, Bruce, I'll die without you!" She looked at him pitifully and reached over to put her hands on his arms, already forlorn as a lost puppy.

"That's what I asked you when you wanted to come to London with me. Or have you forgotten? Listen to me, Amber. There's only one thing for you to do—go back to Marygreen right now. I'll give you as much money as I can. We'll think of some tale or other to tell your aunt and uncle—I know it won't be easy for you, but even in a village a large sum of money doesn't go unrespected. After a while the gossip will run down,

81

and you can get married— Wait a minute, let me finish. I know I'm to blame for having brought you here, and I won't pretend my motives were noble. I wasn't thinking about you or what would happen to you, and to tell the truth I didn't very much care. But I care now; I don't want to see you hurt any more than I can help. You're young and you're innocent and you're beautiful, and all that with your enthusiasm for living can easily ruin you. I wasn't joking when I said that London eats up pretty girls —the town's aswarm with rogues and adventurers of every conceivable breed. You'd be snapped up in a minute. Believe that I know what I'm saying and go back home, where you belong."

Amber's eyes sparkled angrily, and she lifted her chin as she answered him. "I a'nt so innocent, my lord! I warrant you I can look to my own interests as well as the next one! And don't think I can't see what you're about, either! You've grown tired of me now the King's mistress has caught your eye, and think to fob me off with some lame story that I should go back for my own good! Well, you don't know what you're talking about! My Uncle Matt wouldn't so much as let me in the house —money or no! And the constable would likely set me up in the stocks! Every man in the parish would laugh in his fist at me and—" She stopped suddenly and burst into tears again. "I won't do it! I *won't* go home!"

He reached over and took her into his arms. "Amber, my darling, don't cry. I swear it, I don't give a damn about Barbara Palmer. And I was telling the truth when I said I thought you should go back for your own sake. I still do. But it isn't because I've grown tired of you. You're lovely—you're more desirable than you can know. My God, no man could grow tired of you—"

Under his stroking fingers her sobs grew quieter, a warmth began to come over her and she purred like a kitten. "You aren't tired of me, Bruce? I can stay with you?"

"If you want— But I still think—"

"Oh, don't say it! I don't care! I don't care what happens to me—I'm going to stay with you!"

He gave her a light kiss and got up to finish undressing while she sat on her knees watching him, glowing admiration in her eyes. His body was magnificent—with a splendid breadth through chest and shoulders, sleek narrow hips, and handsome muscular legs. His flesh was hard-surfaced, the skin of his torso browned by exposure. Every movement he made had the easy gracefulness of an animal, seemingly unhurried, yet lithe and quick.

He crossed the room to snuff out the candles. And suddenly Amber could restrain herself no longer.

"Bruce! Did you make love to her?"

He did not answer but gave her a glance, half-scowling, that intimated he considered the question a superfluous one, and then his head bent and he blew out the last candle.

From the beginning Amber had both half-hoped and half-feared that she would become pregnant. She hoped because her love for him yearned to be fulfilled in every way. But she feared, too, because she knew that he would not marry her, and it was her vivid memory that a woman who gave birth to a bastard child had no very tender treatment at the hands of the community. Two years before in Marygreen a daughter of one of the cottagers had become pregnant and had either not known or refused to tell the father's name, so that sheer force of public antagonism drove her to leave the town. Amber remembered the circumstance well, for it had been the subject of chatter among the delighted and scandalized girls for weeks on end, and she had been as contemptuous, as jeering as any of them.

Now, that might happen to her.

She was well enough acquainted with the early symptoms of pregnancy for she had often discussed the subject with those of her friends who were married, and she had watched Sarah carry four children during the years since she had been old enough to notice such things. But by the end of June, when they had been in London almost two months, she still had no reason to think herself with child. And so, to settle her own suspense, she went to consult an astrologer.

It was no very difficult matter to find one for they were all over the city, thick as flies in a cook-shop, and she set out one day in Bruce's coach-and-four to learn her fortune from a certain Mr. Chout. She watched as they rode along and when she saw a sign marked with a moon, six stars, and a hand, she called to the driver to stop and sent the footman to knock at the door. The astrologer, who had peeked out the window and seen her crested coach, came forth himself to invite her in.

He did not look to her like a mystic. He had a large red face, dirt-clogged pores covered his nose, and there was a rank odour about him. But he greeted her so obsequiously, bowing as though she were a duchess of the blood royal, that her confidence in him increased.

The footman followed her into the house and waited while she and Mr. Chout retired to a private parlour. The room was filthy and smelt no better than its owner, and Amber glanced dubiously at the chair before she sat down in it. He took a stool opposite her and began talking about the King's return and his own invincible loyalty to the Stuarts. While he talked he rubbed his dirty hands together and his eyes looked at her as though they could penetrate her cloak. Finally, like a doctor who has humoured his patient long enough by gossiping of other things, he asked her what she wanted to know.

"I want to know what's going to happen to me."

"Very well, madame. You've come to the right man. But first there are some things you must tell me."

Amber was afraid that he would ask her some embarrassingly personal questions, but all he wanted was the date and hour of her birth and where she was born. When she had told him he consulted several charts, gazed into a round crystal ball he had on the table, peered occasionally at both her palms—holding her hands in his own moist and grimy ones—and nodded his head gravely. All the while she watched him with anxious eagerness, now and then giving an absent-minded caress to the large grey cat that came and nudged against her skirts.

"Madame," he said finally, "your future is of singular interest. You were born with Venus in separating square aspect to Mars in the Fifth House." Amber solemnly absorbed that, too impressed at first even to wonder what it meant. Then, as she was about to ask, he continued, having reached his conclusions

84

as much by looking at her as at his charts: "Hence you are inclined, madame, to over-ardent affections and to rash impulsive attractions to the opposite sex. This can cause you serious trouble, madame. You are also too much inclined to indulge yourself in pleasure—and hence must suffer the attendant difficulties."

Amber gave a wistful little sigh. "Don't you see something good, too?"

"Oh, indeed, madame, indeed. I was coming to that. I see you in possession of a great fortune, madame—a very great fortune." By the appearance of her clothes and smart coach he had surmised that she must already have access to a large amount of money.

"You do?" cried Amber, delighted. "What else do you see?"

"I see jealousy and discord. But also," he added hastily at a protesting frown from Amber, "I see that the sextiles of Venus to Neptune and Uranus give you considerable magnetism—no man may resist you."

"Ohhh—" breathed Amber. "Gemini! What else do you see? Will I have children?"

"Let me see your palm again, madame. Yes, indeed, a very fair table—the line of riches well extended. The wheels of fortune are large. These intersparsings betoken children. You will have—let me see—several. Seven, I should say, more or less."

"When will I have the first one? Soon?"

"Yes, I think so. Very soon—" His eyes went down over her cloak, but nothing was revealed there. "That is, of course," he added cautiously, "within a reasonable time. You understand, madame."

"And when will I get married—soon, too?" Her voice and eyes were hopeful, almost pleading with him.

"Let me see. Hmmm—let me see. Now, what did you dream last night? I've found there's nothing to compare with a dream for telling a woman when she'll marry."

Amber frowned, trying to remember. She could recall nothing but that she had dreamed of pounding spices, which she had often done for Sarah—particularly after the two annual fairs, when they were purchased in bulk. That fragment, however, was enough for Mr. Chout's purpose.

"That's very important, madame. Very important. To dream of pounding spices always foretells matrimony."

"Will I marry the man I love?"

"Why, truly, madame, that I can't say for certain." But at Amber's stricken expression he again hastened to amend his statement. "Of course, madame, you will marry him one day— perhaps not today or tomorrow—but someday. These lines here betoken husbands. You will have, let me see, some half-a-dozen, more or less."

"Half-a-dozen! I don't want half-a-dozen! I just want one!" She pulled her hand away from him, for he seemed sticky and repulsive to her, and he had been holding on somewhat too tightly. But he was not done yet.

"And one thing more I see—if I may be frank with you?— I see that someday you will have, madame, a hundred lovers." His greedy eyes watched her with obscene calculation, taking vicarious pleasure from her look of surprise and the faint pink blush that spread over her face and neck. "More or less, that is."

Amber gave an excited little laugh. He was making her feel ill-at-ease and she wished that she was out of there; it was difficult to breathe, and though he had moved no nearer he seemed to be oppressively close. "A hundred lovers!" she cried, trying to sound city-bred and casual. "Marry come up! One's enough for me! Is that all, Mr. Chout?" She got to her feet.

"Isn't that enough, madame? I don't often discover as much, let me tell you. The fee is ten shillings."

Amber took a dozen or more coins from her muff and dropped them onto the table. His broad grin told her that most likely she had overpaid, again. But she did not care. Bruce always left a handful of coins for her to use and when one pile was gone another appeared in its place. Ten shillings as a sum of money meant nothing to her at all.

I'm going to have a baby and marry Bruce and be rich! she thought exultantly as she rode home.

That night she asked Bruce what the planet Venus was, though she did not tell him of her visit and did not intend to,

86

until something more definite had come of it. But perhaps he guessed.

"It's a star called Venus after the Roman goddess of love. It's supposed to control the destinies of those who are born under it. I believe such people are thought to be beautiful and desirable and generally dominated by emotion—if you believe in that kind of nonsense." He was smiling at her, for Amber's face showed her shock at this heretical statement.

"Don't *you* believe in it?"

"No, darling, I don't believe in it."

"Well—" She put her hands on her hips and gave her curls a toss. "One day you will, I warrant you. Just wait and see."

But nothing which happened immediately seemed to indicate that any of Mr. Chout's predictions were coming true. And meanwhile her life continued very much as it had been.

Most of the time Bruce was away from home, either gambling at the Groom Porter's Lodge, where the nobles went to play cards and dice, or overseeing the supplying and loading of his ships. Often, too, she knew that he went to balls or suppers given at Court or the homes of his friends. And though she thought wistfully of how wonderful it would be to go with him he did not ask her and she never mentioned it. For she was still strongly conscious of the great gulf which separated his social position from hers—and yet when she lay waiting for him to come back she was lonely and sad, and jealous too. She was morbidly afraid of Barbara Palmer and other women like her.

Almsbury often came to call and, if Bruce was not there, took her out somewhere with him.

One day they went to see a bull-and-bear baiting across the river in Southwark. And Amber leaned out the coach window to gape at the weather-beaten heads, some twenty or thirty of them, exposed above London Bridge on poles that stuck up crazily, like toothpicks in a glass. Another time he took her to a fencing-match, and one of the antagonists lost an ear which flopped off into the lap of a woman sitting down in front.

They went to supper at various fashionable taverns and two or three times he took her to the theatre. She paid no more attention to the play than did the rest of the audience—for she was

87

too much interested, though she pretended not to be, in the havoc she was creating down in the pit. Some of the young men came up to Almsbury in such a manner that he could not avoid presenting them, and two or three made her outrageous proposals beneath his very nose. Almsbury, however, always assumed his dignity at this and let them know she was no whore but a lady of quality and virtue. While Amber, ashamed of her country accent, hoped that they would indeed take her for a Royalist lady who had lived retired with her parents during the Protectorate and had only now come up to Court.

But the greatest adventure of all was her visit to Whitehall Palace.

Whitehall lay to the west, around the bend of the river from the City. It was a great sprawling mass of red brick buildings in the old Tudor style, honeycombed with hallways and having dozens of separate apartments opening one into another like some complex maze or huge rabbit-warren. Here lived the royal family and every court attendant or hanger-on who could wheedle official lodgings on the premises. It fronted directly on the river, so close that at high tide the kitchens were often flooded. And through the grounds ran the dirty unpaved narrow little thoroughfare of King Street, flanked on one side by that part of the Palace called the Cockpit and on the other by the wall of the Privy Garden.

Whitehall was open to all comers. Anyone who had once been presented at Court or who came with one who had could get in, and many total strangers filtered through the carelessly watched gateways. Hence, when Amber and Almsbury arrived in the Stone Gallery they found it so thronged as to be almost impassable.

The gallery was the central artery of the Court, a corridor almost four hundred feet long and fifteen feet wide, and on the walls were hung some of the splendid paintings which Charles I had collected and which his son was now trying to reassemble—paintings by Raphael, Titian, Guido. Scarlet-velvet drapes covered all doors opening into the royal apartments, and Yeomen of the Guard were posted before each one. The crowd was a motley assortment of satin-gowned ladies, languid sauntering young fops, brisk men-of-business hurrying along with an air of having weighty problems to solve, soldiers in uniform, country squires and their wives. Amber could easily recognize these latter for they all wore clothes hopelessly out of fashion—boots, when no gentleman would be seen off his horse in them; high-crowned hats like a Puritan's, though the new mode was for low ones; and knee-gartered breeches, although wide-bottomed ones were now the style. Here and there was even a ruff to be seen. Amber was contemptuous of such provinciality and glad that her own clothes did not betray her origin.

She was less confident, however, about herself. "Gemini!" she whispered, round-eyed, to Almsbury. "How handsome all the ladies are!"

"There's not one of 'em," said the Earl, "half so pretty as you."

She gave him a grateful, sparkling smile and slipped her arm through his. She and Almsbury had become great friends and though he had not asked again to sleep with her he had told her that if she ever needed money or help he would be glad to give it. She thought that he had fallen in love with her.

And then all at once something happened. A ripple of excitement flowed along the Gallery, turning heads as it passed, catching the Earl and Amber in its wake.

"Here comes Mrs. Palmer!"

Amber's head turned with every other. And she saw advancing toward them, with people falling back on either side to make way for her, a magnificent red-haired white-skinned woman, trailing behind her a serving-woman, two pages, and a blacka-moor. Haughty and arrogant, she walked with her head held high, seeing no one, though she could not but be well aware of the excitement she was creating. Amber's eyes began to burn with rage and jealousy and her heart set up a suffocating flutter. She was sickeningly afraid that Madame Palmer would see Almsbury—who she knew was acquainted with her—and stop. But she did not. She went past them without a glance.

"Oh! I hate her!" The words burst out as though driven by some pent-up violence.

"Sweetheart," said Almsbury, "someday you'll learn it's impossible to hate every woman a gentleman may make love to. It wears out your own guts, and that's all the good it does."

But Amber neither could nor wished to accept his Lordship's mellow philosophy. "I don't care if it does!" she insisted stubbornly. "I do hate her! And I hope she gets the pox!"

"No doubt she will."

After that they went to the Banqueting Hall to watch the King dine in state, which he usually did at one o'clock on Wednesday, Friday, and Sunday. The galleries were massed to see him but he did not come and at last they had to go away, disappointed. Amber had been much impressed when she had seen King Charles the day he returned to London; after Bruce she thought him the finest man in England.

About the first of August Amber became convinced that she was pregnant, partly because she had at least one symptom but mostly because it was forever on her mind. For a couple of weeks past she had waited and counted on her fingers and nothing had happened. Now her breasts began to feel stretched and sore and as though pricked by a thousand pins. She wanted to tell Bruce and yet she was half scared, for she guessed that he would not be pleased.

He got up early every morning—no matter how late he might have come in the night before—and Amber would put on her dressing-gown and talk to him until he left, after which she went back to sleep again. On this day she sat at the edge of the bed, swinging her bare feet and pulling a tortoise-shell comb through the tangled snarls of her hair. Bruce stood near her, wearing only his breeches and shoes, shaving with a long sharp-bladed razor.

For several minutes Amber watched him and neither of them spoke. Each time she tried to open her mouth her heart gave a leap and her courage failed her. Then all at once she said: "Bruce—what if I should get with child?"

He gave a slight involuntary start and cut himself, the bright blood showing in a little line on his chin, and then he turned to look at her. "Why do you say that? Do you think you are?"

"Well—haven't you noticed anything?" She felt strangely embarrassed.

"Noticed what? Oh—I hadn't thought about it." He scowled and even though it was not at her she felt a sudden frightened loneliness; then he turned back, took up a small bottle and put a drop of liquid styptic on the cut. "Jesus!" he muttered.

"Oh, Bruce!" She jumped off the bed and ran to him. "Please don't be mad at me!"

He had started shaving again. "Mad at you? It's my fault. I intended to be careful—but sometimes I forgot."

Amber looked at him, puzzled. What was he talking about? She'd heard in Marygreen that it was possible to avoid pregnancy by spitting three times into the mouth of a frog or drinking sheep's urine, but Sarah had warned her often enough that such methods were unreliable.

"Sometimes you forgot what?"

"Nothing it will do any good to remember now." He wiped his face with a towel, tossed the towel onto the table-top and then turned to put on the rest of his clothes. "Oh, Lord, Amber —I'm sorry. This is a devil of a mess."

She was quiet for a moment, but finally she said, "You don't like babies, do you?"

She asked the question so naïvely, looked up at him with so sad and wistful an expression that all at once he took her into his arms and held her head against his chest while one hand stroked tenderly over her hair. "Yes, my darling, of course I like them." His mouth was pressed against the top of her head, but his eyes were troubled and a little angry.

"What are we to do?" she asked him at last.

Held close in his arms with her body against his she felt warm and safe and happy—the problem had dissolved. For though he had told her he would not marry her and she had believed it at first, now she was almost convinced that he would. Why shouldn't he? They loved each other, they were happy together, and during the past several weeks of living with him she had almost forgotten that he was a lord and she the niece of a yeoman farmer. What might once have seemed impossible to the point of absurdity now seemed to her quite natural and logical.

He let her go and stood with his arms hanging at his sides while he talked, his green-grey eyes hard and uncompromising, watching her steadily. There was no doubt he meant every word he said.

"I'm not going to marry you, Amber. I told you that at the first and I've never once said anything to the contrary. I'm sorry this has happened—but you knew it probably would. And remember, it was your idea that you come to London—not mine. I won't just leave you to drift—I'll do everything I can to make it easier for you—everything that won't interfere with my own plans. I'll leave you money enough to take care of yourself and the baby. If you won't go back to Marygreen the best thing is for you to go to one of the women here in London who take care of pregnant women and arrange for their lying-in—some of those places are very comfortable and no one will inquire too closely for your husband. When you're well again you can do as you like. With a few hundred pound in cash a woman as beautiful as you are should be able to marry a country-squire, at the least—or perhaps a knight, if you're clever enough—"

Amber stared at him. She was suddenly furious, all the pride and happiness she had felt at the prospect of bearing him a child was drowned now in pain and outraged pride. The sound of his voice enraged her—talking so coolly, as if falling in love with a man and having his baby was a matter to be settled with money and logic, like provisioning a ship! She almost hated him.

"Oh!" she cried. "So you'll give me money enough to catch a knight—if I'm clever! Well, I don't want to catch a knight! And I don't want your money, either! And as for the matter of that— I don't want your baby! I'm sorry I ever laid eyes on you! I hope you go away and I never see you again! I hate you! —Oh!—" She covered her face with her hands and began to cry.

Bruce stood watching her for a moment, but at last he put on his hat and started out of the room. Amber looked up. And when he had scarcely reached the bedroom door she ran after him.

"Where are you going?"

"Down to the wharf."

"Will you come back tonight? Please come back! Please don't leave me alone!"

"Yes—I'll try to get here early. Amber—" His voice was again warm and smooth, caressing, tender. "I know this is hard for you and I'm truly sorry it's happened. But it'll be over sooner than you expect and you'll be none the worse for it. It's really no great tragedy when a woman has a baby—"

"No great tragedy to a man! You'll go away and forget all about it—but *I* can't go away! *I* can't forget it! I'll never be able to forget it— Nothing will *ever* be the same for me again! Oh, damn men!"

As the days passed she became convinced beyond all doubt that she actually was pregnant.

Less than a week after she had told him, she began to retch the moment she lifted her head in the mornings. She was morose and unhappy and cried upon the slightest provocation, or with none at all. He began coming home even later at night and when he did they often quarrelled; she knew that her ill temper was keeping him from her, but she could not seem to control herself. But she knew also that nothing she had said or could say would make him change his mind. And when he was away once for an entire day and night and until late the next night, she realized that she must give over her haranguing and tantrums or lose him even before he sailed. She could not bear the thought of that, for she still loved him, and she made a tremendous effort to seem once more gay and charming when they were together.

But alone she was no more reconciled than she had been and the hours without him seemed endless, while she trailed idly about the house, steeped in pity for herself. This great world of London to which she had come with such brilliant expectations only four months ago now seemed a dismal place and full of woe. She had not the vaguest idea as to what she would do when he was gone and refused to discuss it with him, even pushing the thoughts out of her own mind when they began to creep in. When that day came she felt that the end of the world would also come, and did not care what happened afterward.

One hot mid-morning in late August Amber was down in the courtyard playing with some puppies that had been born at the inn a month or so before. She knelt on the flag-stones in the mottled shade of a fruit-heavy plum tree, laughing and holding two of the puppies in her arms while the proud mother lay nearby, wagging her tail and keeping a careful eye on her off-spring. And then, unexpectedly, she glanced up and saw Bruce leaning on the rail of the gallery outside their bedroom, watching her.

He had left several hours before and she had not expected him back till evening, at the earliest. Her first reaction was one of delight that he had come home and surprised her and she gave him a wave as she got quickly to her feet, putting the puppies back into their box. But then immediately a slow stealthy fear began to sneak in. It grew ominously, and as she reached the stairs and started to mount them she raised her eyes and met his. She knew it then for sure. He was leaving today.

"What is it, Bruce?" she asked him, warily, as though she could ward off the answer.

"The wind's changed. We're sailing in an hour."

"Sailing! In an hour! But you said last night it wouldn't be for days!"

"I didn't think it would. But we're ready sooner than I expected and there's nothing to wait for."

While she stood there, helpless, he turned and went through the door, and then she followed him. There was a small leather-covered nail-studded trunk of his on the table already packed more than half full, while the wardrobe in which he kept his clothes was opened and empty. Now he took some shirts from a carved oak chest, piled them into the trunk, and as he did so he began to talk to her.

"I haven't much time, so listen to what I say. I'm leaving the coach and horses for your use. The coachman gets six pound a year with his livery and the footman gets three, but don't pay them until next May or they'll likely rub off. I've paid all the bills and the receipts are in the drawer of that table. So are the names and locations of a couple of women who can take care of you—ask them what the charge will be before you move into the house. It shouldn't be more than thirty or forty pound for everything."

While Amber stood staring at him, horrified at the brusque impersonal tone of his voice, he closed the lid of the trunk and walked swiftly to the door of the other room where he made a

94

signal to someone evidently waiting out in the hall. The next moment he was back, followed by a great ruffian with a patch over one eye, who shouldered the trunk and went out again. All the while Amber had been watching him, desperately trying to think of something she could say or do to stop him. But she felt stunned, paralyzed, and no words came to help her.

From the pocket of his doublet Bruce now drew a heavy leather wallet, closed by draw-strings and bulging with coins, and tossed it onto the table.

"There's five hundred pound. That should be enough to take care of you and the baby for several years, if necessary, but I'd advise you to put it with a goldsmith. I'd intended to do that for you, but now I haven't time. Shadrac Newbold is perfectly reliable and he'll allow you six percent interest if you put it with him at twenty days call, or three and a half if you want it on demand. He lives at the Crown and Thistle in Cheapside; his name is written on this piece of paper. But don't trust anyone else—above all don't trust a maid if you take one into service, and don't trust any strangers no matter how much you may like them. Now—" He turned and picked up his cloak. "I've got to go."

He spoke swiftly, giving her no chance to interrupt, and obviously was in a hurry to get out before she started to cry. But he had not taken three steps when she ran to throw herself before him.

"Bruce! Aren't you even going to kiss me?"

He hesitated for only an instant and then his arms went about her with a rough eagerness which suggested some reluctance within himself to leave her. Amber clung to him, her fingers clutching his arms as though she could hold him there by sheer force of superior strength, her mouth avidly against his, and already her face was wet with tears.

"Oh, Bruce! *Don't* go! Please don't go—please don't leave me—! Please—*please* don't leave me—"

But at last his fingers took hold of her wrists and slowly he forced her away. "Amber, darling—" His voice had a sound of pleading urgency. "I'll come back one day—I'll see you again—"

She gave a sudden cry, like a lonely desperate animal, and

then she began to struggle with him, reaching out to grab hold of his arms, terrified. All at once he seized both her wrists, his mouth caught at hers again for an instant, and before she could quite realize what had happened he was gone through the room and out the door and it slammed behind him.

Stunned, she stood for a moment staring at the closed door. And then she ran to it, her hand going out to grab the knob.

"Bruce!"

But she did not quite reach it. Instead she stopped, brought up short by some hopelessness inside herself, and though for a moment her eyes continued to watch the door, at last she slumped slowly to her knees and her head dropped into her hands.

CHAPTER SIX

THE DUKE OF YORK leaned gloomily against the fireplace. His hands were in the pockets of his breeches, his good-looking face was sulky, and he stared down at the floor. Across the room Charles was bent over a table, peering intently into a pewter pan set on an oil-lamp, in which boiled and bubbled a hundred different herbs. Now, carefully, he took up a spoon and measured in three heaping spoonfuls of dried ground angelica, stirring as he did so.

The brothers were in his Majesty's laboratory, surrounded on all sides by crucibles and alembics, retorts and matrasses. There were glass and earthenware jars full of powders, pastes, many-coloured liquids, oil of prima materia. Egg-shaped vessels of every size and substance lined the shelves. Piles of books bound in old leather, stamped with gold, stood on the floor or on the tables. Chemistry—which had not yet secured its divorce from the medieval witch-woman, alchemy—was one of the King's chief interests. Even when he had had to beg a meal he had not been able to resist paying money out of his meagre store for almost every new nostrum recommended him by a passing quack.

"How the devil," said Charles now, stirring the mixture but

not looking around, "did you let her get you into such a mess?"

York gave a heavy sigh. "I wish I knew. She isn't even pretty. She's as ugly as an old bawd. Eyes that pop and a shape like this—" His hands described an ungainly female form.

Charles smiled. "Perhaps that's what fooled you. It's my observation a pretty woman seldom thinks it's necessary to be clever. Anne Hyde is clever—don't you agree?" He seemed amused.

James shifted his weight, scowling. "I don't know what fooled me. I must have been out of my mind. Signing that damned marriage-contract!"

"And in your own blood. A picturesque touch, James, that one. Well—you've signed it and you've had her and she's pregnant. Now what?"

"Now nothing. I hope I never see her again."

"A contract of marriage is as binding as a ceremony, James, you know that. Whether you like it or not, you're married to her. And that child she carries is yours and will bear your name."

James heaved himself away from the fireplace, walked across the room and glanced at the concoction his brother had stirred up. "Ugh!" said the Duke. "How it stinks!"

"It does, I agree," admitted Charles. "But the fellow who sold me the recipe says it's the most sovereign thing for an ague ever discovered—and London and the ague, you know, are synonymous. This winter I don't doubt you'll be glad enough to borrow a dose of it from me."

Restless, discontented, angry, James turned and walked away. After a moment he once more took up the subject of his marriage. "I'm not so sure," he said slowly, "you're right about that, sir. The brat may not be mine after all."

"Now what've you been hearing?"

Suddenly James came back to him; his face was serious and growing excited. "Berkeley came to me two days ago and told me that Anne has lain with him. Killigrew and Jermyn have sworn the same thing since."

For a long moment Charles looked at his brother, searching his face. "And you believed them?"

"Of course I believed them!" declared James hotly. "They're my nearest friends! Why wouldn't I believe them?"

"Berkeley and Jermyn and Harry Killigrew. The three greatest liars in England. And why do you suppose they told you that? Because they knew it was what you wanted to hear. It is, isn't it?" Charles's dark eyes narrowed slightly, his face shrewd. He understood his brother perfectly, much better in fact than James understood himself.

James did not answer him for a long moment but at last he said softly, half-ashamed, "Yes. I suppose it is. But why the devil should I think Anne Hyde is more virtuous than another woman? They all have a price—"

"And hers was marriage." The King set the pan off the flame and turned down the lamp. Then he took his doublet from where it had hung over a chair-back and slipped into it. "Look here, James—I'm no better pleased than you are with this business— The daughter of a commoner, even if he is my Chancellor, is no suitable wife for the heir to the English throne. But it would raise a damned peculiar smell all over Europe if you got her with child and refused to marry her. If she'd been anyone but the Chancellor's daughter we might have found a way around it. As it is I think there's only one course for you: Marry her immediately and with as good a grace as you can."

"That isn't what the Chancellor wants. He's locked her in her rooms and says he'd rather have her thrown into the Tower and beheaded than disgrace the Stuarts by marrying one of them."

"Edward Hyde was a good servant to my father and he's been a good servant to me. I don't doubt he's angry with her, but one thing you may be sure of—it's not only the Stuarts he's worried about. He knows well enough that if his daughter marries you he'll have a thousand new enemies. Jealousy doesn't breed love."

"If you say it's best, Sire, I'll marry her—but what about Mam?" He gave Charles a sudden desperate look that was almost comical.

Charles laughed, but put an arm about his brother's shoulders. "Mam will most likely have a fit of the mother that will go near to killing her." "A fit of the mother" was the common term for hysteria. "She's always hated Hyde—and her family pride is almost as great a passion with her as her religion. But I'll protect you, Jamie—" He grinned. "I'll threaten to hold off her pension."

They walked out together, James still thoughtful and morose, Charles good-humoured as usual. He snapped his fingers at a pair of little spaniels asleep in a square of sunshine and they scrambled to their feet and tore yapping out of the room, scuttling between his legs, turning to prance on their hind legs to look up at him.

James's marriage to Anne Hyde created a considerable excitement. The Chancellor was furious; Anne wept incessantly; and the Duke still thought he might find a way out. With the help of Sir Charles Berkeley he stole the blood-signed contract and burned it, and Berkeley offered to marry her himself and give the child his name. The courtiers were in a quandary, not knowing whether they should pay their respects to the new Duchess or avoid her altogether, and only Charles seemed perfectly at ease.

And then the Duke of Gloucester, who had fallen ill of smallpox but had been thought to be out of danger, died suddenly. Charles had loved him well, as he did all his family, and he had seemed a young man of great promise, eager and charming and intelligent. It was unbelievable that now he lay dead, still and solemn and never to move again. There had been nine children in the family. Two had died on the day of birth, two others had lived only a short while, and now there remained only Charles and James, Mary who was Princess of Orange, and Henrietta Anne, the youngest, still with her mother in France.

But even the death of Henry could not halt the festivities for long. And though the Court managed to show a decent face of sorrow in the presence of Charles or James, the balls and the suppers, the flirtations and the gambling went on as before, wildly, madly, as though it would never be possible to get enough of pleasure and excitement.

The great houses along the Strand, from Fleet Street to Charing Cross, were opened all day and far into the night. Their walls resounded with noisy laughter and the tinkle of glasses, music and chatter, the swish of silken skirts and the tap of high-heeled shoes. Great gilt coaches rattled down the streets, stood lined up outside theatres and taverns, went rambling through the woods of St. James's Park and along Pall Mall. Duels were fought in Marrowbone Fields and at Knightsbridge over a lady's dropped fan or a careless word spoken in jest. Across the card-tables thousands of pounds changed hands nightly, and lords and ladies sat on the floor, watching with breathless apprehension a pair of rolling dice.

The executions of the regicides, held at Charing Cross, were attended by thousands and all the quality went to watch. Those men who had been chiefly responsible for the death of Charles I now themselves died, jerking at the end of a rope until they were half-dead, and then they were cut down, disembowelled and beheaded and their dripping heads and hearts held up for the cheering crowds to see. After that their remains were flung into a cart and taken off to Newgate to be pickled and cured before being set up on pikes over the City gates.

A new way of life had come in full-blown on the crimson wings of the Restoration.

It was only a week after her brother's death that Princess Mary arrived in London. She was twenty-eight, a widow and mother—though she had left her son in Holland—a pretty, graceful gay young woman with chestnut curls and sparkling hazel eyes. She had always hated Holland, that sombre strait-laced land, and now she intended to live in England with her favourite brother and have all the lovely gowns and extravagant jewels for which she longed.

She embraced Charles enthusiastically, but she was cooler with James and only waited until the three of them were alone to speak her mind to him:

"How could you do it, James? Marry that creature! Heavens, where's your pride? Marrying your own sister's Maid of Honour!" Anne and Mary had been close friends at one time, but that was over now.

James scowled. "I'm sick of hearing about it, Mary. God knows I didn't marry her because I wanted to."

"Didn't marry her because you wanted to! Why, pray, *did* you marry her then?"

Charles interrupted, putting an arm about his sister's waist. "I advised him to it, Mary. Under the circumstances it seemed the only honourable course to take."

Mary cocked a skeptical eyebrow. "Mam won't find it so honourable, I warrant you. Just wait until *she* gets here!"

"That," said Charles, "is what we're all waiting for."

It was not long until the Queen Mother Henrietta Maria arrived—not more than a week, in fact, after Anne Hyde's son was born. Most of the Court went to Dover to meet her and they stayed a day or two at the great old castle which for centuries had guarded the cliffs of England.

Henrietta Maria was forty-nine but she looked nearer seventy, a tiny hollow-cheeked haunted-eyed woman with no vestige of beauty left. What little she had possessed had gone early, lost in the bearing of her many children, in the hardships of the Civil Wars, in her grief for her husband whom she had loved devotedly.

In repose her face was ugly, but when surrounded by people she was vivacious and gay, with all the superficial charm of her youth and the delightful manners in which she had so carefully schooled her children. She was dressed in the mourning-clothes which she had worn faithfully since her husband's death and never intended to leave off until her own. The gown was plain black with full sleeves and high neck, broad white linen collar and cuffs, and over her head was hung a heavy black veil. She still wore her dark hair in old-fashioned corkscrew curls; it was her one concession to the love of personal ornament and pretty things which had been so strong in her.

By nature she was domineering and since all her children were stubborn and self-willed there had been continual conflict in the family. Several years before she had quarrelled with Gloucester over his refusal to enter the Catholic Church and had warned him never to see her more; when he died they were still unreconciled. But in spite of her deep hurt over that situation she now accosted James, determined to rule him or to break off their relationship. The Duke and his mother had always been most friendly when apart and he had been dreading this encounter with her, for her tongue could be acid and spiteful when she was angry.

"Well, James," she said at last, when they were alone in her bedchamber to which she had summoned him. Her voice was quiet, and she had her hands clasped lightly before her, but her black eyes sparkled with excitement. "There's talk about you in France—talk of which I was, needless to say, deeply ashamed."

He stood across the room near the door and stared down at his feet, unhappy and ill-at-ease. He said nothing and would not look at her. For a long moment they remained perfectly silent and then he ventured to steal a glance, but instantly dropped his eyes.

"James!" Her voice was sharp and maternal. "Have you nothing to reply?"

With sudden impulsiveness he crossed the room and dropped to one knee at her feet. "Madame, I beg your pardon if I have offended you. I've played the fool, but thank God now I've come to my senses. Mrs. Hyde and I are not married and I intend to think of her no more—I've had proof enough of her unworthiness."

The Queen Mother bent and kissed him lightly on the forehead. She was relieved and very pleased at the unexpected good sense he was showing—for knowing James she had anticipated a stubborn and bitter struggle. And so a part, at least, of what she had come for was accomplished.

She had two other purposes.

One was to secure a pension which would enable her to live out the rest of her life in comfort and security. She had begged too often from the tight-fisted Cardinal Mazarin, had lived too long in privation and want—sometimes without so much as firewood to heat her rooms. It would mean a great deal to her to have money again. Her other purpose was to get a suitable dowry for Henrietta Anne, who had suffered perhaps more than any of them during the years of exile. For with her father dead, her brother hunted out of his country, she had grown up as the poor relation of the grand Bourbons, a mere neglected little waif lost in the glitter of the French Court.

Now, however, King Louis's brother wanted to marry her.

Henrietta Anne, whom Charles called Minette, was just sixteen. Her features were not perfect, her figure was too slender and one shoulder was slightly higher than the other—but almost everyone who met her was immediately struck by her beauty. For they attributed to facial prettiness what was really the glow of a warm and tender charm; it was impossible to resist her. And Charles had for her a deep and sincere devotion which he had never felt for any of his numerous mistresses.

His sister's marriage to Philippe, Duc d'Orléans, would give him a valuable ally in the French Court, because Minette had already shown that she possessed a diplomatic talent which won admiration and respect from the most cynical statesmen. And she loved her brother with a passionate loyalty which would always place his interests first, those of Louis XIV second. Nevertheless Charles hesitated.

"Are you sure," he asked her, "that you *want* to marry Philippe?"

They had left the Banqueting Hall to stroll in the Privy Gardens, along the gravel paths which separated the lawns and hedges into formal squares. Though mid-November it was very warm, and the rose-bushes were still covered with leaves; Minette had not even troubled to throw a cloak over her gold-spangled ball-gown.

"Oh, yes, Sire! I do!" She answered him with an eager smile.

He glanced down at her. "Do you love him?" Charles was so eager for his sister's happiness that it troubled him to think of her marrying, as other princesses must, without love.

"Love him?" Minette laughed. "Mon Dieu! Since when did love have anything to do with marriage? You marry whom you must and if you can tolerate each other—why, so much the better. If not—" She shrugged. But there was no air of precocious cynicism about what she said—merely good common Parisian sense, and a willingness to accept the world for what it was.

"Perhaps," he said. "But nevertheless you're my sister, and I want to know. Do you love him?"

"Why—to tell you the truth, I don't know whether I do or not. I've played with him since we were children, and he's my cousin. I think he's pretty—and I feel a little sorry for him. Yes, I suppose you might say I love him." She put up one hand as a quick little breeze ruffled her hair. "And of course he's mad in love with me. Oh, he swears he can't *live* till we're married!"

"Oh, Minette, Minette—how innocent you are. Philippe's not in love with you—he's not in love with anyone but himself. If he thinks he loves you now it's because he sees that others do and imagines that if he marries you he'll get some of that affection himself. When he doesn't he'll grow jealous and resentful. He's a mean petty man, that Philippe—he'll never make you happy."

"Oh, you judge him too severely!" she protested. "He's so harmless. Why, all his concern is to find a new way of dressing his hair or tying his ribbons. The most serious thought in his life is who takes precedence over whom in a parade or at the banqueting-table."

"Or finding a new young man."

"Oh, well, *that!*" said Minette, dismissing so minor a fault with a graceful little gesture of one hand. "That's common enough—and no doubt he'll change when we're married."

"And suppose he doesn't?"

She stopped directly before him, looking up into his face.

"But, my dear!" Her voice was teasingly reproachful. "You're so serious about it. What if he doesn't? That's no great matter, is it—so long as we have children?"

He scowled. "You don't know what you're talking about, Minette."

"Yes, I do, my dear. I assure you I do, and I think the world overestimates love-making. It's only a small part of life—there are so many other things to do." She spoke now with a great air of confidence and worldly wisdom.

"My little sister—how much you have to learn." He smiled at her but his face was tender and sad. "Tell me, has a man ever made love to you?"

"No. That is, not very much. Oh, I've been kissed a time or

two—but nothing more," she added, blushing a little and drop-ping her eyes.

"That's what I thought—or you wouldn't talk like that." Charles's first son had been born when Charles was Minette's age. "Half the joys and half the sorrows of this world are dis-covered in bed. And I'm afraid you'd find nothing but sorrow there if you married Philippe."

Minette frowned a little and gave a brief sigh; they started to walk again. "That may be all very true for men, but I'm sure it isn't for women. Oh, *please* let me marry him! You know how much Mam wants me to. And I want to too. I want to live in France, Sire—that's the only place I could ever be at home. I know Philippe isn't perfect, but I don't care— If I have France, I'll be happy."

Christmas was England's most beloved holiday, and nowhere was it celebrated with more enthusiasm than at Whitehall.

Every room and every gallery was decorated with holly, cy-press and laurel. There were enormous beaten-silver wassail-bowls garlanded with ivy. Branches of mistletoe hung from chandeliers and in doorways, and a berry was pulled off for each kiss. Gay music sounded throughout the Palace, the staircases were crowded with merry young men and women, and both day and night there was a festival of dancing and games and cards.

The immense kitchens were busy preparing mince-pies, pickled boar's heads to be served on immense golden platters, peacocks with their tails spread, and every other traditional Yule-tide delicacy. In the Banqueting Hall the King's Christmas presents were on display and this year every courtier with a farthing to his name had sent one—instead of retiring into the country to avoid the obligation, as had once been common practice.

And then suddenly the laughter was hushed, the music ceased to play, gentlemen and ladies walked softly, spoke in whispers: Princess Mary was sick of the small-pox. She died the day before. Christmas.

The royal family passed Christmas day quietly and sadly, and

Henrietta Maria began to make preparations for returning to France. She was afraid to leave Minette longer in England for fear she too would contract the disease. And there was no real reason to stay longer, for though she had Minette's dowry and a generous pension for herself, she knew at last that she had failed with James.

Berkeley had finally admitted that his story had been a lie, Killigrew and Jermyn had done the same, and James had recognized Anne as his wife. But he made no mention of his decision to his mother and she was furious when she heard of it, refused to speak to him either in public or in private, and declared that if that woman entered Whitehall by one door she herself would go out by another.

And then all at once her attitude changed completely and she told James that since Anne was his choice in a wife she was ready to accept her, and she asked that he bring the Duchess to her. James was relieved, though he knew what had prompted her sudden softening of heart. Cardinal Mazarin had written to tell her frankly that if she left England while still on bad terms with her two sons she would find no welcome in France. He was afraid that Charles would revoke her pension and that he, Mazarin, would have to support her.

The day before she left London Henrietta Maria received her daughter-in-law in her bedchamber at Whitehall. This was still the custom among great persons for that room was the most opulently furnished of all and differed from a drawing-room only because it contained the immense four-poster tester-covered bed-of-state. The reception was a large one, for Henrietta Maria was popular at Court if nowhere else, and in spite of widespread sickness they had been drawn there by curiosity to see how Queen and Duchess would greet each other. All wore sombre black and most jewels had been reluctantly left at home. The room smelt of unwashed bodies and a nostril-searing stench of burnt brimstone and salt-petre which had been used to disinfect the air. In spite of that precaution Henrietta Maria had not been willing for Minette to run the risk, and she was not there.

The Queen Mother sat in a great black velvet chair, a little mantle of ermine about her shoulders, talking pleasantly with a group of gentlemen. The King stood just beside her, tall and handsome in his royal-purple velvet mourning. But everyone was growing impatient. The prologue had been too long—they were eager for the play to begin.

And then there was a sudden commotion in the doorway. The Duke and Duchess of York were announced.

A hushed expectant murmur ran through the room and many pairs of eyes glanced quickly to Henrietta Maria. She sat perfectly still, watching her son and his wife approach, a faint smile on her mouth; no one could have told what she was thinking. But Charles, glancing down at her, saw that she trembled ever so slightly and that one veined taut-skinned hand had a tight hold on the arm of her chair.

Poor Mam, he thought. How much that pension means to her!

Anne Hyde was twenty-three years old, dark and ugly with a large mouth and bulging eyes. But she walked into the room— stared at by dozens of pairs of curious jealous critical eyes and facing a mother-in-law she knew hated her—with her head held high and a kind of courageous grandeur that commanded admiration. With perfect respect but no slightest hint of servility she knelt at the Queen's feet, bowing her head, while James mumbled a speech of presentation.

Henrietta Maria smiled graciously and kissed Anne lightly on the forehead, apparently as well-pleased as though she had made the choice for James herself. Behind her the face of the King was impassive—but as Anne gave him a quick look of gratitude his black eyes sparkled at her with something that was very like a reassuring and congratulatory smile.

CHAPTER SEVEN

THE DAY AFTER Lord Carlton's departure Amber had moved almost a mile across town to the Rose and Crown in Fetter Lane. She could not stand the sight of the rooms where they had lived, the table where they had eaten, and the bed they had slept in. Mr. Gumble who gave her a bleak, sympathetic look, the chambermaid, even the black-and-white bitch with her litter of pups, filled her with lonely sickness. She wanted to get away from it and, just as much, she wanted to avoid the possibility of seeing Almsbury or any other of his Lordship's acquaintance. The Earl's promise of friendship should she need it meant nothing to her now but the dread of raking over her misery and shame. She wanted to be left alone.

For several days she shut herself up in the single room she had taken.

She was convinced that her life was over and the future that lay before her was arid and hopeless. She wished that she had never seen Bruce, and forgetting her own willful part in what had happened to her, blamed him for all her troubles. She forgot that she had eagerly wanted to have a child and hated him for leaving her pregnant, frightened and baffled by the knowledge that imprisoned within her body, growing with each day that passed, was proof of her guiltiness. One day she would no longer be able to conceal it—and what would happen to her then? She forgot that she had despised Marygreen and wanted to leave it, and blamed him for having brought her to this great city where she had no friends and every strange face looked like an enemy's. A hundred times she decided that she would go back home, but she did not dare. For though she might be able to explain to Sarah what had happened, her uncle, she knew, would very likely refuse her the house. And certainly would turn her out when he found her with child.

Amber mulled wretchedly over her problems, but there seemed no solution to them and no end. She would never again be young and gay and free. And all because of *him!*

But in spite of herself Lord Carlton sometimes—and more often as the days passed—stepped out of his role as Devil. She was still wholly infatuated and she had a passionate painful longing for him that was something more than desire. It was awe, bedazzlement, admiration as well.

But gradually, as time passed, she began again to take an interest in merely being alive. Her meals tasted good to her.

108

There were so many things to eat here in London that she had never had before: elaborate sweets called marchpanes, olives imported from the Continent, Parmesan cheese and Bayonne bacon. And she began to feel a kind of curious wonder at the strange and mysterious functioning of her own body in pregnancy. She even began to care something about her appearance again. And once when she had idly dusted some powder over her cheeks, she went on opening one jar after another, until she had painted all her face, and she could not help being pleased with the result.

She almost felt then that she was too pretty to mope away the rest of her life alone.

Her windows overlooked the street, which was in a somewhat fashionable neighbourhood, and she began to spend more and more time there, wondering who the handsomely gowned lady was, getting out of her coach attended by four gallants, where the good-looking young man who stared up at her was going, and what he thought of her. London was just as exciting as it had ever been.

But *I'm* going to have a baby!

That was what made the difference. Even more than Lord Carlton's departure.

But she could not stay indoors forever, and so one day when Carlton had been gone for about a fortnight she made herself ready again with great care and went out. She had no plan or specific intention but wanted only to get away from her room, perhaps to ramble through the streets in her coach, to feel in some way that she was a part of the world.

The coachman whom Lord Carlton had hired had fallen sick of the small-pox not three days after his Lordship left and Amber had paid him his salary for the year and—scared of the disease—sent the footman away. The host at the Rose and Crown found two others to take their place. Now while she waited for her coach she stood in the doorway of the inn pulling on her gloves, and was unable to keep back a pleased smile as two flaxen-haired beribboned young fops went by and craned their necks to stare at her. She was sure that they thought her some person of quality. And then, to her surprise, she heard her own name spoken and gave a start. Turning quickly she saw that a strange woman had come up behind her.

"Good morning, Mrs. St. Clare. Oh, I'm sorry! I didn't mean to affright you, madame. I wantèd to ask how you were doing. My apartments are just next yours and the landlord told me you'd been abed with an ague. I have a decoction that does wonders for an ague—"

Her eyes and smile were friendly and she looked at Amber as though she admired her beauty and her clothes. Instantly grateful for the attention and glad to have someone to talk to, if only for a moment, Amber made her a little curtsy.

"God-a-mercy, madame. But I think the ague's near gone by now."

At that instant her coach drove up and stopped before them; the footman opened the door, turned down the folding iron steps and stood ready to hand her in. Amber hesitated for just a moment. The jolt her self-confidence had had and two weeks of complete seclusion had made her a little shy. But she was desperately lonely and this lady looked kind—and not too critical. She would have been afraid of one of the glossy tart-voiced young women her own age whom she had seen and admired and half-consciously begun to imitate. But she was not able to think of anything more to say and so made her a slight curtsy and started toward the coach.

"Why!" cried the stranger then. "Is that your family, madame?" She referred to Bruce's crest, which Amber had not removed from the door.

"Aye," said Amber without hesitation. But she was hoping that the woman could not tell one from another. To her, at least, they all looked alike with their absurd clawing dog-faced lions, their checkerboards and stripes.

"Why, then I know your father well! My own country-seat is near Pickering in Yorkshire!"

"I come from Essex, madame. Near Heathstone." She was beginning to wish that she had not lied about it, for it seemed likely she might be caught.

"Why, of course, Mrs. St. Clare! How furiously stupid of me! But your crest is so similar to that of a near neighbour of mine—

110

though now I look closer I see well enough what the difference is. May I present myself, madame? I'm Mrs. Goodman."

"I'm glad of your acquaintance, madame." She bowed, thinking how much like a fine lady she was behaving, for she had learned those little niceties from her French master and by watching Lord Carlton and his friends. "Can't I carry you somewhere?"

"Why, faith, my dear, I wouldn't care to put you to the trouble. I was only going to pick up a trifle or so in the 'Change."

The 'Change, Amber knew, was a fashionable lounge and meeting-place for the gallants and ladies, and that now seemed to her as good a place as any for her excursion. "I'm going there myself, madame. Pray ride along with me."

Mrs. Goodman did not hesitate and they both got in, spreading their full skirts about them, ruffling their fans, commenting on the September heat. The coach started off across town, jogging about on the cobble-stones, and from time to time they were held up in a dispute with a hackney over the right of way or had to wait while a procession of colliers' carts filed slowly by. Amber and Sally Goodman sat inside talking animatedly, and Amber had almost forgotten that she was a jilted woman carrying in her body a bastard child.

Sally Goodman was plump with pink over-fleshed arms and a bosom that bulged out of her low-necked gowns. Her skin was badly pock-marked, though she did what she could to remedy this defect by the application of a thick layer of some pink-white cosmetic, and her hair was two or three shades of light yellow so that it was plain she aided nature in this respect also. She admitted to twenty-eight of her thirty-nine years and, for that matter, she did contrive to look younger than she was. Her clothes had a sort of specious elegance, though a practiced eye might have known immediately that they were made of second-rate materials by a second-rate sempstress, and there was precisely the same quality in her manner and personality. But she had a hearty good-natured joviality that Amber found both warming and comforting.

Mrs. Goodman, it seemed, was a person of quality and means, making a short stay in London while her husband was abroad on business. Evidently judging Amber by her accent, clothes and coach, she assumed her to be a country heiress visiting in the city and Amber—pleased with this identity—agreed that she was.

"But, Lord, sweetheart!" said Mrs. Goodman. "Are you all alone? A pretty young creature like you? Why, there's dozens of wicked men in London looking for just such an opportunity!"

Amber almost surprised herself with the readiness of her reply. "Oh, I'm visiting my aunt—that is, I—I'm going to visit her as soon as she gets back. She's still in France— She was with his Majesty's court—"

"Oh, of course," agreed Mrs. Goodman. "My husband was there too, for a time, but the King thought he could do more good back here, organizing plots. Where does your aunt live, my dear?"

"She lives in the Strand—oh, it's a mighty fine house!" Almsbury had once driven her by his home which was located there, though not yet returned to his possession.

"I hope she comes back soon. I'm afraid your parents would be uneasy to have you here alone for very long, my dear. You're not married, I suppose?"

Amber felt a sudden hot blush at that question and her eyes retreated to her closed fan. But she found another nimble lie conveniently at her tongue's end.

"No—I'm not— But I will be soon. My aunt has a gentleman for me—an earl, I think she said. He's on his travels now but he'll likely come home when she does." Then she remembered what Almsbury had told her about Bruce's parents and added: "My father and mother are both dead. My father was killed at Marston Moor and my mother died in Paris ten years ago."

"Oh, you poor dear child. And have you no guardian, no one to care for you?"

"My aunt is my guardian when she's here. I've been living with another aunt since she went abroad."

Mrs. Goodman shook her head and sympathetically pressed Amber's hand. Amber was passionately grateful for her kindly interest and understanding, for the mere fact that here was another human being she could talk to, share small experiences with—she had always felt miserable and lost when alone.

The Royal Exchange stood at the junction of Corn Hill and Threadneedle Street, not far from the Royal Saracen Inn. The building formed an immense quadrangle completely surrounding a courtyard and the galleries were divided into tiny shops attended by pretty young women who kept up a continual cry: "What d'ye lack, gentlemen? What d'ye lack, ladies? Ribbons, gloves, essences—" The gallants loitered there, flirting with the 'Change women, lounging against a pillar to watch the ladies walk by and calling out boldly to them. The courtyard itself was crowded with merchants, soberly dressed, intent on business, talking of stocks and mortgages and their ventures at sea.

As they went inside and began to mount the stairs Amber reluctantly followed Sally Goodman's example and put on her vizard. What's the good of a pretty face, she thought, if no one's to see it? and she let her cloak fall back, showing her figure. But in spite of the mask there was no doubt she attracted attention. For as they walked along, pausing now and then to examine a pair of gloves, some embroidered ribbons, a length of lace, enthusiastic comments followed them.

"She's handsome—*very* handsome! By God, but she is!"

"Those killing eyes!"

"As pretty a girl, for a fortnight's use or so, as a man could wish."

Amber began to feel pleased and excited and she cast furtive sidelong glances to see how many men were watching her and what they looked like. Mrs. Goodman, however, took another view of the compliments. She clucked her tongue and shook her head.

"Lord, how bawdy the young men talk nowadays!"

Somewhat abashed at this Amber guarded her eyes and frowned a little, to show that she was displeased too. But the frown did not last long—for she was half-intoxicated by the sights and sounds all about her.

She wanted to buy almost everything she saw. She had little sense of discrimination, her acquisitive instincts were strong, and she felt so boundlessly rich that there seemed no reason why

113

she might not have whatever she desired. Finally she stopped before a stall where a plump black-eyed young woman stood surrounded by dozens of bird-cages, painted gold or silver or bright colours; in each one was a brilliant bird, canaries, parrots, cockatoos brought back by the East India Company or some merchant fleet.

While she was making her selection, unable to decide between a small turquoise-coloured parakeet and a large green squawking bird, she heard a man's voice in back of her remark: "By God, she's tearing fine. Who d'ye think she is?"

Amber glanced around to see if he was speaking of her, just as the other replied, "I've never seen her at Court. Like as not she's some country heiress. By God, I'll make her acquaintance though I perish for it!" And with that he stepped forward, swept off his hat and bowed to her. "Madame, if you'll permit me, I should like to make you a present of that bird—which is, if I may be permitted the observation—no more gorgeous than yourself."

Delighted, Amber smiled at him and had just begun to make a curtsy when Mrs. Goodman's voice cut in sharply: "How dare you use a young woman of quality at this rate, sir? Begone, now, before I call a constable and have you clapped up for your impertinence!"

The fop raised his eyebrows in surprise·and hesitated a moment as if undecided whether to challenge the issue, but Mrs. Goodman faced him so stoutly that at last he bowed very cere· moniously to the disappointed Amber and turned to go off with his friend. As they walked away she heard his scornful remark:

"Just as I thought. A bawd out with her protégée. But apparently she intends to save her for some gouty old duke."

At that Amber realized she had seemed too eager to make the acquaintance of strangers, and she began to fan herself swiftly. "Heaven! I swear I thought he was a young fellow I'd seen sometime at my aunt's!" She drew her cloak about her and went back to the business of selecting her bird, but now she kept her eyes decorously within the shop.

She paid for the gilt cage and little turquoise parakeet with a random coin which she fished out of her muff. And once again

Mrs. Goodman's quickness came to her rescue, for as she was scooping the change back into her hand, Sally caught hold of her wrist.

"Hold on, sweetheart. I believe you're lacking a shilling there."

The girl behind the counter quickly produced one, giggling, saying that she had miscounted. Mrs. Goodman gave her a severe frown and she and Amber left, going downstairs then to get into the coach.

On the ride back Mrs. Goodman undertook to warn Amber of the dangers a young and pretty woman, unaccustomed to town life, must encounter in the city. The times were wicked, she said; a woman of virtue had much ado to preserve not only her honesty but even the appearance of it.

"For in the way of the world, sweetheart," she warned, "a woman loses as much by the appearance of evil as she does by the misdeed itself."

Amber nodded solemnly, her own guilty conscience writhing inside her, and she wondered miserably if her behaviour had given the strait-laced Mrs. Goodman some clue to her predicament. And then, as the coach stopped, she looked out the opened window and gave a sharp horrified cry at what she saw: Trudging slowly along was a woman, naked to the waist and with her long hair falling over her breasts, moaning and wincing each time a man who walked behind her slashed his whip across her shoulders. Following in her wake and trailing beside her was a considerable crowd—laughing jeering little boys, grown men and women, who mocked and taunted.

"Oh! Look at that woman! They're beating her!"

Sally Goodman glanced at her and then away, her face complacently untroubled. "Don't waste your sympathy, my dear. Wretched creature—she must be the mother of a bastard child. It's the common punishment, and no more than the wicked creatures deserve."

Amber continued to watch with reluctant fascination, turning her head to look as the procession passed. There were streaks of blood laced across the woman's naked shoulders. And then suddenly she turned back again and shut her eyes hard.

For a moment she felt so sick that she was sure she would faint, but fear of Mrs. Goodman made her take hold of herself again. But all her gaiety was gone and she was aware as never before that she had committed a terrible crime—a punishable crime.

Oh, Gemini! she thought in frantic despair. That might be me! That *will* be me!

The next morning Amber was up, wearing her dressing-gown and eating a dishful of gooseberry jelly, which was supposed to cure her nausea, when there was a rap at the door and Mrs. Goodman's cheerful voice called her name. Quickly she shoved the dish under the bed and ran to let her in.

"I was just putting up my hair."

Mrs. Goodman followed her back to the dressing-table. "Let me help sweetheart. Has your maid gone abroad?"

Amber felt her fingers working competently, making a thick braid, twisting it into a chignon high on her head, then sticking in gold-headed bodkins to hold the heavy scroll in place. "Why—I had to turn my maid off. She—she got herself with child." It was the only excuse she could think of.

Mrs. Goodman shook her head, but her mouth was too full of bodkins to cluck her tongue. "It's a wicked age, I vow and swear. But Lord, sweetheart, how'll you shift, without a maid?"

Amber frowned. "I don't know. But my aunt'll have dozens, when she comes."

Mrs. Goodman had finished now and Amber began combing out the long thick tresses at the sides of her face, rolling the ends into fat curls that lay on her shoulders.

"Of course, sweetheart. But until then—Heaven, a lady can't do without a serving-woman."

"No," agreed Amber. "I know it. But I don't know where to get one—I've never been in London before. And a woman alone must be mighty careful of strangers," she added virtuously.

"She must, my dear, and that's the truth on it. You're a wise young creature to know it. But perhaps I can help you. A dear friend of mine has just removed to her country-estate and left some of her serving-maids here. There's one of 'em I have in mind in particular—a neat modest accomplished

116

young creature she is, and if she's not already found a new place I can get her for you."

Amber agreed and the girl arrived in less than an hour, a plain-faced plump little thing in neat dark-blue skirt, tucked-up fresh white apron and long-sleeved white blouse with a linen cap that covered her hair and tied in a knot beneath her round chin. She curtsied to Amber, her eyes lowered modestly, and she spoke in a soft voice that suggested she would never try to bully whoever took her into service. Her name was Honour Mills and Amber hired her promptly at two pounds a year, with her room and board and clothing.

It made her feel very fashionable and elegant, having a maid to brush her hair and lay out her clothes, run small errands and walk behind her when she went out of doors. And she was grateful, too, for the girl's company. Honour was quiet and well-behaved, always neat in her appearance, always good-tempered, and a most satisfactory audience for her mistress whom she seemed to admire greatly.

But nevertheless Amber remembered Lord Carlton's advice, kept her money well-hidden and did not confide her private affairs to her. She had not, however, taken the five hundred pounds to Shadrac Newbold, as he had suggested, for she had never heard of a goldsmith before and was distrustful of putting her money into the hands of a complete stranger. She thought herself quite competent to manage it. Nor did she intend to go to either of the two women he had suggested until she was forced by her own appearance to do so.

Amber and Mrs. Goodman became constant companions. They ate dinner together, usually in one of their own apartments; they went riding in Hyde Park or the Mall, but did not get out; they shopped in the Royal Exchange or at the East India House. Once Amber suggested that they go to a play, but Mrs. Goodman had some severe things to say about the debauchery of the theatres, and after that she did not dare make any more suggestions.

Mrs. Goodman's husband was detained longer on the Continent, for his business matters were badly tangled. And Amber said that she had received a letter from her aunt, telling her that it would be two weeks or more before she could leave France. If necessary she did not doubt that she could think of another excuse at the end of that time. She was already convinced that people had a better opinion of you if you pretended to be something more than you were than if you used them honestly.

They had been acquainted for perhaps a fortnight when Sally Goodman told Amber about her nephew. Just returned from church, for it was Sunday, they were in Amber's room, eating a dishful of hot buttered shrimps with their fingers and washing them down with Rhenish. Honour was busily using a pair of bellows to make the fire go, for the day had suddenly turned chill and heavy fog hung over the city.

"Faith," said Mrs. Goodman, not looking up, for she ate with an almost impartial attention to her plate, "but I'll vow it was worth a Jew's eye to hear my silly young nephew going on about you last night. He swears you're the most glorious creature he's ever seen."

Amber, popping a crisp plump shrimp into her mouth, glanced over at her swiftly. "When did he see me?"

She had not made the acquaintance of a single young man, though she had had opportunities aplenty; she was convinced that she would never fall in love again but nevertheless she longed for masculine company. Being with a woman she thought was flat and unexciting as a glass of water. But she had almost never met the man who did not seem to have at least one redeeming quality.

"Yesterday, when you alighted from your coach out in the yard. I thought the young simpleton would fall out the window and break his noddle. But I told 'im you're intended for an earl."

Amber's smile disappeared. "Oh. You shouldn't 've done that!"

"Why not?" Mrs. Goodman now turned to a French cake, split and covered with melted butter and rose-water, sprinkled with almonds. "You are, aren't you?"

"Well—yes. But then, he's your nephew. Heavens, you've been mighty kind to me, Mrs. Goodman, and if your nephew wants to make my acquaintance—why, what harm is there in that?"

Luke Channell was to call on his aunt that evening and Mrs. Goodman said that she would bring him to meet her. He was, she said, just returning from his travels and on his way to his country-seat in Devonshire. Amber, very much excited and hoping that he would be handsome, changed her gown and had Honour dress her hair again. She did not expect a man like Lord Carlton, for she had seen none other in London like him, but the prospect of talking to a young man again, perhaps flirting a little, seeing his eyes light with admiration, was an exhilarating tonic.

Luke Channell, however, was a serious disappointment.

Not very much taller than she, he was stockily built with a broad flat snub-nosed face, and his two front teeth had been broken off diagonally; there was a kind of slippery green moss growing along the edges of his gums. But at least he was quite well-dressed, with a profusion of ribbon-loops at his elbows, hips, and knees, his manner was self-assured, and he seemed tremendously smitten by her. He grinned incessantly, his eyes scarcely left her face, and at times he even seemed so nonplussed as to lose his trend of thought in the middle of a sentence.

Like most young men who went abroad he had brought back his quota of French oaths, and every other word was "Mor-blew" or "Mor-dee." He told her that the Louvre was much larger than Whitehall, that in Venice the prostitutes walked the streets with their naked breasts on display, and that the Germans drank even more than the English. When he left he invited Amber and his aunt to be his guest at the Mulberry Gardens the next evening and she accepted the invitation with a smiling curtsy.

They had scarcely closed the door when Honour asked her: "Well, mem, what d'ye think of him? A mighty spruce young fellow, I'd say."

But Amber felt suddenly tired and discouraged; the tendency to gloom and moroseness which had come with her pregnancy began to settle. Listlessly she shrugged her shoulders. "He's no great matters to brag of."

And all at once it washed down over her—the disappointment and loneliness, the aching longing she had for Bruce, the hopelessness of her situation, and she flung herself onto the bed and began to cry. She could feel her pregnancy closing in on her, seeming to shut her into a room from which there was no escape, and she was as terrified as though menaced by some looming monster.

Oh, what'll I do! What'll I *do!* she thought wildly. It's growing and growing and *growing* inside me! I can't stop it! It's going to get bigger and bigger till I swell up like a stuffed toad and everyone will know— Oh! I wish I was dead!

CHAPTER EIGHT

AMBER AND LUKE CHANNELL were married in mid-October, three weeks after they had met, in the old church of the parish where the Rose and Crown was located. As was customary, Amber bought the wedding-ring and she got a very handsome one with several little diamonds, for which she told the jeweller to send a bill. She had discovered that it was possible to do business that way and now made a practice of it, for her ignorance of money-values was otherwise a serious handicap.

Amber had not been at all eager to marry Luke. She considered him to be one of the least attractive men she had ever known and nothing but the eternal nagging awareness of pregnancy could have persuaded her to consider him for a husband. He seemed to have just one redeeming quality, and that was a violent infatuation for her.

But by the next morning she knew that she had been cheated in that too.

His obsequious adoring manner had vanished altogether and now instead he was insolent, crude, and overbearing. His vulgarity shocked and disgusted her and he would allow her neither privacy nor peace but set upon her at any hour of the day or night. From the first day he was gone most of the time, drank incessantly, harangued her to send for the rest of her money, and displayed almost without provocation a violent and destructive bad-temper.

Mr. Goodman's financial affairs continued unsolved and he began to seem almost as nebulous a figure as Amber's aunt, though both women made new excuses to each other whenever the time limit of the old one had run out. As soon as Amber and Luke were married the two apartments were flung together and presently Sally was borrowing Amber's fans and gloves and jewels and even tried without success to squeeze into her gowns. Amber began to feel that somehow she was caught between these two, aunt and nephew, who seemed to have gained an advantage over her—though she was at a loss to know just when or how it had happened.

Honour remained as quiet and self-effacing as ever, though she became slovenly and Amber had to tell her over and over again to wear her shoes in the house and not to go out in a soiled apron. When Luke was at home she stared at him with a sheepish longing that turned Amber sick; when he was drunk she held his head, cleaned up his vomit, undressed him and put him to bed. Such tasks were routine for a servant, but Honour performed them with a kind of fawning wife-like devotion. Luke, however, showed her no gratitude, nagged at her persistently, gave her a cuff or a kick whenever he was annoyed —which was often—and handled her familiarly even before Amber.

When they had been married scarcely two weeks Amber came into the room one day and surprised Honour and Luke on the bed together. Stunned and disgusted Amber stood there for a moment, mouth and eyes wide open, before she slammed the door. Luke gave a startled jump and Honour, with a terrified shriek, scrambled up and ran into Sally's room, whimpering as she went.

Luke glared at her. "What in hell blew you in here?"

She was on the verge of crying, not because she cared if he seduced the maid, but because she was nervous and distraught. "How was I to know what you'd be about!"

He did not answer but got into his doublet, buckled on his

sword and smacking his hat onto his head slammed out of the room. Amber stood for a moment, glaring after him, and then she went to find Honour. The girl was in Sally's room, huddled in a far corner behind the bed, rocking and sobbing with her hands held protectively over her head. A master or mistress had the right to beat unruly servants and that was obviously what she expected.

"Stop that!" cried Amber. "I'm not going to hurt you!" She tossed a coin into her lap. "Here. And I'll give you another for every piece-of-mutton he gets from you. Maybe he won't worry me so much then," she added in a mutter, and swirling her skirts about walked away.

But her own loathing of Luke and his unpleasant personal habits was by no means the only source of Amber's trouble with her husband. Both he and his aunt were spending a great deal of money—almost every day new packages arrived for one or both of them—but they paid for nothing. She brought the subject up one day when she was setting out on a shopping tour with Mrs. Goodman.

"When's Luke going to get some money from home? If he so much as takes his dinner at a tavern or goes to the play he asks me for some."

Sally laughed and fanned herself industriously, looking out into the crowded street. "See that yellow satin gown just across the way, sweetheart? I've a mind to have one like it. Now what's that you were saying? Oh, yes—Luke's money. Well, to tell you truly, sweetheart, we wanted to keep this from you, but since you ask you may as well know: Luke's father is furious he married without his leave. Poor Luke—married for love and now it seems he may be cut off without so much as a shilling. But then, my dear, with all *your* money no doubt the two of you could shift well enough?" She gave Amber an ingratiating grin, but her eyes were hard and searching.

Amber stared at her, shocked. Luke cut off and the two of them to live on her five hundred pounds! She had begun to learn already that five hundred was less than the illimitable fortune she had at first imagined it to be, particularly when spent at the reckless rate they three were going.

122

"Well, now, why the devil *should* he be cut out of his father's will?" The question was a sharp challenge, for she and Sally were by means as polite as they had once been and several times had come close to quarrelling. "I suppose I'm not a good enough match for 'im?"

"Oh, Lord, sweetheart, I protest! I didn't say that, did I? But his father had another girl in mind— Wait till he sees you. He'll come around then fast enough, I warrant. And by the way, my dear, that thousand pound you sent for to your aunt's lawyer—isn't it mighty long in coming?" Sally's voice was once more silky, soothing, as when she asked Luke to curb his temper, not to tear up the cards when he lost a hand, or to treat Honour more gently.

But Amber stuck out her lower lip, refused to look at her, and answered sullenly. "Maybe the lawyer won't send it at all —now I'm married!"

Little by little her money was dribbling away. It went to Luke for pocket-money, to Mrs. Goodman, who always promised to repay the instant her husband returned from France, or to a tradesman who came to the door dunning her for a bill two or three months in arrears.

What'll I do when it's gone? she would think desperately. And overwhelmed with fear and foreboding she would begin to cry again. She had cried more often in the weeks since Lord Carlton had left than in all the rest of her life. If Luke flew into a temper, if the laundress did not return her smocks in time—the slightest upset, the smallest inconvenience was now enough to start the tears. Sometimes she wept dismally, mournfully, but other times the tears came in a torrent, noisy and splashing as a summer storm. Life was no longer a gay and buoyant challenge but had become empty and hopeless.

There was nothing left to look forward to. This baby would be born and others would follow in a succession down the years. Without money, with children to care for, a brutal husband, hard work, her prettiness would soon be gone. And she would grow old.

Sometimes she woke at night feeling as if she were struggling in some growing living net. She would sit up suddenly, so scared that she could not breathe. And then she would remember Luke beside her, sprawled over three-fourths of the bed, and hatred made her long to reach down and strangle him with her own hands. She would sit there staring at him, thinking with pleasure of what it would be like to stab him to death, to have him pinned there to the bed flopping helplessly. She wondered if she could poison him—but she knew nothing of the process and was afraid of being caught. A woman guilty of husband-murder was burnt alive.

So far apparently none of them had guessed at her pregnancy, though it had now passed the end of the fifth month. Her numerous starched petticoats and full-gathered skirts helped to disguise her in the daytime and ever since her stomach had begun to swell she had contrived to dress when no one was around or to keep her back turned. The lights were always out at night because Honour slept in the same room they did, on a little trundle-bed which was pushed under the large one in the daytime. But nevertheless they were sure to find out soon, and she knew she could never make them believe the child was Luke's. She had no idea what she would do then.

From time to time Amber had changed the hiding-place of her money, leaving out only a few coins at one time, and she congratulated herself that the system was a very clever one. One day she went to her cache; the wallet was gone.

She had hung the strings of the leather bag over a nail hammered into the back of a very heavy carved oak chest which stood against one wall and was never moved. Now, with a little gasp, she got down onto her hands and knees to look underneath it, reaching back to feel about in the thick rolls of dust, suddenly scared and sick. She turned and shouted over her shoulder at Honour, who was in the next room, and the girl came on a run, stopping suddenly when she saw Amber glowering there beside the chest. Then she made a demure little curtsy and opened her eyes wide.

"Yes, mem?"

"Did you move this chest?"

"Oh, no, mem!" Her hands were holding to the sides of her skirts, as though for moral support.

Amber decided that she was lying, but thought it most likely that whatever her part in the theft had been she had been prompted by Luke. She got up wearily, discouraged, but still less surprised than she would have expected to be, and went to the door where a tailor stood waiting with his bill in his hand. He was most courteous, however, when she told him that she had no money in the house, and said that he would call again. Mr. Channell had been an excellent customer and he had no wish to antagonize him.

Luke came home late, too drunk to talk, so that Amber had no alternative but to wait. When she woke the next morning, however, the room was empty and the door into Sally's apartment closed, but she could hear low voices coming from it. Quickly she slipped out of bed and ran to get into her clothes, intending to dress and then go in to talk to him before he left.

She had just pulled the sheer linen smock over her head and settled it about her when Luke opened the door. Quickly she reached for a petticoat. But he crossed the room swiftly, grabbed her by one elbow and swung her about, jerking the petticoat out of her hand and flinging it aside.

"Not so quick there. I hope a husband may be permitted a look at his wife sometimes?" He eyed her swollen belly. "You're mighty modest—" he said slowly, his face unpleasant, "for a bitch who was three months gone with child when she got married."

Amber stared at him, unmoving, her eyes cold and hard. Suddenly all her worry and indecision were gone. She felt only a bitter contemptuous hatred so strong it blotted out every other sense and emotion.

"Is that what you married me for, you lousy trull? To furnish a name for your bastard—"

All at once Amber struck him a hard, furious blow, with all the strength of her body, across the side of his face and left ear. Before she could even move he grabbed her by the hair, giving her head a vicious cracking jerk as his free hand smashed across her jaw. Suddenly terrified, seeing murder in his face, Amber screamed and Sally Goodman rushed into the room, shouting at him.

"Luke! Luke! Oh, you fool! You'll spoil everything! Stop it!"

She began to struggle with him as Amber cowered, not daring to fight back for fear some blow or kick would kill the baby, trying to protect herself with her hands and arms. But he struck at her again and again, his hands and fists hitting her wherever he could, swearing between his teeth, his face livid and writhing with rage. And then at last Sally succeeded in dragging him off and Amber crumpled to the floor, retching violently, moaning and gasping and almost hysterical.

"Oh, damn you, Luke!" she heard Sally cry. "Your temper will ruin us all!"

He ignored her, shouting at Amber: "Next time, you damned slut, I won't let you off so easy! I'll break your neck, d'ye hear me?" He made a short vicious kick at her and Amber screamed, arms covering her belly, eyes shut. He left the room, slamming the door with a crash.

The two women rushed immediately to Amber and helped her into the bed. She lay there for several minutes, still sobbing, trembling violently but more with rage and hatred and humiliation than from any pain she suffered. Sally sat on the bed chafing her hands, talking to her in a low soothing tone, while Honour hung over her with a sort of wide-eyed sympathetic stupefaction.

But as Amber began to recover her senses she became conscious of sharp little thrusting movements within her, and putting her hands to her stomach she could feel the baby stir. "Oh!" she cried furiously. "If I lose this baby I swear I'll see that son of 'a whore set up on a gibbet on Tyburn Hill!" Though a great many times she had half-hoped that some accident would bring on a miscarriage, now she realized that more than anything else she wanted to bear this child—for he was all that was left to her of Lord Carlton.

"Lord, sweetheart! How you talk!" cried Sally.

Nevertheless she sent Honour to an apothecary to get something which would prevent abortion and when the girl returned she brewed the packet of herbs into a tea. Amber drank the stinking decoction, holding her nose and making a face. The day wore on and as no symptoms of a miscarriage appeared

126

Amber began to feel easier, for though she was sore and bruised she had not been otherwise seriously hurt. But she could think of nothing but Luke Channell and how she hated him, and she was determined that as soon as she got her money back she would leave him—go away from London to some other town and hide. She lay on the bed for several hours with her eyes shut, absorbed in making her plans.

Sally was most solicitous and even when Amber pretended to be asleep she continued to question her, to bring her something to eat, to suggest that she would feel better if she sat up for a little while and played some game to amuse herself. Finally, with a bored sigh, Amber agreed and they started a game of ombre, playing on a board which rested across their laps.

"Poor Luke," said Sally after a few minutes. "I fear the dear boy inherited his father's fits. Sometimes, I swear, I've seen Sir Walter Channell lie foaming at the mouth and stark rigid for minutes at a time. But when it passes, he's the pleasantest man alive—just like Luke."

Amber, giving Sally a skeptical glance, put down her queen and took the trick. "Just like Luke?" she repeated. "Then I'm mighty sorry for Lady Channell."

Sally pursed her lips primly. "Well, my dear—sure, now, you wouldn't expect any man to be pleased to find his wife with child by another man's offices? And d'ye know—" She played a card, took the trick, and as she was placing it slantwise along the board looked across at Amber. "It would almost seem you must 've known what your condition was when you married 'im."

Amber smiled maliciously. "Oh, would it?" Suddenly her eyes flashed and she snapped out, "Why else would I marry that daggle-toothed lout?"

Sally looked at her, took a deep breath, and then began counting the tricks. She shuffled the cards, dealt, and they played for a while in silence.

All at once Amber said: "I'm missing a wallet that had a deal of money in it. It was on a nail behind that chest and someone stole it."

"Stole it! Thieves in these rooms! Oh, heaven!"

"I think the thief was Luke!"

"Luke? A thief? Lord, child, how you talk! Why, there's never an honester man in London than my nephew! And anyway, my dear, how could he *steal* money from you? A wife's money belongs to her husband the moment they leave the altar. I must say, sweetheart, I'm surprised you'd hide a few paltry pounds from 'im."

"A few paltry pounds! That wasn't a few paltry pounds! It was everything I had in the world!"

Sally looked at her quickly. "Everything you had? Then what about your inheritance? What about your five thousand pound?" She was staring at her, her blue eyes narrowed and hard, all the placid good-humour gone from her face.

"What about *his* inheritance?"

Sally refused to let go of her patience. "I explained that to you, my dear. And now am I to understand that you've swindled my nephew—made him think you were a person of some fortune when five hundred was all you had?"

Suddenly Amber slammed her handful of cards across the room and swept the board onto the floor. "Understand what you damn please! That wretch stole my money and I'll have 'im before a constable for it!"

Sally got up, bowed to her with an air of injured dignity, and went into her own room where she closed the door and remained throughout the rest of the day. Honour stayed with her mistress. Quietly she went about her usual duties. She served Amber her supper on a tray, brushed her hair, and when Amber got up to wash her face and clean her teeth she smoothed out the sheets with a bed-staff. She listened with sympathy but made no comment upon Amber's grumbling about her husband and his aunt and seemed not very much surprised by Amber's statement that she intended to leave him as soon as she could force him to give her money back.

Though she did not intend to, Amber fell asleep before Luke came home. Some time in the middle of the night she wakened to hear voices in the next room—his and Sally's—and though she waited for some time in cold angry apprehension the door between their rooms remained closed. And at last the sound of their voices ceased. She fell asleep again.

When she woke the next morning there was a bright fire going and the room had an almost surprising air of contented domesticity. Sally, humming a tune beneath her breath, was arranging a bowlful of green leaves. Honour was dusting the furniture with more enthusiasm than she usually showed for such tasks. And Luke stood knotting his cravat before a mirror, regarding himself with smug approval.

The moment she pulled back the bed-hangings Sally saw her. "Why!" she cried pleasantly. "Good morning to you, sweetheart!" Briskly she crossed the room and kissed her on the cheek, ignoring the face Amber made. "I hope you've slept well! Luke slept on the trundle in my room so as not to disturb you." She had never been more pleasant and now she turned a beaming smile upon her nephew, like a mother prompting her child in the presence of guests. "Didn't you, Luke?"

Luke gave her a broad grin, the same one he had used during their courtship. Amber lay propped on one elbow and regarded him sourly. She was determined somehow to get her money back, but the mere sight of him infuriated her so that she lost hold of all her schemes and plans. He started toward her, still grinning, though Amber watched him with sullen distrust.

"What d'ye suppose I've got here for you?" He had picked something off the mantel and kept one hand behind his back.

"I don't know, and I don't care! Get away from me!" she cried warningly, as he stooped to kiss her, and she flung the covers up over her head.

An ugly look came swiftly to his face but Sally reminded him with a nudge and jerk of her head. He sat down on the bed and reached out a tentative hand to touch her. "Look here, duckling—look what a fine present I've brought you. Heavens, sweetheart, you a'nt going to stay mad at poor Luke, now are you?"

She could hear him open a box and jingle something which sounded like jewellery and at last out of curiosity she peeked over the top of the blankets. He was holding toward her, temptingly, a bracelet with several diamonds and a ruby or two winking on it. His voice continued to wheedle, though she was looking not at him but at the bracelet.

"Believe me, sweetheart, I'm sorry for what I did yesterday. But truly at times it seems I'm not master of myself. My poor old father had those fits. Here—let me fasten it on your wrist—"

The bracelet was a handsome one, and finally Amber permitted him to clasp it. She knew that she must make him think she liked him, or she would never get her money back. So she let him kiss her and even pretended to giggle with pleasure. She had such contempt for him it was easy to make herself believe that she could outwit him. Finally she got up and dressed and they drank the morning draught of ale, together with a few anchovies. Luke suggested that Amber ride out to Pancras with him and have dinner at a charming little inn he knew, and thinking that most likely he really was sorry for his behaviour and once more infatuated with her, she agreed. She put on her cloak—though at his suggestion she left the bracelet there because of the danger from highwaymen—and they set out.

Pancras, a tiny village to the northwest, was about two miles from the Rose and Crown, or some three-quarters of an hour by coach. But they had scarcely reached High Holborn when it began to rain—though the winter had been a dry and warm and dusty one—and within fifteen minutes the roads were splashing with mud and there was a strong smell of rotten garbage in the air, made more poignant by the wet. Two or three times the wheels stuck and the coachman and footman had to pry them out, using an iron bar, which all coaches carried for that purpose.

To Amber, lurching and jogging inside the springless carriage, the ride seemed interminable and she wished miserably that she had stayed at home. But Luke was cheerful and talkative as he had not been for weeks, and she tried to pretend that she was enjoying the outing and his company. His hands roamed over her persistently, and he urged her to reciprocate his attentions. Amber laughed and tried to push him off, pretending she was afraid that the coach might overturn and spill them out

130

for everyone to see; the touch of his fingers made her flesh crawl and turn cold with loathing.

The inn she found to be a little greasy place and the room to which the host showed them was cold and unaired. He lighted a fire and then Luke went below with him to order the dinner while Amber stood at the window, looking out at the pouring rain and watching the bedraggled red rooster moving majestically across the courtyard, carefully picking up his claws as he went. She kept her cloak on, shivering a little, unhappy and listless, a sense of depression dragging at her.

The dinner was a bad one, a stringy slightly warmed chunk of boiled beef, boiled parsnips, and boiled bacon. Amber was disgusted with such fare and could scarcely force herself to take a bite but Luke, who was never discriminating, ate with gusto, a trickle of greasy juice running over his chin. He smacked his lips noisily, picked at his teeth with his fingernails, and spat on the floor until Amber, queasy with her pregnancy, thought that she would be sick.

He had scarcely done eating when he set upon her again, mauling her and pulling at her clothes. A moment later there was a knock and the landlord called his name; without a word he left her and went out the door.

For a moment Amber lay, surprised and relieved, half wondering what had happened. Suddenly she burst into tears of anger and loneliness and revulsion. I won't do it again! she thought. I won't if he kills me! She rolled over onto her side, crying drearily, and waited for him to come back.

She waited a long time. At last she got up, rinsed her face in cold water and combed her hair. She wondered where he had gone and what kept him, but she did not care very much. For when he did return they would only drive back and she would spend the rest of the afternoon talking to Sally or, if Luke stayed home, playing ombre or gleek and she would be sure to lose because they cheated and she did not know how.

Finally she began to grow uneasy and the suspicion sneaked into her mind that he had taken the coach and gone off, leaving her to get back however she might. It would be like him to take some such means of repaying her for having slapped him.

And she had not so much as a farthing with her. She snatched up her fan and muff and mask, flung on her black velvet cloak, and went out of the room and downstairs. The host was leaning over the counter, talking to some booted muddy stranger, and both men were smoking pipes and drinking ale.

"Where's my husband?" she demanded, halfway down the stairs.

They looked up at her. "Your husband?" repeated the host.

"Of course! The man I came here with!" she cried impatiently, crossing the floor toward him now. "Where is he?"

"Why, he's gone, mem. He said you was a lady wanted to elope with 'im and told me to call 'im at half-after-one. He went off in the coach soon's he came down—said you'd pay the reckoning," he added significantly.

Amber stared at him in astonishment and then she ran to the door to look out. It was true. Her coach was gone. She turned and faced him, angry and worried. "I've got to get back to London! How can I do it? Is there a stage-coach that stops here?"

"No, mem. Few enough of any kind stops here. The dinner was ten shillin's and the room ten shillin's. One pound in all, mem." He held out his hand.

"One pound! Well, I haven't got it! I haven't got a farthing! Oh, damn him!" It seemed to her that no one had ever had such scurvy luck, no one had ever suffered such trials as had beset her constantly since she had come to London. "How 'm I to get home?" she demanded again, desperate now. Certainly she could not walk in that pouring rain and the mud.

For a moment the host was silent, measuring her, deciding at last in her favour because of her fine clothes. "Well, mem, you look an honest lady. I've got a horse I can let you take and my son can show you the way—if you'll pay him the reckoning when you get there."

Amber agreed and she and the innkeeper's fourteen-year-old boy set out on a pair of swaybacked nags that could not be kicked or coaxed out of a plodding trot. Though not yet two-thirty it was dark and the rain came down steadily, soaking both of them through before they had gone a quarter-mile.

They rode silently, Amber clenching her teeth, wretchedly uncomfortable with the heavy jogging of her belly and the feel of wet clothes and hair clinging tight to her skin. She was wholly obsessed with Luke Channell and how she despised him. And the farther they rode, the more her stomach stabbed and ached, the more chilled she became—the more savagely she hated him. She promised herself that she would murder him for this, though she burnt alive for it.

When they got back into the City the streets were almost deserted. Men with their cloaks wrapped up about their mouths and their hats pulled low leant against the wind. Wet skinny dogs and miserable cats crouched in the doorways, and the kennels down the middle of the streets were rushing torrents of water and refuse.

The boy helped her to dismount and followed her as she ran inside, her skirts sticking to her legs, her soaked hair hanging down her shoulders in long twining tendrils. She looked like some weird water-witch. She ran through the parlour without glancing at anyone—though every eye there turned to follow her in amazement—rushed up the steps two at a time, then down the hallway to burst into her room with a hysterical scream.

"Luke!"

No one answered. For the room was empty, her bed still unmade, and everywhere were signs of hurried departure. Drawers were opened and empty; the wardrobe where her clothes had been stood ajar, but nothing was in it; the top of her dressing-table had been wiped clean. The mirrors she had bought were gone from the walls. A pair of silver candlesticks had been taken from the mantel. In his pretty gilt cage the little parakeet cocked an eye at her, and she saw the earrings Bruce had bought at the May Fair lying on the floor, as though flung away in contempt.

She stood there, staring, stunned and helpless. But even while she stared there began to come over her a feeling of relief and she was glad to be rid of them—all three, Luke and Sally Goodman and simple little Honour Mills. Slowly she reached up one hand and took out the bodkins that held up her back hair

—they had gold knobs on the ends with a pattern of tiny pearls. She held them toward him.

"My money's all gone," she said wearily. "Here. Take these."

He looked at her doubtfully for a moment, but finally accepted them. Slowly Amber pushed the door shut. She leaned back against it. She wanted nothing but to lie down on the bed and forget—forget that she was even alive.

PART TWO

CHAPTER NINE

THE FLOOR OF the room was covered with rushes which smelt sour and old, and rats came out boldly to dart about searching for morsels of food, their eyes bright and black as beads. The walls were stone, moist and dripping and green with a mossy slime; sunk into them were great ring-bolts from which hung heavy chains. Boarded beds ranged the walls as in a barracks. Though only mid-morning it was dark and would have been darker but for a tallow-candle which burnt with a low sullen flame, as though oppressed by the stinking air. It was the Condemned Hold at Newgate where prisoners were kept until they had paid the price of better quarters.

There were four women in the room, all of them seated, all of them shackled with heavy chains on wrists and ankles, all of them perfectly quiet.

One was a young Quaker girl in sober prim black, a starched white collar about her throat and a linen cap covering her hair; she sat motionless, concentrating on her feet. Across from her was a middle-aged woman who looked like any of the dozens of housewives seen every day in the streets going to market with a basket over one arm. Not far from her sprawled a morose slattern who stared dully at the others, one side of her mouth screwed up in a faint cynical smile. There were large open sores on her face and breasts and now and again she coughed with a hollow, racking sound as if she would bring up her very guts. The fourth woman was Amber, and she sat wrapped in her cloak, one hand tightly clasping the bird-cage set on her lap, the other inside her muff.

She looked strangely out of place there in that mouldering sty, for though all her garments were somewhat the worse for the soaking they had had two weeks before, the materials were good and the style fashionable. The gown, which had been made by Madame Darnier, was black velvet, caught up in back over a stiff petticoat of dark red-and-white-striped satin. Pleated frills of sheer white linen showed about the low neck-line and at the elbows of the puffed sleeves. Her silk stockings were scarlet and her square-toed shoes black velvet with large sparkling buckles. She wore her back-velvet cloak, carried her fox muff, her gloves and fan and mask.

She had been there for perhaps an hour—though it seemed a great deal longer—and so far no one had spoken a word. Her eyes roamed about restlessly, searching in the darkness, and she was beginning to fidget nervously. From everywhere about them, overhead, beneath their feet, from either side, came the muffled sounds of shouts and groans, screams and curses and laughter.

She looked at the housewife, then at the Quakeress, finally at the dirty slut across the room, and the last she found watching her with grum insolent amusement. "Is this the prison?" asked Amber at last, speaking to her because neither of the others seemed conscious of her or their own whereabouts.

For a moment she continued to squint near-sightedly at Amber and then she laughed and suddenly began to cough, leaning over with her hand against her chest until she spat out a great clot of bloody phlegm. "Is this the prison?" she repeated at last, mimicking. "What the hell d'ye think it is? It ain't Whitehall, me fine lady!" Her accent was strong and harsh and her voice had the dreary whine of a woman who has been tired for years.

"I mean is this *all* the prison?"

"Jesus, no." She gave a weary sweep of one arm. "Hear that? It's over us and under us and all around us. What're *you* here for?" she asked abruptly. "We ain't used to havin' the quality for company." She sounded sarcastic, but too tired to be dangerously malicious.

"For debt," said Amber.

The morning after Luke and his aunt and the maid had left her Amber had wakened with a bad cold, her throat so sore she could scarcely speak. But she was half relieved to be sick, for at least she could do nothing until she got well and it was impossible for her even to imagine what she would do then. She had no clothes but the ones she had been wearing, not a penny in cash, and her only negotiable assets were her wedding-ring, the string of pearls she had worn around her neck, a pair of pearl ear-drops, and the ear-rings Bruce had bought for her at the Fair. Luke had stolen everything of value, including the reconciliation bracelet and the silver-handled tooth-brush Bruce had given her.

As Amber lay in bed, coughing and blowing her nose, her very bones seeming to ache and her head feeling as though it was stuffed with cotton, she began to worry. She knew that she had been a fool, that they had played a trick on her that must be old as time and worn threadbare by usage. With her country-girl gullibility she had walked into their trap, as innocent as a woodcock. And she had nothing for consolation but the sureness that they had been almost as much mistaken in her. For now she was convinced that Luke had thought he was marrying a real heiress and that they had left only when the mistake was discovered.

By the third day the hall outside her room was aswarm with creditors, all of them demanding payment. And when Amber went to the door wrapped in a blanket and told them that her husband had run away and she had no money they threatened to bring action against her. At last she refused to answer any more and shouted at them to go away and leave her alone. Then this morning the constable had come, told her to get dressed and taken her off to Newgate. She would not be tried, he said, until the quarter-session and then—if found guilty of her large debt—she would be sentenced to remain in Newgate until it was paid.

"For debt," repeated the housewife. "That's why I'm here, too. My husband died owin' one pound six."

"One pound six!" cried Amber. "*I* owe three hundred and *ninety-seven pound!*" She felt almost triumphant at being in jail for such a stupendous sum, but that feeling was soon squelched.

"Then," said the slattern, "you ain't goin' out of here till they carry you out in a wooden box."

"What d'you mean? I had the money! I had *more* than that—but my husband rubbed off with it! When they catch him I'll get it back again!" She tried to sound confident but the woman's words had scared her, for it was not the first rumour she had heard of the kind of justice they dealt here in London.

Smiling, the other woman heaved herself away from the wall and came forward, bringing with her a stench that made Amber's nostrils flare in revulsion. She stood for a moment looking down at her with an expression that suggested both weary jealousy of her youth and beauty and an almost friendly contempt for her naïveté and confident optimism. Then she sat down beside her.

"I'm Moll Turner. Where'd you come from, sweetheart? You ain't been long in London, have you?"

"I've been here seven months and a half!" retorted Amber defiantly, for it always hurt her pride when she was recognized for an outlander. "I came from Essex," she added, more meekly.

"Well, now, you needn't take such hogan-mogan airs with me, Mrs. Minx. I'd say anyone's had such a flam put upon 'em as you have stands in need of a little friendly counsel. And you'll need more before you been long in this place."

"I'm sorry. But to tell you truly, Mrs. Turner, I'm in such a mouse-hole I think I'll run mad. What can I *do?* I've got to get out of here! I'm going to have a baby!"

"Are you indeed?" She did not seem very much impressed or concerned. "Well, it won't be the first born in Newgate, believe me for that. Look here, sweetheart, most likely you ain't never goin' out of here. So listen to what I say and you'll save yourself a deal of trouble."

"Never!" cried Amber frantically. "Oh, but I am! I've got to!. I won't stay—they can't keep me in here!"

Mrs. Turner seemed bored and impatient, and ignoring Amber's protests went on with what she had begun to say. "You'll have to pay garnish to the jailor's wife to get better quarters, garnish for lighter chains, garnish if you so much as puke in this place. And you can begin to get the feel of it by giving me them ear-drops—"

Amber gasped in horror and moved back a little. "I won't do it! They're mine! Why should I give 'em to *you,* pray!"

"Because, sweetheart, if I don't get 'em the jailor's wife will. Oh, I'll use you honestly. Give me the ear-drops—they don't look worth more'n a pound at the top—" she added, narrowing her eyes and peering at them closely, "—and I'll tell you how to live in this place. I've been here before, I'll warrant you. Come, now, before we're disturbed."

Amber stared at her for a long moment, frank skeptical distrust on her face, but finally she decided that it would be worth the ear-rings to have a friend who understood this strange place. She slid the pearls from her ears and dropped them into Mrs. Turner's outstretched palm. Moll tucked them into the bodice of her gown, somewhere between her stringy breasts, and turned to Amber.

"Now, my dear, how much money have you got?"

"Not a farthing."

"Not a farthing? My God, how d'you intend to live? Newgate ain't run for charity, you may be sure. You pay for everything you get here, and you pay dear."

"Well, *I* won't. Because I haven't got any money."

Amber's matter-of-fact tone sent Moll into another fit of violent coughing, but at last she straightened, running her fore-arm across her wet mouth. "Don't seem like you're old enough to be out of the house alone, sweetheart. Where's your family—in Essex? My advice to you is to send to 'em for help."

Amber stiffened at that suggestion, defensively lowering her black lashes. "I can't. I mean I won't. They didn't want me to get married and I—"

"Never mind, my dear. I think I know your plight well enough. You found yourself with child and so left home. Now your keeper's left you. Well, in London we don't give a damn —we've got troubles enough of our own without worryin' ourselves with our neighbours—"

"But I *am* married!" protested Amber, determined to have the credit of a respectable woman since she had gone to such lengths to be one. "I'm Mrs. Channell—Mrs. Luke Channell. And here's my ring to prove it!" She stripped the glove from her left hand and thrust it beneath Moll's nose.

"Yes, yes. Lord, my dear, I don't care if you're married or

whore to forty men. I was myself, in better days. Now I'm so peppered a man wouldn't have me upon a pinch." She smiled faintly and shrugged, then stared off into space, forgetting her promise as she began to recall the disappointments of her own life. "That's the way I began. He was a captain in the King's army—a mighty handsome fellow in his uniform. But my dad didn't like to see his daughter bringin' a nameless brat into the family. So I came to London. You can hide anything in London. My boy died—more's the mercy—and I never saw my captain again. But I saw other men aplenty, I'll warrant you. And I had money for a while, too. Once a gentleman gave me a hundred pound for one night. Now—" She turned suddenly and looked at Amber, who had been staring at her with fascinated horror, finding it almost impossible to believe that this ugly emaciated sick creature had once been young and in love with a handsome man, just as she was. "How old d'ye think I am? Fifty? No, I'm thirty-two. Just thirty-two. Well, I've had my day, there's no denyin' that. I suppose I wouldn't trade it for something different—"

Amber was beginning to feel sick, seeing herself several years hence in Moll Turner. Oh, God! Oh, God! she thought frantically. It's just like Aunt Sarah said. Look what happens to a bad woman!

And then all of them started at the sound of a key in the lock; the great iron door began to swing open. Moll, putting her hand to her mouth, muttered quickly: "Sell that ring for whatever she'll give you."

A woman, perhaps fifty years old, came into the room. Her hair, almost white, was lifeless as straw and screwed into a hard knot high on the crown of her head. She wore a soiled blouse, a dark-blue woollen skirt with a long red apron tied over it, and slung about her hips was a leather thong to which were attached several very large keys, a pair of scissors, a wallet and a bull's pizzle—a short heavy wooden cudgel for maintaining discipline. She carried a candle stuck into a bottle, and before turning around to look at them she set it on a shelf.

A huge grey-striped cat followed her in, pushing against her legs, arching its back, giving out a low satisfied rumble. And then all at once it caught sight of Amber's parakeet and moved swiftly forward. But Amber, with a little scream, jumped to her feet and, holding the cage at shoulder-level, kicked out at the cat with one foot while her parakeet fluttered and clung terrified to the bars of its cage.

"Good-morning, ladies," said the woman now, and her shrewd pitiless eyes went over them quickly, resting longest on Amber. "I'm Mrs. Cleggat—my husband is the Jailor. It's my understanding that you are all ladies of refinement who naturally would not care to take up your abode in a vault set aside for thieves, parricides, and murderers. I'm happy to say that from here you may be removed to a chamber the equal of that in any private house and there you'll be furnished with the best of conversation and entertainment—for a consideration."

"There's the rub," commented Moll, sprawled out with her arms crossed, her legs stretched before her.

"How much?" asked Amber, keeping an eye on the cat which now sat patiently at her feet, wide-eyed and flicking just the tip of his tail. If she could sell her wedding-ring she would have money enough to buy very good quarters—and she was still convinced that she would be out within a day or two.

"Two shillings six to get out of here. Six shillings for easement. Two shillings six a week for a bed. Two shillings a week for sheets. Six shillings six to the turnkey. Ten shillings six to the steward of the ward for coal and candles. That's all for now. I'll have one pound ten from each of you ladies." As they all looked at her and no one either moved or spoke she said briskly, "Come, now. I'm a woman of affairs. There's others here too, y'know."

Moll now lifted her skirt and from a pocket in her petticoat produced the required sum. " 'Sblood, it seems I only steal enough to support myself in prison."

Amber looked around, waiting for one of the others to speak, but they did not and so she pulled the wedding-ring from her finger and extended it toward Mrs. Cleggat. "I haven't got any money. How much will you give me for this?"

Mrs. Cleggat took it, held it to the candle and said, "Three pound."

"Three pound! But I paid twelve for it!"

"Values are different here." She unbuttoned the wallet, counted out several shillings, handed them to Amber and dropped the wedding-ring into the leather pouch. "Is that all?"

"Yes," said Amber. She did not intend to part with the string of pearls Bruce had given her not long before he sailed.

Mrs. Cleggat looked at her sharply. "You'd better give me whatever else you've got right now. If you don't I promise you it'll be stolen before you've been here two hours."

Amber hesitated a moment longer and then, with a heavy sigh, she unfastened the clasp and drew the strand out of her cloak. Mrs. Cleggat gave her six pounds for them and promptly turned her attention to the other women. The Quakeress stood up and faced her squarely, but as she spoke her voice was soft and meek.

"I have no money, friend. Do with me as thou wilt."

"You'd better send out for some, Mrs. Or you go into the Common side which, though I say it myself, isn't fit for a baboon."

"No matter. I can get used to it."

Mrs. Cleggat shrugged and her voice was contemptuously indifferent. "You fanatics." (A fanatic, in the common understanding, was anyone who belonged to neither the Catholic nor the Anglican Church.) "Well enough then, Mrs. Give me your cloak for the entrance fee and your shoes for easement."

Out of doors it was almost warm for the winter had been a strange one, but in there it was chill and damp. Nevertheless the girl untied her cloak and took it off. Amber, looking from her to Mrs. Cleggat with growing indignation, now suddenly made up her mind.

"Here! Keep it on! I'll pay for you! You'll fall sick without it!"

Moll glanced at her scornfully. "Don't be a fool! You've little enough for yourself!"

But the Quakeress gave her a gentle smile. "Thank thee, friend. Thou art kind—but I want nothing. If I fall sick, it is the will of God."

144

Amber regarded her dubiously, then extended the coins toward Mrs. Cleggat. "Take it for her anyway."

"The girl will be a damned nuisance to me if she's made comfortable. Keep the money for yourself. It'll go quick enough." She turned to the housewife, who admitted that she had not so much as a farthing. Amber looked at Moll to see if she would not offer to share the woman's expenses with her, but Moll was glancing idly about the room and whistling beneath her breath.

"Well, then—I'll pay for her."

This time the offer was accepted and the woman thanked her profusely, promising to repay her as soon as she was able—which would apparently be never if she was to be kept in prison until her debt was cleared. And then a man came in to put on the lighter shackles. They consisted of bracelets which fitted loosely about the wrists and ankles with long chains stretching between, and though they were awkward and clanked dismally they did not seem to be otherwise uncomfortable.

"Take the fanatic to the Common Felon's side," said Mrs. Cleggat to the man when he had done. "Come with me, ladies." They trooped out of the room after her, first Moll, then Amber holding the bird-cage on her shoulder, and then the housewife.

Mounting a dark narrow stairway they reached a big room where the door stood open; above it was nailed a skull-and-crossbones. Mrs. Cleggat went in first with her candle and as they followed they could see two large flat beds, covered with flock mattresses and some grey rumpled bedding, a table, scarred stools and chairs, and a cold fireplace above and beside which hung some blackened kettles and pans and a few pewter mugs and dishes. Certainly there was nothing in this barren dirty room to suggest the luxurious quarters Mrs. Cleggat had painted.

"This," she said, "is the Lady Debtors' Ward."

Amber looked at her in angry astonishment, while Moll smiled. "This!" she cried, forgetting her manacles and giving a sweep of one arm. "But you told us—"

"Never mind what I told you. If you don't like it I can take you to the Common Side."

Amber turned away, disgusted, and Mrs. Cleggat prepared to leave with Moll, who would go to the Lady Felons' Quarters. Oh! she thought furiously. This nasty place! I won't stay here a day! Then she swung around.

"I want to send a letter!"

"That'll cost you three shillings."

Amber paid it. "Are we the only prisoners?" She could still hear the voices, the incessant sounds that seemed to come from the very walls, but they had seen no one else.

"Most of the others are down in the Tap-Room. It's Christmas Eve."

The letter, written by an amanuensis, was sent to Almsbury, and she was very confident that he would have her out of there within twenty-four hours. When she got no immediate reply she told herself that since it was Christmas Day he had very likely been away from his lodgings. Tomorrow, she promised herself, he'll come. But he did not, and the days passed and at last she was forced to realize that either he had not received the letter or was no longer interested in her.

The Lady Debtors' Ward was the least crowded one in Newgate, but even so she and the housewife, Mrs. Buxted, had to share those scant accommodations with a dozen other women. In many wards, however, thirty or forty were crowded into the same space and there were more than three hundred prisoners in a building intended for half that number. It was impossible for everyone to lie on the beds at once and they had to use cooking utensils and dishes in turn. Usually these were merely scraped off between meals, for water cost money and was always stale and stinking and afloat with vegetation and specks of sewage. This encouraged them to spend what they could on ale or wine.

The entire prison lay in an eternal half-gloom, for the windows, deep-set and narrow, opened only upon dark passages. Links and tallow-candles were bought by the prisoners and they burnt all day long. Large ugly cats and numerous dogs, half-

146

naked with mange, roamed the hallways and contested with the rats for every shred of refuse; Amber had to keep a constant eye on her parakeet. The smells were thick and almost palpable, product of the accumulated rot of centuries, and sometimes there was another strange and sickening odour which she learned came from the heads being boiled by the hangman in his kitchen below their ward. She had not been there an hour when she started scratching furiously. She caught the plump lice between her fingers, squashing them like boiled peas.

Newcomers were automatically assigned the duties of chamber-maid. The first morning Amber and Mrs. Buxted carried the slop-jars down the hall and emptied them into the cess-pool below. The stench of the heavy fumes made Amber almost faint. After that she paid another woman two pence a week to do the job for her.

The prison was considered to be a place of detention, not of correction, and from eight o'clock in the morning until nine at night all inside doors were opened and each was free to follow his inclination.

Those who had been arrested because of their religious beliefs were now permitted to hold services, make what converts they could, or preach sedition. Whoever had money usually spent it in the Tap-Room, drinking and gambling. Well-to-do inmates sometimes gave large entertainments attended by persons of the first quality, for some criminals enjoyed considerable popularity. Visitors were admitted to the Hall and swarmed there by the hundreds. A man might have his wife and children to keep him company—sometimes for years—or, if he preferred and had the price, he could take his choice of the prostitutes who daily came from outside.

Thievery was common and fights went on continually, for discipline was maintained by the prisoners themselves. Some went mad and were heavily chained, but usually not segregated. Babies were born but seldom lived long, and the death-rate among all prisoners was high.

Amber remained as aloof from the life of the jail as she could; this was one place where she desired no popularity. She did not go to the Tap-Room and of course she had no visitors, so that the only time she left her own ward was on Sunday when everyone was herded up to the third-floor Chapel.

Most of the women in the Lady Debtors' Ward were the victims of misfortune and all of them expected soon to be released. They sat by the hour talking of the day when their debt would be paid—by a father or brother or friend—and they would go free. Amber listened to them, wistfully, for she had no one to pay her debt and no reason to hope for freedom, though she continued stubbornly to do so.

With aching homesickness her memories went back to the Goodegroome cottage. She took pleasure in remembering many things she had not known she cared for. She remembered how the dormer windows of her bedroom were wreathed in roses, and the delicious summer scent they had had. She remembered how the overhanging eaves were full of sparrows so that every morning she woke to the sound of their twirring and twittering. She remembered Sarah's wonderful rich food, the clean-scrubbed flag-stones of the kitchen floor and the rows of glossy pewter lining the shelves. She longed passionately for a sight of the sky, a breath of fresh air, the smell of flowers and hay new-mown, the sound of a bird's song.

The holidays were dreary as she had never known they could be.

She remembered what Christmas had been the year before when she had helped Sarah to make mince-pies and plum-pottages; she and all her cousins had dressed up to go mumming; and everyone on the farm had toasted the fruit trees in apple-cider, according to the old old custom. On New Year's Eve she spent several shillings of her fast-dwindling supply for Rhenish wine and the Lady Debtors drank it, proposing a toast to the new year. Just before midnight the bells began to ring from every steeple in London and Amber burst into lonely frightened tears, for she was sure that she would never live to hear them ring in another year.

A week later Newgate was swept with frenzied excitement: A rebellion had broken out in the city, led by a band of religious zealots, and for three days and nights they ran riot through the streets. Bellowing for King Jesus, they shot down whoever op-

148

posed them. Inside the prison they heard the bells banging out an ominous warning, confused shouts and cries and the sound of flying hoofs. The prisoners gathered anxiously in groups, talking of massacre and fire, discussing means of escape; the women became hysterical, screamed at the grates and begged to be set free.

But the Fifth Monarchists were hunted out, killed or captured, and within a few days twenty of them had been hanged, drawn and quartered. Their remains were brought to Newgate and dismembered legs and arms and torsos lay in the courtyard while Esquire Dun was at work in his kitchen pickling the heads in bay-salt and cumin seed. Prison life settled back into the normal rut of drunkenness and gambling, quarrels and venery and theft.

When the quarter-sessions were held Amber was brought to trial along with Mrs. Buxted and Moll Turner and a great many others and—like most of them—found guilty. She was sentenced to remain in Newgate until her debt had been paid in full. She had been so hopeful she would be released after the trial that it was a severe shock and for several days she was sunk in despondency; she would have been almost glad to die. But gradually she began trying to persuade herself that her position was not so desperate as it seemed. Why—any day Almsbury might arrive and rescue her. It always happens, she assured herself, when you least expect it; and she tried very hard to stop expecting Almsbury.

She often saw Moll Turner, who wandered in to talk to her and to urge her to come out and mingle with the others. "Christ, sweetheart, what can you lose? D'ye want to rot in here?"

"Of course not!" said Amber crossly. "I want to get out of this damned place!"

Moll laughed and went to the fireplace to light a pipeful of tobacco. Many of the prisoners, both men and women, smoked incessantly for the tobacco was supposed to protect them against disease. She came back puffing and sat down opposite Amber, ostentatiously drumming one hand on the table-top.

"See that?" On her middle finger she wore a large diamond. "Got that off a lady was here visitin' day before yesterday. We gave her the budge, and when she caught her balance I had the fambles cheat and somebody else had the scout." Moll often talked in an underworld cant, of which Amber had begun to pick up a few words. A "fambles cheat" was a ring and a "scout" was a watch. "Oh, I tell you, my dear, the Hall's a mighty profitable place. At this rate I can buy my way out of here in another month. "Well—" She heaved herself up. "Stay in here if you like—"

Amber, half-convinced by Moll's tales of facile theft, ventured out into the hallway a time or two, but she was always accosted so swiftly and roughly that she would pick up her skirts and run as hard as she could go for the comparative privacy of the Lady Debtors' Ward. Moll laughed at this too and told her that she was a fool not to take advantage of what she could get.

"Some of those gentlemen are mighty rich. In time I don't doubt you could earn your way out. Of course," she would admit, with her lop-sided smile, "four hundred pound ain't come by very quick, and there's a dozen half-crown sluts they can have the pick of any day in the week."

Several times she brought Amber offers of specific sums from one or another of the men, but it was never enough that Amber cared to make the venture. Moll's condition was sufficient warning and she was in mortal fear of being peppered herself. Nevertheless she would have done anything to get out of Newgate—taken any wild chance that might keep her baby from being born there.

By the end of a month her money had dwindled to less than two pounds, for everything had a price and it was invariably a high one. She had been paying to have her food sent in—the alternative was to eat the prison-fare, mouldy bread and stale water, with charity-meat once a week—and she had also paid for Mrs. Buxted's meals because otherwise the woman would have had none. When a midwife who shared the ward told her that she was too thin for a pregnant woman and that the baby was getting all she ate, she decided that she must sell the gold earrings.

Mrs. Cleggat gave them one scornful glance. "Those things? Brass and Bristol-stone! They're not worth three farthings!

Where'd ye get 'em—St. Martin's?" A great deal of cheap imitation jewellery was sold in the parish of St. Martin-le-Grand.

Hurt, Amber did not answer her. But she had begun to notice herself that the thin gilt was wearing and showed a grey metal beneath. She was almost glad that they were too worthless to sell.

At the end of her fifth week in Newgate Amber sat in one of the boxes of the chapel, stared at her dirty finger-nails, and worried about how she would eat a month from then. For days she had been trying to find courage to tell Mrs. Buxted that she could not feed her any longer. But she had not been able to do it, for every day Mrs. Buxted's daughter came and brought her the youngest child to nurse. As usual, Amber had not heard a word of the sermon, though it had been going on for a long while.

Now Moll Turner gave her a sharp nudge. "There's Black Jack Mallard!" she whispered. "And he's got his eye on you!"

Amber glanced sulkily across the room where she saw a gigantic black-haired man sitting staring at her, and as she did so he smiled. Cross at being interrupted in her worries, she scowled at him and looked away. Moll, thoroughly disgusted, nudged her several times but Amber refused to pay her any attention.

"Oh, you and your hogan-mogan airs!" muttered Moll as they left the chapel. "Who d'ye expect to find here in Newgate, pray? His Majesty?"

"What's so fine about him, I'd like to know?" She had thought him too dark and ugly.

"Well, Mrs., whatever you may think, Black Jack Mallard *is* somebody! He's a rum-pad, let me tell you."

"A highwayman?"

Highwaymen, she had discovered, were the élite of the criminal world, though this man was the first she had seen. She did remember, though, one of that brotherhood who had hung, a mere clean-picked skeleton, in a set of gibbet-irons at the Marygreen crossroads, mute warning to others of his kind. And in a slight breeze the bones and irons had had an eerie clank that sent the villagers home before sundown to avoid passing him in the dark.

"A highwayman. And one of the best, too. He's already broke out of here three times."

Amber's eyes opened with a snap. "Broke out of here! How!"

"Ask 'im yourself," said Moll, and went off, leaving Amber at the door of her own ward.

Staring dazedly, Amber walked inside. Here was the chance she had been waiting for! If he'd got out before, he'd get out again—perhaps soon. And when he did— She was suddenly excited and full of optimism— But all at once her hopes collapsed.

Look at me! I'm fat as a barn-yard fowl and stinking dirty. The Devil himself wouldn't have a use for me now.

There was no doubt her appearance had suffered sad changes during the past five weeks. Now, at the end of her seventh month of pregnancy, she could no longer button her bodice, the once pert frills had wilted, and her smock was a dirty grey. Her gown was stained in the armpits, spotted with food, and her skirt hung inches shorter in front. She had long ago thrown away her silk stockings, for they had been streaked with runs, and her shoes were scuffed out at the toes. She had not seen a mirror since she had been there, nor taken off her clothes, and though she had scrubbed her teeth on her smock she could feel a slick film as she ran her tongue over them. Her face was grimy and her hair, which she had to comb with her long finger-nails, snarled and greasy.

Despair on her face, Amber's hands ran down over her body. But she was sharply aware that this might be her one chance, and that made her determination begin to rise. It's dark in here, she told herself. He can't see me very well—and maybe I can do something, maybe I can make myself look a little better someway. She decided that she would do what she could to improve her appearance and then go down to the Tap-Room, on the chance of seeing him, though admission there would cost her a precious shilling and a half.

She was scrubbing her teeth with some salt and a piece torn off her smock—rinsing her mouth out with ale and spitting into the fireplace—when a man appeared at the door, and told her that Black Jack wanted to see her in the Tap-Room. She gave a start and turned quickly.

"Me?"

"Yes, you."

"Oh, Lord! And I'm all unready! Wait a moment!"

Not knowing what to do, she began smoothing her dress and rubbing her hands over her face in the hope of taking off some of the dirt.

"I'm paid to light you down, Mrs., but not to wait here. Come along." He gave a wave of the link and started off.

Amber paused just long enough to open her smock low over her breasts, muttered swiftly to Mrs. Buxted, "Watch my bird," and then picking up her skirts she hurried after him. Her heart was pounding as though she had been going to be presented at Court.

CHAPTER TEN

BARBARA PALMER WAS a woman of no uncertain desires or ambitions. Almost from the moment she had been born she had known what she wanted and had usually contrived to get it, whatever the cost to herself or others. She had no morals, knew no qualms, did not trouble herself with a conscience. Her character and personality were as glittering, as elemental, as barbaric as was her beauty. And now, just twenty-one years old, she had found what she wanted more than anything else on earth.

She wanted to be the wife of Charles Stuart; she wanted to be Queen of England. She refused to believe that such an idea was absurd.

Barbara and Charles had met at the Hague a few weeks before the Restoration, when her husband was sent there to take a gift of money to the King. Charles, who was invariably attracted to beautiful women, was instantly and strongly attracted to her. And Barbara, both flattered to be sought by a king and glad of an opportunity to revenge herself on a jilting lover—the Earl of Chesterfield—quickly became his mistress. Everyone agreed that Charles, not surprisingly, was more deeply infatuated than he had ever been during the many years of his gallantry, and Barbara began to be a woman of considerable importance.

The Roger Palmers, who had been married less than two years, lived in one of the great houses on King Street, a narrow muddy but highly fashionable thoroughfare which ran through the Palace grounds and served to connect the villages of Charing and Westminster. Inns massed the west side of the street, but on the east were great mansions whose gardens led down to the unembanked Thames. It was in her husband's home, at the end of the year, that Barbara began to give suppers which were attended by the King and most of the gay young men and pretty women of the Court, his Majesty's closest companions.

For a while Roger obediently appeared and pretended to be host. But at last he balked at the ridiculous role he was expected to play.

He came one January evening and knocked, as he had been told to do, at the door of his wife's bedroom. He was a medium-sized man of no pretentious appearance or manner but there was a look of good-breeding on his face and intelligence in his eyes. Barbara called out to him to enter and then, as he did so, merely glanced around carelessly over her shoulder.

"Oh. Good-evening, sir."

She was sitting before a table above which hung a mirror with candles affixed, and a maid was brushing her long mahogany-coloured hair while she tried several different pairs of dangling ear-rings to see which effect she liked best. Her elaborate gown was made of stiff black satin so that by contrast the skin of her arms and shoulders and breasts looked chalk-white, and there were diamonds at her throat and about her wrists. She was in the eighth month of her first pregnancy but seemed scarcely conscious of her unusual bulk, and she looked robustly healthy.

Now, as he entered and crossed the room the maid curtsied and went on with her brushing while Barbara turned her head from one side to the other, making the diamond pendants dance and catch the candle-light. At his appearance a subtle boredom, a kind of polite contempt, had come upon her face. And as he stood looking down at her in obvious perplexity she paid him no further attention, though she knew that he was trying to speak and wanted her help.

"Madame," he began at last, after taking a deep swallow into his dry throat. "I find that it will be impossible for me to have supper with you this evening."

"Ridiculous, Roger! His Majesty will be here. He'll expect you."

She had finally satisfied herself as to the ear-rings and now began to stick on several small black patches, hearts and diamonds and half-moons; one went beside her right eye, another on the left side of her mouth, a third high on her left temple. She had not glanced at him again after the first careless greeting.

"I think his Majesty will understand well enough, if I'm not present."

Barbara rolled her eyes, heaving a pained but patient sigh. "Heigh ho! Are we to go through this again?"

He bowed. "We are not, madame. Good-night."

As he turned and went to the door Barbara sat drumming her nails on the edge of the table, her eyes taking on a dangerous sparkle, and then all at once she pulled away from the maid and got to her feet, raising her arm to secure the last bodkin herself.

"Roger! I want to speak to you!"

His hand on the knob, he turned and faced her. "Madame?"

"Get out of here, Wharton." She gave a wave of her hand at the maid but started to talk before the girl had had time to leave. "I think you'd better come tonight, Roger. If you don't his Majesty will think it damned peculiar."

"I don't agree, madame. I think his Majesty must find it more peculiar that a man should be content to go tamely and parade his wife's whoredom before half the Court."

Barbara gave an unpleasant laugh. "The mistress of a King is not a whore, Roger!" Her eyes suddenly narrowed and hardened and her voice rose. "How often must I tell you that!" Then it fell again to become soft, purring, sarcastic. "Or can it be you haven't noticed I'm treated with twice as much respect now as I got when I was only the wife of an honourable gentleman?" The inflection she gave the last two words showed her contempt of him and of her own insignificant station as his wife.

He looked at her coldly. "I think there's a better word for it than respect."

"Oh? And what's that pray?"

"Self-interest."

"Oh, a pox on you and your damned jealousy! I'm sick of your bellow-weathering! But you'll come to the supper tonight and act as host or by Jesus you'll smoke for it!"

Suddenly he crossed to her, his pose of indifference gone, his face flushed and contorted with anger. He caught hold of her fore-arm. "Be quiet, madame! You sound like a fish-wife! I was a fool not to have taken you to the country when I first married you—my father warned me you'd disgrace us all! But I've learned since then, and I've discovered that to some women freedom means license. It seems that you're one of those women."

Her eyes, almost on a level with his, stared at him tauntingly. "And if I am," she said slowly, "what of it?"

All the uncertainty he had shown before her at first had now vanished completely, leaving him poised and determined. "To-morrow we shall leave for Cornwall. I don't doubt that two or three years of country quiet will do much to restore your perspective."

With a sudden swift wrench she jerked away from him. "You damned noddy! Just you try spiriting me away to the country and we'll make a trial of what good it does me to have the King's favour!" They were standing silently, both breathing hard, staring fiercely into each other's eyes, when there was a knock on the door and a voice called:

"His Majesty, King Charles II!"

Barbara looked around. "He's here!" Automatically her hands went to her head to make sure that every hair was in place, her eyes moving swiftly and excitedly, and though her face still showed traces of anger it had cleared considerably. She went to pick up her black-spangled fan and then returned. "Now! Are you coming down to act as host, or no!"

"I am not."

"Oh, you fool!"

Her hand lashed out and slapped him stingingly across the face and then she picked up her skirts and hurried across the

156

room, pausing a moment to compose her features before she opened the door. Then she went out and down the broad portrait-lined hallway, to the staircase.

Below her stood the King in conversation with her cousin, Buckingham, but as she appeared both men stopped talking and turned to give her their attention. She came down slowly, partly because the precarious unbalance of pregnancy made her cautious, partly to let them admire her. And then as she reached the bottom she curtsied while both men bowed and the King, who alone might remain covered in his own presence, swept off his hat.

Barbara and Charles exchanged lingering smiles, deep intimate looks charged with memories and anticipation. And then she turned to the Duke who had been watching them with cynical amusement on his face.

"Well, George. I didn't expect you back so soon from France."

"I didn't expect to be back so soon. But—" He gave a shrug of his heavy shoulders, glancing at the King.

Charles laughed. "But Philippe flew into a jealous rage. I think he was afraid his Grace intended to follow in his father's footsteps."

It was notorious gossip in both kingdoms that the first Buckingham had been the lover of beautiful Anne of Austria, who was now Louis XIV's fat and old and ill-tempered mother. And his son had made no secret of his violent admiration for Minette.

"It would have been a pleasure," said Buckingham, and made the King a half-mocking bow.

"Shall we go into the drawing-room?" asked Barbara then, and as they walked toward it she looked up at Charles, her face appealing, soft and almost childish. "Your Majesty, I'm in a most embarrassing position. There's no host for the supper tonight."

"No host? Where's— You mean he didn't care to come?"

Barbara nodded and dropped her black lashes, as though deeply ashamed of her husband's bad manners. But Charles had another view of the matter.

"Well, I can't say that I blame him, poor devil. Ods-fish, it seems a man with a beautiful wife is more to be pitied than envied."

"If he lives in England, he is," said the Duke.

Charles laughed good-humouredly. He could not be offended on the subject of his own habits for he did not try to fool himself about them.

"Still, every party needs a host. If you'll permit me, madame—"

Barbara's purple eyes gleamed with triumph. "Oh, your Majesty! If you would!"

Now, as they entered the doorway and paused for a moment, the roomful of people swung to face them as though magnetized. The hat of every man came off in a sweeping bow and the ladies bent gracefully to the ground, like full-blown flowers grown too heavy for their stems. Barbara had already become so successful and important a hostess that she did not find it necessary to welcome her guests as they arrived. Everyone of any ambition, whether social or political, was delighted to receive an invitation from Mrs. Palmer and would not have complained whatever her manners might be. For many were convinced she would one day, perhaps soon, be Queen of England.

A year ago Barbara would have thought it incredible that she would ever have in her home all at one time these men and women she now used so carelessly.

There was Anthony Ashley Cooper, small, emaciated and sick, related to many of the most powerful families in the nation. By some sleight-of-hand performance he had contrived to transmute himself into a loyal Cavalier at just about the time of the Restoration. The feat, however, was no very unusual one. Sympathizers with or active workers in the old régime had by no means all been hanged and quartered or harried into exile—many of them now supported the Monarchy and, in fact, formed the basis of the new Government. Charles was too practical and too well-versed in politics to have imagined that his Restoration could mean a complete overthrow of everything that had been done these past twenty years; the recent change had been mostly superficial. Cooper, like many another, had adopted a new set of manners which matched better with Charles's Court, but he had relinquished neither principles nor fundamental intentions.

There was Cooper's good friend, the Earl of Lauderdale, a huge red-faced red-haired Scotsman whose brogue was thick even though most of his forty-five years had been spent in England. He was ugly and coarse and boisterous, but he had an amazing education in Latin, Hebrew, French, and Italian which he had laboriously acquired during his years of imprisonment under the Commonwealth. Charles found him amusing and the Earl had a deep affection for his King.

George Digby, Earl of Bristol, was a good-looking man of almost fifty, vain and unreliable, but he had in common with Cooper and Lauderdale a violent hatred of the Chancellor. That hatred, founded on envy and jealousy, served to unite most of the ambitious men at Court. To put Chancellor Hyde out of the way was their highest aim, their greatest hope. Barbara's house gave them a rallying-ground, for here they might meet the King when he was at his leisure and most accessible.

But many of them were merely gay young people interested in nothing more serious than their love-affairs and gambling, in learning the latest dance or keeping apace with the French fashions.

Lord Buckhurst, only twenty-three, lived at Court but had no use for it, and refused to exert himself to become a man of power. Henry Jermyn was a big-headed spindle-shanked fop who was enjoying a considerable amatory success because many persons believed he had been married to the dead Princess Mary. Among the ladies was the voluptuous cat-like Countess of Shrewsbury; Anne, Lady Carnegie, flagrantly over-painted, now famous because she had shared Barbara's first lover with her; Elizabeth Hamilton, a tall gracious cool young woman, newly arrived at Court, whom it was the fashion to admire. They were all about Barbara's age, twenty or younger, for the men were outspoken in their opinion that a woman had begun to decay at twenty-two.

The immense drawing-room was furnished well, hung with heavy draperies of gold-green, lighted by dozens of candles burning in wall-sconces and in brass chandeliers overhead. The floor was uncovered and the high heels made a melodious tapping upon it. Laughter seemed to fill the air to the very ceiling; a band of musicians played in one corner; silverware and dishes rattled together.

An adjoining room was set with a buffet-table, in the French style which Charles preferred, and footmen swarmed everywhere. The dishes piled upon it might have done justice to a cathedral builder: pompous confections decorated with candied roses and violets; little dolls in full Court dress spinning about on cake tops; great silver porringers containing steaming ragouts of mushrooms, sweetbreads, and oysters. Bottles of the new drink, champagne, crowded the tables. No more was an Englishman to be satisfied with boiled-mutton and pease and ale. He had learnt better in France and would never be reconciled to the old fare again.

The King's role as host created a sensation, for many of them were sure that it was a subtle way of showing his future intentions. Barbara was sure too and she moved about the room like a flame, charming, amazingly beautiful, full of the confidence of her power. Their eyes followed her and their whispers discussed her. But Barbara was not fooled, for she knew well enough that obsequious though they all were now it would take no more than a hint that the King was losing interest and out would come the sheathed claws, every honeyed word would turn to acid, and she would find herself more alone than she had ever been in the days before her dangerous glory.

It had happened before. But it won't happen to me, she told herself. To all the others, perhaps, but not to me.

Gambling-tables were set up in a third room and there they were soon congregated. Charles sat down to play for a short time, but in less than half an hour he had lost a couple of hundred pounds. He glanced up at Lauderdale who hung over his shoulder.

"Take my place, will you, John. I always lose and I'm a bad loser— What's worse, I can't afford it."

Lauderdale guffawed appreciatively, splattering the King as he did so for his tongue was too big for his mouth, but he

160

took his seat and Charles strolled into the next room to listen to the music. Barbara promptly left her own table and met him just as he was going out the door. Her arm linked with his and he bent to kiss her lightly on the temple, while behind them significant glances were exchanged and some wagers laid.

"It's my opinion Mrs. Palmer is mad enough to think she might be Queen," said Dr. Fraser. He was a personal favourite of the King and, since he could with equal dexterity perform an abortion, cure a clap, or administer a physic, his services were much in demand at Whitehall.

"The lady has a husband, you know," murmured Elizabeth Hamilton, not glancing away from her cards.

"A husband is no obstacle where a king has set his heart."

"He'll never marry her," said Cooper positively. "His Majesty is no such fool as that." Cooper had acquired a considerable reputation for sagacity by guessing far ahead of anyone else that York was married to Anne Hyde.

Barbara's old chum, Anne, gave him a malicious smile. "Why, whatever do you mean by that, sir? Sure, now, you don't think she'd be an unlucky choice?"

"I do not, madame," he assured her coldly. "But I think that the King will marry where political expediency dictates—as kings have always done."

By the time they had left, Barbara was thoroughly relieved. She was tired. The muscles in her legs ached and trembled. But she was happier than she had ever been and perfectly convinced that her hopes and expectations—wild as they might have seemed—would soon be fulfilled.

As she and Charles entered the bedroom together Wharton, asleep in a chair by the fire, jumped to her feet and curtsied, looking at her mistress with frightened apprehension. But Barbara smiled and spoke to her kindly.

"You may go, Wharton. I won't need you again tonight." Then, just as the girl was leaving, she called after her, "Wake me by half-after-eight. There's a 'Change woman coming to show me some lace and if I don't get it first, Carnegie will."

Barbara smiled at Charles as though she were a naughty little girl. "Isn't that selfish of me?"

He answered the smile but not the question, and took a chair. "That was good food, Barbara. Haven't you a new head-cook?"

She had gone to the dressing-table and was beginning to unfasten her hair. "Isn't he a marvel? Guess where I got him. I took him away from Mrs. Hyde—she brought him from France with her. D'you know, Charles, that woman hasn't *once* paid me a call?" She shook out her hair and it tumbled in long ripples like dark-fire running down her back; over her shoulder she threw him a quick, petulant glance. "I don't think the Chancellor likes me—or his wife would have called long since."

"Well," said Charles easily, "suppose he doesn't."

"Well! Why shouldn't he! What harm have I done him, pray?" Barbara thought that her new position should command not only the deference but the liking of every man and woman at Court, and she intended to get it, one way or another.

"The Chancellor belongs to the old school of statesmen, my dear. He'll neither pimp nor bribe, but thinks it's possible to get along in this world by honest hard work. I'm afraid there's a new model politician likely to prove too hard for him."

"I don't care what his morals are! He was good friends with my father and I think it's damned bad manners his wife doesn't make me a call! Why, I've heard he even tells you you shouldn't waste your time on a jade like me!"

Charles smiled, one arm over the back of the chair and his legs crossed, his eyes lazily admiring as he sat watching her undress. "The Chancellor has been telling me what I may and may not do for so many years I believe he half thinks I pay him some attention. But he's a very good old man and very loyal, and his intentions are the best even if his understanding is sometimes faulty. However, I wouldn't trouble myself with whether or not his wife calls, if I were you. I assure you she's a dull old lady and no very entertaining company."

"I don't care whether she's dull or not! Don't you understand? It's just that she *should* call on me!"

He laughed. "I understand. Let's forget it—"

He got up and went toward her and Barbara turned, just slipping her smock down over her breasts, to look at him. Her eyes lighted with a bright passion that was perfectly genuine, and as his hands reached out a shudder of expectation shook her, driving everything else from her mind. But not for long.

As they lay in the bed, her head resting on his shoulder so that she could feel beneath her cheek the pulsing of his blood, Barbara said softly, "I heard the most ridiculous rumour today."

Charles was uninterested and merely murmured, "Did you?"

"Yes—someone told me that you're already married to a niece of the Prince de Ligne—and have two sons by her."

"The Prince doesn't even have a niece, so far as I know. None I've married, anyway." His eyes were closed and he lay flat on his back, a faint smile on his mouth. But he was not thinking of what they were saying.

"Someone else told me that you're contracted to the Duke of Parma's daughter."

He did not answer and now, raising herself on one elbow, she said anxiously: "You're not, are you?"

"Not what? Oh, no. No, I'm not married."

"But they want you to marry, don't they? The people, I mean."

"Yes, I suppose they do. Some fat squint-eyed straight-haired antidote, no doubt," he said lazily. "Odsfish, I don't know how I'll ever get an ugly woman with child."

"But why should you marry an ugly woman?" With one pointed forefinger she was tracing a pattern in the matted black hair on his chest.

He opened his eyes and looked up at her, and then his face broke into a grin and he reached out his hand to stroke her head. "Princesses are always ugly. It's a tradition they have."

Barbara felt the excitement begin to mount within her, and her heart was pounding at a furious rate. Unable to look him full in the face, she dropped her eyes before she spoke. "But—Well, why marry a princess if there's none you like? Why not—" She took a deep quick breath and her throat felt dry; a sharp pain stabbed at the base of her skull. "Why not marry me?" Then she raised her eyes quickly and looked at him, searching.

Instantly Charles's face grew wary, the smile faded, and it settled once more into the old lines of moody cynicism. She could feel him draw away from her, though actually he had not moved at all. Barbara was shocked and she looked at him with horrified disbelief on her face. She had been so sure, so perfectly confident that he loved her madly, even enough to make her his wife.

"Sire," she said softly, "hasn't that ever occurred to you?"

He sat up and then left the bed to begin dressing. "Now come, Barbara. You know as well as I do that it's impossible."

"Why?" she cried, growing desperate. "Why is it impossible? I've heard it was you who made the Duke marry Anne Hyde! Then why *can't* you marry me—if you want to. If you love me." She felt her temper getting away from her and caught at it frantically, telling herself that this was too important to throw away because she couldn't hold her tongue. She still thought that she could wheedle him into anything.

Someway I'll make him marry me. I know I will. He's got to. He's got to!

With his breeches on he pulled the thin white linen shirt over his head and fastened the full sleeves at the wrist. He was eager to get away from her, bored and impatient at the prospect of a useless quarrel. He was, and he knew it, thoroughly infatuated with her, for he had never found a woman more exciting to lie with. But if she had been Queen of Naples he would not have cared to marry her—he knew her too well for that, already.

"The two cases aren't exactly comparable, my dear," he said now, his warm voice low and soothing, hoping to lull her into quiet and then get away. "My children will succeed to the throne. James's, most likely, never will."

Certainly that seemed perfectly reasonable for Charles had already recognized at least five illegitimate children, while Barbara herself was convinced that the child she carried was his and not her husband's—or Chesterfield's.

"Oh, but what's to become of *me* if you marry another woman? What will *I* do?" She was close to tears.

"I think you'll do very well, Barbara. I see no reason why

you shouldn't. You're not exactly a helpless person, you know."

"But that isn't what I mean! Oh, you see how they all run after me now—Buckingham and Cooper and the rest of that crew— But if you marry someone else and fob me off— Oh, I'd die! You can't think how they'd use me! And the women would be even worse than the men! Oh, Charles, you can't, you *can't* do that to me!"

He paused now and looked at her sharply; then all at once his face softened and he sat down beside her again, taking her hands into his. Her face was wet with tears that welled out of her eyes and slid over her cheeks in great drops, splashing off onto the satin-covered blankets beneath her.

"Don't cry, darling. What the devil do you take me for— an ogre? I won't desert you, Barbara, you can be sure of that. You've given me a great deal of happiness, and I'm grateful. I can't marry you, but I'll see that you're taken care of—very well."

She was sniffling and her chin quivered but she was again conscious of her appearance and trying to weep attractively. "How? With money? Money won't help—not in the case I'll be in."

"What would help?"

"Oh, Sire, I don't know! I don't see how I can—"

He interrupted her quickly, to stem another flood. "If I make you a Lady of my wife's Bedchamber—would that help?"

He spoke to her like an indulgent uncle holding out a sweet-meat to a small girl who had fallen and skinned her knee.

"I suppose it would. If you really do it. You won't change your mind and just—just— Oh—"

Now, suddenly overwhelmed with the knowledge of her defeat, she burst into shaking sobs and flung herself toward him. He held her against his chest for a moment, patting her shoulder while she cried, and then very gently he disengaged himself and got up.

While she lay on the bed and sobbed he swiftly slid into his doublet, knotted his cravat, buckled on his sword, and taking up his hat came to stand above her. Charles, who could not do without women though he could very easily do without any one woman, was often inclined to wish that it was never necessary to see any of them out of bed.

"Barbara—I swear I've got to go now. Please don't cry any more, darling. Believe me, I'll keep my promise—"

He bent and kissed the top of her head and then turned and went to the door. He glanced back just in time to see her look around at him, red-faced and swollen-eyed; he gave her a hasty wave and went out.

She sat up slowly, her face wrenched into a scowl, one hand to her aching head. And then all at once she opened her mouth and gave a high uncanny scream that made the veins in her neck stand out like purple cords, and picking up a vase from the bedside table she hurled it with all her strength at the mirror across the room.

CHAPTER ELEVEN

To get to the Tap-Room, which was a floor and a half below the Lady Debtors' Ward, Amber had to follow the candleman down a black narrow flight of stairs. But when they had gone only part way he turned suddenly and blocked the passage and she stopped three steps above him, angry and frightened at the look she saw on his face, for her advanced pregnancy gave her a sense of clumsy helplessness.

"Go on!" she cried. "What are you stopping for?"

He made no answer but lunged swiftly forward; one hand caught hold of her skirts and dragged her toward him. With a scream Amber knocked the candle out of his hand. Suddenly she found that he had given way and she was going swiftly down the steps, her hands reaching out blindly toward the walls, but the short chains on her wrists and ankles caught with a jerk. She lost her footing and toppled headlong, twisting desperately to protect her belly and yelling with terror as she plunged toward the bottom of the stairwell.

But even as she stumbled Black Jack Mallard started up, and

he caught her before she had hurt herself. She could not see him but she felt with passionate relief a man's powerful hands and arms, his great protecting body, and she heard the violent angry thunder of his voice bellowing curses at the candleman whose footsteps went pounding on up to the second story.

"What did he do to you? Are you hurt?" he demanded anxiously.

Spent with fear, Amber relaxed against him. "No—" she panted. "I think I'm—"

From above, the candleman shouted something unintelligible and with a snarl of rage Black Jack let her go and started after him. "You stinking son-of-a-whore, I'll—"

Suddenly his warmth and protectiveness were gone. Amber's eyes opened and she reached out frantically. "Don't leave me! Please—don't leave me!" She was afraid of other unseen dangers hiding there in the dark.

Instantly he was back again. "I'm here, sweetheart. Don't be scared. I swear I'll slit his gullet next time I see him, the turd-coloured dog!"

"I wish you would," she muttered, pressing her hands to her swollen stomach.

Fright had left her crumpled and weak and she let him half carry her to the bottom of the staircase where he gently set her on her feet again. The Tap-Room was nearby and they stood in a kind of smoky twilight; she could feel him watching her. And finally, forcing herself to look up, she saw his eyes going over her face and shoulders and breasts with an expression of pleased contemplation. All at once she felt pretty again; she could almost forget her stringy hair and the lice crawling on her skin and the dirt packed beneath her fingernails. The corners of her mouth went up in a faint smile and her eyes slanted flirtatiously.

Black Jack Mallard was the biggest man Amber had ever seen. He was at least six feet five, his shoulders were massive and the muscles in his calves thick and powerful. His coarse black hair, shiny with oil, hung to his shoulders and there was a slight wave in it. She could see the glint of gold as a vagrant light touched the rings he wore in either ear—it was a fashion much affected by the fops, but on this giant the jewels seemed only to accentuate his almost threatening masculinity. His forehead was low and broad, his nose wide at the nostrils, and while his upper lip was narrow and tightly drawn the lower rolled out in a heavy curve.

His clothes were in the latest mode: A blue velvet suit consisting of short doublet and wide-legged knee-length breeches, white shirt, white linen-and-lace cravat. Garnet-coloured satin ribbons hung in loops at his waist and sleeves and shoulders, there was a feather-loaded Cavalier's hat on his head and he wore calf-high riding boots. Only the boots would not have been acceptable in the King's own Drawing-Room. The clothes were obviously expensive and certainly no cast-off garments but they were soiled, somewhat wrinkled, and he wore them with an air which suggested contempt of such finery.

Now he grinned at her, showing even, square teeth so white they glistened, and made a bow. For all his great bulk he was controlled and graceful as a cat. "I'm Black Jack Mallard, madame, of the Press Yard." The Press Yard was the élite quarter of the jail, reserved for the rich.

She curtsied, delighted to be once more in the presence of a man who was not only susceptible to her charms but worthy of them. "And I, sir, am Mrs. Channell of the Lady Debtors' Ward, Master side."

Both of them laughed and bending over he gave her a casual kiss, the customary salute upon formal introduction. "Come in here," he said, "and we'll have a bouse on that."

"A what?"

"A bouse, sweetheart—a drink. I don't suppose you know our Alsatian cant." He took her arm and she noticed that he wore no fetters and even had a sword slung at his hip.

The Tap-Room was dimly lighted with several tallow candles, but the smoke that hung over it was thick as a morning fog on the Thames. At one end was a bar. Stools and tables and chairs were packed in closely, leaving little room to pass between them, and the ceiling was so low that Black Jack had to hunch his shoulders as he walked along, going toward a table in one far corner. He exchanged several greetings as he went and Amber was aware that every eye there turned to survey her, searching curiously over Black Jack's new wench; she caught some whistles from the men and low-murmured spiteful comments from the women.

But he evidently had a position of some authority, for they moved respectfully aside to let him pass, several of the women gave him inviting smiles, and one or two men complimented his choice. His own attitude toward them was that of good-natured camaraderie—he slapped the men on the back, stroked one woman's head and another's cheek as he passed—and seemed as much at his ease as though they had been in the tap-room of the Dog and Partridge.

Amber sat down with her back to the wall, and Black Jack, after asking her what she wanted, ordered Rhenish for her and brandy for himself. When they had examined her thoroughly the others went back to what they had been doing. Bottles were raised, cards shuffled and dice rolled, prostitutes wandered from table to table soliciting business; the room swelled with voices— laughter, songs and shouts, the occasional cry of a child. Amber exchanged a smile with Moll Turner but averted her eyes swiftly from the sight of a blowzy fat woman sprawled at a table, holding a fan of cards in her hand while a sleeping baby had its mouth fastened to one brown teat.

Oh, my God! she thought with horror. Two more months and I'll— She looked quickly at Black Jack, and found him smiling down at her.

"You're a mighty dimber wench," he said softly. "How long 've you been here?"

"Five weeks. I'm here for debt—four hundred pound."

He was less impressed than the Lady Debtors had been. "Four hundred. God's blood, I can take that much in an easy night's work. What happened?"

"My husband stole every penny I had and ran off and left me with the debts—"

"And the lullabye-cheat." He glanced significantly at her belly. "Well—" He poured a glass of white wine for her and a smaller one of brandy for himself and flipped a coin to the waiter, giving a casual salute to the brim of his hat. "Here's to

you! May he come back soon and get you out of crampings."
He tossed it down at a gulp, as a gentleman should, poured
another glass and turned to look at her shrewdly.

Amber drank hers down too, for she was thirsty, but a scowl
puckered her eyebrows. "He'll never come back. And I hope
he never does—the ungrateful pimp!"

Black Jack laughed and gave a low whistle. "You say that
with such spleen I'd go near to believe you really are married."

She stared at him, her eyes sparkling. "Well! And why
shouldn't you believe it, pray! Why the devil does everyone
think that's just some tale I tell!"

He poured another glass for each of them. "Because, sweetheart, a girl like you who says her husband left her, probably
never had one at all."

She smiled then and her voice purred. "The way I look now
I think I'd fright away a better man than a husband."

"My eyes are good, sweetheart. They see under six layers
of dirt—and they see a tearing beauty." For a moment they
sat looking at each other and then at last he said, "I've got a
room with a window on the third floor. Would you like to
smell some fresh air and look at the sky?" He half-smiled at
the invitation but got to his feet and reached down his hand
to help her.

As they walked out the entire room set up a bellowing and
laughing, shouting obscenities and advice to Black Jack, who
waved his hand at them but did not glance around.

The rooms were furnished like those in a low-class tavern
catering to gay parties, the furniture scarred and much initialled,
but certainly luxurious compared to the rest of the jail. The
walls were covered with ribald words and sentences, crude
drawings, names, and dates. Black Jack told her that the quarters had cost him three hundred pounds. Every man who bought
the office of Jailor at Newgate went out of it rich, if not beloved.

Black Jack was often gone, for he had a great many visitors
and social obligations to fulfill. But each time he came back
they would laugh together over the fine lady—masked of course

—who had hinted that she was at the very least a countess and had offered to solace his lonely hours. Once he stole a gold bracelet from some admirer and gave it to her. The highwaymen were the aristocrats of the underworld and they enjoyed a general popularity. Their names were well-known, their exploits discussed in taverns and on street-corners, they were much visited when in jail and when they took their last ride in a cart up Tyburn Hill they were attended by great and sympathetic crowds.

Amber spent most of her time at the window, swallowing in the fresh air as though she could never get enough, standing with her arms braced on the window-sill and looking out over the city. She could see the favoured prisoners down below in the courtyard, walking or standing in groups, some of them playing hand-ball or pitch-and-toss, for though it was now the end of January the weather continued mild and the streets were dusty. The tar-smeared quarters of the men hanged after the fanatic uprising earlier that month still lay exposed there and flies and wasps buzzed over the heap in angry masses.

Four days after Amber had met him Black Jack made another of his miraculous escapes, and she went with him. Every bolt, every door, every gate had been liberally greased with the King's coin and each swung open at a touch. In the street a hackney waited, the door ajar; they got in swiftly and rattled off down Old Bailey Street. Black Jack, settling into the seat beside her, slapped his thigh and gave one of his thunderous laughs.

Suddenly a woman's voice spoke, tart and peevish. " 'Sdeath, Jack! That's a fine stink you've got! You bring it out every time you go into that damned jail!"

That, Amber knew, must be Bess Columbine, whom he called his "buttock." Now he introduced them, saying, "Bess, this is Mrs. Channell."

The two women exchanged cool murmurous greetings and all three of them lapsed into silence. It was only a few minutes, however, until the coach stopped, and as she got out Amber saw that they were at the edge of the river. They climbed swiftly into the barge that waited there and the water-man started upstream; it was perfectly black and moonless and though none of them could see the others Amber felt Bess staring insistently at her and could sense her jealous hostility.

Much I care, she thought, if she likes my company or not!

But she did not expect to stay long with Black Jack. For somehow, she was sure, she could get him to give her four hundred pounds. He seemed to have so much money, and so little use for it, she was convinced she would have it from him in less than a fortnight. And then she would leave him—though what she would do or where she would go she had no idea. She had even lost the names of the women Lord Carlton had said would take care of her during her lying-in.

At the foot of Water Lane they disembarked and Bess started out ahead up the steep stone steps to the street level. Amber, holding the bird-cage in one hand and her skirts in the other, cautiously felt her way along until all at once Black Jack—who had been delayed while he paid the bargeman—came up behind her, swung her into his arms and went up as swiftly as though it had been broad daylight. They passed through the gardens which had belonged to the old Carmelite monastery that had once stood there, and finally came into a narrow street.

Here, there was light and noise, and great street signs indicated that almost every other building was a tavern. Through the square-paned windows they could see men playing cards, a naked woman dancing, two other women stripped to the waist and fighting before a crowd of onlookers that cheered and threw coins. The sound of fiddles blended with screams and laughter and the wailing of babies. They were in Ram Alley, Whitefriars, a part of the district which gave the privilege of sanctuary to criminals and debtors. Those who lived there preferred to call it, ironically, Alsatia.

They stopped before one of the houses, Bess opened the door with a key and Black Jack set Amber down. She stepped inside and instantly the two women turned to look at each other.

Bess, Amber saw, was no more than her own age, and of about the same height. Her hair, which was abundant, was dark brown and curly and fell below her shoulders; her eyes were blue and she had a small piquant face, somewhat too broad at the cheekbones, with a nose that turned up saucily. Her figure was round almost to plumpness and her breasts were full-blown. Amber thought that she looked vulgar—an ill-bred slut.

But she was uneasy and angry herself to be put under the girl's scrutiny. For though she had used Black Jack's comb and scrubbed her face she was still miserably dirty, and now she could feel a louse begin to bite. But she would have died rather than reach down to scratch. As it was, Bess lifted her brows and smiled faintly to indicate that she considered her no very formidable rival.

Pox on her! thought Amber furiously. Just wait till I've had a bath, Mrs.! We'll see whose nose is out of joint then, I'll warrant you! Her speech was taking on the colour of her surroundings, reflecting Lord Carlton and Almsbury, Luke Channell and his aunt, Moll Turner and Newgate, and now, Black Jack and Alsatia.

But if Black Jack was conscious of the resentment crackling between the two women he gave no indication of it. "I'm thirsty," he said. "Where's Pall?"

Bess shouted the name and within a few moments a girl pushed open the door which led into another room and stood sleepily on the threshold. Evidently the kitchen-slavey, she was barefooted and ill-kempt, and her hair hung in greasy yellow streaks about her neck. But at the sight of Black Jack she blushed and smiled self-consciously and dropped him a curtsy.

"Glad t'see ye back, sir."

"Thanks, Pall. I'm glad to be back. Can we have something to drink? I'll have cherry-brandy. What do you want, sweetheart?" He turned to Amber.

Bess scowled swiftly at that and the next instant she was berating Pall, pouring her jealous spleen over her. "What've you been doing, you lazy slut! Why aren't those dishes cleaned?" She pointed to a table littered with dishes and bones and nutshells, glasses and wine-bottles. "By Jesus, you'll mend your ways or I'll give you a flogging— D'ye hear me?"

Pall winced, evidently believing her, but Black Jack interrupted the tirade. "Leave the girl alone, Bess. Maybe she's been busy in the kitchen."

"Busy sleeping, I'll warrant you!"

"Bring a bottle of Rhenish for Mrs. Channell, and Bess will have—"

"Brandy!" snapped Bess, and gave Amber a quick furious glare.

Amber turned her back and went to sit down. She felt tired and listless and suffered acutely from knowing that she had never been less attractive. She wished only that she might get away from them all and go somewhere to sleep, and then in the morning have a fine warm bath with soap-suds enough to float on. Oh, to be really clean again!

Black Jack and Bess began to talk then, but it was in the underworld cant of which Amber had learnt only a few words. She heard their voices but did not try to understand what they were saying. Instead, she looked idly about her at the furnishings of the room. It was crowded with a vast number of chairs and tables and stools. Half-a-dozen cupboards and hutches ranged the walls. There were innumerable portraits in heavy gold frames and several more stood stacked in a pile against the fireplace. Some of the pieces were obviously expensive, but others were so old or so badly scarred and broken as to be of no possible value and very little use.

Pall brought the glasses and bottles and they drank a toast to the night's success. Amber then told Black Jack that she was tired and he asked Pall to light her upstairs to the west-center bedroom, kissing her casually when she left. Even that made Bess fume and draw down her brows. But Amber hoped the girl might have her way that night, for she did not care to be troubled with him.

Amber sat in a great wooden tub full of warm water and soap, sought out the lice and cracked them while they were wet and immobilized. Her hair, just washed, had been wrung out and skewered onto the top of her head. On a gold and white brocade chair beside her Black Jack sat, idly flipping a knife into the floor between his feet. Amber gave a wave of one arm that surveyed the room.

"Why d'you have so much of everything?"

For the bedroom was as overfurnished as the parlour downstairs, and in much the same helter-skelter fashion. The bed was hung luxuriously with violet velvet and the counterpane was yellow satin; several of the chairs were covered with violet velvet and another with crimson, fringed with gold tassels. There were at least two dozen portraits on the walls, a great many mirrors, three wardrobes, and two screens.

"Mother Red-Cap's a pawn-broker. The house is furnished with what she takes in—the portrait of grand-dad always seems to go first." He grinned and gave a lift of one eyebrow to indicate the numerous old gentlemen in stiff black doublets and white ruffs who looked down from the walls.

Amber laughed. Her spirits had revived and she was once more full of energy and optimism and self-confidence. She knew that she should not be in a tubful of hot water, for Sarah had always said that sitting in a warm bath was sure to bring on a baby before its time, but she was enjoying herself so that she had no intention of moving for at least another half-hour.

"Who lives here? Anyone besides Mother Red-Cap and Bess and Pall?" The corridor down which Pall had led her had been a long one and the house seemed to be quite large.

"Mother Red-Cap lets out the four extra bedrooms. A man who coins false money has the third floor and there's a fencing-school on the fourth."

This was not the first Amber had heard of Mother Red-Cap. Mother Red-Cap had sent the money to bribe the Jailor. Mother Red-Cap had just been elected Mayor of Sanctuary and the night before had been hearing a case at the George and Dragon. Mother Red-Cap wanted to see her as soon as she was dressed.

At last Amber stood up, dried herself, and slipped into one of Black Jack's East Indian dressing-robes; both of them laughed to see how it trailed on the floor and the sleeves hung below her knees. Then, giving her a wink, Jack went to a chest and lifted out a large box which he put into her hands. She took it and glanced at him questioningly. He was standing there with his hands thrust into his pockets, rocking back on his heels and grinning broadly, waiting for her to open it.

Excited at the prospect of a present, Amber laid the box on a chest, untied the strings and tossed the crackling papers aside.

With a cry of delight she took out a green taffeta gown sewn with appliquéd scrolls of black velvet. Underneath lay a black velvet cloak, a smock and two petticoats, green silk stockings and green shoes.

"Oh, Black Jack! It's beautiful!" She reached up to kiss him and he bent rather awkwardly, like a bashful boy, for he was always afraid of hurting her. "But how'd you ever get it so quick?" Madame Darnier had never completed a gown in less than a week.

"I was abroad early this morning. There's a second-hand dealer in Houndsditch where the quality sell their clothes."

"Oh, Black Jack—and just the colour I love!" She slipped off the robe and began to dress hastily, chattering all the while. "It looks like the leaves on the apple-tree that used to grow outside my bedroom window. How'd you know green's my favourite colour?"

But a moment later her face fell in disappointment. The gown would not fasten over her stomach and the sight of herself in a mirror—something she had not seen for over a month—made her want to cry. It seemed to her that she had been pregnant forever.

"Oh!" she cried in exasperation, and stamped her foot. "How ugly I look! I *hate* having a baby!"

But Black Jack assured her soothingly that she was the prettiest thing he had ever seen, and they went downstairs to meet Mother Red-Cap. They found her seated at one of the tables with her back to them and a candle at her elbow, writing in an enormous ledger which lay spread open before her. As Black Jack spoke to her she turned and then immediately got to her feet and came forward. She gave Amber a friendly kiss on the cheek and smiled her approval at Black Jack, who stood there proudly beaming over both of them.

"A gentry-more she is, Jack." She glanced over her figure. "When do you reckon?"

"About two months, I think."

Amber was looking at her wide-eyed, amazed to find that she bore no resemblance at all to the dissolute old harridan she had been expecting. She did not, in fact, look any more vicious than Aunt Sarah. Mother Red-Cap was fifty-five years old but her skin was clear and smooth and her eyes snapped brightly. Smaller than Amber, her body was trim and compact, and all her movements suggested a fund of unexpressed energy. The clothes she wore were plain neat ones made of cotton and wool with starched collar and cuffs and apron, and there was not a jewel in sight. A bright red cap covered every wisp of hair and Black Jack had told Amber that in almost ten years he had never seen her without it.

"I'll have a midwife for you in good time, then," she said, "and we'll find a woman to take the baby."

"Take the baby where!" cried Amber, suddenly on the defensive.

"Don't be alarmed, my dear," said Mother Red-Cap reasonably, and the accent with which she spoke reminded Amber of Lord Carlton and his friends. "Who'd want a baby to live in the Friars? Most of those who do, die before their first year is out. We can get a cleanly responsible cottager's wife who will care for the child and let you visit him whenever you like. Oh, it's a very satisfactory arrangement—many women do it," she assured her, as Amber still did not look convinced. "Now," she turned briskly and went back to her ledger. "Tell me your full name."

Black Jack spoke up quickly. "Mrs. Channel is all she wants to give. I'll pay the garnish-fee for her."

Amber had not told even Black Jack her real name and he did not seem to care for he said that his own was assumed and that any person of sense kept his name secret in Alsatia.

"Very well. No one here is interested in prying into the past. Black Jack tells me you're in debt for four hundred pound and want to pay it so that you can leave the Friars. I don't blame you—I think you're too pretty to stay here long, and I assure you I'll put the means of earning that sum in your way, just as soon as you're able to go abroad." Amber started to ask her how, but Mother Red-Cap went crisply on. "Meanwhile, we'll have to do something to get rid of that accent. A girl from the country is generally assumed to be a fool here in London, and that's a handicap to the best laid plans. I think that Michael

Godfrey might make a good tutor for her, don't you, Black Jack? And now, my dear, make yourself comfortable with us and ask for whatever you want or need. I'll leave you now; this is the first of the month and I must call upon my tenants."

She closed the ledger, put it into a drawer of the table, and locked it with a key taken from her apron-pocket. Then tossing a cloak over her arm, she smiled at them both and went to the door. Once again she turned to give Amber a sweeping glance, shook her head slightly, and remarked, "A pity you're so far gone with child. Three months ago you'd have brought a hundred pound as a maidenhead."

She went out and though Black Jack burst into hearty laughter Amber turned to him with an angry light in her eyes. "What the devil does that old woman intend? If she thinks I'm going to earn my way out of here by—"

"Don't get excited. She doesn't—I'll see to that. But once a bawd, always a bawd. And Mother Red-Cap's such a match-maker I'll swear she could have married the Pope to Queen Elizabeth."

What Mother Red-Cap's real name was, Amber never learned, but very obviously Black Jack not only liked her but had a strong masculine admiration for her success, her uncompromising determination, her ability to survive and prosper no matter what happened to others. But Amber could not understand why the woman lived so frugally when she did not need to, or why she had chosen a life of chastity after what must have been an exciting youth. For those reasons she felt a frank but unexpressed contempt for her and decided that she could not be so very clever after all.

But nevertheless she exerted herself to make Mother Red-Cap like her and believed that she was succeeding very well. For Black Jack had flatly refused, the first time she broached the subject, to give her money enough to pay her debt—and it had led to a quarrel between them.

"I think you *want* me to stay in this damned place!"

"I certainly do. What d'ye think I got you out of jail for? You're an ungrateful little bitch!"

"What if I am! Who wants to stay in this filthy hole all their

178

life! I hate it! And I *will* get out! Just you wait and see! If you won't give it to me I'll ask Mother Red-Cap for the money! She doesn't use it and she'll lend me four hundred pound, I warrant you!"

He was a formidable giant who might have snapped her bones like toothpicks, but he threw back his head and laughed. "Go ahead and ask her if you like! But believe me, she'd as soon lend you four hundred of her teeth."

CHAPTER TWELVE

ONE AFTERNOON WHILE Black Jack was away Amber sought out Mother Red-Cap. When she was home, which was not often, she was almost always employed in working on her ledger, entering long columns, filling out bills and receipts by the dozen, and she did not like to be interrupted. Now, as Amber approached, she made her a signal to be silent and continued running her pen up a line of neatly written figures, her lips moving as she did so, and then finally she set down the total and turned to Amber.

"What is it, my dear? Can I do something for you?"

Amber had prepared and rehearsed her speech, but now she cried impulsively: "Yes! Lend me four hundred pound so I can get away from here! Oh, please, Mother Red-Cap! I'll pay it back, I promise you!"

Mother Red-Cap observed her coolly for a moment, and then she smiled. "Four hundred pound, Mrs. Channell, is a large sum of money. What do you offer for security?"

"Why—I'll give you a promise, on paper, or anything you like. And I'll pay it back with interest," she added, for she had learned by now that Interest was both God and Sovereign to Mother Red-Cap. "I'll do anything. But I've *got* to have it!"

"I don't believe you understand the business of pawn-brokerage, my dear. It may seem to you that four hundred pound is an insignificant sum to borrow. It is, however, a very large sum to lend upon no better security than the promise of a young girl to repay. I don't doubt your intentions, but I think you would find it more difficult to come by four hundred pound than you imagine now."

Surprised, disappointed, Amber was angry. "Why!" she cried. "You said yourself you could have got a hundred pound for me!"

"And so I probably could. More than half that hundred, however, would have been mine for arranging the match, not yours. But to be frank with you, it was merely an idle thought. Black Jack's told me very flatly he intends keeping you for himself and I believe, my dear, you should feel some gratitude toward him. It cost him three hundred pound to get you out of Newgate."

"Three hundred— Why, he never told me that!"

"And so I think that while Black Jack's here we won't be using you that way."

"While he's here? Is he going somewhere?"

"Not very soon, I hope. But someday he'll ride up Tyburn Hill in a cart—and he won't come down again."

Amber stared at her, horror-struck. She knew that he had been burnt on the left thumb, which meant he was to hang for the next offense. But he had escaped again in spite of that and he had a reckless audacity which made her think of him as almost indestructible. Now, however, she was thinking not of him but of herself.

"That's what's going to happen to all of us! I know it is! We're *all* going to hang!"

Mother Red-Cap lifted her brows. "We might, I suppose. But we're far more likely to die of consumption here in Alsatia." She turned away and picked up her pen and though Amber lingered a few moments she knew that she had been dismissed, and went to climb the stairs back up to her bedroom.

She was discouraged but not beaten. She still intended to escape somehow, and comforted herself with the reminder that she had made the far more difficult escape from Newgate.

Alsatia lay just east of the Temple Gardens and could be

reached from them by going down a narrow broken flight of steps. Low as it was and close to the river it was perpetually invaded by a thick dingy-yellow fog that hung to the very pavements, seeped into the bones, stuck in the nostrils and made it difficult even to breathe. Ram Alley, where Mother Red-Cap's house was, smelt of stinking cook-shops and the lye-soap used by the laundresses who made that street a headquarters.

Its courts and alleys were crowded with beggars and thieves, murderers and whores and debtors, a wild desperate rabble who lived in a constant internecine warfare but who invariably banded together to beat off any attempted intrusion by constable or bailiff. Children swarmed everywhere—almost as numerous as the dogs and pigs—starving little dwarfs with sunken eyes and husky high-pitched voices. Amber shuddered at the sight of them and looked swiftly away for fear her own baby would be marked before birth because she had seen them. She felt that living here she had left the world—the only world that mattered to her, the world where she might see Lord Carlton again.

It was Michael Godfrey, hired by Mother Red-Cap to teach her to speak as a London lady of quality should, who gave her glimpses back into that life toward which her heart yearned.

He was a student at the Middle Temple where sons of many of England's wealthy families were to be found, supposedly acquiring a liberal education and learning how to manage their estates and preside at the sessions when they came into their property. Most of them, however, spent more time in taverns than they did in the class-room and more money on women than on books. Like many of the others, Michael had sometimes ventured into the Friars, impelled by curiosity and a desire to see how the wicked lived and looked. And also like many others, when his mode of living had far outrun his allowance and he found himself embarrassed with debts, he had come to borrow and thus he had made the acquaintance of Mother Red-Cap, the fabled witch-woman of the Sanctuary. Within a fortnight after Amber's arrival he had been engaged as her tutor.

He was just twenty years old, of medium height and size, with light-brown curling hair and blue eyes. His father was a knight with property in Kent and money enough to give his son all the customary advantages of his class: Michael had gone to Westminster School to learn Latin and Greek. At sixteen, the usual age for entering college, he had been sent to Oxford to master Greek and Roman literature, history, philosophy, and mathematics. That was supposed to be accomplished in three years, for too much education was not considered good for a gentleman, and a year ago he had enrolled in the Middle Temple. Two years or so there and he would go on his tour abroad.

While the rain dripped unceasingly—for the mild winter had been followed by weeks of wet—he and Amber would sit beside the fireplace in the parlour drinking hot-spiced buttered ale and talking. She was an eager and enthusiastic listener, appreciative of his jests, fascinated by the things he did and saw and heard.

She would laugh delightedly to hear of how he and his friends, "somewhat disguised" as the gallants liked to say when they had been drunk, had knocked over a watchman's stand where the old man sat sleeping, serenaded a bawdy-house in Whetstone Park and broken all the windows, and finally stripped naked a woman they met returning home late with her husband. Bands of young aristocrats scoured about the town every night, boisterous and destructive, the terror of all quiet peaceable citizens, who would as soon have been set upon by cut-throats or thieves. But Michael recounted his exploits with a zestful freshness and relish which made them seem the most harmless innocent childish pranks.

He told her that for the past three or four months women had been appearing on the London stage and were now in every play, overpainted, daringly-dressed young sluts, some of them already taken by the nobles as mistresses. He told her of seeing the rotten bodies of Cromwell and Ireton and Bradshaw pulled out of their graves and hanged in chains at Tyburn, and of how their pickled heads were now stuck atop poles on Westminster Hall and chunks of their carcasses exposed on pikes over the seven City gates. And he told her about the plans for his Majesty's Coronation which was to take place in April and was to be the most magnificent in the history of the British throne; he promised to describe for her every robe, every jewel, every word spoken and gesture made, after he had seen it.

Meanwhile she was losing the remnants of her country accent. Her ear was alert and her memory retentive, mimicry was natural to her and she had a passionate eagerness to learn. She stopped pronouncing power as pawer and you as yeow. She gave up both Gemini and Uds Lud and learned some more fashionable oaths. He taught her all the correct ways of making and receiving introductions, a few French phrases and words, that it was the mode to pronounce certain as sartin and servant as sarvant. Vulgarity was high-fashion at Whitehall and pungent words of one syllable interlarded the conversation of most lords and ladies. Amber absorbed all of it, and with it the cant of Alsatia.

Michael Godfrey, who was already sure he loved her, wanted to know her real name, who she was, and where she came from. She refused to tell him the truth but she embroidered upon her story to Sally Goodman and he accepted her for what she said she was: a country heiress run away from home with a man her family disliked, and now deserted by him. He was very sympathetic, indignant that a woman of her gentle breeding should have to live in such surroundings, and offered to get in touch with her family. But Amber shied away from that and assured him that they would never come to her aid in such a place as Whitefriars.

"Then come with me," he said. "I'll take care of you."

"Thanks, Michael, I wish I could. But I can't—not till I've laid-in, anyway. Lord, wouldn't it be a pretty fetch if I fell into labour in your quarters! You'd be turned out in a trice!"

They both laughed. "They've threatened me a dozen times. Mend your ways, sirrah, or out you go!" He drew down his brows and bellowed dramatically. Then all at once he leaned forward and took her hand. "But please—afterward—will you go with me then?"

"There's nothing I'd like better. But what about the constables? If they caught me I'd have to go back to Newgate."

Michael lived on an allowance which did not cover his own expenses; he could never pay her debt.

"They won't catch you. I'll see to that. I'll keep you safe—"

Amber woke early in the morning on the 5th of April, conscious of a dull prodding ache in her back. She turned over to make herself more comfortable and then suddenly she realized what it was. She gave Black Jack a poke.

"Black Jack! Wake up! Go tell Mother Red-Cap it's started! Send for the midwife!"

"What?"

He grumbled sleepily, not wishing to be disturbed. But when she shook him—frantic, for she had heard of babies being born and no preparation made for them—he woke up, stared at her for a surprised instant, and quickly began to get into his clothes.

Mother Red-Cap came to see her and then went out on her perpetual round of business, confident that nothing would happen for several hours. The midwife arrived with her two helpers, made an examination and sat down to wait. Bess Columbine looked in once but was sent away, for there was a strong superstition that the presence of one whom the labouring woman disliked would impede the progress of birth. But Black Jack, though he poured sweat and seemed to suffer at least as much as she did, remained with her constantly, drinking one glass of brandy after another.

At last, about four o'clock in the afternoon, the baby's head began to appear, like a red wrinkled apple, and a few minutes later a boy was born. Amber lay in exhausted collapse on the bed, unable to feel anything but relief.

She was disappointed in the baby for he was long and thin and red and gave scant promise that he would ever resemble his handsome father, though Mother Red-Cap assured her that he would be very pretty in a month or two. But now his tiny face was screwed up in a continuous squall, for he was hungry. Amber had assumed that she would nurse him herself—in the country, women did not expect to look like virgins once they were married—but Mother Red-Cap was horrified at such a thought and told her that no lady of fashion would think of

184

spoiling her figure. A wet-nurse would be found instead. Amber's vanity needed no urging and she agreed readily, but while they interviewed applicants the baby starved.

It took four days to find the woman who answered to Mother Red-Cap's exacting demands, but after that he was quiet and content and slept most of the time, in his cradle beside Amber's bed. She felt a passionate tenderness for him, far greater than she had ever expected or believed possible. Even so, she hoped that she would never have another baby.

She recuperated rapidly and by the time the wet-nurse arrived she was sitting up in bed, propped against pillows and wearing one of Black Jack's shirts, for that was supposed to cause the milk in the breasts to dry quickly. Michael Godfrey came to visit her and brought the baby a lavishly embroidered white-satin gown for his christening, and she received several other presents as well. Apparently she had made more friends in the Friars than she had realized.

One of them was Penelope Hill, a prostitute who lived just across the street. She was a large-boned young woman whose claims to beauty were a head of hair that was like a heavy skein of pale yellow silk, and ample melon-shaped breasts. Rusty sweat-stains showed in the armpits of her soiled blue-taffeta gown and all her body gave out a strangely inviting promise of lushness and fulfillment. She was languid and cynical and regarded all men with a kind of amused contempt; but she warned Amber that a woman had no chance of succeeding in a man's world unless she could turn their weaknesses to her own advantage.

Such philosophical advice, however, meant less to Amber than did her practical information on another subject. From Penelope she learned that there were a great many means of preventing perpetual child-bearing—or abortions—and she learned what they were. In possession of the knowledge, Amber wondered how she had ever been so stupid as not to have guessed at it long since; it seemed so perfectly obvious.

When the baby was two weeks old he was christened with the single name—Bruce. It was customary to give a bastard his mother's surname, but she could not use hers and would not use Luke Channell's. Afterwards she had a christening feast, which was attended by Mother Red-Cap and Black Jack, Bess Columbine and Michael and Penelope Hill, an Italian noble-man who had fled his country for reasons he did not disclose and who knew no word of English, the coiner and his wife from the third floor, two men who accompanied Black Jack on his expeditions out of town—Jimmy the Mouth and Blueskin—and an assortment of cutpurses, bilks, and debtors. While the men drank and played cards the women sat and discussed pregnancy and miscarriages and abortions with the same ravening interest they had in Marygreen.

A week after that the woman Mother Red-Cap had hired to take the baby came for him. She was Mrs. Chiverton, a cottager's wife from Kingsland, a tiny village lying out of London some two and a quarter miles, but almost four miles from Whitefriars. Amber liked and trusted her immediately, for she had known many women of her kind. She agreed to pay her ten pounds a year to feed and care for the baby, and gave her another five so that she could have him brought to see her whenever she wanted.

She did not wish to part with him at all and would have kept him there with her in Whitefriars if it had not been for Mother Red-Cap's insistence that he would probably die in that unhealthy place. She loved him because he was her own—but perhaps even more because he was Bruce Carlton's. Bruce had been gone now for almost eight months, and in spite of the violent feeling she still had for him, he had grown increasingly unreal to her. The baby, a moving breathing proof of his existence, was all that convinced her she had ever known him at all. He seemed to be a dream she had had, a wish that had almost, but not quite, come true.

"Let me know right away if he falls sick, won't you?" she said anxiously as she put him into Mrs. Chiverton's arms. "When will you bring him to see me?"

"Whenever ye say, mem."

"Next Saturday? If it's a good day?"

"Very well, mem."

"Oh, please do! And you'll keep him warm and never let him be hungry, won't you?"

"Yes, mem. I will, mem."

Black Jack went along to see her safely into a hackney, but when he came back Amber was sitting alone in a chair by the table, staring morosely into space. He sat down beside her and took her hands into his; his voice was teasing but sympathetic. "Here, sweetheart. What's the good of all this moping and sighing? The little fellow's in good hands, isn't he? Lord, you wouldn't want 'im to stay here. Would you now?"

Amber looked at him. "No, of course not. Well—" She tried a little smile.

"Now, that's better! Look here—d'ye know what day this is?"

"No."

"It's the day before his Majesty's coronation. He rides through the City on his way to the Tower! How would you like to go see 'im?"

"Oh, Black Jack!" Her whole face lighted eagerly and then suddenly collapsed into a discontented frown. "But we can't—" She had come to feel that she was as much a prisoner here in Whitefriars as she had been in Newgate.

"Of course we can. I go into the City every day of my life. Hurry along now, into your rigging and we'll be off. Bring your mask and wear your cloak," he called after her, as she whirled and started out on a run.

It was the first time Amber had left Alsatia since she had come there two months and a half before, and she was almost as excited as she had been the first day she had seen London. After weeks of rain the sky was now blue and the air fresh and clean; there was a brisk breeze that carried the smell of the outlying fields into the city. The streets along which the King's procession would pass had been covered with gravel and railed off on either side and the City companies and trainbands formed lines to keep back the eager pushing crowds. Magnificent triumphal arches had been erected at the corners of the four main streets and—as the year before—banners and tapestries floated from every house and women massed at the windows and balconies threw flowers.

Black Jack shepherded Amber through the crowd before him, elbowing one man aside, shoving his hand into the face of another, until finally they came to the very front. She dropped her mask—which was kept in place by a button held between the teeth—and could not stop to pick it up. Black Jack did not notice and in her own excitement she soon forgot that it was gone.

When they got to where they could see, the great gilt coaches, filled with noblemen in their magnificent Parliament robes, were turning slowly by. Amber stared at them with her eyes wide open, impressed as a child, and unconsciously she searched over each face, but did not see him. Lord Carlton had ridden the year before with the loyal Cavaliers returning from over the seas. But when the King approached she forgot even Bruce.

His Majesty was on horseback and as he rode along, nodding his head and smiling, hands reached out trying to touch him or the trappings of his horse. From time to time his attention was caught by a pretty woman somewhere in the crowd. And so he glanced once, then again, at a girl whose tawny eyes stared up at him in passionate admiration and awe, her lips parted with a sudden catch of breath as his gaze met hers. And as he passed he smiled at her, the slow lazy smile that—for all its cynicism— was so strangely tender. Her head turned, following him, but he did not look back.

Oh! thought Amber, dizzy with exultation. He looked at me! And he smiled! The *King* smiled at me! In her excitement she did not even see the camel lumbering along bearing brocaded panniers from which a little East Indian boy flung pearls and spices into the crowd.

The King's swarthy sombre face and the expression in his eyes stayed with her for hours as vivid as the moment she had seen him. And now she was more than ever dissatisfied with her life in the Sanctuary. The world of which she had half lost remembrance called to her again like an old and beloved melody and she yearned to follow it—but did not dare. Oh, if only somehow, *somehow* I could get out of this scurvy place!

That evening the four of them sat at the supper-table: Bess sullen and glowering because she had not been to the pageant; Amber eating in silent preoccupation; Black Jack laughing as he showed Mother Red-Cap the four watches he had stolen. Amber was conscious of the conversation but she paid no attention to what was being said until she heard Bess's angry protest.

"And what about me, pray? What am *I* to do?"

"You may stay here tonight," said Mother Red-Cap. "There'll be no need for you to go along."

Bess banged her knife onto the table. "There was a need for me once! But now Mrs. Fairtail's come I find I'm as unwelcome as a looking-glass after the small-pox!" She gave Amber a venomous glare.

Mother Red-Cap did not answer her, but turned to Amber. "Remember the things I've told you—and above all, don't be uneasy. Black Jack will be there when you need him. Keep your wits and there'll be no possibility of mistakes."

Amber's hands had turned cold and her heart was beginning to pound. During the discussions and rehearsals for these hold-ups she had always felt that she was merely pretending, that she would never really have to do any of those things. And now all of a sudden—when she had least expected it—the pretending was done. Mother Red-Cap *did* intend her to go. Amber could feel the noose about her neck already.

"Let Bess go if she wants to!" she cried. "I've no great maw for the business! I dreamed about Newgate again last night!"

Mother Red-Cap smiled. Her temper was never ruffled, she never lost her cool, reasonable tone and manner. "My dear, surely you know that dreams are expounded by contraries. Come, now, I had expected great things of you—not only for your beauty but for your spirit, which I had thought would carry you undismayed through any adventure."

"Undismayed spirit, my arse!" snorted Bess.

Amber gave her a sharp hard stare across the table and then got to her feet. Without another word she left the room and went upstairs to get her cloak and mask, to powder her face and smooth a little rouge on her lips. A few minutes later she came down to find Bess and Black Jack quarrelling. Bess was chattering furiously at him though he merely lounged in his chair with a wine-bottle in his hand, and ignored her. Seeing Amber at the door he smiled and got to his feet. Bess whirled around.

"*You!*" she cried. "You're the cause of all my troubles—you

189

jilting whore!" And suddenly she grabbed a salt-cellar from the table and hurled it to the floor. "There! And the devil go with you!" She turned and rushed out of the room, sobbing as she went.

"Oh!" cried Amber, staring at the spilt salt with scared and anxious eyes. "We're cursed! We *can't* go!"

Black Jack, who had gone after Bess, now gave her a cuff with his great hand that almost knocked her off her feet. "You damned meddling jade!" he roared at her. "If we run into ill-luck I'll cut your ears off!"

But Mother Red-Cap scoffed at Amber's superstitious fears and assured her that it could be no ill omen because it had been done purposefully. She gave them some last-minute admonitions, Black Jack swallowed a glass of brandy and—though Amber was still reluctant and worried—they set out. By the time they had climbed the stairs and entered the Temple gardens she was beginning to feel excited and eager for whatever adventure might lie ahead; Bess and the spilled salt were already far out of her mind.

CHAPTER THIRTEEN

IN THE CITY the bells were ringing, and blazing bonfires sent up a glow against the sky. Every house was brightly lighted and crowds of merrymakers filled the streets; coaches rattled by and there were sounds of laughter and singing and music. Taverns were packed and the inns were turning customers away. It was the night of the Restoration all over again.

The Dog and Partridge was a fashionable tavern located in Fleet Street, frequented for the most part by gallants and the well-dressed, overpainted harlots who tracked them to their habitat. On this night it was jammed full. Every table was crowded with men—those who brought women usually took them to a private room upstairs; waiters were going among them with trays of bottles and glasses and foaming mugs of ale; a tableful of young men were singing; over in one corner some fiddlers scratched away, unheard and ignored. And just as Amber entered the door four young men started out, drunk and excited, going to fight a duel over some petty disagreement or imagined slight. They jostled against her but went on, troubling neither to stop nor to apologize, though by their dress they were obviously gentlemen.

Amber, masked and with her hood up, drew her cloak disdainfully about her and stepped aside. When they had gone she stood in the doorway and looked over the smoke-filled room, as though to find someone, and presently the host approached her.

"Madame?"

She knew by his manner that he took her for what she was supposed to be: a lady—Covent Garden variety. And she felt like one herself. She had spent hours at her window, both at the Royal Saracen and the Rose and Crown, watching them get in and out of their coaches, stop to speak to an admirer, fling a beggar a shilling. She knew how they picked up their skirts, how they pulled on a glove, spoke to a footman, used their fans. They were confident careless ladies, sure of the world and of their position in it, ever so slightly scornful of those who lived apart. But it was not by mere mimicry that she could so successfully pretend to be one; it was an attitude toward life that seemed natural to her.

"I'm looking for a gentleman," she said softly. "He was to meet me here." She scarcely glanced at the host; her eyes were going over the room.

"Perhaps I can help you to find him, madame. What was he wearing? What is his appearance?"

"He's very tall and his hair is black. I think he wears a black suit with a gold braid garniture."

The host turned, looked over the room. "Can it be that gentleman? The one at the far right-hand table?"

"No, no. Not that one. Hang it, the rascal must be late!" She fluttered her fan in annoyance.

"I'm sorry, madame. Perhaps you would prefer to wait in some more private place?"

"I'd prefer it, but if I do he might miss me. I can't tarry long —you understand." He was to understand that she was a married woman come to an assignation with her lover and in some apprehension of being seen by her husband or an acquaintance. "Place me in some discreet corner then. I'll wait on the wretch a few minutes or so."

The host led her across the room, weaving his way through the hot, noisy crowd, and Amber was aware that for all she was concealed from top to toe several of the gallants turned and looked at her. Her perfume was alluring and her cloak—which Black Jack had stolen from some lady of quality—suggested wealth. He seated her at a table in the farthest corner, and though she declined to order anything to drink she put a silver coin into his hand.

"Thank you, sir."

Sitting down Amber let her cloak fall open just enough to reveal something of her low neckline, flared her fan, gave a bored little sigh and then a quick casual glance around the room. She met several pairs of eyes, a few smiles and one broad grin, and instantly she dropped her lashes. They were not to take her for a prostitute.

She was glad now that she had come; a quick excitement flowed through her veins, and she only wished that this was real life, no mere part she was playing.

Within a quarter of an hour she had sorted them over and found at least one young man apparently well suited to her purposes. He sat at a table some seven or eight feet away playing cards with four companions, but his head turned persistently and his eyes looked back at her again and again. When most women went masked in public places a man had to learn to judge beauty by very little detail—the colour and sheen of a curl escaping from a hood, the sparkle of a pair of eyes seen between narrow slits, the curve of a pretty mouth.

Now, as she felt him looking at her again she glanced across and let the faintest smile touch her lips, a smile that scarcely existed at all, and then she looked away. Immediately he put down his cards, shoved back his chair and started toward her, walking unsteadily.

"Madame—" He paused politely to hiccough. "Madame, will you permit me the honour of buying you a glass of wine?"

Amber, who had been looking in another direction, now glanced at him in apparent surprise.

"Sir?"

The boy was flustered. "Oh, I'm sorry, your Ladyship. I meant no offense—hic—but I thought you might be lonely—"

"I'm waiting for someone, sir. I'm not lonely at all. And if you take me for a whore you're quite mistaken. I think you'll find your luck better with that lady over there."

With her fan, which she held clasped in one hand as it lay on the table, she indicated an unmasked woman who had just come in and who stood surveying the room, her cloak open to show a pair of almost naked breasts. As he looked Amber noticed that he wore four rings, had gold buttons on his coat with tiny diamonds in the centers, that his sword case was silver and that he wore a large mink muff attached to a broad twisted satin girdle.

He gave her a bow, very stiff and dignified. "I beg your pardon, madame. That is not my game, I assure you. Your servant, madame." He turned and would have gone off but she stopped him.

"Sir!" He looked around and she smiled up at him, her tawny eyes coaxing. "Forgive my rudeness. I fear the waiting has set me on edge. I'll accept your offer of wine, and thanks."

He smiled, forgiving her instantly, sat down and summoned the waiter to order champagne for her and brandy for himself. He told her that his name was Tom Butterfield and that he was a student at Lincoln's Inn, but when he tried to find out who she was she grew cool and aloof, intimating that she was too well known to dare give her name. And she knew by the way he stared at her that he was trying to place her, wondering if she was Lady This or Countess That, and thinking that he was having a considerable adventure.

They sipped their drinks, chatting idly, and when a little herring-peddler came to the table to ask if she might sing a song for the lady they both agreed. The child was perhaps ten or eleven years old, a slovenly little waif with dirty fingers, snarled

193

blonde curls and shoes worn through at the toes. But her voice was surprisingly clear and mature and there was about her a buoyant happy quality, refreshing as the taste of oranges on a stale tongue.

When she had done, Tom Butterfield munificently gave her several shillings, no doubt to impress her Ladyship. "You've a pretty voice, child. What's your name, pray?"

"Nelly Gwynne, sir. And thank ye, sir." She gave them both a grin, bobbed a curtsy, and was off through the crowd, stopping at another table across the room.

Amber now began to seem impatient. "What provoking creatures men are!" she exclaimed at last. "How the devil does he dare use me at this rate? I'll see that he smokes for it, I warrant you!"

"He's an ignorant blockhead that would keep your Ladyship awaiting," agreed Tom Butterfield soberly, though his eyes no longer focused well and he looked half-asleep.

"Well, he'll not do it again, you may be sure!" She began to gather up her belongings, muff, fan, and gloves. "Thank you for your drink, sir. I'll go along now."

She dropped one glove and bent slightly to pick it up. He stooped at the same time to get it for her and as he did so stared down into her bodice; he was weaving on his feet as he straightened, and gave his head a vigorous shake to clear it.

"Let me see you to your coach, madame."

They went out the door, Tom Butterfield walking solemnly at her heels and ignoring the jocular hoots of his friends. "Where is your coach waiting, madame?"

"Why, I came in a hackney, sir," she replied, implying that no lady going to an assignation would be so foolish as to ride in her own coach which might be seen and reported. "I believe there's one for hire over there. Will you call it for me?"

"I protest, madame. So fine a person as yourself travelling about after nightfall in a hell-cart? Tush!" He waggled an admonitory finger at her. "I have my coach just around the corner. Pray, let me carry you to your home." He put his fingers to his mouth and whistled.

They climbed in and the coach started off, jogging along

Fleet Street to the Strand, and now Tom Butterfield sat in his own corner, hiccoughing gently from time to time and hanging onto the strap beside the window for support. Amber, afraid that he would fall asleep, finally said to him: "You still don't know me, do you, Mr. Butterfield?"

"Why, no, madame. *Do* I know you?" She could feel him lean toward her as though trying to see through the darkness.

"Well—you've smiled and bowed to me often enough at the play."

"How now, have I then? Where were you sitting?"

"Where? In a box, of course!" No lady of quality sat elsewhere and her tone was indignant, but still teasing.

"When were you there last?"

"Oh, perhaps yesterday. Perhaps the day before. Don't you recall a lady who smiled kindly on you? Lord, I never thought you'd forget me so quick—all those amorous tweers you cast."

"I haven't forgot. My mind's been running on you ever since. You were in the fore of the King's box three days ago, dressed in a pretty déshabillé with your hair in a tour and your eyes had the most languishing gaze in all the world. Oh, gad, madame, I haven't forgot—not I. I'm mightily smitten with you, I swear I am. I'm in love with you, madame!"

As his impetuosity mounted Amber grew more coy, moving as far away as she could get and giving a low giggle in the darkness so that he made a grab for her. They started to tussle, she yielding a little and then pushing him off as he tried to draw her against him, giving a cry of dismay as his hand went into her bodice and caught one breast. He was panting excitedly, blowing his sour breath in her face, and all at once she gave him a brisk slap.

"What the devil, sir! Is this the way you handle a person of quality?"

Suddenly abashed, sobered by the slap, he drew away. "Forgive me, madame. My ardour outran my breeding."

"Indeed it did! I'm not accustomed to that kind of courtship!"

"My humblest apologies, madame. But I've admired you for a great while."

"How do you know? Perhaps I'm not the lady you have in mind at all."

"You must be the lady I have in mind. In fact, madame, I find myself so hot for you—" He reached for her again and they had begun to struggle once more, when the coach stopped. "Hell and furies!" he muttered, and she began to push him off.

"Sit up, sir, for God's sake!" She was straightening her clothes, pulling up her bodice, smoothing her hair, and then the door opened and Tom Butterfield staggered out and offered his hand to help her down.

The house before which they were stopped was a new one in Bow Street just a block from Covent Garden Square. At the door he caught hold of her to kiss her again and as he did so she took the key from her muff and slipped it into the lock.

"My husband's abroad tonight," she murmured. "Will you come in, Mr. Butterfield—and drink a glass of wine with me?"

She pushed open the door and went in with him following close behind her. But when he would have detained her in the passage she disengaged herself and went on up the black staircase to another door, which she also opened. She went in first and turned to find him smiling, his eyes full of expectancy as he looked at her; a candle was burning and it gave just enough light to see by. And then as Black Jack's heavy cudgel smashed down upon his skull the smile froze on his face, his eyes glazed over, and he dropped to the floor, folding up in sections like a carpenter's rule. Amber gave an involuntary little scream, one hand to her mouth, for the look of accusation she had seen in his eyes filled her with guilt.

But Black Jack had already stuck the cudgel back into his pocket and was kneeling beside him, cutting the string of cat's gut on which the buttons of his coat were strung. While she stood and stared he went efficiently about his work, rolling him over to get the buttons in back, pulling off the rings, unbuckling the sword and muff, searching through his pockets. And then, as a dark narrow streak of blood began to run out of his hair and over his temple, Amber moaned aloud.

"Oh! You've killed him!"

"Hush! He's not hurt." He looked up, giving her a broad

grin. "What the hell, sweetheart! Scared by a little blood? A broken head may teach him better sense next time—if we hadn't fibbed the young prigster somebody else would have. Look at this scout—" He held up a gold watch. "Fifteen pound if it's worth a sice. It takes fine bait to catch a big fish. Now come along—let's rub off." He had the boy's wrists and ankles tied and they started out. Amber paused to look back once more, but Black Jack hurried her down the backstairs and into a hackney that was waiting.

The night's easy success was reassuring to Amber, who now believed that she might soon get money enough to leave the Friars. And she had enjoyed the adventure, too—all but the clouting of Tom Butterfield, for whose welfare she still felt a certain guilty concern. When she had drunk her morning draught of ale, brought to her by the shuffling Pall, she slipped into her dressing-gown and went downstairs. Mother Red-Cap and Black Jack were in the parlour, talking, and both of them seemed in high spirits.

Amber came in with a breezy greeting and wave of her hand —full of a vast self-confidence and ready to be congratulated. Mother Red-Cap gave her a warm smile.

"Good-morning, my dear! Black Jack's been telling me how like a veteran you handled matters last night! He says it was worth a Jew's eye to see the way you led the young cully into his trap. And now you've seen for yourself how easy it is, and how safe, haven't you?"

Amber, thinking that now they had a need of her, was inclined to be independent. She shrugged. "I suppose so. Well—" She held out her hand. "Tip me my earnest."

"Why, my dear, there's nothing for you this time. I've applied your share on your bill."

"On my bill!"

"Of course. Or did you think it costs nothing to eat and lodge and give birth to a baby?"

She unlocked the drawer where her ledger was kept, took out a neatly written sheet and handed it to Amber who stood for a moment staring at it, nonplussed. She did not know what it said, for she had never been taught to read or write, but she was horrified to think that none of the money she had helped to steal was hers. For those expenses Mother Red-Cap had mentioned were not ones she had ever expected to pay. She felt that she had been cheated, and it made her angry. After a moment she looked up, her mouth opened to speak, and saw Mother Red-Cap just removing her cloak from the peg where it hung beside the door; she put it on and went out.

"Here!" Amber thrust the bill at Black Jack. "Read it to me!"

He took it and read the items slowly. At each one her scowl intensified. Now she was in a fine pickle! Instead of being less in debt she was deeper than ever. A violent despair filled her.

The bill was carefully itemized.

		£.	s.	d.
1.	For 3 months lodging and diet	30	0	0
2.	Suit of childbed linen	4	4	0
3.	For the minister to christen the child	2	10	0
4.	For the midwife's fees	3	3	0
5.	For the christening supper	6	0	0
6.	For the wet nurse for 15 days	1	0	0
7.	For Mrs. Chiverton	10	0	0
8.	For Mrs. Chiverton to bring the child upon request	5	0	0
9.	For the dressmaker for altering the green gown	0	6	2
		£62	3	2

"Lord!" cried Amber furiously. "I'm surprised she doesn't charge me for the use of her pot!"

Black Jack grinned. "Never mind. She will."

Amber was as angry with Black Jack as she was with Mother Red-Cap. For he could have paid her bill—and the debt too—at no hardship to himself. She was so resentful over his refusal that she had lost all sense of gratitude at being out of Newgate. She would have pawned some of the jewellery he had given her, but it was not enough to clear the full debt and if part of it disappeared she knew that she would get no more. It seemed to her that she would be in Whitefriars forever.

And so when Michael Godfrey came the next afternoon and asked her again to go away with him she agreed without hesitating an instant.

"Wait here and I'll be right down. I want to get my cloak and I have a new gown—" She was already out of the room.

Michael called after her: "Let it go! I'll get you another!"

But she pretended not to hear him and ran on, for there were several things she wanted to take with her—a lace fan, a pair of green silk stockings, the imitation gold ear-rings, and her parakeet. She rushed about the room—the house was empty and she wanted to get away before someone should return—flung everything into a sheet and hastily tied it. "Come on," she said to the parakeet. "We've had enough of this damned Sanctuary." And with the cage in one hand, the tied-up sheet in the other, she hurried out and down the stairs. Halfway to the bottom she stopped with a gasp, for the door swung open and Black Jack Mallard stood there, his great frame blocking out the light.

She gave a gasp of dismay. "Jack!"

It was dark down there and she could not see the expression on his face, but his voice was deep and hoarse. "So you were going to scour!" Slowly he started up the stairs toward her, and she could only stand there helplessly, watching him and waiting. All at once she was afraid of him; she had seen him lose his temper with Bess and knew that he could be violent. "You ungrateful little bitch, I should break your head for this—"

Amber's courage came back with a rush. "Get out of my way!" she cried. "I'm leaving this filthy place! I'm not going to stay here and hang with the rest of you!"

He was just below her now and she could see his face, the thin upper lip drawn tight against his teeth, his eyes dark and glittering. "You'll stay here as long as I want you to stay. Go on upstairs now. Go on, I say!"

For a long moment they stood staring at each other. Then suddenly she kicked out at his shins and threw herself against his arm, trying to break through. *"Michael!"* she screamed.

Suddenly Black Jack laughed. He picked her up with one arm, threw her over his shoulder, and started back up the stairs.

"Michael!" he repeated contemptuously. "What good d'ye think that jack-straw could be to you?" He laughed again, a thunderous roar that echoed up the narrow stairwell, and he seemed scarcely to notice that Amber was screaming furiously, kicking and beating at him with her fists.

When he reached the bedroom he set her down, so forcibly that the jar went from her heels up into her head. She recovered quickly.

"God damn you, Black Jack Mallard!" she yelled at him. "You're trying to kill me, *that's* what you're doing! You'll make me stay here till we *all* get caught! But I won't do it, d'ye hear? I'll get out if I have to—" She started for the door again, so furious that she would have run out of Whitefriars and into the arms of the first constable who saw her.

He reached out a hand and caught her as she would have gone by, jerking her to him as easily as if she were one of the dolls bought at Bartholomew Fair. "Stop it, you little fool! You gabble like a magery prater! You're not going out of the Friars —not while I'm here. When I'm gone, do what you damned please—but I didn't give three hundred pound to get you out of Newgate so some other man could have the use of you!"

She stared at him with angry amazement, for she had always believed that he was in love with her; and it had long been her opinion that it was very easy for a woman to take advantage of a man in love. Now she realized that the only distinction he made between her and Bess was that she was newer and more ornamental and evidently pleased him better in bed. It was a sharp and humiliating cut to her pride, and all of a sudden she despised him.

When she answered him her voice was low and tense, full of enraged scorn. "Oh, you gormandizing vermin, Jack Mallard, I despise you! I hope you *do* get caught! I hope they hang you and cut you up in pieces—I hope— Oh!" She whirled about and flung herself on the bed, bursting into sobs, and in a moment she heard the door slam behind him.

She stayed in her room the rest of the day, refused any supper, and was still sulking the next morning when someone knocked. Thinking that it was probably Black Jack, coming with a gift to beg her pardon and try to make up the quarrel, she called out for him to come in. She was at the dressing-table, cleaning her nails, and did not glance around until she saw Bess's face appear in the mirror. Then she turned swiftly.

"What are you doing here!"

Bess was unexpectedly sweet and agreeable. "I only came to wish you a good morning." Amber thought she had most likely come to gloat because Black Jack had spent the night with her, and she turned away. But now Bess leaned over, close to her shoulder.

"I heard you and Jack yesterday afternoon—"

"Did you now!"

"If you really want to leave the Friars—if you'll promise to go away and never come back—I can get that money for you."

Amber jumped to her feet, one hand reaching out to grab Bess's wrist. "If I'll promise to go! My God! I'll go so fast I'll— Where is it?"

"It's mine. I've saved it up to have if Black Jack should ever need it. Mother Red-Cap keeps it for me, but I can get it by tomorrow night. I'll put it in the food-hutch in the kitchen."

But the money was not there and when next Amber saw Bess she had a purple bruise across one eye, and the side of her face and her lower lip was swollen—obviously Black Jack had discovered their plot. After that Bess never troubled to conceal her hatred and jealousy and only a few days later Amber found the house-cat with turquoise-coloured feathers clinging to its jowls and paws. Bess insisted that she was completely innocent of any connection with the cat's crime, but Amber had always kept her parakeet's cage safely out of reach and knew the little bird could not have been caught without help from someone.

CHAPTER FOURTEEN

Though she at first intended to, Amber discovered it would not be possible to stay on bad terms with Black Jack forever. She depended on him for too much. And so—even if she continued to harbour her resentment against him—within four or five days after the quarrel they seemed as close as before.

She had declared to Mother Red-Çap and all of them that she would never venture her carcass again for so paltry a fee—twelve pounds was her share from the first night—but she soon did. For it was the only possible chance she had of ever getting out of the Friars. And in spite of the danger she enjoyed their escapades: playing at being a fine lady, venturing up into the City, even the excitement of running great risks.

For the most part their luck was as good as it had been the first night. It seemed that every young coxcomb in London was ready to believe a beautiful stranger had fallen in love with him at the play or in Hyde Park or the Mulberry Gardens, and was more than eager to help her cuckold her foolish old husband. Both Black Jack and Mother Red-Cap attributed much of their success to Amber's own skill at portraying a fashionable woman. Bess, they said, had too often spoiled the whole scheme by being taken for a whore in disguise—which made the gentlemen wary, for it was well known that those ladies were frequently in league with a gang of bullies.

One of their most consistently successful tricks was the "buttock and twang"—a simpler form of what they had done the first night. Amber would go masked into a tavern, find her victim and lure him outside into some dark alley. When she had picked his pocket a cough or sneeze summoned Black Jack who would come staggering along and pretending to be drunk, knock him over, and make off with whatever she had stolen. Concealed by the darkness she would also disappear, join Black Jack, and return to Alsatia. A time or two she went "upon the question lay." Dressed well, though discreetly, and carrying in her hand an empty bandbox she would go to some great house and pretend to be the 'Change-woman come with the ribbons my lady had bespoke the day before. While the maid was gone to see if the lady was awake she could put a few small valuable objects into her box and depart.

But Amber did not care for that kind of sport. She preferred to play the lady of quality herself and told them flatly this dodge was a trick better suited to Bess's talents than her own.

Once Amber went into a house in Great Queen Street where

a masquerade was in progress, and after a while she and one of the young men sought a quiet room. But as they were walking down a dark hallway she felt stealthy fingers at the nape of her neck and moved swiftly away. "You're a thief!" she whispered, afraid to cry out for fear a constable actually would come. He protested and was about to run off when he discovered that the buttons on his coat had been cut. They both laughed, he admitted he had been mistaken in her too, and so they parted, to cast for other fish.

She had only one serious scare and that occurred the night she went to an upstairs-room in a tavern with their victim and found that Black Jack had not yet arrived. For more than half an hour she was capricious and teasing, holding him off; but at last he grew impatient, began to suspect what she was about and when he tried to pull off her mask she grabbed up a pewter candlestick and struck him with it. Then, not stopping for his sword or watch or even to see whether or not he was dead, she rushed out of the room, down the hallway and the stairs and was halfway through the tap-room when she heard a voice bellow: "Stop that woman! She's a thief!" He had recovered consciousness and come after her.

Amber felt an agonizing terror that seemed to freeze blood and muscle, but somehow in spite of herself she ran on at full speed through the roomful of dumfounded patrons. She had just reached the door to the street when a man sprang up from one of the tables and started after her, shouting that he would bring her back. It was Black Jack. They got safely to the Sanctuary where he told the story to everyone with shouts of laughter —but Amber refused to stir out of the Friars again for more than a fortnight. She had felt the gallows noose too plain that time.

But in spite of all these activities she was not able to save much money. She had to have numerous gowns and cloaks, so that she could not come to be recognized by what she wore, and though she bought them second-hand in Houndsditch or in Long Lane and soon sold them again, she spent a good deal. She also had to defer the cost of her lodging and food and other incidental expenses. And every time Mrs. Chiverton brought the baby in she had a dozen gifts for him. She had come to feel that there was a wall around Alsatia over which it would never be possible to climb—most who came there, she knew, stayed.

Black Jack was himself a good example.

Whatever his real name, he was the son of a country-squire and had come to London eleven years before to attend the Middle Temple. At that time the King had just been beheaded and the Puritans were rabidly punishing vice and praising virtue; but the young men nevertheless contrived to live very much the same carefree reckless lives they always had. A hypocritical cloak of modesty served its purpose for them. Thus he ran himself into debt, far beyond his father's ability to pay even had the old man wished to do so. It was never permissible for impecunious gentlemen to beg of their relatives and friends, and so when his creditors became too pressing he moved into Whitefriars to avoid arrest. And there he had found, as did many another bankrupt young man of good family, that the King's highway offered an easy and exciting livelihood.

"When it's so easy to steal money," he said, "a man's a fool to work for it." Amber was half inclined to agree with him —or would have had she been able to keep all and not merely a small part of what she took.

Early in June Black Jack went back to the roads again. Winter was the gay social season in London and many of the nobility returned to their country homes to spend the summer months. Then the roads swarmed with highwaymen and numerous innkeepers were in their pay; but in spite of the well-known dangers most persons rode without sufficient protection.

Amber's part was a simple and safe one. With Bess, who went along dressed as her serving-woman, she would ride out to the inn from which Mother Red-Cap had had information and there make the acquaintance of the traveller and his family. Pretending to be a lady of quality just going out of or coming into town, she would tell them that her coach had been overturned and wrecked; and when they offered to let her ride with them she could manage the time of departure to Black Jack's advantage. For though many inn-keepers were willing to give information, very few would allow a robbery on the premises—too many such incidents would put them out of business. Amber was well satisfied with this arrangement, but Bess was not—for she had been accustomed to acting the part of lady herself and was furiously resentful at having been demoted.

There was seldom any scuffle when the bandits appeared, for even if all members of a party were armed they usually preferred giving up the master's valuables to risking a wound. One man, however, told Black Jack that he would never have got the money if he had not taken him unawares, and Black Jack offered to shoot it out with him. Armed with pistols, they walked into the nearby field, counted off ten paces, and fired. The man dropped dead. Amber, who had been watching with anxiety and trying to think what she should do if Black Jack was killed, felt a passionate relief—but afterward she was more in awe of him than she had been.

But he was a good-natured thief and always left the coachman half-a-crown to drink his health. Once he robbed an old Parliamentarian just returning from a trip into the country with his whore, stripped them both naked and tied them to a tree, back to back; over their heads he put a sign informing all passers-by that here were two Adamites.

As the summer weeks passed Amber's savings began to mount; by mid-August she had accumulated two hundred and fifty pounds. They had had no new scares and she became brazenly confident and almost began to enjoy the life she was living. She still had an uneasy restlessness to leave Alsatia, a feeling that she was missing something of great importance going on out in the real world, but the days faded one into another and she was half content.

Then one day she got a rude and sickening shock.

Coming into the parlour she found Black Jack standing between Blueskin and Jimmy the Mouth—leaning with his great arms upon their shoulders—while they looked at something laid out on the table before them. Their backs were to her and she could not see what it was but they were talking together in low voices which now and then burst into a laugh.

Amber walked up and saw that it was a large sheet of paper

with his Majesty's coat-of-arms and two long lines of printing upon it. She frowned, suddenly suspicious.

"What's that?"

They looked around, surprised to find her there.

"Black Jack's a famous man," said Blueskin. "He's been named first in a proclamation for taking twenty-two highwaymen." Black Jack grinned, pleased with the honour.

But Amber stared, open-mouthed and horrified. She wanted violently to live, and at a time like this, when she saw how close death stood beside her, she grew frantic with terror.

"What's the matter?" demanded Black Jack, a kind of sharpness in his voice.

"You know what's the matter! They're looking for you and they'll catch you! They'll catch all of us, and hang us! Oh, I wish I'd never come to this damned place! I wish I was still in Newgate! There at least I was safe!"

"And so do I wish you were still in Newgate! Of all the complaining jades I've ever known— What the hell did you expect when I brought you here? You'd better get it through your head the whole world doesn't function for your benefit! But you can stop worrying about your neck! A woman's always got one alibi—you can plead your belly. Why," he continued—and now his voice had turned sarcastic, his eyes went over her with mocking amusement—"I once knew a woman put off the hangman for ten years—no sooner was she delivered of one brat than they found her quick again."

Amber scowled and her mouth gave a sneer of repugnance. "Oh, did she, indeed? Well, that's all very well—but not for me!" She finished the sentence with a shout, leaning toward him, fists clenched and the cords in her throat straining. "I've got other things to do with *my* life, I'll have you know—!"

At that moment Bess came in the door, and saw that there was trouble between them. She grinned maliciously. "What's the quarrel here? Sure, now, Jack, you've not fallen out with our fine Mrs. Fairtail?"

Amber turned, her nostrils flaring with anger, and gave her a sweeping glance of lazy insolence. "Marry come up, Bess Columbine, but you're as jealous as a wife of her husband when she lies-in!"

206

"Jealous? *Me* jealous of *you!*" yelled Bess. "I'll be damned if I am, you scurvy wench!"

"Don't call *me* names!"

Suddenly Amber reached out, grabbed her by the hair, and gave a violent jerk. With a shriek of rage Bess seized a fistful of curls and the two women would have flown into deadly battle—but for the unexpected appearance of Mother Red-Cap. The men merely stood looking on and smiling, but she rushed forward, took them by the shoulders and gave each a vigorous shake.

"Stop!" she cried. "I won't have any brawling under my roof! Just once more, Bess Columbine, and out you go!"

"Out *I* go!" protested Bess, while Amber, with a superior smile, reached up to pin back the long heavy curls that had come loose. "What about her! What about that—"

"Bess!"

For a long moment Bess and Mother Red-Cap stood with locked stares, but Bess was finally forced to yield. Nevertheless, as she turned to leave the room she knocked into Amber, giving her a hard jar. Without an instant's hesitation Amber turned her head and spat onto her gown. Bess stopped abruptly, the two women once more face to face like a pair of bristling cats; but at another warning from Mother Red-Cap Bess whirled around and stalked out.

For several days after that Black Jack ignored Amber as though she did not exist, and Bess was insultingly triumphant; she flouted his preference whenever they met. But however little Amber cared for Black Jack or his company, she did not intend to let Bess get the better of her. She began a new flirtation with him which was presently successful—and after that Bess's hatred was so intense and so sullen that she half expected to get a knife stuck into her ribs. She believed, and with good reason, that it was only Bess's fear of Black Jack which secured her own life.

Early in September Bess, convinced that she was pregnant, told Black Jack about it and asked him outright to marry her. He gave her an insulting snort.

"Marry you? You must take me for a dommerer. I suppose

you think I don't know every man that's come into this house has had a lick at you!"

He was sitting at the dinner-table, as he always did, long after everyone else had left, gnawing at a chicken-leg he had in one hand and washing it down with swallows from a wine-bottle held in the other. He was slumped far down on his spine, perfectly easy and relaxed and unconcerned, not even troubling to glance up at her.

"That's a damned lie and you know it! I never so much as spoke to another man until you brought that slut in here! And anyway I haven't laid with anyone but Blueskin—and that only a few times! This brat is yours and you know it, Black Jack Mallard, and you'll own it or I'll—"

He tossed the bone aside and leaned forward to pick up a cluster of purple Lisbon grapes. "For God's sake, Bess, stubble it! You sound like a beggar's clack-dish! I don't care what you do. Lay with who you damned please, but don't bother me about it."

His back was half turned and for a moment she stood staring at him, her eyes like glass, her whole body beginning to tremble with rage. And then with an animal-like cry she lunged for him, snatching up a knife off the table. A quick look of surprise crossed his face as he saw the swift descending flash of the blade and his arm went up to defend himself, thrashing out then and giving her a violent blow that sent her sprawling across the room.

She was crouched on the floor, staring ferociously up at him where he loomed above her, when Mother Red-Cap rushed in from her room down the hallway. "What is it?" she cried. "Oh!" She put her hands on her hips. "Well, I've warned you before, Bess, and now you go. Get your belongings and leave this house!"

Bess glared up at her with sulky defiance, but got slowly to her feet. For a long moment she stood there without moving.

"Go on!" repeated Mother Red-Cap. "Get out of here!"

Bess started to protest and then she gave a sudden furious scream. "Don't say it again! I'm going! I'm going away from here and I'll never come back! I wouldn't come back if you got on your knees and begged me! I hate you! I hate every one of you and I hope you—" Suddenly she whirled about and ran from the room and they could hear her feet pounding up the stairs.

Black Jack gave a low whistle and glanced at the knife where it lay on the floor, knocked out of her hand when he had struck her. "Whew! The crafty little gypsy. She'd have slit my throat, I think." He gave a shrug and went back to take up the cluster of grapes, picking them off and tossing them one at a time into his mouth.

Mother Red-Cap went to the table, got out her ledger, and sat down to settle Bess's account. "I'll be glad to be done with her. She's never been much use to me, and ever since Mrs. Channell came she's been an infernal nuisance. Oh, well—you can't make a whistle of a pig's tail."

Presently Black Jack went into the kitchen to tease Pall, who adored him though she blushed and stammered and scratched nervously at her lice whenever he appeared. The house was quiet for several minutes and then Amber came in the front door. She was wearing a thin pale-green silk dress with her hair tumbling about her shoulders and tied with a ribbon, and she had two of Penelope Hill's choicest yellow roses stuck into the low-cut neckline.

"Ye gods! I swear this is the hottest day in an age!" She dropped into a chair, fanning herself with her lace-trimmed handkerchief, and Mother Red-Cap went on with her work. After a few moments Amber got up and started for the doorway that led into the hall where the stairs were.

"I don't think you'd better go up there, my dear," said Mother Red-Cap, dipping her pen into a pewter inkwell, but neither turning nor looking around. "I just sent Bess to pack her rigging and she's in a tearing rage."

Amber glanced back, smiling. "Bess is going?" She shrugged. "Well, much I care if she's in a rage or no. Let her just say something to me and I'll—"

"Never mind, my dear. I don't want another brawl in my house. Go into the kitchen with Black Jack and Pall until she's gone."

Amber hesitated for a moment but finally turned and went into the other room. After a few minutes they heard Bess's high-heeled shoes coming down the stairs, Mother Red-Cap's voice talking to her, though Bess did not answer, and then with a bang she was gone. Black Jack proposed a toast to the peaceful life, and he and Amber presently wandered back into the parlour and sat down to play a game of cards.

They had spent interminable hours at cards and dice, for they did not go out on business more than once or twice a week—sometimes even less—and the long days and nights had to be passed somehow. Black Jack had taught her every trick in a gambler's repertoire—palming, slurring, knapping, the brief—and in seven months she had attained to a very creditable proficiency. She felt that she could hold her own now at a table with any lord or lady in the kingdom.

After a while Blueskin came in and they started to play at putt, the favourite tavern game and one which had probably been the undoing of more country-squires' sons than any other. It was three or four hours before she went upstairs to her own room, and there she found Bess's final gesture to the rival she despised. Her smocks and gowns and petticoats littered the room, ripped and slashed to pieces. There were torn fans, gloves cut in two, cloaks hacked by scissors, and she had dumped the contents of the chamber-pot onto the remnants of Amber's finest gown.

Black Jack promised to find Bess and give her the beating she deserved, but she had disappeared from Sanctuary and left not a trace, and they all knew it would never be possible to seek her out in the great sprawling city with its half-million inhabitants. She could lose herself in the warrens of Clerkenwell or St. Pancras, in the glutted seafaring center of Wapping, or in the alleys and courts of the Mint across the river in Southwark.

It was a bad shock to Amber; she decided that her life was cursed and that she would never get out of Whitefriars. She became gloomy and despondent, trailed listlessly about the house, and was sullenly bad-tempered with all of them. She hated Bess and Black Jack and Mother Red-Cap, Pall and Blue-skin and the house-cat, even herself.

No matter what I do, she thought, no matter how hard I work and how much I save, there's always *something* happens! I'll never get out! I'll die in this stinking hole!

Three days after Bess had gone Mother Red-Cap came into the bedroom and found Amber lying on her back, stretched out straight with her hands behind her head. She had been awake for at least two hours, mulling over her troubles, and the longer she thought about them the more insurmountable they became. She gave Mother Red-Cap a sulky glare, annoyed at being interrupted, but she did not speak.

"Well, my dear," said Mother Red-Cap, as cheerfully as though Amber had greeted her in good humour. "This is no ordinary day for us, you know."

Every morning she got up punctually at five, like an apprentice, put on her plain, neat dress, and began to go about her numberless tasks. From the moment she woke she was brisk and alert and ready for the day. The sight of such determined activity was irritating to Amber.

"It's an ordinary day for me," she said crossly.

"How now! Surely you've not forgot this is the day you're going to Knightsbridge."

"It's not the day *I'm* going to Knightsbridge!"

"But, my dear child, this is most important. There's a great deal of money involved."

"It isn't the first time there's been a great deal of money involved—but *I* never saw much of it!" The subject had been discussed between them before, always with considerable bitterness, for though Amber protested she was being cheated of her rightful share Mother Red-Cap insisted that she got exactly what her services warranted, and Black Jack agreed. "Anyway, it'd be like Bess Columbine to have the constables waiting on us. She knows all our plans."

"Nonsense, my dear. I think I know Bess better than you do, and I assure you she's no such desperate creature as that. She hates the sight of a constable worse than a fishmonger hates a hard frost. But as for the money—I came up here to tell you

I'll double your earnest this time, to make up for the loss of your clothes." Considering the matter settled she started toward the door. "Black Jack is below with Jimmy and Blueskin. They intend setting out within the hour."

But as she went Amber flounced over on her side, scowled and called after her, "I'm *not* going!"

Mother Red-Cap did not reply, but within a few minutes Black Jack appeared and after half-an-hour's coaxing and wheedling and assuring her that they had changed their plans so that Bess could not catch them if she tried, she got up and began to dress. Even so she would not leave before she had gone to consult an astrologer who lived in Mitre Court. Upon his assurance that the day was a propitious one for her she borrowed a cloak from Mother Red-Cap and, still sulking, left the Sanctuary with Pall and the three men.

Knightsbridge was a quiet little village on the West Bourne, just two miles and a half out of the city, and they reached it by taking a barge up the river to Tuthill Fields and then hiring a coach to the village. Because of its convenient situation Knightsbridge was much frequented by highwaymen who attacked travellers leaving or entering the city. Mother Red-Cap had had a message from the inn-keeper in her employ there that an old gentleman, Theophilus Bidulph, who came into London twice a year, was expected on the 8th of September.

Sometimes they had to wait two or three or more days for a victim to appear, but Amber heartily hoped that this time it would not be necessary. They went upstairs to the room assigned them and Pall immediately took off her shoes, complaining—as she had ever since leaving home—that they hurt her feet. Having nothing else to do Amber sat down to arrange her hair all over again, a process which could easily take half-an-hour, and when that was done she plagued Pall until the miserable girl finally admitted that she was with child by Black Jack Mallard. By nightfall she was distractedly bored, pacing uneasily about the room, hanging out the window and tapping her fingers on the sill, wishing she were anyone but who she was and anywhere in the world but there.

But at last she heard the pounding of horses' hoofs, the clatter and bang of a coach; dogs began to bark and the ostlers ran out into the courtyard to greet the arriving guest. A few moments later there was a hasty tap at her door and the host told her Theophilus Bidulph had come and was ordering his supper downstairs. Amber waited about a quarter of an hour and then she went down herself.

Mr. Bidulph was standing beside the fireplace drinking a glass of ale and talking to the host and he did not see her until she spoke his name. Then he turned about in some surprise. He was a short merry-faced old gentleman with great bushy pointed eyebrows and the look of a good-natured imp.

"Why, Mr. Bidulph!" she cried, giving him a sparkling smile and holding out her hand.

He took it and made her a bow. "Your servant, madame." In spite of his courtesy he was frankly puzzled, though he looked at her with interest.

"I vow I think you've forgotten me, sir."

"By the mass, madame, I fear I have."

"I'm Balthazar St. Michel's eldest daughter, Ann. Last time we met I was no more than so high." She bent a little, indicating with her flat palm a very tiny girl. "Surely you remember me now, sir? You used to dandle me on your knee." She continued to smile at him.

"Why—uh—of course, madame—my dear, I mean. And how is your father, pray? It's some years since we've met and—uh—"

Her face fell a little. "Oh, Mr. Bidulph, he's not well. The old gout again. Sometimes he's in bed for days." She gave him another quick smile. "But he speaks so often of you— He'll be so pleased I chanced to see you."

Mr. Bidulph drank down his ale. "You must give him my regards, child. But what are you doing all alone out here?"

"Oh, I'm not alone, sir. I'm travelling with my woman. I'm going into town to visit Aunt Sarah—but one of our horses lost a shoe and we stopped here for the night. They say the ways are thick with highwaymen nowadays."

"It's true the wretches are everywhere—much worse than when I was a young fellow, let me tell you. But then, of course, nothing is as it was. But won't you ride in with me in the morning? I'll see you get there safe and sound."

"Oh, thank you, sir! How kind that is! For the truth on it is, those cut-throats everywhere about have me uneasy as a witch."

While they talked Amber saw some of his footmen going through the room bearing trunks and boxes on their backs; evidently the old gentleman did not intend to trust his belongings to the surveillance of the stable-boys. But at least that would make it possible for Black Jack to take what he wanted, while she occupied Mr. Bidulph's attention. And, long before morning, all five of them would be in Whitefriars again. Amber was eager to have it over and done and to be back in safety once more—for Bess's jealousy hung above her like an ominous threat. She thought the girl was mad enough to do anything for her revenge.

At Mr. Bidulph's invitation Amber sat down to have supper with him, and they lingered there afterward while she listened to his tales of the Civil Wars. She heard of numerous instances demonstrating his and everyone else's heroic valour, of the dead King's nobility and martyrdom, the magnificent leadership of Prince Rupert. Nothing, he assured her again and again, could have been more glorious than the way the Royalists had lost the war.

Amber kept an eye on the clock.

By ten she was beginning to grow nervous and had to force herself to sit still and smile and ask questions. They had been there at the table for more than three hours, and certainly Black Jack should have finished his work by now and made her a signal to join them. A feeling of panic was rising in her, and her stomach turned over and over, fluttering like a captive bird.

Oh! she thought wildly. Where is he! Why doesn't he come! *What* can have happened!

Then all at once she heard a noisy commotion from outside. The dogs began to bark again, horses' hoofs beat along the roadway, and there was a babble of voices—men shouting, a woman's scream. Pall opened their door at the head of the stairs to wave frantically at her. And Amber, suddenly terrified, thinking that Bess had arrived with a party of constables, leaped to her feet.

"Good Lord, madame! What's amiss?"

"It's thieves!" cried Amber wildly. "Quick! Put out the lights!"

She darted across to snuff out the candles burning in wall-sconces, and as she did so Pall burst from the room above and came running down, wailing with fear. "Shut up!" cried Amber frantically. At that moment she heard the unmistakable sound of Bess Columbine's voice and a bellow of rage from Black Jack.

The voices were nearer now and Amber—able to think of nothing but saving herself—started for the front door. She heard Pall bawling her name, and Mr. Bidulph, catching the contagion of excitement, went stumbling around in the dark, calling out, "Mrs. Ann! Mrs. Ann! Where are you!" By mistake he grabbed hold of Pall and she shrieked with terror.

Amber rushed on and then, just as she got outside, she heard footsteps coming that way and saw the flare from their torches. Bess's voice screamed: "She's in here! Let him go—*He's* not the one! The woman's inside!"

Amber whirled and ran back inside, heading for the kitchen. Mr. Bidulph was still floundering about and calling her name while Pall screamed but could not decide what to do; as Amber ran by he reached for her and caught hold of her skirt. She jerked it free, hearing it tear, and rushed on, reaching the narrow little hallway below the stairs just as a torch brightened the room. Pall gave a shriek of agony as she was seized and Mr. Bidulph indignantly demanded to know what was going on.

Amber burst into the kitchen, panting so that she could scarcely breathe, and gave a scared start as she heard a voice.

"Mrs. Channell? It's the host."

She stopped still. "Oh, my God! Where can I go! Where can I hide? They'll be here next!" Her teeth were chattering and her very bones seemed to shake.

"Quick! Get into this food-hutch! Give me your hand!"

Amber reached out gropingly. He caught hold of her hand,

threw up the top of a great oaken chest, and she climbed in. The lid had just shut down when Bess and the constables came through the hallway; the host turned and ran out of the room, slamming the door behind him.

"There she goes!" yelled Bess. And through the air-holes bored in the chest Amber saw a flare of light and heard the rush of their feet as they went by, Bess swearing when she knocked her ankle against a stool.

Amber waited only until the last one was gone and then she flung back the lid and got out, picked up her skirts, and ran after them. Still on the trail of the host they had rounded the corner into the courtyard, and since the kitchen formed a separate wing of the house it was dark when she got outside. The confusion was greater than ever and she knew they had captured all three men for she heard Bess yelling: "Let him go, you damned fools! He's the ostler here! Get that woman!"

Amber did not pause an instant but struck off in the other direction, toward the river, hoping only to get away where it was so dark she could not be seen. Reaching the bank she plunged down it. She was unable to see at all, for the moon had disappeared and the sky was black with storm-clouds, but she ran blindly ahead—like one in a dream who, no matter how hard the legs churn, cannot seem to make any progress. The sounds were growing fainter, but she dared not stop or look back.

Her shoes were soaked through in a moment and the rocks on the stream-bed bruised the soles of her feet. Her wet skirts flopped and clung to her ankles; brambles scratched her face and bare arms and caught in her hair. A hard pain seared her left side, her legs felt wooden and her lungs were beginning to burn. But she ran on and on.

It was quiet down there and after several minutes she could hear nothing at all from the inn, only the occasional plop of a frog into the water or the frightened scurrying of an animal. At last she could run no more and stopped, heaving, sagged helplessly against a tree.

But as she began to get her breath she also began to think and to wonder how she would get back. Following the Bourne, she knew, would lead her down to the Thames a great way from Whitefriars. She must go back to the road and hope to find a hackney—or walk; it was only about two miles and a quarter. She climbed the bank and started off across the fields, but did not return at once to the road, for fear they would come along searching for her. She alternately ran and walked, constantly looking back. Whenever a coach or a man on horseback approached, she flung herself flat and waited, but for the most part the night was quiet and she met no one.

Within a few minutes she had reached St. James's Park. She skirted the edge of it, and though here there were some late walkers, by keeping in the shadows and moving softly, she got through without molestation. Reaching the Strand she hurried along, holding onto her skirts to keep them from dragging in the street, clotted and littered as it was with animal dung and decaying vegetable refuse. She was afraid to be alone in the city, for she knew the menace of it and wished violently that a hackney would come along. And then all at once the banging clatter of a coach resounded through the night, lumbering heavily toward her as though in a great hurry to run her down and be on.

Seeing that it was a public vehicle she shouted. The driver hauled on the reins, came to a stop some yards beyond, and turned on his perch. "Want to hire a coach?"

Amber had already reached the door and pulled it open. "Temple Bar!" she cried. "And quick!" She jumped in and slammed it shut, so glad to be safe inside that she scarcely noticed how it smelt.

He drove so fast and so recklessly that she could only try to keep her seat as the coach careened along. The wooden seat on which she sat was covered with a thin hard pad and the jarring and vibrating of the springless compartment shook her to the heels. At Temple Bar he stopped. Almost before the wheels had quit turning she was down and off on a run toward the Temple, for she had not a farthing with her.

"Hey!" he yelled furiously. "Come back here, you cheating drab!"

And then as she ran on, disappearing into the darkness, he

climbed down and started after her. But at the sight of a party of gay and drunken students, he apparently decided it.was not worth the risk of losing his coach-and-horses for a one-shilling fare. He got back up on his perch and started off again.

Amber ran down Middle Temple Lane and cut into the Pump Court. Many lights were still burning, there were sounds of music and singing and laughter, and people were going and coming everywhere. Her head was down, because she was now too tired to hold it up, and she ran headlong into a group of some half-dozen students, one of whom caught her in his arms.

"Hey, there, sweetheart!" he cried gaily. "Where're you going in such haste!"

Amber did not answer him but began to struggle frantically, pounding at his chest with her fists, crying with exhaustion and terror. But the more she struggled the tighter he held her. And all the others had gathered around now, laughing and joking, thinking that perhaps they had caught a whore, since no respectable woman would be running about the streets at eleven o'clock in only a thin silk dress, and that torn and wet.

He bent her head back to kiss her and Amber felt them crowding closer and closer until such a terror swept over her she was close to fainting. Every one of them looked like a constable. At that moment she heard a familiar voice.

"Hey, just a minute! What's going on here! I know this lady— Let her go, you varlets!" It was Michael Godfrey, whom Amber had not seen for more than four months.

Reluctantly the young man released her. Amber looked up at Michael with tears streaking down her scratched and dirt-stained face, but she did not speak to him. Giving a quick shove she broke free and started off, but he followed her. When he caught her they had reached a dark corner leading into Vine Court, away from the light of the torches.

"Mrs. Channell! For God's sake, what's the matter? What's happened? It's Michael—don't you remember me?"

He grabbed hold of her arm and brought her to a stop but she jerked at him furiously, sobbing. "Let me go! Oh, damn you! Let me go or I'll get caught!"

218

"Caught by who! What is it? Tell me!" He gave her a little shake for she was not looking at him but tugging to free herself, trying to pry his fingers loose from her wrist, wild and desperate.

"The constables, you fool! Let me go!"

He turned suddenly, dragging her after him, and entered a doorway, which he closed. Amber slumped against the wall.

"Where's Black Jack?" he demanded.

"They've caught him. We were at Knightsbridge and the constables came—I got away but they're coming after me—" She made a sudden lunge. "Let me go! I've got to get back!"

He grabbed her shoulders, thrusting her against the wall, and she felt his arms go about her. "You can't go back there. Mother Red-Cap'll send you out again, and someday you'll get caught for sure. Come with me—" His mouth sought hers, his arms held her close, and Amber relaxed gratefully, so tired she could struggle no longer. He picked her up and started through the dark hallway toward the stairs.

CHAPTER FIFTEEN

THE THREE MEN, Black Jack and Jimmy the Mouth and Blueskin, were all hanged from the same arm of the three-cornered gallows, just ten days from the night they were taken. When the processes of justice worked at all it was with devastating swiftness; they left him no time to pay his way out. Bess was sent to Bridewell, the house-of-correction for female offenders, to improve her morals. Pall, who pleaded her belly, was sent to Newgate to await the birth of her child and probable transportation to Virginia.

At the time of the execution Amber was alone in Michael Godfrey's rooms in Vine Court. Michael had gone to watch and when he came back he told her that all three men had been cut down and taken to lie at a tavern—where they might be viewed by mourners or whoever had a curiosity to look at them.

All the corpses had been treated with respect and not, as often happened, carried through the streets and tossed about until mangled beyond recognition. Black Jack, he said, was very nonchalant to the end, and the last words of his farewell speech were: "Gentlemen, there's nothing like a merry life—and a short one."

But even then she could not believe it.

How could Black Jack Mallard be dead when she remembered him so well, everything he had done and said over the months she had known him? How could he be dead when he was so big, so powerful, so obstinately indestructible? She remembered his six feet five inches of male strength, hard-muscled and hard-fleshed, covered with wiry black hair that matted on his chest. She remembered the thunderous rumble of his laugh; his enormous capacity for wine—he had said that his nickname originated one night when he won a wager by drinking a blackjack of Burgundy without once putting down the vessel. She remembered a thousand things more.

And now he was dead.

She remembered how some of the men had wept at Chapel the day before they were to be executed. And, though she thought she had forgotten, she could, all too well, recall the expressions on their faces. She wondered how Black Jack had looked—and how she would have looked herself had she been sitting there beside him. She suffered agonies thinking of it. Whatever she was doing—enjoying her dinner, brushing her hair, leaning on the windowsill and laughing at the pranks of the young men down in the courtyard—the thought would come like the sudden shocking impact of a physical blow: I might not be here! I might be *dead!*

At night she would wake up, crying with terror and clutching at Michael. She had seen two of her cousins die, but this was the first time that any personal realization of death had come to her. She became very pious and repeated all the prayers she knew a dozen times a day.

But for the grace of God I'd not be here right now but in Hell, she would think, for she knew she had not been good enough to get into Heaven. Even before she had left Marygreen

Uncle Matt had not thought it likely that Heaven was her destination. She believed in the existence of those two places with superstitious intensity, just as she believed that a hare was a witch in disguise, but the prospect of eternal damnation could not deter her from anything she really wanted to do.

For almost a month she did not once leave Michael Godfrey's apartment of two rooms. He bought a second-hand suit of boy's clothes for her to wear and she strutted about, swaggering, clacking her heels on the floor in imitation of the young fops she had seen in the streets, while he roared with laughter and told her that she was as good an actor as Edward Kynaston himself. She was supposed to be Tom, his nephew from the country, but none of his friends who visited them were very much fooled, though they all made a great jest of it and obligingly called her by that name.

He told her, however, that it would probably not be a great deal longer before her presence there became known and that when it did they would be forced to leave. But that threat did not trouble him for he seldom studied as it was and had no more interest in learning law than did most of the other young men whose fathers sent them to the Inns of Court. Now, more than ever, life was too distracting for a young man to give much time to books and lectures.

She told him her own name and the story of her misfortunes, though she omitted altogether Lord Carlton's part in it and pretended that the baby had been gotten by her husband. Luke Channell's name, since she had used it in Whitefriars, was no longer of any value to her and she made Michael promise to keep secret the fact that she had ever been married; she considered that that mistake was over and done and absolutely refused to think of Luke as her husband.

About a fortnight after Black Jack's death Michael went down to Ram Alley to visit Mother Red-Cap and convince her that Mrs. Channell had gone from London and would never return. He went partly out of curiosity, to see what the old woman's reaction to the recent events had been, and also because Amber begged him to get the imitation gold ear-rings she had left behind, telling him that her aunt had given them to her just before she had gone away. He brought them back, and some news as well.

"She's satisfied you're gone. I told her I'd had a letter from you and that you were back with your family and would never so much as think of London again."

Amber laughed, taking a bite out of a big red apple. "Did she believe you?"

"She seemed to. She said that you should never have left the country in the first place—and that London was no place for a girl like you."

"I'll warrant she's running distracted to have lost me. I made her a mighty good profit, let me tell you."

"Sweetheart, Mother Red-Cap wouldn't run distracted if she lost her own head. She's got another girl she's training to take your place—a pretty little wench she found somewhere who's with child and unmarried and full of gratitude for the kind old lady who's promised to help her out of her difficulties."

Amber made a sound of disgust, throwing the apple-core across the room into the fireplace. "That old flesh-broker would pimp for the devil himself if there was a farthing to be got by it!"

Most of her time, when she was alone, she spent learning to read and to write and she undertook both with the same enthusiasm she had had for her dancing and singing and guitar lessons. Hundreds of times she wrote her name and Bruce's, drawing big hearts around them, but she always burnt the papers before Michael should see them—partly because she knew it would not be tactful to let the man who was keeping her find that she was in love with someone else, but also because she could not bear the thought of discussing Bruce with anyone. Her own signature was a long sprawl of which only the initial letters were made large and distinguishable, and when she showed Michael specimens of her handwriting he laughed and told her it was so illegible it might be mistaken for that of a countess.

One wet early October afternoon she lay stretched out flat on her stomach on the bed, mouthing over the text of one of the bawdy illustrated books which he had given her to practice on, an English edition of Aretino's sonnets. Hearing the key turn in the lock and the door of the other room open, she called over her shoulder: "Michael? Come in here! I can't make this out—"

His voice, solemn for once, answered her. "Come here, nephew."

Thinking that he was playing some joke she leapt off the bed and ran to the doorway, but stopped on the threshold with a gasp of astonishment and dismay. For with him was an old man, a sour prim thin-nosed old gentleman with a forbidding scowl and a look of having been preserved in vinegar. Amber took a startled step backward and one hand went to the throat of her deeply opened white shirt, but it was too late. He could never mistake her for a boy now.

"You said that you were entertaining your nephew, sirrah!" said the old man sternly, drawing down his tufted brows and frowning back at Michael. "Where is he?"

"That is he, Mr. Gripenstraw," said Michael, respectfully, but nevertheless with an air of whimsical unconcern.

Mr. Gripenstraw looked at Amber again, over the tops of his square-cut green spectacles, and he screwed his mouth from side to side. Amber's hand dropped and she spoke to Michael, pleading.

"I'm sorry, Michael. I thought you were alone."

He made a gesture, motioning her into the bedroom, and she went, closing the door but standing next to it so that she could hear what was said between them. Oh, God in Heaven! she thought despairingly, rubbing the palms of her hands together. *Now* what will happen to me? What if he finds out who I— Then she heard Mr. Gripenstraw's voice again.

"Well, Mr. Godfrey—and what excuse have you to make this time?"

"None, sir."

"How long has this baggage been on your premises?"

"One month, sir."

"One month! Great God! Have you no respect for the ancient and honourable institution of English law? Because of my regard for your father I have overlooked many of your past misdemeanours, but this is beyond anything! If it were not for the honour and esteem in which I hold Sir Michael I would have you sent to the Fleet, to learn a better view of the conduct befitting a young man. As it is, sirrah, you are expelled. Never show me your face again. And get that creature out of here—within the hour!"

"Yes, sir. Thank you, sir."

The door opened. "Let me tell you this, sirrah—there is nothing a young man may get by wenching but duels, claps, and bastards. Good-day!" The door closed noisily.

Amber waited a moment and then flung open her own door. "Oh, Michael! You're expelled! And it's all my fault!"

She began to cry but he came swiftly across to take her into his arms. "Here, here, sweetheart! What the devil! We're well rid of this scurvy place. Come now, put on your hat and doublet and we'll find us lodgings where a man may live as he likes."

He took two rooms in an inn called the Hoop and Grapes, situated in St. Clement's Lane, which wound up out of Fleet Street. It was outside the City gates in the newer and more fashionable west-end of the town. Drury Lane was nearby, and Covent Garden, and not five minutes walk away was Gibbon's Tennis Court in Vere Street, which had become the Theatre Royal.

He bought her some clothes, second-hand at first because she needed them immediately—though later she had some made—and she found herself precipitated into a whirl of gaiety and pleasure. She had met several of his friends while they were still at the Temple, but now she met many more. They were young men of good family, future barons and lords; officers in the King's or the Duke's guards; actors from one of the four public theatres. And she met, too, the women they kept, pretty girls who sold ribbons or gloves at the Royal Exchange, professed harlots, actresses, all of them wise and gay and no more than Amber's age—flowers that had bloomed since the Restoration.

They went to the theatres and sat in the pit where the women wore their masks and sucked on China oranges, bandying pleasantries with everyone in earshot. They went to the gambling-houses in the Haymarket and once Amber was thrown into a frenzy of excitement when a rumour swept through that the King was coming. But he did not and she was bitterly disappointed, for she had never forgotten his expression that day he had looked at her. They went to the New Spring Gardens at Lambeth and to the Mulberry Gardens, which was temporarily the height of fashion. They went to dinner at all the popular taverns, Lockets near Charing Cross which was always filled with young officers in their handsome uniforms, the Bear at the Bridgefoot, the notorious Dagger Tavern in High Holborn, a rough-and-tumble place that abounded in riots and noise but was famous for its fine pies. They went to see the puppet-play in Covent Garden, currently the resort of all the fashionable world. At night they often drove about town in a hackney, contesting as to who could break the most windows by throwing copper pennies through them.

And when they were not out their rooms were full of young people who came in at all hours of the day and night, ordered food and drink sent up, played cards and got drunk and borrowed their bed for love-making. None of them had a serious thought or occupation, beyond avoiding their creditors. Pleasure was their creed. The old views of morality had gone as much out of fashion as high-crowned hats and, like them, were now disdained and ridiculed. Indifference, cynicism, selfishness and egoistic opportunism were the marks of quality. Gentleness, honesty, devotion—these were held in contempt.

The gentlemen of the old school, of the decorous Court of Charles I, were blaming the present King for the manners and behaviour of the new generation. And while it was true that Charles neither wished nor tried to set up strict standards, the same conditions had existed during the late years of the Protectorate, though then more than half concealed under a mantle of hypocrisy. The Civil Wars, not his Majesty, had sowed the seeds for plants suddenly shot to full growth since his return.

But Amber was not even remotely aware of the force of trends and currents.

She was in love with this life. She liked the noise and confusion, the continual bustle and disorder, the reckless devil-may-care gaiety. She knew that it was wholly different from the country and was glad that it was, for here she might do as she liked and no one was shocked or admonitory. It never even occurred to her that this was perhaps not the usual life of all gentlemen of all times.

None of the young men was interested in matrimony, which had fallen into such disrepute that it was considered only as the last resort of a man so far encumbered by debt he could see no other way out. Good manners forbade a man and wife to love—scarcely permitted them even to like—each other, and a happy marriage was regarded with scorn, not envy. This was Amber's view, for Luke Channell had convinced her that marriage was the most miserable state a woman could endure, and she talked as glibly as any rake about the absurdity of being a wife or husband. In her heart she held a secret reservation, for Bruce Carlton—but she was almost willing to believe now that she would never see him again.

Only once did her confident audacity receive a jar and that was when, about mid-October, she discovered that she was pregnant again. Penelope Hill had warned her that the most careful precautions sometimes failed, but she had never expected that they might fail her. For a time she was wildly distracted. All her pleasures would be ruined if she had to go again through the tedious uncomfortable ugly business of having a baby, and she determined that she would not do it. Even in Marygreen she had known women who had induced abortions when pregnancy recurred too often. She had wanted Bruce Carlton's child, but she did not want another man's now, or ever.

She talked to one of the girls she had met, a 'Change woman named Mally, who was rumoured to have been given a great sum of money by no one less than the Duke of Buckingham: the girl directed her to a midwife in Hanging Sword Alley who she said had a numerous clientèle among young women of their class and way of life. Without telling Michael anything about it she went to the midwife, who set her for an hour or more over a pot of steaming herbs, gave her a strong dose of physic, and told her to ride out to Paddington and back in a hackney. To Amber's immense relief some one, or all, of the remedies had been successful. Mally told her that every twenty-eight days she followed the practice herself of taking an apothecary's prescription, a long soaking in a hot tub, and a ride in a hell-cart.

"Gentlemen nowadays," said Mally, "you'll find, have no patience with a woman who troubles 'em in that way. And, Lord knows, with matters as they stand a woman needs what good looks she can be mistress of." She lifted up her plump breasts and crossed her silken ankles, giving a. smug little smile.

At first Amber was in considerable apprehension whenever she left the house—even though she habitually went cloaked and hooded and masked—for fear a constable would stop her. The memory of Newgate weighed on her like an incubus. But even more terrifying was the knowledge that if caught again she would very likely be either hanged or transported, and she was already so rabid a Londoner that one punishment seemed almost as bad as the other.

And then one day she learned something which seemed to offer her a solution, and an exciting new adventure as well. She had been surprised at the elegant clothes worn off-stage by all the actors she had seen, and one night she commented idly about it to Michael.

"Ye gods, they all look like lords. How much money do they get?"

"Fifty or sixty pound a year."

"Why, Charles Hart had on a sword tonight must have cost him that much!"

"Probably did. They're all head over ears in debt."

Amber, who was getting ready for bed, now backed up to have him unlace the tight little boned busk she wore. "Then I don't envy 'em," she said, jingling the bracelet on her right wrist. "Poor devils. They won't look so spruce in Newgate."

Michael was concentrating on the busk, but at last he had it unlaced and gave her a light slap on the rump. "They won't go to Newgate. An actor can't be arrested, except on a special warrant which must be procured from the King."

She swirled around, sudden eager interest on her face. "They can't be arrested! Why?"

"Why—because they're his Majesty's servants, and enjoy the protection of the Crown."

Well—

That *was* something to think about.

This was not the first time, however, that she had cast covetous eyes toward the stage. Sitting with Michael in the pit, she had seen how the gallants all stared at the actresses and flocked back to the tiring-room after the play to paw over them and take them out to supper. She knew that they were kept by some of the greatest nobles at Court, that they dressed magnificently, occupied handsome lodgings and often had their own coaches to ride in. They seemed—for all that they were treated with a certain careless contempt by the very men who courted them—to be the most fortunate creatures on earth. Amber was filled with envy to see all this attention and applause going to others, when she felt that she deserved it at least as much as they.

She had looked them over narrowly and was convinced that she was better looking than any of them. Her voice was good, she had lost her country drawl, and her figure was lovely. Everyone was agreed as to that. What other qualifications did an actress need? Few of them had so many.

Not many days later she got her opportunity.

With Michael and four other couples she was at supper in a private room on the "Folly," a floating house of entertainment moored just above the ruined old Savoy Palace. They sat over their cheesecake and wine, cracking open raw oysters and watching the performance of a naked dancing-woman.

Amber sat on Michael's lap; he had one arm hung over her shoulder with his hand slipped casually into the bodice of her gown. But all his attention was on the dancing-girl, and Amber, offended by his interest in the performance, got up and left him to sit down beside the one man who had his back turned while he continued to eat his supper. He was Edward Kynaston, the fabulously handsome young actor from the King's Theatre, who had taken women's parts before the hiring of actresses had begun.

He was very young, no more than nineteen, with skin like a girl's, loosely waving blonde hair and blue eyes, a slender but well-proportioned body. There was nothing to mar his perfection but the sound of his voice which, from long practice of keeping it high-pitched, carried a kind of unpleasant whine. He smiled at her as she took a chair next to his.

"Edward, how d'you go about getting on the stage?"

"Why? Have you a mind to acting?"

"Don't you think I could? I hope I'm pretty enough." She smiled, slanting her eyes.

He looked her over thoughtfully. "You certainly are. You're prettier than anyone we have—or anyone Davenant has, either, for the matter of that." Davenant managed the Duke of York's Theatre, for there were only two licensed companies (though some others continued performing), and rivalry was sharp between His Majesty's and His Highness's Comedians. "I suppose you think to show yourself on the boards and get some great man for a keeper."

"Maybe I do," she admitted. "They say there's a mighty fine profit to be got that way."

Her voice had a soft tone of insinuation, for Kynaston, everyone knew, had numerous admirers among the gentlemen and had received many valuable gifts from them, most of which he shrewdly turned into money and banked with a goldsmith. Among his lovers he was said to number the immensely rich Buckingham, who had already begun the ruin of the greatest fortune in England, squandering what he had as recklessly as if it came out of a bottomless well.

Kynaston did not take offense at her suggestion, but he had a kind of feminine modesty which, for all that he sold himself in the open market, lent him the appearance of dignity and virtue.

"Perhaps there is, madame. Would you like me to present

you to Tom Killigrew?" Thomas Killigrew was a favourite courtier and manager of the King's Theatre.

"Oh, would you! When?" She was excited, and a little fearful.

"Rehearsal will be over about eleven tomorrow. Come then if you like."

Amber dressed with great care for her interview and, though it was a cold dark early-November morning with no shred of sun filtering through the heavy smoke and fog, she put on her finest gown and cloak. All morning long her stomach had been churning and the palms of her hands felt wet. In spite of her eagerness she was miserably nervous, and at the last moment such a panic of doubt swept through her that she had to bully herself into going out the door.

When she reached the theatre, however, and took off her mask the attendant gave a low whistle; she laughed and made him an impudent face, suddenly relieved.

"I've come to see Edward Kynaston. He's expecting me. Can I go in?"

"You're wasting your time, sweetheart," he told her. "Kynaston doesn't give a hang for the finest woman that wears a head. But go along if you will."

The stage was just clearing and Killigrew was down in the pit talking to Kynaston and Charles Hart and one of the actresses who stood on the apron-shaped stage above them. It was dark inside, for only the candles in the chandelier that hung above the stage were lighted, and the cold seemed to bring out a strong sour smell. Orange-peelings littered the aisle and the green-cloth-covered benches were dirty with the foot-marks of the men who had stood upon them. Empty now of people and of noise there was something strangely dismal and shabby, almost sad, about it. But Amber did not notice.

For a moment she hesitated, then she started down the aisle toward them. At the sound of her heels they looked around, Kynaston lifting his hand to wave. They watched her come, Kynaston, Charles Hart, Killigrew, and the woman on the stage, Beck Marshall. She had met Charles Hart, a handsome man who had been on the stage for many years, often risking imprisonment to act during the dour years of the Commonwealth. And once she had been casually introduced to Beck Marshall who stood now, hands on her hips, looking her over, not missing anything about her gown or hair or face, and then with a switch of her skirt walked off. The three men remained.

Kynaston presented her to Killigrew—an aristocratic, middle-aged man with bright-blue eyes and white hair and an old-fashioned, pointed chin-beard. He did not look as though he would be the father of the notorious Harry Killigrew, a bold rash drunken young rake whose exploits caused some surprise even at Court. Amber had seen Harry once, molesting the women in St. James's Park, but she had been masked and well muffled and he had not seen her.

She made her curtsy to Killigrew, who said: "Kynaston tells me that you want to go on the stage."

Amber gave him her most alluring smile, which she had practiced several times in the mirror just before leaving home. But the corners of her mouth quivered and her chest felt tight. "Yes," she said softly. "I do. Will you give me a part?"

Killigrew laughed. "Take off your cloak and walk up onto the stage, so I can have a look at you."

Amber pulled loose the cord which tied in a bow at her throat, flung back the cloak, and Charles Hart offered his hand to lift her onto the platform. Ribs held high to show off her pert breasts and little waist, she walked the length of the stage, turning, raising her skirts above her knees to let him see her legs. Hart and Killigrew exchanged significant glances.

At last, having appraised her as carefully as any man buying a horse, he asked: "What else can you do, Mrs. St. Clare, besides look beautiful?"

Charles Hart, stuffing his pipe with tobacco, gave a cynical snort. "What else *should* she do? What else can any of 'em do?"

"What the devil, Hart! Will you convince her she needn't even *try* to learn to act? Come, my dear, what else do you know?"

"I can sing, and I can dance."

"Good! That's half an actress's business."

"God knows," muttered Charles Hart. He could act himself and thought the theatre was running amuck these days with its emphasis on nothing but female legs and breasts. "I don't doubt to see 'Hamlet' put on one day with a Gravediggers' dance."

Killigrew gave her a signal and Amber began to dance. It was a Spanish saraband which she had learned more than a year before and had since performed many times, for Black Jack and his friends in Whitefriars, more recently for Michael and all their acquaintance. Twirling, swaying, dipping, she moved swiftly about the stage, all her self-consciousness gone now in her passionate determination to please. After that she sang a bawdy street-ballad which burlesqued the old Greek fable of Ariadne and Theseus, and her voice had a full voluptuous quality which would have made a far more innocent song seem sensual and exciting. When at last she sank to a curtsy and then lifted her head to smile at him with eager questioning, he clapped his hands.

"You're as spectacular as a show of fireworks on the Thames. Can you read a part?"

"Yes," said Amber, though she had never tried.

"Well, never mind about that now. Next Wednesday we're going to give a performance of 'The Maid's Tragedy.' Come to rehearsal tomorrow morning at seven and I'll have a part in it for you."

Half delirious with joy, Amber ran home to tell Michael the great news. But though she did not expect to play the heroine, she was nevertheless seriously disappointed the next morning to learn that she was to be merely one of a crowd of Court ladies-in-waiting, and that she had not so much as a single word to speak. She was disappointed, too, at her salary, which was only forty-five pounds a year. She realized by now that the five hundred pounds given her by Bruce Carlton had been a considerable sum of money, if only she had had the wit to keep it.

But both Kynaston and Charles Hart encouraged her, saying that if she attracted the attention of the audience as they knew she would, he would put her in more important parts. An actress had no such period of long training and apprenticeship as did an actor. Pretty young women were very much in demand for the stage, and if the men in the audience liked them they could sound like screech owls and act no better than puppets.

232

She quickly established a gay friendliness with the actors and was prepared to do likewise with the women, but they would have none of it. Despite the fact that women had been on the stage no more than a year they had already formed a tight clique, and were jealous and distrustful of any outsider trying to break into their closed ranks. They ignored her when she spoke to them, tittered and whispered behind her back, hid her costume on the day of the dress rehearsal, all in the obvious hope of making her so miserable that she would quit. But Amber had never believed that other women were important to her success and happiness, and she did not intend to let them trouble her now.

The stage fascinated her. She loved everything about the theatre: The hours of rehearsal, when she listened and watched intensely, memorizing the lines of half the other characters. The thrilling day when she was sworn in at the Lord Chamberlain's Office as his Majesty's servant. The occult mysteries of stage make-up, into which she was now initiated, black and white and red paint, false-noses, false-beards, false-hair. The marvellous collection of scenery and other apparatus which made it possible to show the moon coming up at night, to reveal the sun breaking through a mist, to simulate a bird's song or the rattle of hail. The costumes, some of which were gorgeous things given by the nobles, others mere cheap imitations made of shoddy and bombazine. She took it to her heart, made it a part of her, in the same way she had London.

At last the great day arrived and, after a restless turning night full of apprehension and doubts, she got up and dressed and set out very early for the theatre. On the way she saw one of the play-bills nailed up on a post and stopped to read it: "At the Theatre Royal this present Wednesday, being the Ninth day of December will be presented a play called: The Maid's Tragedy beginning exactly at three after Noon. By His Majesty's Servants. Vivat Rex." And when she reached the theatre a flag was already flying from the roof to announce that there would be a performance that day.

Oh, Lord! she thought. What ever made me think I wanted to go on the stage?

It was still so early that she found the entire theatre empty but for a couple of scene-shifters and the tiring-woman, Mrs. Scroggs, a dirty profane drunken old harridan whose daughter Killigrew hired at twenty shillings a week for the use of his actors. With her easy camaraderie and frequent gifts of money Amber had purchased her friendship at least, and Scroggs was as ardently partisan in her favour as the women were violently antagonistic. By the time the other actresses began to arrive she was painted and dressed and had gone out to watch the audience from behind the curtains.

The pit was already crowded, fops, prostitutes and orange-girls, all of them noisy and laughing, shouting to acquaintances all over the theatre. The galleries were spotted with men and women, and 'prentices were trying out their cat-calls. Finally the boxes began to fill with splendidly gowned and jewelled ladies, languid dreamy creatures who were bored with the play before it had even begun. The very boards and walls seemed now to have changed, enchanted by the glamour and richness of the audience.

Amber stood looking out, her throat dry and her heart beating with anticipation, when suddenly Charles Hart appeared behind her, slipped an arm about her waist and kissed her cheek. She gave a startled little jump.

"Oh!" She laughed nervously and swallowed.

"How now, sweetheart!" he said briskly. "Ready to lay the town by its ears?"

She gave him a pleading look. "Oh, I don't know! Michael's in the pit with a score of friends to cry me up. But I'm scared!"

"Nonsense. What are you scared of? Those high-born sluts and fop-doodles out there? Don't let them scare you—" He paused, as suddenly the fiddlers in the music-room above the stage struck up the first bars of a gay country air. "Listen! His Majesty's come!" And he drew back the curtains so that he and Amber could look out.

There was a scraping of benches and a low running murmur as they got to their feet, turning to face the King's box which was in the first balcony in the center just above the stage, gilded and draped with scarlet velvet and emblazoned with the royal coat-of-arms. And then, as the King appeared, the music swelled and the hats of the men swept off with a flourish. The tall and swarthy Charles, smiling easily, lifting one hand in greeting, dominated the group of men and women who surrounded him; but no one overlooked Barbara Palmer at his side, glittering with jewels, haughty and beautiful and a little sullen. They seemed very magnificent and awe-inspiring; and staring at them from behind the curtains Amber was suddenly overcome with an agonizing sense of her own insignificance.

"Oh," she breathed unhappily. "They look like gods!"

"Even gods, my dear, use a chamber-pot," said Charles Hart, and then he walked away, back to the tiring-room to get his cloak, for he was to speak the prologue. Amber looked after him and laughed, somewhat relieved.

But her eyes returned immediately to Mrs. Palmer, who was leaning back in her chair, smiling and speaking to a man who sat behind her. As she looked Amber's face hardened with hate. Her fingers with their long nails curled involuntarily and she had a sharp satisfying image of clawing across the woman's face, tearing away her beauty and confident smile. The jealousy she felt was as violent and painful as on that far-away night when she had looked down into the street and seen Bruce Carlton's head bend to kiss a red-haired woman leaning out of her coach and laughing.

Soon, however, she was surrounded by the other actresses, who came trooping up behind her, giggling, elbowing her aside —until she gave one of them a sharp jab in the ribs—lifting back the curtain to wave at their admirers below. All of them seemed as merrily unconcerned as though this were nothing but another rehearsal. But Amber was wishing desperately that she might bolt and run, out of the theatre, back to the quiet and security of her own rooms, and hide there. She knew that she could never force herself to go out onto the stage and face those hard smart critical people whose eyes and tongues would go over her like rakes.

The prologue was done, the curtains had swung back, and Charles Hart and Michael Mohun had started to speak their lines. The theatre was settling down, quieting as much as it ever did, though the buzzing and murmuring went on and there were occasional laughs or loud-spoken comments. Amber, who knew most of the lines by heart, now discovered that she was not able even to follow the dialogue, and the ladies-in-waiting had already started out when Kynaston gave her a little shove.

"Go on!"

For an instant she hung back, unable to move, and then, with her heart pounding so hard she thought it would burst, she lifted her head high and walked out. During the rehearsals the other women had always maneuvered to keep her in the background, despite the fact that Killigrew said he wanted the audience to see her, but now because of her late entrance she stood in the front, closer to the audience than any of them.

She heard a man's voice from nearby, in the pit. "Who's that glorious creature, Orange Moll?"

Another one spoke up. "That must be the new wench. By Jesus, but she's handsome, I swear she is!"

And from the gallery the 'prentices sent up a low appreciative hum.

Amber felt her cheeks begin to burn and sweat start in her armpits, but at last she forced herself to sneak a glance out of the corner of one eye. She saw several upturned faces beneath her, grinning, and all at once she realized that these were only men like any other men. Just before the ladies-in-waiting went off the stage she threw them a dazzling smile, and heard another rising hum of approval. After that she stood in the wings and fretted because her part was done. By the time the play was over she was incurably stage-struck.

Beck Marshall spoke to her as they were going into the tiring-room. "Look here, Mrs. What-d'ye-call," she said, pretending to have forgotten Amber's name. "You needn't strut up and down like a crow in the gutter. Those gentlemen will have a swing at anything new—"

Amber smiled at her, superior, very well satisfied with herself. "Don't concern yourself for me, madame. I'll have a care of my own interests, I warrant you."

But she was more than a little disappointed when Michael and three of his friends appeared promptly, surrounding her and shutting her off from any possible outside interference, for several of the young men were watching her, asking about her, curious and interested and admiring.

Oh, well, she thought. I won't always be troubled with Michael.

CHAPTER SIXTEEN

THE NEXT DAY Amber was given the part of the first Court lady, and had four short lines to say. Not very long after that she was taking important roles, singing songs and, dressed in a tight pair of breeches and thin white blouse, performing the dance at the end of the play. It was her chief qualification as an actress that she could easily achieve an accurate and only piquantly exaggerated imitation of almost any kind of woman, whether great lady or serving-wench. And little more was expected, for the audience had no interest in the subtleties of character delineation. The taste was for crude gorgeous exciting effects, whether in women, scenery, or melodrama.

They liked the bloody noisy terrifying tragedies of Beaumont and Fletcher, considered Ben Jonson the greatest playwright of all time, thought Shakespeare too realistic and hence deficient in poetic justice. He required considerable altering before he could qualify for presentation. A great deal of singing and dancing, frequent changes of scenery and costume, battles and deaths and ghosts, profanity and smut and seminudity was what they liked and what they got. At every murder or suicide sheep's-blood spurted from concealed bladders and covered the actor with gore; ghosts rose and sank on trap-doors; scenes of torture by rack, wheel and fire filled the theatre with anguished screams and groans. But through it all the fops in the pit kept up a stream of banter with the actors and prostitutes and orange-girls, and the ladies in the boxes waved their fans and cast lazy smiles at the gallants below.

Amber's popularity was considerable—because she was new,

237

the women insisted—and every day after the performance she was surrounded by a flock of gallants who kissed her, tied her garters, watched her dress, and invited her to spend the night with one or all of them. She listened and laughed, flirted with everyone, but went home with Michael Godfrey.

She was afraid of arousing his jealousy, for he knew all her secrets and could ruin her if he chose. But even had she been free of him, she had not yet heard the offer which could interest her. She was looking for a man of both importance and wealth, who would keep her according to the manner in which she intended to live—clothes and jewels and a coach, a generous annual allowance, handsomely furnished lodgings, a serving-woman, and a footman. The man who could supply those things was not to be found every day, even among the tiring-room gallants, and when found he was not likely to be a ready dupe. Amber was impatient, eager to better her status, but determined to make no rash change which might precipitate her down the steep narrow road leading to common prostitution. Penelope Hill's advice meant more to her now than when she had first heard it—and she intended to turn some man's weakness to her own advantage.

More than a month went by and still Amber was on no better terms with the other actresses than she had been at first. They missed no opportunity to confuse or embarrass her, either on the stage or in the tiring-room, circulated rumours that she had the French-pox and that she was living incestuously with her brother—Michael—and were more annoyed than ever when she treated them all with cool, superior contempt. But nothing they said seemed to discourage the men, who brushed it all aside as mere jealous female slander.

"Well," said Beck Marshall to her one day, "they may poach after you here in the tiring-room, but I don't notice *one* of 'em's made you an offer of more than half-a-crown."

Amber sat on one of the tables, legs crossed while she looked into a hand-mirror and carefully drew a black line along the edge of her eyelid. "And what about you, madame? Who's your stallion? The Duke of York, I doubt not?"

Beck gave her a smug, complacent smile. "Not his Highness,

238

perhaps. But then, Captain Morgan's a man of no mean consequence."

"And who the devil's Captain Morgan? That straight-haired nincompoop I saw you with at Chatelin's the other night?" She got up and turned her back, beckoning Scroggs to come help her into her gown.

"Captain Morgan, Mrs. Double-tripe, is an officer in his Majesty's Horse Guard—and a mighty handsome fellow into the bargain. And he's so mad in love with me he's going to make me a settlement and take me off the stage. I don't doubt he'd marry me quick enough—if I could make up my mind to endure matrimony," she added, examining her nails.

Amber stepped into her gown and stooped over to pull it up. "You'd better make up your mind to endure it before long," she said, "or you'll be leading apes in hell." Leading apes in hell was supposedly the destiny of an old maid, and Amber liked to taunt Beck with the fact that she was two or three years her senior. "But where d'you keep this wonder? Under lock and key?"

"He's been out of town these two months past—his family's got a great estate in Wales, and his father just died. But he wrote me he expects to return within the week and then—"

"Oh, I don't doubt I'll be in a green-sickness of jealousy at the very sight of 'im."

At that moment a boy stuck his head in the door calling, "Third music, ladies! Third music!" and they all began to troop out, for the third music meant that it was time for the curtains to be drawn. Amber thought no more of Beck's Captain Morgan and several days went by. But late one afternoon as she was dressing after the performance, surrounded by her circle of impudent gallants, a man appeared in the doorway who instantly arrested her attention.

He was well over six feet tall with wide, square shoulders, lean hips, and magnificent legs. Powerful and virile, in his red and blue uniform he was an exciting contrast to the pale effeminate young fops who talked incessantly of their claps and poxes and carried a box of turpentine-pills wherever they went. His face was crudely handsome, with well-defined features; he had

239

waving brown hair and skin tanned to a tawny-gold. Amber stared at him in surprise and admiration, wondering who he was, and then as he smiled slowly the corners of her eyes went up and she gave him a faint answering smile.

At that moment there was a scream from Beck.

"Rex!"

And she rushed over to throw herself into his arms, took his hand, and led him to the opposite side of the room. She dressed hastily then and hurried him out, but as he went he gave Amber a backward glance.

"Well!" said Beck the next morning, as they sat in the pit watching a rehearsal. "What d'ye make of him?" But her eyes were slightly narrowed and she was more defiant than triumphant.

Amber smiled innocently and gave a little shrug. "Oh, no doubt he's a very fine person. I don't wonder you rushed 'im out as fast as if you were going for a midwife." Her eyes took on a malicious sparkle. "It'd never do to let a fellow like that make the acquaintance of other ladies, would it?"

Beck flared. "I smoke your design, madame! But let me tell you this—if I find you spreading your nets for him I'll make you sorry for it! I'll carbonado you, I swear I will!"

"Pooh!" said Amber, and got up to leave her. "Your bellow-weathering doesn't scare me!"

Still, Captain Morgan did not appear backstage again for several days, and when Amber gibed at her for not daring to show her prize not only Beck but her older sister Anne flew into a rage and threatened her with the wrath of God, as well as their own. "Just you dare meddling with Captain Morgan!" cried Anne dramatically, for she was the tragedienne of the company. "You'll wish you hadn't!"

But Amber was so little impressed by their threats that whenever she saw him in the pit, as she often did, she flirted openly with him. It would have pleased her a great deal to steal Beck Marshall's admirer, even if he had been much less attractive than he was.

She was going into the theatre early one afternoon when a ragged little urchin came limping up, glanced hastily around,

240

and thrust a wax-sealed paper into her hand. Curious, Amber tore it open. "For Madame St. Clare," she read. ("Madame" was the title applied to all actresses.) "I must confess I am hopelessly smitten by you, for all that a lady known to us both has warned me you're not to be trusted and already belong to another man. Still, I have made so bold as to reserve a table for us at the Fox-Under-the-Hill at Ivy Bridge. I shall hope to see you there tomorrow evening at seven. Your most humble obliged servant, madame, I am, Captain Rex Morgan." And he added a postscript: "May I ask you, madame, to have the kindness for me as not to mention this note to anyone?"

Amber smiled slyly to herself, and after a moment tore the paper into little bits, tossed them up over her head and went on into the theatre. She had no intention of telling Beck about the note. Not, at least, until she was sure that he was captured; but she could not resist giving her a fleering little smile that annoyed the other girl even if it told her nothing.

She had no performance the next afternoon and spent the day washing her hair—in spite of the almanac, which said that the time was astrologically unfavourable—deciding what she would wear, and trying to think of an excuse to give Michael. She was still undecided when she took a hackney and rode to the Royal Exchange to buy some ribbons and gloves and a bottle of scent. Coming back with her arms full of parcels, her cloak and hood covered with raindrops, she opened the door and found Michael standing in conversation with another man.

He was much older than Michael and as he turned to look at her there was a stern scowl on his face. She knew instantly who he was: Michael's father. For some time past Michael had been getting letters from his father, demanding to know why he had been expelled from the Middle Temple, insisting that he return home at once. Michael had read each one to her, laughing, saying gaily that his father was a formal old coxcomb, and had thrown them into the fire without ever sending an answer. Now, however, he wore a hang-dog expression and a look of cowed helplessness.

"Amber," he said at last, "this is my father. Sir, may I present Mrs. St. Clare?"

Sir Michael Godfrey merely stared at her without speaking, and after a moment she crossed the room, laid down her packages, and spread her cloak on a chair before the fire. That done she turned to find both men still watching her, and Sir Michael's hostile eyes made her aware that her neckline was cut very low and her face obviously painted. He turned away.

"Is this the woman you kept in the Temple?" As he said it Amber had an uncomfortable feeling that she was the commonest kind of whore.

"Yes, sir."

Michael was not flippant with his father as he had been with Mr. Gripenstraw. The wild gay boy who had delighted in getting drunk every night and breaking the windows of sleeping citizens had quite disappeared in the chagrined, embarrassed dutiful son.

Sir Michael Godfrey turned to Amber. "Madame, I fear you shall have to cast about elsewhere for a young fool to meet your expenses. My son is returning with me into the country and you shall get not a farthing more by his misplaced generosity."

Amber merely stared at him coolly and curbed her impulse to give him a tart answer because she remembered all that Michael had done for her, and all that he could still do, if he chose, to injure her. With a gesture of his hand Sir Michael signalled his son from the room. And though he hesitated for a moment he went, turning back once to give Amber a wistful pleading look of good-bye, which Sir Michael cut short by thrusting him sharply out and banging the door after them. Amber was sorry for Michael; evidently his life would now be sadly changed, but her pity soon gave way to relief—and then to eagerness for the night.

My stars are lucky! she thought exuberantly. Just when I had no more use for 'im—he's gone!

Amber was only a little late, but as she was ushered upstairs to the private-room, Captain Morgan flung open the door and greeted her with happy enthusiasm. "At last you're here! How kind of you to come!" His eyes glistened with pleasure as they looked down at her and he took her muff and cloak, tossed them over a chair, and turned her about by one hand. "You look wonderful! By God, you're the most glorious creature I've ever seen!"

Amber laughed. "Come now, Captain Morgan! Beck Marshall tells me you've said kinder things to her by far."

But she luxuriated in his admiration, feeling a warm glow of pleasure go through all her body at the expression on his face. It had been a long while since she had seen a man so infatuated —not, in fact, since she had left Marygreen. And she was glad that he had the sense to appreciate a pretty gown, for she had worn her best and newest one; too many of the young fops were so concerned with their own "garnitures" and "petite-oie" they scarcely knew what a woman was wearing. The dress was made of bright green velvet, with the skirt slit down the front and draped up over a black-satin sequin-spattered petticoat, and she had one pert black-satin bow tied at either temple.

He snapped his fingers. "The devil with Beck Marshall. She's nothing to me, I assure you."

"That's what every man says about his old doxy when he has a mind to a new one."

Rex Morgan laughed. "I see you have wit as well as beauty, madame. That makes you perfect."

At that moment there was a loud rap at the door. Morgan called out for them to enter, and in marched the host and three waiters, loaded down with covered pewter dishes, knives and spoons, napkins, glasses and salt-dishes, and two bottles of wine. They set the places, removed all covers with a flourish so that Captain Morgan might inspect the contents, and then marched out again. Amber and Rex sat down to eat.

There was a great steaming bowlful of crayfish bisque, a well-seasoned leg-of-mutton stuffed with oysters and chopped onion, a chicken-pie covered with a flaky golden crust, and a pudding made of thick pure cream and pounded chestnuts. They sat side by side, facing the fireplace where sea-coals burnt brightly, and as they ate they fell into easy comfortable talk, enjoying the good meal and admiring each other.

He told her that she had the most fascinating eyes in the world, the loveliest hair he had ever seen, the most beautiful breasts, and the prettiest legs. His voice had an authentic sincerity she did not even care to question, and he looked at her with frank adoration and desire. Why, he's mad in love with me already! thought Amber delightedly, and had an image of herself parading him into the tiring-room tomorrow like a tame monkey on a chain.

"Is it true," he asked her at last as they were beginning to eat the hot baked chestnut pudding, "that you're in the keeping of someone from the Middle Temple?"

"Lord Almighty! Who told you that?"

"Everyone I asked about you. Is it true?"

"Certainly not! Lord, I swear a woman can be raped here in London without losing her maidenhead! I'll admit I was occupying lodgings with a gentleman for a time—but he was my cousin, and he's gone back to Yorkshire now. Heavens, I can't think what my father would say, to hear the bawdy talk that goes on here—about nothing at all!" She gave him a look of wide-eyed indignation.

"Lucky for him he's only your cousin. I'd have had to send him a challenge to get him out of my way. But I'm glad he's gone anyway. Tell me, who are you? Where'd you come from? Everyone told me a different story."

"I'm Mrs. St. Clare and I came from Essex. What else d'you want to know?"

"What are you doing on the stage? You don't look as though you belong there."

"Oh, don't I? I've been told different."

"That isn't what I mean. You look like a person of quality."

"Oh. Well—" She gave him a sidelong glance as he began to pour the champagne. "To tell you truly, I am."

She took the glass as he handed it to her, leaned back in her chair and began to spin for him the story upon which she had been embroidering almost since she had first come to London, improving upon it whenever she got a new idea. "My family's old and honourable and they had a good estate in Essex—but they sold everything to help his Majesty in the Wars. So, when an old ugly earl wanted to marry me my father was going to insist, to help repair his loss. I wouldn't have the stinking old goat—my father said I should have him, and he locked me into the house. I broke out and came to London— Of course I changed my name—I'm not *really* Mrs. St. Clare." She smiled at him over the rim of her glass, pleased to see that he apparently believed her.·

He got up then, moved their chairs closer to the dying fire, and they sat down side by side. Amber lifted her legs, bracing her feet on one side of the narrow fireplace so that her skirts fell back above her knees and showed her legs in black silk stockings and lacy garters. He reached over to take her hand in his and they sat for several moments, perfectly still and silent, but with the tension mounting between them.

What shall I do? she was thinking. If I do, he'll take me for a harlot—and if I don't, maybe he won't ever come back again.

At last she turned to face him and found his eyes on her, intense and serious, glowing with desire. One arm reached out and went around her waist, drawing her slowly toward him, and she slid over onto his lap. For a moment she hesitated, and then her face bent to his and she felt the pressure of his mouth, moist and warm and eager; his hand moved over her breasts, and she could feel the heavy beating of his heart against her own. Her blood began to rush, filling her with warmth and quick passion—she felt herself sliding toward surrender and had no inclination to stop.

But as he would have knelt before her she jumped up suddenly and left him, crossing the room to stand before the black windows, her head buried in her hands. Instantly he was behind her, his fingers taking hold of her shoulders, pressing her back against him. His voice whispered to her, pleading, and as his lips touched the back of her neck a thrill ran along her spine.

"Please, darling—don't be angry. I'm in love with you, I swear I am. I want you, I've *got* to have you!" His fingers cut into her shoulders and his voice in her ear was hoarse with intensity. "Please—Amber, please! I won't hurt you—I won't let anything happen— Come here—" He swung her around to face him.

Amber wrenched herself free; her own eyes were a little wild and her face was flushed. "You've got the wrong opinion of me, Captain Morgan! I may be on the stage, but I'm no whore! My poor father would die of shame if his daughter gave herself up to a sinful life! Now let me go—" She brushed past him, starting to get her cloak, and when he turned swiftly, catching her arm, his jaw set and hard, she cried warningly, "Have a care, sir! I'm not one of your willing rapes, either!"

She jerked away and getting her cloak, flung it on, took up her muff and went to the door. "Good-night, Captain Morgan! If you'd told me why you brought me here I could've saved you the cost of a supper!" She looked at him haughtily, but the cold angry expression on his face alarmed her.

Now! she thought. If he doesn't really like me I've spoiled everything.

One eyebrow went up as he stared at her and his mouth twisted slightly, but as she took hold of the knob he crossed over and stopped her. "Don't go away like this, Mrs. St. Clare. I'm sorry if I've offended you. I'd heard— Well, never mind. But you're a damned desirable woman. A man must be gelt if he wouldn't want you—and to tell the truth, I'm not." He grinned down at her. "Let me see you home."

After that she saw him often, but not at the theatre, for she was not sure of him yet and did not care to give Beck the opportunity of jeering at her. Beck, meanwhile, continued to boast and brag of his attentions to her, showed Amber his gifts, and gave her the intimate details of his visits. Amber was receiving some gifts, too: A pair of exquisite black-lace stockings from France, garters with little diamond buckles, a muff made of wide bands of gold brocade hooped at either end with black fox—but she was very mysterious about the giver.

She used every trick she knew—and by now they were several —to heighten his desire for her. But each time he imagined himself about to succeed she pushed him off and insisted again that she was a woman of virtue. Fortunately for her, he did not suggest that such behaviour seemed quite the opposite of virtuous. Sometimes he bellowed that she was a jilting baggage and stormed off, swearing that he would never see her again. Other times he stayed and pleaded, doggedly, with real desperation, and then finally went away defeated. But each time he came back.

And then one evening, his face haggard and his cravat askew, he slumped down into a chair, demanding, "What the devil *do* you want, then? I can't go on like this. I'm fretting my bowels to fiddle-strings over you!"

She had a sense of quick poignant relief. At last! And though a moment before she had been feeling tired and discouraged and all too inclined to be virtuous no longer, now she laughed, got up, and went to the mirror to smooth her hair.

"That isn't what Beck says. She was telling me today how last night you came to see her, so hot you wouldn't be put off for an instant."

He scowled, like an embarrassed boy. "Beck prattles too much. Answer me! What are you holding me off for? What do you want? Marriage?" She knew that he had been dreading to ask that, that he was no more eager to get married than were any of the other young men, and that even though he believed or pretended to believe her story about her aristocratic family, he would not marry an actress.

"Marriage!" she repeated in mock astonishment, staring at him in the mirror. "That's enough to give one the vapours! What woman in her right senses wants to get married?"

"Any woman, it seems."

"Well, they wouldn't if they'd ever *been* married!" She turned around and stood looking at him, her hands easily on her hips.

"Ye gods! Are you married?"

"No, of course not! But I'm not blind. I've seen a thing or two. What's a wife, pray? The men use 'em worse than a dog nowadays. They think they're good for nothing but to breed up their brats—and serve as a foil to a mistress. A wife gets a full belly every year, but a mistress gets all the money and attention. Be a wife? Pooh! Not me! Not for a thousand pound!"

"Well!" he said, obviously much relieved. "You talk like a woman of rare good sense. But you don't seem very anxious to be a mistress, either. Surely you don't expect to be that worthless object, a virgin, all your life? Not a woman like you."

"Have I said I did? If a man I liked made me a fair offer, I assure you I'd do him the kindness to think it over."

He smiled. "Well, now—we're getting somewhere at last. And what's your notion of a fair offer, pray?"

She leaned her elbow back on the mantelpiece and stood with her weight on one foot, the other bare knee sliding out of her satin dressing-gown; she began to count on her fingers. "I'd want a settlement of two hundred pound a year. I'd want lodgings of my own choosing, and a maid, and a neat little coach-and-four—and of course a coachman and footman—and leave to keep on acting." She had no intention of quitting the stage, for she had met him there and hoped someday to meet another and more important man. As she saw what was possible for a young and beautiful and obliging woman, her ambitions soared.

"You set a damned high price on yourself."

"Do I?" She smiled a little and gave a faint shrug. "Well—a high price, you know, serves to keep off ill company."

"If I take you at that figure I'll expect it to keep off *all* company, but mine."

It took Amber several days to find the lodgings that suited her and she rattled all over town in a hackney, searching, whenever she could be free from the theatre. But at last she found a three-room suite on the third floor of the Blue Balcony, down at the fashionable Strand end of Drury Lane. The rent was high, forty pounds a year, but Captain Morgan paid it in advance.

Everything here was in the latest fashion, reflecting the light gay colourful taste of the new age. The parlour was hung in emerald-green damask. There were French tables and chairs of walnut, some of them gilt, and all very different from the heavy old oaken pieces she was accustomed to seeing in inns. A long walnut couch had thick green cushions, fringed with gold, and there were several green-and-gold lacquered mirrors. She decided immediately that she would have her portrait painted and sink it flush with the wall above the fireplace, like one she had seen in the apartments of another actress, who was in the keeping of a lord.

The walls of the dining-room were covered with hand-

248

painted Chinese paper, flaunting peonies and chrysanthemums, all aswarm with brilliant-hued birds and butterflies. The chairs and stools had thick bright-green cushions tied to them. In the bedroom the hangings were also of damask, patterned in green and gold; there was a five-leaved screen, two leaves red and three green, and green-and-red-striped chair cushions.

"Oh!" cried Amber, when Captain Morgan went with her to see it and agreed that she might have it. "Thank you, Rex! I can't wait to move in!"

"Neither can I," he said. But she gave him a quick pout and then a smile.

"Now, Rex—remember what you said! You promised you'd wait."

"And I will. But for God's sake—not much longer."

She insisted on having the whole of her allowance in advance and, when she got it, hunted out Shadrac Newbold—whose name, she remembered, Bruce Carlton had told her—and put it with him at six percent interest. In Cow Lane they found a second-hand coach which, though small, was freshly painted and in good condition. It was glossy black with red wheels and red reins and harness, and he bought four handsome black-and-white horses to draw it. The coachman and footman were named, respectively, Tempest and Jeremiah, and she ordered red livery trimmed with silver braid for them.

She hired her maid from an old woman Mrs. Scroggs recommended with the absolute assurance that the girl was honest, demure, and well-bred, that she could carve and sew and clean, would not sleep late or gossip to the neighbours or run about in slovenly dress. She was a plain-faced girl whose teeth had wide spaces between them and whose face was entirely covered with little pale freckles. Prudence was her name, which Amber did not like, for she remembered simple harmless Honour Mills' who had been in league with a pair of thieves to rob her. But still the girl seemed anxious to please and looked so pitiful at the prospect of not being hired that Amber took her.

The first night at her new apartments she and Rex had an elaborate supper sent in from the Rose Tavern nearby and opened a bottle of champagne, but they scarcely drank a glass, for he picked her up impetuously and carried her into the bedroom. And yet for all his passionate fervour he was tender and considerate, as eager to give pleasure as to take it, and Amber thought that this was far more like a wedding-night than that wretched experience she had had with Luke Channell. For the first time in a year and a half she was wholly and completely satisfied, for Rex had the same combination of experience, energy, controlled violence, and instinctive understanding which Lord Carlton had also had.

There's a world of difference, she told herself, between being a man's mistress and his wife. And as far as she was concerned that difference was all for the better.

The next afternoon Amber found the women's tiring-room buzzing like a swarm of angry hornets, and Beck Marshall was the centre of their chattering indignation. She realized instantly that they had heard about her and Rex. And though they all turned at once to fix upon her their cold wrathful stares, she sauntered into the room and pulled off her gloves with a great show of unconcern. Scroggs waddled over to her immediately, a self-satisfied grin on her ugly old face.

"Damn me, Mrs. St. Clare!" she said now, and her deep hoarse rough voice carried above all the noise of the room. "But it pleased me mightily to hear of your good fortune!" She leaned close, smelling strongly of brandy and spoilt fish, and gave Amber a jab in the ribs. "When ye asked me t'other day where ye might hire a woman I says to m'self, 'Aha! Mrs. St. Clare's a-goin' into keepin', I'll warrant you!' But I'll swear I never guessed the gentleman'd be Captain Morgan!" She leered and nudged, and jerked her thumb in the direction of the glowering group across the room.

Scroggs had taken Amber's cloak and fan and muff and was helping her out of her gown. "Neither did anyone else, I see," murmured Amber, glancing toward them with a significant lift of one eyebrow. She bent over to step out of her petticoats.

"Foh! Ye should've seen the look on the face of Mrs. Snotty-nose when she heard the news!" She laughed heartily, showing the holes in her mouth where teeth had been, and slapped her great thigh. "Damn me! I thought she'd bust a gut!"

Amber smiled, taking the combs out of her side curls and giving her hair a shake. And then, as she looked at her, Beck's head turned and their eyes met directly. For a long moment they stared, Amber exultant, taunting, Beck seething with rage, and then all at once Beck turned away, raising her right hand to show Amber the stiff middle finger. Amber laughed out loud at that and picked up the black wig she was to wear for her part as Cleopatra in Shakespeare's tragedy, sliding it down over her own coarse bright silken hair.

She knew well enough herself that she was ill-suited to play the Egyptian queen—the part might much better have gone to Anne Marshall—but the idea had been Tom Killigrew's and in her black wig with her eyes elongated by black pencil, a sleeveless sequin-spotted vest which just covered her breasts and a thin scarlet silk skirt slit to the knees in front, she had attracted an overflowing house for the past week and a half. Most productions were limited to three or four days, because so small a part of the London population attended plays, but some of the young men had been back four or five times to see this Cleopatra. They were used to a woman's breasts being displayed in public, but not her hips and buttocks and legs. Every time she walked onto the stage there were whistles and murmurs and the most unabashed comments, but the boxes had been noticeably empty and the ladies were said to have protested they could not tolerate so lewd and immodest a display.

Amber more than half expected trouble and was prepared for it, but though the atmosphere was undoubtedly tense, everything went as usual until the last scene of the last act. Then, as she stood waiting at the side of the stage for her cue to go on, both Beck and Anne Marshall came to stand beside her, Beck on her right, Anne slightly in back. Amber gave Beck a careless glance but continued to watch the stage where the men—in their great plumed head-dresses which told an audience that this was tragedy being performed—were deciding Cleopatra's fate.

"Well, madame," said Beck. "Let me offer my congratulations. You've progressed mightily, they tell me—to be kept by only one man now."

Amber looked at her sharply, and then said with an air of profound boredom: "Lord, madame, you should see your 'pothecary. I swear you're turned quite green."

At that instant a pin pricked her from behind and she gave an angry start, but before she had time to say anything Mohun came off the stage, scowled, and muttered at them to go on. With Beck on one side and Mary Knepp on the other Amber walked out, proclaiming in a loud clear voice:

> "My desolation does begin to make
> A better life. 'Tis paltry to be Caesar . . ."

But for the commotion in the audience, the last scene progressed smoothly—through Cleopatra's dialogue with Caesar, her decision to end her life, the trial suicide of Iras, and then Cleopatra's own seizure of the pâpier-maché asp, which she addressed in full dramatic tones:

> "With thy sharp teeth this knot intrinsicate
> Of life at once untie; poor venomous fool . . ."

While Beck, as the faithful serving-woman who could not bear her mistress's death, ran distractedly about the stage, Amber applied the asp beneath her vest and heard a young man down in Fop Corner remark, "I've seen this six times. That viper should be weaned by now."

She clenched her teeth and shut her eyes as in a sudden spasm of pain. But she did not take her tragic parts very seriously and had to resist the inclination to laugh.

After standing motionless for a long moment she began to turn slowly in her death agony. Halfway around, she was arrested by a sudden barking shout of laughter from nearby. And then the sound was repeated from hundreds of throats. It swept on up through the boxes to the galleries beneath the roof, growing ever louder and noisier as it rose, until it seemed to fill the theatre and to come from all sides at once, hammering against her with an almost physical force.

Instinctively conscious that the laughter was directed at her,

252

Amber swung quickly about, putting her hand to the back of her skirt. And though she half expected to find it torn open, she felt there instead a piece of cardboard and ripped it off, sailing it furiously across the stage. Beneath and before and above her she saw a blur of faces, a seemingly endless vista of opened mouths, and at the same instant the apprentices began to beat their cudgels and stamp their feet and a roaring chant went up:

"My tail's
For sale.
Half-a-crown
Will lay me down!"

Half-crown pieces had begun to ring upon the stage and Amber felt them pelting her sharply, hitting her from every side. The men were climbing onto their benches, shouting at the top of their lungs; the ladies had put on their masks but were shaking with laughter; from top to bottom the theatre was a bedlam of noise and confusion—though not more than forty seconds had passed since Amber's unlucky turn.

"You lousy bitch!" Amber ground the words through her clenched teeth. "I'll break your head for this!"

With a hysterical titter Beck started off the stage at a run and, just as the curtains swished frantically together, Amber went after her as fast as she could go, yelling, "Come back here, you damned coward!"

Anne, waiting in the wings, stuck out a foot to trip her, but Amber jumped over it, gave Anne a backhand swipe that sent her staggering, and rushed on. Flying down the narrow dark hallway Beck turned to look back just as she reached the tiring-room, gave a shriek when she saw how close her pursuer was, and dashing in slammed the door. But before she could throw the bolt Amber had burst against it, shoved it open, and with a violent push was inside. In one movement she flung the bolt herself and turned to grapple with Beck.

Clawing and biting, screaming and kicking and pounding at each other with their fists, they rocked and swayed from one side of the room to the other. Their flimsy costumes were soon torn to shreds; their wigs came off and the black eye-paint smeared their faces; bloody scratches appeared on cheeks and arms and breasts. But for the time they were engrossed in rage, unfeeling, unhearing, unseeing.

Outside a crowd had gathered and was pounding at the door, clamouring to be let in. Scroggs moved straddle-legged after them, keeping just out of reach of thrashing arms and legs, cheering and shouting for Madame St. Clare. Once, when she came too close, Beck gave her a vicious kick in the belly that knocked her into a breathless groaning quivering heap on the floor.

At last Amber locked one leg behind Beck's knee and they went down together, clasped as tight as lovers, rolling over and over with first one on top and then the other. Amber's nose was streaming and her throat was beginning to feel raw from the blood she had swallowed, but at last she got astride Beck and pummelled her head and face with her fists while Beck fought her off with teeth and clawing nails. Thus they were when Scroggs opened the door and half-a-dozen men rushed in to drag them apart, hauling Amber off and pulling Beck away in another direction. Both women collapsed from sudden nervous exhaustion, and neither protested at the interference. Beck began to cry hysterically, babbling an incoherent stream of accusations and curses.

Amber lay stretched out flat on a couch, Hart's cloak flung over her, and now while Scroggs sopped at the blood and muttered her fierce congratulations she began to feel the sting and smart of her wounds. Her nose was numb and seemed to have swollen immensely and one eye was beginning to close.

Faintly she heard Killigrew's loud angry voice: "—the laughing stock of all the town, you damned jades! I'll never dare show this play again! Both of you are suspended for two weeks—no, three weeks, by God! I'll have some discipline among you impudent players or know the reason why! And you can pay the cost of replacing your costumes—"

The voice went on but Amber's eyes were closed and she refused to listen. She was only relieved that Rex, who held his commission in his Majesty's regiment of Horse Guards, had been on duty at the Palace that day.

Still, when she came back at the end of her enforced vacation she found that though the other women probably liked her no better and envied her no less, she had been accepted as one of them. There was tension and amusement in the tiring-room the first day that she and Beck met face to face, but they merely looked at each other for a moment, then nodded and exchanged cool greetings.

A few days later Scroggs slyly gave Amber a new blue-velvet miniver-lined hood which some countess had just presented to the wardrobe. Blue was not Amber's colour and she knew it. "Thanks a million, Scroggs," she said. "But I think Beck should have it. It matches her gown."

Beck, standing only a few feet away and pulling on a stocking, heard her. She glanced around in surprise. "Why should I have it? My part's but a small one." Killigrew persisted in his punishment, and neither of them had yet been put into the roles they had played before.

"It's as big as mine," insisted Amber. "And anyway I've got a new petticoat to wear."

Still skeptical, Beck took it and thanked her.

In the comedy that day they played two frivolous girls, close friends, and halfway through the first act each suddenly discovered toward the other a new warmth which grew quickly into liking. At the end of the act everyone was astonished to see them coming off the stage arm in arm, laughing gaily. After that they were as good friends as most women, and Beck even flirted sometimes with Captain Morgan when he came to the tiring-room—though she knew as well as Amber that nothing would ever come of it. It was merely a gesture of good will.

CHAPTER SEVENTEEN

CHARLES II WAS married to the Infanta Catherine of Portugal two years after his Restoration.

She had been decided upon by Charles and Chancellor Hyde

—now Earl of Clarendon—very shortly after his return; the delay in the wedding had been political, designed to coerce a larger dowry from desperate little Portugal, just recently free but still menaced by Spain. In the end the Portuguese paid a high price for marrying English sea-power: they gave 300,000 pounds; the right of trade with all Portuguese colonies; and two of their most prized possessions, Tangier and Bombay.

The Earl of Sandwich had been sent to Portugal with a fleet to escort the princess back to England, but Charles could not leave London until he had prorogued Parliament, and that was several days after she had arrived at Portsmouth. But once it was dismissed he set out immediately and rode through the night. He arrived there early the next afternoon and went first to his own apartments to change his clothes.

Charles sat down and his barber lathered his face, then began to swipe across it with swift clean strokes of a sharp-edged razor. There were black circles beneath his eyes but he looked happy and alert, and somewhat amused, for the room was full of courtiers and he knew that the same thought was in every head.

They were wondering what kind of husband he was going to make, how this marriage would affect the status of each of them, and whether or not he really would, as he had said, keep no mistresses once he was married. For his own part he was glad to be away from London and the melancholy Barbara, who had sulked and pouted and cried for weeks past, though she bragged to acquaintances that she was going to lie-in of her second child at Hampton Court, while the King was spending his honeymoon there.

Now Charles glanced up at Buckingham who stood beside him, stroking the head of a little brown-and-black spaniel. Buckingham had been there for some time and had already seen the Infanta.

"Well?"

"Well," said the Duke.

Charles laughed. "I think you're jealous, my lord." Buckingham's wife was a plain, plump little woman with odd, slanted eyes and a large turned-up nose. When the barber was finished the King got up and submitted to being dressed. "Well

—for the honour of the nation I only hope I'm not put to the consummation tonight. I haven't had two hours rest in the past thirty-four, and I'm afraid matters would go off somewhat sleepily."

Dressed at last he slapped his hat onto his head and strode rapidly from the room, a pack of his spaniels running at his heels, a pack of courtiers following after them. The Infanta, he had been told, had caught a cold and been sent to bed; and that was where he found her, sitting propped against white silk pillows embroidered with the Stuart coat-of-arms, wearing a dressing-gown of pale pink satin with belled wrist-length sleeves. He paused in the doorway, bowing, and saw her eyes staring at him wide and half-frightened, her fingers twisting the counterpane nervously.

She was surrounded on all sides by her attendants, banked two or three deep about the bed as though for her protection. There were half-a-dozen long-robed priests, their tonsured heads shining, their eyes measuring and skeptical. There were the Countesses of Penalva and Ponteval, her Majesty's chaperons, two ugly, muddy-skinned, punctilious old women. And the six maids-of-honour, young but just as dark, sallow, and hideous to the eye of an Englishman. Instead of the sweeping, graceful low-cut gowns then in fashion, they were without exception dressed in stiff-bodiced, old-fashioned farthingales which had not been worn in England for thirty years. If they had breasts they were so tightly cased as to appear perfectly flat, and their skirts jutted out from the waist on either side like shelves that swung and teetered clumsily whenever they moved.

As the King appeared in the doorway, his gentlemen crowded behind him, peering over his shoulders; the women stood motionless and waiting, a look of alarm on their faces. Portuguese etiquette was as rigid as the clothes they wore and the girls, having seldom seen men who were not members of their own families, regarded the entire sex with suspicion and distrust. They had been creating a good deal of trouble by refusing to sleep in any bed which had ever been occupied by a man, and at the sight of one of the creatures approaching had covered their faces and run off in another direction, cackling and gabbling. Now, unable to run, they stood and stared—defensive, nervous, wretchedly ill-at-ease. They would have been more so if they had guessed what the men thought of them.

Charles's face did not change and immediately he came forward, taking her hand to kiss. "My apologies to you, madame," he said in soft Spanish, for she knew no English. "Business kept me until late last night. I hope you've been made comfortable?" He straightened then and looked down at her.

Catherine was twenty-three but she looked no more than eighteen. Her hair was beautiful, a cascading mass of dark brown waves, and her eyes which were also brown were large and bright, gentle and just a little wistful as she looked up at him. They seemed to beg for kindness and to ask apology for her own shortcomings. For her skin was inclined to sallowness; her front teeth protruded a little. And he had been told that she was scarcely five feet tall.

Still—he thought—for a princess, she's not bad.

Catherine had been bred in a convent, embroidering, praying, singing hymns, waiting for her mother to find her a husband. When she did, Catherine was already far beyond the age when most princesses married and still she knew nothing at all of men, was almost as ignorant of their natures as if they had been members of another species. She had expected to learn to love her husband because it was a woman's duty to do so; but now as she looked up at Charles she realized that she had already fallen in love with him. Everything about him seemed wonderful to her: his swarthy good-looks, the powerful grace of his body, the deep smooth gentle tones of his voice which lapped over her like a warm tide, stilling some of her terrors, echoing in her heart.

The next morning they were married, first by a secret Catholic ceremony in her bedchamber, again in the afternoon according to the rites of the Church of England. A few days later they set out for Hampton Court. And though there was much gossip to the effect that Charles was disappointed in his marriage and ready to accept Barbara Palmer back again as soon as she had recovered from her confinement, both their Majesties seemed

258

perfectly happy and content and as much in love as though they had not married for reasons of political expediency.

But if Catherine was satisfied, there were others in her suite who were not.

Penalva, an ailing, near-sighted old virgin, disliked England the moment she set foot upon it. It was too different from Portugal to be good. The women, she decided immediately, were wanton and bold, the men unscrupulous and dishonourable, and she undertook to warn the naïve little Queen of these facts.

"The Court of England," she said sternly, "must needs be much remodelled before it is fit for the occupancy of your Majesty."

Catherine, who was still admiring her splendid crimson-and-silver-hung apartments, examining the massive toilet and mirror made out of pure beaten gold, looked at her in surprise, but with a happy little smile.

"Why, perhaps it should be. I've not heard what condition it's in, but I don't doubt his Majesty will be glad to make any repairs I ask—he's so kind to me." Her dark eyes went out the windows, looking across the stretches of green lawn, the blooming flower-plots, and something dreamy and thoughtful came into them that evidently annoyed Penalva.

"You misunderstand, your Majesty! I was not speaking of the *furnishings* of the Palace. Quite possibly it will be as barbarous as this—" She gestured quickly, for she did not like English taste either. "I was speaking of the manners and morals of the courtiers and ladies themselves."

"Why," said Catherine, "what's wrong with them?"

"Can it be your Majesty has not noticed how these women dress? All of them go half naked from morning till night."

"Well—" she admitted with some reluctance, for she did not want to be disloyal to her new land and husband. "They are— different—from what we're used to seeing at home."

"Different! My dear, they're indecent! No woman whose intentions were innocent would display herself before a man as these creatures do. Your Majesty, you have an opportunity to earn for yourself the gratitude of all England—by reforming the Court."

"I wouldn't know how to begin. Perhaps they wouldn't like to have an outsider—"

"Nonsense, your Majesty! What does it matter what they would like! You're not their subject! They are yours, and must be made to understand so immediately—or you will find yourself a mere hanger-on at your own Court."

Catherine smiled gently, thinking that the poor old lady was so concerned for her happiness that she saw a great deal of evil where none existed. "I think you've misjudged them, my lady. They all look so fine—I'm sure they must be good."

"Unfortunately, your Majesty, that is not the way of the world. The good are never ostentatious—these creatures are. Now, your Majesty, you must listen to the advice of an old woman who has lived a long while and seen a great deal. Be mistress in your own Court! Be a leader, not a follower, or they'll leave you alone for whoever does undertake to lead, and Heaven knows, in this abandoned place it could be no one of good character. Begin, your Majesty, by putting off those absurd English clothes his Majesty gave you. Return to your native costume, and others will be forced to follow."

Catherine looked down, somewhat dismayed, at her pink-and-blue taffeta gown with its full-gathered skirt, billowing sleeves, the neckline cut more discreetly than were those of most ladies, but still quite daring, she had thought. She felt that in it she was prettier than she had ever been before in her life.

"But," she protested softly, "I like it."

"It doesn't become you, my dear, as your native costume does. Go back to your farthingales, or these English will think they've converted you to their ways already. They're an arrogant race, and will have scant pity or respect for whoever is easily tamed by them. And one thing more, your Majesty—*don't* learn the language. Let them speak to you in your own tongue—"

Catherine had listened to Penalva all her life, and she knew that the old lady had nothing but love and affection for her. She bowed to the wisdom of age and that night she appeared

260

at a banquet in her bobbing, black-silk farthingale. She gave Charles a quick anxious glance, to see whether or not he disapproved of the change, but his face was inscrutable. He smiled, bowing, and offered her his arm.

The honeymoon was celebrated with endless entertainment and gaiety. There were banquets and balls and cock-fights, picnics, rides on the canal in the luxurious royal barges, plays performed by actors who came down from London. All day long the staircases, the chain of great rooms and galleries, were crowded with a brilliantly dressed throng of men and women. In plum-coloured velvet, blue satin, gold brocade, they clattered and swished from room to room, strolled down the cradle-walk of interlaced hornbeam, drifted lazily on the river. And the sound of their voices, calling to one another, laughing, chattering eternally, reached Catherine whether she was with them or —more often—when she was in her own apartments at prayer or talking to her ladies and priests. She liked to hear them, for though she felt shy and lonely when she was among them, from a distance it gave her a sense of being part of their gay, debonair, heedless world.

She did not guess what they thought of her.

"She's ugly as a bat," they told one another, after the first glimpse, and greatly magnified her defects because she did not look like an Englishwoman.

They dissected her among themselves, the women giggling and murmuring behind their fans even when she was in the room, for they knew she could understand nothing of what they said. And if by chance the Queen's brown eyes rested upon one of them and she smiled, they quickly composed their faces to smile back, curtsying faintly, and gave a wink and a nudge to the nearest lady.

"Gad! But she looks as demure as a dog in a halter!"

"I'll be damned if I can bring myself to admire a woman with such a dingy skin! Why the devil doesn't she give it a plastering of powder?"

"Oh, heavens, my lord! Her monster would never allow it! They say the old witch thinks we're a pack of infidels and counsels her Majesty to have a care we don't corrupt her."

"Look! how she gives the king the sheep's eye! Ugh! I swear it makes me queasy to see a woman who dotes so upon her husband—and in public in broad daylight!"

"I say it's a mark of his Majesty's good-breeding he can make such a tolerable show of seeming to endure her."

"Well—I'll wager he won't make such a tolerable show much longer. Castlemaine laid-in last week. She'll be here in another fortnight—and *then* we'll see—" Barbara Palmer had been created Countess of Castlemaine some six months before.

"It runs through the galleries the King promised long ago he'd make her a Lady of the Bedchamber when he married—"

"And she says he will or she'll know why!"

Much as they disliked Barbara for her insolence and airs, hot though jealousy of her flared among the other women, still she was one of them and they were united in her favour against this newcomer who outraged them with her modesty and reticence, her obstinate clinging to the fashions of her own country, her persistent devotion to her church. But it was not only the frivolous and cynical whom Catherine had offended. By seeming from the first to like Chancellor Clarendon she had unwittingly drawn upon herself the enmity of the most ambitious and able and influential men at Court.

But Catherine could know nothing of all this. And in spite of Penalva's repeated warnings she looked at her new subjects and saw only women dressed in beautiful gowns, with glossy golden hair and a look of sleek complacency—women she envied though she knew it was wicked to do so—and men with suave easy manners bowing over her hand, sweeping off their hats as she appeared, their closed faces telling her nothing. She was still a little frightened by England, but so much in love with her husband and so eager to please him that she tried to conceal her awe and uncertainty and thought that she was succeeding very well.

And then one evening, while she was being made ready for bed, Lady Suffolk, aunt of Lady Castlemaine, and the only English attendant thus far appointed, handed the Queen a sheet of paper with a list of names written upon it. "These are the persons proposed for your Majesty's attendants," she said. "Will your Majesty be pleased to sign?"

Catherine, now in her flowing night-gown of white silk, took it and went to her little writing-table. She picked up a pen and had bent to write her signature, when suddenly Penalva's hawk-nosed face appeared over her shoulder.

"Don't sign without reading it first, your Majesty!" she whispered.

.Catherine gave her a glance of mild surprise, for she had assumed that if the King had chosen these ladies to attend her they could not be otherwise than acceptable. But already her old chaperon was mumbling them over.

"—Mrs. Price. Mrs. Wells. Mother of the Maids: Bridget Saunderson. Ladies of the Bedchamber: my Lady Castlemaine—" At the last name her voice became audible, suddenly sharp and indignant, and her face turned to Catherine's.

It was the only name which meant anything to her. For before she had sailed her mother—who had given her so little advice as to how to be happy, either as wife or queen—had warned her never to allow Lady Castlemaine to so much as come into her presence. She was, the old Dowager Queen had said, an infamous hussy for whom the King had shown a deplorable kindness during the days of his bachelorhood.

"Why!" said Catherine, horrified. Then quickly she glanced about to catch the cool eyes of Lady Suffolk upon her, and turned so that only her back was to be seen. "What shall I do?" she whispered, pretending to study the list.

"Scratch the creature's name *out,* of course!" With a quick motion she snatched up the pen which Catherine had dropped, dipped it into the inkwell and handed it to her. "Scratch it out, your Majesty!"

For a moment longer Catherine hesitated, her face troubled and hurt, and then resolutely she crossed her pen over the name with several dark broad strokes, until it was completely obliterated. She felt that by so doing she had also obliterated this menace to her happiness. She turned then and spoke to her interpreter.

"Tell my Lady Suffolk that I shall return the list to her in the morning."

Half an hour later Charles arrived to find her alone and, as usual, on her knees before the little shrine which had been set up next to the great scarlet-velvet bed-of-state. He waited quietly, but already his eye had caught sight of the paper on the writing-table and the black bar which marked out Lady Castlemaine. However, he said nothing, and when she turned and smiled at him he crossed over to help her to her feet; but as he stooped to kiss her he could feel her tiny body stiffen defensively.

For a few moments they talked, discussing the play they had seen that night—a performance of "Bartholomew Fair" done by the King's Company—but all the while Catherine was wondering nervously how she should broach the subject and wishing that he would mention it first. At last, in desperation, just as he excused himself to go into the dressing-room, she spoke quickly.

"Oh—and Sire—before I forget. My Lady Suffolk gave me the list tonight—it's over there—" She swallowed and took a deep breath. "I crossed out one name. I'm sure you know which one," she added hastily, a little note of defiance coming into her voice, for Penalva had warned her that she must let him know once and for all she was not to be treated like that again.

Charles stopped, glancing carelessly across his shoulder, for he was just passing the writing-table. He turned slowly to face her. "Have you an objection to a lady you've never seen?"

"I've heard of her."

Charles gave a shrug and one finger stroked his mustache, but he smiled. "Gossip," he said. "How people love to gossip."

"Gossip!" she cried, shocked now to see how crassly unconcerned he was at having been taken in this bold attempt. "It can't be just gossip! Why, my mother told me—"

"I'm sorry, my dear, that my personal affairs are known so far afield. And yet since you seem so well advised of my shortcomings, I hope you'll believe me when I tell you that that episode is past. I have not seen the lady since we were married, and I intend having nothing more to do with her. I only ask you to accept her so that she may not have to suffer the indignities sure to be otherwise imposed upon her by ladies and gentlemen who were her friends only a short while since."

"I don't understand you, Sire. What else does a woman of that kind deserve? Why, she was nothing but your—your concubine!"

"It's always been my opinion, madame, that the mistresses of kings are as honourable as the wives of other men. I don't ask you to make her your friend, Catherine, or even to have her about you—but only that she be allowed the title. It would make her life much easier—and could scarcely hurt you, my dear." He smiled, trying to convince her, but nevertheless he was surprised at her stubbornness, for he had never suspected that this quiet adoring little woman had so much spirit.

"I'm sorry, your Majesty, but I must refuse. I would gladly do anything else you ask—but I can't do this. Please, Sire—try to understand what it would mean to me, too."

A week later Charles, on the pretext of going hunting, went to see Barbara at her uncle's nearby estate. She had just arrived and had sent him a desperate, humble imploring letter which, however, touched him less than did the fragrance it carried— that heavy musky compelling odour with which she always surrounded herself.

Breathless from running, she met him just as he stepped into the great hallway where stag-horns decorated the walls and ancient armour and firearms hung in every corner. He looked at her and saw a woman more beautiful than the one he remembered—his memory was short for such things—with brilliant violet eyes, her hair in a lavish cluster of curls about her face, dressed in a becoming gown of deep-red silk.

"Your Majesty!"

She made him a sweeping curtsy and her head dropped gracefully. Her eyes closed and she gave a little sigh as he bent casually to kiss her upon the cheek. Then she took his arm and they walked on into the house and up the flight of stairs which led to the main apartments.

"You're looking very well," he said, determinedly ignoring

her obvious efforts to enchant. "I hope your confinement was not difficult."

She laughed gaily and pressed his arm, as sweet and merry as she had ever been in the early weeks of their acquaintance before the Restoration. "Difficult! Heavens, Your Majesty, —you know how it is with me! I'd rather have a baby than a quartan ague! Oh, but wait till you see him! He's ever so handsome—and everyone says he's the image of you!" That was not what they had said about her first child.

In the chapel the bishop was waiting with Lord Oxford and Lady Suffolk and the baby. When the ceremony of baptism was over Charles admired his son, took it up into his arms with an air of knowing exactly what he was about. But presently it began to cry and was sent off back to the nursery. The others went into a small private room to have wine and cakes, and here Barbara maneuvered him off to one side, under the pretext of showing him a section of the garden.

But she soon turned from the roses and flowering lime.

"And now you're married," she breathed softly, looking up at him with her eyes sad and tender. "And I've heard you're deep in love."

He stood and stared at her moodily, his eyes flickering over her face and hair and down to her breasts and small-laced waist. He caught the faint lascivious odour of her perfume, and his eyes darkened. Practiced voluptuary as he was, Charles had begun to long for a woman whose senses he could arouse, and who could arouse his. Catherine loved him, but he was finding her innocence and instinctive reticence a bore.

He sucked a quick breath through his teeth and his jaw set. "I'm very happy, thank you."

A faint mocking smile crossed her face. "For your sake, Sire, I'm glad." Then she sighed again and looked wistfully out the window. "Oh, you can't think what a wretched time I had in London after you'd left! The very porters and 'prentices in the streets insulted me! If you hadn't promised to make me a Lady of the Bedchamber—Lord, I don't know how I'd shift!"

A scowl crossed his face, for this was what he had been

expecting and dreading. Of course her aunt had told her the whole story. "I'm sure you exaggerate, Barbara. I think you'll get along very well, in spite of everything."

Her head turned swiftly, the black centers of her eyes enlarging. "What do you mean—in spite of everything?"

"Well—it's unfortunate, but my wife crossed out your name. She says she doesn't want you for an attendant."

"Doesn't want me! Why, that's ridiculous! Why doesn't she want me? My family's good enough, I hope! And what harm can *I* do her now?"

"None," he said, very definitely. "But all the same she doesn't want you. She doesn't understand the way we live here in England. I told her that I would—"

Barbara stared at him aghast. "You told her she needn't have me!" she repeated in a horrified whisper. "Why, how could you do such a thing!" Tears had swum into her eyes and already, in spite of Lady Suffolk's frantic signalling, her voice was rising and a quaver of hysteria had come into it. "How can you do such a thing to a woman who has sacrificed her reputation, been deserted by her husband, and left to the scorn of all the world—to give you happiness! Oh, ——!" She turned and leaned her forehead against the window, one closed fist pressed to her mouth. She took a deep sobbing gasp. "Oh, I wish I'd died when the baby was born! I'd never have wanted to live if I'd known you'd do a thing like this to me!"

Charles looked more annoyed than sympathetic or conscience-smitten. All he wanted was to have the matter settled one way or another—and whether Barbara won or Catherine did made little difference to him. There was something to be said for both sides of the question, he thought, but a woman could never see more than one.

"Very well," he said. "I'll speak to her again."

But instead he sent the Chancellor to do the delicate business for him, though the old man protested vehemently, for he thought that Castlemaine would be well served if she were sent into exile overseas. Clarendon came out of his interview wiping his red face and shaking his head, limping slightly to favour his gout-stricken right foot. Charles was waiting for him in his laboratory and that was where he went—but as the short, round, pompous little man passed through the galleries he was followed by a trail of smirks and whispers. The contest between their Majesties was giving amusement to the entire Court.

"Well?" said the King, getting up from where he had sat writing a letter to Minette—she was now Madame, Duchess of Orléans and third lady at the Court of France.

"She refuses, your Majesty." He sat down, ignoring ceremony, because he was tired and discouraged and his foot ached. "For a little woman who looks meek and obliging—" He mopped his wet face again.

"What did you tell her? Did you tell her that—"

"I told her *everything*. I told her that your Majesty no longer had commerce with the Lady—nor ever intends to. I told her that your Majesty has the greatest affection for her and will make her a very good husband if she would but agree to this one thing. Oh, I beg of your Majesty, don't send me again! I have no maw for this business—you know what my opinion is—"

"I don't care what your opinion is!" said Charles sharply, though usually he listened with a lazy patient smile to whatever criticism of his manners, morals or intellect the Chancellor cared to make. "What was her attitude when you left?"

"She was in such a passion of tears, I think she may be wholly dissolved by now."

Charles went to his wife's room that night in a mood defiant and determined. He had had a domineering mother; he had unwittingly chosen a domineering mistress; but he did not intend to be hen-pecked at home. He was less interested now in the fate of Barbara Palmer than he was in convincing his wife that he and not she would make the decisions. Catherine met him with an equally defiant air—though only an hour before they had been smiling politely at each other and listening to a choir of Italian eunuchs.

He bowed to her. "Madame, I hope that you are prepared to be reasonable."

"I am, Sire—if you are."

"I ask this one favour of you, Catherine. If you'll grant it,

I promise it shall be the last hard thing I'll ever expect of you."

"But the one thing you do ask is the hardest thing a man *could* ask of his wife! I can't do it! I won't do it!" Suddenly she stamped her tiny foot and cried in a flare of angry passion that astonished him, "And if you speak of it again I'll go home to Portugal!" She stared at him for a moment, and then bursting into tears turned her back and covered her face with her hands.

For a long moment both of them were silent, Catherine struggling to control her sobs but wondering miserably why he did not come to her, take her into his arms, and tell her that he realized how impossible it would be for her to accept his cast-off whore as an attendant. He had seemed so kind and gentle and tender, she could not understand what had happened to change him. Surely if he cared so much about the woman's having that place he must still love her.

But Charles, his stubbornness now thoroughly aroused, had a vision of himself going through life the meek, uxorious husband of a tyrannizing little despot. She could never learn earlier that he would rule his own household.

"Very well, madame," he said at last. "But before you go I think it would be wise to determine first if your mother will have you—and to find out, I'll send your attendants before you."

Catherine whirled around and stared at him with unbelieving astonishment. Those men and women of her own country were all she had to cling to in this strange terrifying land. Now, more than ever, when he was against her too, she needed them.

"Oh, please, Sire!" Her hands went out imploringly.

He bowed. "Good-night, madame."

To the amused relief of the Court most of Catherine's ugly train departed within a few days, for Charles allowed only Penalva, the priests, and a few kitchen attendants to remain. He did not trouble to send so much as a letter of explanation with them, but he hoped the Dowager Queen would know that he was displeased because she had paid most of the dowry—at the last moment—in sugar and spices instead of in gold.

For days the contest between them persisted.

Catherine remained most of the time in her own rooms and,

when she did appear, she and Charles scarcely spoke. When the courtiers met in the garden or at the cockpit they asked each other: "Are you going to the Queen-baiting this afternoon?" The young and gay wanted to see Barbara Palmer triumphant because she represented their own way of living; the older and more circumspect sympathized with the Queen but wished that she understood men better and had been taught that tact could often accomplish what blustering and threats could not. As usual, Charles heard advice from both camps, but though he listened politely to everyone he was no more influenced than usual. In any matter which he considered to be of importance to his comfort he made his own decisions—and he did so now.

Queen Henrietta Maria was coming to pay her son another visit, and Charles did not intend that she should arrive to find his wife pouting and his house in a turmoil. Determined to settle the issue for once and all, he sent for Barbara to come to Hampton Court.

One warm late-July afternoon Catherine's drawing-room was crowded to capacity and many who could not force their way in stood in the anteroom. There was a sharp tension in the air which she felt but could not understand, unless it was because Charles had not yet appeared. In spite of herself she continued to look anxiously for him, over their heads toward the doorway. For he was always there, and even when he ignored her she could find some comfort in the mere fact of his presence. But now, feeling lonely and forsaken, she had to force herself to smile, bit the inside of her lower lip so that it would not tremble, swallowed hard over the lump in her throat.

Oh! she was thinking desperately, how I wish I'd never come to England! I wish I wasn't married! I wish I was back home again! I was happy then—

Her memory returned with longing to the lazy still afternoons in the convent garden, washed with the hot Portuguese sun, when she had sat with her brush and palette trying to catch the sharp contrast of white walls and blue shadows, or had worked her needle and listened to the murmurous chant of prayers in the chapel. What a quiet safe world that was! She envied that Catherine for the things she had not known.

And then suddenly she saw him and her back stiffened, a cold wave washed over her and the sadness and the dreamy languor was gone. Alert, glad to see him though she knew he would pay her no attention, a little smile touched her mouth. How tall he is, she thought, and how handsome! Oh, I do love him! She had scarcely noticed that a woman—dressed in white lace that sparkled with silver sequins—walked by his side.

As they came forward the room fell into a hushed waiting silence, every eye watching, every ear straining to hear. It was not until Charles, in a low but perfectly distinct tone, had spoken the lady's name that Catherine turned to look at her, holding out her hand to be kissed as the woman dropped to one knee.

At the same moment she felt a grasp on her shoulder and heard Penalva's hiss in her ear: "It's *Castlemaine!*"

Catherine's hand jerked involuntarily, and her eyes turned to Charles, surprised, incredulous, questioning. But he was merely watching her, his face hard and speculative, his whole manner coolly defiant, as though daring her to refuse him now. She looked then at Lady Castlemaine, who had risen, and had a quick unforgettable glimpse of a beautiful face—the lips curled faintly, the eyes shining with triumph and mockery.

She turned suddenly sick and weak. The world began to swim and rock dizzily, a ringing in her ears drowned out every other sound, and the room blackened before her eyes. She pitched forward out of her chair, but was kept from falling by the quick restraining hands of two pages and the Countess of Penalva, who glared at Charles with cold and unrelenting hatred. A sudden look of horror crossed his face and involuntarily one hand went out. But he quickly remembered himself, stepped back, and stood there silently while the Queen was carried from the room.

CHAPTER EIGHTEEN

BECAUSE OF REX MORGAN's place at Court, Amber was able to watch the King and Queen's state entry into London from the roof of one of the Palace buildings along the Thames.

For as far as it was possible to see in both directions the shores were packed; on the water the barges lay so thick a man could have walked from Westminster Hall to Charing Cross Stairs on them. Banners whipped out in the brisk breeze, and garlands of flowers trailed in the water. Music played, and as the first of the great gilded state-barges appeared cannon went off, roaring along the river-front, while shouts echoed back from shore to shore and every bell-tower in the city began to rock clamorously.

Amber, her hair blowing about her face, was standing over in one corner, very close to the edge and trying hard to see everything. With her were three young men who had just come from Hampton Court and who had been telling her the story of how the Queen had fainted when Castlemaine was presented to her, and how angry the King had been, thinking she had done it on purpose to embarrass him.

"And since then," one of them was saying, "the Lady's gone to all the balls and entertainments and they say his Majesty is sleeping with her again."

"Can you blame him?" demanded another. "She's a mighty delicate creature—but as for that olivader skinned—"

"Well, damn me!" interrupted the third. "If there isn't the Earl himself!"

Elbow-nudges and glances passed along the roof, but Roger Palmer ignored them all; and presently they turned their attention back to the pageant, for the great City barges were now moving by just below. A few minutes later, however, Barbara herself came up the stairway. She was followed by her handsome waiting-woman, Mrs. Wilson, and a nurse carrying her little son. She made a perfunctory curtsy to her husband, who bowed coldly, and immediately she was surrounded by the three young gallants who had left Amber with never a word of apology.

Angry and resentful, hot at the mere sight of this woman she despised, Amber gave her head a toss and turned away. At least *I'll* not stare like a country-bumpkin at a puppet show! she thought furiously. But no one else seemed to have any such compunctions.

Not very much later she was surprised by the sound of a strangely familiar masculine voice, a hand on her shoulder, and she looked swiftly about to see the Earl of Almsbury grinning down at her. "Well, I'll be damned!" he was saying. "If it isn't Mrs. St. Clare!" He bent then and kissed her, and she was so charmed by the warmth of his smile, the admiration she saw in his eyes, that she forgave him on the instant for having neglected her when she was in Newgate.

"Why, Almsbury!"

The questions rose immediately to her tongue: Where's Bruce? Have you seen him? Is he here? But her pride bit them down.

He stepped back now and his eyes went over her from head to toe. "You're looking mighty prosperous, sweetheart! Matters have gone swimmingly with you, I doubt not—"

Amber forgot Luke Channell and Newgate and Whitefriars. She gave him a little smile with the corners of her mouth and answered airily. "Oh, well enough. I'm an actress now—in the Theatre Royal."

"No! I'd heard they have females on the stage now—but you're the first I've seen. I've been in the country for two years past."

"Oh. Then maybe you never got my letter?"

"No—did you write me?"

She made a light gesture of dismissal. "Oh, it was a great while since. In December, a year and a half gone."

"I left town just after—at the end of August in '60. I tried to find you, but the host at the Royal Saracen said you'd packed and gone to parts unknown, and the next day I left myself for Herefordshire—his Majesty granted me my lands again."

At that moment the noise about them swelled deafeningly, for the Royal barge had reached the pier and the King and Queen were getting out, while the Queen Mother came forward to meet them.

"Good Lord!" shouted Amber. "What the devil is her Majesty wearing?" From the distance the Queen's propped-out skirts made her look almost as wide as she was tall, and as she moved they rocked and swayed precariously.

"It's a farthingale!" bellowed Almsbury. "They wear 'em in Portugal!"

When at last the crowds began to break up Almsbury took her arm, asking if he might carry her to her lodgings. They turned, to find Barbara with a man's wide-brimmed hat on her head, standing only a few feet away, and she gave Almsbury a wave and a smile, though her eyes slid with unmistakable hostility over Amber. Amber lifted her chin, lowered her lashes, and sailed by without a glance.

Her coach was waiting in King Street with a great many others, just outside the Palace Gate, and at sight of it Almsbury gave a low whistle. "Well! I didn't know acting was such a well-paid profession!"

Amber took the cloak which Jeremiah handed her and tossed it over her shoulders, for evening had set in and it was growing cool. Picking up her skirts she gave him a sly smile over her shoulder.

"Maybe acting isn't. But there's another that is." She climbed in, laughing as he sat down heavily beside her.

"So our innocent country-maid has listened to the Devil, after all."

"What else could I do after—" She stopped quickly, colouring, and then hastily added, "There's only one way for a woman to get on in the world, I've found."

"There's only one way for a woman to get on very well—or very far. Who's your maintainer?"

"Captain Morgan, of his Majesty's Horse Guard. D'you know 'im?"

274

"No. I think I'm somewhat out of the fashion, in keepers and clothes alike. There's nothing will run a man out of the mode so quick as a wife and a home in the country."

"Oh! So now you're married!" Amber gave him a roguish grin, almost as though he had just admitted some indiscretion.

"Yes, now I'm married. Two years the 5th of next month. And I've got two boys—one a little over a year and another just two months. And—a—weren't you—" His eyes went down over her questioningly, but he hesitated.

"I have a boy, too!" cried Amber suddenly, unable to control herself any longer. "Oh, Almsbury, you should see him! He looks just like Bruce! Tell me, Almsbury: Where is he? Has he been back to London? Have you seen him?" She did not care any longer about seeming flippant and independent. She was happy with Rex and had almost thought that she was no longer in love with Bruce Carlton—but the mere sight of Almsbury had brought it all churning up again.

"I've heard that he's in Jamaica and sails from there to take Spanish ships. Lord, sweetheart, don't tell me you're still—"

"Well, what if I am!" cried Amber, tears in her voice, and she turned her head quickly to look out the window.

Almsbury's tone was soothing. He moved closer and put an arm about her. "Here—darling. Good Lord, I'm sorry."

She dropped her head onto his shoulder. "When do you think he'll come back? He's been gone two years—"

"I don't know. But I suppose one of these days when we least expect it he'll be putting into port."

"He'll stay here then, won't he? He won't go away again, will he?"

"I'm afraid he will, sweetheart. I've known Carlton for twenty years, and most of that time he's been just coming home or just going away. He doesn't stay long in one place. It must be his Scottish blood, I think, that sends him off adventuring."

"But it'll be different—now that the King's back. When he has money he can live at Court without having to crawl on his belly—that's what he said he didn't like."

"It was more than that. He doesn't like the Court."

"Doesn't like it! Why, that's ridiculous! That's where every-body would live—if they could!"

Almsbury shrugged. "Nevertheless he doesn't like it. No one does—but few of 'em have got the guts to leave."

Amber shook her shoulders, pouting, and leaned forward to get out as the coach drew up before her lodging-house. "That sounds like damned nonsense!" she muttered crossly.

Her maid, Gatty, was not in, for Amber had given her per-mission to see the pageant and then pay a visit to her father. Prudence she had long since dismissed when she had come home unexpectedly to find the girl parading about in her best and newest gown. And there had been two others before Gatty, one sent away for pilfering and the other for laziness. Amber sent Jeremiah to bring them some food from the Bear, an excellent nearby ordinary which sold French food cooked by English-men. Her meals were all sent in, from taverns or cook-shops.

She showed him her rooms with great pride, pointing out every detail so that he should miss nothing. Rex was generous and gave her almost everything she asked for; consequently he spent much of his time when not on duty gambling in the Groom Porter's Lodge or at a tavern.

Among her recent acquirements was a chest of drawers from Holland made of Brazilian kingwood—chocolate brown with black veins, decorated with a great deal of florid Dutch carv-ing. There was a lacquered black Chinese screen, and in one corner stood a what-not loaded with tiny figures: a tree of coral, a blown-glass stag, an old Chinese knife-grinder worked in sil-ver filigree. And over the fireplace hung a three-quarter portrait of Amber.

"What d'you think of me?" she asked, gesturing toward the portrait, tossing her muff and fan aside.

Almsbury put his hands in his pockets and leaned back on his heels, examining it with his head to one side. "Well, sweet-heart, I'm glad I saw you in the flesh first, or I should have been troubled to think you'd grown so plump. And who sat for the mouth? That isn't yours."

She laughed, beckoning him into the bedroom where she began to unpin her back hair. "Being in the country hasn't

276

changed you so much, Almsbury. You're still as great a courtier as ever. But you should see the miniature Samuel Cooper did of me. I'm supposed to be Aphro—I forget what he called it—Venus, anyway, rising from the sea. I stand like this—" she struck an easy graceful pose, "and haven't got a thing on."

Almsbury, sitting astride a low chair with his arms folded across the back, gave a low appreciative hum. "Sounds mighty pretty. Where is it?"

"Oh, Rex has it. I gave it to him for his birthday and he's carried it ever since—over his heart." She grinned mischievously and began untying the bows down the front of her gown. "He's mad in love with me. Lord, he even wants to marry me now."

"And are you going to?"

"No." She shook her head vigorously, indicating that she did not care to discuss the matter. "I don't want to get married."

Picking up her dressing-gown, she went behind the screen to put it on. Just her head and shoulders showed over the top of it, and as she took off her garments, tossing them out one by one, she kept up a merry chatter with the Earl.

Finally the waiter arrived and they went into the dining-room to eat. Rex had sent her a message that he would be on duty at the Palace until late, or she would never have dared eat her supper with a man, wearing only a satin dressing-gown. For she had discovered long ago that Rex was not joking when he said that if he took her into keeping he would expect a monopoly of her time and person. He kept the beaus from crowding her too closely or impudently at the theatre and discouraged them from visiting her—though all the actresses held their levées at home just as the Court ladies did and entertained numbers of gentlemen while they were dressing. The result was that during the last few months they had quite given up Mrs. St. Clare. Rex had a formidable reputation as a swordsman, and most of the tiring-room fops would rather see an apothecary for a clap, than a surgeon for a flesh-wound.

Throughout the meal Amber and the Earl talked with all the animation of old friends who have not met for a long while and who have a great deal to say to each other. She told him about her successes, but not her failures, her triumphs but not her defeats. He heard nothing of Luke Channell or of Newgate, Mother Red-Cap or Whitefriars. She pretended that she still had left a good deal of Lord Carlton's five hundred pounds, deposited with her goldsmith, and he admitted that she had been far more clever than most young country girls left to shift for themselves in London.

It was two hours later as they sat on her long green velvet-cushioned settle, empty wine-glasses in their hands and staring into the last glow of the sea-coal fire, that Almsbury drew her into his arms and kissed her. For a moment she hesitated, her body tense, thinking of Rex and how furious he would be if another man kissed her, and then—because she liked Almsbury and because he meant Bruce Carlton to her—she relaxed against him and made no protest until, at last, he asked her to go into the bedroom.

Then suddenly she shook back her hair and pulled the front of her gown together. "Oh, Lord, Almsbury! I can't! I should never have even let you think I would!" She got up, feeling a little dizzy from the wine, and leaned her head against the mantelpiece.

"Good God, Amber! I thought you were grown up now!" He sounded exasperated and more than a little angry.

"Oh, it isn't that, Almsbury. It isn't because I'm still—" She was about to say "waiting for Bruce," but stopped. "It's Rex. You don't know him. He's jealous as an Italian uncle. He'd murder you in a trice—and turn me out of keeping."

"He wouldn't if he didn't know anything about it."

She smiled, skeptically, turning her head to look at him, though her hair fell forward over her face. "Was there ever a man yet who could lie with a woman and not tell all his acquaintance within the hour? The gallants say that's half the pleasure of fornication—telling about it afterwards."

"Well, I'm no gallant, and you damned well know it. I'm just a man who's in love with you. Oh, maybe I shouldn't say that. I don't know whether I'm in love with you or not. But I've wanted you since the first day I saw you. You know now that what I told you that night is true, so don't put me off any longer.

278

How much do you want? I'll give you two hundred pound—put it with your goldsmith, toward the day when you'll need it."

The money was a convincing argument, but the thought that someday Bruce Carlton might hear about it—and be hurt—was even more so.

It was true, as Amber had told Almsbury, that Rex Morgan wanted to marry her. During the past seven months they had been happy and content, leading a life of merry companionable domesticity. They took an instinctive pleasure in doing the same things, and it was heightened always by a warm suffusing glow of happiness at the mere fact of being together.

The summer just past they had been together most of the time, for with the King out of town Rex had no official duties and the theatres were always closed for a vacation period of several weeks—though twice Amber had gone down with the rest of the Company to perform before their Majesties at Hampton Court. With Prudence or Gatty or whomever she might have in service, they would pack a hamper and ride out Goswell Street on warm June evenings to eat a picnic supper at the lonely, pretty little village of Islington. Several times they found a quiet spot in the river and pulled off their clothes to go swimming, laughing and splashing in the cool clean water, and afterwards while she dried her hair Rex would catch a few fish for them to take home.

Or they rowed up the river in a hired scull, Amber with her shoes and stockings off and her ankles trailing in the water, screaming with delighted laughter to hear Rex bandy insults and curses with the watermen—caustic-tongued old ruffians who amused themselves by hooting and jeering obscenely at everyone who ventured upon the river, whether Quakeress or Parliament man. At Chelsea they would get out to lie dreamily in the thick meadow grass, watching the clouds as they formed and passed overhead, and Amber would fill her skirt with wildflowers, yellow primroses, blue hyacinths, white dogwood. Then she would open the hamper and spread a clean white linen cloth, laying on it the potted neat's tongue, the salad which the cele-brated French cook at Chatelin's had made for her with twenty different greens, fresh ripe fruits, and a dusty bottle of Burgundy.

They seldom quarrelled—only when, rightly or wrongly, Rex's jealousy was aroused, though before she had seen Almsbury she had never been unfaithful to him. But she did drive out to Kingsland to see the baby once a week. For a long while she contrived to keep her visits secret from him, but one day, to her astonishment, he accused her of having been with another man. During the violent quarrel which ensued she told him where she had been—and told him also that she was married.

For two or three days he was angry, but no matter what lies he caught her in he did not seem to love her less, and even after that he asked her again to marry him. She had refused before, pretending that she thought he was only joking, but now she objected that it was impossible. Bigamy was punishable by death.

"He'll never come back," said Rex. "But if he does—well, you let me alone for that. I'll see to it you're a widow, not a bigamist."

But Amber could not make up her mind to do it. She still had a lingering horror of matrimony, for it seemed to her a trap in which a woman, once caught, struggled helplessly and without hope. It gave a man every advantage over her body, mind and purse, for no jury in the land would interest itself in her distress. But neither that horror nor the greater one she had of being prosecuted for bigamy was the real reason behind her refusal. She hesitated because in her heart she still nursed an imp of ambition, and it would not let her rest.

If I marry Rex, she would think, what will my life be? He'd make me quit the stage and I'd have to start having babies. (Rex resented the child she had had—he thought by her first husband—even though he had never seen the little boy, and had a sentimental desire for her to bear him a son.) And then most likely he'd grow more jealous than ever and if I so much as came home a half-hour late from the 'Change or smiled at a gentleman in the Mall he'd tear himself to pieces.

He probably wouldn't be as generous as he is now, either, and if I spent thirty pound for a new gown there'd be trouble and he'd think last year's cloak could do me again. First thing you know I'd grow fat and pot-bellied and dwindle into a wife —and before I was twenty my life would be over. No, I like it better this way. I've got all the advantages of being a wife because he loves me and won't put me aside, and none of the disadvantages because I'm free and my own mistress and can leave him any time I like.

She had heard that King Charles had remarked more than once he considered her to be the finest·woman on the stage, and that in particular after her last performance at Hampton Court he had told someone he envied the man who kept her.

A fortnight or so after Almsbury's return to town Amber got a new maid. She dismissed Gatty one day when the girl surprised her taking a bath and talking to his Lordship, sending her away with the warning that Almsbury had a great interest at Court and would order her tongue cut out if she spoke to anyone at all of what she had seen. She told Rex that she had turned the girl away because she was pregnant, and sent Jeremiah to post a notice for a serving-woman in St. Paul's Cathedral, where a good deal of such business was done.

But that same morning as she was riding from the New Exchange to a rehearsal, her coach stopped at the golden-crowned Maypole, and while Tempest was bellowing abuse at the driver and occupants of the coach that blocked his way, the door was flung open and a girl leaped in. Her hair was dishevelled and her eyes looked wild.

"Please, mam!" she cried. "Tell 'im I'm your maid!" Her pretty face was intense and pleading, her voice passionate. "Oh, Jesus! Here he comes! *Please,* mam!" She gave Amber ·a last imploring look and then retreated far back into one corner, pulling the hood of her cloak up over her red-blonde curls.

Amber stared at her in amazement and then, before she could speak a word, the door was thrown open and a blue-coated constable, carrying his staff of office, pushed his head in at them. At this Amber gave an involuntary backward start. But, remembering that a constable could mean nothing to her now, she quickly recovered herself.

He made her a half salute, evidently mistaking her for a lady of quality. "Sorry to trouble you, mam, but that wench just stole a loaf of bread. I arrest you," he shouted, "in the King's name!" And he lunged across Amber toward the girl, who cowered far into one corner, skirts drawn close about her. Even from where she sat, Amber could feel her tremble.

Suddenly furious, all her memories of Newgate rising like a tide, Amber brought her fan down with a hearty smack on the constable's wrist. "What are·you about, sir? This girl is my serving-woman! Take your hands off her!"

He looked up at her in surprise. "Well, now, mam—I wouldn't care to be calling a lady a liar—but she just stole a loaf of bread from off that bulk over there. I seen 'er myself."

He leaned far in now, grabbing hold of the girl's ankle and dragging her toward him. A curious restless crowd was beginning to gather outside in the street—and as Amber gave him a kick in the chest with the toe of her shoe and a violent shove that sent him staggering, a loud joyous laugh went up. He lurched back; she leaned forward and slammed the door shut.

"Drive on, Tempest!" she shouted, and the coach rolled off, leaving justice to pick itself up from a swimming kennel of rain-washed filth.

For a moment both women were silent, the girl staring at Amber with gratitude, Amber breathing heavily from anger and the nervousness which the sight of a constable still roused in her.

"Oh—mam!" she cried at last. "How can I ever thank you? But for you, he'd have carried me off to Newgate! Lord, I didn't see 'im till he made a grab for me, and then I ran—I ran as fast as anything but the old fat pricklouse was right on my heels! Oh, *thank* you, mam, a million times! It was mighty kind for a great lady like yourself to care what happens to the likes of me. It wouldn't 've been any skin off your arse if I'd gone to Newgate—"

She rattled along in a quick light musical voice, the expressions playing vivaciously over her pretty face. She could have been no more than seventeen, fresh and dainty with clear blue eyes, light lashes and brows, and a golden sprinkle of freckles over her little scooped nose. Amber smiled at her, liking her immediately.

"These damned impertinent constables! The day's a loss to 'em that they don't throw half-a-dozen honest citizens into jail!"

The girl lowered her lashes guiltily. "Well—to tell you truly, mam, I did steal that loaf of bread. I've got it here." She tapped her cloak, beneath which it was concealed. "But I couldn't help it, I swear I couldn't! I was so hungry—"

"Then go ahead and eat it."

Without an instant's hesitation she took out the crusty split-topped loaf, broke a piece off one end and crammed it into her mouth, chewing ravenously. Amber looked at her in surprise.

"How long since you've eaten?"

The girl swallowed, took another great bite and answered with her mouth full. "Two days, mam."

"Ye gods! Here, take this and buy yourself a dinner."

From a little velvet bag inside her muff she emptied several shillings and dropped them into the girl's lap. By now they had drawn up before the theatre and the footman came to open the door. Amber gathered her skirts and prepared to get out and the girl leaned forward, staring through the glass windows with great interest.

"Lord, mam, are you goin' to the play?"

"I'm an actress."

"You are!" She seemed both pleased and shocked that her benefactress should be engaged in so exciting and disreputable a profession. But immediately she jumped out on her own side and ran around to make her curtsy to Amber. "Thank you, mam. You were mighty kind to me, and if ever I can do a good thing for you, I wish you'd be pleased to call on me. I'll not forget, you may be sure. Nan Britton's my name—serving-woman, though without a place just now."

Amber stopped, looking at her with interest. "You're a serving-woman? What happened to your last place?"

The girl lowered her eyes. "I was turned out, mam." Her voice dropped almost to a whisper and she added, "The lady said I was debauchin' her sons." But she looked up quickly then and added with great earnestness, "But I wasn't, mam!

I vow and swear I wasn't! 'Twas just the other way around!"

Amber laughed. "Well, my son's not old enough to be de-bauched. I'm looking for a woman myself, and if you want to wait in the coach after you've had your dinner we'll talk about this later."

She hired Nan Britton at four pounds a year and her clothes and lodging and food. Within three or four days they were good friends—Amber felt that Nan was the first real woman friend she had ever had—and Nan did her work quickly and well, taking the same delight in polishing a pewter pitcher or arranging Amber's hair that she did in riding to the 'Change or accompanying her and Rex on a visit to the Spring Gardens.

She was energetic, vivacious, and unfailingly good-natured, and as she became more sure of her place and accustomed to it, these qualities remained. Nan and Amber found much to dis-cuss, exchanging the most unabashed feminine confidences, and while Nan learned almost all there was to know about her mistress (except that she had been in Newgate and White-friars) Amber likewise heard the tale of Nan's adventures as a girl-servant in a household where there were four handsome boys. Her dismissal had come when one of them, deciding that he had fallen in love with Mrs. Nan, announced to his horrified parents that he intended to marry her.

When Rex was not there Nan shared the bed, but other-wise she slept on the trundle. As was customary, she was as much his personal servant as she was Amber's, helped him in and out of his clothes, was not embarrassed to be in the room when he was naked, and soon decided that Captain Morgan was the finest gentleman she had ever known. He enlisted her on his side and she urged Amber again and again to marry him.

"How Captain Morgan loves you, mam!" she would say in the mornings, while she brushed Amber's hair. "And he's the handsomest person, and the most genteel! I vow, he'd make any lady a mighty fine husband!"

But Amber, who merely laughed at first and teased Nan with having fallen in love with him herself, grew less and less inter-ested in such advice. "Captain Morgan's well enough, I sup-

284

pose," she said finally. "But after all, he's only an officer in the King's Guard."

"Well!" cried Nan, offended at such disloyalty. "And who will you have, mam? The King himself?"

Amber, smiling at this sarcasm, gave a superior lift of her eyebrows. She was just setting out for the theatre and now began pulling on her gloves. "I might at that," she drawled and, when Nan gasped, repeated, "Yes, I might at that." She strolled toward the door, leaving Nan staring pop-eyed after her, but just with her hand on the knob she turned suddenly. "But don't you dare breathe a word of this to Captain Morgan, d'ye hear me!"

After all, it might be only gossip that King Charles had told Buckingham who had told Berkeley who had told Kynaston who had told Amber that the King had a mind to lay with her.

CHAPTER NINETEEN

AMBER UNLOCKED THE door and started up the steps two at a time. She was eager to look at herself in a mirror, for she was sure that she must be very much changed. She had almost reached the top when the door to her apartments was flung open, and Rex loomed there above her. The light was at his back and she could not see the expression of his face, but knew by his voice that he was angry.

"Where in hell have you been?" he demanded. "It's half after two!"

Amber paused for one astonished moment, staring at him almost as if he were some intruding stranger. And then, with a haughty lift of her chin, she came on toward him and would have gone by without a word, but he grabbed her wrist and snatched her up close to him. His eyes had the dangerous glitter she had seen before when his ready jealousy was aroused.

"Answer me, you jilting little baggage! The plays at Whitehall are done by eleven! Who've you been with since then!"

For a long moment they stared at each other, and then at last Amber gave a pout and winced. "You're hurting me, Rex," she whimpered.

His face relaxed, and though he hesitated a moment he released her. But just as she moved away a heavy bag dropped out of her muff and fell clanking to the floor; by the sound it could only contain money. Both of them looked down at it, and then as Amber raised her eyes she saw that his were narrowed and gleaming with rage, and that the veins in his neck stood out.

"You God damned whoring little bitch," he said softly.

And then suddenly he grabbed her by the shoulders and began to shake her, harder and harder, until her head snapped back and forth so fast she felt that the top of it would come off.

"Who was it?" he shouted. "Who've you been laying with! Tell me, or by Jesus I'll break your neck!"

"*Rex!*" she cried imploringly. But the moment he let her go and she began to recover her senses her own rage mounted to heedless violence. "I was with the King!" she yelled at him. "*That's* where I was!" She began massaging her neck, and ended with a mutter, "Now what've you got to say!"

For a long moment he stared at her, incredulous at first, and then slowly, gradually, she saw the crumpling of his hopes and confidence. "You weren't," he said at last. "I don't believe it."

Her hands went up to arrange her hair where it had come loose, and she gave him a cruel superior little smile. "Oh, don't you?"

But he did and she knew it.

Then without another word he turned, took his cloak and sword and hat from the chair where he had left them, and started across the room. He gave her a last look of contempt and disgust before he went out, but she met it with merely a cool lift of the eyebrows. And as the door slammed behind him she gave a snap of her fingers, swirled about quickly and ran into the bedroom to a mirror.

For surely a woman who had been made love to by a king could not look like any common mortal. She half expected a glow, a luminous shimmer to her skin and hair, and was dis-

286

appointed to see that she looked no different except that her hair was tumbled and there were tired shadows beneath her eyes.

But I'm not the same! she assured herself triumphantly. I'm somebody now! I've lain with the King!

When Nan tried to wake her the following morning she shooed her away, rolling over onto her stomach, saying she'd sleep as long as she liked and they could do without her at rehearsal. By the time she finally did wake up it was almost noon and the rehearsal long since over. She yawned and stretched, sliding back the heavy draperies which had made the bed so hot and sultry that she was wet all over, and then suddenly she reached beneath the feather mattress and brought out the bagful of coins, dumping them onto the pillow so that she could count them again.

There was fifty pounds. Only to think of it—fifty pounds as a gift for the greatest honour a woman could have.

Before going to the theatre she took the money to deposit with Shadrac Newbold, and when she finally got there it was after two. As she had expected, her appearance in the tiring-room created a considerable sensation; all the women began to babble and shriek at once. Beck ran to throw her arms about her.

"Amber! We thought you weren't coming at all! Quick! Tell us about it—we're a-dying to hear! What was it like?"

"How much money did he give you?"

"What did he say?"

"How long were you there?"

"What did he do?"

"Was it different than it is with ordinary men?"

It was the first time that King Charles had sent for a player and their feelings were divided between personal jealousy and occupational pride. But curiosity over-rode both.

Amber was not reticent; she answered all their questions. She described the rooms of Edward Progers where she had been received first, the appearance of the King in his brocade dressing-robe, the new-born puppies which had slept beside their mother on a velvet cushion near the fireplace. She told them that he had been as kind and easy, as courteous as though she were a lady of the highest rank. But she did not add that she had been so scared she thought she would faint, and she hinted that he had given her at least a thousand pounds.

"When are you going again?" Beck asked at last, as Scroggs began to help Amber out of her clothes.

"Oh," she said casually, "sometime soon, I suppose. Maybe next week."

She was very confident, for though she had not spent more than an hour with him she had come away feeling that of all the women he had known she had pleased him best. It did not occur to her that perhaps the others had thought the same.

"Well, madame!" It was Tom Killigrew's voice, sounding cold and sarcastic as he made his way through the crowded room toward her. "So at last you've come."

Amber looked up in surprise, and then gave him a friendly smile. She was prepared to be no different from usual, in spite of her changed status—at least until she was more secure in her new place. "I'm a little late," she admitted, ducking her head into the gown which Scroggs held for her.

"You were not at rehearsal this morning, I believe."

"No." She thrust her arms through the sleeves and as Scroggs pulled the dress down her head appeared once more. "But that's no matter. I've played the part a dozen times—I know it well enough without rehearsing." She took up a mirror and half turned to face the light, examining the paint on her face and wiping away a little smear of lip-rouge rubbed onto her chin as she had struggled into the gown.

"With your permission, Madame St. Clare, I shall decide who will rehearse and who will not. I've given your part to Beck Marshall—I don't doubt you'll be able to play the strumpet well enough without rehearsal."

There was a concerted giggle at that. Amber shot Beck a quick glare and caught a smug look of mischief on her face. She was on the verge of bursting out that she would play her own part or none at all, when caution warned her. "But I know my lines! I know every one of 'em if I never rehearsed again! And the other's but a small part!"

"Perhaps it is, madame, but those who are too much occupied elsewhere must learn to be content with small parts—or with no part at all." He glanced around at the sparkling, smiling faces, on which malicious pleasure was but ill concealed. "And I advise all of you to keep that in mind—should another head be turned by attention from high places. Good-day." He swung about and left the room.

Amber was furious that he should have dared to treat her like that, and consoled herself with the promise that one day she would be even with him. I'll get his patent and run him out of the theatre, that's what I'll do! But for the benefit of the others she gave a shrug and a pout of her mouth.

"Pooh! Much I care! Who wants to be a player anyway?"

As the days began to pass, however, her disgrace was not alleviated by another request from the King. She continued to play small roles—and to wait for another invitation. No one let her forget that she had been sent for once and had expected to go again; the other women, even some of the actors, and the gallants who came back to the tiring-room, all knew about it and taunted her slyly. They seemed to have grown more insolent than ever. And Amber, though she tried to toss off the gibes with a laugh or counter them with some impertinence of her own, was sick at heart, disappointed and miserably unhappy. She felt that after all her bragging she would die of shame if he sent for her no more.

And though she had thought in her first high-flown confidence that she did not care whether or not she ever saw Rex again, she soon began to miss him. It was not quite a week after their quarrel that Beck told her he had given a diamond ring to Mrs. Norris of the rival playhouse and that she was saying he had offered to take her into keeping.

"Well, why tell me about it! It's nothing to me if he gives diamond rings to every tawdry little whore in Whetstone Park!"

But it was all bravado.

She was learning that Rex Morgan was more important to her happiness than she had ever suspected he could be. Though she had not realized it before, she knew now that he had protected her from much that would otherwise have been unpleasant. The tiring-room fops, for example, would never have dared patronize and bait her as they were doing. Without him she felt that she had been plunged suddenly into a hard and bleak world which hated her and wished her nothing but misfortune. There was no kindness or sympathy in any of them—they enjoyed her failure, battened upon her humiliation, were amused by her not-well-concealed anger and frustration.

She began to wish again that she had never seen Lord Carlton and never come to London.

Nan, however, continued optimistic even when ten days had gone by. She could think of more reasons why the King had been too busy to see her than he could possibly have found himself. "Don't be downcast, mam," she would say. "Lord, it takes up one's time—being a king."

But Amber refused to be comforted. Slumped in a chair before the fireplace, she muttered petulantly: "Oh, nonsense, Nan! You know as well as I do if I'd pleased 'im he'd have sent long ago!"

Nan sat beside her on a stool, working on a piece of embroidered satin, pale green with a whole English gardenful of flowers on it, which she intended as a petticoat for Amber. Now she gave a little sigh and made no answer, for she was finally beginning to grow discouraged herself. But when, just a few minutes later, there was a knock at the door she leaped up and rushed across the room.

"There!" she cried triumphantly. "That must be him now!"

Amber, however, merely looked around over the back of her chair toward the door, expecting to see one of the gallants or perhaps Hart or Kynaston come to visit her. But as Nan threw open the door she saw that a young boy stood there, dressed in some unfamiliar livery, and she heard him ask:

"Madame St. Clare?"

"I'm Madame St. Clare!" She jumped up and ran across the room. "What is it?"

"I come from Mr. Progers, madame. My master presents his service to you and asks if you will wait upon him at his lodgings tonight at half-after-eleven?"

It was the royal summons!

"Yes!" cried Amber. "Yes, of course I will!"

She picked up a coin off the table and gave it to him, and when he was gone she turned to throw her arms about Nan. "Oh, Nan! He did like me! He did remember! Only think! Tonight I'm going to the Palace!"

Suddenly she paused, made a stiff little bow and said: "Madame St. Clare? My master presents his service to you and asks if you will wait upon him tonight at his lodgings." And then she spun around and danced off across the room, laughing joyously. But in the midst of a whirl she stopped, her face serious again. "What shall I wear!" And chattering excitedly the two women ran into the bedroom. The clock on the mantel pointed to nine.

This time she was more sure than ever that he liked her.

Some of her earlier awe and self-consciousness was gone and they laughed and talked like old friends; she thought him the most fascinating man she had met since Lord Carlton. When she left he said, as he had the time before, "Good-night, my dear, and God bless you," gave her a playful slap on the buttocks, and another bagful of coins.

Tempest and Jeremiah were waiting for her at the Holbein Gate and they set off swiftly for home, rattling and clanging through the night.

But the coach had no sooner turned into the Strand than a party of horsemen rushed at them from out of the shadows. Before Amber knew what was happening Tempest had been hauled down from his perch and Jeremiah knocked to the ground. The horses began to rear and neigh with excitement. Amber was looking around her, wondering what she should do, when the door was flung open. A masked man leaned in, seized her by the wrist and began dragging her toward him. Amber screamed and started to struggle, though she knew well enough what little good that could do.

He gave her a rough shake. "Stop that! I won't hurt you— just hand me that bagful of coins his Majesty gave you! Quick!"

Amber was kicking at him and trying to tear his fingers loose from her wrist. But now as she leaned over to bite his hand he gave her a violent shove that knocked her across the coach and half onto the floor and she could see the gleam of moonlight on his levelled pistol. "Give me that bag, madame, or I'll shoot you! I have no time for playful tricks!"

Amber continued to hesitate, expecting to be rescued somehow, but as she heard the sound of the pistol cocking she took the bag from her muff and tossed it at him. He caught it, gave her a bow and backed away. But just before the door shut she heard a woman's triumphant laugh and a voice cried: "Many thanks, madame! Her Ladyship appreciates your charity! I promise you the money will be laid out in a good cause!" The door slammed and there was a sound of prancing horses' hoofs as they wheeled about and then started off again at a gallop—riding back down King Street toward the Palace.

Amber lay for a moment without moving, dumfounded. That voice! she thought. I've heard it somewhere before! And then suddenly she remembered: It was the same laugh, the same aggressive, high-pitched feminine voice she had heard that night outside the Royal Saracen—it was Barbara Palmer!

That was the last of Amber's visits to Whitehall.

The King, it was well known, liked to live in peace and quiet, and a jealous woman's sharp venomous tongue could make that impossible. Fortunately for her though, gossip spread that Charles had said he liked Madame St. Clare well enough—but not to the point of sacrificing his ease for her. And that was all that saved her. As it was they kept at her for several days, stinging and biting like malicious insects, but at last they grew tired of baiting her and found another victim.

By the time a fortnight had passed her life had settled back to normal. Everyone but Amber had forgotten that the King had ever sent for her.

But she did not forget or intend to forget. She nursed her new grievance against Barbara Palmer as carefully as she had the old. Someday, she promised herself, I'll make her sorry she ever was born. I'll find a way to get even with her if it's the last thing I do on earth! She spent much time and found much pleasure in imagining her revenge, but those images, like every-thing else she could not see or touch, slid gradually into some back compartment of her mind to be saved and brought out again when she had a use for them.

She had been entertaining, one night, a dozen young men and women whom she had invited to supper and they had just gone home, leaving the tables littered with dishes, the floors covered with nut-shells and fruit-peelings and a torn deck of cards. There were wine-bottles and glasses, with only a sticky sediment in the bottoms, the air was thick with tobacco smoke, and the furniture had all been pushed out of place.

While Nan began to pile up dishes and pick up nut-shells Amber went to stand with her back to the fireplace, raising her skirts to warm her buttocks. It was mid-December and the ground was covered with snow, the first in three years, and even the Thames was frozen over. For a while they talked idly about who had said what, whether a certain lady was now hav-ing an affair with a certain gentleman or with another, or with both, and discussed at some length the gowns and coiffures and figures of the women who had been present, to the detriment of each.

Amber had taken off her gown and stood yawning and stretch-ing in her puff-sleeved smock and frilly petticoats, when a low knock sounded at the door. Both of them started and then looked at each other, and Amber waited tensely as Nan crossed the room and flung back the bolt. Can it be—can it—

It was Captain Morgan who stood there, his long riding-cloak thrown across his shoulder, his hat pulled low. He looked in and his eyes met hers, pleading, his expression that of a small boy who has run away and now returns to his home. Instantly forgetting that she had hoped it might be the King's messenger, Amber ran to him with her arms outstretched.

"Rex!"

"Amber!" He swung her up off the floor, kissing her face again and again, and at last he gave a kind of sobbing exultant laugh. "Oh, my God! I'm *glad* to see you!" He put her onto her feet again but kept her in his arms, stroking her head, run-

293

ning his hands eagerly over her back. "Jesus, darling! I couldn't
stay away any longer! I love you—oh, God, I love you so much!"

There were tears in his eyes and from behind them came
Nan's surreptitious sniffle as she stood and watched them, smiling and crying at the same time. They both turned to look at
her and suddenly all three of them began to laugh.

"Come in, Rex darling! Close the door. Oh, how sweet of you
to come back! Why— Have you been waiting outside for the
others to leave?"

He smiled, gave a nod.

"But you knew them all! Why didn't you just come in! Lord,
it's bitter-cold out there!"

He hesitated. "Well—I wasn't sure you'd—let me in."

"Oh, Rex!"

Suddenly and thoroughly ashamed of herself Amber stood
staring at him, fully aware for the first time how kind and
generous and good he had been to her, and great tears rolled
down her cheeks.

"Here, darling! What are you crying for, you little minx?
This is a night for celebrating! Look at this—" He reached into
his pocket and drew out a jeweller's box, holding it toward her.

Slowly Amber took it from him and as she opened it Nan
edged forward so that she could see too. As she lifted the lid
both women gave a cry of astonished delight: there was a great
topaz stone set in a golden heart, depending from a heavy golden
chain. She looked up at him, doubtfully, for it must have cost
a great deal. "Oh, Rex!" she said softly. "It's beautiful—but—"

He gave a wave of his hand, dismissing her objections. "I had
a run of luck with the dice not long ago. And here, Mrs. Nan,
is something for you."

Nan opened the box he handed her to find a pair of gold
ear-rings set with tiny pearls. She gave a little scream of pleasure
and jumped up to kiss him on the cheek—for he was at least a
foot taller than she—and then quickly recovering herself she
blushed and curtsied and turned in confusion to run into the
bedroom.

"Hey!" called Rex. "Just a moment there, Mrs. Nan! Your
mistress and I have a fancy to that place." He swung Amber up

in his arms and started toward it. "You'll have to sleep out here tonight, sweetheart. This is a very special occasion."

The months began to go by swiftly, for she was happy and popular and thought herself very famous. The winter was unusually cold and through December, January and February there were hard frosts with much snow and ice, but at last the frost broke and there came the slush and mud and the new green buds of spring. Killigrew had put her into leading parts again, and she was very busy with her singing and dancing and guitar lessons.

When they played at Court or when he came to the Theatre Amber saw King Charles, and though he sometimes smiled at her, that was all. She heard the gossip that he was less interested in Castlemaine than he had been and was now engrossed in lovely Frances Stewart, though so far, they said, he had not succeeded in overcoming her scruples. Some thought that Mrs. Stewart was a fool and others that she was very clever, but there was no doubt she had captured the fickle heart of the King, and that was distinction enough in itself. Amber did not care whom he fell in love with if only Barbara Palmer lost by it.

In the middle of February Amber found herself pregnant again. And though she hesitated for some time, not telling Rex but arguing with herself as to whether or not she should marry him, in the end she went to Mrs. Fagg and had an abortion. This time it took more than a pot of herbs and a ride in a hackney and made her so sick that she had to spend most of a week in bed. Rex was wild with anger and fear when he found what she had done and begged her to marry him immediately.

"Why won't you, Amber? You say you love me—"

"I do love you, Rex, but—"

"But what?"

"Well, what if Luke—"

"He'll never come back and you know it as well as I do! Even if he did, it wouldn't matter. I could either kill him or get someone at Court to have the marriage annulled. What is it, Amber? Sometimes I think you put me off in hopes the King will send for you again. Is that it?"

She was sitting half propped up in bed, pale and sick and discouraged, staring at nothing. "No, Rex, that's not it. You know it isn't."

She was lying, for she did still hope, but nevertheless she was almost convinced that if she did not marry Rex Morgan now she would regret it in the future. What did it matter if she left the stage? She had been playing for a year and a half and could not see that she had got anything by it. Her nineteenth birthday was less than a month away and she felt that the time was passing rapidly, leaving her in a backwash. And it was true, as she had said, that she loved him, though she could never quite force from her heart the memory of Lord Carlton or her ambitions for a more glorious and exciting life.

"Let me think about it, Rex—just a little longer."

Her son was to be two years old on the 5th of April and, because she would not be free that day, Amber planned instead to go out on the 1st and take him the gifts she had bought. Rex left at seven while it was still dark outside, and the eaves dripped with rain that had fallen during the night.

He kissed her tenderly. "Twelve hours until I'll see you again. Have a good trip, darling, and give the little fellow a kiss for me."

"Why, Rex! Thank you!" Amber's eyes sparkled with pleasure, for usually Rex ignored her trips as he wanted to ignore the fact that she had a child; but since she had almost agreed to marry him he had evidently decided that he must reconcile himself to his step-son. "I'll bring one back from him to you!"

He kissed her again, gave a wave of his hand to Nan Britton, and was gone. Amber closed the door softly, leaning back against it for a moment, smiling. "I think I'll marry him, Nan," she said at last.

"Lord, mam, you should! A finer, kinder gentleman never lived—it makes my heart ache to see how he loves you. You'd be happy, mam, I know you would."

"Yes," she agreed. "I suppose I would be happy. But—"

"But what?"

"But that's all I'd be."

Nan stared at her, shocked and uncomprehending. "Good God, mam! What else d'ye want?"

It was not long before the singing-master arrived, and after him came the dancing-master to put her through the steps of the minuet—a new French dance which everyone was busily learning. Meanwhile Jeremiah trudged again and again through the parlour carrying buckets of hot water to pour into the wooden tub in the bedroom for her bath.

Nan washed her hair and rubbed it almost dry, piling it on top of her head where she secured it with half-a-dozen bodkins. It was now close to ten and at last the sun had come out, for the first time in many days, so that where she sat in her tub the warmth fell across her bare shoulders and filled her with pleasure. She felt, as she usually did, that it was a wonderful thing to be alive, and was urging herself to leave the soapy luxury of her bath when there was a knock at the door.

"I'm not home," called Amber after Nan. She had no intention of having her plans for this day disturbed, for anyone at all.

Nan returned a moment later. "It's my lord Almsbury, mam."

"Oh. Well, bring 'im in then." Almsbury had not stayed long in town the last autumn but had recently come again for the spring session of Parliament and he visited her frequently—though he had given her no more money. But Amber did not care, for she was very fond of him. "Is he alone?"

"No, there's another gentleman with him." Nan rolled her eyes, but Nan was easily impressed by men.

"Have 'em wait in the parlour—I'll be out in a trice."

She stood and began to dry herself with a towel. From the other room came the low sound of the men's voices; occasionally Nan giggled or burst into a peal of delighted laughter. Amber slipped into a green satin dressing-gown, took the bodkins out of her still slightly damp hair and ran a comb through it, stuck her feet into a pair of golden mules and started out. But she turned back again. After all—he might have someone of some consequence with him. She patted a little powder over her face, touched a perfume stopper to her wrists and throat, and smoothed some carmine into her lips. Then, pulling the neckline apart to show her breasts, she went to the door and opened it.

Almsbury stood before the fireplace and leaning against the mantel, smiling down at Nan, was Bruce Carlton.

CHAPTER TWENTY

HE RAISED HIS head quickly as she came in and their eyes met. Amber stood perfectly still, one arm braced against the door-jamb, staring at him. She felt her head begin to whirl and her heart to pound and she was suddenly paralyzed, unable to move or speak. He bowed to her then but Amber merely stood and trembled, cursing herself for a fool, but utterly helpless.

Almsbury came to her rescue. He crossed the room, kissed her casually, and slipped one arm about her waist. "What d'you think, sweetheart! The scoundrel put into town yesterday!"

"Did you?" said Amber weakly.

Bruce smiled, his eyes going swiftly down over her body. "The sailor's home from the sea."

"To stay?"

"No—at least not for long. Amber, may I go with you today?"

She glanced at Almsbury in surprise, for she had forgotten that she had told him her plans for the baby's birthday. "Yes, of course. Will you wait while I dress?"

With Nan she went back into the bedroom and when the door was shut she sank against it, her eyes closed, as exhausted as though she had just finished some tremendous physical labour. Nan looked at her in alarm.

"Lord, mam! What is it? You don't look well. Is *he* your husband?"

"No." She gave a shake of her head, and started for the dressing-table, but her legs felt as though every bone and muscle had dissolved. "Will you get out that new gown Madame Drelincourt just finished?"

"But it's raining again, mam. You might spoil it."

298

"Never mind!" snapped Amber. "Just do as you're told!" But she was instantly apologetic. "Oh, Nan, I'm sorry. I don't know what's the matter with me."

"Neither do I, mam. I suppose you'll not be wanting my company today?"

"No. Not today. I think you'd better stay here and polish the silver—I was noticing last night it's somewhat tarnished."

But as she painted her face and Nan dressed her hair she began to grow calmer, the blood seemed to flow in her veins again, and a passionate happiness replaced the first stunning sense of shock. She had thought him more handsome than ever, and the sight of him had filled her with the same intense irrational excitement she had felt the first time she had ever seen him. The past two years and a half had dissolved and vanished. Everything else in her life seemed suddenly unimportant, and dull.

Her new gown was made of chartreuse-coloured velvet and her shoes and stockings matched it exactly; her hooded cloak was topaz velvet, almost the same honey-rich colour as her eyes and hair, and she wore Rex Morgan's topaz heart around her neck. She picked up her great mink muff and started for the door, but Nan stopped her: "When will you be home, mam?"

Amber tried to answer casually, from over her shoulder. "Oh, I don't know. Maybe I'll be a little late."

She saw disapproval on Nan's face and knew that she was jealous for Rex, thinking that she ought not to go out there with another man, particularly a man who affected her as this one did.

"What about Captain Morgan?"

"The devil with Captain Morgan!" muttered Amber, and went back in to join Almsbury and Bruce.

When they were all in the coach, several gaily wrapped packages piled beside Amber, Almsbury gave a sudden snap of his fingers. "By God, I'm engaged to play at tennis with Sedley! Damned lucky thing I remembered!" With that he climbed out again, grinning back at them from the doorway. Bruce laughed and slapped him on the shoulder, Amber blew him a kiss, and the coach started off.

Behind them the Earl and Nan exchanged looks. "Well," said his Lordship, "there's no friend to love like a long voyage at sea," and he climbed into his own coach and rattled off in the opposite direction.

Amber turned instantly to Lord Carlton. "Bruce! Oh—is it really and truly you! It's been such a long time—oh, darling, it's been two years and a half!"

She was close beside him as she looked up, her eyes seeming to swim in some luminous light, and his arm went around her. He bent his head swiftly and his mouth came down hard upon hers. Amber returned his kiss with wild abandon, forgetting where they were, straining toward him with a longing to be crushed and enveloped. She had a sense of plunging disappointment when he released her, as if she had been cut off in the midst of a dream, but he smiled and his fingers passed over her face, lightly caressing.

"What a charming little witch you are," he said softly.

"Oh, Bruce, *am* I? Do you think so? Did you ever think about me—way over there?" She was intensely serious.

"I thought about you a great many times—more than I expected. And I worried about you too. I was afraid that someone might get that money away from you—"

"Oh, no!" protested Amber immediately. She would have died rather than let him know what had happened to her. "Don't I look well enough?" A wave of her hand indicated her expensive clothes, the coach they rode in, her own triumph over the great world. "I can shift for myself, I'll warrant you."

He grinned, and if he saw through her bluff he gave no indication of it. "So it seems. But I should have known you would. You've got the world's most marketable commodity—enough for ten women."

"What's that?" she asked him, putting on a demure face.

"You damned well know what it is, and I'm not going to flatter you any more. Tell me, Amber: What does he look like? How big is he?"

"Who?" She looked at him in sudden surprise, thinking that he meant Rex Morgan, and then they both burst into laughter. "Oh, the baby! Oh, Bruce, wait till you see him! He's grown so big I can hardly lift him. And he's so handsome! He looks just like you—his eyes are the same colour and his hair is getting darker all the time. You'll adore him! But you should have seen 'im at first. Lord, he was a fright! I was almost glad you weren't there—"

Both their faces sobered at that. "I'm sorry, darling. I'm sorry you had to be alone. You must have hated me for leaving you."

She put her hand over his and her voice was low and tender. "I didn't hate you, Bruce. I love you and I'll always love you. And I was glad I had him—he was a part of you that you'd left with me, and while I carried him I wasn't as lonely as I'd have been otherwise. But I don't want any more babies—it takes too long. Maybe someday when I get old and don't care how I look I'll have some more then."

He smiled. "And when will that be?"

"Oh, when I'm about thirty." She said it as though she would never be about thirty. "But tell me what you've been doing. What's it like in America? Where did you live? I want to know everything."

"I lived in Jamaica. It's an island, but I went to the mainland too. It's a wonderful country, Amber—wild and empty and untouched, the way England hasn't been for a thousand years. And it's over there waiting—for whoever will come to take it." He sat staring ahead now, talking softly and almost as though to himself. "It's bigger than anyone knows. In Virginia the plantations are spreading back from the coast, hundreds of thousands of acres, and still there's more land. There are wild horses and herds of wild cattle, and they belong to whoever can catch them. The forests are full of deer and every year the wild pigeons come over in clouds that blot out the sky. There's more than enough food in Virginia alone to feed everyone in England better than he's ever been fed before. The soil is so rich that whatever you plant grows like weeds. It's something to catch your imagination—something you never dreamed of—" He looked at her suddenly, his eyes glittering with passionate enthusiasm.

"But it isn't England!"

He laughed, relaxed again, the tension gone. "No," he agreed. "It isn't England."

As far as Amber was concerned that settled the matter, and they began to talk, instead, of his adventures at sea. He told her that the life was unpleasant, that nothing could make a man uglier than being shut up for weeks at a time on a ship with other men, but that it was not very dangerous and was a sure road to riches. That was why so many seamen preferred sailing with the privateers to joining the British navy or the merchant fleets. At that moment the Thames was crowded with prizes just brought into port and more were arriving every day.

"I suppose you're a mighty rich man, now."

"My fortunes are considerably improved," he admitted.

It took an hour and a half to reach Kingsland, for the road was unpaved most of the way and the recent heavy rains had turned it into a slough. Tempest and Jeremiah had to pry the wheels free a dozen times.

But at last they arrived and went around to the kitchen-door of Mrs. Chiverton's pretty little thatched cottage, where they found her just cleaning the remains of the noon-day meal. Amber had given her frequent and generous gifts of money, for she wanted her son to live in a comfortable home, and the cottage now had an air of pleasant warmth and friendliness that it had not had at first.

The baby lay in his cradle, which he had now almost outgrown, flat on his back and sleeping soundly. Amber put up a cautioning finger as they came in and, walking softly, went over to look at him. His cheeks were flushed and there was a sheen of moisture on his eyelids, his breathing came quietly and regularly. For a long moment Bruce and Amber stood staring down at him, and then their eyes turned and met in a look of mutual pride and congratulation. Lord Carlton's slender, hard aristocratic hands reached down and closed under his son's armpits and he lifted him to his chest.

He woke up then, yawning, looked in some surprise at the man who held him, and then catching sight of Amber broke into a sudden smile and reached out for her.

"Mother!"

After a while, when they had eaten a bowl of hot pottage which Mrs. Chiverton insisted they have, they began to unwrap the baby's presents. There were numerous toys, including drums and soldiers and a Jack-in-the-Pulpit—a Puritan preacher which popped out of a box and swayed comically from one side to the other. And there was a doll with real blonde hair and an extensive wardrobe which Amber had bought for Mrs. Chiverton's four-year-old daughter. They stayed until mid-afternoon, but when finally they got ready to leave, the baby cried and wanted to go with them. While Amber tried to quiet him Bruce gave Mrs. Chiverton fifty pounds, telling her that he was grateful for the good care his son had received.

It was raining again as they started back, Amber chattering with the greatest enthusiasm and excitement about the baby. For she had been pleased and a little surprised to find that Bruce—who she had half expected would be an indifferent father—seemed to love the child as much as she did. But even while she talked she was conscious again of the rising surge of passion in both of them, temporarily calmed and forced back while they had been at the cottage. Now it was once more wild and violent, immediately demanding, determined to sweep away two years and a half in a few moments of savage union.

Stopping in the midst of a sentence she turned and looked up at him. Bruce gave a swift glance out the window, and as one arm went about her he leant forward to rap on the side of the coach. "We're coming to Hoxton," he said quickly to Amber. "I know a good inn there. Hey!" he raised his voice to a shout. "Stop up here at the Star and Garter!"

When Amber got home, after nine o'clock that night, she found Nan sitting beside the fireplace mending one of Rex's shirts while he stood next to her, his hands jammed into his pockets and a scowl on his face. Amber paused, looking at him with a sense of surprise, for he seemed almost unreal to her— and then he had crossed the room and had her hands in his.

"My God, darling! What happened! I was just going out to try to find you!"

She forced a smile. "Nothing happened, Rex. The baby didn't

want me to go and I kept staying on—and then the coach got stuck and once it almost turned over." She reached up to caress his cheek, a little sorry to have cheated him as she had, for he looked at her with such adoration and not the faintest hint of doubt or suspicion. "You mustn't worry about me all the time, Rex."

"I can't help it, darling. I love you, you know."

Amber turned away to escape the expression in his eyes and as she did so she saw Nan's look of disapproval and resentment.

Early the next morning, when they were alone, Amber asked her if she had told Rex about the visit of Almsbury and Lord Carlton. Nan was making the bed, smoothing out the sheets with a bed-staff, and she answered without looking at Amber.

"No, mam, I did not," she said crisply. "Lord, I'm sure I don't know why you should think I'd meddle in your business. I never have before. What's more, I wouldn't tell Captain Morgan ,you were playing him false for a thousand pound. It would break his heart!" She turned around all at once and the two women stood staring at each other; there was a gleam of moisture in Nan's eyes.

"You weren't so finical when it was the King I was playing him false with!"

"That was different, mam. That was serving the Crown. But this—this is wicked. Captain Morgan loves you beyond his own life— It's—it's not kind!"

Amber gave a sigh. "No, Nan, it's not kind. But I can't help it. I'm in love with Lord Carlton, mad in love with him. Nan! He's Bruce's father! Not my husband—I married Luke after Lord Carlton had gone to America. Oh, you've got to help me, Nan! Help me to keep Rex from finding out. While he's here I've got to see him—and I will see him!—but he'll be gone soon, in a month or two, and when he's gone Rex will be none the wiser. I'll marry him then—to make it up to him. *Will* you help me, Nan? Will you promise?"

As Amber talked Nan's flexible face changed, her expressions shifting like the play of sunlight over water, and at the end she ran to throw her arms about Amber. "Oh, I'm sorry, mam! I didn't know—I didn't guess—I thought he was just some gentleman you'd taken a fancy to." Suddenly she smiled broadly, holding onto Amber's arms. "And so he's little Bruce's father! Oh, of course! Why, they look alike!" She gave a gasp and put one hand to her mouth. "Lord, but it's mighty lucky the Captain would never go out with you to see 'im! If he ever saw his Lordship—"

Carlton was staying at Almsbury House and two days later Amber sent a note inviting him, with Almsbury and his countess, to see the play—she wheedled Killigrew into reserving four seats in the front row of the King's Box—and she asked them to have supper with her in her apartments afterward. Lord and Lady Almsbury were intended as decoys in the event that Captain Morgan should arrive unexpectedly.

They accepted, and for the next forty-eight hours Amber was in a flurry of excited preparation. She had Nan call in a woman to help her clean so that every speck of dust was brushed from the drapes and the walnut furniture oiled and polished until it gleamed. She went herself to the New Exchange to buy a great supply of artificial silk flowers, since the fresh ones were not yet in bloom, and she badgered Madame Drelincourt into finishing a new gown for her several days before it had been promised. She consulted the head-cook at Chatelin's about the supper and the wine, trying to remember everything that Bruce liked best, and just before she left for the theatre she repeated once more to Nan the multifarious instructions which covered each smallest detail.

Halfway down the stairs she stopped suddenly, turned about, and ran back again. "Don't forget to put a decanter of water on the tray with the brandy, Nan! Lord Carlton likes it that way!"

She got there very early and, once dressed and painted, went down into the pit to circulate about among the young men. She made a great show of all her charm and gaiety, hoping that Lord Carlton would see her and be impressed and perhaps a little jealous to find how popular she was with all the fops. But it was almost three-thirty and she was once more back behind the curtains when she saw him come in.

Lord and Lady Almsbury walked ahead, going to the seats

which Amber had sent some boys to keep for them; but as one of the ladies leaned back and put out a hand to take hold of Bruce's wrist he stopped, smiling, and bowed. Amber watched with anxious alarm while he bent over to hear what she was saying and saw her languid-eyed stare, the lazy intimate grasp which her hand kept on his, as though they had been long and well acquainted.

"Hey!" She heard Beck's voice suddenly just beside her. "Who's the handsome fellow my Lady Southesk is giving an assignation to?" Carnegie's husband had recently succeeded to the earldom of Southesk.

"That's Lord Carlton and he's *not* making her an assignation!"

Beck looked at her in mild surprise and then smiled. "Well—" she drawled. "And if he is or isn't—what's that to you, pray?"

Quick anger at her own foolishness rushed over Amber, for she knew well enough that in spite of the half-hearted friendship which existed between them nothing would please Beck so much as an opportunity to create trouble between her and Rex Morgan. "It's nothing at all to me! But I happen to know he's laid his affections elsewhere."

"Oh? And where's that?" Beck's voice was a musical purr and her eyes gleamed with sly malice.

"On my Lady Castlemaine!" snapped Amber, though it burnt her tongue to say it, and she flounced off.

She wished then that she had not invited Bruce to come back to the tiring-room after the play—for she knew that Beck's sharp eyes would be upon them—and just before the last act she sent a boy to their box with a note asking him to meet her at Almsbury's coach instead. She was not on the stage at the end of the play, and she rushed through her dressing to be ready to go by the time the crowds began streaming out of the theatre.

She left before anyone had returned to the tiring-room and made her way over to Almsbury's coach, where Bruce stood waiting at the opened door. "Bruce! I'm so glad to see you!" She lowered her voice and glanced quickly around, for she did not want to be seen or overheard by anyone who might know Rex. "I sent you that note because I thought—"

He smiled. "Never mind, Amber. No excuses are necessary. I believe I know what you thought. May I present you to Lady Almsbury?"

She gave him a quick glance of indignation—for she wished he would not understand her motives so readily, or would be more offended by them when he did. But he seemed not to notice the look, took hold of her arm and began to make the introductions.

As Amber saw at once, Emily, Lady Almsbury, was by no means a beauty. Her hair, her eyes, even the clothes she wore, seemed indefinite in colouring, though there was nothing otherwise amiss in her features, and her teeth were white and even. Paint and false curls, a few patches and a low-necked gown, as well as a little natural audacity, might have made quite another woman of her. And it was noticeable that she was pregnant again.

Lord! thought Amber. How unprofitable it is to be a man's wife!

Bruce and Amber went to ride in her coach and with them went a little Negro boy who could have been no more than five or six and who had much ado to keep his master's cloak, which he carried, from getting into the mud. He was perfectly black and shiny, so that the whites of his eyes gleamed in his face, and as Amber smiled at him he gave her a broad ingratiating grin.

"This is Tansy," Bruce explained. "I got him a year ago in Jamaica."

Some of the nobility owned black servants, but Amber had never seen one of them at close range before and she examined him as though he were some small inanimate object or a new dog, looking at the pale-coloured palms of his hands and admiring the dazzling whiteness of his teeth. He wore a splendid suit of sapphire-blue satin and his head was wound in a silver-cloth turban, stuck through with a large ruby pin. But his shoes were shoddy and much too large for him and he was then easing the heel of one down off his foot with the toe of the other, while his big solemn eyes stared up at her.

"Oh, Bruce, what a pretty little moppet he is!" cried Amber. "Can he talk?" And without waiting for an answer she immediately asked him, "Why do they call you Tansy?"

" 'Cause my mother ate a tansy puddin' before I was born." He had a soft liquid voice which it was difficult for her to understand. He stood up in the coach, leaning with one elbow on the seat beside Bruce, and he did not once glance out the window at the busy streets through which they were passing.

"What does he do? What's he for?"

"Oh, he's very useful. He plays the merry-wang—that's a kind of guitar the Negroes have—and makes coffee. And of course he sings and dances. I thought perhaps you'd like to have him."

"Oh, Bruce, is he for me! You brought him across the ocean for me! Oh, thank you! Tansy—how would you like to stay here in London with me?"

He looked from Amber to Bruce, then shook his head. "No, sir, mam. I's goin' back to see Mis' Leah."

Amber looked questioningly at Bruce, and caught a quick passing smile on his face. "Who's Miss Leah?"

"She's my housekeeper."

Instant suspicion showed in her eyes. "Is she a blackamoor too?"

"She's a quadroon."

"What the devil's that?"

"It's one who has a quarter Negro blood and the rest white."

Amber gave a mock shudder. "They must be a scurvy lot!"

"Not at all. Some of them are very beautiful."

"And do they call 'em all 'miss'?" she demanded sarcastically. "Or only yours!"

He smiled. "That's the way Tansy pronounces 'Mrs.' "

She gave him a sidewise glance of jealousy and mistrust, and though she wanted to ask him point-blank if the woman had been his mistress he was still a little strange to her and she did not quite dare. I'll ask Tansy, she decided. I can find out from him some way.

308

At that moment they stopped before her lodging-house. Bruce helped her out and whatever she was about to say to him was cut short by the appearance of Almsbury's coach, which had followed close behind them. She and the countess walked upstairs together, chatting about the weather and the play and the audience, and Amber found herself liking her very well, for she seemed kind and generous and apparently had none of the envy or malice which Amber habitually expected in a woman.

The meal was everything that Amber had hoped it would be.

There was a hot thick pea soup, steamingly fragrant, with leeks and chopped bacon and small crusty meat-balls that floated on the surface. There was roast duck stuffed with oysters and onions and walnuts; fried mushrooms; sweet biscuits; and an orange pudding baked in a dish lined with a crisp flaky puff-paste and decorated with candied orange-blossoms. And she had ordered a potful of black coffee because she knew that Bruce liked it—it was becoming a fashionable, though still an expensive, drink. The men were enthusiastic and Amber was as pleased as though she had cooked it all herself.

When supper was done they went into the parlour to talk; Amber and Lady Almsbury sat on the couch before the fire while the men took chairs, one on either side of them. For a few minutes Amber and her Ladyship discussed the new fashions —gowns were now being made with trains three feet long—and Bruce and the Earl talked of the Dutch war, which both were sure would come soon. But Amber presently grew tired of that. She had not invited Bruce there to talk to Almsbury.

"You say you're not here to stay, my lord," she said now, turning to him. "What do you intend doing?"

Bruce, who sat with both elbows resting on his wide-spread legs, holding his brandy glass in his two hands, glanced across at Almsbury before he answered her.

"I'm going back to Jamaica."

"Why there, for Heaven's sake? I've heard it's a nasty place."

"Nasty or not, it's a very good place for my purpose."

"And what's your purpose, pray?" She was thinking of Mrs. Leah.

"To get some more money."

"Some more? Aren't you rich enough by now?"

"Is anyone ever rich enough any time?" Almsbury wanted to know.

Amber ignored him. "Well, now, sure you don't intend to be a pirate all the rest of your life!" She knew well enough what was the difference between a pirate and a privateer, but liked to make his profession sound as disreputable as she could.

Bruce smiled. "No. Another year or two, perhaps, depending on what luck I have—and then I'm through."

Her face brightened. "Then you'll come back here to stay?"

He drew a deep breath, drained his glass, and as he answered her he started to get up. "Then I think I'll go to America and plant tobacco."

Amber stared at him, nonplussed. "Go to America!" she cried, and then added, "To plant tobacco! Why, you must be out of your head!" Suddenly she sprang up and ran after him where he had gone to pour himself another glass of brandy. "Bruce! You're not serious!"

He looked down at her. "Why not? I don't intend to stay here and play at cross-or-pile with the Court politicians for the next thirty years."

"But why America! It's so far away! Why not plant your tobacco here—in England?"

"For one thing, there's a law against planting tobacco in England. And even if there were not it would still be impractical. The soil isn't suitable and tobacco culture requires a great deal of ground—it exhausts the land quickly and you've got to have room to spread out."

"But what will you get by it? You won't need money over there—money's no good if you're not where you can spend it!"

He did not answer her, for just then the door opened and Rex Morgan came in; and paused in surprise to find her staring up so intensely at a man he had never seen before. Amber was disappointed and a little troubled, wondering what her expression had been at the moment he had opened the door, but immediately she ran to take his hand, welcoming him gaily.

"Come in, darling! I wasn't expecting you and we've eaten

everything but the nut-shells! Here—let me present my guests—"

Rex had already met Almsbury but neither the Countess nor Bruce, and once the introductions were acknowledged Amber made a quick suggestion that they play cards. She did not want the men to begin talking. They sat down to a five-handed game of lanterloo and as Almsbury began to shuffle the cards Amber saw Rex and Lord Carlton exchange glances across the table that sent a chill down her spine.

Oh, Lord! she thought. If he guesses!

She played badly, unable to keep her mind on her cards, and the room seemed too hot and close. But Bruce paid her no particular attention and was as casual in his manner as though he were merely the friend who had come along because he happened to be staying at Almsbury's house. And in her turn Amber tried desperately to convince Rex of her undivided interest in him. She flirted with him as flagrantly as though they had just met, asked his opinion on several matters of no importance, called Nan to fill his wine-glass the moment it was empty, and scarcely looked at Bruce. For he had given her no reason as yet to think she would not continue to need Rex Morgan.

But she was uncomfortably nervous and the back muscles of her neck were beginning to ache when Almsbury, giving his wife's pregnancy as an excuse, suggested that it was time to go home. She threw him a look of grateful relief.

Nan brought out the men's cloaks and plumed hats and Amber walked into the bedroom with Lady Almsbury, telling her how pleased she was to have made her acquaintance. She held her cloak for her and took her fan while Emily adjusted her hood, then gave back her own instead. Emily did not notice the change and they went back into the parlour. The three men were having a last drink and all of them seemed to be on perfectly friendly terms; when they left Rex invited them to come again.

Nan went out with a candle to light them to the bottom of the stairs and Amber waited a minute or two. "Oh!" she cried then. "I've got her Ladyship's fan!" And before Rex, who had gone into the dining-room to pick up a cold biscuit, could offer to take it down for her she had run out of the room. She reached them when they had just gotten to the bottom of the stairs, for Emily had to move with care, and all of them laughed politely as they made the exchange.

But as she turned to go back up again she gave a swift glance around, and then whispered to Bruce, "I'll come to Almsbury House tomorrow morning at eight," and before he could reply or object she had picked up her skirts and was running up the stairs once more.

Bruce was busy most of the time.

The days he spent down at the wharves overseeing the cleaning and repairing and supplying of his ships, signing new men, and talking to the merchants from whom he ordered provisions, for many of them had a monetary share in his ships. Privateering was the greatest speculative business of the nation, and not only the King and courtiers but most of the great merchants and many of the lesser ones were engaged in it, usually through money invested in a venture such as his. At night he went to Whitehall, saw the plays there, gambled in the Groom Porter's Lodge, attended the never-ending succession of balls and supper-parties.

Consequently Amber saw him for only an hour or two in the morning when she visited his apartments at Almsbury House, and she did not go every day because, when he could, Rex waited until she was ready to start for the Theatre before he left. But as far as she knew he had no slightest suspicion that she had seen Lord Carlton either before or since that one night. And she intended to make sure that he never would suspect it.

But contending against her determination to be cautious and clever, to keep Rex Morgan's confidence and his love, was the violent infatuation which made her reckless in spite of herself. She had begged Bruce again to take her with him when he went and again he had refused, nor would any amount of tears and imploring change his mind. She was accustomed to Rex, who could usually be coaxed, and his obdurate refusal filled her with frantic, impotent fury.

"I'll stow away on your ship then!" she told him one day, half-joking, but thinking nevertheless that if she did there would be nothing he could do about it. She would be there and he couldn't very well throw her overboard.

"And I'll send you back again when I find you, no matter how far out we are." His eyes had a warning glitter as he looked at her. "Privateering's no game of handy-dandy."

Amber worried because she knew that soon he would be gone and she would not see him at all—perhaps for years—but she worried even more because now, while he was here, the days were getting away from them one by one and they were able to be together only for a snatched hour or two at a time. She longed to spend whole days and nights with him, uninterrupted by either his obligations or hers. And at last she discovered the solution—a plan so simple and obvious it seemed incredible she had not thought of it weeks ago. They would go away together into the country.

"And what about Captain Morgan?" Bruce wanted to know. "Is he going along too?"

Amber laughed. "Of course he isn't! Don't you trouble yourself about Rex. I'll take care of him, I warrant you. I know just what I'm going to tell him—and he'll never suspect a thing. Oh, please, Bruce! You will go, won't you?"

"My dear—I'd like to, of course. But I think you'd be taking a very great risk for a very small reward. Suppose that he—"

But she interrupted him swiftly. "Oh, Bruce, he won't! I know Rex better than you do—he'll believe anything I tell 'im!"

He gave her a slow smile. "Darling, men aren't always as gullible as women think they are."

He finally agreed, though, to go away with her for five or six days, after he had settled his business. A Spanish merchant-fleet was known to be returning from Peru, heavily laden with gold and silver, and he hoped to intercept it sometime at the end of May, which meant that he must leave London in the middle of the month.

And, as when he had agreed to bring her to London, Amber thought that she had persuaded him. She still did not realize

313

that selfishness and cynicism made him indifferent to what might happen to her. He had warned her, but he did not believe that he either could or should protect her from the risks of living and of her own headstrong temper.

They took the main road down through Surrey toward the sea-coast. As in London it was raining—and had been almost every day for a month and a half—so that they travelled slowly and had to make frequent stops to haul the coach out of mud-bogs, for the roads were now nothing more. But the countryside was beautiful. This was the rich agricultural heart of England and prosperous farms lay spread over the rolling hills; many of them were enclosed by hedges, though that practice was as yet an uncommon one. The cottages and manor-houses were made of cherry-coloured brick and silver oak and the luxuriant gardens were massed with purple-and-white violets, tulips, crimson ramblers.

Amber and Bruce sat side by side, hands lightly clasped, looking out the glass windows and talking softly. As always his presence gave her a sense of finality, a sureness that this was all she wanted from life and that it would last as it was forever.

"It makes me think of home," she said, gesturing to take in the village through which they were passing. "Marygreen, I mean."

" 'Home'? Does that mean you'd like to go back?"

"Go back—to Marygreen? I should say *not!* It gives me the vapours to so much as think of it!"

The first night they stopped at a little inn, and since the rain continued they decided to stay there. It was warm and comfortable and friendly and the food was good. The host was a veteran of the Civil Wars, a bluff old fellow who cornered Bruce every time he saw him and went into lengthy reminiscences of Prince Rupert and Marston Moor. They were the only guests there.

But the week which she had expected would pass so slowly seemed to pick up speed as it went and the precious minutes and hours rushed along, slipping out of her hands as she tried to catch at them and drag them back. So soon now it would be over—he would be gone—

"Oh, *why* does the time go by so fast, just when you want it to go slow!" she cried. "Someday I hope the clock will stand still and never move!"

"Haven't you learned yet to be careful of what you wish for?"

They spent the days idly, lay long in the mornings, and went to bed early at night. While the rain poured down outside they sat before the fire and played card games, costly-colours, putt, wit-and-reason; invariably he won and, though she thought that she had become very clever, he always seemed to know when she was cheating. If the evenings were nice, as two or three of them were, they bowled on the green beside the inn.

They had brought the baby with them—as well as Nan and Tansy—and Bruce told her that he had arranged with Almsbury to take him from Mrs. Chiverton and put him into the nursery with the Earl's two sons. Amber was delighted to see how intensely fond he was of the child she had borne him. It encouraged her to think that sooner or later he would give up his roving life, and marry her—or take her to America with him.

Until the last day she kept her resolution not to argue with him, and then she could not resist making one more effort to convert him. "I don't see why you want to live in America, Bruce," she said, pouting a little before he had even had time to answer. "What can you like about that country—full of nothing but wild Indians and blackamoors! Why, you said yourself there isn't a town the size of London in the whole of it. Lord, what can you find to do? Why don't you come back to England and live when you're done privateering?"

The rain had stopped and the sun come out hot. They had spread a blanket beneath a beech-tree, heavily laden with long drooping clusters of purple blossoms, and Amber sat cross-legged on it while Bruce lay stretched out on his stomach. As she talked she kept an eye on the baby who had wandered some yards away to watch a duck and several little tawny ducklings swimming on a shallow pond; from his hand trailed a neglected wooden doll tied to a cord. She had just cautioned him not to go too close, but he was absorbed in the ducks and paid her scant attention.

Bruce, with a stalk of green grass between his teeth and

his eyes narrowed against the sun, looked up at her and grinned.

"Because, my darling, the life I want for myself and my children doesn't exist in England any more."

"Your children! How many bastards have you, pray? Or are you married?" she asked suddenly.

"No, of course not." He gave a quick gesture as she started to open her mouth. "And let's not talk about that again."

"Oh, I wasn't going to! You have such a damned high opinion of yourself! I don't have to go begging for a husband, let me tell you!"

"No," he agreed. "I don't suppose you do. I'm only surprised that you aren't married already."

"If I'm not it's because I've been a silly fool and thought that you'd— Oh, I'm not going to say it! But *why* don't you like England? Lord, you could live at Court and have as fine a station as any man in Europe!"

"Perhaps. But the price is too high for my purse."

"But you'll be rich as anything—"

"It isn't money I mean. You don't know anything about the Court, Amber. You've only seen it from the outside. You've seen the handsome clothes and the jewels and the fine manners. That isn't Whitehall. Whitehall's like a rotten egg. It looks good enough until you break it open—and then it stinks to the heavens—"

She did not believe that and was about to tell him so, when there was a sudden splash and a loud howl from the baby as he tumbled into the pond. Bruce was on his feet at a bound and running, with Amber close behind, to pick his son out of the water. And when the little boy found himself unhurt and safe in his father's arms all three burst into laughter. Bruce set him up on one shoulder and they started for the inn to get him out of his wet clothes.

It was late the next night when she left Bruce at Almsbury House. A nurse he had already hired came out to get the baby and disappeared with him. But for a moment Bruce stood in the rain beside the opened door of the coach, while Amber struggled with her tears. This time she was determined that he should go away with a pleasant memory of her, but her throat ached painfully and she thought that she would never be able to bear the parting. For hours she had kept herself talking and thinking of other things, but now she could pretend no longer. This was goodbye.

"I'll see you when you come back, Bruce—" she whispered, for she could not trust her voice.

He stood looking at her, but for a moment did not answer. Then he said, "I've put a thousand pound with Shadrac Newbold in your name—you can have it on twenty days' notice. If you have any trouble with Morgan because of this, that will help take care of you." He leaned forward quickly, kissed her, and turned to walk away. She watched him go, fading from sight in the wet darkness, and then suddenly she could control herself no longer and she began to cry.

She was still crying when she reached the Blue Balcony. She felt as though she had been away for a great while, it was almost strange to her, and she climbed the stairs slowly. The door, as she tried it, was already unlocked and she went in. Rex was there.

His eyes were bloodshot and he looked as though he had not shaved for days, nor perhaps slept either, for his face was haggard and his clothes rumpled. Surprised to find him there and in that condition she stood perfectly still for a moment, sniffling unconsciously though the tears had stopped at sight of him, and one hand went up to wipe her streaked face.

"Well," he said quietly at last. "So your Aunt Sarah died. Nothing else, I suppose, could make you look like that."

Amber was wary, for she could not be sure if that was sarcasm in his voice. But she did not think—if he knew where she had been—that he would be so still and calm. "Yes," she said. "Poor Aunt Sarah. It was a mighty bad shock to me—she was the only mother I ever—"

"Don't trouble yourself to lie to me. I know where you've been and who you've been with." He spoke between his teeth, biting off each word with a savage snap, and though his voice did not rise she saw all at once that he was insanely, murderously angry. She opened her mouth to make some denial but he cut her off. "What kind of a fool do you take me for? Don't you suppose it ever occurred to me to wonder why that brat of yours had the same first name he has? But you'd made me so many promises— Oh, you'd never be unfaithful to the man who loved you, not you! I was determined to believe in you and trust you no matter what happened. And then both of you went out of town at the same time— You ungrateful jilting little slut—I've been here four days and nights, waiting for you to come back— Do you have any idea what I've been through since you went? Of course you don't! You've never thought about anyone but yourself in all your life— You've never cared who you hurt if you got what you wanted— You selfish, mercenary, whoring little bitch, I should kill you—I'd *like* to kill you—I'd like to watch the breath go out of you—"

His voice went on in a low monotonous tone that did not sound like him and his face was twisted with rage and sickness and jealousy into something she could scarcely recognize. This was a man she had never known existed beneath the quiet gentle Rex Morgan she had taken so casually for granted; this was some malevolent, savage stranger.

Amber stared at him in terror. She took a step or two backward, intending to turn and run if he made the slightest move. Slowly he started toward her. And like a frightened animal she whirled, but he was quicker; before she knew what was happening he had grabbed her arm and jerked her back again. She screamed, but he clapped one hand over her mouth and gave her head a vicious shake.

"Shut up, you lousy little coward! I'm not going to hurt you!" He was straining every nerve and muscle, exhausted by jealousy and sleeplessness, to hold his fury in leash. Amber's eyes looked up at him, big and glittering with fear, but the grasp he had on her was so tight she could not have moved if she had tried. "I want you to live—I want you to live long enough to know how I've felt—I want you to live and wish you were dead because he is—" Suddenly he let her go.

Relieved, Amber shook herself a little. She had scarcely realized what he was saying but now, as he started out, she looked up suddenly. "Where are you going?" All at once she understood what he had meant. "Rex! You're not going to fight him!"

"I'm going to fight him, and kill him."

318

Confident that her own life was no longer in danger, Amber gave him a scowl of contemptuous disgust. "You're crazy, Rex Morgan, if you do! He's a better swordsman than you are—"

He slammed his hat onto his head, picked up his cloak and went swiftly out of the room. At the door he knocked into Nan and Tansy and Jeremiah just coming in with their arms full of boxes, but he brushed on by without a word of apology.

Nan caught her balance and her blue eyes widened as she turned to watch him running down the stairs. "Where's he going in such a rage, mam?" She looked back anxiously at Amber. "He's not going to fight Lord Carlton!"

"He's a fool if he does!" muttered Amber, and turned away.

But Nan whirled about, and started down the stairs after him, crying, "Captain Morgan! Captain Morgan! Come back here!"

CHAPTER TWENTY–ONE

AN HOUR LATER Bruce came to her rooms.

He walked in swiftly when Nan opened the door, and there was a dark scowl on his face that did not clear when Amber came running out of the bedroom in her dressing-gown. Her eager expectant smile disappeared as she saw his angry expression.

"Why, Bruce! What is it? What's happened?"

He crossed to her and gave her a folded sheet of paper on which the seal had been broken. "Look at this! It was just brought to me at Almsbury House!"

She took it and began to read:

"Sir: You have done me an injury which one gentleman may not accept from another. I will see you tomorrow morning at five in Marrowbone Fields, where Tyburn Brook meets the road. Have your sword in your hand. Or I shall be at your service at the earliest time you shall appoint.

"Your servant, sir,

"CAPTAIN REX MORGAN."

The handwriting was scratchy and the pen had splattered several times, streaking the page with black ink.

In his rage Rex had ignored half the formal appointments for a duel, for it was customary to let the challenged name the time and the place and the weapon. Nor had he said anything of seconds, either one or two of which were usually selected by each man, according to the French style of fighting imported into England and already responsible for many unnecessary deaths.

Amber looked up at him, giving back the note. "Well?"

"Well! Is that all you have to say! for the love of God, Amber, what's the matter with you! You know that he'll lose his rank and have to go into exile— He might never come back again! If you don't care what happens to him you should at least have the sense to consider your own future! Get hold of him tonight and tell him there's no reason for this ridiculous meeting!"

Amber was astonished, and then offended, for he obviously did not consider her sufficient cause for a duel. Her pride hurt, she wanted to hurt him, and now a mocking smile curled the corners of her mouth.

"You surprise me, Lord Carlton," she said softly.

Bruce looked at her, his eyes narrowed. "What do you mean by that?"

She gave a little shrug. "I wouldn't expect to find you troubled about a meeting with swords. I should think a privateer could defend himself as well as any other man."

Nan gasped, one hand going to her mouth as though to stop the words her mistress had just spoken. But Bruce's face had a sort of angry contempt on it.

"I'm not afraid to meet him and you damned well know it! But I don't care to fight a man without a better reason than this!"

"If you mean me, Lord Carlton, Rex thinks I'm reason enough!"

"Tell him you've already had a son by me and see what he thinks about it then!"

"He knows it—and he still wants to fight you! Anyway, I don't know where he's gone! If you don't want to fight, you'll have to make your own excuses!"

She turned away from him, but as she did so she caught a glimpse of his face staring at her with an expression that was almost frightening, and without another word he wheeled and left the room, his long riding-cape swirling about him.

"Oh, mam!" cried Nan despairingly. "Now what 've you done!"

"I don't care! He needn't expect me to beg him off!"

"But it wasn't because he's afraid, mam! You know that!"

Irritably Amber gave a kick at a low stool and went back into the bedroom, slamming the door hard to ease her feelings. For a few minutes she paced back and forth, angry with Bruce and Rex and herself and all the world. A pox confound all men! she told herself furiously, and flung off her dressing-gown to get into bed, even though she knew she would not be able to sleep.

When Nan came in an hour or so later Amber was still awake and tossing restlessly, but the anger was beginning to wear off and worry was taking its place. The prospect of the duel did not trouble her, for in spite of the fact that duels were forbidden by law they took place every day and hot-tempered young men fought over the flimsiest pretexts: a quick thoughtless word, bad luck at the gaming-table, the giving or taking of the wall as they passed on the streets, a difference of opinion over religion or wine or a woman. Every gentleman learned to handle his sword almost as soon as he learned to walk, and he knew that the art was acquired to be used.

She was not afraid of having them fight. She was, in fact, flattered and almost pleased—or would have been had Bruce been less frankly insulting—for a duel was not often fatal and was usually stopped at the first drawing of blood. But she was afraid now of what would happen to her when it was over.

Suppose Rex would not forgive her this time? Suppose he did have to leave the country and never came back again? Then what would become of her? She had no illusions left about a woman's place in Restoration London—she knew that she had been lucky to find a man like Rex Morgan who had loved her. For love was not in fashion any more, and without it a man had no obligations, a woman no rights. She realized all at once that she had been a fool to take such a chance— Of course he was sure to know— Her lame story about Aunt Sarah falling sick! And yet, how else could she have done it? She was forced now to admit to herself that there was only one way she could have avoided this—she should never have left London with Bruce. She had wanted too much, she had been too greedy —and this was what she got for it.

What was the matter with me? she asked herself furiously. I had Rex—and I had Bruce, too—now what have I got! But swiftly her anger reverted to Bruce. Damn him! He's never been anything but trouble to me!

As she heard Nan tiptoeing about in the dark, she spoke to her.

"Light a candle if you want, Nan. I can't sleep."

Nan went back to the other room, returned with a wax candle, and lighted three or four others in wall-sconces while Amber sat with one arm across her knees and her hand clenched in her hair.

"Lord, Nan! What'll I do?"

Nan, who was beginning to undress, heaved a sigh. "To tell you truly, mam, I don't know. It's the devil's own mess we're in."

Both of them looked worried and disconsolate. At last Nan blew out the candles and got into bed and they lay side by side, talking; neither one of them was able to sleep for a long while. Finally Nan fell asleep but Amber continued to toss and turn from one side to the other and she heard the bell-man go by, calling out each hour as it passed: one, two, three.

I'm not going to just lie here, she thought, and let my life be ruined! And when she heard, "God give you good morrow, my masters! Past three o'clock and a fair morning!" she flung back the covers and got out of bed, turning to shake Nan.

"Nan! Wake up! Get up! I'm going to Marrowbone Fields!"

"Good Lord, mam! I thought the house was afire—"

Amber dressed quickly but carefully, as though she was aware that this would be a dramatic moment in her life and wanted to look ready for it. She painted her face and stuck on a couple of patches, combed out her hair and let it fall in deep loose waves down over her shoulders. She wore a scarlet velvet suit, the coat of which was cut exactly like a man's. It fitted her snugly and the neck-line opened in a low V, and there were elaborate scrolls of gold braid decorating the deep cuffs and borders of the coat and skirt. The brim of her low-crowned Cavalier's riding-hat billowed with scarlet ostrich plumes and she had a pair of red-velvet boots lined with miniver. She had had a tailor make this suit and expected to set a new fashion, but she had not worn it before.

While Jeremiah went to hire four riding-horses Amber drank some hot coffee which Tansy had just made and, well laced with brandy, it tasted good to her for once. It was after four when Jeremiah returned and they set out for Marrowbone Fields, Amber and Nan, with Tempest and Jeremiah. It was just beginning to grow light but a heavy mist was falling which blurred the outlines of houses and trees and made it impossible to see more than a few feet ahead; Amber was annoyed, for the dampness would probably spoil her gown.

She soon forgot her appearance, however, and the closer they came the more her anxiety mounted.

It took them no longer than twenty minutes to reach the place in the road where Tyburn Brook ran under a little stone bridge—and looking off toward the east they could dimly see a party of men and several horses, half obscured by a spacious group of Lombardy poplars. Amber immediately turned her horse and started toward them. Presently she could distinguish Bruce and Rex, Almsbury, Colonel Dillon whom she knew slightly, and two others who were apparently the surgeons. But only Bruce and Rex had removed their outer coats, to show that no armour had been worn.

At the sound of horses' hoofs pounding across the field they all turned; it was not uncommon for a party to be sent to stop such meetings. But as Amber pulled on her reins and they saw who it was Bruce looked quickly away—though not before she had seen the angry annoyance on his face. Rex, however, stood and stared at her.

"Oh, Rex, darling!" she cried, stopping only a few feet from him and holding out her hand. "Thank God I got here in time! You mustn't fight this duel—you mustn't, Rex! Please, darling, for my sake!" Her eyes turned swiftly to the corners and she saw Bruce look across at her; his expression was sombre and a cynical half-smile touched one side of his mouth. Sick with fury she wanted to hurt him, any way she could. "There's no reason for you to fight, Rex! Why, I don't care any more for him than the man in the moon!" There! she thought savagely, and flung him a vindictive glance; he met it with cold contempt, impervious as stone.

But as her eyes shifted across to Bruce and back again she missed altogether the look on Rex's face, and when she looked down at him it had gone. The wild unreasoning rage of despair had disappeared. Now he was quiet, self-possessed, and seemed cool. In her preoccupation with her own worries Amber did not realize that his seeming calm was a deadly determination and that his own tension quivered like the thin blade in his hand. Misunderstanding, she still thought that she could make him do what she wanted.

"You shouldn't have come out here, Amber," he said. "A duelling-ground is no place for a woman. Go on back." He turned away and walked toward the rest of the group.

"Rex!" she cried, really alarmed now, and as Jeremiah came to help her dismount she got down as quickly as she could and ran after him, grabbing him by the arm. "Rex! I don't want you to fight! I don't want you to, d'you hear me?"

He neither looked at her nor answered, but jerked his arm free and went on. Amber would not have stopped even then, but suddenly Almsbury caught hold of her. "Come back here. You'll be in the way up there."

"But I can't let them fight! I won't—"

"Amber, for the love of Christ!" he growled at her. "Now stay here! Don't move!"

Helplessly she stood where he had left her. Bruce and Rex both had unsheathed their swords, and with Almsbury and the officer they were talking in low tones. At last, giving a shrug of his shoulders, Almsbury moved back; Dillon took out a white handkerchief and indicated where each man was to stand. The Earl looked at her with a scowl.

"What is it?" she asked him anxiously. "What's the matter?"

"Carlton wants to consider it settled when blood has been drawn, but your noble champion won't be satisfied until one of them is dead."

"Dead! Why, he's out of his mind! He can't! I won't let him!" She broke away from Almsbury and started forward at a run. "Rex!"

Almsbury caught her arm before she had gone three steps and brought her up with a jerk. "Stop it, you little fool! A duel's no game between children! Keep your mouth shut or go back home! You've got no business here in the first place!"

Surprised, she obeyed him, and stopped perfectly still. The two men now stood facing each other, poised, sword-tips touching, and Colonel Dillon held the handkerchief over his head.

"All's ready!" called Bruce and Rex in the same voice.

"All's ready!" Dillon brought the handkerchief down with a sweep.

Both of them were quick, fierce, and graceful, expert swordsmen. But the English style of fencing was to cut rather than to thrust, as the French did, and as they were almost of a height neither had the advantage in that respect. Rex, however, was not fencing but fighting with reckless fury, and obviously intended to kill or be killed, while Bruce was on the defensive—protecting himself but making no effort to wound his antagonist.

Amber stood watching them, her eyes darting from one to the other; her throat was dry and she twisted her skirt in her fingers. But her fears were all for Bruce—she might not have even known the man he was fighting. And when Rex's sword pierced his right upper-arm, just below the shoulder, and drew a quick streak of blood she gave a scream and started forward. Almsbury threw one arm about her waist and dragged her back.

Bruce had lowered his sword and Rex, refusing to seize an unfair advantage, dropped his own to his side. The blood from the small gash was streaming down Bruce's right arm, staining

325

his shirt and making red rivers along the exposed brown skin, and the sight of it filled Amber with terror and remorse.

"Oh, Bruce!" she wailed. "You're hurt!"

Rex's jaw set tensely, but Bruce ignored her.

"There," he said to Rex. "That should satisfy you."

More furious than ever since Amber's impulsive cry, Rex answered him through clenched teeth. "Nothing could satisfy me but to see you dead."

Amber gave a terrified scream that momentarily drew all eyes to her but Almsbury clapped his hand to her mouth and gave her a rough shake.

"If you don't shut up you'll distract him and he *will* get killed!"

Already the swords had begun to ring and clash again; now there was no doubt that Bruce was fighting in earnest, no longer merely defending himself. For several minutes the men moved rapidly back and forth, slashing and hacking, without either one being able to touch the other.

And then all at once the swords met, engaged, and locked. For a long tense moment they strained to get free, both men pouring sweat, their faces contorted with the intensity of effort. Then, so swiftly that it was not possible to see it happen, Bruce forced his sword free and thrust it into Rex's chest until the tip showed through his shirt in back; and then he withdrew it, red with blood.

For an instant Rex stood as though stunned, and then he fell slowly, crumpling. The surgeons ran toward him and Amber rushed forward, dropping to her knees beside him where he lay on the grass. Her throat muscles were so stiff with horror that for a moment she could not even say his name, but she took his head into her arms, cradling it against her breast, and then suddenly a mournful frightened sob broke from her and her tears splashed onto his face.

"Oh, Rex! Rex!" she moaned. "Speak to me, darling! Speak to me—please!" Her mouth touched his forehead, his temples and eyelids, with frantic passionate kisses.

Behind her, Bruce took Almsbury's handkerchief and wiped the blood from his sword, jammed it back into its case and buckled the belt around his hips once more. By tradition the sword of the defeated man was forfeit, but he made no move to take it and Rex's fingers were still loosely clasped on the hilt. Bruce's surgeon was tearing open his shirt and binding the wound with a strip of white cloth while Bruce stood, hands on his hips and feet spread, looking down at Rex. His face was dark and grim, bitter but not triumphant.

Rex was moving restlessly, as if to escape the pain, and though he coughed and turned his head to spit out blood there was very little blood coming from the wound in his chest. Amber was sobbing hysterically, covering his face with kisses and stroking his head with her hands.

"Rex, darling! Look at me! Speak to me!"

He opened his eyes at last, very slowly, and as he saw her he tried to smile. "I'm ashamed, Amber," he said softly, "that you saw me—beaten."

"Oh, Rex! I don't care about that! You know I don't! All I care about is you— Are you in pain? Does it hurt you?"

A quick spasm crossed his face and the sweat started suddenly, but his features relaxed again as he looked up at her. "No— Amber. It doesn't hurt. I'll be—" But at that moment he coughed again and turned his head to spit out a great glob of clotted blood. His mouth was splattered with it; his eyes shut and one hand pressed hard against his chest in an effort to stop the gurgling cough.

Bruce slid his arms into the doublet Almsbury held for him, gave Rex a last look and then tossing his cloak over his arm started off, with the Earl and his surgeon, toward where a young page held their horses.

Amber looked around suddenly and saw him walking away. She glanced swiftly at Rex. He lay now quiet and with his eyes closed; she hesitated only an instant and then, very gently, she laid his head onto the grass. Hurriedly she got to her feet and ran after Bruce, calling his name in a soft voice so that Rex would not hear.

"Bruce!"

He swung around and looked at her, incredulity on his face and violent anger. When he spoke his teeth were clenched and the muscles at one side of his mouth twitched with nervous rage. "There's a man dying over there— Go back to him!"

Amber stared at him for a moment in stunned helplessness, unable to believe the contempt and loathing she saw on his face. As though from a distance she heard Rex's voice, calling her name. Blind fury raged in her and before she knew what she was doing she had drawn back her hand and slapped him squarely across the mouth with all the force in her body. She saw his eyes glitter as the blow struck but at the same moment she whirled, picking up her skirts, and was running back to kneel beside Rex. His eyes were opened now but as she bent over him she saw that they stared without seeing, his face was expression-less—he was dead. And in his hand, held closely as though he had been trying to lift it high enough to see, was the miniature of herself which she had given him the year before.

PART III

CHAPTER TWENTY–TWO

GROPING LANE WAS a narrow dirty disreputable little alley on Tower Hill. The houses were crazily built and old, and the overhanging stories leaned across the street, almost touching at the top and shutting light and air from the festering piles of refuse that lay against each wall. The great gilded coach tried to turn into the lane but, finding it too narrow, was forced to stop at the entrance. A woman, completely covered by a black hooded cloak and with a vizard over her face, got out and with two footmen on either side of her hurried several yards farther up the alley and disappeared into one of the houses. The footmen remained below, waiting.

Running swiftly up two flights of stairs she paused and knocked on the door just at the top. For a moment there was no reply and she knocked again, hammering impatiently, glancing around as though some unseen pair of eyes might be watching her there in the pitch-dark stairwell. Still the door did not open, but a man's voice spoke from behind it, softly:

"Who is it?"

"Let me in! It's Lady Castlemaine, you logger-head!"

As though she had given the magic formula the door swung wide and he bowed from the waist, sweeping out one hand with a gesture of flourishing hospitality as Barbara sailed in.

The room was small and bare and dark, furnished with nothing but some worn, cane-bottomed stools and chairs and a large table littered with papers and piled with books; more books and a globe of the world stood beside it on the floor. Outside the night was frosty, and the meagre sea-coal fire which burnt in the fireplace warmed only a small area around it. An ugly mongrel dog came to reassure himself by a curious sniff at Barbara's velvet-booted feet, and then returned to gnaw at a bone.

The man who admitted her looked little better than his dog. He was so thin that his chamois breeches and soiled shirt hung upon him as though on a rack. But his pale blue eyes were quick and shrewd and his face for all its gauntness had a look of enthusiasm and intelligence, combined with a certain slyness that was revealed in the shifting of his eyes and the unctuous quality of his smile.

He was Dr. Heydon—the degree he had bestowed upon himself—astrologer and general quack, and Barbara had been there once before to find out whom the King would marry.

"I apologize, your Ladyship," said Heydon now, "for not opening the door immediately. But to be honest with you I am so hounded by my creditors that I dare not open to anyone unless I first make certain of his identity. The truth of it is, your Ladyship," he added, heaving a sigh and flinging out his arms in a gesture of despair, "I scarcely dare leave my lodgings these days for fear I shall be seized upon by a bailiff and carried off to Newgate! Which God forbid!"

But if he hoped to interest Barbara in his problems he was very much mistaken. In the first place she knew well enough that there was no ribbon-seller or perfumer or dressmaker in London with a trade at Court who did not hope to enrich himself at the expense of the nobility. And in the second she had come there to tell him her troubles, not to listen to his.

"I want you to help me, Dr. Heydon. There's something I *must* know. It means everything to me!"

Heydon rubbed his dry hands together and picked up a pair of thick-lensed spectacles which he perched midway down his nose. "Of course, my lady! Pray be seated." He held a chair for her and then took one himself just across the table, picking up a pen made of a long goose quill and beginning to caress his chin with the tip of it. "Now, madame, what is it that troubles you?" His tone was sympathetic, inviting confidence, implying a willingness and ability to solve any problem.

Barbara had removed her mask and now she tossed back the hood and dropped the cloak down from her shoulders. As she did so the diamonds at her throat and in her ears and hair caught

332

the light and struck off brilliant sparks; Dr. Heydon's eyes widened and began to glow, focusing upon them.

But Barbara did not notice. She frowned, stripping off her gloves, and for several moments she remained silent and thoughtful. If only there was some way she could get his advice without telling him! She felt like a young bride going to consult a physician, except that her scruples were those nòt of modesty but of angry and humiliated pride.

How can I tell him that the King's grown tired of me! she thought. Besides, it's not true! I know it isn't! No matter what anyone says! It's just that he's so pleased at the prospect of having a legitimate child—for once! I know he still loves me. He must! He's just as cold to Frances Stewart as he is to me—! Oh, it's all because of that damned woman—that damned Portuguese!

She raised her eyes and looked at him. "You've heard, perhaps," she said at last, "that her Majesty finally proves with child?" She accentuated the word "finally," giving it an inflection which suggested that the delay was due to Catherine's own malicious procrastination.

"Ah, madame! Of course! Haven't we all heard the happy news by now? And high time it is—but then, better late than never, as they say. Eh, your Ladyship?" But at Barbara's quick disapproving scowl he sobered, cleared his throat, and bent over his papers. "Now, what were you saying, your Ladyship?"

"That her Majesty proves with child!" snapped Barbara. "Now, it seems that since it was learned the Queen is pregnant, his Majesty has fallen in love with her. That must be the reason, since no one noticed that he paid her any undue attention before. He neglects his old friends and scarcely goes near some of them. I want you to tell me"—suddenly she leaned forward, staring at him intently—"what will happen once the child is born. Will he go back to his old habits then? Or what?"

Heydon nodded his head and bent to his work. For some time he was silent, poring over an extremely complicated map of the heavens which was spread before him, pursing his lips and frowning studiously. From time to time he sucked air through a space between his two front teeth and drummed his fingers on the table. Barbara sat and watched him, her excitement mounting and her hopes, as well, for she could not believe that he would give her any really bad news. Somehow, this would all work out to her satisfaction—as everything had always done.

"Faith, madame," he said at last, "you ask me a very difficult question."

"Why? Can't you see into the future? I thought that was your business!" She spoke to him as though he were a glove-maker who had just told her that he would be unable to get the kind of leather she wanted.

"My years of study have not been in vain, madame, I assure you. But such a question— You understand—" He shrugged, spreading his hands, and then made a gesture as of a knife being run across his throat. "If it should be known I had made a prognostication in a matter so important—" He glanced down at his charts again, frowning dubiously, and then he murmured softly, as though to himself: "It's incredible! I can't believe it—"

Barbara, in a froth of sudden excitement, sat far forward on the edge of her chair and her eyes blazed wildly. "What's incredible? What is it? You've got to tell me!"

He leaned back, putting his finger-tips lightly together and contemplating the bony joints. "Ah, madame—it is information of too much importance to be disposed of so casually. Give me a few days to think it over, I pray you."

"No! I can't wait! I've got to know now! I'll run mad if I don't! What do you want—? I'll give you anything! A hundred pound—"

"Have you a hundred pound with you?"

"Not with me. I'll send it tomorrow."

He shook his head. "I'm sorry, madame, but I can no longer do business on credit. It was that practice which brought me to the condition you now see. Perhaps it would be best if you returned tomorrow."

"No! Not tomorrow! I've got to know now! Here—take these ear-rings, and this necklace, and this ring—they're worth more than a hundred pound any day!" She took off her jewels swiftly, tossing them across the table to him as though they were glass

334

baubles bought at a fair or from some street vendor. "Now—Tell me quick!"

He gathered up the jewellery and slipped it into his pocket. "According to the stars, madame, the Queen's child will be born dead."

Barbara gasped. One hand went to cover her mouth and she sank back into her chair, her face shocked and unbelieving. But presently there began to creep into her eyes a look of cunning and of malignant satisfaction.

"Born dead!" she whispered at last. "Are you sure?"

"If the stars are sure, madame, I am sure."

"Of course the stars are sure!" She got up swiftly. "Then he'll come back to me, won't he?" In her sudden joy and new confidence she spoke recklessly.

"It would seem likely, would it not—under the circumstances?" His voice had a soft purring sound and his face was smiling and subtle.

"Of course he will! Good-night, Dr. Heydon!" She lifted the hood up over her head once more as she walked to the door and he followed her, opening it and standing back to bow her out. The dog came too to see the visitor off. She took one step down, holding up her skirts so that she would not stumble in the darkness, and then all at once she glanced back over her shoulder and gave him a dazzling smile. "I hope the diamonds keep you out of Newgate, Doctor! *That* news was worth far more than a thousand pound to me!"

He bowed again, still smiling and nodding his head, and as she got to the landing and disappeared he closed the door and slowly fastened the bolt. Then he bent to stroke his dog and the animal went meekly down onto its back, its long rat-like tail thumping the floor.

"Towser," he said, "at least we'll eat for a while."

Barbara, however, took the Doctor absolutely at his word and from then on the Queen's health was her greatest concern. She went to her levée every morning, invited her to supper in her own rooms, bribed some of the pages to bring her immediate word if the Queen should fall sick—she kept a constant close but secret watch on everything she did. But Catherine seemed to thrive. She looked healthy and happy and prettier than she ever had.

"Your Majesty is not feeling well?" Barbara asked her at last in desperation. "You look so pale, and tired."

But Catherine laughed and answered in her heavily accented English: "Of course I'm well, my lady! I've never been more well!"

Barbara began to grow discouraged and even considered demanding the return of her jewels from Dr. Heydon. And then, in mid-October, sometime in the fifth month of Catherine's pregnancy, a rumour swept through the Palace corridors: her Majesty had fallen ill, and had miscarried of the child.

Catherine lay flat on her back in bed, surrounded on all sides by her maids and waiting-women. Her eyes were closed tightly to keep back the tears, for she was desperately sick and afraid. But as she heard Penalva turn and tell one of the women in a whisper to call the King she looked up swiftly.

"No!" she cried. "Don't do that! Don't send for him! It's nothing— I'll be better presently— Wait until Mrs. Tanner comes."

Mrs. Tanner was the midwife who had been taking care of her Majesty, and the moment Catherine had begun to feel sick and faint they had sent for her. She arrived a few minutes later, and as she went toward the bed her cheerful vulgar face contrived to appear both alarmed and optimistic. Mrs. Tanner resembled nothing so much as a fish-wife masquerading as a great lady. Her hair was dyed the fashionable silver-blonde colour that was almost white, her cheeks were so brightly painted with Spanish paper that they looked like autumn apples, and her fingers and wrists and neck were loaded with expensive jewellery —tokens of appreciation from her patients and a convenient and portable form of advertising.

Catherine opened her eyes to find the woman bending over her. "Your Majesty is feeling unwell?"

"I've been having pains—here—and I feel as though—as though I'm bleeding—" She looked up at her with the great mournful eyes of a puppy who begs a favour.

336

Mrs. Tanner swiftly masked the horrified surprise that came to her face and immediately began to take off her rings and bracelets. "Will your Majesty permit me to make an examination?"

Catherine nodded and Mrs. Tanner gave a signal for the curtains to be pulled about the bed. Then oiling her hands thoroughly with sweet-butter which an assistant had brought, she disappeared for several moments behind the curtains. Once there was a tormented little cry and a softly drawn groan from the Queen, and the face of every woman there winced with sympathetic pain. Finally Mrs. Tanner parted the curtains, dipped her right hand into a basin of water, and whispered to another woman: "Her Majesty has miscarried. Send for the King." A wave of excited murmurs and significant glances rushed around the room.

A few minutes later Charles came in on the run and went immediately to Mrs. Tanner, who was now wiping her hands while two maids sponged blood from the floor. He had been called from the tennis-court and wore only his open-necked shirt and breeches; and his brown face—streaked with sweat—was drawn taut by anxiety.

"What's happened? They told me her Majesty had fallen sick—"

Mrs. Tanner could not meet his eyes. "Her Majesty has miscarried, Sire."

A look of horror struck across his face. Swiftly he parted the curtains and knelt beside her bed, out of sight of the roomful of curious watching eyes. "Catherine! Catherine, darling!" His voice was urgent, but low, for she lay with her eyes closed and appeared to be unconscious.

But at last her lashes lifted slowly and she saw him. For a moment there was scarcely even recognition on her face, and then the tears came and she turned her head away with an agonized sob.

"Oh, Catherine! I'm sorry—I'm so sorry! Have they given you something to ease the pain?" His face looked tired and as haggard as hers, for above all things on earth he wanted a legitimate son; but pity made him yearn to protect her.

337

"It isn't the pain. I don't care about that. Pain doesn't matter— But, oh, I so wanted to give you a son!"

"You will, darling—you will someday. But you mustn't think about that now. Don't think about anything but getting well."

"Oh, I don't want to get well! What good am I on earth if I can't do the one thing I'm put here for? Oh, my dear—" Her voice now sank so low that he had to lean forward to hear it and she stared up at him, her eyes flooded with self-reproach. "Suppose it's true what they say—that I'm barren—"

Charles was shocked and his breath caught sharply. He had not known she had heard that gossip, though it had been circulating through the Court and even out in the town from the first month of their marriage, perhaps earlier.

"Oh, Catherine, my darling—" His long fingers stroked her hair, caressed her pale moist cheeks. "It isn't true; of course it isn't true. People will talk maliciously as long as they have tongues in their heads. These accidents happen so often, but they mean nothing. You must rest now and grow well and strong—for my sake." He smiled tenderly, and bent his head to kiss her.

"For your sake?" She looked up at him trustingly, and at last she gave him a grateful little smile. "You're so kind. You're so good to me. And I promise—this won't happen the next time."

"Of course it won't. Now go to sleep, my dear, and rest, and presently you'll be well again."

He remained kneeling beside her until her breathing was deep and regular and the little frown of pain had left her forehead, and then he got up and without a word walked from the room and back to his own apartments where he went into his closet alone.

Catherine was no better the next day and she grew steadily worse with each day that passed. They did everything they knew to cure her: They bled her until she was white as the sheets she lay on. They cut live pigeons in two and tied them to the bare soles of her feet to draw out the poison. They gave her purgatives and sneezing-powders, pearls and chloride of gold. Her priests were with her constantly, groaning and wailing and

338

praying, and at every hour the room was filled with people. Royalty could neither be born nor die in quiet and privacy.

Hour after hour Charles sat there beside her, anxiously watching each move that she made. His grief and devotion amazed them all; but for that one episode regarding Castlemaine, he had been a kind but by no means adoring husband.

They were all convinced that she would die, most of them hoped she would, and the talk was not so much of the dying Queen as of the new one. Whom would he marry next? For of course he must and would marry, after a decent interval of mourning.

Frances Stewart was the bride they had selected. She had some royal blood in her veins, enough to make such a match possible, she was beautiful—and she was still a virgin. That, at least, was the opinion of the best-informed, even though his Majesty had been pursuing her for months, ever since she had come from France to take a place as one of Queen Catherine's Maids of Honour.

She was not quite seventeen but rather tall, and slender as a candle-flame; she had about her an air of tranquil poise which could be suddenly broken by a bubbling merry laugh that gurgled up out of a happy well of youth and confidence. Her beauty was pure and perfect, flawless as a cut gem, delightful as the sight of a poplar glistening in the sun.

Charles had been first attracted by the irresistible lure of beauty, and then, discovering in her a modest shyness that was to him as incredible as it was genuine, he began a systematic program of seduction. So far, it had been unsuccessful. But her fresh youth and naïveté appealed to him strongly, sent him yearning toward the lost years as though in her he could catch again for a moment something of that perishable and precious charm.

During the past four months, since the discovery of her Majesty's pregnancy, Charles had seemed to lose interest in Frances; he had been as coolly polite as though he had never desired her at all—or as though he had already had her. But now he seemed to return to Frances again for comfort in his despair. They were so positive she would be the next Queen of England that it was not even possible to find betting odds. Frances believed it herself.

But certainly not even the King's sorrow was more extravagant or more seemingly sincere than that of the least likely of all mourners, Lady Castlemaine. She kept a continuous stream of pages running from the Queen's apartments to her own at every hour of the day and night, went there frequently herself, and was reliably reported to pray for her Majesty's recovery five or six times a day. Barbara was alarmed.

It had never occurred to her, when Heydon had made his astounding prophecy, that the Queen would be as sick as she was. Certainly not that she would die. And she had not even considered the possibility that if she did she might be replaced by a woman like Frances Stewart, whose marriage to the King could mean nothing but Barbara's own ruin and, more than likely, her exile into France. She and Frances had not been friendly for some time, not, in fact, since Barbara had become convinced that his Majesty's infatuation for the girl was a serious one. She had always underestimated all women but herself, and it had taken her a long while to discover that Frances was really a formidable rival. Now she lived in terror that the Queen would die.

The gatherings in Barbara's rooms were sober affairs now, for though the King came almost every night at supper-time his mood was a morose and silent one, and discretion kept them from seeming to be as indifferent as they were.

On the tenth night after Catherine had fallen sick he stood in Barbara's drawing-room, over against the fireplace, thoughtfully swirling the red wine in his glass and talking in quiet tones which the most intent ears could not catch, to Frances Stewart. For Frances, though her own hopes of glory depended upon the Queen's death, was genuinely sympathetic and sorrowful for the quiet unhappy little woman who had befriended her.

"How was she when you left her, Sire?"

Charles scowled, a drawn and worried scowl which seldom left his face nowadays, and stared down into his glass. "I don't think she even knew me."

340

"Is she still delirious?"

"She hadn't spoken for more than two hours." He gave a quick shake of his head as though to drive away the painfully vivid image of her that dogged his memory. "She talked to me this morning." A strange sad and cynical smile touched his mouth. "She asked me how the children were. She said that she was sorry the boy·was not pretty. I told her that he was very handsome and she seemed pleased—and said that if I was satisfied then she was happy."

Frances gave a sudden hysterical sob, her fist pressed against her mouth, and Charles looked at her in quick surprise, as though he had forgotten that she was there. Just then a page entered the room, running in without ceremony, and went immediately to the King.

Charles whirled around. "What is it?"

"The Queen, Sire, is dying—"

Charles did not wait for the boy to finish his sentence but with a swift movement he flung the glass into the fireplace and ran out of the room. The Queen's bed-chamber was in the same miserable condition it had been in for days: All windows were closed and had been since she had first fallen sick, so that the air was heavy and hot and stinking; the darkness was complete, but for a few low-burning candles about the bed; and the priests hung over her like bald malefic ravens, their voices eternally wailing and moaning.

Catherine lay flat on her back. Her eyes were closed and sunken in dark pits, her skin was yellow as wax, and she breathed so faintly that at first he thought she was dead. But before he had even spoken she became aware of his presence beside her, her eyes opened slowly and she looked up at him. She tried to smile and then, painfully, she began to talk to him, falling back into Spanish.

"Charles—I'm glad you came. I wanted to see you just once more. I'm dying, Charles. They told me so, and I know it's true. Oh, yes it is." She smiled gently as he started to open his mouth to protest. "But it doesn't matter. It will be better for you when I'm dead. Then you can marry a woman who will give you sons—I want you to promise me that you won't wait.

Get married soon— It won't matter to me where I'll be—"

As she talked he stared at her, horrified and sick with shame. He had not realized before that she was dying because she had no wish to live. He had never wanted or tried to understand what this past year had been for her. The enormity of his selfish thoughtlessness, the guilty awareness that in his secret heart he had hoped for her death, struck him like a blow from a mighty fist. He had a moment of passionate regret, of devout promises for a better future.

Suddenly he leapt to his feet and turned to face the priest who was standing just beside him, interrupting the old man in the midst of his clamorous prayer.

"Get out of here." His voice was low and tense with fury. "Get out of here, I say! All of you!"

Priests and doctors stared at him in astonishment, but made no move to go.

"But, your Majesty!" protested one. "We must be here when her Majesty dies—"

"She's not going to die! Though God knows what you've put her through would kill a stronger woman! Now, get out, or by Jesus, I'll throw you out myself!" His voice rose to an enraged shout and one arm swept out in a violent gesture of dismissal. His face was dark as a devil's and his eyes glittered savagely; he hated them for his own errors as much as for theirs.

They began to straggle out, puzzlement on their faces as they looked back again and again, but he paid them no more attention and turning away dropped once more to his knees beside her. For a long minute her eyes remained closed and he watched her, his own breathing almost stopped; at last she looked up at him again.

"Oh—" she sighed. "It's so quiet now—so peaceful. For a moment I thought I must be—"

"Don't say it, Catherine! You're not going to die! You're going to live—for me, and for your son!"

But she shook her head, a vague almost imperceptible movement. "I have no son, Charles. I know I haven't. But, oh, I did so want to give you one—I wanted to be part of your life. But now, before very long, I'll be gone— And when you marry again you'll have sons— You'll be happier, and so I'm glad I'm going—"

Charles gave a sudden sob. The tears were streaming from his eyes and his two hands crushed her tiny one between them. "Catherine! Catherine! Don't talk that way! Don't say those things! You've got to want to live! If you want to you can— And you've got to—for me—"

She stared up at him, a new look in her eyes. "For *you*, Charles? You want me to?" she whispered.

"Yes, I do! Of course I do! My God, whatever made you think— Oh, Catherine, darling, I'm sorry—I'm *sorry!* But you've got to live—for me— Tell me that you'll try, that you will—"

"Why, Charles— I didn't know you— Oh, my darling, if you want me to— I can live— Of course I can—"

CHAPTER TWENTY-THREE

IT WAS NOT until after he was dead that Amber realized how much Rex Morgan had meant to her. She missed the sound of his key turning in the lock and the feeling of warmth and happiness he had always brought with him, as though a fire had just been lighted in a cold dark room. She missed waking up in the morning to find him half-dressed and shaving, screwing his face this way and that as he scraped the beard off. She missed the evenings when they had been alone and had played cribbage or crambo and he had listened to her strum her guitar and sing the popular bawdy street ballads. She missed his smile and the sound of his voice and the reassuring adoration in his blue eyes. She missed him in a thousand ways.

But most of all, though she scarcely knew it herself, she missed the comfortable sense of security with which he had surrounded her.

For now she found herself suddenly adrift, lost, and filled with a cold apprehension for the future. She had almost seventeen hundred pounds with Shadrac Newbold; so there was no immediate cause for concern on that score, and she could not be arrested for debt anyway. But even seventeen hundred pounds, she knew, would not last very long if she continued to live on her present scale, and when it was gone she would be at the mercy of the tiring-room gallants.

The thought was not pleasant—for after a year and a half of association she saw them naked now and unvarnished with the gilt of a naïve young girl's illusions. To her they were no longer gallant and gay and valiant, fine gentlemen because they wore fine clothes and could trace their families to followers of William the Conqueror—but only a half-breed species of Frenchified Englishman, shallow, malicious, and absurd. They had all the trappings of cynicism, careless ill-breeding and light-hearted cruelty, which were now the marks of quality. There was not another man like Rex Morgan to be found among them.

"Oh, if I'd only known this would happen!" she thought, over and over again. "I'd never have gone away! And I wouldn't have gone to the King that time, either. Oh, Rex, if I'd known, I'd have been kinder to you—I'd have made you happy every minute—"

The first visitor she admitted after Rex's funeral—though many others had come—was Almsbury. He had been there before but she had been unfit to see anyone at all, and so Nan had sent him away. But one afternoon, ten days after the duel, he came again and this time she said that she would see him.

She was sitting on a couch before a burning fire, for the weather was cold and wet, and her head was bent in her arm. She did not even glance up until he sat down and reached over to put one arm about her, and then she looked at him with red and swollen eyes. Her dress was plain black and she wore not a ribbon or a jewel, her hair was tumbled and only carelessly combed, and her face was shiny with tears; her head ached and she looked thinner than she had.

"I'm sorry, Amber," he said softly, tenderness and sympathy in his eyes and the tone of his voice. "I know how little it means to hear that when you've lost someone—but I mean it with all my heart, and please believe me when I say that Bruce—"

344

She gave him a venomous glare. "Don't you dare speak of him to me! Much I care how sorry *he* is! If it hadn't been for him Rex would still be alive!"

Almsbury looked at her in surprise and an expression of impatience crossed his features, but she had covered her face with her hands and was crying again, wiping at the tears with a wet wadded handkerchief.

"That isn't fair, Amber, and you know it. He asked you to stop the duel; he even let Captain Morgan cut his arm in the hope that that would satisfy him. There was nothing more to do unless he had let Morgan kill him—and surely even you couldn't have expected that."

"Oh, I don't care what he did! He killed Rex! He murdered him—and I loved him! I was going to marry him!"

"In that case," said the Earl, with unmistakable sarcasm, "it would have been better judgement not to go off on a honeymoon with another man—even if he was an old friend."

"Oh, mind your own business!" she muttered, and though he hesitated for a moment, Almsbury got to his feet, made her a polite bow and went out of the room. Amber neither spoke nor tried to stop him.

She did not feel able to go back to the theatre immediately, and then shortly after the first of June it closed for two months. But as soon as she began to admit visitors her own apartments became almost as crowded as the tiring-room. She found, somewhat to her surprise, that the duel had made her as much the fashion as red-heeled shoes or Chatelin's Ordinary. Lord Carlton was handsome, his family one of the oldest and most honourable, and his exploits as a privateer had made him a spectacular figure, not only at Court but throughout the city.

Amber knew how much such popularity meant, but she determined to take every advantage of it that she possibly could. Somewhere among those clamoring beaus, those beribboned fops and wit-imitators, there must be a man—a man who would fall in love with her as Rex had done; and if she could but single him out, this time she would know what to do. Marriage she did not expect, for the social position of an actress was no better than that of the vizard-masks in the pit, and with Rex dead her earlier opinion of matrimony had revived. But the brilliant lavish exciting life of an exclusive harlot seemed to her a most pleasant one.

She saw herself occupying a magnificent house in St. James's Field or Pall Mall, driving about town in her gilt coach-and-six, giving fabulous entertainments, setting the styles which would be taken up at Whitehall. She saw herself famous, admired, desired and—most of all—envied.

It was what she had wanted for a long time; and now that she had begun to reconcile herself to the fact of Rex Morgan's death, the wish opened once more into quick full blossom. Optimistically, she decided that he was all that had kept her from having those things.

But though she encouraged them all, flirted with them and laughed at their jokes, she never accepted their proposals. She knew that they held constancy in contempt, but also that they valued a woman more if she pretended concern for her virtue and made a great issue of surrender—just as they would rather win money from a man who hated to lose it. And so far no one had offered what she wanted.

"Phoo, pox, Mrs. St. Clare!" said one of them to her. "A virtuous woman is a crime against nature!"

"Well," retorted Amber, "then there aren't many criminals nowadays."

But nevertheless she was growing uneasy and discouraged and in spite of her insistence that she intended never to err again, the other actresses taunted her because she had not found another keeper.

"I hear the young gentlemen are grown mighty shy of keeping these days," remarked Knepp one afternoon when she and Beck Marshall had come to call on Amber. Over her glass of clary—a potent drink made of brandy and clary-flowers flavoured with sugar and cinnamon and ambergris—she flipped Beck a sly wink. "They say three months is the limit a man will keep now, for fear of losing his reputation as a wit."

"Oh, gad, a man is as much laughed at for keeping as ever

he was for taking a wife," said Beck. "More, I believe, for at least a wife brings a dowry to settle his debts, while a whore gives him nothing but a bastard and more debts."

"Especially," said Amber, "if she's being kept by three or four at once."

Beck looked at her sharply. "What d'you mean by that, madame?"

"Heavens, Beck." Amber opened her eyes wide in pretended innocence. "I'm sure it isn't my fault if your conscience troubles you."

"My conscience doesn't trouble me at all! Don't you agree it's better to be kept by three men at once—than by none at all?" She gave Amber a malicious tight-lipped smile, and then defiantly downed her drink at one gulp.

"Well," said Amber, "I'm glad I learnt my lesson on that score. I intend never to go into keeping again."

"Hah!" Knepp gave a sudden short barking laugh, and then she and Beck got up and prepared to leave.

As Amber closed the door after them she heard Knepp say, "She intends never to go into keeping again—until she can find the man who'll make her an indecent proposal at a high figure!" And the giggling voices of the two women faded away down the stair-well.

Amber turned back to Nan, who rolled her eyes and shook her head.

"Oh, Nan, maybe they're right! I half believe it's harder to find a man who'll keep than one who'll marry."

"Well, mam—"

"Now don't tell me again I should have married Captain Morgan!" she cried warningly. "I'm sick of hearing it!"

"Lord, mam, I wasn't going to say anything about that. "But I have been thinking of a plan you might try."

"What?"

"If you quit the theatre, took lodgings in the City and set yourself up for a rich widow, I'll warrant you'd find a husband with a good portion within the month."

"My God, Nan! Can you imagine me married to some stinking old alderman with nothing to do but breed his brats and

visit his aunts and cousins and sisters and go to church twice
on Sundays for my diversion? No thanks! I'm not that discouraged—yet!"

For three months it had rained, and then on the last day of
June the sun came out brilliantly, the puddles in the streets
began to dry, and the air was fresh and sparkling-clean. Children
appeared, like a ragged legion sprung up overnight, in every
alley and lane and courtyard in London, running and shouting
joyously at their gutter games. Vendors and ballad-singers and
housewives swarmed out-of-doors to feel the sun, and in St.
James's Park and the Mall courtiers and ladies strolled
again.

Since his Majesty's Restoration St. James's Park was open to
the public and not only the nobility but other idlers were free
to saunter through its broad tree-lined avenues and stop to watch
the King playing at pall mall, which he did with the same enthusiasm and skill he showed at every kind of athletic contest.

Amber went there that pleasant sunny afternoon with three
young men—Jack Conway, Tom Trivet and Sir Humphrey Pere-
pound—who had come to invite her to supper. It was scarcely
four o'clock when they left her apartments and so they had some
time to waste until the supper hour. At the Park entrance they
got out of their hired coach and started off up Birdcage Walk,
so called because the trees were full of cages containing singing
and squawking birds from Peru, the East Indies, and China.

The three fops were all younger sons who lived far above their
means and much in debt. Up at noon, they escaped by some
back door or window to avoid their creditors. They strolled
then to the nearest ordinary for dinner, went next to the play-
house where they got in free under the pretext of intending to
stay for but one act, spent part of the evening in a tavern playing cards and the rest in a bawdy-house, and started for home
at midnight, noisy and surly and drunken. Not one of them
was over twenty, they would never inherit an estate, and the
King probably was not even able to recognize them at sight.
But Amber had been alone when they had called and she would
rather be seen with anyone than no one—for obviously if a

woman lay shut up in her house she could not bring herself to the attention of a great man.

She always hoped and expected that this day might be the day for which she had been waiting. But her hopes had been sorely buffeted these past six weeks and were beginning to show signs of wear.

They kept up an unceasing chatter, gossiping about everyone who passed, bowing obsequiously to the lords and ladies of higher rank but judging them vindictively once they had gone by. Amber scarcely listened to them, but her eyes saw every detail of a lady's gown and coiffure, compared it mentally with her own, and went on to the next. She smiled at the men she knew and was amused to see how much it annoyed the women they were attending.

"There's my Lady Bartley with her daughter fast in tow, as usual. Gad, she's exposed the girl at every public mart in town and still they haven't found a taker," Sir Humphrey informed them.

"Nor ever will, as far as I'm concerned. Curse my tripes, but they made a mighty play for me not long since. I vow and swear the old lady is hotter for a son-in-law than the daughter is for a husband—there's never a more eager bed-fellow than your wanton widow. It was her design I should marry her daughter but devote my manhood to her. She told me as much one day when— Now! What d'ye think! She went by like she'd never seen me before! Damn my diaphragm, but these old quality-bawds grow impertinent!"

"Who's that rare creature just coming? She looks as if she would dissolve like an anchovy in claret. Damn me, but she has the most languishing look—"

"She's the great fortune from Yorkshire. They say she hadn't been in town a week when she was discovered in bed with her page. Your country-wench may never learn the art of dressing her carcass, but it doesn't take her long to find out how to please it." Sir Humphrey, as he talked, had taken a bottle of scent from his inner pocket and was touching the stopper to his eyebrows and wrists and hair.

"For my part, gentlemen," said Jack Conway, who was lazily

fanning himself with Amber's fan, a trick the beaus all had to show their gentility, "I consider every woman odious but the finest of her sex—" He made Amber a deferential bow. "Madame St. Clare."

"Oh, gad, and I too! I only spoke of the slut to give Sir Humphrey the opportunity of railing at her. I vow, there's no one has the art of wiping out a reputation almost in one breath as it were, like Sir Humphrey."

Jack Conway had begun to comb his hair with a great carved ivory comb and now Tom Trivet took a flageolet from his pocket and started to play a tune on it. Obviously, he had played in company more than he had practiced. Sir Humphrey took advantage of the noise to whisper in her ear.

"Dear madame, I'm most confoundedly your slave. What d'you think I've done with the ribbon you gave me from your smock?"

"I don't know. What did you do? Swallow it?"

"No, madame. Though if you'll give me another to take its place I will. I've got it tied in a most pretty bow—I'd be most glad to show you. The effect is excellent, let me perish—"

Amber murmured "Hm—" in an absent-minded tone.

For advancing through the crowd with people bowing to him on every side sauntered the gorgeous figure of his Grace, Duke of Buckingham, an equipage of several pages following close in his wake. Everyone turned and stared as he passed, whispers ran along behind the raised fans of elegant ladies, ambitious mothers, eager young girls—all of them hoping for an extra moment's notice from the great Duke.

Oh, damn! thought Amber frantically. Why didn't I wear my new gold-and-black gown! He'll *never* see me in this!

The Duke was advancing steadily. The green plumes on his hat swayed with every nod of his head, the sun glittered on the diamond-buttons of his suit, his handsome, arrogant face and splendid physique gave every other man a look of drab insignificance. Amber had seen Buckingham in the pit and in the tiring-room, she had been presented to him casually once, and she had heard endless gossip about his amorous and political exploits—but he had never paid her any particular attention.

Now, however, as he came closer she saw his eyes run over her swiftly and go on and then her heart gave a plunge as they returned again—and this time lingered. He was no more than four yards from her.

"Madame St. Clare?"

The Duke had stopped and was making her a flourishing bow while Amber quickly recovered herself and swept out her skirts in a deep curtsy. She was conscious that other men and women were watching them, turning their heads as they passed, and that her three gallants were stammering foolishly and making desperate efforts at nonchalance. The Duke's mouth was smiling beneath his blonde mustache, and his eyes travelled down her body and back up again, as though measuring her by his own private yardstick.

"Your servant, madame."

"Your servant, sir," mumbled Amber, almost suffocated with excitement. She stabbed about wildly for something to say, something to arrest his attention—witty and amusing and different from what any other woman would have said, but she did not find it.

His Grace, however, was at no loss for words. "If I mistake not, you're the lady over whom Lord Carlton fought some officer, a month or so since?"

"Yes, your Grace. I am."

"I've always admired Lord Carlton's taste, madame, and I must say that you're so fine a person I can see no reason to differ from his judgement now."

"Thank you, your Grace."

"Oh, gad, your Grace!" interrupted Sir Humphrey, suddenly bold and swaggering. "Every man in town is adying to be the lady's servant. I vow and swear, her health is drunk as often as the King's—"

Buckingham gave him a brief glance, as though he had noticed him for the first time, and Sir Humphrey wilted instantly. Neither of the two others ventured to speak.

"My coach is at the north gate, madame. I stopped to take a turn in the Park as I was going to supper— It would please me mightily if you would be my guest."

"Oh, I'd like to, your Grace! But I—" She paused, her eyes indicating that she was obligated to the three fops who were now bridling and grinning in anticipation of being invited to sup with the Duke of Buckingham.

The Duke bowed to them, a bow which was at once polite and condescending, which showed his own breeding even while it contrived to belittle theirs. "Sure, now, gentlemen—you've enjoyed the lady's company all afternoon. I know you're all too·much men of wit and understanding to wish to deprive others of that privilege. With your permission, gentlemen—"

He offered his arm to Amber, who could not conceal her delight and pride, and making a quick bobbing curtsy to the three beaus she sailed off. She had never been so stared at or felt so full of importance in her life as she did now, for wherever he went the Duke attracted as much·attention as the King himself and more than his Highness ever had. On the way to the north gate they passed the Mall where Charles was playing before a gallery crowded with ladies and a packed row of courtiers and beggars and loitering tradesmen. The King—who had just struck the little wooden ball into a hoop suspended from a pole at the opposite end of the Mall—saw them going by and waved. Buckingham bowed.

"If the King would spend as much time in the council-room as he does at the tennis-court and Mall," murmured the Duke as they went on, "the country might be in a better state than it is."

"Than it is? Why, what's the matter with it? It seems well enough to me."

"Women, my dear, never understand such matters and should not—but you may believe me, England's in a most miserable condition. The Stuarts have never been good masters. Here's my coach—"

They circled around the Park and stopped at Long's, a fashionable ordinary in the Haymarket, which was a narrow little suburban lane lined with hedges and surrounded by green fields. The host led them upstairs to a private room and supper was served immediately, while below in the courtyard the Duke's fiddlers played and people gathered from neighbouring cottages to sing and dance to the music. From time to time a cheer went up for the Duke, who was popular with the Londoners because he was well known to be a violent anti-Catholic.

The food was excellent, well-cooked and seasoned, and served hot by two quiet unobtrusive waiters. But Amber could not enjoy it. She was too much worried about what the Duke was thinking of her, what he would do when the meal was over and what she should do in her turn. He was such a great man, and so rich— If only she could please him enough it might be the making of her fortune.

But it did not seem likely the Duke would be an easy man to please.

He was thirty-six years old, and his life had left him nothing of either illusion or faith. He had raked and probed his emotions, experimented with his senses until they were deadened and dull and he was forced to whip them up by whatever voluptuous device occurred to him. Amber had heard all this and it was what made her uneasy. She was not afraid of what he would do—but that she would never be able to interest this bored and jaded libertine.

Now, once the table had been cleared and they were left alone, he merely took a pack of cards from his pocket and began to shuffle them idly; they flew through his fingers with a speed and sureness which proclaimed the accomplished gamester.

"You look uneasy, madame. Pray compose yourself. I hate to see a woman on edge—it always makes me feel that she expects to be raped, and to tell you truly I'm not in the mood for such strenuous sport tonight."

"Why, I didn't think the woman breathed who couldn't be persuaded by your Grace by an easier means than that." In spite of her awe and eagerness Amber could not keep a certain tartness from her voice; something in the personality of the Duke set her teeth on edge.

But if he noticed the sarcasm he ignored it. He dealt himself two putt hands, one from the top and the other from the bottom of the deck, inspected each with satisfaction and began to shuffle again.

"She doesn't," he said flatly. "Women are all inclined to make two mistakes in love. First, they surrender too easily; second, they can never be convinced that when a man says he is through with them he means it." As he talked he continued to watch the cards, but there had spread over his face a look of brooding discontent, a self-occupied bitterness. "It's long been my opinion the world would run far smoother if women would not insist on expecting love to be a close relation of desire. Your quality whore is always determined to make you fall in love with her—by that means she thinks she justifies the satisfaction of her own appetite. The truth of the matter is, madame, that love is only a pretty word—like honour—which people use to cover what they really mean. But now the world has grown too old and too wise for such childish toys—thank God we're beyond needing to deceive ourselves."

He looked up at her now and tossed the cards away. "I take it you're for hire on the open market. How much do you ask?"

Amber looked at him, her eyes narrowed slightly and slanting at the corners. His harangue, made obviously for the sole purpose of amusing himself, since it was plain he did not consider it necessary to convince her of anything, had made her angry. She had been listening to that kind of talk from the tiring-room gallants for a year and a half, but the Duke was the first man she had met who wholly believed what he said. She would have liked to get up, slap his face and walk out of the room—but he was George Villiers, Duke of Buckingham, and the richest man in England. And her morals were dictated rather by the expediency of the moment than by any abstract formula of honour.

"What am I bid?"

"Fifty pound."

Amber gave a short unpleasant langh. "I thought you said you weren't in the mood for a rape! Two hundred and fifty!"

For a long moment he sat and stared at her, and then he got up and walked to the door. Amber turned, watched him apprehensively, but he merely spoke to a footman who was waiting just outside and who ran off down the steps. "I'll give you your two hundred and fifty, madame," he said. "But pray don't flatter

354

yourself it's because I think you'll be worth it. I can give you that sum without missing it any more than you would miss a shilling flung to a whining Tom o' Bedlam. And when all's said and done, I doubt not you'll be more surprised by this night's business than I."

Amber was surprised; it was her first experience with perversion. And it would, she swore, be her last if she starved in the streets.

Shocked and disgusted, she conceived a violent loathing for the Duke which not even one thousand pounds could dispel. For days she thought of nothing but how she could contrive to pay him back. But in the end all she could do was put him in her list of enemies to be dealt with at some future date— when she should be powerful enough to ruin them all.

The theatre reopened late in July, and Amber found that she now had among her admirers the finest beaus in town. Buckingham had done that much for her, at any rate.

There was Lord Buckhurst and his plump black-eyed friend Sir Charles Sedley. The huge and handsome Dick Talbot, wild Harry Killigrew, Henry Sidney whom many thought to be the finest-looking man in England, and Colonel James Hamilton who was generally considered the best-dressed man at Whitehall. All of them were young, from Sidney who was twenty-two to Talbot who was thirty-three; all of them came of distinguished families and were allied through marriage or blood to the country's ruling houses; all of them frequented the innermost circles of the Court, associated on familiar terms with the King and might have been men of more consequence if they had cared to spare the time from their amusements.

Almost every night she went to supper with one or more of them, sometimes in a crowd of young men and women— actresses and orange-girls and other professed whores—often it was an intimate group of only two or three. They drank toasts to her and strained wine through the hem of her smock, and anatomized her among themselves. She went to the bear-baitings and cock-fights and spent three or four days at Banstead Downs with Buckhurst and Sedley, attending the horse-races—

for the old passionate English love of field sports had returned three-fold since the Restoration.

She went several times to Bartholomew Fair during the three weeks it was in progress, saw every puppet-show and rope-dancer, gorged herself on roast pig and gingerbread and made a great collection of Bartholomew Babies—the pretty dolls which it was customary for a gentleman to buy and present to the lady he admired.

One Sunday afternoon she visited Bedlam to see the insane hung up in cages, their hair matted and smeared with their own filth, raving and screaming at the sight-seers who jeered at and tormented them. At Bridewell, where they went to watch the prostitutes being beaten, Talbot recognized a woman he had known some time since and she began to yell at him, pointing her finger and accusing him of being the cause of her present shame and misery. But when they wanted to stop at Newgate to visit the great highwayman, Claude de Vall, who was holding his court there, Amber declined.

After the play she often drove in Hyde Park with four or five young men, and sometimes she saw a copy of her latest gown on one of the Court ladies. She slept short hours, neglected her dancing and singing and guitar lessons, and was so little interested in the theatre that Killigrew threatened to turn her out and would have done so but for the intervention of Buckhurst and Sedley and his own son. When he chided her for missing rehearsal or forgetting her lines—or not even troubling to learn them—she laughed and shrugged her shoulders or flew into a fit of anger and went home. The fops threatened to boycott the theatre if Madame St. Clare was not there, and so Hart and Lacy and Kynaston would be sent to coax her back again. Her popularity made her arrogant and saucy.

At first she had intended to be just as independent and unattainable as she had been at the beginning of her acquaintance with Rex Morgan. But the gentlemen were not subtle. They told her frankly that they would never spend the time courting an actress which they would lavish on a Maid of Honour. And Amber, faced with the alternative of abandoning either her

356

resolutions or her popularity, did not hesitate long in her choice. When Sedley and Buckhurst offered her one hundred pounds to spend a week with them at Epsom Wells she went. But she was never offered so large a sum again.

To each of her lovers she gave a bracelet made from her abundant hair, and some who did not get them had imitations made which they swore were hers. Her name began to appear in the almanack records of half the young fops in town, many of whom she did not even know. Buckhurst gave her a painted fan with a dreamy sylvan scene on one side and on the other the loves of Jupiter which depicted the god in the guise of a swan, a bull, a ram, an eagle, with various women—all of whom looked like Amber. Within a week copies of it were hiding blushes and veiling smiles in the Queen's Drawing-room.

In December a filthy verse which was unmistakably about her—though the woman in it was called "Chloris" and the man "Philander," after the old pastoral tradition—began to circulate through the tiring-room and the taverns and bawdy-houses. Amber, who was becoming tired, resented it deeply though she knew many similar poems had been written with far less provocation than she had given, but she could never find out whose it was. She suspected either Buckhurst or Sedley, both poets and very creditable ones, but when she accused them they smiled blandly and protested their innocence. Harry Killigrew followed the insult by flipping her a half-crown piece one night when she tardily suggested a settlement.

Early in January she spent two nights in succession at home without a caller or an invitation, and she knew all at once that her vogue was passing. And only a few days later Mrs. Fagg confirmed her fears that she was again with child. She felt suddenly sick and discouraged and exhausted. It was all but impossible for her to force herself to get out of bed in the morning, her appetite was gone, she looked pallid and thin and there were dark smudges beneath her eyes. Almost anything could bring forth a passionate flood of tears or a hysterical tantrum.

"I wish I was dead!" she told Nan. For her future was only too clear.

Nan suggested that they go away from London for a few weeks and when Mrs. Fagg advised a long ride in a coach, to be taken with her own special medicine, she agreed. "If I never see another fop or another play as long as I live I'll be glad!" she cried violently. She hated London and the play-house, all men and even herself.

CHAPTER TWENTY-FOUR

AMBER DECIDED TO go to Tunbridge Wells in the hope that drinking the waters would make her feel better. She set out early the next morning in her coach with Nan and Tansy, Tempest and Jeremiah. As it was raining, they could travel at but little more than a foot-pace, and even then the coach almost turned over several times.

Amber rode along in sullen silence, eyes tight shut and teeth clenched, not even hearing the chattering of Nan and Tansy. She had taken Mrs. Fagg's evil-tasting medicine and her belly was full of grinding cramps which seemed worse than those of child-birth. She wished that the earth would open and swallow them all, that a thunderbolt from heaven would strike her, or merely that she would die and be relieved of her misery. She told herself that if a man ever dared make her an indecent proposal again, though for a thousand pound in gold, she would have him kicked like a common lackey.

They stopped at an inn late that afternoon and went on the next morning. The medicine had taken its effect but she felt even worse than she had the day before, and at each turn of the wheels she longed to open her mouth and scream as loud as she could. She scarcely noticed when the coach came to a stop and Nan began wiping at the steamy window with her sleeve, putting her face against it to look out.

"Lord, mam! I hope we're not set upon by highwaymen!" She had had the same apprehension almost every time Tempest and Jeremiah had stopped to pry the wheels out of the mud.

Amber scowled crossly, but kept her eyes shut. "My God, Nan! You expect a highwayman behind every tree! I tell you they don't go abroad in weather like this!"

At that moment Jeremiah opened the door. "It's a gentleman, mam, who's been stopped by highwaymen and his horses taken."

Nan gave a little cry and turned to her with an accusing stare. Amber made a face. "Well, ask him if he wants to ride with us. But tell 'im we're only going to the Wells."

The màn who returned with Jeremiah was perhaps sixty, though his skin was clear and smooth and fresh-coloured. His hair was white, cut much shorter than a Cavalier's, and was not curled but had merely a slight natural wave. He was handsome, somewhat above six feet, erect and broad-shouldered. The clothes he wore were old-fashioned but well made of fine materials, sober black and untrimmed with ribbon or gold braid.

He bowed to her politely, but his manner suggested nothing of the French-tutored courtier. This was some plain City-bred man, very likely a Parliamentarian who thought the worst of Charles Stuart and all his beribboned cursing whoring sword-fighting crew—a substantial merchant, perhaps, or a jeweller or a goldsmith.

"Good afternoon, madame. It's very kind of you to invite me into your coach. Are you quite sure I won't be making you uncomfortable?"

"Not at all, sir. I'm glad to be of service. Pray get in, before the rain soaks you through."

He climbed in, Nan and Tansy moved over to make room for him, and the coach started off. "My name is Samuel Dangerfield, madame."

"Mine is Mrs. St. Clare."

Mrs. St. Clare obviously meant nothing to him, and for once she welcomed the anonymity. "Did my coachman tell you that I'm only going as far as Tunbridge? I don't doubt you can hire horses and another coach there."

"Thank you for the suggestion, madame. But as it happens I too am going to Tunbridge."

They talked little after that and Nan explained her mistress's silence by saying that she was suffering wretchedly from a quartan ague. Mr. Dangerfield was sympathetic, said he had had that ailment himself, and suggested bleeding as a sovereign remedy. Within three hours they arrived at the village.

Tunbridge Wells was a fashionable spa and the previous summer her Majesty and all the Court had paid it a visit; but now, in mid-January, it was a dreary deserted scattered little village. Not a person was in sight, the elms that lined the single main street were naked and forlorn, and only the smoke drifting from several chimneys gave evidence of life.

Amber and Samuel Dangerfield parted at the inn, where he had accommodations, and she promptly forgot him. She rented a neat little three-room cottage, furnished with very old polished oak, chintz curtains, and an array of shining brass and copper utensils. For four days she did not get out of bed but lay sleeping and resting, and by the end of that time her vitality and energy began to return. She started worrying again about what was to become of her.

"Well, I can't go back to London, that's sure as the smallpox," she told Nan as she sat morosely in bed, propped against pillows and plucking at her brows with a silver-plated tweezer.

"I'm sure I don't see why, mam."

"Don't see why! D'you think I'd ever go back to that scurvy theatre again, and have every town-fop laughing in his fist at me? I will not!"

"Well, after all, mam, you can go back to London without going back to the stage, can't you? It's a sorry mouse that has but one hole." Nan liked well-worn aphorisms.

"I don't know where else I'd go," muttered Amber.

Nan drew in a deep breath to prepare for her next speech, but kept her eyes on her deftly stitching needle. "I still think, mam, that if you'd take lodgings in the City and set yourself up for a rich widow you'd not be long a-catching a husband. Maybe you don't want to—but beggars should be no choosers."

Amber looked at her sharply. Then suddenly she flung the tweezers away, tossed the mirror aside and slumped back against the pillows with her arms folded. For several moments both women remained silent and Nan did not even glance at her glowering mistress. But at last Amber smoothed out her face and gave a sigh.

"I wonder," she said, "if Mr. What-d'ye-call—who had his horses stolen—is rich enough to bother with." Mr. Dangerfield had sent two days earlier to inquire if her ague was improving; she had returned a careless ungracious reply and had thought nothing of him since then.

"He might be, mam. He's got a mighty handsome young footman I could go talk to for a while."

Nan came back a couple of hours later flushed and excited—not altogether, Amber suspected, by the news she had heard. "Well?" asked Amber, who was lying out flat with her arms braced behind her head. She had spent the time since Nan's departure gloomily mulling over her past errors and disliking the men she considered to have been responsible for them. "What did you find out?"

Nan swept into the room, bringing with her a gust of cool fresh air from the outside and a buoyant energy. "I found out *everything!*" she declared triumphantly, untying the strings of her hood and throwing it into a chair. With her cloak still on she rushed to the bed and sat down beside Amber, who stubbornly refused to catch her enthusiasm. "I found out that Mr. Samuel Dangerfield is one of the richest men in England!"

"One of the richest men in—England!" repeated Amber slowly, still incredulous.

"Yes! He's got a fortune! Oh, I can't remember! Two hundred thousand pound or something like that! John says everybody knows how rich he is! He's a merchant and he's—"

"Two hundred thous— Is he married?" demanded Amber suddenly, as her wits began to revive.

"No, he isn't! He was but his wife died—six years ago I think John said. But he's got fourteen children; some other ones are dead—I forget how many. He comes up here every year to drink the waters for his health—he had a stroke. And he's just getting ready now to go down to the wells—Big John's going with 'im!"

Suddenly Amber flung back the covers and began to get out of bed. "I think I'll go drink some waters myself. Get out my green velvet gown with the gold braid and the green cloak. Is it muddy enough to wear chopins?"

"I think it is, mam." Nan was scurrying busily about, searching through unfamiliar drawers for smocks and petticoats, ransacking the still half-unpacked trunk for garters and ribbons, chattering all the while. "Only to think, mam! What luck we're in! I vow and swear you must have been born with a caul on your head!" Both women were gayer and in better spirits than they had been for some weeks past.

It had stopped raining the day before and the night had been cold, so that there was a crust on the mud. A pale sun sifted down through the grey-blue sky and there were whiffs of clouds overhead, too white and thin to threaten more immediate rain. Country girls in straw hats and short skirts, with baskets over their arms, appeared in the street crying their wares of poultry and fresh butter, milk and vegetables. And when Amber, with Nan and Tansy, strolled to the well two young men in ribboned suits and plumed hats, with long curling wigs and elaborate swords, bowed ceremoniously and begged leave to present themselves. It was the custom of such resort-places, where a man might with propriety introduce himself.

They were Frank Kifflin and Will Wigglesworth and they told her that they had come down from London to avoid a lady who was beginning to insist that Will marry her. Amber had never seen either of them at the theatre and decided that they were most likely a pair of rooks who posed as men of quality, or perhaps younger sons who had to live like gentlemen without being given the means to do so. Card-sharpers, pick-pockets, forgers, they preyed upon the naïve and unsuspecting—young country squires and heiresses were their easiest dupes. Luke Channell had been a crude specimen of the breed; Dick Robbins who had lived at Mother Red-Cap's a subtler and more clever one. Probably, since Tunbridge could not be a very fertile field for such activities at that time of the year, they had been run out of London or some other city and were in temporary retirement here.

To Amber's dismay they perked up immediately when she told them her name. "Mrs. St. Clare?" repeated Will Wigglesworth, an ugly pock-marked weasel-toothed young man. "I vow to gad the name's familiar, madame. What about you, Frank? Haven't we met Mrs. St. Clare somewhere before?"

"Why, yes, I'm sure we have, madame. Where could it have been, I wonder? Were you at Banstead Downs last year, perhaps?"

Oh, damn! thought Amber. If these fools find out who I am and Mr. Dangerfield hears about it, I wouldn't have any more chance with him than the man in the moon!

But she smiled at them very sweetly. "No, gentlemen, I'm sure you've got some other lady in mind. Neither of you looks at all familiar to me—and I know I'd never have forgotten your faces if we'd ever met."

Both of them took that for a compliment, grinned and coughed and made simultaneous bows. "Your servant, madame." But even then they would not let the subject drop and, probably for lack of other conversation, galloped along in relentless pursuit. Frank asked Will if they hadn't seen her in the Mall, and Will assured Frank it must have been in the Drawing-Room. Amber denied having been anywhere at all and was casting about for a means of escape when Mr. Dangerfield arrived and came to speak to her.

"You're looking very well, madame. I hope your ague is improved?"

She curtsied and smiled at him, and wished she could blow Kifflin and Wigglesworth away like two puffs of smoke. However, while Amber and Mr. Dangerfield talked of the weather, the taste of the well-water, and Tansy's scuffed shoes, they fiddled with their ribbons and combs and rolled their eyes about, obviously wishing that the old dotard would go away. But when Amber presented them to him she was amused to see the great change in their manners. She knew for sure then that she had guessed them for what they really were.

"Samuel Dangerfield, sir?" repeated Will Wigglesworth, as both of them jerked suddenly to attention. "I know a Bob Dangerfield. That is, we met once at the home of a mutual friend. He's a member of the great merchant family. Are you, by any chance, sir, a relative?"

"I'm Bob's father."

"Well, well. Only fancy, Frank. This is Bob's father."

"Hm, only fancy. Pray take our regards to Bob, sir, when you return to London."

"Thank you, gentlemen, I will."

Amber was growing nervous for she did not want them to begin talking and guessing at her identity again before Mr. Dangerfield. "If you'll excuse me, gentlemen, I must be getting back now. Your servant, sir." She curtsied again to Mr. Dangerfield, but as she would have left, the two young men insisted that they be allowed to see her home.

"Faith and troth, Will," said Frank Kifflin, as soon as they were out of Mr. Dangerfield's hearing. "Only think of meeting Bob's old father here. He seems a close acquaintance of yours, Mrs. St. Clare."

"Oh, no. I happened upon him just after his coach had been held up and his horses stolen, and carried him the rest of the way."

Will was indignant. "Lord, to see the effrontery of the highwaymen nowadays! I vow it's barbarous! They'll stop at nothing to gain their ends. And only to think of the scurvy rascals daring to attack a man of Mr. Dangerfield's consequence!"

"Barbarous!" agreed Frank.

As Amber stood in her doorway bidding them goodbye, Wigglesworth, who had been studying her face carefully for some moments, suddenly gave a snap of his fingers. "I know who you are now, Mrs. St. Clare! You're the player from His Majesty's Theatre!"

"Of course! That's who she is, Will! I knew all along we'd seen you before, madame. But why so modest, pray? Most actresses are—"

"An actress!" protested Amber. "Lord, whatever put that unlucky notion into your heads! It may be I resemble one of the wretches, but then it's the practice of all of 'em to try to look like quality, they tell me. No, gentlemen, you've made

364

a mistake. I assure you I've never been nearer the stage than the middle-box. And now, good-day."

But she knew by the sly looks they exchanged and the smiles on their faces when they bowed, that she had not convinced them. When the door was shut Amber leaned back against it with a low whistle.

"Whew! Blast those two paper-skulled nuisances! I've got to find a way to be rid of *them*, that's flat!"

When they came that night and invited her to go with them to the gaming-house Amber's first impulse was to refuse. But it occurred to her then that she might be able to catch them at something and scare them away from the Wells, and so she agreed. On the way Frank Kifflin suggested that they stop and ask Mr. Dangerfield to join them.

"Most likely the poor old gentleman's lonely, and though gad knows I hate to play with an old man I can't bear to think of Bob's old father being lonely."

But Amber did not intend to have Mr. Dangerfield told that she was an actress. "Mr. Dangerfield never plays cards, gentlemen. He hates the sight of 'em worse than a Quaker hates a parrot. You know these old Puritans."

The men, obviously disappointed, agreed that they did.

There were not a score of persons gathered about the tables in the gaming-house, and of those some were obviously natives of the town playing for only a few pence or shillings. Amber and the two men watched for a while and finally Frank Kifflin suggested that they try their luck at raffle—a dice-game which they assured her was the most harmless in the world and depended upon nothing but a turn of the wrist. "Oh; heavens, gentlemen," said Amber with an air of surprised innocence. "I can't play. I only came along to watch and keep you company. I never carry money with me when I'm travelling."

That seemed to please Mr. Kifflin. "Very wise, Mrs. St. Clare. Travel is full of too many hazards these days. But pray let me lend you ten or twenty pound—it's but dull entertainment watching others play."

Amber pretended to hesitate. "Well—I don't know if I should or not—"

"Tush, madame! Why shouldn't you? And let's not speak a word of interest, I beg of you. Only a rook would accept interest from so fine a person as yourself."

"What a courtier you are, Mr. Kifflin!" said Amber, thinking that if they did not want interest for their money they must have some other game.

Between them Mr. Kifflin and Mr. Wigglesworth produced a great many shiny shillings from their pockets and put them on the table before her. There was not a guinea or a penny or another coin in the pile, nothing but shillings. It was not very difficult to guess that they must be hired by some counterfeiter to pass his false money and get back true. Amber obligingly lost several pounds and when she quit said that she would send a note to her goldsmith immediately so that they could collect next time they were in London.

"But remember, Mrs. St. Clare," said Wigglesworth the last thing before they parted. "We'll accept not a penny in interest. Not a penny."

Amber examined some of the coins and was sure that they were "black-dogs"—double-washed pewter discs; they looked and sounded exactly like those made by the counterfeiter who had lived on the third-floor at Mother Red-Cap's. She tossed one of them up and caught it, laughing and giving a wink to Nan.

"I'll take care of those two young fop-doodles, I warrant you. Send Jeremiah the first thing tomorrow morning to invite Mr. Dangerfield to take his dinner with me. Let's see—I believe I'll wear that black velvet gown with the white lace collar and cuffs—it gives me a maidenly air, don't you think?"

"If anything could, mam."

When Samuel Dangerfield arrived Amber met him at the door. Her gown was high-necked but the bodice fitted snugly. She had her hair combed into deep waves and held at each temple by a black velvet bow; and her face was painted so subtly that even a woman could not have been sure the colouring was not natural.

"It was kind of you to invite me to dinner, Mrs. St. Clare."

"I know it isn't proper," she said demurely, "but I sent such a barbarous reply to your note—pray forgive me, sir. It was the sickness made me churlish."

Amber knew that her invitation was unconventional but hoped she could affect sufficient modesty to fool him. He smiled at her now much as he might have smiled at a pretty little kitten.

They discussed her ague for a few moments, and then took their places at a table which Nan had set in the parlour next the fireplace. The footman had informed Nan that his master had a hearty appetite—though he was now under his physician's orders to eat sparingly—and the meal Amber had had sent down from the inn was an ample one. She thought it would be more to her interest to please Mr. Dangerfield than his doctor.

Without much difficulty Amber had soon maneuvered the conversation around to Mr. Kifflin and Mr. Wigglesworth. Off-handedly, she told him how they had come to her house last night to ask her to change some money for them. She said that she had only brought fifteen or twenty guineas to Tunbridge, but that she had given them to the young men to pay their gambling debts with, and was now wondering how she would ever pack all those shillings into her trunk.

Mr. Dangerfield, as she had hoped, seemed somewhat alarmed by this innocent tale. "Are you well acquainted with Mr. Kifflin and his friends?"

"Heavens, no! I met them yesterday morning at the well. They introduced themselves. You know how little one goes upon ceremony in places like this."

"You're very young, Mrs. St. Clare, and I don't imagine you understand the ways of the world so well as an old man. If I may I'd like to give you some advice—and that is not to accept too much money from those gentlemen. They may be honest as they pretend, but when you've lived as long as I you'll know it's best to be cautious with a new acquaintance—particularly if you happen upon him at a public resort."

"Oh," said Amber, suddenly crestfallen. "But I thought that Tunbridge Wells was frequented by persons of the best quality! My physician who sent me here told me that her Majesty was here with all her ladies only last summer."

"Yes, I believe she was. But where there's quality there are sure to be rooks. And it's unworldly young persons like yourself of whom they'll take the greatest advantage."

While he talked Amber reached up to adjust the bow in her hair, as a signal for Nan who was waiting just outside and peeking in the window. "Oh!" she said, with a troubled frown, "how could I have been so foolish! I hope—"

At that moment Nan came in, out of breath, and stood in the doorway taking off her chopins. "Heavens, mam!" she cried excitedly. "The landlord at the inn refused the money! He says it's a false coin!"

"A false coin! Why, that was one Mr. Kifflin gave me last night!"

Samuel Dangerfield turned in his chair. "May I see it?" He took it from Nan, rung it upon the table and felt of the edges while both women watched him. "It is a false one," he said seriously. "So the young coxcombs are counterfeiters. That's a sorry business—and a dangerous one. I wonder how many others they've got to change money with them?"

"Everyone who looked simple enough, I suppose!" said Amber indignantly. "Well, I think we should call the constable and put 'em where they belong!"

Mr. Dangerfield, however, was less inclined to be vindictive. "The laws are too harsh—they'd be hanged, drawn, and quartered." That would not have troubled Amber but she thought it best not to say so. "I believe we can manage them some other way. Do you think, Mrs. St. Clare, that you could get them to come here on some pretext or other?"

"Why, they should be along any minute—they asked me to walk to the well with them."

When they arrived, not much later, Nan opened the door. At sight of Mr. Dangerfield their mouths opened into broad grins—and then closed suddenly when he said: "Mrs. St. Clare and I have just been discussing the fact that there seem to be counterfeiters at Tunbridge."

Kifflin raised his eyebrows. "Counterfeiters? Gad! It's unthinkable! I swear the wretches grow bolder every day!"

368

While Wigglesworth exclaimed, as though he could not believe his own ears, "Counterfeiters at Tunbridge!"

"Yes," said Amber. "I have a shilling that was just refused at the inn and Mr. Dangerfield says it's not a true coin. Perhaps they'd like to see it, sir."

He gave it to Wigglesworth and both young men examined it closely, frowning, while Kifflin cleared his throat. Their faces were beginning to shine with sweat.

"It looks good enough to me," said Kifflin at last. "But then I'm such a simple fellow someone has always got me on the hip."

Wigglesworth laughed, not very enthusiastically. "That's exactly my case, to the letter." He returned the coin.

"The constable," said Mr. Dangerfield gravely, "will be along soon to look at this coin. If he finds it to be false I suppose he'll examine every person in the village."

At that moment a country girl went by outside carrying a basket over her arm and crying, "Fresh new eggs! Who'll buy my new fresh eggs?"

Kifflin turned about quickly. "There she is, Will. I hope you'll excuse us, Mrs. St. Clare, but we came to ask if we might wait upon you later in the day. We overslept and came out in search of some eggs for our dinner. Good-day, madame. Good-day, sir."

He and Wigglesworth bowed, backed their way out of the room, and once outside turned and started off in all haste. Their pace increased, they passed the girl without giving her so much as a glance, and when they had gone two hundred yards broke into an open run and at last cut off the main street and disappeared from sight. Amber and Mr. Dangerfield, who had gone out to watch, looked at each other and then burst into laughter.

"Look at 'em go!" cried Amber. "I vow they won't stop for breath till they've reached Paris!"

She shut the door again and gave a little sigh. "Well, I hope I've learnt my lesson. I vow I'll never put my trust in strangers again."

He was smiling down at her. "A young lady as pretty as

you are should be suspicious of all strangers." He said it with the air of a man who intends to be very gallant, without ever having had much practice. And when she answered the compliment with a quick upward slanting glance he cleared his throat and his ruddy face darkened. "Hem—I wonder, Mrs. St. Clare, if you'd care to put your trust in this stranger long enough to walk to the well with him?"

Confidence was beginning to sweep through Amber, and the intoxication she always felt when she knew a man was attracted to her. "Of course I would, sir. I think I know an *honest* man when I see him—even if I can't always tell one who isn't."

Amber had acted in numerous plays depicting the rigid austere hypocritical life of the City families and, though all of them had been bitter and satirical and slanderously exaggerated, she had taken them for literal truth. Consequently, she thought she knew exactly what Samuel Dangerfield would admire in a woman; but she soon discovered that her own instinct was a surer guide.

For as she became better acquainted with him she began to realize that even though he was a City merchant and a Presbyterian he was nevertheless a man. And she found to her surprise that he bore no resemblance at all to the sanctimonious severe dour old humbugs who had occasioned such derisive laughter at His Majesty's Theatre.

If he was not frivolous, neither was he grimly sober; his disposition was a happy one and he laughed easily. He had worked hard all his life, for he had accumulated most of that vast fortune himself, but he was all the more susceptible to a young woman's gaiety now. His family life had been a close one, but that had given him perhaps a sense of loss, and of curiosity. Amber came into his life like a spring gale, fresh, invigorating, a challenge to whatever he had of dormant venturesomeness. She was everything he had never known before in a woman, and much he had scarcely suspected.

It was not long before they were spending hours out of every day together, and though Samuel insisted that she must grow bored with the company of an old man and urged her to become acquainted with the few young people who were there, Amber insisted that she hated young fellows who were always so silly and empty-headed and thought of nothing but dancing or gambling or going to the play. She kept in close and never went out when she could avoid it, for she was afraid that someone else might recognize her.

And she thought that she could guess pretty well what he would think of an actress, by his opinion of the Court in general. For one day, after some mention of King Charles, he said: "His Majesty could be the greatest ruler our nation has ever had but, unfortunately, not only for him but for all of us, the years of exile were his ruin. He learned a set of habits and a way of living during that time from which he can never escape—partly, I'm afraid, because he doesn't want to."

Amber, stitching on a piece of embroidery borrowed from Nan's work-basket, observed soberly that she had heard Whitehall had grown a most wicked place.

"It is wicked. Wicked and corrupt. Honour is a sham, virtue a laughing-stock, marriage the butt for vulgar jests. There are still decent and honest men aplenty at Whitehall, as everywhere else in England—but knaves and fools elbow them aside."

Most of their conversation, however, was less serious, and he seldom cared to discuss ethical or even political matters with her. Women were not interested in such things, and pretty ones least of all. Besides, she was his escape from them.

But Amber did often ask him to advise her about financial matters; and listened wide-eyed and with her head nodding every so often to his talk of interest and principal, mortgages, title-deeds, and revenue. She talked of her goldsmith and when she mentioned Shadrac Newbold's name was glad to see how favourably impressed he seemed. She said that it was a great responsibility for her to handle her husband's money—she represented herself as a rich young widow—and that she worried a great deal for fear someone would cheat her out of it. That was another reason, she said, why she was always suspicious of young men who wished to strike up an acquaintance. She also talked frequently about her family and what terrible things they had suffered in the Wars—recounting, with elaboration, tales she had heard from Almsbury about his own or Lord Carlton's difficulties. By these devices she hoped to discourage him, had he been so inclined, from taking her for a fortune-hunter.

They played dozens of games of wit-and-reason, and she always let him win. She made him laugh with her mimicry of the fat middle-aged women and gouty old men who were there taking the waters. She played for him on her guitar and sang songs—not ribald street-ballads, but gay country tunes or the old English folk-songs: "Chevy Chase," "Phillida Flouts Me," "Highland Mary." She pampered and flattered and teased him, treated him at all times as though he was much younger than he was, and yet was as solicitous for his comfort as if he had been much older. She guessed his age one day at forty-five and when he told her that his eldest son was thirty-five, insisted he could never make her believe that Banbury-story. She gave a lively imitation of a woman most thoroughly infatuated.

But at the end of three weeks he had not tried to seduce her and she was growing worried.

She stood at the window one evening just after he had gone and traced idle patterns on the frosted pane with her finger-nail. Her lower lip stuck out and there was a scowl on her forehead.

Nan, who was lifting hot embers out of the fireplace with a pair of tongs and putting them into a silver warming-pan, glanced sideways at her. "Something amiss, mam?"

Amber swung around, giving a petulant switch to her skirt. "Yes, there is! Oh, Nan, I'm ready to run distracted! Three weeks I've been coursing this hare—and haven't caught 'im yet!"

Nan closed the warming-pan and started into the bedroom with it. "But he's getting winded, mam. I know he is."

Amber followed her in and began to undress, but her face was gloomy and from time to time she gave an impatient ill-tempered sigh. It seemed to her that she had been trying all her life to make Samuel Dangerfield propose to her. Nan came to help her undress and stood behind her, unlacing her busk.

"Lord, mam!" she protested now. "You've got no cause for

such vapourings! I know these formal old Puritans—I've worked in their houses. They think fornication's a serious matter, let me tell you! Why, I'd bet my virginity he hasn't laid with any woman save his wife these twenty years past! Heavens, give the gentleman leave to overcome his modesty! And what's more, don't forget you've gone to the greatest pains to make him take you for a woman of virtue. But I've watched him like a witch and I know he's mighty uneasy—there's fire in the flax and it'll be quenched," she added with a sage nod. "Only give 'im the right opportunity and you'll have 'im—secure as a woodcock in a noose." She made her two hands into a trap and put them about her own neck.

While Amber stepped out of her smock Nan whisked the warming-pan over the sheets, held back the covers and Amber jumped in, pulling them up quickly about her chin. Then she lay there in luxurious warmth and considered her problem.

This was, and she knew it, her last chance to take the world by its ears and climb on top. If she failed now—but she could not fail. She did not dare. She had seen too much at first hand of what happened to the women who, like her, made a livelihood by their wits and physical attractions but who had somehow let the years and the opportunities pass without achieving security.

Somehow, somehow, she thought desperately, I've got to do it; I've *got* to make him marry me!

And as she lay there thinking, it occurred to her all at once that perhaps she had been wrong, trying to make him marry her out of remorse and a sense of guilt. Why, she thought, with a sudden feeling of discovery, that would never even enter his head! Of course he's not going to seduce me! He thinks I'm innocent and virtuous and he respects me! He'll never marry me any way at all but from his own free will. That's what I've got to do—I've got to get him to make me an *honest* proposal of marriage! Why didn't I think of that long ago? But how can I do it—how can I do it—?

Amber and Nan put their heads together over that problem, and at last they worked out a plan.

About a week later Amber and Samuel Dangerfield set out

373

for London in his coach. He had told her several days before that he must return and she had said that since she was leaving soon they might as well travel together; she would feel much safer riding with him. Her own coach, carrying Nan and Tansy, followed them. They had had a breakfast together at her cottage that morning—a substantial meal to prepare them for the journey—and though Amber had been gay and playful while they ate, now she had subsided into wistful and pensive quietness. From time to time she gave a little sigh.

The day was grey and dark and the rain seeped steadily down through the leafless branches of the forest. The air had a wet and penetrating chill, but they had fortified themselves against it with fur-lined cloaks and a fur-lined robe spread across their laps. Beneath their feet each one of them had a little brazier, like the ones people took to church, full of burning coals. So it was warm and moist inside the great lurching and rocking coach, and the warmth with the steam on the windows gave it a strange intimacy, making it a private little island shut off from the world.

Perhaps it was that seclusion and aloneness which made him bold enough to reach for her hand beneath the robe and say, "A penny for your thought, Mrs. St. Clare?"

For a moment Amber said nothing, and then she looked at him with her tenderest and most appealing smile. She gave a faint shrug of her shoulders. "Oh," she said, "I was just thinking that I'm going to miss our card games and suppers and walking up to the well in the afternoons." She gave another soft little sigh. "It's going to seem mighty lonely now I've grown used to company." She had told him how retired she lived in London, where she had no relatives, only a few friends, and was wary of making new acquaintances.

"Oh, but, Mrs. St. Clare, I hope you won't think our friendship is over. I— Well, to be honest, I've been hoping we might meet sometimes in London."

"That's kind of you," said Amber sadly. "But I know how busy you'll be—and you have all your family about you." Most of the children, she knew, grown and small alike, still lived at the great family mansion in Blackfriars.

"No, I assure you I won't. My physician wants me to do less work and as for the matter of that, I find I've a taste for idleness —if it's spent in pleasant company." She smiled, and lowered her eyes at the compliment. "And I'd like to have you meet my family. We're all very happy together and I think you'd like them—I *know* they'd like you."

"You're so kind, Mr. Dangerfield, to care about what— Oh! is something amiss?" she cried, as a sudden spasm of pain shot across his face.

For a moment he was silent, obviously embarrassed to be caught with an ailment at a moment so delicately romantic. But at last he shook his head. "No—" he said. "No, it was nothing."

But presently the look of agony came again and his face flushed dark. Amber, now greatly alarmed, seized hold of his arm.

"Mr. Dangerfield! Please! You must tell me—What is it!"

He now looked wretchedly uncomfortable and was finally forced to admit that something, he could not imagine what, was causing him great abdominal discomfort. "But don't trouble yourself for me, Mrs. St. Clare," he pleaded. "It will pass presently, it's only— Oh!" A sudden uncontrollable grunt escaped him.

Amber's own face reflected sympathetic pain as she watched him. But instantly she was in practical charge of the situation. "There's a little inn not far up the road—I remember we passed it on the way down. We'll stop there. You must get into bed right away, and I'm sure I have some— Oh, now don't make any objections, sir!" she said as he began to protest, and though her tone would permit no argument it was tender as a mother's speaking to her sick child. "I know what's best for you. Here—I've got some hawkweed and camomile in this little bag, I always carry it with me. Wait till I get this water-flask open so you can wash it down—"

It was not long before they reached the inn, at which Amber called out to order the coachman to stop, and Mr. Dangerfield's gigantic footman, Big John Waterman, helped him to make his way inside. Big John offered to carry him, and no doubt could easily have done so, but he flatly refused and resented such assistance as he was forced to receive. Amber was busy as a hen with chicks. She rushed ahead to bid the hostess get a chamber ready, directed Tempest and Jeremiah which trunks to unload, ran back a half-dozen times to make sure Mr. Dangerfield was all right. At last they had him upstairs and, against his will, lying down in the great testered bed.

"Now," said Amber to the hostess, "you must make a hot fire and bring me a kettle and crane so that I can heat water. Bring me all the hot-water bottles you have and some more blankets. Nan, open that trunk and get out the boxful of herbs —Jeremiah, go find my almanac—it's in the bottom of the green leather trunk, I think. Now get out of here, all of you, so Mr. Dangerfield can rest—"

Amber loosened his clothes, took off his cloak and hat, cravat and doublet, piled hot-water bottles around him and covered him with blankets. She was quick and gentle, cheerful but concerned; an outsider would have thought she was already his wife. He begged her not to trouble herself with him, but to go on to London and send back a doctor. And, apparently in some apprehension that this might be another and perhaps final stroke, he asked her to notify his family. Amber firmly refused.

"It's nothing serious, Mr. Dangerfield," she insisted. "You'll be hearty as ever in a few days, I know you will. It wouldn't be right to scare them that way—especially with Lettice about to lie-in." Lettice was his eldest daughter.

"No," he agreed meekly. "It wouldn't be right, would it?"

And in spite of his discomfort it soon became clear that he was enjoying his illness and the attentions it brought him. No doubt he had always felt obliged to be stoical before; now, far from home and those who knew him, he could luxuriate in the care and endless concern of a beautiful young woman who seemed to think of nothing at all but his comfort. She refused even to leave him alone at night, for fear the attack might recur, and slept there on the trundle only a few feet away.

The slightest sound from him and she was out of bed and beside him, her rich heavy hair falling about her face as she bent over him, the faint light from the candle throwing shadows across her arms and into her breasts. Her murmuring voice was like a caress; her flesh was warm whenever she happened to touch him; the heat in the room brought out an intoxicating fragrance of jasmine flowers and ambergris in her perfume. No illness had ever been so pleasant. And, half because she persuaded him he was pale and not strong enough to be moved, he remained in bed many days after all the pain had gone.

"Ye gods!" said Amber to Nan one day as she was dressing in the room which adjoined his chamber. "I think when I marry this old man I'll be a nursemaid and not a wife!"

"Heavens, mam, it's you've insisted he can't get out of bed! And it was your idea in the first place to feed 'im those toadstools—"

"Shhh!" cautioned Amber. "You've got no business remembering such things." She got up, gave herself a last glance in the mirror, and went toward the door into the next room; an expression of sweet tenderness spread over her face before she opened it.

CHAPTER TWENTY-FIVE

BARBARA'S HEAD LAY on James Hamilton's shoulder.

And both of them lay motionless, half between waking and sleeping, eyes closed, faces smooth and peaceful. But slowly Barbara began to grow uneasy. Her nose wrinkled a little and then the nostrils flared; she sniffed once or twice. What the devil's that smell? she thought irritably. And then all at once she realized.

Smoke!

The room was on fire!

She sat up with a start and saw that an entire velvet drapery was aflame, apparently having been lighted by a candle into which it had blown. She put her fists to her mouth and screamed.

"James! The room's on fire!"

The handsome colonel sat up and glared resentfully at the flaming drapery. "Good Lord!"

But Barbara was pushing him out of bed, sticking her feet into mules, reaching for her dressing-gown. And now, suddenly wide awake, Hamilton rushed across the room and with a swift movement jerked the hanging from its rod and started to stamp the flame out. But already it had spread to a chair and as he flung it onto the floor a Turkish rug caught fire.

Barbara ran to him with his clothes in her hand. "Here!" She thrust them at him: "Get into these! Quick—down that stairway before someone comes! Help! Help!" she screamed. "Fire! Help!"

James got out of the room just as Barbara admitted half-a-dozen servants from the other door. By now the flames were licking up the walls, the opposite drapery was afire and smoke was beginning to fill the room and make them cough.

"Do something, some of you!" yelled Barbara furiously, but though the room was filling with people—footmen, pages, blackamoors, serving-women, courtiers who had been passing by— no one had yet made a move to put out the fire. They all stood for several seconds, looking on in stupefied amazement, each waiting for someone else to decide what should be done.

And then a couple of footmen arrived carrying buckets full of water and pushed their way in; they gave a mighty sling and sent the water splashing over one burning chair and carpet. There was a hissing and the smoke rolled out and everyone retreated, squinting his eyes and coughing. Several now began to run for more water.

Dogs were barking. A scared monkey leaped chattering from one shoulder to another and in his terror bit the hand of a woman who tried to knock him aside. Men rushed in and out with buckets of water, most of the women ran around distractedly, doing nothing. Barbara was trying to give orders to everyone at once, though no one paid her much attention. And now she seized a page by the arm as he went hurrying by, huge buckets slopping with water in either hand.

"Boy! Wait a moment—I want a word with you!" The young

378

man stopped and looked at her; his eyes were bloodshot and his face wet with sweat and smeared with soot. She lowered her voice. "There's a cabinet in there—a small one over in this corner—with a guitar atop it. Bring it out and I'll give you twenty pound."

His eyes flickered in surprise. Twenty pounds when his pay for the year was three! She must want it badly. "The whole side's aflame, your Ladyship!"

"Forty pound, then! But bring it out!" She gave him a shove.

Two or three minutes later he came back carrying the cabinet easily in one hand, for it was very small. One side had been charred and as he set it down it fell apart and several folded letters dropped to the floor. He stooped quickly to retrieve them but Barbara cried: "Leave them alone! *I'll* pick them up! Go back to your work!"

She knelt on one knee and began to gather them swiftly, when all at once a hand reached across and took one from beneath her very fingers. Looking up she saw the Duke of Buckingham standing there smiling down at her. Her purple eyes narrowed and her teeth closed savagely.

"Give that to me!"

Buckingham continued to smile. "Certainly, my dear. When I've had a look at it. If it's so important to you, perhaps it's also important to me."

For a moment they continued to stare at each other, Barbara still half crouching, her tall cousin looming over her, both impervious to the noise and confusion all about them. And then suddenly she sprang at him, but he stepped lightly aside and warded her off with one raised arm, meanwhile sliding the letter into an inside pocket of his doublet.

"Don't be so hasty, Barbara. I'll return it to you in good time."

She gave him a sullen glare and muttered some impolite curse beneath her breath, but evidently realizing that she would have to wait until he was ready she went back to directing the workmen. The fire was almost out by now and they were carrying from the bedroom all the furniture which had not been scorched. But the entire apartment was black with smoke and the bedchamber a wet charred mess. The windows were flung open to air the rooms, though it was a gusty rainy night, and Wilson brought Barbara a mink-lined cloak to put over her dressing-gown.

When at last they had gone she turned back to Buckingham, who was strumming at a guitar. Barbara stared at him from across the room. "Now, George Villiers—give me that letter!"

The Duke made an airy gesture. "Tush, Barbara. You're always so brisk. Listen to this tune I pricked out the other morning. Rather pretty, don't you think?" He smiled at her and nodded his head in time to the gay little melody.

"A pox on you and your damned tunes! Give me that letter!"

Buckingham sighed, tossed the guitar into a chair and took the letter from his pocket; as he began to unfold it she started toward him. He held up a warning hand. "Stay where you are, or I'll go elsewhere to read it."

Barbara obeyed him and stood there, her arms folded and the toe of her mule tapping impatiently. The crisp parchment crackled in the quiet room, and then as his eyes went rapidly over the contents a smile of amusement and contempt stole onto his face.

"By God," he said softly, "Old Rowley writes as lewd a love-letter as Aretino himself." Old Rowley was his Majesty's nickname, after a pet goat that roamed the Privy Gardens.

"*Now* will you give me that letter!"

Buckingham slipped it once more into his own pocket. "Let's talk this over for a moment. I'd heard his Majesty wrote you some letters just after you'd met. What do you expect to do with 'em?"

"What business is that of yours!"

The Duke shrugged and started for the door. "None, I suppose, strictly speaking. Well—a very fine lady has made me an assignation and I should hate to disappoint her. Good-night, madame."

"Buckingham! Wait a minute! You know what I intend doing with them as well as I do."

"Publishing them some day perhaps?"

"Perhaps."

"I've heard you've threatened him with that once or twice already."

"Well, what if I have? He knows what a fool he'd look if the people were ever to read them. I can make him jump through my hoop like a tame monkey by the mere mention of 'em." She laughed, a gleam of reflective gloating cruelty in her eyes.

"A time or two, perhaps, but not for long. Not if he really decides to put you by."

"Why, what do you mean? Age won't stale these! Ten years will only give 'em a higher savour!"

"Barbara, my dear, for an intriguing woman you're sometimes uncommonly simple. Has it never occurred to you that if you really tried to publish those letters you wouldn't be able to find 'em?"

Barbara gasped. It had not, though she kept them under lock and key and until tonight no one but herself had known where they were. "He wouldn't do that! He wouldn't steal them! Anyway, I keep them well hidden!"

Buckingham laughed. "Oh, do you? I'm afraid you take Old Rowley for a greater fool than he is. The Palace swarms with men—and women too—who make it their business to find anything that will bring a good price. If he really decided that he wanted those they'd disappear from under your nose while you had your eye on 'em."

Barbara was suddenly distraught. "Oh, he wouldn't do that! He wouldn't play me such a scurvy trick! You don't *really* think he would, do you, George?"

He smiled, very much amused at her distress. "I know he would. And why not? Publishing them wouldn't be exactly a gesture of good faith on your part, would it?"

"Oh, good faith be damned! Those letters are important to me! If he ever gets tired of me they'll be all I have to protect myself—and my children. You've got to help me, George! You're clever about these things. Tell me what I can do with them!"

Buckingham heaved himself away from the wall against which he had been leaning. "There's only one thing to do with them." But as she started eagerly toward him he made a gesture of one hand, and shook his head. "Oh, no, my dear. You'll have to puzzle this out for yourself. After all, madame, you've not been my best friend of late—unless I've heard amiss."

"*I've* not been *your* best friend! Hah! And what good turns have you done me, pray? Oh, don't think I don't know about you and your Committee for Getting Frances Stewart for the King!"

He shrugged. "Well, a man must serve his King—and pimping's often the high-road to power and riches. However, it all came to nothing. She's a cunning slut, if I've ever seen one."

"Well," said Barbara, beginning to pout. "If it had it might have undone me for good and all. I thought you and I were pledged to a common cause, Buckingham." She referred to their mutual hatred of Chancellor Clarendon.

"We are, my dear. We are. It's my fondest wish to see that old man turned away in disgrace—or better yet to see his head on a pole over London Bridge. It's time the young men have a swing at governing the country." He smiled at her, a friendly ingratiating smile, all malice and scorn gone from his face. "I can't think why we're so often at odds, Barbara. Perhaps it's because we both have Villiers blood in our veins. But, come— let's be friends again— And if you'll do your part I'll try what luck I can have to bring you back into his Majesty's favour again."

"Oh, Buckingham, if only you would! I swear since her Majesty's recovery he's done nothing but trail after that simpering sugar-sop, Frances Stewart! I've been half-distracted with worry!"

"Have you? I'd understood there were several gentlemen who'd undertaken to console you—Colonel Hamilton and Berkeley and Henry Jermyn and—"

"Never mind! I thought we were going to be friends again— but that doesn't give you leave to slander my reputation to my face!"

He made her a bow. "My humblest apologies, madame. I assure you it was but an idle jest."

They had similarly quarrelled and made friends a dozen

times or more, but both of them were too fickle, too mercurial, too determinedly selfish to make good partners in any venture. Now, however, because she wanted his help she gave him a flirtatious smile and was instantly forgiving.

"Gossip will travel here at Whitehall, be a woman never so innocent," she informed him.

"I'm sure that's your case to a cow's thumb."

"Buckingham—what about the letters? You know I'm but a simple creature, and you're so clever. Tell me what I shall do."

"Why, when you ask so prettily of course I'll tell you. And yet it's so simple I'm half ashamed to say it: Burn 'em up."

"Burn them! Oh, come now, d'you take me for a fool?"

"Not at all. What could be more logical? As long as they exist he can take them from you. But once they're burned he can turn the Palace upside down and never find 'em—and all the while you're laughing in your fist."

For a moment she continued to regard him skeptically, and then at last she smiled. "What a crafty knave you are, George Villiers." She took a candle from the table and going to the cold fireplace tossed into it those letters which she held in her hand. Then she turned to him. "Give me the other one."

He handed it to her and she tossed it too on the heap. The candle-flame touched one corner and in a moment the slow fire began to creep up the paper, making it curl as it turned black. And then suddenly they broke into a bright blaze which burned for a moment or two, the sealing-wax crackling and hissing, and began to die out. Barbara looked up over her shoulder at Buckingham and found him staring into the low fire, a thoughtful enigmatic smile on his handsome face. She had a quick moment of misgiving, wondering what he could be thinking; but it soon passed and she got to her feet again, relieved to have the troublesome letters safe at last.

About a week later most of the Court went to the opening performance of John Dryden's new play, "The Maiden Queen."

The house was full when the Court party arrived and there was a great buzzing and scraping as the fops in the pit climbed onto their benches to stare, while the women hung over the balconies above. One of them impudently dropped her fan as the King passed beneath and it landed squarely on top of his head. It began to slide off and Charles caught it and presented it with a smile to the giggling blushing girl above, as a spattering of handclaps ran over the theatre.

The King, York, and the young Duke of Monmouth were all in royal mourning—long purple cloaks—for the Duchess of Savoy.

Monmouth, the King's fourteen-year-old bastard by an early love affair, had come to England in the train of Queen Henrietta Maria a year and a half before. Some said he was not really the King's son, but at least he looked like a Stuart and there could be no doubt that Charles thought he was one. Almost since the day of the boy's arrival he had shown him the most conspicuous affection and as a result of the title conferred upon him by his father he took precedence over all but York and Prince Rupert. The year before, his Majesty had married him to Anne Scott, eleven years old and one of the richest heiresses in Britain. Now the boy was appearing publicly in royal mourning—to the scandal of all who reverenced the ancient proprieties or who believed that blood was not royal unless it was also legitimate.

Down in Fop·Corner one of the sparks commented: "By God, if his Majesty isn't as fond of the boy as if he were of his own begetting."

"It runs through the galleries he intends to declare him legitimate and make him his heir now it's been proved the Queen's barren."

"Who proved it?"

"Gad, Tom, where d'ye keep yourself? My Lord Bristol sent a couple of priests to Lisbon to prove that Clarendon had something given her to make her barren just before she sailed for England."

"A pox on that Clarendon's old mouldy chops! And will you have a look at his mealy-mouthed daughter up there—as smug and formal as if she was *Queen* Anne!"

"And so she may be one day—if it's true what they say about her Majesty."

384

Another fop, catching the last phrase, perked up. "What's that? What about her Majesty?"

All over the theatre the gossip went on, hissing and murmuring, while the royal party found its seats. Charles took the one in the center, with Catherine on his right and York on his left. Anne Hyde was beside her husband, and Castlemaine at the opposite end of the row next the Queen. Around and all about them were the Maids of Honour, both her Highness's and the Queen's. They were a group of pretty, eager, laughing girls, white-skinned, blue-eyed, with shining golden curls, their satin and taffeta skirts making a rustle as they arranged the folds and fluttered their fans, whispering and giggling together over the men down in the pit. They had arrived at Court during the past year and almost all of them were lovely—as though nature herself had sought to please the King by creating a generation of beautiful women.

On Barbara's right sat one of the Queen's Maids, Mrs. Boynton, a lively little minx who liked to affect an air of great languor and who grew faint three or four times a day when there were gentlemen about. Now Barbara spoke to her in an undertone which was nevertheless loud enough for Frances Stewart, just behind them, to overhear.

"Mrs. Stewart is looking wretchedly today, have you noticed? I would swear her complexion has a greenish cast."

It was a well-known fact that Frances had been suffering from jealousy over the sensation created by the recent arrival at Court of Mrs. Jennings, a fifteen-year-old blonde who was currently being admired by all gentlemen and criticized by all ladies. Barbara was delighted that someone had come to catch interest from Frances Stewart, since that was what had happened to her the year before when Frances appeared.

Boynton waved her fan lazily, lids half-closed, and drawled, "She doesn't look green to me. Perhaps it's something in your Ladyship's eye."

Barbara gave her a look that once might have troubled her and turned to talk to Monmouth who leant forward eagerly, obviously much smitten by his father's flamboyant mistress. He was tall and well-developed for his age, physically precocious as the King had been, and so extraordinarily handsome that grown women were falling in love with him. He had not only the Stuart beauty but also the Stuart charm—a merry gentle lovable disposition, and something in his personality so dazzling that he arrested attention wherever he went.

Boynton glanced around over her shoulder to exchange smiles with Frances, and Frances leaned forward, whispering behind her fan: "I just saw his Highness slip another note into Mrs. Jennings's hand. Wait a moment and I'll warrant you she tears it up."

Jennings had been amusing the Court for some weeks by refusing to become York's mistress, an office which was generally included in the appointment of Maid of Honour to his wife. She tore up his letters before everyone and scattered the pieces on the floor of her Highness's Drawing-Room. And now, as Boynton and Frances Stewart watched her, she tore this note into bits and tossed them high in the air so that they drifted onto the Duke's head and shoulders.

Boynton and Stewart burst into delighted laughter and York, glancing around, saw the scraps on his shoulder. Scowling, he brushed them off, while Mrs. Jennings sat very straight and prim-faced and looked down over his head at the stage, where the play was beginning.

"What!" said Charles, glancing at his brother as he brushed himself, and he laughed outright. "Another rebuff, James? Odsfish! I should think you'd have taken the hint by now."

"Your Majesty doesn't always take hints, if I may say so," muttered the Duke, but Charles merely smiled good-naturedly.

"We Stuarts are a stubborn race, I think." He leaned closer to James and murmured beneath his breath: "I'll wager my new Turkish pony against your Barbary mare that I break in that skittish filly before you do."

York raised a skeptical eyebrow. "It's a wager, Sire." The two brothers shook hands and Charles settled down to watch the play.

For two acts Barbara remained seated. She smiled at Buckingham and other gentlemen down in the pit. She twisted her pearls and fiddled her fan and put her hands to her hair. She took out a mirror to examine her face, stuck on another patch, and then tossed the mirror back to Wilson. She was, very ostentatiously, bored. And all the while Charles seemed unaware that she was nearby; he did not trouble to glance at her even once.

At last she thought she could bear this no longer, and fixing a determined smile on her face she leaned across Catherine and touched his arm. "It's a wretched performance, don't you think. Sire?"

He glanced at her coldly. "No, I don't think so. I'm enjoying it."

Barbara's eyes glittered and the blood rushed to her face, but in a moment she had recovered herself. All at once she stood up, smiling sweetly, and crossing behind the Queen went to force a place for herself between Charles and York. The two men gave her surprised and angry glances and turned instantly away while Barbara sat, her face impassive and motionless as stone, though humiliated rage was making her sweat. For a moment she thought that her heart would explode, so bursting-full of blood it seemed.

And then, out of the corners of her eyes, she looked at Charles and saw the ominous flicker of his jaw-muscles. She stared at him, longing violently to reach over and rake her nails across that dark smooth-shaven cheek until she drew blood—but at last with a determined effort she dragged her eyes away and forced them down to the stage once more. All she could see was a blur that shifted and rocked; there were faces, faces, faces, turned up and grinning, smirking, sneering at her—a whole sea of enemy faces. She felt that she hated each one of them, with a murderous savage hatred that turned her sick and trembling.

It seemed to her that the play went on for hours and that she would never be able to endure the next minute of sitting there —but at last it was over. She waited a moment, under the pretense of pulling on her gloves, still hoping that Charles would invite her to ride in his coach. But instead he went off with Harry Bennet to call on the Chancellor who was again sick in bed with his gout.

Barbara lifted her hood up over her head, put on her mask

and with an impatient gesture to Wilson started out as fast as she could go—the people stepped back to make a path, for her name still had magic to part the waves. Outside she got into her coach, and though it blocked the traffic she kept it waiting while her coachman yelled and swore at whoever complained, telling them to be silent—my lady would go in her own good time. It was several minutes before Buckingham appeared.

But finally he came strolling out of the theatre with Sedley and Buckhurst, and she gestured her footman to open the door. Frantically she signalled to him, but he was talking to an orange-girl, a merry laughing young wench who chattered with the three great men, no more awed than if they had been porters or carmen. At last, completely exasperated, Barbara shouted at him:

"Buckingham!"

He glanced carelessly in her direction, waved, and turned back to continue his conversation. Barbara ripped her fan across. "Lightning blast him! I'll cut off his ears for this!" But finally he took an orange from the girl, kissed her, and dropping his coin into her low-necked bodice strolled toward the coach, tossing the orange to a tattered little ragamuffin who begged him for it.

"Get out and take a hackney," Barbara muttered hastily to Wilson, and as his Grace got in on one side the waiting-woman got out on the other.

"That little wench has the readiest wit in London," he said, sitting down beside her and waving out the window at the girl, while Barbara glared at him with a look so malignant he should have wilted. "She was put out into the streets at six to sell herring and was a slavey in Mother Ross's brothel at twelve. Hart keeps her now, but I say she belongs on the stage. Nell Gwynne's her name and I'd be willing to bet—"

Barbara had not listened to him but was yelling at her coachman to drive off, though now the traffic was so snarled on every side of them that it was impossible to move at all.

"A pox on you and your damned orange-girls!" she cried furiously, turning from the coachman back to her cousin. "A fine service you've done me! I've never been so humiliated—

388

and in plain view of all the world! What 've you been about this past week?"

Buckingham stiffened, all his natural pride and arrogance rising in resentment at her hectoring tone and manner. "D'you expect miracles? Pray remember, madame, it's taken you some time to get so far out of his Majesty's favour. Even I can't put you back in all at once. You should have stayed in your own seat—you wouldn't have been humiliated there. And henceforward, madame, please don't shout at me on street-corners as though I were your footboy."

"Why, you impertinent dog! I'll have you—"

"You'll what, madame?"

"I'll make you sorry for this!"

"I beg your pardon, madame—but you'll never make me sorry for anything again. Or have you forgotten already that I can undo you whenever I care to take the trouble? Don't forget, madame, that only you and I know that you burned his Majesty's letters."

Barbara's mouth fell open and for several seconds she sat staring at him with horror which turned slowly to writhing impotent rage. She was about to speak when he flung open the door and got out, gave her a careless wave of his gloved hand and climbed into the next coach. It was full of young women who sat in a billowing sea of silk and satin skirts, and they welcomed him with screams of delight and kisses as he sat down among them. While Barbara stared, her eyes burning purple in a white face, the coach started slowly and rolled off, but the Duke did not give her so much as a backward glance.

CHAPTER TWENTY–SIX

DANGERFIELD HOUSE WAS in the aristocratic old quarter of Blackfriars and had been built twenty years before on the site of a great fourteenth-century mansion. It formed a broad sprawling H, with courtyards both in front and in back, and was four stories high with a fifth half-story; the ground floor and the basement served for offices and warehouse. Made of red brick it was perfectly symmetrical with innumerable large square-paned glass windows, several gables cutting into the roof-line and a forest of chimney-tops. It stood on the corner of Shoemaker Row, facing Greed Lane, and was surrounded on every side by a tall iron picket-fence, guarded by massive gates where servants waited at all hours of the day or night.

Climbing out of the coach before the twin staircases which led to the main entrance on the second floor, Amber looked up at it with wide wondering eyes.

This house was something bigger, more imposing, more formidable than she had expected. Two hundred thousand pounds was an even greater amount of money than she had realized. Until now she had thought of Samuel Dangerfield merely as a kind simple old gentleman whom she had contrived to hoodwink, but now he took on something of the awe-inspiring quality of his home, and she began to feel a little nervous at the prospect of meeting his family. She wished that she felt as convinced as he did that they were going to welcome her with open arms— love her at sight.

And now, as they stood for a moment in the February drizzle while he gave instructions to the footmen regarding the disposal of their trunks and baggage, a third-story window was flung open and a woman appeared in it.

"Dad! At last you're back! We were so worried—you've been gone so long! But did it help you? Are you feeling better?" She did not, or pretended not to notice that there was a woman with her father.

But Amber looked up at her curiously. That, she thought, must be Lettice.

She had heard a great deal about Lettice—as she had heard a great deal about all his children—but more, perhaps, of Lettice than any of the others. Lettice had been married for several years, but at her mother's ·death she had returned to Dangerfield House with her husband and family to take charge of the housekeeping. Without intending to, Samuel had portrayed a prim energetic domineering woman, whom his wife was already prepared to dislike. And now Lettice was ignoring her, as though she were a lewd woman whom it was not necessary to notice.

"I'm feeling very well," said Samuel, obviously annoyed by his daughter's bad manners. "How is my new grandson?"

"Two weeks old yesterday and thriving! He's the image of John!"

"Come down into the front drawing-room, Lettice," Samuel said crisply. " I want to see you—immediately."

Lettice, after giving a quick stealthy glance at Amber, closed the window and disappeared and Amber and Samuel—with Nan and Tansy following—went up the staircase and into the house. The door was opened for them by a gigantic Negro in handsome blue livery and they stepped into a great entrance-hall out of which opened other rooms; a pair of broad curved staircases ran up either side of it to the railed-off hallway above.

Everywhere about them were the evidences of lush comfort and wealth: the beautifully laid floors, the carved oak furniture and tapestry-hung walls. And yet, somehow, the impression created was one of soberness, not frivolity. An almost ponderous conservatism marked each velvet footstool and carved cornice. It was possible to know at a glance that quiet and well-bred and moderate people lived in this house.

They walked off to the left into a drawing-room more than fifty feet long and Samuel saw immediately, to his regret, that he had made a careless mistake. For there, over the fireplace, hung a portrait of him and his first wife, painted some twenty years before; it had been there so long that he had forgotten it. But Amber, looking at the powerful prim unlovely face of the first Mrs. Dangerfield, understood immediately why it had been possible to induce Samuel to marry her—though she doubted whether his family would understand as well.

At that moment there were footsteps behind them and she turned to see a replica of the woman on the wall standing facing her. For an instant Lettice's eyes met hers in a quick fierce womanly stare, all-seeing, and condemning, and then she turned to her father. Amber gave her a sweeping glance which discovered that she knew nothing about clothes, was too tall, and looked older than her thirty-two years. The gown Lettice was wearing was like those Killigrew had put on the actresses when he had wished to show a hypocritical Puritan, and against which they had always protested violently. It was perfectly plain black and fitted neither snugly nor too loosely, had a deep white-linen collar which covered her to the base of her throat, and broad linen cuffs. Her light-brown hair was almost entirely concealed beneath a starched little cap with shoulder-length lappets, and she wore no jewellery but a diamond-studded wedding-band. Against such simplicity Amber, who had thought herself very demure, felt suddenly gaudy and flamboyant.

"My dear," said Samuel to Amber, and he took her arm, "may I present my eldest daughter, Lettice? Lettice, this is my wife."

Lettice gasped and turned paste-white. Amber—once the ceremony was performed—had suggested to Samuel that they send a messenger ahead to notify the family. But he had insisted upon giving them what he was sure would be a most happy surprise.

Now Lettice stood and stared at her father for several stark quiet moments, and then as she turned to look at Amber there was an expression of frank horrified shock on her face. She seemed aware of it herself, but unable to help it, and this unexpected reaction on her part was making Samuel angry. Amber, who had prepared herself for it, smiled faintly and nodded.

At last Lettice managed to speak. "Your—wife? But, Dad—" She put one hand distractedly to her head. "You're married? But your letters never mentioned— We didn't— Oh, I—I'm sorry— I—"

She seemed so genuinely and painfully stunned that Samuel's rigid hauteur collapsed. He put one arm about her. "There, my dear, I know it's a surprise to you. But I was counting on you, Lettice, to help me tell the others. Look at me— And please smile. I'm very happy and I want my family to be happy with me."

For a long minute Lettice buried her head against her father's chest and Amber waited with a feeling of annoyance, expecting hysterics. But at last she stood erect, kissed Samuel's cheek and smiled. "I'm glad you're happy, Dad." She turned about quickly.

"I'll make arrangements for dinner," and she ran out of the room.

Amber glanced at Samuel and saw a strange thoughtful look on his face as his eyes followed Lettice. She put her hand into his. "Oh, Samuel—she doesn't like me. She didn't want you to get married."

His eyes came back to her. "Well, perhaps she didn't," he agreed, though before he had never admitted such a possibility. "But then Lettice never likes anything new—no matter what it is. But wait until she knows you. She'll love you then—no one could help it."

"Oh, Samuel, I hope so! I hope they'll *all* like me. I'll try so hard to make them like me."

They went upstairs then to his apartments which were in the south-west wing of the building, overlooking the rear court and the garden. The suite consisted of a string of rooms opening one into another, all of them furnished in much the same style as the others she had seen. There were reminders of his first wife everywhere: another portrait of her above the fireplace, a wardrobe which must have held her clothes and perhaps still did; there was the impress of her personality on every rug and piece of furniture. Amber felt as though she had walked into a room which still belonged to the dead woman, and decided immediately that she would make some changes here.

Promptly at one o'clock Samuel and Amber entered the dining-room. They found every member of the family who was home and old enough to walk assembled there to meet her. Almost thirty persons stood about the huge table, several of them children who would ordinarily have been eating in the nursery. Such large families were common among the richer middle-classes, for their children did not die in as large proportion as did those of the poor and their women made no effort to prevent child-bearing as did the fashionable ladies of Whitehall and Covent Garden.

Now, as Amber and Samuel stood in the doorway, one little moppet inquired loudly: "Mother, is *that* the woman?" Her mother administered a hasty embarrassed slap and followed it with a shake to keep her from crying.

Samuel ignored this incident and began to make the introductions. Each person, when presented, came forward to bow, if a man, or to curtsy and give her a peck on the cheek if a woman. The children, staring round-eyed, likewise made their awkward bows and curtsies. It was obvious from their interest and awe that much had already been said among the grown-ups about the new Mrs. Dangerfield.

On the whole they were handsome people; Lettice's plain face was almost conspicuous. There was the eldest son, Samuel, with his wife and six children. Robert, the next son, whose wife was dead, and his two children. Lettice's husband, John Beckford, and their eight children. The third son, John, who also lived in the house with his wife and five children and was engaged as were the older sons in their father's business. A daughter who had come from her nearby home with her children for the occasion. James, with his wife and two children. And three younger children, girls fifteen and thirteen, and a twelve-year-old boy. There were others—one travelling abroad, one at Grey's Inn and one at Oxford, a girl who lived in the country and another whose first pregnancy had kept her from attending the great event.

Lord! thought Amber. So many people to divide a fortune between! Well, there's one more now.

They were all instructed to call her "Madame"—Samuel could not bring himself to tell them her first name—and a troop of footmen began to march into the room carrying great silver trays, porringers and tankards, steaming with the most deliciously fragrant food and brimful of good golden ale. The dining-room was as solemnly impressive as the rest of the house. The stools they sat on were covered with tapestry; a great carved-oak cupboard was loaded with silver plate that made Amber's eyes pop; they drank from fragile crystal glasses and ate from silver dishes. And yet in the midst of all that splendour they sat in their quiet unpretentious clothes, black and grey and dark green, with white collars and cuffs, drab as sparrows. Ribbons and lace, false curls and powder and patches were nowhere to be seen and Amber, even in her simple black velvet

394

gown with the white lace collar, felt strangely conspicuous—and she was.

She had expected them to be hostile, and they were, for by law in the City of London one-third of a man's fortune must go to his widow, and if she bore him a child—as she hoped to do—she might get even more.

But that was not the only reason they disliked her. They disliked her first because their father had married her, and every grievance stemmed from that, though it was not probable they would have had a good opinion of her under any circumstances. She was, though she tried not to seem so, an alien, different from them in all the wrong ways.

Her beauty, even without obvious paint, was too vivid to be decent in their eyes. The women were convinced that she was neither as sweet nor as innocent as she seemed, for they recognized though they did not discuss her blatant quality of sexual allure. A woman's eyes should not have that wicked slant, nor her body an air of being unclothed even when thoroughly covered. They learned what her first name was and were shocked; their own names were the old-fashioned and trustworthy ones, Katherine, Lettice, Philadelphia, Susan.

And Amber, in spite of her protestations to Samuel that she wanted nothing on earth but the love of his family, did from the start many things which they could only resent and criticize.

She had already possessed an extensive wardrobe, but nevertheless she was constantly ordering and buying new things—elaborate gowns, fur-lined cloaks, dozens of pairs of silk stockings, fans and shoes and muffs and gloves by the score. For weeks at a time she never appeared twice in the same costume. And she wore her jewels, emeralds, diamonds, topazes, as carelessly as if they were glass beads. Her portrait, faintly smiling in a gold-lace gown, replaced that of Samuel and the first Mrs. Dangerfield in the drawing-room. The bedroom in which many of them had been born was refurnished and gold-flowered crimson-damask hangings went up at the windows and around the bed; the old fireplace was torn out and a new black Genoese marble mantel put in its stead; Venetian mirrors and lacquered

East Indian cabinets and screens supplanted the respectable pieces of English oak.

But even those things they might have forgiven her had it not been for their father's obvious and shameless infatuation. For once married to him Amber was able to make use of a great many means for increasing his passion which she had not dared employ during the courtship. She knew that her chief hold over him was her youth and beauty and flagrant desirability—qualities his first wife had utterly lacked and would have scorned as more suitable to a man's whore than to his lawful wife. And, because she wanted a child to bind him even closer, she pandered in every way she could to his concupiscence. He neglected his work to be with her, lost weight, and—even though he made an effort to behave decorously before his family—his eyes betrayed him whenever he looked at her. They were aware of all this, aware in fact of more than any of them cared to mention, and their hatred grew.

At his age it seemed to them not only disgusting but actually treacherous, a desecration of the memory of their own mother. And it was incomprehensible, to the men as well as the women, for Samuel had lived so continently, had worked so hard and seemed so little interested in pretty women or any other form of divertissement, that they could not understand why he should now suddenly reverse all the habits of a lifetime.

But it was Lettice, more than any of the others, who resented her. She felt that Amber's presence in the house was a shameful thing, for she could not regard a wife of barely twenty as anything other than her sixty-year-old father's mistress, taken in his declining and apparently immoral years.

"That woman!" she whispered fiercely one day to Bob and the younger Sam as the three of them stood at the foot of the stairs and watched Amber run gaily up, curls tossing, skirts lifted to show the embroidered gold clocks on her green-silk stockings. "I vow she's no good! I'm sure she paints!" They always criticized her for the things they dared to say out loud to each other, though the rest was well if silently understood among them.

Twenty-year-old Henry, who was a student at Grey's Inn, had

just sauntered up and stood watching her too. He was so much younger than the others that his share in the fortune would not be a large one and so he had no prejudice on that score. For the rest, he had a sly admiration for his step-mother which he often humoured in fanciful day-dreams.

"It wouldn't be so bad if she wasn't a raving beauty into the bargain, eh Lettice?" he said now.

Lettice gave her brother a look of scorn. "Raving beauty! Who wouldn't be a beauty with paint and curls and patches and ribbons and all the rest of it!"

Henry shrugged, looking back to his sister now that Amber had disappeared down the upper hallway. "It's a pity more women aren't then, since it's so easy."

"Faith and troth, Henry! You're getting all your ideas from the playhouse!"

Henry coloured. "I am not, Lettice! I've never been inside a playhouse and you know it!"

Lettice looked skeptical, and the other two brothers threw back their heads and laughed. Henry, growing redder, turned hastily and walked off; and Lettice with a sigh went out toward the kitchens to resume her work. For Amber had made no attempt to take over the running of the household and though Lettice would have liked to force it upon her Samuel had asked her to continue in charge and she could not refuse him. But it was no easy task to organize and direct an establishment consisting of thirty-five children and adults and almost a hundred and fifty servants.

Upstairs Amber was getting into her cloak, putting the hood up over her hair, tucking a black-velvet vizard inside her muff. Her movements were quick and her eyes sparkled with excitement.

"I tell you, mam," said Nan, helping her but shaking her red-blonde curls, "it's a foolhardy thing to do."

"Nonsense, Nan!" She began pulling on a pair of embroidered, elbow-length gloves. "No one could recognize me in this!"

"But suppose they *do,* mam! You'll be undone—and for what?"

Amber wrinkled her nose and gave Nan's cheek a little pat. "If anyone wants me I've gone to the 'Change. And I'll be back by three."

She went out the door and down a narrow spiralling flight of stairs which led her into the back courtyard where one of the great coaches stood waiting. She got in quickly and the heavy vehicle lumbered about and drove out of the yard to turn up Carter Lane; she had kept Tempest and Jeremiah with her and they drove her wherever she went.

At last they stopped. She put on her mask and got out, crossed the street and turned into a lane which led through a teeming noisy courtyard and thence to the back of the King's Theatre. She glanced around, then went in and down to the door of the tiring-room which she found, as always, full of half-naked actresses and beribboned gallants, most of whom were wearing the brand-new fashion of periwigs.

For a moment she stood unnoticed in the doorway and then Beck Marshall spoke to her. "What d'you want, madame?"

With a triumphant laugh and a flourish Amber took off her mask and dropped back her hood. The women shrieked with surprise and Scroggs waddled forward to greet her, her ugly old face red and grinning, and Amber put an arm about her shoulders.

"By Jesus, Mrs. St. Clare! Where've ye been? See!" she crowed. "I told ye she'd be back!"

"And here I am. Here's a guinea for you to drink, Scroggs, you old swill-belly—that should keep you foxed for a week."

She came on into the room and was instantly surrounded on every side by the women who kissed her, asking a dozen questions at once, while the gallants hung close and insisted they had been adying for her company. There had been rumours that she had gone into the country to have a baby, had died of the ague, had sailed for America, but when she told them she had married a rich old merchant—whose name she did not disclose— they were much impressed. The actors heard that she was there and came in too, claiming a kiss each, examining her clothes and jewels, asking her how much money she would inherit and if she was pregnant yet.

398

Amber felt wholly at her ease for the first time in more than four months. At Dangerfield House she was constantly dogged by the feeling that she would inadvertently do or say something improper. And she was made more uncomfortable by a nagging mischievous desire to suddenly throw off her air of sweet naïveté, make a bawdy remark, wink at a footman, shock them all.

Then all at once she caught sight of a face which, for an instant, she did not recognize, seeing it in this unfamiliar environment. And suddenly she clapped her mask back on, turned up her hood and began to make her goodbyes. For there across the room, talking to one of the new actresses, was Henry Dangerfield. In less than a minute she was on her way down the dimly-lighted corridor, but she had not gone far when footsteps came up behind her.

"I beg your pardon, madame—"

Amber's heart jumped and she stopped perfectly still, but only for an instant and then immediately she went on again.

"I don't know you, sir!" she snapped, changing her voice to a higher pitch.

"But I'm Henry Dangerfield and you're—"

"Mrs. Ann St. Michel, sir, and travelling alone!"

"I beg your pardon, madame—"

To her intense relief Amber found that he had stopped and when she got outside and glanced back he was not in sight. Nevertheless she did not get into the coach but said softly to Tempest as she walked by, "Meet me at the Maypole corner."

Amber spent the rest of the afternoon in her room, nervous and restless. She paced back and forth, looked out the window dozens of times, wrung her hands and asked Nan over and over why Samuel was late. Nan had not said that she knew this would happen, but she looked it.

But when he came in, late in the afternoon, he greeted her with a smile and kiss, just as he always did. Amber, who had put on a dressing-gown and nothing else, laid her head against his chest.

"Oh, Samuel! Where 've you been! It's so late—I've been so worried about you!"

He smiled and, glancing around to make sure that Nan was

not looking, he slipped one hand into her gown. "I'm sorry, sweetheart. A gentleman had come from out of town on business and we talked longer than I expected—" His head bent to kiss her again, and from behind his back Amber signalled at Nan to leave the room.

At first she thought she would stay there that night and not go down to supper, but finally she decided that it would do no good. If Henry had recognized her he could mention it tomorrow as well as today, and she could not hide in their apartments forever.

But the supper went exactly as it usually did and afterward, as was their custom, they all went into one of the small parlours to spend an hour or two before retiring. Again Amber thought of pleading a headache and getting Samuel to go upstairs with her, but again she decided against it. If Henry was suspicious and she stayed—perhaps he would think that he had been wrong.

Lettice, with Susan and Philadelphia and Katherine, sat before the fireplace talking quietly and working on pieces of embroidery. The younger children started a game of blind-man's-buff. Samuel sat down to a chess game which had been going on for several nights between him and twelve-year-old Michael, and Henry pulled up a chair to watch. The older brothers smoked their pipes and discussed business and the Dutch and criticized the government. Amber, beginning to feel comfortable again, sat in a chair and talked to Jemima, prettiest of all the good-looking Dangerfield children.

Jemima, just fifteen, was the one friend Amber had made in her new home; and Jemima admired her whole-heartedly. She was too unsophisticated to understand much more regarding her father's recent marriage than that he had brought a new woman to live in the house. And this woman looked and dressed and behaved exactly as she would have liked to do herself. She could not understand the animosity felt toward Madame by her older brothers and sisters, and had often repeated to Amber the things she had heard them say about her. Once she told her that Lettice, upon hearing of how devotedly Madame had nursed him through his illness, had said that she would just as soon think she had made him sick herself to have the opportunity of making him well. Amber, somewhat uneasy to hear this, was relieved that the oldest brother had cautioned Lettice against being carried too far by her own jealousy. After all, he had said, the woman might be of dubious character—but she couldn't be *that* bad.

Amber—who usually got along well with girls too young or unattractive to compete with her—encouraged the friendship. She found Jemima's naïve admiration and talkativeness a convenient means of informing herself on the others—as well as a source of entertainment to help her pass the long dull days. Furthermore, she took malicious delight in annoying Lettice. For Lettice had warned Jemima repeatedly against the association, but Lettice was no longer head of the house and Jemima was spirited enough to enjoy disobeying her.

She was about the same height Amber was, but her figure was slight and less rounded. Her hair was rich dark brown with sparks of copper in it; her skin fine and white and she had blue eyes with a sweep of curling black lashes. She was eager, vivacious, spoiled by her father and elder brothers, independent, stubborn and lovable. Now she sat on a stool beside Amber, her fingers clasped over her knees, eyes shining in fascination while Amber told her a story she had heard at second hand of the King begging my Lady Castlemaine's pardon on his knees.

Across the room Susan glanced at them and raised her eyebrows significantly. "How devoted Jemima is to Madame! They're all but inseparable. I should think you'd be more careful, Lettice. Jemima might learn to paint."

Lettice gave her a sharp glance but found her looking down at her embroidery, taking tiny precise stitches. For several years, ever since Lettice had returned home and assumed management of the household, there had been a low-current feud going on between her and this wife of the eldest brother. The other two women smiled faintly, amused, for they were all secretly a little pleased that at last Lettice had found someone she could not dominate. But they were not so pleased it sweetened the bitter gall of lost money: the new wife was still the common enemy of them all, and their little personal animosities of but minor importance.

Lettice answered her quietly. "I am going to be more careful in the future—for that isn't all the child might learn from her."

"Low-necked gowns without a scarf too, perhaps," said Susan.

"Much worse than that, I'm afraid."

"What could be worse?" mocked Susan.

But Katherine sensed that Lettice knew something she had not told them, and her eyes lighted with the prospect of scandal. "What've you heard, Lettice? What's she done?" At Katherine's tone the other two instantly leaned forward.

"What do you know, Lettice?"

"Has she done something *terrible?*" They could not even imagine what could be terrible enough.

Lettice threaded her needle. "We can't discuss it now with the children in the room."

Immediately Philadelphia rose. "Then I'll send them to bed."

"Philadelphia!" said Lettice sharply. "I'll handle this! Wait until she begins to sing."

For every night, after the children had gone to bed and just before they all retired, Amber sang to them. Samuel had instigated the custom, and now it was a firmly-established part of household routine.

The women fidgeted nervously for almost an hour, begging Lettice in whispers over and over again to send the children to bed, but she would not do so until exactly the time when they went every night. She returned from seeing them into the custody of their nurses to find Amber strumming her guitar and singing a mournful pretty little song:

> "What if a day, or a month, or a year,
>   Crown thy delights
> With a thousand glad contentings?
> Cannot the chance of a night or an hour
>   Cross thy delights
> With as many sad tormentings?"

When it was done the listeners applauded politely, all but Jemima and Samuel, who were enthusiastic. "Oh, if only I could sing like that!" cried Jemima.

And Samuel went to take her hand. "My dear, I think you have the prettiest voice I've ever heard."

Amber kissed Jemima on the cheek and slipped her arm through Samuel's, smiling up at him. She was still holding her guitar which had been a gift from Rex Morgan and was decorated with a streamer of multicoloured ribbons he had bought for her one day at the Royal Exchange. She was relieved to have the evening done and was eager to get upstairs where she could feel safe. Never again, she had promised herself a dozen times, will I be such a fool.

Lettice sat leaning forward in her chair, tense, her hands clasped hard, and now Katherine gave her an impatient nudge with her elbow. Suddenly Lettice's voice rang out, unnaturally clear and sharp: "It's not surprising that Madame's voice should be pleasant."

Henry, standing across the room, gave a visible start and his adolescent face turned red. Amber's heart and the very flowing of her blood seemed to stop still. But Samuel had not heard, and though she continued to smile up at him she was wishing desperately that she could stop up his ears, push him out of the room, somehow keep him from ever hearing.

"What do you mean, Lettice?" It was Susan.

"I mean that any woman who used her voice to earn her living should have a pleasant one."

"What are you talking about, Lettice?" demanded Jemima. "Madame has never earned her living and you know it!"

Lettice stood up, her cheeks bright, fists clenched nervously at her sides, and the lappets on her cap trembled. "I think that you had better go to your room, Jemima."

Jemima was instantly on the defensive, looking to Amber for support. "Go to my room? Why should I? What have I done?"

"You've done nothing, dear," said Lettice patiently, determined that there should be no quarrel within the family itself. "But what I have to say is not altogether suitable for you to hear."

Jemima made a grimace. "Heavens, Lettice! How old do you think I am? If I'm old enough to get married to that Joseph Cuttle I'm old enough to stay here and listen to anything you might have to say!"

By now Samuel was aware of the quarrel going on between his daughters. "What is it, Lettice? Jemima's grown-up, I believe. If you have something to say, say it."

"Very well." She took a deep breath. "Henry saw Madame at the theatre this afternoon."

Samuel's expression did not change and the three women about the fireplace looked seriously disappointed, almost cheated. "Well?" he said. "Suppose he did? I understand the theatre is patronized nowadays by ladies of the best quality."

"You don't understand, Father. He saw her in the tiring-room." For a moment she paused, watching the change on her father's face, almost wishing that her hatred and jealousy had never led her to make this wretched accusation. She was beginning to realize that it would only hurt him, and do no one any good. And Henry stood looking as if he wished he might be suddenly stricken by the devil and disappear in a cloud of smoke. Her voice dropped, but Lettice finished what she had begun. "She was in the tiring-room because she was once an actress herself."

There was a gasp from everyone but Amber, who stood perfectly still and stared Lettice levelly in the eye. For an instant her face was naked, threatening savage hate showing on it, but so quickly it changed that no one could be certain the expression had been there at all. Her lashes dropped, and she looked no more dangerous than a penitent child, caught with jam on its hands.

But Susan pricked her finger. Katherine dropped her sewing. Jemima leaped involuntarily to her feet. And the brothers were jerked out of their lazy indifference to what they had thought was merely another female squabble. Samuel, who had been looking younger and happier these past weeks than he had in years, was suddenly an old man again; and Lettice wished that she had never been so great a fool as to tell him.

For a moment he stood staring ahead and then he looked down at Amber, who raised her eyes to meet his. "It isn't true, is it?"

She answered him so softly that though everyone else in the room strained to hear her words they could not. "Yes, Samuel,

404

it's true. But if you'll let me talk to you—I can tell you why I had to do it. Please, Samuel?"

For a long minute they stood looking at each other, Amber's face pleading, Samuel's searching for what he had never tried before to find. And then his head came up proudly and with her arm still linked in his they walked from the room. There was a moment of perfect silence, before Lettice ran to her husband and burst into broken-hearted tears.

CHAPTER TWENTY-SEVEN

No FURTHER MENTION was ever made, in the presence of Samuel Dangerfield, of his wife's acting.

The morning after Lettice had made her sensational disclosure, he called her into a private room and told her that the matter had been explained to his own satisfaction, that he did not consider an explanation due the family, and that he wanted no more talk of it among themselves, nor any mention to outsiders. Henry was told that he could either forgo visiting the theatre or leave home. And to all outward appearances everything went on exactly as it had before.

The first time Amber appeared at dinner after that she was as composed and natural as if none of them knew what she really was; her coolness on this occasion was considered to be the boldest thing she had yet done. They could never forgive her for not hanging her head and blushing.

But though Amber knew what they thought of her she did not care. Samuel, at least, was convinced that she was wholly innocent, the victim of bad luck which had forced her into the uncongenial surroundings of the theatre, and that she had been tainted neither physically nor morally by the months she had spent on the stage. His infatuation for her was so great, his loyalty so intense, that none of them dared criticize her to him, even by implication. And they were all forced by family pride and love of their father to protect her against outsiders. For though, inevitably, gossip spread among their numberless relatives and friends that old Samuel Dangerfield had married an actress—and one of no very good repute—they defended her so convincingly that Amber became acceptable to the most censorious and stiff-necked dowagers in London.

But if the rest of the family was shocked and ashamed to be related, even by marriage, to a former actress, there was one of them who thought it the most exciting thing that had ever happened. That was Jemima. She teased Amber by the hour to tell her all about the theatre, what the gentlemen said, how my Lady Castlemaine looked when she sat in the royal box, what it felt like to stand on the stage and have a thousand people stare at you. And she wanted to know if it was true—as Lettice had said—that actresses were lewd women. Jemima was somewhat puzzled as to exactly what a lewd woman was, but it did sound wickedly exciting.

Amber answered her questions, but only part of each one. She told her step-daughter of all that was gay and colourful and amusing about the theatre and the Court—but omitted those other aspects which she knew too well herself. To Jemima fine gentlemen and ladies were fine because they wore magnificent clothes, had an elaborate set of mannerisms, and were called by titles. She would not have liked to be disillusioned.

And for all that Lettice could say or do she began to imitate her step-mother.

Her neck-lines went lower, her lips became redder, she began to smell of orange-flower-water and to wear her hair in thick lustrous curls with the back done up high and twisted with ribbons. Amber, motivated by pure mischief, encouraged her. She gave her a vial of her own perfume, a jar of lip-paste, a box of scented powder, combs to make her curls stand out and seem thicker. At last Jemima even stuck on two or three little black-taffeta patches.

"Faith and troth, Jemima!" said Lettice to her sister one day when she came down to dinner in a satin gown with huge puffed sleeves that left her shoulders and too much of her bosom bare. "You're beginning to look like a hussy!"

406

"Nonsense, Lettice!" said Jemima airily. "I'm beginning to look like a lady!"

"I never thought I'd see the day my own sister would paint!"

But Sam put his arm about Jemima's tiny laced-in waist. "Let the child be, Lettice. What if she does wear a patch or two? She's pretty as a picture."

Lettice gave Sam a look of scornful disgust. "You know where she learns all this, don't you?"

Jemima sprang hotly to the defense of her step-mother. "If you mean I learned it from Madame, I did! And you'd better not let Father hear you speak of her in that tone, either!"

Lettice gave a little sigh and shook her head. "What have we Dangerfields come to—when the feelings of a common actress are—"

"What do you mean a 'common actress,' Lettice?" cried Jemima. "She isn't common at all! She's a lady of quality! Of better quality than the Dangerfields are, let me tell you! But her father—who was a knight, I'll have you know—turned her out when she married a man he didn't like! And when her husband died she was left without a shilling. Tom Killigrew saw her on the street one day and asked her to go onto the stage, and so she did—to keep from starving! And as soon as her husband's father died and left her some money she quit and went to Tunbridge Wells where she could live quiet and retired! Well—what are you both smirking at?"

Sam sobered immediately, for it was his opinion that Jemima would be less injured by her association with the woman if she did not know what she really was. "Is that the story she told Father?"

"Yes, it is! You believe it, don't you, Sam? Oh, Lettice! You make me sick!"

Suddenly she swirled about and lifting up her skirts started off up the stairs and as she went Lettice saw that with everything else she had begun to wear green silk stockings. Sam and Lettice looked at each other.

"Do you suppose he really believed that wild tale?" he asked at last.

Lettice sighed. "I know he did. And if he thought that we

didn't—well, he mustn't ever think it, that's all. I don't know what happened to him to make him change, but something did and we must hide our feelings and thoughts for his sake. We still love him even if—even if—" She turned about quickly and walked away, though Sam gave her arm a brief pressure as she went. And at that moment Samuel and Amber walked into the room, Jemima triumphantly beside them with one arm linked through her step-mother's.

By June Amber, who was not yet pregnant, was beginning to worry frantically. For Samuel, she knew, was anxious to have a child—mostly, she suspected, to justify his marriage to her in his own and his family's eyes. And she wanted one herself. He had already redrawn his will to give her the legal one-third, but she thought that a baby might induce him to give her even more. He had grown almost comically sentimental about babies, considering that his first wife had borne him eighteen children. And perpetually aware as she was of the hostility they all felt toward her, she believed that a baby would protect her as nothing else could.

Enveloped in a cloak, her face covered with a vizard, she went to consult half the midwives and quacks and physicians in London, asking their advice. She had a chestful of oils and balsams and herbs and a routine of smearing and anointing which occupied a great deal of time. Samuel's diet included vast quantities of oysters, eggs, caviar, and sweetbreads—but still the maddening fact persisted, she was not pregnant. She finally went to an astrologer to have her stars read and was encouraged when he told her that she would soon conceive.

One very hot day late in June she and Jemima returned from a visit to the Royal Exchange and came into her apartments to drink a syllabub cooled in ice. The streets had been dusty and the crowds bad-tempered. There were so many flies in the house that though Tansy was detailed with a swatter to kill them they zoomed and buzzed everywhere. Amber tossed aside her fan and gloves and the hood she had been wearing and dropped onto a couch, beginning immediately to unfasten the bodice of her gown.

Jemima was less interested in the heat than in the exciting adventure they had just had. For two very fine and good-looking gentlemen had stopped her step-mother in the Upper Walk of the 'Change and one of them had asked, with charming impudence, to be presented to "that pretty blue-eyed jilt"—meaning Jemima. And then he had kissed her on the cheek; bowed most graciously, and invited her to drive to Hyde Park with him and have a syllabub.

"Imagine!" cried Jemima delightedly. "Mr. Sidney saying that after meeting me the day seemed hotter than ever!" She giggled and sipped her drink. "I vow I've never seen such handsome men—at least not in a great while. And the other one, Colonel Hamilton, is my Lady Castlemaine's lover, isn't he?" She felt flattered to have been looked at admiringly by a gentleman her Ladyship loved. Barbara's notoriety was now so extensive that she had become a kind of myth, known even to innocent and sheltered girls like Jemima.

"That's the gossip," said Amber lazily.

"Of course I know you were right to tell them we couldn't go—and yet they seemed so fine, and so genteel and well-bred. I vow we'd all have been mighty merry."

Amber exchanged a sly glance with Nan, who was across the room behind Jemima. "No doubt," she agreed and got up to begin undressing. The Dangerfields entertained a great deal—more than ever since Samuel was so eager to display his lovely young wife—and it was her chief diversion to change one beautiful gown for another.

"You know," said Jemima now, not watching her step-mother but staring reflectively down into her glass. "I think it would be a mighty fine thing to have a lover—if he was a gentleman, I mean. I hate common fellows! All the Court ladies have lovers, don't they?"

"Oh, some of 'em do, I suppose. But to tell you truth, Jemima, I don't think Lettice would like to hear you talk that way."

"Much I care what Lettice would like! What does she know about things like that? The only man she ever knew was John Beckford—and she married him! But you're different. You know everything—and I can talk to you because you won't tell me I'm wanton. Husbands are always such dull fellows—the gentlemen never seem to get married, do they?"

"Not while they can get—not while they can help it," amended Amber.

"Why not? Why don't they?"

"Oh," she shrugged into a dressing-gown, "they say they'll lose their reputations as men of wit. But come, Jemima, you don't really mean all this. I thought that you were going to marry Joseph Cuttle."

Jemima made a violent face. "Joseph Cuttle! You should see him! Don't you remember— He was here last Wednesday. He's got teeth that stick out and skinny legs and pimples all over his face! I hate him! I won't marry him! I don't care what they say! I won't!"

"Well—" said Amber soothingly. "I don't think your father will make you marry a man you hate."

"He says I have to marry him! They've been planning it for years. But, oh, I don't want to! Amber!" she cried suddenly, and rushed to kneel before her where she sat in her dressing-gown, stroking a great purring tortoise-shell cat. "Father will do anything you say! *You* make him promise I don't have to marry Joseph Cuttle, will you? *Will* you, Amber, please?"

"Oh, Jemima," protested Amber, "you mustn't say such things! Your father doesn't do what I tell him to, at all." She knew that even Samuel would not want his family to think he was hen-pecked. "But I'll speak to him about it for you—"

"Oh, if only you would! Because I won't marry him! I can't! I'm— Do you want to know something, Amber? I'm in love!"

Amber seemed duly impressed, and asked the expected question. "How fine. Is he handsome?"

"Oh," breathed Jemima fervently. "The handsomest man I've ever seen! He's tall and his hair's black and his eyes—I forget what colour they are, but when he looks at me I get such a queer feeling right here. Oh, Amber, he's wonderful! He's everything in the world that I admire!"

"Hey day!" said Amber. "Where's this wonder to be seen?"

Jemima grew wistful at that. "Not here—not in London. At

least not now—but I hope he'll be back one day soon. I've been waiting for him for thirteen months and a week—and I'll never love another man till he returns."

Amber was amused, for Jemima's enthusiasm seemed quite childish to her, considering that the girl did not guess what the primary business of love was about. Naïve kisses and queer feelings were the limit of her experience. "Well, Jemima, I hope he comes back to you. Does he know you're waiting?"

"Oh, no. I suppose he scarce knows I'm alive. I've only seen him twice—he was here one night for supper and another time I went down with Sam and Bob to see his ships, just before he sailed for America."

"Sailed for America! Who is this man! What's his name!"

Jemima looked at her in surprise. "If I tell you will you promise not to tell a soul? They'd all laugh at me. He's a noble-man—Lord Carlton— Oh! What's the matter? Do *you* know him?"

It was like a smack in the face with cold water, rude and shocking, and it made her angry because it scared her. But why should it? she thought, annoyed by her own uneasy lack of confidence. This girl can't mean anything to him— Why, she's just a child. Besides, she's not half as pretty as I am— Or is she? Amber's eyes were going swiftly over her step-daughter's face—seeing there now a threat to her own happiness. Don't be such a fool! she told herself wrathfully. Do you want her to guess— Only seconds had passed before she managed to answer, with a show of casualness:

"Why, I think I met him once at the Theatre. But how d'you come to be entertaining a lord and visiting his ships?"

"He does some business with Father—I don't know just what."

Amber lifted her eyebrows. "Samuel doing business with a pirate?"

"But he's not a pirate! He's a privateer—and there's a world of difference between 'em. It's the privateers we have to thank for keeping England on the seas—his Majesty's navy won't do it!"

"You talk like a merchant yourself, Jemima," said Amber tartly, but brought herself up with another quick warning.

"Well—" She contrived a smile. "So you're in love with a nobleman. Then I hope for your sake he'll come back to England soon."

"Oh, I hope so too! I'd give anything to see him again! D'you know—" she said with sudden confiding shyness, "last Hallowe'en Anne and Jane and I baked a dumb-cake. Anne dreamed that night about William Twopeny—and now she's married to him! And *I* dreamed about Lord Carlton! Oh, Amber, do you think he could ever fall in love with me? Do you think he'd ever marry me?"

"Why not!" snapped Amber. "You should have a big enough dowry!" The instant she heard the words she was furious with herself and quickly added, "That's what men always think about, you know."

In less than an hour she broke her promise to Jemima, for Samuel came in and she could not resist the temptation to speak to him of Bruce, though she began by saying innocently, "I heard today in the 'Change that the Dutch have told his Majesty their fleet is only to defend their fishing trade, and that he's angry they should think he's stupid enough to believe it."

Samuel, who was putting off his outer clothes, laughed at that. "What a ridiculous lie! The Dutch fleet is for just one purpose—to run England off the seas. They've captured our ships, beaten our men in the East Indies, hung the St. George under their own flag, granted letters-of-marque against us, and done everything but dare us to fight them."

"But we've been granting letters against them too, ever since the King came back, haven't we?"

"If we have it's not supposed to be known—the letters were mostly against the Spanish, though I don't doubt that Dutchmen have been stopped too. Which is no better than they deserve. But how does it happen you know so much of our politics, my dear?" He seemed tenderly amused to hear his wife discussing serious matters.

"I've been talking to Jemima."

"To Jemima? Well, I suppose she has the latest news at her finger-tips."

412

"When it concerns privateers she does. She says you do business with 'em."

"I do, with three or four. But I never knew Jemima to be very much interested in my business affairs." He smiled as he stood before her, hands in his pockets while his eyes ran over her admiringly.

"It isn't your business she's interested in so much as the privateers."

"Oh, so that's it, is it? The little minx. Well—I suppose she thinks she's in love with Lord Carlton."

"How did you guess?"

"It wasn't very difficult. He was here for supper once about a year ago. She could hardly eat a bite and talked about nothing else for days. Well, she'd better get him out of her head."

"She says she's waiting for him to come back."

"Nonsense! He doesn't know she's on earth! His family's one of the oldest in England and he's made himself enormously rich privateering. He's not interested in marrying some upstart merchant's daughter."

Samuel had no illusions about his social relationship to the aristocracy. His family was a new one, just come into power and wealth during the last two generations, and he had no snobbish ambition to buy his way into the peerage—as some men he knew were doing—at the price of his own self-respect.

"I wouldn't want her to marry Lord Carlton if he'd have her. As a man, I like and admire him, but as a husband for my daughter—I wouldn't consider it even if he wanted to marry her, which I know he doesn't. No, Jemima's going to marry Joseph Cuttle and she may as well get such ridiculous notions out of her head. The Cuttles and I have done business together for years and it's a suitable marriage for her in every respect. I'll speak to her directly about such nonsense."

"Oh, please, Samuel—don't do that! I promised her I wouldn't tell you. But of course I thought you should know. Why not let me talk to her?"

"I wish you would, my dear. She has more respect for your opinion than for anyone's." He smiled and offered her his arm. "I don't want to force her, and yet I know that it's best for her and for all of us. The boy is young, but he's very fond of her and is a quiet hard-working lad, exactly the kind of man she should marry."

"Of course she should! But young girls have such silly ideas about men—" They started out of the room and Amber asked casually, "By the way, Samuel, is Lord Carlton coming to London soon?"

"I don't know. Why?"

"Oh, I was only thinking that the contract should be signed before she sees him again—or heaven only knows what foolishness she might do."

"That's a very good idea, my dear. I'll see the lawyers tomorrow. It's kind of you to take an interest in my family."

Amber smiled modestly.

Joseph Cuttle was among the guests they had that night and though Amber had met him before she had not remembered him. He was a tall awkward boy, eighteen years old, with a face which looked unfinished. His manners were clumsy and embarrassed, as though he always wished that he might run away and hide. It was almost ridiculous to think of dainty effervescent little Jemima married to so gauche a creature.

But Amber sought him out and though at first he was desperately uncomfortable she succeeded so well in putting him at his ease that presently he was confiding his troubles to her and begging her to help him. She promised that she would and hinted that Jemima liked him much better than she seemed to but that shyness kept her from showing her feelings. Once she caught Jemima's eyes on her, surprised and hurt and accusing. It was not long before Jemima, pleading that she had a headache, left the company and went upstairs to her own apartments.

She rushed into Amber's room early the next morning, while Amber lay drowsily sunk in her feather-mattress, contemplating the tufted satin lining of the tester over her head. She was indulging, as she often did when not quite awake, in a sensual reverie, half memory, half wishful imagining, about herself and Bruce Carlton. She had long since forgiven him for Captain Morgan's death and did not doubt that he had likewise forgiven her. And, since Jemima had talked about him, she felt that he was closer than he had been, that perhaps she would see him again before so very long. Now Jemima's appearance jerked her rudely from her voluptuous musing.

"Heavens, Jemima! What's the matter?" She half sat up.

"Amber! How could you be so civil to that nasty Joseph Cuttle last night!"

"I don't think he's nasty at all, Jemima. He's a good kind-hearted young man, and he adores you."

"I don't care! He's ugly and he's a fool—and *I* hate *him!* And you promised you'd help me!" All at once she began to cry.

"Don't cry, Jemima," said Amber, rather crossly. "I'll help you if I can. But your father told me to talk to him, and I couldn't very well refuse."

"You could if you wanted to!" insisted Jemima, wiping the tears from her face. "Lettice says you make him do anything you want—like a tame monkey!"

Amber repressed a burst of laughter at this, but said severely, "Well, Lettice is wrong! And you'd better not say things like that, Jemima! But make yourself easy—I'll help you all I can."

Jemima smiled now, for her tears were sudden and light and left no traces. "Oh, thank you! I knew you wouldn't turn against me! And when Lord Carlton comes—you will help me then, won't you?"

"Yes, Jemima, of course. Every way I can."

Amber, crossing the front courtyard to get into her coach, stopped suddenly and stared at another coach which was standing there. It was Almsbury's. And since it was not likely the Earl could have any business with Samuel, it must mean that Bruce was back. He was there, at that very moment, inside with Samuel!

For an instant she stood, stunned, staring at the crest; and then without a word she whirled and ran back across the courtyard. She had been in Samuel's offices no more than three or four times and the various men working there looked at her in some surprise and curiosity as she rushed through the outer rooms toward his private office. Without stopping for an instant to decide what she would say or do, to try to gather her composure, she flung open the door.

The room was large and handsomely furnished with carved oak tables and chairs and stools, dark rich velvet hangings, panelled walls, and numerous candles burning in brass sconces. Samuel and Lord Carlton stood before a great framed map of the New World, and though Samuel was facing her Bruce had his back turned. He had on one of the new cassock-coats, made of dark-green-and-gold brocade and reaching to his knees, with a broad twisted satin sash about the waist and a belt slung from one shoulder to hold his sword. A broad-brimmed hat was on his head and he wore a periwig which was not, however, much different in appearance from his own hair; only the fops wore the long extravagantly-curled wigs.

Even from the back he looked different to her from any other man, and her heart was beating so violently she was almost stifled. I'm going to faint! she thought desperately. I'm going to do something terrible and make a fool of myself!

"Oh, I'm sorry, Samuel," she said, still standing in the opened doorway and holding to the knob. "I thought you were alone."

"Come in, my dear. This is Lord Carlton, of whom you've heard me speak. My lord, may I present my wife?"

Bruce turned and looked at her and his eyes showed first surprise and then amusement. You—he seemed to say—of all people. You, married to a respectable rich old merchant. And she saw too that he had not forgotten their last parting, made in anger and tragedy.

But he merely took off his hat and bowed to her gravely. "Your servant, madame."

"Lord Carlton is just returned from America with his ships —and several others, as well," Samuel added with a smile, for the merchants were proud of the privateers, and grateful to them.

"How fine," said Amber nervously, and she had a terrible feeling that she was going to fall apart, collapse in little pieces from head to toe. "I just came to tell you, Samuel"—she spoke rapidly—"that I won't be home in time for dinner. I've got a call to make." She gave Carlton a swift uncertain glance. "Why don't you come to supper this evening, Lord Carlton? I'm sure you must have a great many exciting tales to tell of your adventures at sea."

He bowed again, smiling. "I don't believe sea-going stories hold much interest for ladies, but I shall be very glad to come, Mrs. Dangerfield. Thank you."

Amber gave them both an abrupt smile, curtsied, and went out in a rush of taffeta petticoats; the door banged noisily behind her. She ran back across the courtyard as if afraid that her legs would not carry her all the way to the coach. She climbed in, dropped down onto the seat, and closed her eyes.

Excitedly Nan seized her hand. "Is he there, mam?"

"Yes," she whispered weakly. "He's there."

Half an hour later she was at Almsbury House and Emily was greeting her with eager enthusiasm. Together they started upstairs toward the nursery.

"How kind of you to call! We've been in town less than a fortnight and we tried to find you but at the Theatre they could only tell us you'd married, but didn't know where you were living. Lord Carlton is here with us—"

"Yes, I know. I just saw him at my husband's office. Do you think he'll come back here for dinner?"

"I don't know. I believe that he and John were to meet somewhere at one."

They had reached the nursery and found the children having their porridge. Amber's disappointment over the prospect of missing Bruce was partly eased by her reunion with her son, whom she had not seen since the previous September. He was an extraordinarily beautiful child, healthy and happy and friendly, with dark waving hair and green eyes. She picked him up in her arms, laughing gaily when he kissed her and got cream on her cheeks and mouth and tangled his spoon in her curls.

"Daddy's here too, Mother!" he announced loudly. "Aunt Emily brought me all the way to London to see him!"

"Oh," said Amber, a little jealous resentment pricking at her. "You knew he was coming?"

"He wrote to John," explained Emily. "He wanted to see the baby."

"He isn't married, is he?"

It was the one question she dreaded to ask, each time he came back, though she could not imagine whom a man could find to marry in that barbarous empty land across the ocean.

"No," said Emily.

Amber sat down on the floor with Bruce and a fat barking spotted puppy which belonged to him, while Emily's two sons came to join them. Between playing with the puppy and talking to her son, she managed to ask Emily some questions.

"How long is he going to stay this time?"

"A month or so, I believe. He's going to volunteer his ships for the war."

"The war! It hasn't begun yet, has it?"

"Not yet, but soon, I believe. At least that's what they're saying at Court."

"But what's he going to do that for? He might lose them all—"

Emily looked faintly surprised. "Why, he wants to. England needs every ship and every experienced seaman she can get. Many privateers will do the same thing—"

At just that moment Bruce came through the opened doorway and walked toward them. While Amber sat speechless and helpless, the baby broke out of her arms and ran to his father, who swung him up onto one shoulder. He was standing above her now, looking down and smiling.

"I thought I might find you here."

CHAPTER TWENTY–EIGHT

JEMIMA CAME RUNNING into the bedroom that evening as Amber was getting dressed for supper. "Amber!" she cried joyously. "Oh, Amber, thank you!"

Amber turned and saw to her annoyance that Jemima, dressed in a gown of cornflower-blue satin, with the skirt caught up by artificial roses and real roses pinned into her glossy curls, was looking prettier than she ever had.

"Thank you for what?"

"For inviting Lord Carlton to supper, of course! Father told me he was coming and that you had asked him!"

"Joseph Cuttle's coming too, remember," said Amber crossly. "And if you're not nice to him your father will be mighty displeased."

"Oh, Joseph Cuttle! Who cares about him! Oh, Amber, I'm so excited. What'll I do? What'll I say? Oh, I do want to make a great impression! Tell me what I shall do, Amber, please— You know about those things."

"Just be quiet and modest," advised Amber, somewhat tartly. "Remember, men never like a pert woman."

Jemima was instantly subdued, struggling to compose her face. "I know it! I've got to be very formal and languishing— if only I can! But, oh, I think I'll faint at the sight of him! Tell me—how do I look?"

"Oh, tearing fine," Amber assured her. She got up to put on her gown.

Amber was unhappy and worried and sickeningly jealous, desperately afraid of her step-daughter. She and Bruce had been together all afternoon, and the glow of those hours still lingered, throbbing and reverberating through every chord of her being. But now here was Jemima, young, lovely, audacious, who suddenly seemed to her a dangerous rival. For by her own marriage to a rich old merchant Amber had acquired a sort of counterfeit respectability which she felt made her less alluring. She was married but Jemima was not; and for all Samuel's certainty that Lord Carlton would not care to marry into the Dangerfield family, Amber was scared.

Don't be a fool! she had told herself a hundred times. He wouldn't marry a simpleton like Jemima for *all* the gold in England! Besides, he's rich enough himself now. Oh, why doesn't Jemima look like Lettice!

She did not look at Jemima as she got into her gown but she could feel the girl watching her, anxiously, and her own confidence began to return. The gown was made of champagne-coloured lace over champagne satin, and was spangled with thousands of golden stars. She turned, still avoiding Jemima's eyes, and walked back to the dressing-table to put on her emeralds.

"Oh!" cried Jemima at last. "How beautiful you are!" Her eyes wistfully sought out her own reflection in a mirror. "He won't even see me!"

"Of course he will, sweetheart," said Amber, better-natured now. "You've never looked half so pretty."

At that moment Jemima's woman, Mrs. Carter, stuck her head in the door. "Mrs. Jemima!" she hissed. "His Lordship's here! He just came in!"

Amber's heart gave a bound, but she did not turn her head or move. Jemima, however, looked as distraught as a girl summoned to her execution. "He's here!" she breathed. "Oh, my God!" That alone was enough to show her mortal desperation, for blasphemy was no more allowable in Dangerfield House than was bawdry.

And then Jemima picked up her skirts and was gone.

Five minutes later Amber was ready to go downstairs herself. She was eager to see how he looked at Jemima, what he seemed to think of her—but most of all she wanted nothing but to see him again, to hear his voice and watch his face, to be in the same room with him.

"Take care, mam," cautioned Nan softly, as she gave her her fan.

Amber saw him the moment she entered the drawing-room. He was standing across from her talking to Samuel and two other men, and Jemima was there at his side, staring up at him like a flower with its face turned to the sun. She started toward them but had to stop a great many times on the way to greet her other guests, most of whom were familiar to her for they had been there often during the past five months.

They were merchants and lawyers and goldsmiths, part of that solid body of upper-middle-class rich which was rapidly becoming the greatest force in England. More and more they were able to control governmental policies both at home and overseas, because they now controlled the largest share of the

420

country's money. Almost without exception they had been on the winning side in the Civil Wars, and their fortunes had continued to grow during the years that the defeated Royalists suffered imprisonment and ruinous taxes at home or lived in desperate poverty abroad. Even the Restoration had not been able to bring about a return of the old conditions; these were the rich strong men of the kingdom now.

It was the merchants who were loudest and most insistent in demanding a war against the Dutch, which was necessary to protect England's commerce and trade from the most formidable rival she had in that sphere. And Lord Carlton, as a privateer who had been sinking Dutch ships and capturing Dutch merchandise, was vastly respected and admired by them, in spite of the fact that he was an aristocrat.

At last Amber came up to the small group which stood framed by the new gold-embroidered velvet draperies she had put in the drawing-room. She made a deep curtsy and Bruce bowed to her. Jemima watched them both.

"I'm glad you were able to come, Lord Carlton." She could face him more calmly now, though her inner excitement was still intense.

"I'm extremely happy to be here, Mrs. Dangerfield."

No one could have guessed that only three hours ago they had lain together. Now they were cool and polite—strangers.

Supper was announced and the guests began to straggle into the dining-room where the meal was being served in French buffet style. There was food enough to feed three times the hundred people there were to eat it, and gallons of white and red wine. Wax candles cast a soft bright light on the women's hair and shoulders; music of fiddles drifted from the rooms beyond. Some of the women were dressed with as great splendour as the Court ladies; the men were for the most part in sober dark velvets or wool.

Amber and Bruce were immediately separated, for she had her duties as hostess and he was captured by a circle of merchants who wanted to know when the war would begin, how many ships he had taken, and if it was true that there was a plague in Holland which would lay her so low she would be an easy victim. They asked him why the King did not mend his ways, how long the idleness and corruption at Court would continue and, privately, whether it was a safe investment to loan his Majesty a large sum of money. "Our ships," "our trade," "our seas," were the words that sounded over and over. The women gathered in groups to talk of their children, their pregnancies and their servants. Almost everyone would remark, sometime during the course of the evening, that England had been far happier under Old Oliver; they forgot how they had grumbled about that same Old Oliver.

They drifted out of the dining-room and back to the drawing-room to seat themselves about little round tables or on chairs and benches. And Amber, whose eyes followed Bruce wherever he went, even when she seemed most occupied with something else, was furious when Jemima at last succeeded in maneuvering him away from his questioners and into a corner alone with her. They sat down, plates on their laps, and began to talk.

Jemima was chattering at him and smiling, her eyes ashine with happiness and passionate admiration as she plied on him all the pretty tricks of a natural flirt. Bruce sat and watched her and now and then he said something, but though he seemed only lazily amused Amber was in a state of anguished jealousy.

She made several starts to go over and interrupt them, but each time someone stopped her. At last one old dowager with a bosom like a shelf and the face of a petulant spaniel said to her: "Jemima seems mightily smitten with his Lordship. She's been making sheep's-eyes at him all evening. Let me tell you, Mrs. Dangerfield, if Jemima was my daughter I'd find a way to get her out of his company—I admire his Lordship's exploits on the sea as much as anyone, but his reputation with women is none of the best, you can take my word for that."

Amber was horrified. "Oh, heaven! Thank you for telling me, Mrs. Humpage. I'll take a course with her this instant."

And immediately she was off across the room to where Joseph Cuttle stood in a corner talking to Henry and trying to pretend he did not know Jemima was with a man who was not only handsome and titled but a hero into the bargain.

"Why, Joseph!" she cried. "Where have you been all evening? Whatever are you doing over here? I'll wager you haven't spoke so much as a word to Jemima!"

Joseph blushed and shuffled one foot awkwardly, while Henry looked into his step-mother's neckline. "I'm having a fine time Mrs. Dangerfield. Jemima's busy."

"Nonsense, Joseph! Why, she'll never forgive you if you serve her at this rate!" She took his wrist, kindness and encouragement in her eyes. "Come along, Joseph—you can't help your cause with her by standing over here."

They began to make their way across the room and Amber kept a firm hold on Joseph's hand, as though afraid that he would bolt and run. But Amber dragged him up to Bruce and Jemima, ignoring the reproachful accusing stare Jemima gave her, and presented him to Lord Carlton.

"I'm going to let you and Joseph start the dancing, Jemima," she said sweetly. "You can begin with a coranto."

Reluctantly Jemima got to her feet, but her face began to sparkle again as she turned to Bruce. "Excuse me, your Lordship?"

Bruce bowed. "Certainly, madame. And I thank you for your company at supper."

Jemima gave him a long smile, one he was not intended to forget—ignoring the tormented boy by her side—and then with a brief curtsy to Amber she went off toward the ballroom, but she did not take Joseph's arm or seem aware that he was with her.

Amber waited until they were out of ear-shot and then she turned to Bruce, to find him smiling down at her. He seemed to know exactly what she was thinking. "Well!" she said. "And did you have a pleasant evening!"

"Very pleasant. Thank you for inviting me. And now—" He glanced across the room at a clock. "I must be going."

"Oh, you must be going!" she repeated sarcastically. "As soon as *I* come along you must be going!"

"I have business at Whitehall."

"I can imagine what *your* business is!"

"Smile a little, Amber," he said softly. "Some of your guests are beginning to wonder at your familiarity with me. A woman never quarrels with a man she doesn't know well."

His mocking tone made her furious, but what he said scared her even more. And now she forced a bright smile onto her mouth if not into her eyes, and gave a quick sweeping glance to 'see if they were being watched. I've *got* to be careful! she warned herself. If anyone guessed— Oh Lord, if they ever guessed!

She raised her voice a little, smiling. "I'm so glad you could come tonight, Lord Carlton. It isn't often we have the company of a man who's done so much for England."

Bruce bowed, bending with his careless, light feline grace. "Thank you, madame. Good-night."

He left her then and made his way across the room to speak to Samuel. Suddenly Amber, who had turned about to talk to a white-haired old gentleman, left him with the excuse that she must see about replenishing the wine. In the hallway she picked up her skirts and ran as fast as she could go, out the door and round to the front courtyard where she saw Bruce just getting into a coach.

"Lord Carlton!" she cried breathlessly, her high heels clicking as she ran across the brick pavement toward him.

He stopped, turning to look at her. "Did you call me, Mrs. Dangerfield?"

"I have a message from my husband, your Lordship." With that she climbed into the coach and beckoned him to follow her, motioning the footman then to close the door. "Bruce— when can I see you again?"

"Amber, you little fool! What are you thinking about?" His voice was impatient and there was an angry look in his eyes. "You've got to use more sense this time!"

She frowned a little as she glanced out the window, wishing that that stupid footman would go away with his torch, for it sent a flaring light in upon them. "I'll be careful! Only I've got to see you, Bruce! When? I can come any time."

"Come to the ships tomorrow, then. We'll be unloading and no one will be surprised if you're there."

"I'll be there in the morning."

She leaned a little toward him, longing for a kiss.

"Amber!"

Reluctantly she got out of the coach and ran back into the house again. To her horrified amazement she found the drawing-rooms in an uproar of excitement and turmoil, though she had left her guests talking and laughing and beginning to dance.

"What is it? What's happened?" She rushed up to the first person she saw.

"It's your husband, Mrs. Dangerfield. He's fainted."

"Fainted!"

The terrible thought went through her mind that he had somehow guessed or been told about her and Bruce and that the shock had brought on a stroke. She was more worried for herself than for Samuel, as she ran up the stairs.

She found the outer rooms full of people, servants and members of the family, but without stopping to speak to them she went directly into the bedroom. Samuel lay at full length on the bed and Lettice knelt beside him, while the four oldest brothers stood anxiously nearby. None of them glanced at her. Dr. de Forest, who was his physician and who had been at supper, was holding his wrist and taking the count of his pulse.

Instinctively Amber lowered her voice to whisper. "What happened? I went out to see about the wine and when I came back they said he had fainted."

"He *has*," said Sam curtly.

Amber went to stand beside the bed, on the opposite side from Lettice. She did not dare look at her or at the others, but she sensed that none of them was paying her any attention; all interest was focused on their father. And though it seemed to her that she waited there for an endless time, it was actually but a few minutes. When he opened his lids he was looking up at Lettice; his eyes shifted, searching for Amber, and when he found her he smiled. She was watching him breathlessly, afraid that now he would say something that would tell her she was caught.

She bent across the bed and kissed him gently. "You're here, Samuel, with us. There's nothing to worry about."

"I don't remember what happened—I thought we were—"

"You fainted, sir," said Dr. de Forest.

Lettice was crying, very softly so that she would disturb no one, and her eldest brother reached down and took her by the shoulders to raise her to her feet. At the doctor's request they left the room, all but Amber. He began to talk to them both then, very seriously, of the necessity for Samuel to be perfectly quiet for a few days, to avoid exertion of any kind—and he particularly addressed himself to Amber who looked at him solemnly and nodded her head.

"You must help your husband, Mrs. Dangerfield," he said privately to Amber when she was showing him out. "His life's in jeopardy if you don't. You understand me?"

"Yes, Dr. de Forest. I will."

When she came back Samuel took her hand and smiled. "Dr. de Forest is full of ridiculous notions. We won't pay any attention to him, will we?"

But Amber answered him firmly. "Yes, we *will*, Samuel. He says it's for your good and we will. We must. Promise me, Samuel—promise you'll do as he says."

He was obviously embarrassed, but Amber was insistent. She would allow him to do no thing, not the smallest, which might be injurious to his health. And they would be just as happy as before—he must never think that it mattered to her in any way at all. Nothing mattered to her but his safety and well-being. Samuel, deeply touched by this manifestation of tender devotion, could not restrain a few tears. But while she sat beside him and talked and stroked his head Amber was thinking that if she became pregnant now the child would be Lord Carlton's —and if only it happened soon, Samuel would think it his own.

The next morning he was feeling somewhat better, but Amber insisted that he remain in bed as the doctor had said he should, and much against her will she stayed in the room with him. About one o'clock Jemima came in with her two oldest brothers to say that they were going down to watch Lord Carlton's ships being unloaded.

"Why don't you go with them, my dear?" Samuel asked Amber. "You've been shut up here with me all day."

Jemima looked at her anxiously, obviously hoping that she

would not come, and though for a moment or two Amber insisted that she could not leave him she allowed herself to be persuaded. But the trip was a disappointment. They had not so much as a word alone together and Bruce was so busy he seemed scarcely aware of her presence. Her only consolation was that Jemima was as much disappointed as she was, and did not conceal it so well.

He did, however, make each of them a handsome present. To Jemima he gave a magnificent length of material which looked as though molten gold had been poured over a piece of silk, and a pattern etched in it by sensitive fingers holding a feather; to Amber he gave an elaborate necklace of topaz and gold. Both gifts had been captured from one of the Dutch ships returning from the East Indies.

But early the next morning she slipped out of the house in a black cloak and mask and took a hackney to Almsbury House. They spent half an hour in the nursery with the baby and Emily and Almsbury, and then they went back to his apartments.

"Suppose someone finds out about this," he said.

Amber was confident. "They won't. Samuel was asleep and Nan was to say I went to have a gown fitted, so I wouldn't have to trouble him with women about in the room." She smiled up at him. "Oh, I'm a marvellously devoted wife, I'll warrant you."

"You're a hard-hearted little bitch," he said. "I pity the men who love you."

But she was too happy to get angry about anything, and there was a light in his green eyes as he sat looking at her which would have made her forgive anything. She went over and sat on his lap, putting her arms about his neck and her mouth against his smooth-shaven cheek.

"But you love me, Bruce—and I've never hurt you. I don't think I could if I tried," she added with a pout.

He gave a lift of one eyebrow and smiled. He had never indulged in the extravagant compliments which were a fashion among the gallants, and she sometimes wondered jealously if he paid them to other women. Jemima, perhaps.

"What do you think of Jemima?" she asked him now.

"Why, she's very pretty—and naïve as a Maid of Honour her first week at Court."

"She's mad in love with you."

"A hundred thousand pound or so, I've discovered, will make a man more attractive than he'd ever suspected himself of being."

"A hundred thousand! My God, Bruce! What a lot of money! When Samuel dies I'll have sixty-six thousand. Think what a fortune that would be if we put it together! We'd be the richest people in England!"

"You forget, darling. I won't be in England."

"Oh, but you—"

Suddenly he stood up and swung her into his arms; his mouth closed over hers. Amber sailed away dizzily, her arguments effectively stopped. But he had not heard, by any means, the last of it. For now she had contrived to get something which she knew he valued, money, and she hoped to bargain with it. If only he would marry her—if only she could have him forever. There was nothing else she wanted, really. All her other great ambitions would vanish like a piece of ice dropped on a red-hot stove.

She did not go back to Almsbury House the next two mornings, for Bruce had warned her that unless she was very careful she would be found out. "If you're sailing that ocean under false colours," he said, "and I suppose you must be—you'd better remember it won't take much to make them suspicious. And if they ever caught you—your sixty-six thousand might dwindle considerably." She knew that it was the truth and determined to be cautious.

But when Jemima asked her what she had thought of Lord Carlton the blood shot suddenly to her face and she had to bend over to retie her garter. "Why—he's mighty handsome, of course."

"I think he liked me—don't you?"

"What makes you think so!" Her voice was sharp in spite of herself, but she hastily changed its tone. "You mustn't be

428

so bold, Jemima. I'm sure everyone thought you were flirting with him—and courtiers are all the same."

"All the same? In what way?"

Worried and annoyed by what seemed to be Jemima's stupidity she snapped: "Just remember this—take care he doesn't do you some harm!"

"Harm, pish!" said Jemima scornfully. "What harm *could* he do me when I love him?"

Amber had an impulse to run after her and grab her by the hair and slap her face, but she restrained herself. It would certainly not be in keeping with the character she had built for herself, a structure put together at too much pain and cost to kick it over carelessly now because of a silly girl who meant nothing to him. Nevertheless, she and Jemima were henceforward somewhat cool when they met and Jemima—who was even now puzzled as to what had caused this change in their friendship—again began to call her "Madame."

The next afternoon she returned from visiting some of Samuel's innumerable relatives and found Jemima waiting in the entrance hall with Carter, both of them dressed to go out. Jemima was painted and patched and perfumed, her hair was curled and her buttercup-yellow satin gown cut so low that it seemed her small round breasts might escape at any moment. There were yellow roses in her hair and she wore her yellow-lined black-velvet cloak hung carelessly on her shoulders, to cover as little of her as possible. She looked for all the world like a Court beauty or the town's reigning harlot.

"Ye gods, Jemima!" said Amber, pausing in shocked amazement to look at her step-daughter. "Wherever are you going dressed like that?"

Jemima's eyes sparkled and her voice was triumphant, almost defiant. "Lord Carlton is coming to take me for a drive in Hyde Park."

"I suppose you asked him?"

"Well, maybe I did! You don't get what you want by sitting and waiting for it!"

Amber had told Jemima something like that once, but now Jemima said it without remembering its source. She thought it was her own idea. And Amber, who had meddled in a spirit of malicious mischief, encouraging Jemima's rebellion against family traditions, was faced with the prospect of having her own advice turned against her. Three months ago Jemima would never have dared ask a man to take her riding. Amber was not thinking of retributive justice, however, as she stood staring at Jemima with her hatred showing plain in her eyes. Oh! if only I wasn't married to her father! she thought, furious at her own impotence.

"Jemima, you're making a fool of yourself! You don't know the kind of man Lord Carlton is!"

Jemima lifted her chin. "I beg your pardon, Madame, but I know exactly. He's handsome and he's fascinating and he's a gentleman—and I love him."

Amber's lip curled and she repeated the words, mimicking her with cruel accuracy. "He's handsome and he's fascinating and he's a gentleman—and you love him! Hoity-toity! And if you're not mighty careful you'll find that your maidenhead is missing!"

"I don't believe you! Lord Carlton isn't like that at all! Besides, Carter is going along!"

"She'd better! And see that she stays along, too!"

She was now so angry that, in spite of Nan's frantic nudges and grimaces, she might have gone on to say much more, but the knocker clattered and the footman who answered it admitted Bruce. He swept off his hat to both of them, and his eyes glittered with amusement to find Amber and her step-daughter so obviously engaged in a quarrel.

Damn him! thought Amber. Men always think they're so superior!

"This is a pleasant surprise, Mrs. Dangerfield," he said now. "I hadn't expected to have your company too."

"Oh, Madame isn't coming!" said Jemima hastily. "She's just returned from a drive!"

"Oh," said Bruce softly. "I'm sorry, Mrs. Dangerfield. I'd have enjoyed having you with us."

Amber's eyes stared at him, hard and shining and slanting like a cat's. "*Would* you, Lord Carlton?"

And she turned and ran up the stairs, but as she heard the door close behind them she stopped abruptly on the balcony above, swirling about to look down. They were gone. Suddenly she raised her arm and threw her fan as hard as she could at the floor below. She had not realized that anyone was about, but at that moment a footman appeared and looked up in some surprise; her eyes met his for an alarmed angry instant and then she rushed off.

She was still somewhat excited when Samuel came up from the office where he had gone to spend an hour or two. But she kissed him affectionately, made him sit down, and then took a stool beside him and put her hand into his. For a few moments they chatted of various small things and then she gave a troubled little frown, and stared off pensively into space.

He stroked the smooth crown of her head, where the hair lay in burnished satin waves. "What is it, my dear? Nothing's amiss?"

"No, Samuel, nothing. Oh, Samuel—I must tell you! It's about Jemima! I'm worried about her!"

"You mean about Lord Carlton?"

"Yes. Why, only an hour ago I met her in the hall and she'd asked him to take her driving in Hyde Park!"

He gave a heavy tired sigh. "I can't understand her. She's been as carefully brought up as could be possible. Sometimes I think there's a taint in the air nowadays—the young people fall sick of it. Not all of them, of course," he added with a smile of fondness. "I don't think he's at all interested in her—Jemima isn't the kind of woman he can be used to associating with—and I think that if she had let him alone he'd never have given her a second thought."

"Of course he wouldn't!" agreed Amber, very positively.

"I don't know what's to be done—"

"I do, Samuel! You must make her marry Joseph Cuttle—right now! Before something much worse happens!"

CHAPTER TWENTY–NINE

THAT WAS THE end of Jemima's friendship with her step-mother. For by an unerring feminine instinct she knew immediately who was responsible for her father's sudden determination to marry her to Joseph Cuttle without more delay. It was the one thing Amber had done of which the family approved, for they had been worried too about Jemima's infatuation for a Cavalier —though they considered that it was Madame's fault Jemima had ever fallen in love with him. They did not believe it would have occurred to Jemima to admire such a man, but for the bad example of false values Amber had set. But Bruce seemed somewhat shocked when Amber told him that the contract had been signed and the marriage date set for August 30th—forty days from the time of betrothal.

"Good Lord!" he said. "That awkward spindle-shanked boy! Why should a pretty little thing like Jemima have to marry him?"

"What difference does it make to you who she marries!"

"None at all. But don't you think you're meddling rather impertinently in the affairs of the Dangerfield family?"

"I am not! Samuel was going to make her marry him anyway. I just got the matter settled—for her own good."

"Well, if you think I intend seducing her, I don't. I took her driving because she asked me to and it would have been an affront to her father if I'd refused." He gave her a long narrow look. "I wonder if you have any idea what a very fine old gentleman Samuel Dangerfield is. Tell me—how the devil did you manage to marry him? The Dangerfields aren't people who would welcome an actress to the hearth-side."

She laughed. "Wouldn't you like to know!" But she never told him. ·

It was not long before Amber refused altogether to heed Bruce's admonitions—she went to Almsbury House three or four

432

mornings in every week. Samuel left for his office at about seven and returned between eleven and noon; she was there when he left and there when he got back. But even if she had not been it would have occasioned no comment. He trusted her implicitly and when he asked her where she had been it was never from motives of suspicion, but only to make conversation or because he was interested in the little things which occupied her day. Whatever off-hand tale she told him, he believed.

And Jemima, meanwhile, turned sulky and bad-tempered, refused to take an interest in the elaborate preparations for her wedding. Dressmakers and mercers filled her rooms at all hours; she was to be married in cloth-of-gold and her wedding-ring was studded with thirty diamonds. The great ballroom in the south wing of the house where the wedding-feast and masque were to take place would be transformed into a blooming, green-leafed forest, with real grass on the floor. There would be five hundred guests for the ceremony and almost a thousand for the festivities afterward. Fifty of the finest musicians in London were being hired to play for the ball and a noted French chef was coming from Paris to oversee the preparation of the food. Samuel was eager to please his daughter and her persistent sullenness troubled him.

Amber magnanimously took Jemima's part. "There's nothing wrong with her, Samuel, but what's wrong with all girls old enough to be married who aren't. She's got the green-sickness, that's all. Wait till after the wedding, she'll be herself again then, I warrant you."

Samuel shook his head. "By heaven, I hope so! I hate to see her unhappy. Sometimes I wonder if we're not making a mistake to insist that she marry Joseph. After all, there are suitable matches enough for her in London if she—"

"Nonsense, Samuel! Who ever heard of a girl choosing her own husband! She's too young to know *what* she wants. And Joseph is a fine young man; he'll make her mighty happy." That settled it. And Amber thought that she had managed everything with great cleverness—Jemima was no source of worry to her now. Silly girl! she thought scornfully. She should have known better than to cross swords with me!

433

Scarcely six weeks had gone by since Bruce's arrival in London when she told him that she was sure she was pregnant, and explained why she believed the child must be his. "I hope it'll be a girl," she said. "Bruce is so handsome—I know she'd be a beauty. What do you think we should name her?"

"I think that's up to Samuel, don't you?"

"Pish—why should it be? Anyway, he'll ask me. So you tell me what name you'd like—please, Bruce, I want to know."

He seemed to give it a few moments' serious consideration—but the smile that lurked about his mouth showed what he was thinking. "Susanna's a pretty name," he said at last.

"You don't know anyone named Susanna, do you?"

"No. You asked me for a name that I liked, and I told you one. I had no ulterior motives."

"But you've named your share of bastards, I doubt not," she said. "What about that wench—Leah, or what d'ye call her? Almsbury said you'd had two brats by her."

By now Bruce had been back long enough and she had seen him so often that the jealousies and worries that beset her when he was away had begun to encroach upon the pleasure she found in being with him. She had begun to feel more discontented over what she was missing than grateful for what she had.

His voice answered her quietly. "Leah died a year ago, in childbirth."

She looked up at him swiftly, saw that he was serious and a little angry. "Oh, I'm sorry," she lied. But she turned to another subject. "I wonder where you'll be when Susanna's born?"

"Somewhere giving the Dutch hell, I hope. We'll declare war on them as soon as Parliament votes the money for it. While we're waiting I'll try what I can do to keep the peace the way his Majesty wants it kept." England and Holland had been at war everywhere but in the home seas for almost a year, and during the past two months the fight had blazed into the open; it needed only to be declared, but Charles had to wait on further preparation and Parliamentary grants.

They were lying on the bed, half-dressed. Bruce had his

434

periwig off and his own hair had been cut short so that now it was no more than two or three inches long, and combed back from his forehead in a wave. Amber rolled over onto her stomach and reached for a bunch of purple Lisbon grapes in a bowl on the table.

"Heigh ho! I suppose it's a dull day for you when there isn't a town to burn or a dozen Dutchmen to kill!"

He laughed, pulled a small cluster of grapes from the bunch she held, and began to toss them into his mouth. "Your portrait's somewhat bloodthirsty."

She gave a sigh. "Oh, Bruce! If only you'd listen to me!" And then all at once she bounced up and knelt facing him, determined that he should listen to her. Somehow he had always managed to stop her before—but not this time. This time he was going to hear her out. "Go off to the wars if you must, Bruce! But when it's over sell your ships and stay here in London. With your hundred thousand and my sixty-six we'd be so rich we could buy the Royal Exchange for a summer pavilion. We could have the biggest finest house in London—and everyone who was anybody at all would come to our balls and suppers. We'd have a dozen coaches and a thousand servants and a yacht to sail to France in if we took the notion. We'd go to Court and you'd be a great man—Chancellor, or whatever you wanted, and I'd be a Lady of the Bedchamber. There wouldn't be anyone in England finer than us! Oh, Bruce, darling—don't you see? We'd be the happiest people in the world!"

She was so passionately convinced herself that she was positive she could convince him; and his answer was a painful disappointment.

"It would be fine," he said. "For a woman."

"Oh!" she cried furiously. "You men! What *do* you want then!"

"I'll tell you, Amber." He sat up and looked at her. "I want something more than spending the next twenty-five years standing on a ladder with one man's heels on my fingers and mine on the man's beneath. I want to do something besides plot and scheme and intrigue with knaves and fools to get a reputation with men I despise. I want a little more than going from the

435

theatre to a cock-fight to Hyde Park to Pall Mall and back over the same round the next day. Playing cards and poaching after anything that goes by in petticoats and a mask and serving my turn as the King's pimp—" He made a gesture of disgust. "And finally dying of women and drink."

"I suppose you think living in America will keep you from dying of women and drink!"

"Maybe not. But one thing I know— When I die it won't be from boredom."

"Oh, won't it! I don't doubt it's mighty exciting over there with blackamoors and pirates and Newgate-birds and every other kind of ragamuffin!"

"It's more civilized than you imagine—there are also a great many men of good family who left England during the Commonwealth, remember. And who are still leaving—for the same reason I am. It isn't that I'm going there because I think the men and women in America are better or different from what they are in England; they're the same. It's because America is a country that's still young and full of promise, the way England hasn't been for a thousand years. It's a country that's waiting to be made by the men who'll dare to make it—and I intend getting there while I can help make it my way. In the Civil Wars my father lost everything that had belonged to our family for seven centuries. I want my children to have something they can't lose, ever."

"Well, then, why trouble yourself to fight for England— since you love her so little!"

"Amber, Amber," he said softly. "My dear, someday I hope you'll know a great many things you don't know now."

"And someday I hope you'll sink in your damned ocean!"

"No doubt I'm too great a villain to drown."

She jumped off the bed in a fury, but suddenly she stopped, turned and looked at him as he lay leaning on his elbow and watching her. And then she came back and sat down again, covering his hand with both of hers.

"Oh, Bruce, you know I don't mean that! But I love you so —I'd die for you—and you don't seem to need me at all, the way I need you! I'm nothing but your whore—I want to be your

436

wife, *really* your wife! I want to go where you go, and share your troubles and plan with you for what you want, and bear your children—I want to be part of you! Oh, please, darling! Take me to America with you! I don't care what it's like, I swear I don't! I'll live in anything! I'll do anything! I'll help you cut down trees and plant tobacco and cook your meals—Oh, Bruce! I'll do *anything,* if only you'll take me with you!"

For a moment he continued to stare at her, his eyes glittering, but just when she thought she had convinced him he shook his head and got up. "It would never work out that way, Amber. It's not your kind of life and in a few weeks or months you'd get tired of it, and then you'd hate me for bringing you."

She ran after him, throwing herself before him, grabbing frantically at the happiness that seemed just to elude her fingers but which she was sure she could catch. "No, I wouldn't, Bruce! I swear it! I promise you! I'd love anything if you were there!"

"I can't do it, Amber. Let's not talk about it."

"Then you've got another reason! You have, haven't you? What is it?"

He was suddenly impatient and faintly angry. "For the love of God, Amber, let it go! I can't do it. That's all."

She looked at him for a long minute, her eyes narrowed. "I know why," she said slowly at last. "I know why you won't take me over there, and why you won't marry me. It's because I'm a farmer's niece and you're a nobleman. My father was only a yeoman, but *your* family was sitting in the House of Lords before there was one. My mother was just a plain simple woman, but *your* mother was a Bruce and descended from no one less than Holy Moses himself. My relatives are farmers—but *you've* got some Stuart blood in you, if you look hard enough to find it." Her voice was sarcastic and bitter, and as she talked her mouth twisted, giving an ugly expression to her face.

She turned angrily away and began to pull on the rest of her clothes, while he watched her. There was a kind of tenderness on his face now and he seemed to be trying to think of something to say to her that would help take away the painful sense of humiliation she felt. But she gave him no opportunity to speak. In only two or three minutes she was dressed

437

and then as she picked up her cloak she cried: "That's why, isn't it!"

He stood facing her. "Oh, Amber, why must you always make things hard for yourself? You know as well as I do that I couldn't marry you if I wanted to. I can't marry just for myself. I'm not alone in the world, floating in space like a speck of dust. I've got relatives by the score—and I've got a responsibility to my parents who are dead and to their parents. The Bruces and Carltons mean nothing to you—and there's no reason why they should —but they're damned important to the Bruces and Carltons."

"That wheedle won't pass with me! You wouldn't marry me even if you could! *Would* you!"

They stared at each other; and then his answer cracked out, surprising as the sharp report of a pistol.

"No!"

For an instant Amber continued looking at him, but her face had turned beet-red and the blue cords throbbed in her throat and forehead. "Oh!" she screamed, almost hysterical with rage and pain. "I hate you, Bruce Carlton! I hate you—I—" She turned and rushed from the room, slamming the door after her. "I hope I never see you again!" she sobbed to herself as she dashed headlong down the stairs. And she told herself that this was the end—the last insult she would take from him—the last time he would ever—

Amber ran out of Almsbury House and straight to her coach. She jumped in. "Drive away!" she yelled at Tempest. "Home!" She flung herself back and began to cry distractedly, though with few tears, her teeth biting at the tips of her gloved hands.

She was so excited that she did not notice another coach waiting just outside the gates, with its wooden shutters closed, which started up and came rumbling along behind her own. And it stayed there, just behind her, following every turn, halting when her coach halted, proceeding at exactly the same rate of speed and never letting another coach come between them. They were almost home before Amber noticed that two of her footmen, who were hanging on the side, kept looking back and gesturing, apparently both puzzled and amused. She turned and glanced through the back window, saw the hackney behind them, but was not much concerned.

And then, as they turned through the great south gate of Dangerfield House, the impertinent hackney turned in also. Amber got out, still scowling in spite of her struggles to compose her face, and confronted Jemima who had just stepped down from the hackney. Carter was paying the driver.

"Good morning, Madame," said Jemima.

Amber started off, and tossed Jemima what she hoped was a careless greeting. "Good morning, Jemima." But her heart was pounding and she had a sick feeling of despair. The damned girl had been spying! And, what was worse, had caught her!

"Just a moment, Madame. Haven't you time for a word with me? You were glad enough to be my friend—before Lord Carlton came."

Amber stopped still, and then she turned around to face her step-daughter. There was nothing to do but try to brazen it out with her. "What's Lord Carlton got to do with this?"

"Lord Carlton's staying at Almsbury House. That's why you were there just now—and day before yesterday and twenty other times this past month, for all I know!"

"Mind your own business, Jemima! I'm no prisoner here. I'll come and go as I like. As it happens Lady Almsbury is a dear friend of mine—I was visiting her."

"You didn't visit her before Lord Carlton came to town!"

"She wasn't here! She was in the country. Now look here, Jemima, I've a mighty good idea why you've been following me—and I've a mind to tell your father. He'll take a course with you, I warrant."

"*You'll* tell Father! Suppose *I* tell him a few things I know—about you and Lord Carlton!"

"You don't know a thing! And if you weren't as jealous as a barren wife you wouldn't have such suspicions, either!" Her eyes went swiftly from Jemima to Carter and back again. "Who puts these ideas in your head? This old screech-owl here?" Carter's guiltily shifted glance told her that her guess was right and Amber, with a great show of independent virtue, gave her a last warning and went off. "Don't let me hear any more of your bellow-weathering, Jemima, or we'll try which one of us your father will believe!"

Jemima evidently did not care to make the test, and Danger-field House remained quiet. Amber pretended to have the ague so that her step-daughter could not ask why she had stopped going to visit Lady Almsbury. The time was drawing nearer for Jemima's wedding, though the date had been postponed a few days at her almost hysterical demand, and Amber was eager to have it over and the girl out of her way.

A week after her quarrel with Bruce Samuel told her that Lord Carlton had been in his office that morning. "He's sailing tomorrow," he said, "if the wind serves. I hope that once he's gone Jemima will—"

But Amber was not listening. Tomorrow! she thought. My God—he's going tomorrow! Oh, I've got to see him—I've got to see him again—

His ships lay at Botolph Wharf and Amber waited inside her coach while Jeremiah went to find him. She was excited and anxious, afraid that he would still be angry, but when he returned and found who it was waiting there for him he smiled. The afternoon was hot and he wore no periwig but only his breeches and bell-sleeved white shirt, and his tanned face was wet with perspiration.

She leaned forward eagerly and put her hand on his as he stood in the door, and her voice spoke swiftly and softly. "I had to see you again, Bruce, before you went."

"We're busy loading, Amber. I can't leave."

"Can't we go on board? Just for a minute?"

He stepped back and took her hand to help her down.

Everywhere about them was activity. Tall-masted ships, elabo-rately carved and gilded, moved gently with the water, and the wharf was crowded. There were sailors who had been so many years at sea that they walked with a rolling gait which would distinguish them anywhere. Husky-shouldered porters were trundling casks or staggering along bent beneath great wooden boxes and iron-hooped bales. Well-dressed merchants strolled up and down, pestered by the beggars—broken old seamen who had given a leg or an arm or an eye for England. There were

440

wide-eyed boys, loitering old men and blatantly painted harlots—a noisy variegated crowd.

As they walked along the wharf every eye glanced at or followed them. For her clothes and her hair and her jewels glittered in the sunlight; she was beautiful and she had a look of breeding to which they were not very much accustomed. The prostitutes looked Bruce over with an interest not wholly professional.

"Why didn't you come to see me?" she asked him in an undertone, and then crossed over the wide roped-off plank which led to one of his ships.

Following her, he murmured, "I didn't think my company would be very welcome," and turned to talk for a moment or two to another man. Then he led her around the deck and down a flight of stairs to a small cabin. It looked comfortable, though not luxurious, and was fitted with a good-sized bunk, a writing-table and three chairs. Maps were nailed to the dark oak-panelled walls and on the floor were stacks of leather-bound books.

Inside she turned about swiftly to face him. "I'm not going to quarrel with you, Bruce. I don't want to talk—just kiss me—"

His arms had scarcely gone around her when there was a sharp knock. "Lord Carlton! A lady to see you, sir!"

Amber looked up accusingly at him, and as he released her he muttered a soft curse. But before he started for the door he gestured at her, and picking up her cloak and the muff she had dropped she hurried through the door he had indicated into the adjoining cabin. And then, as Bruce opened the other door, she heard a pair of high heels coming down the stairway and Jemima Dangerfield's lilting young voice.

"Lord Carlton! Thank Heaven I found you! I've got a message from my father for you—"

Amber heard Jemima's feet walk into the cabin and the door swing shut. She stood close behind her own door, her ear against the wooden panels and her heart hammering violently as she listened. Her excitement was caused as much, just now, by fear of being caught as by jealousy.

441

"Oh, Bruce! I found out you're going tomorrow! I had to come!"

"You shouldn't have, Jemima. Someone might see you. And I'm so busy I haven't an extra moment. I came down here to get some papers—here they are. Come, and I'll walk back to your coach with you."

"Oh, but Bruce! You're going away tomorrow! I've *got* to see you again! I can meet you anywhere—I'll be at the Crown tonight at eight. In our same room."

"Forgive me, Jemima. I can't come. I swear I'm too busy—I've got to go to Whitehall, and we'll sail before sun-up."

"Then *now!* Oh, Bruce, please! Just this once more—"

"Hush, Jemima! Sam and Robert will be here at any moment. You don't want them to find you here alone with me." There was a pause, during which she heard him turn and walk to the door and open it, and then he said: "Oh, I'm sorry. I didn't see you drop your glove." Jemima did not answer and they walked out.

Amber waited until she was sure that they were gone and then she went back into his cabin again.

Apprehension for her own safety, now that it was secured, dissolved instantly into a jealous fury against both Jemima and Bruce. So he *had* been making love to her! The dirty varlet! And that puling little milk-sop, Jemima! She'll smoke for this!

Bruce returned to find her sitting on the writing-table, her feet braced against the bunk and both hands on her hips. She looked at him as though expecting him to hang his head and blush.

"Well!" she said.

He gave a shrug, closing the door.

"So that's what you've been about this past week!" Suddenly she got up, walked across the room and turned her back on him. "So you didn't intend to seduce her!"

"I didn't."

She swung around. "You didn't! She just said—"

"I didn't intend to. Now look here, Amber, I haven't time for a quarrel. A fortnight or so ago Jemima came one morning to Almsbury House and sent up your name. You may think I should have indignantly ordered her out of my bedroom, but I didn't. The poor child was unhappy and disappointed over being made to marry Joseph Cuttle and she thinks, at least, that she's in love with me. That's all there is to it."

"Then what about the Crown—and our same room?" The last three words mocked Jemima's voice as she had said them.

"We met there three or four times afterwards. If you want to know anything else about it, ask Jemima. I haven't the time. Come on—I'm going back up on deck."

As he turned she ran forward and grabbed his arms. "Bruce! Please, darling— Don't go till we've said goodbye—"

Half an hour later they returned to her coach and he handed her in. "When will you come back to London again?" she asked.

"I don't know. It'll be several months anyway. I'll see you when I do."

"I'll be waiting for you, Bruce. And, oh, darling, be careful! Don't get hurt. And think of me sometimes—"

"I will."

He stepped back, swinging the door closed, and made a signal to the coachman to start. The coach began to move and he smiled back at her as she stuck her head out the opened window.

"Sink a thousand Dutchmen!" she called.

He laughed. "I'll try!" He gave her a wave and turned to go back onto the ship. The coach moved on and the crowds closed between them; he disappeared from her sight.

Amber entered her apartments, still too full of the warm luxuriant afterglow of Bruce's love-making to have begun thinking of Jemima again. It was an unpleasant shock to find the girl there, waiting for her.

Jemima was tense and excited. "May I see you alone, Madame?"

Amber felt very superior; triumphant. "Why, of course, Jemima."

Nan herded the other servants out of the room, all but Tansy who stayed where he was, sitting cross-legged on the

443

floor absorbed in working a Chinese puzzle which Samuel had brought him more than a week ago. A servant took Amber's muff and fan and gloves, one of which Amber had lost. She was careless with her belongings, they were so easily replaced; and if she lost something it gave her an excuse to buy another.

Amber turned and faced her step-daughter. "Now," she said casually, raising her hands to her hair. "What d'you want?"

The two women, both of them beautiful and expensively dressed, with well-bred features, presented a strange contrast. For one was obviously unsophisticated and essentially innocent, while the other was just as obviously the reverse. But it was not the way she looked, nor was it anything in her manner. It was rather a certain indefinable aura which hung about her, like a wickedly fascinating perfume, redolent of passion and recklessness and a greed for living.

Jemima was too overwrought, too disappointed and unhappy and angry to try to be subtle. "Where 've you been!" It was no question, but an accusation.

Amber gave her eyebrows a lift, and twisted around to straighten the seams in her stockings. "That's none of your business."

"Well, whether it's any of my business or not, I know! Look at this—it's yours, isn't it!" She held out a glove.

Amber glanced at it and then her eyes narrowed. She snatched it away. "Where'd you get that!"

"You know where I got it! It was lying on the floor in the master-cabin of the *Dragon!*"

"Well, what if it was? I hope I can visit a man who's gone to sea to fight the Dutch!"

"Visit him! Don't try to put that upon me! I know what kind of visiting you do! I know what *you* are! You're a harlot—! You've cuckolded my father!"

Amber stood and stared at Jemima and her flesh began to crawl with loathing and hatred. "You whining little bitch," she said slowly. "You're jealous, aren't you? You're jealous because I got what you wanted." She began to mimic her, repeating exactly the words and tone Jemima had used scarcely an hour before, but giving to them a savage twist that mocked and

444

ridiculed. "Then *now!* Oh, Bruce, please! Just this once more—" She laughed, enjoying the horror and humiliation that came onto Jemima's face.

"Oh," said Jemima softly. "I never knew what you were like before—"

"Well, now you do but it won't do you any good." Amber was brisk and confident, thinking that she would settle Jemima's business for her now, once and forever. "Because if you're thinking to tell your father what you know about me, just stop long enough to consider what he'd say if he knew that his daughter had been sneaking out of the house to meet a man at public taverns! He'd be stark staring mad!"

"How do you know that!"

"Lord Carlton told me."

"You couldn't prove it—"

"Oh, couldn't I? I could call in a midwife and have you examined, remember!"

Amber had been about to order Jemima triumphantly from the room, when her next words came with the unexpected shock of a mid-summer thunderclap. "Call in anyone you like! I don't care what you do! But I can tell you this much—either you make Father stop my wedding to Joseph Cuttle or I'll tell him about you and Lord Carlton!"

"You wouldn't dare! Why it—it might kill him!"

"It might kill him! Much you'd care! That's what you want and you know it! Oh, the rest of them were right about you all along! What a fool I was not to see it! But I know what you are now—you're nothing but a whore."

"And so are you. The only difference between us is that I got what I went for—and you didn't."

Jemima gasped and the next instant lashed out with the palm of her right hand and smacked Amber on the cheek. So swiftly that it seemed to be part of the same movement Amber returned the slap, and with her other hand she grabbed a fistful of hair and gave a jerk that snapped Jemima's head back like a chicken's. Jemima screamed in sudden fright and viciously Amber slapped her again. Her self-control had slipped away and she was not even wholly conscious of what she was doing.

Jemima began to struggle to free herself, now genuinely terrified and screeching for help. The sight of her scared eyes and the sound of her cries infuriated Amber; she had a sudden savage determination to kill her. It was Nan, who rushed into the room and threw herself between them, who saved Jemima from a serious mauling.

"Mam!" she was shouting. "Mam! For God's sake! Are you mad!"

Amber's hands dropped to her sides and she gave an angry shake of her head to toss the hair back from her face. "Get out of here!" she cried. "Get out and don't trouble me again, d'ye hear?" The last words were a hysterical shriek, but Jemima had already fled, sobbing.

It was not easy to convince Samuel that Jemima's wedding must be postponed. But she did, at last, succeed in making him agree to put it off for a few more weeks to let the poor child recover from her grief at Lord Carlton's departure. Amber, nervous and worried and lonely for Bruce, was made even more morose and irritable by pregnancy. But she had to conceal her ill-humour from everyone but Nan, who listened patiently and with sympathetic concern to her mistress's perpetual grumbling and sighing.

"I'm so damned sick and tired of being virtuous," she said wearily one day as she came in from having paid several afternoon calls.

She spent a great deal of time visiting the wives and daughters of Samuel's friends, sitting about and discussing babies and servants and sickness with them until she wanted to yell. She worked hard at being a respectable woman. Now all at once she arranged her mouth into a smug smile and began to mimic the elderly aunt upon whom she had just called. No one—not even the immediate family—had yet been told that she was pregnant, though Samuel knew it and was almost absurdly delighted.

"My dear, I do hope you'll soon prove with child. Believe me, no woman can know what it is to be truly happy until she

446

holds her first little one in her arms and feels its tiny mouth at her breast." Amber screwed up her face and gave a noisy rattle with her tongue: "I'll be damned if I can see where the pleasure is to throw-up every morning and look like a stuffed pig and blow and puff like an old nag going up Snow Hill!" She slammed her fan onto the floor. "Crimini! I'm sick of this business!"

To make matters worse, when Bruce had been gone four weeks Samuel firmly announced that the wedding-date was definitely set for October 15th. Nothing at all, he assured her, would induce him to change his mind again. The Cuttles were growing impatient, people were beginning to wonder at the delay, and it was high time Jemima stop her foolishness and behave like a grown woman. Amber was frantic with worry and though she mulled over her problem most of the day and half the night she could discover no solution. Jemima warned her again that if she did not do something to stop it she would tell her Father, even though he threw both of them into the streets.

"Oh, Lord, Nan! After everything I've been through to get that money I'm going to lose it! I'll never get a shilling! Oh, I always knew *something* would happen! I knew I'd never *really* be that rich!"

"Something 'll save you, mam," insisted Nan cheerfully. "I know it will. Your stars are lucky."

"Something?" demanded Amber, her voice sliding up an octave. "But what! And when?"

By the tenth Amber was half-wild with worry and remorse. She wished that she had never seen Bruce Carlton. She wished that she was back home in Marygreen and married to Jack Clarke or Bob Starling. She paced the floor and beat her hands together and bit her knuckles.

Oh, my God, my God, my God, what am I to do!

Thus she was one morning, still in her dressing-gown and walking distractedly about the bedroom, when Nan came rushing in. Her cheeks were pink and her blue eyes sparkled triumphantly. "Mam! What d'ye think? I just saw one of Mrs.

Jemima's women and she told me Mrs. Jemima's been in a green-sickness all this past fortnight—but no one's supposed to know it!"

Amber stared at her. "Why, Nan!" she said softly.

And then all at once she ran out of the bedroom, down the long hallway toward the opposite wing of the house, and into Jemima's chamber. She found it crowded with dressmakers, maids, several mercers and other tradesmen. Amber had told her that if she would go ahead and pretend she was going to be married, she would somehow find another excuse at the last moment—if she had to throw herself out the window. And Jemima, not because she wished to oblige her step-mother, but because she really was confused and helpless, had done so.

There were gowns heaped on every chair and stool, lengths of brocade and satin and sheer tiffany ran like rivers over the floor, fur-skins lay in soft shining piles. Jemima stood in the midst of the crowded, noisy room, her back turned to the door, having her wedding-gown fitted; it was made of the gold cloth Lord Carlton had given her.

Amber came in breezily. "Oh, Jemima!" she cried. "Such a marvellous gown! How I envy you—getting married in that!"

Jemima gave her a sullen, warning glance from over her shoulder. But Amber saw to her satisfaction that the girl was pale and seemed tired.

"Are you almost done now?"

Jemima spoke wearily to two of the dressmakers who were kneeling about her on the floor, pins in their mouths, arranging each smallest fold and crease with the most meticulous care.

"In a moment, madame. Can't you bear it just a little longer?"

Jemima sighed. "Very well. But hurry—please."

Amber went to stand before Jemima, her head cocked to one side as she examined the dress, and her eyes ran tauntingly up and down the girl's figure. She saw Jemima begin to fidget nervously, a faint shine of sweat came to her forehead; and then all at once her arms dropped and she sank to the floor, her head falling back, her eyes rolling. The dressmakers and maids gave excited squeaks and the men stepped aside in alarm.

Amber took charge. "Pick her up and lay her on the bed.

448

Carter, bring some cold water. You—run for some brandy."

With the help of two of the maids she got Jemima out of her gown, took the pillow from under her head and began to unlace her busk. When Carter brought the cold water she sent them all out of the room—though Carter was obviously reluctant to leave Jemima in the care of her step-mother—and wrung out a cloth to lay on Jemima's forehead.

It was not more than a minute before Jemima regained consciousness and looked up at Amber, who leaned above her. "What did I do?" she asked softly, her eyes going uncertainly about the empty room.

"You fainted. Take a sip of this brandy and you'll feel better." Amber put her hand behind Jemima's head and tipped it forward. Both of them were silent for a moment, and Jemima made a face as she tasted the brandy.

"The dizzy feeling's gone," she said at last. "You can call the others back in now." She started to sit up.

"Oh, no, Jemima. Not yet. I want to talk to you first."

Jemima glanced at her swiftly, her eyes guarded. "What about?"

"You know what about. There's no use trying to pretend. You're pregnant—aren't you?"

"No! Of course I'm not! I can't be! It's just that— Well, I've had the vapours, that's all."

"If you thought it was only the vapours why didn't you tell anyone? Don't try to fool me, Jemima. Tell me the truth and maybe I can help you."

"Help me? How could *you* help me?"

"How long has it been since your last flux?"

"Why—almost two months. But that doesn't mean anything! Oh, I know I'm not pregnant! I can't be! I'd die if that happened!"

"Don't be a fool, Jemima! What the devil did you think when you laid with him? That you had a charm of some kind— it couldn't happen to you? Well, it has, and the sooner you admit it the better for you."

Suddenly Jemima began to cry, scared and distracted now that she was finally forced to confront the fact from which she had been fleeing for weeks. "I don't believe you! I'll be well again in a few days, I know I will! You're just trying to scare me, that's all! Oh—go away and leave me alone!"

Amber gave her an angry shake. "Jemima, stop it! Most likely some of the servants are listening! D'you want everyone to know what's happened? If you'll keep your mouth shut and be sensible you can save yourself and your family too. Don't forget what a disgrace this will be for them if it's ever found out—"

"Oh, that's what I'm afraid of! They'll hate me! They'll—Oh—I wish I was dead!"

"Stop talking like an idiot! If you marry Joseph Cuttle on the 15th—"

Jemima snapped out of her hysteria as if she had been dashed with cold water. "Marry Joseph Cuttle! Why, I won't marry Joseph Cuttle and you know it! I wouldn't marry him for—"

"You've got to marry him! There's nothing else you can do now! It's the only way you can keep the Dangerfields from being disgraced."

"I don't care! I don't care about them! I won't marry him! I'm going to run away from home and take lodgings somewhere and wait till Lord Carlton comes back. He'll marry me then, when he knows what happened."

Amber gave a short brutal laugh. "Oh, Jemima, you silly green foolish girl. Lord Carlton marry you! Are you cracked in the head? He wouldn't marry you if you had triplets. If he'd married every woman he's ever laid with I don't doubt he'd have as many wives as King Solomon. Besides, if you ran away from home you wouldn't even have a dowry to offer him! Marry Joseph Cuttle while you've still got time—it's the only thing you can do now."

For a long moment Jemima lay perfectly still and stared up at her.

"So at last you're going to get your way," she said softly. Her eyes glittered, but her next words merely formed on her mouth:

"Oh, how I *despise* you—"

CHAPTER THIRTY

JEMIMA'S WEDDING WAS a social event of considerable importance.

Between them the Dangerfields and the Cuttles had friends or relatives in almost every one of the great City families. Gifts for the bride and groom had been pouring into the house for weeks past, and had almost filled one large room set aside to receive them. The bride walked on a golden tapestry to the improvised altar which had been set up in the south drawing-room, while her aunts and female cousins sniffled and the mighty music of three great organs made the walls tremble. She wore her dark coppery hair flowing over her shoulders—symbol of virginity—and a garland of myrtle and olive and rosemary leaves; she was sober-faced and dry-eyed, which was unfortunate, for it was believed to be bad-luck if the bride did not weep. But she seemed preoccupied and almost unaware of what she was doing or saying, and when the ceremony was over she accepted the kisses of her eager happy groom and her friends and relatives with an air of absent-minded indifference.

The newly married couple opened the ball, and when the first dance was over they retired, as was customary, to the decorated bridal-chamber above. She began to cry when the women were undressing her, and everyone was pleased at this happy omen. When the two young people sat side by side in the great bed, Jemima's eyes now wide and troubled like those of a frightened animal which has been trapped, the spouted posset-pot was handed ceremoniously from one to another, all around the room.

There was no unseemly laughter, no bawdy jests or boisterous singing as was common at many weddings, but an atmosphere of quiet good-natured but serious responsibility. They went out then, leaving Jemima and her groom alone—and Amber heaved a grateful sigh of relief. There! she thought. It's done at last! And I'm safe.

But once she knew that she was secure, boredom began to settle on her like the gloomy fogs that hung over the river. She had bought too many gowns and too much jewellery to be satisfied by that any longer, particularly since she felt contemptuous of the opinion of those who saw them. Consequently she moped over her pregnancy, worried about the colour of her skin and the circles beneath her eyes, wept when her belly began to enlarge, and was sure that she was hideous and would always be so. For amusement she spent a great deal of time wishing for out-of-the-season foods—it was now winter—and since everyone knew that when a pregnant woman "longed" she must be satisfied or the child might be lost, it kept Samuel and all the household in a pother to supply her with the things she wanted. Usually by the time she got them the longing was gone, or another had taken its place.

She slept ten or eleven hours every night, no longer getting up at six with Samuel, but often drowsing till ten; and then she lay in bed another half-hour, thinking discontentedly of the day before her. By the time she had dressed it was noon and dinner-time. If he stayed home after that she did too; otherwise she went to visit some of the dozens of Dangerfield relatives or the hundreds of Dangerfield friends, and sat talking talking talking of babies and servants, servants and babies.

"When do you reckon, Mrs. Dangerfield?" they asked her everywhere she went, and time after time. And then came the discussion of Cousin Janet and the frightful labour she had had—fifty-four hours of it—or of Aunt Ruth who had been brought to bed of triplets twice in succession. And all the while they sat and munched on rich cakes, thick pastries, cream and curds, plump good-natured happy satisfied women whom Amber thought the most absurd creatures in the world.

Weeks went by very quickly this way.

Ye gods! thought Amber dismally. I'll be twenty-one in March! I'll most likely be too old to enjoy it when I finally get that damned money.

Christmas was a welcome diversion to her. The house

swarmed with children, more of them than ever: Deborah who lived in the country had come to spend the holidays, bringing with her a husband and six children. Alice and Anne, though they both lived in London, followed the Dangerfield tradition and came home with their families. William returned from abroad and George came down from Oxford. Only Jemima preferred to stay at her husband's home, but even she paid them a visit almost every day, with Joseph always beside her—full of pride for his pretty wife and so happy at the prospect of parenthood he must tell everyone he saw the wonderful news. And Jemima seemed, if not in love with Joseph, at least tolerant of his adoration—which she had not been before; pregnancy had given her a kind of serene contentment. Her rebellion against the manners and morals of her class was over, and she was beginning to accept and settle into her place in that life.

Laurel and cypress and red-berried holly decorated every room and filled them with a spicy winter fragrance. An enormous silver bowl of hot-spiced wine, garlanded with ivy and ribbons and floating roast apples, stood ever ready in the entrance hall. And there was food in all the glorious ancient tradition: plum-porridge and mince-meat pies, roast suckling pig, a boar's head with gilded tusks, fat geese and capons and pheasants roasted to a crusty golden brown. Every dinner was a feast, and whatever was left was distributed to the poor who crowded at the back gates in vast numbers, baskets over their arms, for the Dangerfield generosity was well-known.

Gambling for money was traditionally permitted in all but the strictest households at Christmas-time, and from early morning till late at night cards were shuffled and dice rolled and silver coins clinked merrily across the tables. The children played hot-cockles and blind-man's-buff and hunt-the-slipper, shouting and laughing and chasing each other from one room to another, from garret to basement. And for more than two weeks a stream of guests poured continuously through the house.

Amber gave Samuel a heart-shaped miniature of herself (fully clothed) set in a frame of pearls and rubies and diamonds. She gave gifts almost as expensive to every other member of the family, and her generosity to the servants convinced them that she was the best-natured woman in the world. She received as much as she gave, not because the family liked her any better than before, but to keep up appearances for their father and for outsiders. Amber knew this but she did not care, for nothing could have dislodged her now that he thought she carried his child. He gave her a beautiful little gilt coach, upholstered in padded scarlet velvet trimmed with swags of gold rope and numerous tassels, and six fine black horses to draw it. She was not, however, allowed to ride in it but must go everywhere in a sedan-chair—Samuel would take no chances with her health or the baby's.

Twelfth Night marked the end of the celebrations. It was late in the evening that Samuel suffered another severe stroke, his first since the previous July.

Dr. de Forest, who was sent for immediately, asked Amber in private if Samuel had obeyed his earlier advice and she reluctantly admitted that for some time past he had not. But she defended herself, insisting that she had tried to persuade him but that he had refused to listen and had said it was ridiculous to think a man of sixty-one too old for love, and swore he felt more vigorous than he had in years.

"I don't know what else I can do, Dr. de Forest," she finished, giving the responsibility back to him.

"Then, madame," he said gravely, "I doubt that your husband will live out the year."

Amber turned about wearily and left the room. If she was ever to get rich Samuel must die, and yet she shrank from the thought of being his murderess, even indirectly. She had developed a genuine, if superficial, love for the handsome, kind and generous-spirited old man she had tricked into marriage.

In the anteroom to the bedchamber she came upon Lettice and Sam, and Lettice was in her brother's arms, crying mournfully. "Oh, Sam! If only it had happened any night but this one! Twelfth Night—that means he'll die before the year is out, I know it does!" Twelfth Night was the night of prophecy.

Sam patted her shoulders and talked to her quietly. "You mustn't think that, Lettice. It's only a foolish superstition.

454

Don't you remember that last year Aunt Ellen had the ague on Twelfth Day? And she's been merry as a grig all year." He caught sight of Amber, pausing in the doorway, but Lettice did not.

"Oh, but it's different with Dad! It's that terrible woman! She's killing him!"

Sam tried to shush her beneath his breath, as Amber came on into the room. Lettice spun around, stared at her for a moment as though undecided whether to apologize or speak her mind. And then suddenly she cried out:

"Yes, *you're* the one I meant! It's all your fault! He's been worse since you came!"

"Hush, Lettice!" whispered Sam.

"I won't hush! He's my father and I love him and we're going to see him die before his time because this brazen creature makes him think he's five-and-twenty again!" Her eyes swept over Amber with loathing and contempt; Samuel's announcement of his wife's pregnancy had been a serious shock to her, as though it were the final proof of her father's infidelity to their dead mother. "What kind of woman are you? Have you no heart in you at all? To hurry an old man into his grave so that you can inherit his money!"

"Lettice—" pleaded Sam.

Amber's own sense of guilt stopped her tongue. She had no stomach for a quarrel with his daughter when Samuel lay in the room beyond, perhaps dying. She answered with unwonted gentleness.

"That isn't true, Lettice. There's a great difference in our ages, I know. But I've tried to make him happy, and I think I have. He was sick before I came, you know that."

Lettice, avoiding her eyes, made a gesture with one hand. Nothing could ever make her like this woman whom she distrusted for a hundred reasons, but she could still try to show her at least a surface respect for her father's sake. "I'm sorry. I said too much. I'm half distracted with worry."

Amber walked by, toward the bedroom, and as she passed gave Lettice's hand a quick grasp with her own. "I am too, Lettice." Lettice looked at her swiftly, a questioning puzzled look, but she could not help herself; the woman's smallest gesture would always seem false-hearted to her.

Samuel refused to make his annual trip to Tunbridge Wells that January because his wife's advanced pregnancy would not allow her to accompany him. But he did rest a great deal. More and more he stayed in his own apartments with her, while the eldest sons took over the business. She read to him and sang songs and played her guitar, and with gaiety and affection tried to soothe her own conscience.

It was customary for men with financial responsibilities to check over and settle their accounts at the end of the year, but because of his stroke Samuel postponed doing so until early in February. And then he worked on them for several days. He had his wealth in goldsmiths' bills, stock in the East India Company—of which he was one of the directors—assignments upon rents, mortgages, shares in privateering fleets and other similar ventures, cargoes in Cadiz and Lisbon and Venice, jewels and gold-bullion and cash.

"Why don't you let Sam and Bob do that?" Amber asked him one day, as she sat on the floor playing a game of cat's-cradle with Tansy.

Samuel was at his writing-table, dressed in an East Indian robe which Bruce had given him, and there was a many-branched candlestick lighted above his head, for though mid-day it was dark as twilight. "I want to be sure myself that my affairs are in order—then if anything should happen to me—"

"You mustn't talk like that, Samuel." Amber got to her feet, dropping the cradle, and with a pat on the head for Tansy she walked over to where he sat. "You're the picture of good health." She gave him a light kiss and bent over, one arm about his shoulders. "Heavens! What's all that? I couldn't puzzle it out to save my bacon. My senses seem to run a-wool-gathering at the sight of a number!" She could, in fact, not do much more than read them.

"I'm arranging everything so that you won't need to worry about it. If the baby's a boy I'm going to leave him ten thousand pound to start in a business for himself—I think that's better than for him to try to go in with his half-brothers—and if it's

456

a girl I'll leave her five thousand for a marriage portion. How do you want your share? In money or property?"

"Oh, Samuel, I don't know! Let's not even think about it!"

He smiled at her fondly. "Nonsense, my dear. Of course we shall think about it. A man with any money at all must have a will, no matter what his age. Tell me—which would you prefer?"

"Well—then I suppose it would be best for me to have it in gold—so I won't get cheated by some sharp rook."

"I haven't that much cash on hand, but in a few weeks' time I think it can be arranged. I'll put it with Shadrac Newbold."

He died very quietly one evening early in April, just after he had gone upstairs to rest from a somewhat strenuous day.

In a great black mourning-bed, Samuel Dangerfield's body lay at home in state. Two thousand doles of three farthings each were distributed to the poor, with biscuits and burnt ale. His young widow—much pitied because it was so near the time of her confinement—received visitors in her own room; she was pale and wore the plainest black gown, with a heavy black veil trailing from her head almost to the floor. Every chair, every table and mirror and picture in the entire apartment had been shrouded in black crape, every window was shut and covered, and only a few dim candles burned—Death was in the house.

The guests were served cold meats, biscuits and wine, and at last the funeral procession set out. The night was dark and cold and windy and the torches streamed out like banners. They moved very slowly, with a solemn stumping tread. A man ringing a bell led them through the streets and he was followed by the hearse, drawn by six black horses with black plumes on their heads. Men in black mounted on black horses rode beside it, and there followed a train of almost thirty closed black coaches carrying all members of the immediate family. After that there came on foot and in their official livery the members of the guilds to which he had belonged and other mourners in a straggling line almost two miles long.

Amber could not go to sleep that night in her black room

457

alone but insisted that Nan sleep with her and that a torchère be left burning beside the bed. She was not as glad to be a rich woman as she had expected she would be, and she was not as sorrowful at Samuel's death as she thought she should be. She was merely apathetic. Her sole wish now was that her pains would begin so that she could bear this child and be freed of the burden which grew more intolerable with each hour.

CHAPTER THIRTY–ONE

THE ANTEROOM WAS crowded. Young men stood about in groups of two and three and four, leaning on the window-sills to look down into the courtyard where a violent mid-March wind racked the trees, bending them almost double. They wore feather-loaded hats and thigh-length cloaks, with their swords tilting out at an angle in back; lace ruffles fell over their fingers and flared out from their knees and clusters of ribbon loops hung at their shoulders and elbows and hips. Several of them were yawning and sleepy-eyed.

"Oh, my God," groaned one, with a weary sigh. "To bed at three and up at six! If only Old Rowley would find the woman could keep him abed in the mornings—"

"Never mind. When we're at sea we can sleep as long as we like. Have you got your commission yet? I'm all but promised a captaincy."

The other laughed. "If you're a captain I should be rear-admiral. At least I know port from starboard."

"Do you? Which is which?"

"Port's right, and starboard's left."

"You're wrong. It's the other way around."

"Well—it won't make much difference, this way or that. There never was a man so plagued by sea-sickness as I. If I so much as take a pair of oars from Charing Cross to the Privy Stairs I'm sure to puke twice on the way."

"I'm a fresh-water sailor myself. But for all of that I'm mighty damned glad the war's begun. A man can live just so long on actresses and orange-girls, and then the diet begins to pall. Curse my tripes, but I'll welcome the change—salt air and waves and fast gun-fire. By God, there's the life for a man! Besides, my last whore begins to grow troublesome."

"That reminds me—I forgot to take my turpentine pills this morning." He brought a delicate gem-studded box out of one pocket and snapped it open, extending it first to his friend who declined the offer. Then he tossed two of the large boluses into his mouth and gave a hard swallow to get them down, shaking his head mournfully. "I'm damnably peppered-off, Jack."

At that moment there was a stir in the room. The door was flung open and Chancellor Clarendon entered. Frowning and preoccupied as usual, his right foot wrapped in a thick bandage to ease his gout, he spoke to no one, but walked straight across and through the other door which led into his Majesty's bed-chamber.

Eyebrows went up, mouths twisted, and sly secret smiles were exchanged as the old man passed.

Clarendon was rapidly becoming the most hated man in England—not only at Court but everywhere. He had been in power too long and the people blamed him for whatever went amiss, no matter how little he might have had to do with it. He would accept no advice, allow no opposition; whatever he did was right. Even those faults might have been overlooked but that he had others which were unforgivable. He was inflexibly honest and would neither take nor give bribes, and not even his friends profited by his favour. Though he had lived most of his life at courts he was contemptuous of courtiers and scorned to become one.

And so they watched, and waited. If his hold on Parliament should once slip they would be at his throat like a pack of starving jackals.

"Have you been out Piccadilly to see the Chancellor's new house?" asked someone, when he had gone.

"Judging by the foundations I'd say he'll have to sell England to finish it. What he got from Dunkirk won't build the stables."

"How many more times does the old devil think he *can* sell England? Our value won't hold up much longer at the present rate of exchange."

The door into the King's private chambers opened again and Buckhurst strolled out with another young man. Two or three others crossed over to speak to them.

"What's the delay? I've been waiting here half-an-hour. Nothing but the hope of speaking to his Majesty about a place for my cousin could have induced me to get out of bed on a morning like this one. Now I suppose he's gone by way of the Privy Stairs and left us all to shift for ourselves."

"He'll be along presently. He's dickering with a Jesuit priest over the price of a recipe for Spirit of Human Skull. Have you got a tailor's bill in your pocket, Tom? If it's illegible enough sell it to Old Rowley for a universal panacea and your fortune's made. He's giving that mangy old Jesuit five thousand pound for his scrap of paper."

"Five thousand! Good God! What can an old man have to spend five thousand on?"

"What do you think? On a remedy for impotence, of course."

"The best remedy for impotence is a pretty wench—"

The voices grew temporarily quiet as the King appeared, strolling through the door with his dogs and sycophants behind him. He was freshly shaved and his smooth brown skin had a healthy glow; he gave them a smile and a nod of his head and started on out. The jostling for place began immediately as they streamed along in his wake, but Buckingham already had one elbow and Lauderdale the other.

"I suppose," said Charles to the Duke, "that by tomorrow it will be running up the galleries and through the town I'm a confirmed Catholic."

"I've heard those rumors already, Sire."

"Well—" Charles shrugged. "If that's the worst rumour that goes abroad about me I think it's no great matter for concern." Charles was not inclined to worry about what anyone said of him, and he knew his people well enough to know that grumbling was a national sport, not much more subversive than football or wrestling. He had been home almost five years now, and the honeymoon with his subjects was over.

Leaving his own apartments he crossed the Stone Gallery and started down a maze of narrow hallways which led along the Privy Garden, over the Holbein Gateway and into St. James's Park. He walked so rapidly that the shorter men had to half run, or be left behind, and since most of them had a favour to ask they did not intend to let that happen.

"I think there's time," said Charles, "for a turn through the Park before Chapel. I hope the air's cold enough to make me sleepy."

They had reached the old stairway which led down into the Park when suddenly one of the doors up the corridor to the left burst open and Monmouth came out in a rush. The men stopped and while his father laughed heartily the Duke ran toward them; he arrived breathless, swept off his hat and made a low bow. Charles dropped an arm about the boy's shoulders and gave him an affectionate pat.

"I overslept, Sire! I was just going to attend you to Chapel."

"Come along, James. I've been wanting to talk to you."

James, who was now walking between the King and Lauderdale, gave his father an apprehensive glance. "What about, Sire?"

"You must know, or you wouldn't have such a guilty face. Everyone's been telling me about you. Your behaviour's a favourite subject of conversation." James hung his head and Charles, with a smile he could not wholly conceal lurking at the corners of his mouth, went on. "They say you've taken to keeping a wench—at fifteen, James—that you've run deep into debt, that you scour about the streets at night disturbing peaceful citizens and breaking their windows. In short, son, they say you lead a very gay life."

Monmouth looked swiftly up at his father, and his handsome face broke into an appealing smile. "If I'm gay, Sire, it's only to help me forget my troubles."

Several of the others burst into laughter but Charles looked

461

at the boy solemnly, his black eyes shining. "You must have a great many troubles, James. Come along—and tell me about them."

The morning was cold and frosty and the wind blew their periwigs about, as it did the spaniels' ears. Charles clamped his hat firmly onto his head, but the others had to hold to their wigs—for they carried their hats beneath their arms—or lose them. The grass was hard-matted and slippery, and there was a thin sheet of ice over the canal; it had been an unusually cold dry winter, and there had been no thaw since before Christmas. The other men looked at one another sourly, annoyed that they must go walking in such weather, but the King strode along as unconcernedly as if it were a fine summer day.

Charles walked in the Park because he liked the exercise and the fresh-air. He enjoyed strolling along the canal to see how his birds, in cages hung in the trees on either side, were standing the cold weather. Some of the smaller ones he had had removed indoors until the frost should break. He wanted to know if the cold had hurt the row of new elms he had had set out the year before and whether his pet crane was learning to walk with the wooden leg he had had made for it when its own had been lost in an accident.

But he did not walk only for amusement and exercise; it was a part of the morning's business. Charles had always preferred that his unpleasant tasks be done under pleasant conditions—and there were few duties he disliked more than hearing petitions and begging for favours. If it had been possible he would gladly have granted every request that was made him, not so much from the boundless generosity of his nature as to buy his own peace from whining voices and pleading eyes. He hated the sound and the sight of them, but it was the one thing from which there never could be escape.

Some of them wanted a place at Court for a friend or relative, and there were always a hundred askers for each place that fell vacant. However he chose he left many disgruntled and jealous and the one who got it was seldom as well pleased as he had expected to be. Another would want a grant for a Plate Lottery —royal permission to sell tickets at whatever price he could command for a lottery of some crown plate. Others were there to beg an estate: it was common practice to bear the expense of arrest and prosecution of other persons in the hope that a cash-fine or confiscated property could be begged from the King. Another man wanted to go to sea to fight the Dutch, and he wanted to go as a captain or a commander, though his sea experience had been limited to a crossing from France in one of the packet-boats.

Charles listened to them patiently, tried when he could to refer the supplicant to someone else, and when he could not usually granted the request, though well aware that it might be impossible of fulfillment. And as he walked and listened to the petitions of his courtiers he was often approached by a sick old man or woman, sometimes a young mother with her child, who begged him to touch and heal them. The courtiers resented the intrusion, but Charles did not.

He liked his people and, though he had lived so long out of the country, he understood them. They grumbled about his mistresses and the extravagance of the Court, but when he smiled and stopped to talk to them and laughed with them in his deep booming voice they loved him in spite of everything. His charm and accessibility were potent political weapons and he knew it.

They walked along the Canal that crossed the Park from one end to another and back along Pall Mall, turning down King Street into the Palace grounds. The chapel bells began to ring and Charles increased his rapid pace, relieved that soon he would be where they could pester him no longer. Monmouth was far ahead of them. All along the way he had been running and leaping, calling the spaniels to follow him until now their long ears were soggy and wet and their paws clotted with mud.

Ah! thought Charles, and drew a deep breath as they came into the courtyard which led to the chapel. Another hundred yards and I'm safe!

At that moment Buckingham, who had given his place to others, caught up with him again. "Sire," he began. "May I present—"

Charles threw a quick comical glance at Lauderdale. "How is it," he murmured, "that every one of my friends keeps a tame knave?"

But he turned back with a smile to hear the man out, and stopped just at the chapel doors with the courtiers clustered around him. But the ladies were going in, and his eyes wandered. Frances Stewart came along with her waiting-woman and gave him a wave of her hand. Charles grinned broadly and made a quick move to follow her, but remembered that he was listening to a petition and checked himself.

"Yes," he interrupted. "I appreciate your position, sir. Believe me, I'll give it serious thought."

"But, Sire—" protested the man, holding out his hands. "As I told you, it's most urgent! I must know soon or—"

"Oh, yes," said Charles, who had not been listening at all. "So it is. Very well, then. I think you may."

Gratefully the man started to drop to his knees, but the King gave him an impatient signal not to, for he was eager to get away. And then, just before he entered the great carved oak doors he turned and said over his shoulder, "As far as I'm concerned, you may have your wish. But you'd best make sure the Chancellor has no other plans on that score."

The man opened his mouth again, the smile disappearing in a sudden look of dismay, but it was too late. The King was gone. "Catch him as he comes out," whispered Buckingham, and went on himself.

The chapel was already well filled and the music of the great organ thundered in the walls. Charles did not like going to church and sermons bored him, but he did contrive to please himself while there with some of the finest music to be had. And, much to the scandal of the conservative, he had introduced violins, which he loved better than any other instrument.

He sat alone in the Royal Closet in the gallery—Catherine attended her own Catholic mass—looking down over the chapel. Curtains at either side closed off the portion of the gallery where the ladies sat, though he knew that Frances was there just beside him, so close that he could whisper to her. The young clergyman who was to speak for the day had taken his

464

place and was mopping his perspiring cheeks and forehead with his black-gloved hands, until as the dye came off he looked more like a chimney-sweep than a divine. Titters went up here and there and the young man looked more wretchedly uncomfortable than ever, wondering why they had begun to laugh before he had spoken so much as one word.

It was almost as difficult to preach to the Court as it was to act to it. The King invariably went to sleep, sitting bolt upright and facing the pulpit, as soon as the subject of the sermon had been announced. The Maids of Honour whispered among themselves, waved their fans at the men below, giggled and tried on one another's jewellery and ribbons. The gallants craned their necks back up at the ladies' gallery and compared notes on the previous night's activities or pointed out the pretty women present. The politicians leaned their heads together and murmured in undertones, keeping their eyes ahead as though no one could guess what they were doing. Most of the older ladies and gentlemen, relics of the Court of the first Charles, sat soberly in their pews and listened with satisfaction to the warnings repeatedly given by the pulpit to a careless age; but even their good intentions often ended in noisy snores.

At last the young chaplain, newly preferred to his place by an influential relative, proclaimed the subject of his first sermon before the King and Court. "Behold!" he announced, giving another swipe of his black glove along his cheek, "I am fearfully and wonderfully made!"

Instantly the chapel was filled with laughter, and while the bewildered frightened young man looked out over his congregation, tears starting into his eyes, even the King had to clear his throat and bend over to examine his shoe-lace to conceal a smile. A finger poked him gleefully through the curtains, and Charles knew that it was Frances whom he could hear gasping with laughter. But the chapel finally grew quiet again, the terrified clergyman forced himself to go on, and Charles composed himself to sleep.

Frances Stewart had replaced Barbara Palmer as the most popular and successful hostess at Whitehall. The suppers she gave in her apartments overlooking the river were crowded with all the powerful and clever men and pretty women of the Court. Both Buckingham and Arlington were trying to enlist her support for their own projects, for they were convinced as was everyone else that the King could be led through a woman.

Buckingham strummed his guitar for her and sang songs, mimicked Clarendon and Arlington, played with her at her favourite game of building card-castles, and flattered himself that she was falling in love with him. The Baron had no such social tricks at his command, but he did unbend enough to talk to her with a certain air of gracious condescension which was the best he could do toward charming a woman. And when Louis XIV sent his new minister, Courtin, to try to persuade Charles to call off the Dutch War, the merry little Frenchman immediately applied himself to Mrs. Stewart.

"Oh, heavens!" she said one evening to Charles, when he had finally maneuvered her into a corner alone. "My head's awhirl with all this talk of politics! One tells me this and another that and a third something else—" She stopped, looked up at him and then gave a sudden mischievous little burst of laughter. "And I don't remember any of it! If they only guessed how little I listen to their prittle-prattle I warrant you they'd all be mightily out of sorts with me."

Charles watched her, his eyes glowing with passionate admiration, for he still thought that she was the most perfectly lovely thing he had ever seen. "Thank God you don't listen," he said. "A woman has no business meddling in politics. I think perhaps that's one reason why I love you, Frances. You never trouble me with petitions—your own or anyone else's. I see asking faces everywhere I look—and I'm glad yours doesn't ask." His voice dropped lower. "But I'd give you anything you want, Frances—anything you *could* ask for. You know that, don't you?"

(Across the room one young man, watching them, said to another: "His Majesty's been in love with her for two years and she's still a virgin. I tell you, it's beyond credence!")

Frances smiled, a gentle wistful smile so young and artless that it clutched at his heart. "I know that you're very generous,

466

Sire. But truly, there's nothing I want but to live an honourable life."

A look of quick impatience crossed his face and his eyebrows twisted with a kind of whimsical anger. But then he smiled. "Frances, my dear, an honourable life is exactly what he who lives it thinks it to be. After all, honour is only a word."

"I don't know what you mean, Sire. To me, I assure you, honour is much more than a word."

"But nevertheless it must be one or several qualities you associate with a certain word. His Grace of Buckingham, for instance, over there at the card-table, has quite another definition from your own."

Frances laughed at that, somewhat relieved that she could, for she did not like serious conversations and felt uneasy in the presence of an abstraction. "I don't doubt that, your Majesty. I think that's one subject where his Grace and I think no more alike than you and I do."

"Oh?" said the King, with an air of mild and amused interest. "And has Buckingham been trying to persuade you over to his interpretation?"

Frances blushed and tapped her fan on her knee. "Oh, that wasn't what I meant!"

"Wasn't it? I think it was. But don't trouble yourself about it, my dear. It's an old habit of the Duke's—falling in love along with me."

Frances looked offended. "Falling in love along with you! Heavens, Sire! You sound as if you've been in love mighty often!"

"If I tried to pretend I'd never noticed a woman until you came along—well, Frances, after all—"

"Just the same you needn't speak as though it's a common everyday occurrence!" She tilted her chin and turned a haughty profile to him.

Charles laughed. "I almost think you're prettiest when you're just a little—just ever so little—angry with me. You have the loveliest nose in the world—"

"Oh, have I, Sire?" She turned eagerly and smiled at him, unable to resist the compliment.

But suddenly the King glanced across the room and muttered in annoyance, "Good Lord! Here comes Courtin to lecture me about the war again! Quick! Let's go in here!"

He took her arm and though she started to protest he swiftly ushered her through the door and closed it. The room was dark but for the moonlight reflecting off the water, but he led her across it and into another beyond.

"There!" he said, closing the second door. "He'll never dare follow us in here!"

"But he's such a nice little man. Why don't you want to talk to him?"

"What's the use? I've told him a thousand times. England and Holland are at war and that's all there is to it. The fleet's at sea—I can't very well call it back for all the nice little men in France. Come here—"

Frances glanced at him dubiously, for each time they were alone the same thing happened. But after a moment of hesitation she walked to the window and stood beside him. White swans were floating there close to shore in the early spring dusk, and the reeds grew so tall the tips of them touched the glass. The water looked dark and cold and a brisk wind had whipped up the waves. He slipped one arm about her waist and for a minute or more they stood silently, looking out. And then slowly he turned, drew her close against him, and kissed her mouth.

Frances submitted, but she was unresponsive. Her hands rested lightly on his shoulders, her body held taut and her lips were cool and passive. His arms tightened and his mouth forced her lips apart; the blood seemed to vibrate through his veins with the intensity of his passion. He felt sure that this time he could bring her to life, make her desire him as violently as he did her.

"Frances, Frances," he murmured, a kind of pleading rage in his voice. "Kiss me. Stop thinking—stop telling yourself that this is wicked. Forget yourself—forget everything and let me show you what happiness can be—"

"Sire!"

She was beginning to push at him now, a little frightened, arching her back and trying to bend away from him, but his

468

body curved over hers, his hands and his mouth seeking. "Oh, Frances, you can't put me off any longer—I've waited two years —I can't wait forever—I love you, Frances, I swear I do! I won't hurt you, darling, please—please—"

It was true that he was in love with her. He was in love with her beauty and her femininity, the promise of complete fulfillment which she seemed to offer. But he did not really love her any more than he had ever loved any other woman; and he believed furthermore that her show of virtue was a stubborn pretense, designed to get something she wanted. In his relations with women as in all other phases of his life, his selfishness took refuge in cynicism.

"Sire!" she cried again, really alarmed now, for she had never realized before how powerful was his strength, how easy it would be for him to force her.

But he did not hear. His hands had pushed the low-cut gown far off her shoulders, and he held her hard against him, as though determined to absorb her body into his own. She had never seen him so blindly excited and it terrified her, for her emotions did not answer his but fled to the opposite extreme—she was scared and disgusted. And all at once she hated him.

Now she put her crossed arms against his shoulders and pushed, and at the same time she gave a sobbing desperate cry. "Your Majesty, let me go!" She burst into tears.

Instantly he paused, his body stiffening, and then he released her, so swiftly that she almost lost her balance. While he stood there in the darkness beside her, so quiet she would have thought she was alone but for the sound of his breathing, she turned away and continued to cry—not softly but with whimpering sobs so that he would hear her and regret what he had done. And also so that he would realize she was even more offended than he could possibly be. For she was afraid now that he might be angry.

It seemed a long time, but at last he spoke. "I'm sorry, Frances. I didn't realize that I was repulsive to you."

Frances whirled around. "Oh, Sire! Don't think that! Of course you're not! But if I once give myself up to you I'll have lost the only thing I have that's any value to me. A woman can no more be excused because she gives herself to a king than if he were any other man. You know that your own mother says that."

"My mother and I do not always think alike—and certainly not on that point. Answer me honestly, Frances. What is it you want? I've told you before and I tell you again—I'll give you anything I have. I'll give you anything but marriage—and I'd give that if I could."

Frances's voice answered him crisply. "Then, Sire, you will never have me at all. For I shall never give myself to a man under any other conditions than marriage."

He stood with his back to the windows and his face in darkness, and she could not see the expression of savage anger that brushed across it. "Someday," he said, in a soft voice, "I hope I'll find you ugly and willing." He went past her swiftly and out the door.

CHAPTER THIRTY-TWO

AMBER DID NOT like being shut up in a black room; it made her melancholy. But at least the fact that she was supposed to be in mourning secured her from what would otherwise have been an intolerable number of visits from every friend, acquaintance and remote relative of the entire family. Her child, a girl, had been born just a few days after Samuel's death. And she would have been expected to give a gossips'-feast, a child-bed feast, and a great reception following the christening.

As it was she received calls only from close relatives and friends of the family, though many others sent gifts. During these she sat half propped in bed, looking very pale and fragile against all that sombre black. She smiled wistfully at her visitors, sometimes squeezed out a tear or two or at least a long sigh, and looked fondly at the baby when someone said that she was as much Samuel's image as if she had been spit out of his mouth. She was polite and patient and as decorous as ever, for she felt that she owed Samuel that much at least in return for the great fortune he had left her.

She scarcely saw the immediate family at all. Each of them came just once to her room, but Amber knew that it was only out of a persistent sense of duty to their father. She realized that now he was dead they expected and wanted her to leave as soon as she could get out of bed. And she did not intend to linger there any longer than necessary.

But it was only Jemima who said what the others were thinking. "Well—now that you've got Father's money I suppose you expect to buy a title with it and set yourself up for a person of quality?"

Amber gave her an impudent mocking smile. "I might," she agreed.

"You may be able to buy a title," said Jemima, "but you can't buy the breeding that goes with it." That sounded to Amber like something she had heard one of the others say, but the next words were Jemima's own: "And there's something else you can't buy, either, not if you had all the money there is. You never *can* buy Lord Carlton."

Amber's jealousy of Jemima had faded, since she knew her to be securely trapped in marriage, to lazy contempt. There was nothing she had to fear from her now. And she gave her a slow, sweeping insolent glance. "I'm very sensible of your concern, Jemima. But I'll shift for myself, I warrant you. So if that's all you came for, you may as well go."

Jemima answered her in a low tense voice, for Amber's smugness and indifference made her furious. "I *am* going—and I hope I never see you again as long as I live. But let me tell you one thing—someday you're going to get the fate you deserve. God won't let your wickedness thrive forever—"

Amber's superiority dissolved into a cynical laugh. "I vow and swear, Jemima, you've grown as great a fanatic as the rest of them. If you had better sense you'd have learned by now that nothing thrives so well as wickedness. Now get out of here, you malapert slut, and don't trouble me again!"

Jemima did not trouble her again, and neither did anyone

471

else in the family. She was left as strictly alone as if she were not in the house at all.

She sent Nan about the town searching for lodgings—not in the City but out in the fashionable western suburbs that lay between Temple Bar and Charing Cross. And about three weeks after the baby's birth she went herself to look at one Nan had found.

It was a handsome new building in St. Martin's Lane, between Holborn, Drury Lane, and Lincoln's Inn Fields, where she would be surrounded by persons of the best quality. The house was four stories high with one apartment on each floor and there was a top half-story for the servants. Amber's apartment was on the second floor; a pretty young girl just in from the country with her aunt to find a husband was above her, and a rich middle-aged widow occupied the fourth. The landlady, Mrs. de Lacy, lived below Amber. She was a frail creature who sighed frequently and complained of the vapours, and who talked of nothing but her former wealth and position, lost in the Wars along with a husband whom she had never been able to replace.

The house was called the Plume of Feathers and a large wooden sign swung out over the street just below Amber's parlour windows—it depicted a great swirling blue plume painted on a gilt background and was supported by a very ornate wrought-iron frame, also gilded. The coach-house and stables were up the street only a short distance. And the narrow little lane was packed with the homes and lodgings of gallants, noblemen, titled ladies and many others who frequented Whitehall. Red heels and silver swords, satin gowns and half masks, periwigs and feathered hats, painted coaches and dainty high-bred horses made a continuous parade beneath her window.

The apartments were the most splendid she had ever seen.

There was an anteroom hung in purple-and-gold-striped satin, furnished with two or three gilt chairs and a Venetian mirror. It opened into one end of a long parlour which had massed diamond-paned windows overlooking the street on one side and the courtyard on another. The marble fireplace had a plaster overmantel reaching to the ceiling, lavishly decorated with

472

flowers, beasts, swags, geometrical figures and nude women. The chimney-shelf was lined with Chinese and Persian vases, there was a silver chandelier, and the furniture was either gilded or inlaid with ivory and mother-of-pearl. Nothing, Mrs. de Lacy explained proudly, had been made in England. The emerald-and-yellow satin draperies were loomed in France, the mirrors came from Florence, the marble in the fireplace from Genoa, the cabinets from Naples, the violet-wood for two tables from New Guinea.

The bedroom was even more sybaritic. The bedstead was covered with cloth-of-silver and all hangings were green taffeta; even the chairs were covered with silver cloth. Several wardrobes were built into the walls and there was a small separate bench-bed with a canopy and tight-rolled bolster for lounging, surely the most elegant little thing Amber had ever seen. And there were three other rooms, nursery, dining-parlour and kitchen, which last she did not expect to use.

The rent was exorbitant—one hundred and twenty-five pounds a year—but Amber had the merest contempt for such small change and paid it without a word of protest, though she hoped and expected that she would not be there even half that long. For Bruce should be back soon; he had been gone now more than eight months and the Pool was crowded again with captured merchant-shipping.

She moved her belongings from Dangerfield House before she herself left, and though the process took three or four days no one came near or commented on what she was taking, not all of which strictly belonged to her. She had hired a wet-nurse and a dry-nurse for the baby, and now she hired three maids, which completed the equipage necessary to a woman of fashion living alone. The day she left, the great house was perfectly silent; she scarcely saw a servant and not even one of the children appeared in the hallways. Nothing could have told her more plainly than this silent contempt how they hated her.

But Amber did not care at all. They were nothing to her now—those stiff precise formal people who lived in a world she despised. She sank back onto the seat of her coach with a sigh of relief.

"Drive away! Well—" she turned to Nan. "That's over—thank God."

"Aye," agreed Nan, softly but with real feeling. "Thank God."

They sat quietly, looking out the windows as the coach jogged along, enjoying everything they saw. It was a dirty foggy day and the moisture in the air made stronger than ever the heterogeneous and evil smells of London. Along one side of the street swaggered a young beau with his arm in a sling from a recent duel. Across the way a couple of men, obviously French, had been caught by a group of little boys who were screaming insults at them and throwing refuse picked up out of the kennels. The English hated all foreigners, but Frenchmen most of all. A ragged one-eyed old fish-woman lurched drunkenly along, holding by its tail a mouldering mackerel and bawling out her unintelligible chant.

All at once Nan gave a little gasp, one hand pressed to her mouth and the other pointing. "Look! There's another one!"

"Another what?"

"Another cross!"

Amber leaned forward and saw a great red cross chalked on the doorway of a house before which they were stalled. Beneath it had been printed the words, in great sprawling letters: LORD HAVE MERCY UPON US! A guard lounged against the house, his halberd planted beside him.

She leaned back again, giving a careless wave of her gloved hand. "Pish. What of it? Plague's the poor man's disease. Haven't you heard that?" Barricaded behind her sixty-six thousand pounds she felt safe from anything.

For the next few weeks Amber lived quietly in her apartments at the Plume of Feathers. Her arrival in the neighbourhood, she knew, created a considerable excitement and she was aware that every time she stepped out of the house she was much stared at from behind cautiously drawn curtains. A widow as rich as she was would have aroused interest even if she were not also young and lovely. But she was not so eager to make friends now as she had been when she had first come to

London, and her fortune made her suspicious of the motives of any young man who so much as stepped aside to let her pass in the street.

The courtiers were all out at sea with the fleet and—though she would have enjoyed flaunting to them her triumph over the conditions which had once put her at their mercy—she had no real interest in anyone but Bruce. She was content waiting for him to return.

Most of the time she stayed at home, absorbed in being a mother. Her son had been taken away from her so soon, and she had seen him so infrequently since, that this baby was as much a novelty to her as if it were her first. She helped the dry-nurse bathe her, watched her while she fed and slept, rocked her cradle and sang songs and was fascinated by the smallest change she could discover in her size and weight and appearance. She was glad that she had had the baby, even if it had temporarily increased her waist-line by an inch or so, for it gave her something of Bruce's which she could never lose. This child had a name, a dowry already secure and waiting, an enviable place of her own in the world.

Nan was almost as interested as her mistress. "I vow she's the prettiest baby in London."

Amber was insulted. "In London! What d'you mean? She's the prettiest baby in England!"

One day she went to the New Exchange to do some unnecessary shopping, and happened to see Barbara Palmer. She was just leaving when a great gilt coach drove up in front and Castlemaine stepped out. Barbara's eyes went over her clothes with interest, for though Amber was still dressed in mourning her cloak was lined with leopard-skins—which Samuel had bought for her from some African slave-trader—and she carried a leopard muff. But when her eyes got as far as Amber's face and she saw who was wearing the costume she glanced quickly and haughtily away.

Amber gave a little laugh. So she remembers me! she thought. Well, madame, I doubt not you and I may be better acquainted one day.

As the days went by red crosses were seen, more and more frequently, chalked on the doors. There was plague in London every year and when a few cases had appeared in January and February no one had been alarmed. But now, as the weather grew warmer, the plague seemed to increase and terror spread slowly through the city: it passed from neighbour to neighbour, from apprentice to customer, from vendor to housewife.

Long funeral processions wound through the streets, and already people had begun to take notice of a man or a woman in mourning. They recalled the evil portents which had been seen only a few months before. In December a comet had appeared, rising night after night, tracing a slow ominous path across the sky. Others had seen flaming-swords held over the city, hearses and coffins and heaps of dead bodies in the clouds. Crowds collected on the steps of St. Paul's to hear the half-naked old man who held a blazing torch in his hand and called upon them to repent of their sins. The tolling of the passing-bell began to have a new significance for each of them:

Tomorrow, perhaps, it tolls for me or for someone I love.

Every day Nan came home with a new preventive. She bought pomander-balls to breathe into when out of doors, toad amulets, a unicorn's horn, quills filled with arsenic and quicksilver, mercury in a walnut shell, gold coins minted in Queen Elizabeth's time. Each time someone told her of a new preservative she bought it immediately, one for each member of the household, and she insisted that they be worn. She even put quicksilver-quills around the necks of their horses.

But she was not content merely with preventing the plague. For she realized sensibly, that in spite of all precautions one sometimes got it, and she began to stock the cupboards with remedies for curing the sickness. She bought James Angier's famous fumigant of brimstone and saltpetre, as well as gunpowder, nitre, tar and resin to disinfect the air. She bought all the recommended herbs, angelica, rue, pimpernel, gentian, juniper berries, and dozens more. She had a chestful of medicines which included Venice treacle, dragon water, and a bottle of cow-dung mixed with vinegar.

Amber was inclined to be amused by all these frantic preparations. An astrologer had told her that 1665 would be a lucky

476

year for her, and her almanac did not warn her of plague or any other disease. Anyway it was true, for the most part, that only the poor were dying in their crowded dirty slums.

"Mrs. de Lacy's leaving town tomorrow," said Nan one morning as she brushed Amber's hair.

"Well, what if she is? Mrs. de Lacy's a chicken-hearted old simpleton who'd squeak at the sight of a mouse."

"She's not the only one, mam, you know that. Plenty of others are leaving too."

"The King isn't leaving, is he?" They had had this same argument every day for the past two weeks, and Amber was growing tired of it.

"No, but he's the King and couldn't catch the sickness if he tried. I tell you, mam, it's mighty dangerous to stay. Not five minutes' walk away—just at the top of Drury Lane—there's a house been shut up. I'm getting scared, mam! Lord, I don't want to die—and I shouldn't think you would either!"

Amber laughed. "Well, then, Nan—if it gets any worse we'll leave. But there's no use fretting your bowels to fiddle-strings." She had no intention at all of leaving before Bruce arrived.

On the 3rd of June the English and Dutch fleets engaged just off Lowestoft, and the sound of their guns carried back to London. They could be heard, very faintly, like swallows fluttering in a chimney.

By the 8th it was known that the English had been victorious —twenty-four Dutch ships had been sunk or captured and almost 10,000 Dutchmen killed or taken prisoner, while no more than 700 English seamen had been lost. The rejoicing was hysterical. Bonfires blazed along every street and a mob of merrymakers broke the French Ambassador's windows because there was no fire in front of his house. King Charles was the greatest king, the Duke of York the greatest admiral England had ever known—and everyone was eager to continue the fight, wipe out the Dutch and rule all the seas on earth.

The red crosses had now entered the gates of the City.

Nan came in a few days later with a bill-of-mortality in her hand. "Mam!" she cried. "Mam! There was 112 died last week of the sickness!"

477

Amber was entertaining Lord Buckhurst and Sir Charles Sedley who—along with the other gentlemen—had just returned from sea, all of them sunburnt heroes. Nan stopped on the threshold in surprise to find them there.

"Oh," she said. "I'm sorry, gentlemen." She made a curtsy.

"Never mind, Mrs. Nan. Damn me, Sedley! She's as pretty as ever, isn't she? But what's this? Sure *you're* not worried about the plague?"

"Oh, but I *am*, sir! I'm scared out of my wits! And all these other things they've got marked! I'll warrant you at least *half* of 'em died of the plague!" She began to read from the fresh-printed bill, for they were scarcely off the press before Nan had one. "Griping of the guts—3! Worms—5! Fits—2! How do we know those weren't all the plague too and not reported by the searcher because somebody greased 'em in the fist to give another cause of the death!"

Amber and the two men laughed but Nan was so excited she began to choke on the gold-piece she had in her mouth and ran out of the room. Only nine days later, however, the Queen and her ladies set out for Hampton Court, and the gentlemen intended to follow very shortly. Buckhurst and some of the others who had heard of her inheritance tried to persuade Amber to go along, but she refused.

Then at last, very much to Nan's relief, she began to make preparations for leaving town herself. She had the maids begin packing her clothes, and most of her jewellery she took to Shadrac Newbold, for she did not want to carry it about the countryside with her and had no idea as to where she would go. She found the street before his house crowded with carts and wagons and all the household in a turmoil.

"It's fortunate you came today, Mrs. Dangerfield," he told her. "I'm leaving town tomorrow myself. But I had assumed you were in the country with the rest of the family. They left at least a fortnight ago." The Dangerfields had a country home in Dorsetshire.

"I don't live at Dangerfield House any more. I think I'll take just a hundred pound. That should be enough, don't you think?"

"I think so. The ways will be more crowded than ever with highwaymen. And the plague must be near spent by now. Excuse me a moment, madame."

While he was gone Amber sat fanning herself. The day was hot and she could feel her high-necked black-satin gown sticking to 'her skin; her silk stockings, moist with perspiration, clung tight to her legs. Presently he returned and sat down to count out the pieces of gold and silver for her, stacking them in piles on the table while she watched him drowsily.

"That was a fine boy little Mrs. Jemima had, wasn't it?" he said conversationally.

Amber had not known that Jemima's child was born, but now she said sarcastically: "So soon? She was only married last October."

He gave her a glance of surprise, and then smiled, shrugging his shoulders. "Well, yes, perhaps it is a little early. But you know how young people are—and a contract is as binding as the ceremony, they say."

He scooped the money into a purse and handed it to her as she got up to go. At the door she turned. "Any word of Lord Carlton?"

"Why, yes, as it happens, I have. Some ten days ago one of his ships put into port and a man came to tell me that his Lordship would be here soon. I've waited for him now longer than I'd intended, but I can't wait any longer. Perhaps he's heard of the sickness and decided not to come. Good-day, madame, and the best of luck to you."

"Thank you, sir. And to you."

Everyone was wishing everyone else good luck these days.

She drove immediately down to the wharves and sent Jeremiah to inquire for Lord Carlton. After half-an-hour or so he returned to say that he had found a man who had been on the ship which had come in and that he was expected at any time. The men who had manned the first ship were all waiting impatiently, for they wanted their shares of the venture.

Back home she saw that several carts piled with her own gilt leather trunks and boxes stood before the house, and Nan came running down the stairs to meet her. "A man died this morning only four doors up the street!" she cried. "I've got everything ready! We can leave this instant, mam! Can't we, please?"

Amber was annoyed. "No, we can't! I've just heard that Lord Carlton is expected in port any day and I'm not going till I've seen him! Then we'll all go together."

Suddenly Nan began to cry. "Oh, we're all going to catch it and die! I know we are! That's what happened to a family in Little Clement's Lane—every one of 'em died! Why can't you meet his Lordship in the country? Leave 'im a message!"

"No. He might not come at all then. Oh, Nan! For Heaven's sake! Stop your blubbering then. You can go tomorrow."

Nan set out very early the next morning with the baby, her nurses, Tansy, two of the maids, and Big John Waterman— who had come with them from Dangerfield House because he was in love with Nan. She was to go to Dunstable and wait there or, if there was plague in the town, to continue on until she found a safe place and sent back a message. Amber gave them a great many instructions and admonitions regarding the care of the baby and protection of her belongings and they rattled off, waving back at her. Then she sent Jeremiah back to the wharves—but Bruce had not come.

London was emptying rapidly now.

Trains of coaches and carts started out early every morning: twenty-five hundred had died the week before. The sad faces of the plague prisoners—shut in with the sick—appeared at many windows, and bells tolled from almost every parish church in the city. People held their noses when they passed a cross-marked house. Some families were storing their cellars with great supplies of food and then sealing the house, stuffing every crack and keyhole, boarding the doors and windows to keep out the plague.

The weather continued hot and there was no fog; it had not rained for almost a month. The flowers down in the courtyard, roses and stocks and honeysuckle, were wilting and the meadows about the town were beginning to dry up and turn brown. Street vendors hawked cherries and apples and early pears, though oranges were scarce since the war had begun, and

480

everyone who could afford it bought ice—cut off the lakes and rivers in the winter and stored underground packed in straw—to cool their wine and ale. They talked almost as much about the heat as they did about the war or the plague.

Amber was finally beginning to feel nervous herself. The long funeral processions, the red crosses on every hand, the tolling bells, the people passing with their noses buried in a pomander or bottle of scent had at last made her uneasy. She wanted to get away, but she was sure that if she left, Bruce would arrive the same day. And so she waited.

Tempest and Jeremiah were complaining about being kept so long in town and did not like being sent to the wharves. Jane—the serving-girl who had stayed with Amber—whined and wanted to go to her father's home in Kent and so Amber let her. When Nan had been gone four days she asked Tempest and Jeremiah to look for Lord Carlton once more and told them that if they found him she would give them each a guinea. But for the money, she knew, they would merely drive around or go to a tavern for a couple of hours and then come back. By noon they were home again. Lord Carlton had come in the night before and they had just seen him down at the wharves, unloading his ships.

PART IV

CHAPTER THIRTY-THREE

THE WHARVES WERE busy as an ant hill.

Ships with their gilded hulls gleaming, their tall masts mere bare skeletons, lay on the quiet water in great numbers. Many of them were men-of-war back from fighting the Dutch and in the process of being overhauled and cleaned. Broken seams were being mended with boiling-pitch, and the ropes bound with tarpaulin. Sailors and porters were everywhere, unloading the plundered treasure which had recently been seized, while captured Dutch flags snapped out bravely from the Tower. But there were also great numbers of crippled and wounded men, hobbling about, sitting, lying flat on their backs, all reaching out their hands to beg. For the most part they were ignored. The navy had not been paid and already some of the seamen were starving.

Amber got out of her coach and walked along the wharf between Tempest and Jeremiah, one hand shading her eyes against the hot sun. The beggars tried to touch her as she passed and some of the sailors whistled or made audible comments, but she was too absorbed in looking for Bruce even to hear them.

"There he is!" She started to run and the sound of her high heels on the boards made him turn. "Bruce!"

She came up to him, smiling eagerly and out of breath, expecting to be kissed. But instead he looked down at her with a scowl and she saw that his face was tired and his skin wet with sweat.

"What the devil are you doing down here?"

As he spoke he glanced around truculently at the men who were staring at her, for her cloak was opened over her black-satin gown and emeralds sparkled in her ears and on her fingers.

Disappointed, offended by his surly tone, she had an instant of angry self-pity. But his look of exhaustion was real and her eyes went over him anxiously, tender as a mother's caress. She had seldom seen him tired and now she longed to take him into her arms, kiss away the scowl and the weariness—her love for him rose up like a painful throbbing ache.

"Why, I came to see you, darling," she answered softly. "Aren't you glad?"

He gave a faint smile, as though ashamed of his ill temper, and ran the back of one hand across his moist forehead. "Of course I am." His eyes went down over her figure. "The baby's been born?"

"Yes—a little girl. I named her Susanna— Oh!" She remembered with a sudden sense of guilt. "Samuel's dead."

"I know. I heard about it this morning. Why aren't you out of town?"

"I waited for you."

"You shouldn't have—it's not safe in London. Where's the baby?"

"I sent her and Nan and Tansy into the country. We can go too—and meet them—" She looked at him questioningly, afraid he might tell her that he already had other plans.

Bruce took her arm and they started back toward the coach. As they went he began talking in an undertone. "You've got to get away from here, Amber. You shouldn't have come down at all. Ships carry disease, you know."

"Oh, I'm not worried about that. I've got a unicorn's horn."

He laughed, but without much humour. "Unicorn's horn— my God! A cuckold's horn would do you as much good."

They reached the coach and he handed her in. Then he braced one foot on the step, rested his arms on his knees and as he leaned forward to talk to her his voice was no more than a murmur. "You've got to get away from here as fast as you can. Some of my men are sick of the plague."

Amber gasped in horror, but he made her a quick negative motion with his head. "But Bruce!" she whispered. "*You* might catch it too!"

"There've only been three cases. There was sickness on some

486

of the Dutch ships we took and when we found it we sank them with everyone on board—but three of my own sailors have fallen sick since. They were moved off the ships last night and there haven't been any new cases so far today."

"Oh, Bruce! You can't stay here! You've got to come away— Oh, darling, I'm scared! Have you got an amulet or something to protect yourself?"

He gave her a look of exasperated impatience, and ignored the last question. "I can't leave now—I can't leave until everything's been unloaded and stored. But you've got to go. Please, Amber, listen to me. I've heard a rumour they're going to lock the gates and forbid anyone's leaving. Get out while there's still time."

She looked at him stubbornly. "I won't go without you."

"Holy Jesus, Amber, don't be a fool! I'll meet you somewhere later."

"I'm not afraid of the plague—I never get sick. When will you be through unloading?"

"Not before night."

"Then I'll come back here for you at sundown. Nan and the baby are at Dunstable and we can meet them there. I'm not living at Dangerfield House any more—I've got lodgings in St. Martin's Lane."

"Then go there and stay. Keep off the streets and don't talk to anyone."

He turned away and then, as she watched anxiously, her face wistful as a child's, he looked around and gave her a smile and a slow weary wave of his hand. He walked off down the wharf and disappeared into the crowds.

But she did not stay at home as he had told her to do.

She knew that he was skeptical about a great many things in which she believed, and a unicorn's horn was one of them. Wearing it pinned inside her smock she felt perfectly safe as she went out to make arrangements for their supper, for she thought that tomorrow morning would be early enough to leave. She ordered their supper at the Blue Bells, a very fine French tavern in Lincoln's Inn Fields, and then went back to set the table herself. All her silver had been stored with Shadrac

487

Newbold but there was pewter enough in the kitchen to make a handsome show and she amused herself for most of an hour experimentally folding the napkins to resemble weird birds. In the courtyard she gathered a great armful of limp yellow roses that climbed over the walls and onto the balconies, and arranged them in a large pewter bowl for the dining-room table.

She took delight in each small detail, each unimportant little thing which she did, with the hope that later it would make him comfortable or cause him to smile. The plague began to seem almost a blessing to her now, for it meant that they would be together for several weeks, perhaps months—perhaps, forever. She thought that she had never been so happy, or had so much cause for happiness.

The last hour before she set out she spent brushing and arranging her hair, polishing her nails, and painting her face—very subtly, for she did not want him to look at her with the smile she knew so well, which always made her feel that she was both foolish and wrong. She was standing at the window fastening a bracelet when she saw a funeral procession turn the corner. There were banners floating, horses and men tramped solemnly, and though it was still light several torches burned. She turned quickly away—resenting the intrusion of death into her happiness—threw on her cloak and went downstairs.

The wharf was half deserted now and as she rode out along it the wheels of her coach rumbled noisily. He was talking to two other men, and though he gave her a nod he did not smile and she saw that he looked even more tired than before. After a few minutes all three returned to one of the ships and disappeared from sight.

By the time a quarter of an hour had gone by she was beginning to grow impatient. Now, just *what* can be keeping him all this time! Here he hasn't seen me for ten months and what does he do? Goes back to his damned boat for a drink, I suppose! She began to tap her foot and flutter her fan. From time to time she sighed and scowled, and then she smoothed her features again and tried to compose herself. The sun had set, dark red over the water, and now there was a slight breeze

488

which seemed refreshing after the hot day just passed.

It was at least another half-hour before he came back and by then her eager anticipation had turned to angry pique. He got in and sat down heavily. She gave him a sideways glance and said tartly:

"Well, Lord Carlton! Have you come at last! Pray don't let me keep you from something important!"

The coach began to move again. "I'm sorry, Amber—I've been so damned busy I—"

She was instantly contrite and ashamed of her meanness, for she could see that his eyes were bloodshot and even though the air was cool now, little drops of sweat stood on his forehead. She had never seen him look so tired, and her hand reached over to his. "*I'm* sorry, darling. I know you didn't keep me waiting on purpose. But why did you have to work so hard and so long? Sure now, those men aren't such fools they can't unload a ship by themselves."

He smiled, stroking her fingers. "They could have unloaded it alone, and would have been only too glad to. But these prizes are the King's, and God knows he needs them. The sailors haven't been paid and the men are refusing to work any more for tickets that can't be cashed— Contractors won't supply commodities they know they won't be paid for. God, you don't have to be here three hours to hear a tale of woe that would make a lawyer weep. And I might as well tell you—the three men who were sick yesterday are dead, and four more got it today."

She stared at him. "What did you do with them?"

"Sent them to a pest-house. Someone told me that the gates are guarded now and that no one can leave without a certificate-of-health. Is that true?"

"Yes, but don't trouble yourself about it. I got a certificate for you when I got mine and Nan's and all the others. Even Susanna had to have one. And what a bother it was! The streets were packed for a half-mile around the Lord Mayor's house. I think everyone in town is leaving."

"If they issue them for people they've never seen they can't be worth much."

Amber held out her hand, rubbing her thumb and first two

fingers suggestively together. "For enough money they'd give a dead man a certificate-of-health. I offered them fifty pound for the lot and they didn't ask a question." She paused. "I'm mighty rich now, you know."

He sat slumped low, as though every muscle was tired, but he gave her a faint smile. "So you are. And is it as pleasant as you'd expected?"

"Oh, much more! Lord, everyone wants to marry me now! Buckhurst and Talbot and I can't think how many others. What a pleasure it was to laugh in their faces!" She laughed now, thinking of it, and there was a malicious sparkle in her eyes. "Oh, gad, but it's a fine thing to be rich!"

"Yes," he agreed. "I suppose it is."

Both of them were silent for a few minutes and then he said, "I wonder how long this plague will last."

"Why?"

"Well, I'd hoped to be back at sea in another month—but the men won't sign now. And anyway it would be foolish—they've found some Dutch ships with everyone aboard dead."

Amber did not reply, but she felt that if there must be a plague at all it could not have happened more to her advantage.

When they reached her lodging-house she ran on up the stairs ahead of him, full of a trembling eager excitement. Sometimes she felt that moments like this one were almost compensation enough for the long periods of time when she did not see him at all. Such wild frantic happiness, ecstasy that was almost torture, pleasures that racked and exhausted—these things could be no everyday occurrence, no matter how truly you loved. They fed on loneliness and longing, and came to full blossom over slow months of separation.

She unlocked the door and flung it open, then turned about quickly to face him.

But he was still only halfway up the staircase, mounting it with slow heavy steps that were strangely and almost frighteningly unlike him. As he reached the top he paused for just an instant, one hand lifting as if to touch her, but he did not and walked on, into the parlour. A cold wet chill went over her and for a moment Amber stood, sick with disappointment, star-

490

ing at the wall. She turned slowly then and saw him drop wearily into a chair, and at that moment her selfish feeling of jilted expectation was gone in a shock of horror.

He's sick!

But instantly she pushed the thought away, superstitiously furious with herself for having allowed it into her mind. No! she thought fiercely. He isn't sick! He's just tired and hungry. When he's rested a while and had something to eat he'll be well and strong again.

Determined that he should not suspect what treacherous fear she had had, she now came toward him with a broad gay smile, taking off her cloak and throwing it over one arm. He looked up at her with an answering grin, but gave a short involuntary sigh.

"Well—" she said. "Aren't you even going to say that you like my lodgings? Everything's in the latest style—and nothing's English." She made a comical little face and gave a sweep of one hand, but as he looked out over the room her eyes watched him anxiously.

"It's lovely, Amber. Forgive my bad manners. To tell the truth I'm tired—I was up all night."

The news relieved her. Up all night! Why, who wouldn't be tired? Then he wasn't sick at all. Oh, thank God—thank God!

"I've got just the thing for that. Here, darling, let me take your cloak and hat—and the sword, too, you'll be more comfortable without it."

She would have bent to unbuckle it for him, but he did so himself before she could, and handed it to her. Then, laying everything on a nearby chair, she brought him a tray on which were two decanters, one of water and one of brandy. He gave her a grateful smile and picked up a bottle while she turned to take their wraps into the bedroom.

"I'll be back in a trice. And we can eat right away. Everything's here."

She ran into the bed-chamber, which opened out of the parlour, and while she took off her gown and unpinned her hair she talked to him from the doorway—still hoping that he was not so tired as he seemed, that he would get up and come to

491

her. But he merely sat, watching her and drinking the brandy, saying very little. She stepped out of her dress, untied the bows on her shoes and stripped off her stockings, let her petticoats drop to the floor and bent to pick them up.

"I've got everything you like best for supper: Westphalia-style ham and roast duck and an almond pudding and champagne. It isn't easy to get French wines any more, either, since the war. Lord, I don't know how we'll shift for new styles if we go to war with France! Do *you* think we will? Buckhurst and Sedley and some of the others say we're sure to—" She talked fast, to keep both of them from thinking. She disappeared from sight for a moment and then came into the room wearing a white silk dressing-gown and a pair of silver mules.

She walked toward him, slowly, and his green eyes darkened like water. He swallowed the rest of the brandy and got to his feet, and though for a moment they stood staring at each other he made no move to touch her. Amber waited, almost afraid to breathe; but as he scowled and turned half away, picking up his glass and the brandy decanter again, she said softly: "I'll put the food on the table."

She went through the dining-room and into the kitchen where the waiter who had brought the food had left the hot soup simmering over some embers in the fireplace. When she had served the soup they sat down to eat and though both of them tried to keep up a lively conversation, it stumbled and lagged.

He told her that he had taken five Dutch merchant-vessels, all of them valuable prizes. He said that he thought there would be war with France because France did not want England to win a decisive victory, and had to protect Holland to keep her from forming an alliance with Spain. Amber told him some of the gossip she had heard from Buckhurst and Sedley: that the Lowestoft victory would have been a much greater one but that Henry Brouncker gave orders in York's name to slacken sail, so that the battered Dutch fleet escaped. And—more exciting, she thought—she told him how the Earl of Rochester had kidnapped the great heiress, Mrs. Mallet, and been put in the Tower by the King for his effrontery.

He said that the meal was delicious, but he ate slowly and obviously had no appetite. At last he laid down his fork. "I'm sorry, Amber, but I can't eat. I'm not hungry."

She got up from the table and went around to him, for her fears had been growing steadily. He did not look tired; he looked sick. "Perhaps you should sleep, darling. After staying up all night you must be—"

"Oh, Amber, there's no use pretending about this. I've got the plague. At first I thought it was only lack of sleep. But I've too many symptoms the other men had—no appetite, headache, dizziness, sweating, and now I begin to feel nauseated." He flung down his napkin and pushed back his chair, slowly heaving himself to his feet. "I'm afraid you'll have to go alone, Amber."

She looked at him steadily. "I won't go without you, Bruce, and you know it! But I'm sure it isn't the plague. It can't be! You're well and strong— When you've had a night's sleep I *know* you'll feel better."

He smiled faintly, but shook his head. "No, I'm afraid you're wrong. I only hope to God I haven't exposed you. That's why I didn't kiss you. I was afraid—" He looked around. "Where's my hat and cloak?"

"You're not going anywhere! You're going to stay here with me! Lord, I've looked and felt as bad as you do a hundred times and next day I was up and about! *Everybody* who gets a pain or ache can't have the plague! If you're not sick we'll leave tomorrow morning. And if you are—I'm going to take care of you."

"Oh, Amber, my dear— You don't think I'd let you? I might be dead by—"

"Bruce! Don't say that! If it *is* the plague I'll take care of you and make you well again. I learned how to take care of a sick person from my Aunt Sarah."

"But it's infectious—you might catch it too. And it's highly fatal. No, darling, I'm going. Get my hat and cloak—go on."

He turned away and the look of worried anger he had tried to conceal before now showed plainly. His face was wet with sweat, so that the drops slid along his jaw, and he moved like a man half drunk. His muscles seemed almost useless. There was a pounding headache over his eyes and a dull aching pain had filled his back and loins and went down into his legs. At a sudden chill he shuddered involuntarily, and the feeling of nausea was overwhelming.

Amber took hold of his arm, determined to keep him there somehow if she had to knock him unconscious. For if he went out onto the street she knew that he either would be taken up by a constable for drunkenness—a mistake which was frequently made—or would be sent to a pest-house. If he was sick, and she was finally convinced that he was, she intended to take care of him.

"Lie down here for a moment on the settee by the fireplace and rest while I make you a tea of some herbs. You can't stir a step in this state. It'll make you feel better, I swear it, and I'll have it ready in a trice."

She took his arm and he crossed the room with her to the corner fireplace. He was still obviously reluctant to stay but was rapidly losing the ability to make a decision; by the minute he grew more dazed and weak. Now he dropped onto the cushioned couch with a heavily drawn sigh, his eyes already closed. He shuddered frequently, as though very cold, but sweat had soaked through the back of his coat—Amber left him and ran swiftly and softly into the bedroom, returning with a satin quilt which she flung over him.

Then, sure that he could not get up and would probably fall asleep, she ran into the kitchen and began to search the cabinets for the herbs Nan had stocked there. As she found them she sprinkled some of each that she needed into a kettle: hawkweed and hound's-tongue and sorrel for the nausea; marigold and purslane for fever; hellebore, spikenard and nightshade for headache. Each had been gathered according to astrological tables, under exactly the right planetary influences, and she had considerable faith in their efficacy.

She poured some warm water into the kettle and hung it on a crane, but the fire had almost gone out and she threw on some more coals from the scuttle and a few chips of wood to make it burn, kneeling while she worked the bellows. At last a bright flame sprang up and she ran back into the parlour to make sure that he was all right, though she had not heard any sound.

He was lying flat on his back but the quilt had fallen off and he was moving restlessly, his eyes closed but his face contorted. As she bent over him, tucking in the quilt again, he looked up at her; and then suddenly he reached out and grabbed her wrist, giving it a savage jerk.

"What are you doing!" His voice was thickened and hoarse and the words slurred one over another. The green-grey irises of his eyes glittered, but the eyeballs were congested and red. "I told you to get out of here— Now, get out!" He almost shouted the last words and flung her arm from him furiously.

Amber was scared, for she thought he was losing his mind, but she forced herself to answer him in a calm reasonable voice. "I'm brewing the tea for you, Bruce, and it'll be ready in a little while. Then you can go. But lie still till then, and rest."

He seemed to return all at once to full rationality. "Amber— please! *Please* go and leave me alone! I'll probably be dead by tomorrow—and if you stay you'll get it too!" He started to sit up but she forced him down again with a sudden swift shove and he collapsed back onto the cushions. At least, she thought, I'm stronger than he is; he *can't* get away.

For a moment she waited, hanging over him anxiously, but he lay perfectly still, and at last she turned and tip-toed swiftly from the room. She was so nervous that her hands and even her knees shook; she picked up a pewter mug and dropped it with a loud clatter that made her heart jump sickeningly. But as she stooped to get it, she heard noises from the other room.

Grabbing up her skirts she rushed back to the parlour and found him standing in the middle of the floor, looking about in a dazed bewildered way. With a cry she ran toward him.

"Bruce! What are you doing!"

He turned and gave her a defiant glare, raising one arm to ward her off, muttering a curse beneath his breath. She grabbed hold of him and he gave her a shove that almost knocked her off her feet, but as she staggered backward she clutched frantically for him and dragged him along with her. He stumbled, tried to save himself from falling, and both of them crashed to the floor, Amber half pinned beneath him. He lay there perfectly still, eyes and mouth open, unconscious.

For a moment Amber remained where she was, stunned, and then she crawled out from beneath him and got to her feet. Bending, she put her hands under his arm-pits to try to drag him to the bed-chamber; but he was a foot taller and eighty pounds heavier than she and she could scarcely move him. She pulled and tugged frantically and was beginning to cry with terror and desperation, when she remembered that Tempest and Jeremiah were most likely upstairs in their quarters.

Whirling about she sped through the kitchen and up the back flight of stairs, bursting into their room without even a knock. They were lounging, looking out the windows and smoking, and they stared at her in amazement.

"Tempest! Jeremiah!" she cried. "Come with me!"

She turned and rushed back out of the room and down the stairs so fast she seemed almost to glide. The two men knocked out their pipes and followed her, through the kitchen and the dining-room back into the parlour where they found Bruce once more standing erect, though his feet were spread wide to brace himself and his shoulders weaved slowly from side to side. Amber ran to place herself before him and the two men followed, but remained at a timid distance, watching him uncertainly. He started forward, glaring menacingly from one to the other, as though to clear a path for himself. He looked like a man so drunk that he was about to pitch forward onto his face.

Amber watched him like one hypnotized, and as he came toward her she stepped aside to let him pass. Her hands went out involuntarily, for he looked as though he would fall at any moment, but she did not touch him. He went through the door-way and into the anteroom, then out onto the landing and for a moment he stood at the top of the staircase, like a colossus looking down. He took one step and then another, but suddenly he gave a groan and staggered, clutching at the railing. Amber screamed and the two men rushed past her in time to keep him from falling headlong. Supported by one on either side, he allowed himself to be half dragged back into the apartment;

his head had dropped forward onto his chest and he was again in an almost unconscious stupor.

She led the way into the bedroom, throwing back the counterpane and quilts and indicating that they were to lay him there on the white silk sheets. Then immediately she pulled off his shoes and peeled down his stockings. They were, she noticed, coloured strangely yellow by his sweat which had a sharp unpleasant smell that was not natural to him. She unwound the sash from about his waist and had begun to work off the coat, when all at once she remembered Tempest and Jeremiah and glanced up swiftly to find them staring at her with white-faced horror. They had just realized, she knew, that they had been helping a man who was not drunk—but sick of the plague.

"Get out of here!" she muttered at them, furious to see the craven terror on their faces, and with their mouths still open they turned and dashed from the room, slamming the door violently behind them.

His shirt was so wet that it clung to his skin and she picked up her smock which had been left lying on the floor to wipe him dry. When she had removed all of his clothes she covered him again and took the pillow from beneath his head, for she knew that he never used one. He lay quietly on his back now, though from time to time he muttered something unintelligible beneath his breath.

She left him again and ran swiftly back to the kitchen. The water on the herbs had boiled down, but not far enough, and while she waited she searched the cupboards for what provisions might be on hand. But she had had all her meals sent in and could find only some orange-cakes, a bowl of cherries, several bottles of wine and one of brandy. While she made a mental list of the things she must get she stood and watched the bubbling mess, her ears alert for any sound he might make. And then at last she swung the crane out and filled the pewter mug she had ready. The smell was nauseating, but she wrapped the handle in a towel and went back to the bedroom.

Bruce was lying there, leaning on one elbow and looking at her as she came in. She saw that he had just vomited onto the

497

floor. His expression was humble and contrite and as guilty as though he had just done some shameful thing, for the sickness humiliated him. He seemed to want to speak to her, but could only drop back exhausted onto the bed. Amber had heard of men who felt well in the morning and were dead of the plague by night—but until now it had not seemed possible to her that a disease could make such swift terrible progress.

The sense of her own inadequacy seemed suddenly to overpower her.

Sarah had taught her how to take care of someone sick of an ague or the small-pox, what to do for a burn or the stomach-ache—but the plague was a mysterious thing, strange and evil. Some thought it rose out of the ground like a poisonous exhalation, entering through the pores of the skin, and that it spread thereafter by personal contact. But no one knew or pretended to know what really caused it, why it sometimes came in a great epidemic, or how to cure it. Still, she felt that she *must* have help of some kind, advice from someone.

Kneeling, she began to mop up the vomit with his shirt. I'll send Jeremiah for a doctor, she thought. At least he'll know more than I do.

When she tried to get Bruce to drink some of the tea he pushed it away, muttering thickly, "Some water? Thirsty. Thirsty as hell." He put his tongue between his lips as if to wet them, and she saw that it was swollen and the tip bright red.

She brought a pewter pitcher of cool water from the kitchen and he drank three glassfuls, swallowing avidly as though he could not get enough; and then with a deep sigh he dropped back onto the bed. When he had lain quietly for a few moments Amber ran up to the garret once more and pounded at the door. She waited impatiently for a few seconds but when she got no answer flung it open.

No one was there. A few soiled articles of clothing were strewn about the floor but an old wooden chest which stood open was completely empty, as were the pulled-out drawers of a dresser. They had packed and gone.

"Scoured!" muttered Amber. "Damn them for a pair of ungrateful pimps!" But she turned that instant and ran back down the stairs, for she was afraid to leave him alone even a minute.

He was lying as she had left him—moving about restlessly and muttering beneath his breath, but it was no longer possible to understand him and he seemed in a low delirium. She wrung out a cloth in cold water and laid it across his forehead, smoothed the sheets and blankets which were already disordered, and wiped away the sweat which continued to pour from him. Then she began to clean up the room. She picked up her own clothes and put them away, spread his over some chairs to dry, brought a basin to use next time he vomited, and a silver urinal. She did not dare stop working or let herself begin to think.

It was now almost ten and the streets had grown quiet but for the occasional rumble of a passing coach or the sound of a link-boy singing as he walked along. And after a while she heard the watchman go by, ringing his bell and crying: "Past ten o'clock of a fine summer's night—and all's well!"

Once or twice Bruce began to retch and each time she ran to hold the basin and help him sit up, covering his chest with a clean white linen towel, and at last he vomited again. When he tried to get out of bed she forced him back and brought the urinal, and now she saw that there was a tender-looking red swelling in his right groin—the beginning of the plague-boil. The last of her hopes died quietly.

CHAPTER THIRTY-FOUR

THE NIGHT PASSED with incredible slowness.

When she had cleaned the room and brought fresh water from the big jug which stood in the kitchen she washed her face and scrubbed her teeth, brushed her hair vigorously, and finally wheeled the trundle out from under the bed. But, though she lay down, a sense of guiltiness followed her—and each time

499

she began to slide off to sleep she woke up with a sudden start and the terrible feeling that something had happened to Bruce.

But when she got up and held the candle down close so that she could look at him he was always lying as he had been, moving constantly, muttering from time to time beneath his breath, his face twisted into an expression of angry anxiety. She could not tell whether he was conscious or not, for though his eyes were partly opened he did not seem to hear her when she spoke to him or to be in any way aware of her. Sometime in the middle of the night the sweating stopped and his skin became hot and dry and his face and neck violently flushed. His pulse beat rapidly and his breath came in quick shallow gasps, and sometimes he gave a slight cough.

About four it began to grow light and Amber decided to stay up, though her eyeballs ached and she was dizzy with tiredness. She put on her smock and one petticoat, stuck her bare feet into a pair of high-heeled shoes, and got into the dress she had been wearing the day before which, without her busk, she could not fasten all the way up the front. She pulled a comb hastily through her hair and rinsed her face, but she did not powder it or stick on a patch. For once it made no difference how she looked.

The room stank, for all the windows were closed. She was not afraid of the night air herself but she shared the common belief that it was fatal to a sick man. And she clung superstitiously to the country belief that if there was serious illness in the house death would not come if all doors and windows were kept tight shut and bolted. The smells were thick and heavy. She did not realize how overpowering they had become until she opened the door into the parlour and took a breath of clean air. Then she lighted the fire in the bedchamber and flung on a handful of dried herbs.

She made up the trundle and shoved it back out of sight and then, while he seemed to be somewhat quieter than usual, she took the slop-pans and went down to empty them into the courtyard privy and rinse them out. She made two more trips to bring up pails of fresh water. It had been a long while since she had remembered how tedious and how inconvenient were the simplest tasks of keeping house.

His intense thirst persisted, but though she gave him one glass of water after another the thirst was not allayed and he soon threw it up. Again and again he vomited, retching with a violence it seemed would tear out his bowels; each time it left him pouring sweat, exhausted and all but unconscious. Amber, who ran to hold the pan and to support him, watched him with horror and pity, and a growing rage.

He's going to die! she thought, holding the pan beneath his chin, pushing herself against his back to help him sit upright. He's going to die, I know he is! Oh! this filthy rotten plague! *Why* did it come! Why did *he* get it? Why should *he* be the one—and not somebody else!

He dropped down once more, flat on his back, and suddenly she flung herself across him, her fingers clutching at his arms— the muscles, though useless now, still looked hard and powerful beneath the brown skin. She began to cry, holding onto him defiantly and with all her strength, as though determined she would not give him up to Death. She murmured his name, mingled with curses and endearments, and her sobs grew wilder and more frantic until she was almost hysterical.

She was jerked out of her orgy of self-pity, back to reality by Bruce, whose fingers took hold of her hair and pulled her head slowly upward. She looked at him, her face smeared with tears, her eyes oddly slanted as his grip on her hair dragged at her scalp. Sick with shame and remorse she stared at him, wondering desperately what she had been saying—and if he had heard her.

"Amber—"

His tongue had swollen now until it almost filled his mouth, and it was covered with a thick white fur, though the edges were red and shiny. His eyes were dull, but he looked at her with recognition for the first time in many hours, scowling with the agonized effort to seize hold of his thoughts and express them.

"Amber— Why—why—aren't you—gone—"

She looked at him warily, like a trapped animal. "I am, Bruce. I am going. I'm just going now." Her fingers, spread out on the quilt before her, moved backward a little, but she could not stir.

He let go of her hair, gave another deep sigh, and his head rolled over sideways. "God go with you. Go on—while—" The words slurred off and he was almost quiet again, though still softly mumbling.

Slowly and carefully she moved away from him, genuinely afraid, for she had heard many awful tales of plague-victims gone mad. She was sweating with relief when at last she stood on her feet again and out of his reach. But the tears were gone and she realized that if she was to be of any use to him she must hold herself in control, do what she could to make him comfortable and pray that God would not let him die.

With quick resolution she went to work again.

She bathed his face and arms and combed his hair—he had not been wearing a periwig when she had met him at the wharf—smoothed the bed and laid another cold compress on his forehead. His lips were parched and beginning to split from the fever, and she covered them with pomade. She brought fresh towels from the nursery, and gathered all the soiled articles into a great bag, though of course no laundress would take it if it became known that there was plague in the house. And all the while she kept one eye on him, tried to understand him when he muttered something and to anticipate what he wanted so that he would not have to make the effort of reaching or moving himself.

About six the streets began to take on life. Across the way an apprentice let down the shutters of a small haberdashery shop, a coach rattled by, and she heard the familiar cry: "Milk-maid below!"

Amber threw open the window. "Wait there! I want some!" She glanced at Bruce and then ran out, scooping a few coins from the dressing-table as she went past, rushed into the kitchen for a pail and down the stairs. "I want a gallon, please."

The girl, pink-cheeked and healthy, was one of those who came in every day from Finsbury or Clerkenwell. She grinned at Amber and slid the yoke off her shoulders to pour the fresh warm milk. "Going to be another mighty hot day, I doubt not," she said conversationally.

Amber was listening for some sound from Bruce—she had left the window open just a crack—and she answered with an absent-minded nod. At that moment a deep boom filled the air. It was the passing-bell and it tolled three times—somewhere in the parish a man lay dying, and those who heard it were to pray for his soul. Amber and the milk-maid exchanged quick apprehensive glances, then both of them closed their eyes and murmured a prayer.

"Three pence, mam," said the girl, and Amber saw her eyes going over her black gown with a sharp glint of suspicion.

She gave her the three pennies, picked up the heavy pail and started to go back into the house. At the door she turned. "Will you be here tomorrow?"

The woman had shouldered her yoke and was already several feet away. "Not tomorrow, mam. I'll not be comin' into town for a while. There's no tellin' these days which one might have the sickness." Her eyes went down over Amber again.

Amber turned away and went inside. She found Bruce lying just as she had left him, but even as she came to the doorway he suddenly began to retch and tried to sit up. She put down the pail and ran toward him. His eyeballs were no longer bloodshot but had turned yellow and sunk into his skull. He had obviously lost all contact with things outside himself and seemed neither to hear nor to see; he moved and acted only by instinct.

Later she made several more purchases. She got cheese, butter, eggs, a cabbage, onions and turnips and lettuce, a loaf of sugar, a pound of bacon, and some fruit.

She drank some milk and ate part of the cold duck left from supper the night before, but when she suggested food to Bruce he did not answer and when she put a glass of milk to his lips he pushed it away. She did not know whether to insist that he eat or not, and decided that it would be best to wait for a doctor—she hoped to see one going past the house, for they carried gold-headed canes to distinguish them. Surely, with so many people sending for them at every hour of the day and night, she would see one soon. She was afraid to leave him alone long enough to go for one herself.

And then at last she found that his vomit was streaked with uncoagulated blood. That scared her violently and she decided that she could wait no longer.

She took her keys, left the building and ran along the street toward where she remembered having seen a doctor's sign, pushing her way through the crowds of porters and vendors and housewives. A passing coach left such a cloud of dust that she could taste the grit in her mouth; an apprentice bawled out some impertinent compliment which reminded her that her gown was undone; and a filthy old beggar, his hands and face covered with running sores, reached out to catch at her skirts. She passed three houses which were marked with the red cross and had a guard before each.

She arrived at the doctor's house out of breath and with hard dry pains in her chest, gave the knocker an impatient clatter and then, when no one answered, banged it furiously. She waited for at least a minute and was just picking up her skirts to leave when a woman answered. She held a pomander-ball to her nose and stared at Amber suspiciously.

"Where's the doctor? I've got to see 'im this instant!"

The woman answered her coldly, as though resentful that she had come at all. "Dr. Barton is making his calls."

"Send him the moment he gets back. The Sign of the Plume in St. Martin's Lane, up the street and around the corner—"

She raised her arm and pointed, and then she whirled and ran off, pressing her hand against the sharp pain that stabbed in her left side. But to her immense relief she found that Bruce, though he had vomited again—bringing up more blood—and had flung off the blankets, was otherwise as she had left him.

She waited nervously for the doctor. A hundred times she looked out the window, swearing beneath her breath at his slowness. But it was mid-afteroon before he arrived and she flew down the stairs to let him in.

"Thank God you've come! Hurry!" Already she was on her way back up again.

He was a tired old man, smoking a pipeful of tobacco, and he started wearily after her. "Hurrying won't do any good, madame."

She turned and looked at him sharply, angry that he apparently did not consider this patient to be of unusual importance. But nevertheless she was relieved to have him there. He could tell her how Bruce was, and what she should do for him. Ordinarily she shared the popular skepticism regarding doctors, but now she would have believed implicitly the idlest words of any quack or charlatan.

She arrived at the bedside before he did and stood there, watching him walk slowly into the room, her eyes big and apprehensive. Bruce lay now in a coma, though he was still mumbling and moving restlessly about. Dr. Barton stopped short of the bed by several feet, and he held a handkerchief to his nose. For a moment he looked at him without speaking.

"Well?" demanded Amber. "How is he?"

The doctor gave a faint shrug. "Madame, you ask me to answer the impossible. I do not know. Is there a bubo?"

"Yes. It started to rise last night."

She turned back the quilts so that he could see the lump in Bruce's groin, enlarged now to the size of a half-submerged tennis-ball; the skin over it looked stretched and red and shining.

"Does it seem to cause him much pain?"

"I touched it once, by accident, and he gave a terrible yell."

"The rising of the plague-boil is the most painful stage of the disease. But unless there is one they seldom live."

"Then he will live, Doctor? He'll get well?" Her eyes glistened eagerly.

"Madame, I can promise you nothing. I don't know. No one knows. We must simply admit that we don't understand it—we're helpless. Sometimes they die in an hour—sometimes it takes days. Sometimes it's easy, without a convulsion, other times they go in a screaming agony. The strong and healthy are as vulnerable as the frail and weak. What have you been giving him to eat?"

"Nothing. He refuses everything I try to feed him. And he vomits so often it wouldn't do any good."

"Nevertheless, he must eat. Force it down him someway, and feed him often—every three or four hours. Give him eggs and meat-broth and wine-caudles. And you must keep him as hot as possible. Wrap him in all the warm blankets you have and don't let him throw them off. Heat some bricks and pack them at his feet. If you have some stone water-bottles use those. Start a good fire and don't let it go out. He must be induced to sweat as profusely as possible. And make a poultice for the boil—you can use vinegar and honey and figs if you have them and some brown bread-crumbs and plenty of mustard. If he throws it off tie it on someway, and keep it there. Unless the boil can be brought to break and run he'll have but little chance of recovery. Give him a strong emetic—antimony in white wine will do, or whatever you may have on hand, and a clyster. That's all I can tell you. And you, madame—how are you?"

"I feel well enough, except that I'm tired. I had to stay up most of the night."

"I'll report the case to the parish and a nurse will be sent to help you. To protect yourself I'd advise you to steep some bay-leaves or juniper in vinegar and breathe the fumes several times a day." He turned and started to go and Amber, though keeping an eye on Bruce, walked along with him. "And by the way, madame, you'd better hide whatever valuables you may have in the house before the nurse arrives."

"Good Lord! What kind of a nurse are you sending?"

"The parish has to take whoever volunteers—we have too few already—and though some of them are honest enough, the truth of it is that most of them are not." He had reached the anteroom now and just before he started down the steps he said: "If the plague-spots appear—you may as well send for the sexton to ring the bell. No one can help them after that. I'll stop again tomorrow." Even as he spoke they heard the bells begin to toll, somewhere in the distance, two tenor notes struck for a woman. "It's the vengeance of God upon us for our sins. Well—good-day, madame."

Amber went back and set immediately about her new tasks,

for tired as she was she was glad to have work to do. It helped her to keep from thinking, and each thing that she did for him gave her a sense of satisfaction and accomplishment.

She poured some of the water which she kept hot in the kitchen into several stone bottles, wrapped them in towels and packed them all about him, and she brought out half-a-dozen more blankets from the nursery. He protested, pushing them down again and again, but each time, patiently, she covered him and went on with what she had been doing. The sweat began to run off his face in rivers, and the sheets beneath him were soaked and yellow. The fire roared and she heaped it with coals, making the room so hot that though she took off her petticoat, pushed her sleeves high and opened her gown, the silk clung to her ribs and there were wet spots beneath her breasts and in her arm-pits. She pulled the heavy hair up off her neck and skewered it on top of her head, and she mopped at her face and chest with a handkerchief.

She poured the emetic into his mouth and then, without waiting for it to take effect, administered the clyster. This was a difficult and painful process, but Amber was beyond either disgust or fastidiousness—she did what was necessary as well as she could, and without thinking about it. Afterwards she cleaned up the mess it had made, washed her hands, and went out to the kitchen to prepare the mustard-plaster and to make a sack-posset of hot milk, sugar and spices and white wine.

He made no protest when she laid the poultice on the boil and did not seem to know that it was there. Relieved—for she had been afraid that it might hurt him—she went back to finish making the posset.

She tasted the curdled drink, sprinkled on just a bit more cinnamon, and then tasted again. It was good. She poured it into the double-spouted posset pot and started for the bedroom. At that moment she heard a yell, a strange terrible sound that sent a quivering chill along her spine. Then there was a thud and a loud crash.

She slammed the pewter pot onto the sideboard and ran toward the bedroom. He was half-crouched on the floor, just getting to his feet—he had apparently fallen as he climbed out of bed, and overturned the table beside it. "Bruce!" she screamed at him, but he was not conscious of her or of what he was doing. Slowly he lunged to his feet and turned to push open the casement window which she had left unlocked. She rushed on toward him, grabbing up a candlestick from a chest-of-drawers and just as he put one foot on the recessed sill she grabbed his arm and swung the heavy stick, striking him hard across the base of the skull. Vaguely she realized that there were people below in the street, looking up, and she heard a woman scream.

He started to fall, sagging slowly, and she flung her arms about him, trying desperately to push him back onto the bed. But he was too heavy for her and in spite of her efforts slid slowly toward the floor. Knowing that she would never be able to lift him from there onto the high bed, she gave a sudden violent shove and he fell sideways, sprawled half across it; she stumbled and pitched down onto him. Swiftly she was on her feet again, and she jerked a quilt from the bed to fling over him, for he was naked and streaming sweat. Pulling and hauling, swearing with fright and rage, at last she got him back into the bed. She collapsed then into a chair beside it, completely exhausted, her muscles quivering and jumping resentfully.

Then, as she looked at him, she saw that a dark streak of blood was beginning to make a crooked path down his neck, and she got wearily to her feet again. With cotton and cold water she sponged it off, and wrapped a clean linen band—torn from a towel—around his head.

"Pox on that nurse!" she thought furiously. "*Why* doesn't she get here?" She replaced the mustard-plaster and filled the hot-water bottles again, for they had begun to cool.

On her way back to the kitchen she stopped and took a long drink of the posset. It was supposed to be highly invigorating and, at least for a time, did make her feel stronger. Putting the pot down she wiped her mouth with the back of her hand. If only that pestilent wench would arrive! she thought. Maybe I could sleep then. I'll die if I don't get some sleep. Exhaustion came over her in waves and for several minutes she would think she could not make another move, or take another step. And then it would pass, leaving her no less tired but able to do what had to be done.

It was several minutes before Bruce regained consciousness and then he was even more restless and violent. He tossed and threshed about, throwing off the blankets; his voice was loud and angry, and though she could not understand very much of what he said she knew that he swore continuously. She was not able to pour much of the posset down him before he gave a sudden swing of his arm that sent the pot clattering violently to the floor.

When at last he grew quieter she took a pen and paper and sat down at a table close by the bed to write a letter to Nan. It was difficult, for she wanted to tell the girl the truth without scaring her, and she worked over it for half an hour, scrawling out the words laboriously, making several drafts before she had one that suited her. She blew it dry and dripped on a great blob of gold sealing-wax. Then, picking up a shilling from the table, she went to the window and opened it, thinking that if she could find some youngster passing in the street below she could give him the coin to take it to the post-office for her. The price of postage would be paid upon delivery.

The sky was turning pale blue and a star or two had come out. There were not very many people abroad now, but as Amber leaned out she saw a boy, going down the middle of the street, hold his nose as he passed her house.

She looked down and saw a guard there, lounging against the wall with his halberd on his shoulder. That meant the red cross had been marked on her door too and they were shut in together for forty days and nights, or until both of them were dead. A few days before she would have been terrified; now she accepted it almost with indifference.

"Guard!" She spoke softly, and he heaved himself away from the wall and stood out from it to look up at her. "Will you give this letter to someone to post for me? I'll give you a shilling." He nodded his head, she tossed down the letter and the coin, and closed the window again. But for a moment she stood looking out, like a prisoner, at the sky and the trees. Then she turned and once more spread the quilts up over Bruce.

It was almost nine when the nurse arrived. Amber heard someone below talking to the guard and then a rap on the door. She took a candle and hurried down to admit her. "Why are you so late?" she demanded. "The doctor told me he'd send you here in the middle of the afternoon!"

"I come from my last patient, mam, and he wasn't a quick one to die."

Amber ran up the stairs ahead of the nurse, holding the candle high to make a light for her, but the old woman mounted slowly, breathing hard and bracing her hands on her knees at every step to boost herself. At the top Amber turned and looked down, surveying her narrowly. What she saw was not reassuring.

The woman was perhaps sixty, and fat. Her face was round and flabby, but she had a sharp-pointed nose and her mouth was compressed into a thin line. She was wearing a gnarled yellow wig set crookedly on her head and a dark-red velvet dress, soiled and worn shiny, which exposed her sloping shoulders and fitted too tight across the great loose breasts. She had an evil smell, reasty and stale.

"What's your name?" Amber asked her, as she came puffing to the top.

"Spong, mam. Mrs. Spong."

"I'm Mrs. Dangerfield. The patient's in here." She walked into the bedroom and Mrs. Spong waddled after her, her stupid blue eyes rolling over the splendid furnishings. She did not even glance at Bruce until at last, in exasperation, Amber said, "Well!"

Then she started slightly and gave a foolish half-grin, exposing a few blackened teeth in her gums. "Oh—that's the patient." She observed him for a moment. "He don't look so good, does he?"

"No, he doesn't!" snapped Amber, angry and disappointed to have been sent this stupid old woman. "You're a nurse, aren't you! Tell me what to do. How can I help him? I've done everything the doctor said—"

"Well, mam, if you've did everything the doctor said there's nothin' more I can tell ye."

"But how does he look? You've seen others sick of it—how does he look compared with them?"

Spong stared at him for a moment, sucking on her teeth. "Well, mam," she said at last, "some of 'em looked worse. And some of 'em looked better. But I tell you truly—he don't look good. Now, mam, have ye got some food for a poor starvin' old woman? Last place I was they didn't have nothin' to eat. I vow and swear—"

Amber gave her a glare of disgust, but as Bruce suddenly began to retch again she rushed to hold the pan for him, motioning toward the kitchen with one hand. "Out there."

She felt more tired than ever, and completely discouraged. This filthy vulgar old creature would be no use to her at all. She would not have let her touch Bruce, and it did not seem likely the nurse would do so anyway. The best Amber could hope would be that she might induce her to watch him tonight so she could have a few hours of sleep, and tomorrow send her away and get someone better.

Half an hour went by and she heard not a sound from Spong. At last, in a fury, she rushed out to find her immaculate kitchen littered and dirty. The food hutch stood open; there was a broken egg on the floor; great chunks had been cut from the ham and the quarter-wheel of cheese. Spong looked around at her in surprise. She had a piece of ham in one hand and the bottle of stale champagne—which they had opened the night before—in the other.

"Well!" said Amber sarcastically. "I hope you won't mighty near starve here!"

"No, mam!" agreed Spong. "I'd rather nurse the quality, let me tell you. They always got more to eat."

"Go in there and watch his Lordship. I've got to get some food ready for him. Call me if he throws off the blankets or starts to vomit—but don't do *anything* yourself."

"His Lordship, is it? And you're her Ladyship, I doubt not?"

"Mind your own business, and get on in there. Go on!"

Spong shrugged her shoulders and went off, and though Amber clenched her teeth together, a sullen scowl on her face, she began immediately to prepare the tray. A few hours earlier she had given him a bowlful of the soup left over from their supper. Resentful at being disturbed, he had sworn at her and tried to shove the spoon away, but she had persisted until she poured it down him. Within a quarter of an hour he vomited it up again.

This time, as she held the basin beneath his chin while he threw up the soup, she was so filled with frustration and despair that she wept softly. Spong was not at all concerned. She sat sprawled in a chair five or six feet from the bed, drinking her wine and gnawing at the last of the cold duck. She flipped the bones out the window, exchanging bawdy pleasantries with the guard below, until Amber rushed in from the kitchen in a blazing anger.

"Don't you dare open that window again!" she cried, and slammed it shut and locked it. Spong jumped. "What are you trying to do?"

"Lord, mam, I wasn't doin' the gentleman no harm."

"Do as I say and keep the window closed—or I'll make you sorry for it! Filthy old sot!" she muttered beneath her breath, and went back to finish washing the dishes and putting her kitchen in order. Sarah Goodegroome had been a meticulous housekeeper, and now that Amber had the work to do herself again she intended to have her rooms spotless if it meant working eighteen hours a day—which it probably would.

Bruce was increasingly restless and violent, which Spong informed her was most likely the effect of the rising carbuncle. Two of her patients, she said placidly, had been unable to stand the pain and had gone mad and killed themselves.

To watch him suffer and to be unable to help or ease his pain was an agony. She hung over him constantly, trying to anticipate his every need. She replaced the blankets each time he flung them off and put the mustard-plaster back again and again—once, as she bent above him, he struck out violently at her with his clenched fist, and if she had not moved quickly the blow would have knocked her down. The plague-boil had risen steadily out of his groin until now it was the full size of a tennis-ball and the taut-stretched skin over it had thickened and turned dark.

512

Spong sat humming or chanting to herself, softly beating her thigh with an empty wine-bottle. Most of the time Amber was so busy, or so haunted with worry over Bruce, she forgot that she was there—and otherwise she ignored her.

But at eleven o'clock, when she had everything clean for the night and was herself undressed and washed, she turned to the old woman. "I only got about three hours sleep last night, Mrs. Spong, and I'm tired as a dog. If you'll watch his Lordship for three or four hours you can call me and then I will. We'll have to take turns, because someone's got to be with him every moment. Will you cover him again if he throws the blankets off?"

"Aye, mam," agreed Mrs. Spong, and as she nodded her head the wig slipped, showing some of her own thin dirty grey hair. "Ye can count on me, mam. I warrant you."

Amber pulled out the trundle on the opposite side of the bed and lay down on her stomach, wearing her dressing-gown but otherwise uncovered, for the room was still hot and close. She did not want to sleep—she was afraid to leave him—but she knew that she must, and she could not help herself. In only a few seconds she had lost consciousness.

Sometime later she was wakened by a sudden stunning blow across the face and weight of a heavy body falling over her. Involuntarily she screamed, a wild terrible sound that filled the night; and then she realized what had happened and began to struggle fiercely to free herself. Bruce, in his restless agony, had gotten out of bed again and stumbled across her; he lay there now, a massive, inert weight.

She shouted for Spong but got no answer. And as she pulled herself out and saw the old woman just lifting her head and opening one eye something seemed to swell and explode inside her. Swiftly she rushed around the bed, slapped her furiously across the face, and grabbed hold of one flabby arm.

"Get up!" she yelled at her. "Get up! you miserable old slut and help me!"

Shocked wide awake, Spong hoisted herself out of the chair much faster than she usually did. It took them several minutes, but at last they got him back into the bed and he lay stretched out, perfectly quiet, collapsed. Amber bent anxiously over him, putting her hand to his heart, pressing her fingers against his wrist—the pulse beat there, faintly.

And then she heard a whine from Spong. "Oh, Lord! *What've* I done! I touched 'im and now I'll get the—"

Amber whirled around furiously. "What've you done!" she cried. "You pot-bellied old bawd! You fell asleep and let him get out of bed! You may've killed him! But by Jesus, if he dies you'll *wish* you had the plague! I'll strangle you, God help me, with my own two hands!"

Spong started back, quivering. "Oh, Lord, mam! I'd but dozed off that instant. I vow and swear! Please, for God's sake, mam, don't hit me—"

Amber's clenched fists dropped and she turned away in disgust. "You're no damned good. I'm going to get another nurse tomorrow."

"Ye can't do it, mam. Ye can't turn out a nurse. The parish-clerk sent me here and he said to stay till all of you was dead."

Amber blew out her cheeks in a sigh of utter exhaustion, throwing the hair from her face with the back of one hand. "Very well. Go to sleep. I'll watch him. There's a bed in there." She pointed toward the nursery.

Through the rest of the long night she stayed beside him. He was quieter than he had been and she did not want to disturb him to make him eat, but she prepared some black coffee to keep herself awake and now and then she took a swallow of cherry-brandy, but she was so tired that it made her dizzy and she dared not drink much. In the next room Spong lay spewing and hawking; an occasional late coach rattled by, the horses' hoofs clopping rhythmically on the pavement; and the night guard stamped wearily up and down. Somewhere a cat squalled in nocturnal ecstasy. The passing-bell tolled three separate times and the watchman went by with his musical call:

"Take heed to your clock, beware your lock,
  Your fire and your light, and God give you good-night.
  One o'clock!"

CHAPTER THIRTY-FIVE

MORNING CAME AT last, the sun rising bright and hot in a cloudless sky. Amber, looking out, wished desperately for fog. The brilliant joyous sunlight seemed a cruel mockery of the sick and dying who lay in a thousand rooms all over the city.

Toward dawn the look of angry worry which had been on Bruce's face, from the first morning she had seen him at the wharf, changed to one of listlessness and apathy. He seemed to have no consciousness whatever of his surroundings or of his own actions. When she put a glass of water to his mouth he swallowed involuntarily, but his eyes stared dully, seeing nothing. His quietness encouraged her and she thought that perhaps he was better.

She got into the dress she had worn yesterday and began to clean up the night's accumulated filth. Her movements were slow, for her muscles felt heavy and aching and the rims of her eyeballs burned. She carried the slop-jars—all but that which Mrs. Spong had used—down to the courtyard privy and there she had to stand and wait, for there was a man inside and he seemed leisurely.

At six she went to wake Spong, shaking her roughly by the shoulder. The old woman smacked her lips together and looked up at Amber with one eye. "How now, mam? What happened?"

"Get up! It's morning! Either you'll help me or I'll lock the food away and you can starve!"

Spong looked at her resentfully, her feelings hurt. "Lord, mam! How was I to know it's mornin'?"

She flung back the quilt and got out of bed, fully dressed but for her shoes. She buttoned the front of her gown, pulling and twisting at the skirt, and cocked her wig back to approximately where it had been. She leaned backward, stretching and yawning noisily, massaging her fat belly, and she stuck one finger into her mouth to pick out some shreds of meat, wiping what she extracted on the soiled front of her gown.

Amber stopped her as she was going through the bedroom on her way to the kitchen. "Come here! What d'you think? He's quieter now—does he look better?"

Spong came back to look at him, but she shook her head. "He looks bad, mam. Mighty bad. I've seen 'em like that not a half-hour before they're dead."

"Oh, damn you! You think everyone's going to die! But *he* isn't, d'ye hear me? Go on—get out of here!"

Spong went. "Lord, mam—ye but asked me and I told ye—"

An hour later, when she had finished cleaning the bedroom and had fed him the rest of the soup, Amber told Spong that she was going to a butcher-shop for a piece of beef and would be gone perhaps twenty minutes. There was one, she knew, not a quarter of a mile away near Lincoln's Inn Fields. She fastened her gown as high as she could and filled in the neck-line with a scarf. It was too hot to wear a cloak but she took a black-silk hood out of the chest and tied it beneath her chin.

"The guard won't allow ye to go, mam," predicted Spong.

"I think he will. You let me alone for that. Now listen to what I say: Watch his Lordship and watch him close, because if I come back to find you've let him harm himself in any way or so much as throw off the blankets—believe me, I'll slit your nose for it!" Her tawny-coloured eyes glared, the black centers swelling, and her lips drew tight against her teeth. Spong gaped, scared as a rabbit.

"Lord, mam, ye can trust me! I'll watch 'im like a witch!"

Amber went through the kitchen, down the back staircase, and started off along the narrow little alley that ran behind the house. She had not gone twenty yards when there was a shout, and she turned to see the guard running toward her.

"Escaping, eh?" He seemed pleased. "Or maybe ye didn't know the house is locked?"

"I know it's locked and I'm not escaping. I've got to buy some food. Will a shilling let me out?"

"A shilling! D'ye think I can be bribed?" He lowered his voice. "Three shillings might do it."

Amber took the coins from inside her muff and flipped them

to him—he did not venture to step up close and he had a pipe of tobacco in his mouth, for that was thought a plague preventive. She walked swiftly down the lane and turned into a main street. There seemed to be even fewer people out today than yesterday and those who were did not loiter or stop to gossip but moved along briskly, pomanders held to their noses. A coach followed by a train of loaded wagons went by and several heads turned wistfully; it was only the prosperous ones who could afford to leave, the others must stay and take their chances, put their faith in amulets and herbs. And there were several houses shut up along the way.

At the butcher's stall she bought a good-sized chunk of beef, taking the meat from the hooks on which he extended it to her and dropping the money into a jar of vinegar. She put the meat, wrapped in a towel, into her market-basket and on the way back she stopped to buy a couple of pounds of candles, three bottles of brandy and some coffee. Coffee was so expensive that it was not hawked on the streets and while Amber did not drink it often she hoped that it would help her get through the day.

She found Bruce just as she had left him, and though Spong protested that she had not so much as taken an eye off him Amber strongly suspected that she had been foraging, at least in the bedroom, for money or jewels. But it was all locked up behind a secret panel, where neither Spong nor anyone else was likely to find it without a long search.

Spong would have followed her to the kitchen to find out what she had bought, but Amber sent her back to stay with Bruce. She locked the brandy away, for she knew that otherwise it would disappear, but first she took a good swallow herself. Then she tied back her hair, pushed up her sleeves and went to work. Into a great blackened kettle full of hot water went the meat, cut up in cubes, and some of the bacon she had bought the day before. She split the bones with a heavy cleaver and added them with the marrow and when the vegetables were ready they went in too: a quartered cabbage, leeks, carrots, peas and a handful of crumbled herbs, and she ground in some rock-salt and peppercorns.

The soup had to be cooked for several hours until it was boiled down and thickened, and meanwhile she prepared a caudle of sack, spices, sugar and eggs for him to drink. She crushed each egg-shell to tiny bits, remembering the old country belief that otherwise a witch would write your name on it. She had trouble enough now, without inviting more.

She found, as she poured the drink down his throat, that the fur on his tongue was beginning to peel, leaving raw red patches, and that his teeth had made deep indentations in it. His pulse had quickened, his breathing was more rapid and sometimes he coughed slightly. He lay in a deep coma, not sleeping but wholly unconscious, and it was no longer possible to rouse him at all. Even when she touched the plague-boil, now a soft doughy mass, he gave no indication of awareness. It did not seem possible, even to her, that a man could be so sick and live very long.

But she refused to think about it. She was, in fact, so tired that it was almost impossible to think at all.

She went back to the kitchen to finish the cleaning there. Then she swept the other rooms and dusted the furniture, put the towels to soak in hot soapy water and vinegar, brought up some more water and finally—when she felt that she could not make another move—she went into the bedroom and dragged out the trundle. Her lids felt rough and seemed to scratch against the eyeballs and there were muddy circles around her eyes.

It was about noon when she lay down and though the draperies were pulled the hot sun beat into the room. She woke up several hours later, wet and with a heavy aching head, feeling as though the house was rocking. It was Spong shaking her shoulder.

"Get up, mam! The doctor's below a-knockin'."

"For God's sake," muttered Amber, "can't you do anything without being told? Go let 'im in."

Spong was offended. "Ye told me not to leave his Lordship—no matter *what* happened!"

Amber got up wearily. She felt as though she had been drugged, her mouth had a vile taste, and days seemed to have gone by since she had lain down. But it was only five o'clock and though the room was darker the fire kept it as hot as ever. She pushed back the curtains and bent to look at Bruce, but he seemed not to have changed, either for better or worse.

Dr. Barton came into the room, looking tired and sick himself, and once more he merely looked at Bruce from a distance of several feet. Amber knew with despair that he had seen so many sick and dying men he could no longer distinguish one from another.

"What do you think?" she asked him. "Will he live?" But her own face showed no hope or expectation.

"He may; but to be truthful, I doubt it. Has the carbuncle burst?"

"No. It's soft now but it feels hard deep inside. He doesn't seem to even know when I touch it. Isn't there *anything* we can do? There must be some way to save him."

"Trust in God, madame. We can do no more. If the carbuncle breaks, dress it—but take care to get no blood or pus on yourself. I'll come tomorrow and if it hasn't opened by then I'll have to cut it open. That's all I can tell you. Good-day, madame."

He bowed slightly and started out but Amber went along with him. "Isn't there someway I can get another nurse?" she asked, her voice soft and urgent. "That old woman is useless. She doesn't do a thing but eat and drink up my supplies. I could get along as well alone."

"I'm sorry, madame, but the parish-clerk is too busy now to consider the problems of each individual. The nurses are all incompetent and most of them old—if they could get a living any other way they wouldn't be doing this. The parish sends them out to nurse to avoid the charge of keeping them on charity. Still, madame, as you must know, you may fall sick yourself at any time—it's better not to be alone."

He left and Amber, shrugging and deciding that since she could not get rid of Spong she would find some use for her, went into the kitchen. The soup was ready now, a rich heavy pottage with the fat swimming in hot oily circles on top of it, and she ladled out a bowlful to eat herself. It made her feel better. Her headache disappeared and she felt almost optimistic again. She was sure once more that she could keep him alive by sheer force of will-power.

I love him so much, she thought, he *can't* die. God won't let him die.

When she was ready to go to bed she decided to try bribing Spong. "If you'll stay awake till three and then call me I'll give you a bottle of brandy." If the old woman would watch and let her sleep at night she was willing to have her drunk all day.

The arrangement satisfied Spong who vowed again that she would not so much as close an eye. Once Amber woke suddenly and sat bolt upright, glaring accusingly at her—it was light in the room for the fire was kept burning all night. But the nurse was sitting there beside him, arms folded on her belly, and she grinned across at Amber.

"Fooled ye, mam, eh?"

Amber flopped back down and instantly fell asleep again. She was wakened by a gurgling scream that brought her to her feet at a leap, her heart pounding sickeningly. Bruce, kneeling on the edge of the bed, had grabbed Spong by the throat and she was lashing and flailing about, helpless as a flounder. With his face contorted, teeth bared savagely, shoulders hunched, he was forcing all the strength of his arms into his fingers and they were crushing out the old woman's life.

Quickly throwing herself onto the bed behind him Amber grabbed his arms and tried to drag him backwards. Cursing, he dropped the nurse, and turned on Amber, his fingers closing around her throat—squeezing the blood into her face and temples until the top of her head felt ready to burst. Her ears cracked and she went blind. Desperately she put up her hands and finding his eyeballs she gouged her thumbs into them. His grip weakened slowly, and then all at once he collapsed onto the bed, sprawling weirdly.

Amber slowly sank to the floor, helpless and stupidly dazed. It was several seconds before she realized what Spong was trying to tell her.

"—it's broke, mam! It's broke—that was what drove 'im mad!"

She dragged herself to her feet then and saw that the great swollen mass of the carbuncle had burst, as though the top had been blown off a crater. There was a hole deep enough and large enough to thrust a finger into, and the blood poured out in a dark scarlet stream that ran into a spreading pool on the bed and clotted thickly. A watery gland-fluid came with it, and yellow pus was beginning to work its way upward.

Amber sent Spong to the kitchen for some warm water and began immediately to wash off the blood, wiping it away as it ran out. The bloody rags accumulated in a heap and the nurse was kept busy tearing bandages from some clean sheets. But it would have done no good to bind them on; they would have soaked through in less than a minute. Amber had never seen a man lose so much blood, and it scared her.

"He's going to bleed to death!" she said desperately, throwing another red sopping rag into the pail beside her. His face was no longer flushed but had turned white beneath the short growth of black bristle and it felt cold and wet to the touch.

"He's a big man, mam—he can lose a lot of blood. But ye can thank God it broke. He's got a chance to live now."

At last the blood stopped flowing, though it continued to seep slowly, and she bound up the wound and turned to wash her hands in a basin of clean warm water. Spong approached her with an ingratiating whine.

"It's half-after-three now, mam. Can't I go to sleep?"

"Yes, go on. And thanks."

"It's almost mornin', mam. Could I have the brandy now, d'ye think?"

Amber went out to the kitchen to get it for her; and though for a while she heard her behind the closed door, droning a song, finally she fell silent and then set up a clattering snore that went on hour after hour. Amber was kept busy changing the bandages and refilling the hot-water bottles. Along toward morning to her enormous relief the colour began to return to his face, his breathing became more regular, and his skin was dry again.

By the eighth day she was convinced that he would live, and Mrs. Spong agreed with her, though she said frankly that she had expected him to die. But the plague took them quickly, if at all. Those who lived until the third day could be reasonably

hopeful, and whoever lived a week was almost certain to recover. But the period of convalescence was long and tedious
and characterized by a deep physical and mental depression, an
almost complete prostration, during which any sudden or undue exertion could have rapidly fatal results.

Since the night the carbuncle had opened Bruce had lain
supine, never making a voluntary move. The restlessness, the
delirium, the violence were gone and his strength had wasted
until he was not able even to stir. He swallowed obediently
whatever food or drink she put into his mouth, but the effort
seemed to exhaust him. Much of the time, she knew, he slept,
though his eyes were always closed and it was never possible
to tell when he was awake or even whether he was conscious
of being awake.

Amber worked ceaselessly, though after the bursting of the
carbuncle she was able to get enough sleep, and she did her
tasks with enthusiasm and even a kind of pleasure, certainly
with satisfaction. Everything that Sarah had ever taught her
about cooking and nursing and housekeeping came back to
her now and she prided herself that she did a better job of
all three than her maids could have done.

She did not dare bathe Bruce, but otherwise she kept him
as clean as possible, and with Spong's help she managed to
change the sheets on the bed. The rest of the apartment was
kept as immaculate as if she expected a visit from a maiden-
aunt. She mopped the kitchen floor, washed the towels and
sheets and napkins and her own smocks and ironed everything;
every day she scoured the pewter dishes with bran and soap
and set them before a hot fire to dry, which was the way Sarah
had taught her to keep them shining and spotless. Her hands
were beginning already to roughen and she had several small
blisters, but that mattered no more to her than did the fact that
her hair was oily and that she had not worn a speck of powder
for a week and a half. When he begins to notice me, she told
herself, I'll take time for those things. Meanwhile, her only
audience was Spong and the shop-keepers she saw when she
went out to buy provisions, and they did not matter.

She had heard nothing at all from Nan and though she

worried about her and the baby she tried to make herself believe that they were all right. As far as she knew there was no plague in the country. And of course it was very likely that the letter had not reached her at all. She knew Nan well enough to know that she could trust her loyalty and resourcefulness, and now she must do so and refuse to think anything but that they were safe and well.

Her own health continued as good as ever, a fact which she attributed to the unicorn's horn, the Elizabethan gold coin she kept in her mouth, and her daily practice of taking a snip of her own hair, cutting it up fine and drinking it in a glass of water. This last was Spong's suggestion and both of them followed it religiously, for it had seen Spong safely through eight houses full of plague. Occasionally she said a prayer, for good measure.

Dr. Barton had not come since his second call, and both Spong and Amber decided that he had either died or run away —as the plague got worse more and more of the doctors were leaving. But, as Bruce continued to improve, she did not trouble to find another one.

Every morning when she had fed Bruce his breakfast— usually a caudle—she changed the bandage on the great sloughing wound, washed his hands and face, cleaned his teeth as well as she could, and then sat down beside him to comb his hair. It was the moment she enjoyed most in each day, for her work kept her so busy that she had very little time to spend with him. Sometimes he looked up at her, but his eyes were dull and expressionless; she could not tell whether he even knew who it was bending over him. But each time that he looked at her she smiled, hoping for an answering smile.

And at last it came.

It was the tenth day after he had fallen sick and she sat on the bed facing him, intent on combing his hair, which was as crisp and healthy as it had ever been. She laid the flat side of her hand gently into one of its waves, smiling as she did so, deeply and truly happy. She realized then that he was watching her and that he actually saw her, knew who she was and what she was doing. A swift thrill ran over her flesh and as his mouth tried to smile at her she touched his cheek with her fingers, caressing.

"God bless you, darling—" His voice was soft and hoarse, scarcely more than a whisper, and he turned his head to kiss her fingers.

"Oh, Bruce—"

She could just murmur his name, for her throat had swollen until it ached, and a tear splashed down onto his cheek. She brushed the next one away before it could fall, and then his eyes closed again, his head turned wearily and he gave a light sigh.

But after that she always knew when he was conscious, and little by little he began to talk to her, though it was many days before he could say more than a few words at a time. And she did not urge him to talk for she knew how great was the exertion and how tired it left him. His eyes often followed her when she was in the room and in them she saw a look of gratitude that wrenched her heart. She wanted to tell him that she had not done so very much—only what she had to do because she loved him, and that she had never been happier than during these past days when she had used all her energy, all the strength she had, every thought and waking minute for him. Whatever had been between them in the past, whatever was to come in the future, she had had these few weeks when he belonged to her completely.

Day by day London was changing.

Gradually the vendors disappeared from the streets, and with them went the age-old cries which had rung through the town for centuries. Many shops had closed and the 'prentices no longer stood before their stalls, bawling out their wares to the passerby—the shop-keepers were afraid of the customers, the customers were afraid of the shop-keepers. Friends looked the other way when they passed, or crossed the street to avoid speaking. Many were afraid to buy food, for fear it might be contaminated, and some of them starved to death.

The theatres had closed in May and now many taverns and inns and cook-shops were shut up. Those which continued to do business were ordered to lock their doors at nine o'clock and to put all loiterers off the premises. There were no more bear-baitings, cock-fights, jugglers' performances, or puppet-shows; even the executions were suspended, for they invariably drew great crowds. Funerals were forbidden, but nevertheless long trains of mourners were to be seen winding through the streets at almost every hour of the day or night.

And in spite of the great fear of the disease, the churches were always crowded. Many of the orthodox ministers had fled, but the Nonconformists remained and harangued the confused, miserable multitudes for their sins. The prostitutes had never been busier. A rumour began to spread that the surest protection against plague was a venereal disease and the whore-houses of Vinegar Yard, Saffron Hill, and Nightingale Lane were open twenty-four hours a day. Harlots and customers often died together, and their bodies were carried out by a back door to avoid offending those who waited in the parlour. An increasing attitude of fatalism made many say that they would enjoy whatever was left to them of life, and die when their turn came. Others rushed to consult astrologers and fortune-tellers and anyone might set himself up as a soothsayer with the prospect of a very good business.

Searchers-of-the-dead walked in every street. It was their duty to inspect the dead and to report to the parish-clerk the cause of death. They were a group of old women, illiterate and dishonest as the nurses, forced to live apart from society during a time of sickness and to carry a white stick wherever they went so that others might know them and stop up their mouths as they passed.

The town grew steadily quieter. The busy shipping of the Thames lay still—no ships might enter or leave the river—and the noisy swearing impudent boatmen had all but disappeared. Forty thousand dogs and two hundred thousand cats were slaughtered, for it was believed that they were carriers of the sickness. It was possible to hear, far up into the City, the roaring of the water between the starlings of London Bridge—a noise which usually went unnoticed. Only the bells continued to ring—tolling, tolling, tolling for the dead.

It soon became impossible to bury the dead in separate graves, and huge pits—forty feet long and twenty feet deep—were dug at the edge of the city. Every night the bodies were brought there, some of them decently in coffins, more and more shrouded only in a sheet or naked, as they had died. In the grave they found a common anonymity. During the day crows and ravens settled there, but at the approach of a man they swarmed up into the air, circling and hovering, waiting until he was gone, and then they drifted earthward again. As the bodies began to rot a foul stench crept into the town, and there was no breath of moving air to dispel it.

There had never been a hotter summer. The sky was bright as brass, blue and without a shred of cloud; they thought of the cool soothing fog as a blessing. Large birds flew heavily and laboriously. The church-vanes scarcely turned. In the meadows about London the grass lay burnt and the earth was hard as brick, flowers withered and dried. Amber transplanted some of the stocks, pink and white ones with a spicy cinnamon smell, into pots and kept them shaded on the balcony, but they did not prosper.

She protected herself against the plague by refusing to think about it. It was all that any of them could do, who were forced to stay in the town, to keep their sanity.

Often, when she went out to shop—she had to buy almost everything herself now that the vendors were gone—she heard cries and groans and terrible screams from the closed houses. Pitiable faces appeared at the windows and hands reached out pleadingly: "Pray for us!"

It became more and more common to see the dead and dying in the streets, for the plague struck swiftly. Once she saw a man huddled by a wall, beating his bloody head against it and moaning in delirium. She stared a moment in horror and then she hurried by, holding her nose and making a half-circle around him. Another time she saw a dead woman slumped in a doorway, a baby still sucking at her breast, and the small blue plague-spots showed plainly on her white flesh. She saw a woman walking slowly, crying, and carrying in her arms a tiny coffin.

One day, as she was busy in the bedroom, she heard from

outside a man's loud voice shouting something which she could not at first understand. But he drew nearer, evidently coming up St. Martin's Lane, and his words became more distinct. "Awake!" he bawled. "Sinners, awake! The plague is at your doors! The grave yawns for you! Awake and repent!" She pushed back the curtains and looked out. He was walking swiftly by, just beneath her window, a half-naked old man with matted hair and a long dark beard, and he brandished his closed fist at the still houses.

Amber looked at him with disgust. "Devil take him!" she muttered. "The blasted old fool! There's trouble enough without that caterwauling!"

And then one night, at the end of July, she heard another and far more terrible cry. There came a rumbling of cart-wheels over the cobblestones, the sound of a hand-bell, and a man's deep voice calling: "Bring out your dead! Bring out your dead!"

She looked swiftly at Spong, for Bruce was asleep, and then she rushed to the window. Spong waddled after her, crowding up close. Below they saw a cart, moving slowly, one man in the driver's seat and another ringing the hand-bell and walking beside it. In the light from the torch carried by a third they could see that the cart was half-filled with bodies, piled indiscriminately, flung one on top of another. Arms and legs stuck out at weird angles; one corpse hung over the side, her long hair pouring half-way to the ground.

"Holy Virgin Mary!" breathed Amber, and then she turned away with a shudder, sick at her stomach, cold and wet.

Spong's teeth were chattering. "Oh, Jesu! To be dumped in like that, helter-skelter, with every Jack Noakes and Tom Styles! Oh, Lud! It's more than flesh can bear!"

"Stop your blubbering!" muttered Amber impatiently. "There's nothing the matter with you!"

"Aye, mam," agreed Spong gloomily. "There's nothin' the matter with either of us today. But who's to tell? By tomorrow we may both be—"

"Shut up, will you!" cried Amber suddenly, whirling around, and then, as the old woman gave a startled jump, she added crossly, somewhat ashamed of her nervous ill-temper: "You're as melancholy as a bawd in Bridewell. Why don't you go out in the kitchen and get a bottle to drink?"

Spong went, gratefully, but Amber could not push the picture of the dead-cart from her mind. The sick men and women she had seen, the dead bodies in the streets, the constant tolling of the bells, the stench from the graves, the city's unnatural quiet, the news (given by the guard) that two thousand had died of plague that past week—the cumulative effect of those things was beginning to overpower her. She had held off fear and despair during the time that Bruce had been most hopelessly sick, for then she had not had time to think. But now a kind of superstitious dread was beginning to work in her mind.

Why should *I* still be well and alive when all these others are dying? What have *I* done to deserve to live if *they* must die? And she knew that she deserved life no more than anyone else.

Fear was as contagious as the plague, and it spread as the plague spread. The well expected to be sick; hope of escape was small. Death was everywhere now. You might inhale it with a breath; you might take it up with a bundle of food; you might pass it in the street and bring it walking home beside you. Death was democratic. It made no choice between the rich and the poor, the beautiful and the ugly, the young and the old.

One morning in mid-August Bruce told her that he thought they would be able to leave London within another fortnight. She was spreading up his bed, and though she answered him as casually as she could she had been worrying about it for some time.

"No one is allowed to leave the city now, whether they have a certificate-of-health or not."

"We'll go anyway. I've been thinking about it and I believe I know a way we can get out."

"There's nothing I'd like more. This city—God, it's a nightmare!" She changed the subject quickly, smiling at him. "How would you like a shave? I'm a mighty good barber—"

Bruce ran his hand across the five-weeks growth of beard on his chin. "I'd like it. I feel like a fishmonger."

She went out to the kitchen for a basin of warm water and found Spong sitting morosely, a half-eaten bowl of soup in her lap. "Well!" said Amber merrily. "Don't tell me that you've got enough to eat at last!" She swung the crane out from the fire and poured some water into the pewter basin, testing it with her finger.

Spong gave a heavy discouraged sigh. "Lord, mam. Seems like I'm off the hooks today. Don't feel so good."

Amber straightened, looking at her sharply. If that old bawd's going to be sick now, she thought, I'll put her out in a trice and the parish clerk be damned!

But she was eager to get back to Bruce and returned to the bedroom where she laid her implements on a table, wrapped a great white linen towel about his chest, and sat down beside him. Both of them enjoyed the operation, and were much amused by it. Amber felt a deep current of joy running through her and once, as she leaned close to him, she saw his eyes on her breasts. Her heart gave a beat and she was aware of a slow creeping warmth.

"You must be feeling *much* better," she said softly.

"Well enough," he agreed, "to wish I felt much better than I do."

When at last his face was clean again, but for the mustache he had always worn and which she left, it was easy to see how sick he had been, and how sick he still was. The smooth brown colour of his skin, habitually tanned before, had faded to a light pallor, his cheeks were lean and drawn and new faint lines showed at his eyes and mouth; all his body was much thinner. But to Amber he seemed as handsome as ever.

She began to pick up after herself, dumping the water out the window, gathering towels and scissors and razor. "In a few days," she said, "I think you can have a bath."

"God, I hope so! I must stink like Bedlam!"

He lay down then and presently fell asleep, for he was still so weak that a very small exertion was fatiguing. Amber took up her hood, locked the bedroom door so that Spong could not go in during her absence, and went out through the kitchen. The old woman was wandering aimlessly, a stupid staring look in her eyes. She reminded Amber of the long-snouted rats which sometimes came out of their holes and stood dazedly, or squeaked with distraction when she went after them with a broom, sick creatures with patches of fur fallen out of their blue-black coats.

"Are you feeling worse?" Amber was tying on her hood, watching the nurse in the mirror.

Spong answered her with a whine. "Not much, mam. But don't it seem cold in here to you?"

"No, it doesn't. It's hot. But go sit by the fire in the kitchen.'

Amber was annoyed, thinking that if Spong was sick she would have to throw away all the food she had in the house and fumigate the rooms. And she felt, as she had not when Bruce was sick, resentful on her own behalf, afraid that she would be exposed herself. When I get back, she thought, if she's worse I'll tell her to leave.

Spong met Amber at the door as she came in. She was winding her hands in her skirt and her expression was worried and depressed, almost comically self-pitying. "Lud, mam," she began immediately, whining again, "I'm feelin' mighty bad."

Amber looked at her, her eyes narrowed. Spong's face was red, her eyes blood-shot, and as she talked it was possible to see that her tongue was heavily coated with a white fuzz, the tip and edges bright red. It's plague, right enough, thought Amber, and turned away so as not to get the woman's breath in her face. She put the basket onto a table and began to unpack the food, transferring it immediately to the food-hutch so that Spong could not touch it.

"If you want to leave," said Amber, as casually as she could, "I'll give you five pound."

"Leave, mam? Where could I go? I got no place to go, mam. And how can I leave? I'm the nurse." She leaned heavily against the wall. "Oh, Lord! I never felt like this before."

Amber swung around. "Of course you haven't! And you know why—you've got the plague! Oh, there's no use pretending you haven't it, is there? It won't make you well again. Look here, Mrs. Spong, if you'll leave and go to a pest-house I'll give you ten pound. You'll be taken care of there. But I warn you, if you stay here. I won't raise a hand to help you. I'll get the money now—wait here."

She started out of the room, but Spong stopped her.

"It's no use, mam. I won't go to a pest-house. Lord, I've got no mind to die if I can help it. A body might as well go to a burial-pit as the pest-house. You're a cruel-hearted woman, to want to turn a poor sick old lady out of your house after she helped you nurse his Lordship back to life. You ain't a Christian, mam—" She shook her head wearily.

Amber gave her a glare, full of disgust and hatred. But she had already decided that when night came she would force the old woman out if she had to do it at the point of a knife. Now, it was only two o'clock, and time to prepare another light meal for Bruce. Spong wandered back into the parlour, uninterested in food for once, and Amber began to set his tray.

As she carried it into the bedroom she passed Spong who lay on a couch before the long range of windows, mumbling beneath her breath and shivering convulsively. She reached out a hand to her. "Mam—I'm sick. Please, mam—"

Amber went by her without a glance, her jaw muscles setting, and took the key from her apron to unlock the bedroom door. The old woman started to get up and in a sudden panic of terror Amber rattled the key, flung the door open and rushed inside, slamming it again and turning the lock swiftly. She heard Spong collapse back onto the couch, whining some unintelligible words.

Amber blew a sigh of relief, thoroughly scared, for she had heard the tales of those sick from plague who roamed the streets, grabbing others into their arms and kissing them. She looked over to find Bruce propped upon his elbow, watching her with a strange expression of puzzlement and suspicion.

"What's the matter?"

"Oh. It's nothing." She gave him a quick smile and came forward with the tray. She did not want him to know that Spong was sick, for she was afraid that it would worry him, and he was not strong enough for worry or any other exhausting emotion. "Spong's drunk again, and I thought she was going to come in here and trouble you." She was setting down the dishes

531

and now she gave a nervous little laugh. "Listen to her! She's drunk as David's sow!"

He did not say anything more, but Amber thought that he had guessed it was not drunkenness but the plague. She ate with him but neither of them talked very much or with any gaiety, and Amber was relieved when he fell asleep again. But she dared not go out and stayed there, occupied with changing his bandage and cleaning the room—her ears were constantly alert for sounds from the parlour, and again and again she tiptoed to the door to listen.

She could hear her moving restlessly about, groaning, calling for her, and at last, late in the afternoon, she heard a heavy thud and knew that she had fallen to the floor. By her cursing she was evidently struggling to get up again but could not do so. Amber felt discouraged and frightened and she watched Bruce constantly, but he was sleeping soundly.

What can I do? How can I get her out? she thought. Oh, damn her, the filthy old fustiluggs!

She stood looking out at a bright setting sun that lighted the trees with red and orange patches and struck a window-pane down the street so that it gave back a blinding reflection. Then, rather slowly, she began to be conscious of a strange new sound and for a few moments she listened curiously, wondering what it was and where it came from. She realized, finally, that it was coming from the other room. It was a sort of bubbling rattle. As she listened it stopped and then, just when she had begun to think her own imagination was playing tricks, it began again. It filled her with pure terror, for it was an evil eerie sound, but she was impelled almost against her will to cross the room and—very softly—turn the lock and open the door, just a crack, to look out.

Mrs. Spong lay on her back on the floor, arms and legs flung wide. Her mouth was open and a thick bloody mucus poured out of it, bubbling from her nose as she breathed, coming out in a gush with each collapsing rattle of her throat muscles. Amber stared, chill with horror, stiff and motionless. Then she closed the door again, more loudly than she had intended, and sank back against it. The sound evidently attracted Spong's attention for Amber heard a choked, gurgling noise as though the old woman was trying to call her—and with a whimper of terror she rushed into the nursery, her hands over her ears, and banged the door.

It was several minutes before she could force herself to return to the bedroom. There she found that Bruce was awake. "I wondered where you were. Where's Spong? Is she worse?"

The room had darkened and as yet she had lighted no candles, so that he could not see her face. She waited for a moment, listening, but as she heard no sound she decided that the nurse must be dead. "Spong's gone," she said, trying to sound unconcerned. "I sent her away—she went to a pest-house." She picked up a candle. "I'll light this from the kitchen-fire."

In the semi-darkness of the parlour she could see the bulk of Spong's body but she went by without stopping, lighted the candle, and then returned. Spong was dead.

Amber picked up her skirts with an automatic gesture of revulsion, and walked back into the bedroom to light the candles. Her face was white and she had an intense desire to vomit, but she went about her tasks, determined that Bruce should not guess. And yet she could feel him watching her and she dared not meet his eyes, for if he should speak she felt that she could not trust herself. She seemed to be hanging on the ragged edge of hysteria but knew that she must keep herself in control, for when the dead-cart came by she would have to get the woman down the stairs and outside.

A pale velvety blueness still lingered in streaks in the sky when she heard the first call, from a distance: "Bring out your dead!"

Amber stiffened, like an animal listening, and then she seized a pewter candle-holder. "I'll get your supper ready," she said, and before he could speak she went out of the room.

Without looking at Spong she set the candle on a table and went to open the doors leading through the anteroom. The call came again, nearer now. She paused there a moment and then with sudden violent resolution she came back, flung up her skirts, unfastened her petticoat and stepped out of it. Wrapping it about her hands she bent and took hold of Spong by her thick swollen ankles, and slowly she began to drag her toward the door. The old woman's wig came off and her flesh slid and squeaked over the bare floor.

By the time Amber reached the head of the stairs she was sick and wet with sweat and her ears were ringing. She reached backward with one foot for the step, found it and sought the next; it was perfectly dark in the stair-well but she could hear the nurse's skull thump on each carpeted stair. She reached the bottom at last and knocked at the door. The guard opened it.

"The nurse is dead," she said faintly. Her face looked out at him, white as chalk in the twilight, and the linen petticoat trailed from one hand.

There was the sound of the dead-cart rattling over the cobblestones, the clop-clop of the horses' hoofs, and then the unexpected cry: "Faggots! Faggots for six-pence!"

It seemed strange to her that anyone should be selling faggots in this weather, and at this hour. But at that moment the dead-cart drew up before the house. A link-man came first, carrying his smoky torch, and he was followed by the dead-cart, beside which walked a man ringing a bell and chanting: "Bring out your dead!" In the driver's seat sat another man, and now Amber saw that he was holding the naked corpse of a little boy, no more than three years old, by the legs.

It was he who shouted, "Faggots for six-pence!"

While Amber stared at him with incredulous horror he turned, flung the child back into the cart, and climbed down. He and the bell-man started forward to get Spong.

"Now," he said, grinning at Amber, "what've we got here?"

Both men bent over to pick Spong up. Suddenly he seized the bodice of her gown and ripped it down the front, exposing the old woman's gross and flabby body. From neck to thighs she was covered with small blue-circled spots—the plague tokens. He made a noise of disgust, hawked up a glob of saliva and spat it onto the corpse.

"Bah!" he muttered. "What a firkin of foul stuff she is!"

Neither of the other men seemed surprised at his behaviour; they paid him no attention at all, and obviously were accustomed to it. Now they picked Spong up, gave a heave and

534

dumped her into the cart. The link-man started on, the bell-man took up his bell again, and the driver climbed back into his seat. From there he turned and surveyed Amber.

"Tomorrow night we'll come back for you. And I doubt not *you'll* make a finer corpse than that stinking old whore."

Amber slammed the door shut and started slowly up the stairs, so weak and sick that she had to hold onto the railing as she went.

She entered the kitchen and began the preparation of Bruce's supper, thinking that as soon as that was done she must take hot water and a mop and clean the parlour floor. For the first time she felt resentful that there was so much work to do, such an endless number of tasks reaching before her. She wished only that she might lie down and sleep and wake up some place far away. All at once responsibility seemed an unbearable burden.

And the driver of the dead-cart was still with her. She could not get rid of him, no matter what she tried to think of. It did not seem that she was there in the kitchen, but still downstairs, standing in the doorway watching him—but it was not Spong whose gown he tore open, and it was not Spong he thrust into the dead-cart. It was herself.

Holy Jesus! she thought wildly. I think I'm stark raving mad! Another day and I'll be ready for Bedlam!

As she went about her work, mixing the syllabub, setting the tray, her movements were slow and clumsy and finally she dropped an egg onto the floor. She scowled wearily but took a cloth and bent to wipe it up, and as she did so there was a sudden splitting pain in her forehead and she was seized by a swirl of dizziness. She straightened again, slowly, and to her amazement she staggered and might have fallen but that she grabbed the side of a table to brace herself.

For a moment she stood and stared at the floor, and then she turned and walked into the parlour. No, she thought, shoving away the idea that had suddenly come to her. It can't be that. Of course it can't—

She took the candle-holder, carried it to the little writing-table and set it there. Then she placed the palms of her hands flat onto the table-top and leaned forward to look at herself in the small round gilt mirror which hung on the wall. The candle-flame cast stark shadows up onto her face. It showed the deep hollows beneath her eyes, flung pointed reflections of her lashes up onto her lids, heightened the wide staring horror of her eyes. At last she put out her tongue. It was coated with a yellowish fur but the tip and edges were clean and shiny, unnaturally pink. Her eyes closed and the room seemed to sway and rock.

Holy Mother of God! Tomorrow night it *will* be me!

CHAPTER THIRTY-SIX

GOD'S TERRIBLE VOICE was in the city.

But twenty miles away at Hampton Court it could scarcely be heard at all; there were too many distracting noises. The whir of shuffled cards and the clack of rolling dice. The scratching of quills writing letters of love or diplomacy or intrigue. The crashing of swords in some secret forbidden duel. Chatter and laughter and the sibilant whisper of gossip. Guitars and fiddles, clinking glasses raised in a toast, rustling taffeta petticoats, and tapping high-heeled shoes. Nothing was changed.

They did, occasionally, discuss the plague when they gathered in her Majesty's Drawing-Room in the evenings, just as they discussed the weather, and for the same reason—it was unusual.

"Have you seen this week's bills?" Winifred Wells would ask as she sat talking to Mrs. Stewart and Sir Charles Sedley.

"I can't bear to look at 'em. Poor creatures. Dying like flies."

Sedley, a dark short plump young man with snapping black eyes and a taste for handsome lace cravats, was scornful of her tender heart. "Nonsense, Frances! What does it matter if they die now or later? The town was overcrowded as it was."

"You'd think it mattered, my Lord, if the plague got you!"

Sedley laughed. "And so it would. Sure, my dear, you'll allow there's some difference between a man of wit and breeding and a poor drivelling idiot of a baker or tailor?"

At that moment another gentleman approached them and Sedley got up to welcome him, throwing one arm about his shoulders. "Aha! Here's Wilmot! We've been sitting here most damnably dull, with nothing to talk on but the plague. Now you've come we can be merry again. What've you got there? Another libel to spoil someone's reputation?"

John Wilmot, Earl of Rochester, was a tall slender young man of eighteen, light-skinned and blonde with a look of delicacy which made his handsome face almost effeminate. Only a few months before he had come to Court direct from his travels abroad, precocious and sophisticated, but still a quiet modest lad who was just a little shy. He adapted himself to Whitehall so quickly that he was but recently released from the Tower for the offense of kidnapping rich Mrs. Mallet with intent to marry her fortune.

Writing was the fashion. All the courtiers wrote something, plays, satires, lampoons on their friends and acquaintances, and the Earl had already shown that he had not only a quick talent but a flair for malice. Now he had a rolled-up sheet of paper stuck beneath his arm and the other three glanced at it expectantly.

"I protest, Sedley." Rochester's smile and manner were deceptively mild, and he bowed to Stewart and Wells so courteously that it was impossible to believe he had not the most charitable opinion of all women. "You'll convince the ladies I'm an ill natured sot. No—it's no libel I have here. Just a silly thing I scratched out while I was waiting for my periwig to be curled."

"Read it to us!" cried both women at once.

"Yes, for God's sake, Wilmot. Let's hear it. The silly things you scratch out while you sit at stool are better than anything Dryden can do though he eat a peck of prunes and put himself into a course of physic."

"Thanks, Sedley. I'll be in the front row to cry up your play if you ever bring yourself to finish it. Well, here's what I've writ—"

Rochester began to read his poem, a long half-idyllic, pseudo-serious rambling tale of a shepherd and his love. The virgin was reluctant, the swain over-ardent, and when at last he brought her to consent he found himself powerless to satisfy either of them—and so it pointed a moral to laggard young maidens, like Frances, perhaps. Winifred Wells and Sedley were much amused, but though Frances could follow the trend of thought the subtleties escaped her. When at last he had finished he suddenly crumpled the paper and flung it into the fireplace. None of the gentlemen would let it be thought they had any regard for their scribbling.

"You write well on that subject, my lord," said Sedley. "Can it be you've had the misfortune yourself?"

Rochester was not offended. "You always seem to know my secrets, Sedley. Is it possible you're lying with my whore?"

"And will you be angry if I am?"

"By no means. I say a man who won't share his whore with his friends is damned ill-natured and deserves the pox."

"Well," said Sedley, "I wish you'd treat your ladies with more kindness. She complains to me constantly that you're unfaithful and use her barbarously. She swears she hates you and never wants to see your face again."

Rochester gave a sudden laugh. "Ye gods, Sedley! You're out of the fashion! That's my last whore!"

At that moment a quick change came over Rochester's face; his blue eyes darkened and an odd smile touched his mouth. The others turned curiously to see that Barbara Palmer had just appeared in the doorway. For an instant she paused, and then she swept in upon them, gorgeous, sultry, impressive as a tropical storm. She was dressed in green satin and she glittered everywhere with the darting shafts thrown from her jewels.

"By God," said Rochester softly, "she's the handsomest woman in the world!"

Frances made a face and turned her back. The King's attention had accustomed her to the flattering notion that she was the most beautiful creature alive and she did not like to hear others praised; and Winifred and Castlemaine, rivals for the same man, had never been more than superficially polite to each other. While they watched, Barbara crossed the room and went to take her place at one of the card-tables.

"Well," said Sedley, "if you have a mind to lie with her you must cure yourself of your nervousness. She'd have no patience with a man who found himself in such a predicament. Anyway, I don't think your Lordship is the type she admires."

They gave a hearty burst of laughter at this, for no one would ever forget how Barbara had given Rochester a blow that had sent him reeling when he had once tried to snatch a kiss.

The Earl joined in the laughter but his eyes had a malicious gleam. "No matter," he shrugged. "Another five years and I warrant she'll be willing to pay even me a round sum."

The two women looked pleased, if a little surprised. Had Barbara actually begun to pay her lovers? Sedley, however, was frankly skeptical.

"Come now, John. You damned well know her Ladyship can have whatever man she sets her mind to, with no more than the lift of an eyebrow. She's still the handsomest woman at Whitehall—or in all London, for the matter of that—"

Frances, now thoroughly hurt, gave a wave of her hand at someone across the room. "Your servant, madame—gentlemen—I must speak a word with my Lady Southesk—"

Rochester and Sedley and Winifred exchanged smiles. "I still hope," said the Earl, "that some day that little milksop Stewart will come to blows with Castlemaine. Gad, I could write an epic on it!"

Several hours later Frances and Charles stood beside an open casement window above the garden, and the soft night breeze carried to them a faint smell of roses and the waxen sweet scent of potted orange-trees. It was almost midnight and many of the ladies and gentlemen had left already. Others were counting up their losses, arranging loans, grumbling about bad luck or exulting if it had been good.

Queen Catherine was talking to the Duchess of Buckingham and pretending not to notice how engrossed her husband was in Mrs. Stewart. She had learned her lesson well three years before, and though she loved Charles sincerely and hopelessly, she had never again objected to his interest in another woman. Now she played cards and danced, wore English clothes and dressed her hair in the latest French mode; she was as much an Englishwoman as her early training would allow. Charles always showed her the most perfect courtesy and insisted that the members of his Court do likewise. She was not happy, but she tried to seem so.

Frances was saying, "What a beautiful beautiful night! It doesn't seem possible that only twenty miles away there are thousands of men and women—sick, and dying."

Charles was quiet for a moment, and then he spoke very softly. "My poor people. I wonder why this has happened to them. They can't deserve it—I can't make myself believe in a malignant God who would punish a nation for the faults of its ruler—"

"Oh, Sire!" protested Frances. "How can you talk like that! They're not being punished for *your* faults! If they're being punished for a fault it's for their own!"

Charles smiled. "You're loyal, Frances. I think *you* must be my loyal subject— But of course you're not my subject at all. I'm yours—"

At that moment the high flaunting voice of Lady Castlemaine interrupted them. "Lord, what wretched cards I held tonight! I lost six thousand pound! Your Majesty, I swear I'm stark in debt again!"

She gave a gurgling laugh, staring up at him with her great purple eyes. Barbara was not so docile as the Queen. Charles visited her in private; she was then carrying his fourth child, and she did not intend that he should slight her in public. Obviously resenting her intrusion, he looked at her coldly with something of the forbidding hauteur he could so well assume when he had a use for it.

"Are you, madame?"

Frances now took up her skirts, with a gesture which delicately conveyed her distaste. "Excuse me, Sire. Your servant, madame." She scarcely looked at Barbara, and then she started away.

Quickly Charles touched her arm. "Here, Frances—I'll walk

540

along with you, if I may. You have an escort, madame?" His question to Barbara did not demand or want an answer.

"No, I haven't! Everyone's gone." Her lips pouted and she had an injured air which was probably the beginning of a crackling tantrum. "And I don't see why I should shift for myself while you—"

Charles interrupted. "With your leave, madame, I shall see Mrs. Stewart to her chamber. Good-night." He bowed, very politely, offered Frances his arm, and the two of them walked off together. They had gone only a few feet when Frances turned her head and looked up at him; suddenly she burst into a gleeful giggle.

They walked back to her apartments and at the door he kissed her, asking if he might come in while she made ready for bed—which he often did, sometimes with a herd of his courtiers. But now she gave him a wan little smile and a look of pleading.

"I'm tired. And my head aches so."

He was instantly alarmed, for though there had been no plague at Court the slightest sign of an indisposition was enough to set up unpleasant fears. "Your head aches? Do you feel well otherwise? Have you any nausea?"

"No, Your Majesty. Just a headache. Just one of my headaches."

"You have them often, Frances."

"All my life. Ever since I can remember."

"You're sure they're not just a convenience—for putting off unwelcome visitors?"

"No, Sire. I really have them. Please—may I go now?"

Quickly he kissed her hand. "Certainly, my dear. Forgive my thoughtlessness. But promise me that if it gets worse or if you have any other symptoms you'll send for Dr. Fraser—and let me know?"

"I promise, Sire. Good-night."

She backed into the room and closed the door gently. It was true that she had always had violent headaches. Her gaiety and high spirits were part nervousness, for she had none of Castlemaine's robust hearty vigour.

In her bedroom the long-tailed green parrot which she had

brought from France was sleeping, his head tucked under his wing, but at her entrance he woke instantly and began to dance up and down on his perch, squawking with delight. Mrs. Barry, the middle-aged gentlewoman who had been with Frances since babyhood, had also been dozing in her chair; now she too woke, and came hurrying forward to help her mistress undress.

Alone now and off her guard, with no need to impress anyone, she looked frankly tired. Slowly she got out of her gown, unfastened the laces of her busk and with a sigh of relief sat down while Barry began to unpin the jewels and ribbons twisted in her hair.

"Another headache, sweetheart?" Mrs. Barry's voice was worried, soft and maternal, and her fingers worked with loving tenderness.

"Terrible." Frances was close to tears.

Barry took a cloth now and wrung it out in a bowl of vinegar which was kept on a shelf nearby, convenient for frequent use. She laid it across Frances's forehead and held it with her fingers at either temple, while Frances closed her eyes and let her head rest gratefully against the cushion of Barry's bosom. They continued silent for a few moments.

Suddenly there was a sound of commotion from outside. A little page spoke, quietly, and an angry feminine voice answered; the door of the bedroom burst open and there stood Barbara Palmer. For an instant she glared at Frances and then she slammed it closed, with such violence that the noise seemed to reverberate in Frances's brain, making her wince.

"I have a crow to pluck with you, Madame Stewart!" declared the Countess.

Frances's pride rose, ready to do combat, and sweeping the weariness from her face she stood up, lifting her chin. "Your servant, madame. And what can I do for you, pray?"

"I'll tell you what you can do for me!" replied Barbara, and she crossed the room swiftly, until she stood just three or four feet from her. Barry was glaring pugnaciously from over Frances's shoulder and the parrot had begun to squawk his resentment, but Barbara ignored them both. "You can stop trying to make me appear a fool in public, madame! *That's* what you can do!"

Frances looked at her with obvious distaste, wondering how she had ever been so stupid as to consider this wild uncontrolled harpy her best friend. And then she sat down again, motioning Barry to continue undressing her hair.

"I'm sure I don't know how I can make you look a fool, madame—in public or anywhere else. If you do, you have only yourself to thank."

Barbara stood with her hands on her hips, eyes slightly narrowed. "You're a cunny gypsy, Mrs. Stewart—but let me tell you this: I can be a mighty dangerous enemy. You may find you've got the bear by the nose. If I set my mind to it, I could have you out of Whitehall like that!" She gave a quick sharp snap of her fingers.

Frances smiled coolly. "Could you, madame? You're welcome to try— But I think I please his Majesty quite as well as you—even though my methods may not be the same—"

Barbara made a sound of disgust. "Bah! You squeamish virgins make me sick! You're no good to any man, once he's had you! I'll wager you my right eye that once his Majesty lays with you he'll—"

Frances gave her a bored look and as Barbara chattered on, the door behind her swung slowly open. His Majesty appeared in it. He motioned her to silence and stood lounging against the door-jamb, watching Barbara, his dark face moody, displeased and glowering.

Barbara was beginning to shout. "There's one place where you can never get the better of me, Madame Stewart! Whatever my faults, there's never a man got out of my bed—"

"Madame!"

The King's voice spoke, sharply, from the doorway, and Barbara swung about with a horrified gasp. Both women watched him come into the room.

"Sire!" Barbara swept him a deep curtsy.

"That's enough of your bawdy talk."

"How long have you been there?"

"Long enough to have heard a great deal which was unpleasant. Frankly, madame, at times you exhibit the worst imaginable taste."

"But I didn't know you were there!" she protested. And then suddenly her eyes narrowed, she looked from Charles to Frances and back again. "Oho!" she said softly. "Now I begin to see something. How cleverly the two of you have hoodwinked us all—"

"Unfortunately, you're mistaken. As it happened you passed me in the hall without seeing me, and when I found where you were going I turned around and followed you back. You looked as though you were about some mischief." He smiled faintly, amused at her discomposure, but instantly his face sobered again. "I thought we had agreed, madame, that your behaviour toward Mrs. Stewart was to be both polite and friendly. What I heard just now sounded neither."

"How can you expect me to be polite to a woman who slanders me!" demanded Barbara, quick to her own defense.

Charles gave a short laugh. "Slanders you! Ods-fish, Barbara, you don't imagine it's still possible? Now, Mrs. Stewart is tired, I believe, and would like to rest. If you'll make her an apology we'll both go and leave her alone."

"An apology!" Barbara stared at him with horrified indignation, and turning she swept Frances contemptuously from head to foot. "I'll be damned if I do!"

All good humour was gone from his face now, replaced by that sombre bitterness which lurked there at all times. "You refuse, madame?"

"I do!" She faced him defiantly, and both of them had forgotten Frances who stood looking on, tired and nervous, wishing that they would quarrel elsewhere. "Nothing under God's sky can make me apologize to that meek simpering milk-sop!"

"The choice is your own. But may I suggest that you retire from Hampton Court while you consider the matter? A few weeks of quiet reflection may give you another view of good manners."

"You're sending me from the Court?"

"Put it that way if you like."

Without a moment's hesitation Barbara was in tears. "So this

544

is what it's come to! After the years I've given up to you! It's a shame before all the world that a king should turn away the mother of his children!"

He lifted one eyebrow, skeptically. "My children?" he repeated softly. "Well, some of them, perhaps. But there's nothing more to be said. Either make Mrs. Stewart an apology—or go elsewhere."

"But where can I go? The plague's everywhere else!"

"For the matter of that, the plague's here too."

Even Frances snapped out of her weary lethargy and both women repeated at once: "Here!"

"The wife of a groom died of it today. Tomorrow we move to Salisbury."

"Oh, my God!" wailed Barbara. "Now we'll all get it! We'll all die!"

"I don't think so. The woman has been buried and everyone who was with her is shut up. So far there've been no new cases. Come, madame, make your choice. Will you be going with us tomorrow?"

Barbara looked at Frances who, feeling her eyes shift to her, suddenly straightened and raised her head—meeting her glance with cold hostility. Suddenly Barbara slammed her fan to the floor.

"I will not! I'll go to Richmond and be damned to you!"

CHAPTER THIRTY-SEVEN

AMBER WENT BACK into the kitchen and continued getting Bruce's meal. She wanted to do as much as she could for him, while she was still able to do anything at all. For by tomorrow she would be helpless and a new nurse would be there—someone perhaps much worse than Spong had been. She was more worried about him than about herself. He was still weak and in need of competent care, and the thought of a stranger coming in, someone who would not know him or care what happened to him, filled her with desperation. If she'd only come in time, she thought, maybe I could bribe her.

Once the first horror of discovery was gone she accepted with resignation and almost with apathy the fact that she was sick. She did not, actually, expect to die. If one person fell ill of the plague in a house and lived, it was thought a good omen for all others in that same house. (Spong's death she ignored and had almost forgotten; it seemed to have occurred in some distant past unconnected with either her or Bruce.) But apart from superstition she had strong faith in her own temporary immortality. She wanted so much to go on living, it was impossible for her to believe that she could die now, so young and with all her hopes still to be realized.

She had the same symptoms Bruce had had, but they came in swifter succession.

By the time she started into the bedroom with the tray her head was aching violently, as though a tight steel band had been bound about her temples and was drawing steadily tighter. She was sweating and there were stabbing pains throughout her stomach and along her legs and arms. Her throat was as dry as if she had swallowed dust, but though she drank several dipperfuls of water it did no good. The thirst increased.

Bruce was awake, sitting propped up as he could often do now, and though there was a book in his hands he was watching the door anxiously. "You've been gone so long, Amber. Is anything wrong?"

She did not look at him but kept her eyes on the tray. Dizziness swept over her in waves, and when it came she had a weird sensation of standing in the midst of a whirling sphere; she could not tell where the floors or walls were. Now she paused for a moment, trying to orient herself and then, setting her teeth, she came determinedly forward.

"Nothing's wrong," she repeated, but even to her her voice had a strange fuzzy sound. She hoped that he would not notice.

Slowly, for she felt very tired and her muscles seemed heavy, she set the tray on the bedside table and reached down to pick up the bowlful of syllabub. She saw his hand reach out and close over her wrist and when at last she forced her eyes to lift and meet his, she found on his face the look of self-condemning horror she had been dreading.

"Amber—" He continued to stare at her for a moment, his green eyes narrowed, searching. "You're not—sick?" The words came out with slow forced reluctance.

She gave a little sigh. "Yes, Bruce. I am—I guess I am. But don't—"

"Don't what!"

She tried to remember what she had started to say. "Don't—worry about it."

"Don't worry about it! Good God! Oh, Amber! *Amber!* You're sick and it's my fault! It's because you stayed here to take care of me! Oh, my darling—if *only* you'd gone! If only you'd— Oh, Jesus!" He let go of her wrist and distractedly ran one hand through his hair.

She reached down to touch his forehead. "Don't torture yourself, Bruce. It's not your fault. I stayed because I wanted to. I knew it was a chance—but I couldn't go. And I'm not sorry—I won't die, Bruce—"

He looked at her then with a kind of admiration in his eyes she had never seen before. But at that moment she felt the nausea begin to rise, flooding up irresistibly, and even before she could reach the basin halfway across the room she had started to vomit.

Each time it happened it left her more exhausted, and now she hung for a minute longer over the basin, leaning on her hands, with her burnt-taffy hair concealing her face. All at once she gave a convulsive shudder; the room seemed cold, and yet the fire was burning, all the windows were closed, and the day had been an unusually hot one. At that moment there was a sound behind her. She turned slowly and saw Bruce beginning to get out of bed. With a last desperate surge of her strength she ran toward him.

"Bruce! What are you doing! Get back—" She began to push at him, frantically, but her muscles seemed useless. She had never felt so weak, so helpless, not even after her children had been born.

"I've *got* to get up, Amber! I've got to help you!"

He had been out of bed only once or twice since he had fallen sick, and now his body was shining with sweat and his face was violently contorted. Amber began to cry, almost hysterical.

"Don't, Bruce! Don't, for God's sake! You'll kill yourself! You *can't* get up! Oh, after everything I've done you're going to kill yourself—"

Suddenly she dropped to her knees on the floor, put her head in her arms and sobbed. He fell back against the pillows, wiping his hand over his forehead, surprised to find that he was dizzy and that his ears rang, for he had thought himself farther recovered than he was. He reached over to stroke Amber's head.

"Darling—I won't get up. Please don't cry—you need your strength. Lie down and rest. The nurse will be here soon."

At last, with an intense feeling of weariness, she forced herself to get to her feet and stood looking about the room as though trying to remember something. "What was I going to do—" she murmured at last. "Something— What was it?"

"Can you tell me where the money is, Amber? I'll need it for supplies. I had none with me."

"Oh, yes—that's it, the money." The words slurred, one over another, as if she had drunk too much cherry-brandy. "It's in here—I'll get it—'sin secret panel—"

The parlour seemed a great distance away, farther than she could possibly walk. But she got there at last, and though it took her a while to locate the panel, she finally found it and scooped out the leather wallet and small pile of jewellery that lay there. She brought them back in her apron and dropped them onto the bed beside Bruce. He had managed to lean over and pull out the trundle and now, when he told her to lie down, she collapsed onto it, already half unconscious.

Bruce lay awake through the night, cursing his own helplessness. But he knew that any violent strain now would only make him worse and might kill him. He could help her best by saving his strength until he was well enough to take care of her. He lay there and heard her vomit, again and again, ·

and though each time when she had done she gave a heavy despairing groan, she was otherwise perfectly quiet. So quiet that he would listen, with mounting horror, for the sound of her breathing. And then the retching would begin again. The nurse did not come.

By morning she lay flat on her back, her eyes fixed and wide open but unseeing. Her muscles were perfectly relaxed and she had no consciousness of him or of her surroundings; when he spoke to her she did not hear. The disease had made much swifter progress than it had with him, but it was characteristic of plague to vary its nature with each victim.

He decided that if the nurse did not appear soon he would get out of bed and talk to the guard, but at about seven-thirty he heard the door open and a woman's boisterous voice called out: "The plague-nurse is here; Where are ye?"

"Come upstairs!"

Within a few moments a woman appeared in the doorway. She was tall and heavy-boned, perhaps thirty-five, and Bruce was relieved to see that she looked strong and at least moderately intelligent. "Come in here," he said, and she walked forward, her eyes already on Amber. "I'm Lord Carlton. My wife is desperately sick as you can see, and needs the best of care. I'd give it to her myself, but I'm convalescing and not able to get up yet. If you take good care of her—if she lives— I'll give you a hundred pound." He lied about their marriage because he thought the truth was none of the woman's business, and he offered a hundred pounds because he believed it might impress her more than a larger sum which she would probably not expect to get.

She stared at him in surprise. "A hundred pound, sir!"

She drew closer to the trundle then and looked at Amber, whose fingers were picking restlessly at the blanket Bruce had thrown over her, though but for the nervous movements of her hands she would have seemed to be totally unconscious. There were dirty green circles beneath her eyes and the lower part of her face was shiny with the bile and saliva which had dried there; she had not vomited at all for the past three hours.

The woman shook her head. "She's mighty sick, your Lordship. I don't know—"

"Of course you don't know!" snapped Bruce with angry impatience. "But you can try! She's still dressed. Take her clothes off, bathe her face and hands—get her into the sheets. She'll be more comfortable at least. She's been cooking for me and you'll find soup and whatever else you need in the kitchen. There are clean towels and sheets in that room— The floor must be mopped, and the parlour cleaned. A woman died there yesterday. Now get to work! What's your name?" he added, as an afterthought.

"Mrs. Sykes, sir. Yes, sir."

Mrs. Sykes, who told Bruce that she had been a wet-nurse but had lost her job because her husband had died of the plague, worked hard throughout the day. Bruce gave her no opportunity to loaf or to rest, and despite the fact that she knew he was helpless and unable to get out of bed she obeyed his commands meekly—whether from respect of the nobility or one hundred pounds he did not know or care.

But by nightfall Amber seemed, if possible, to be even worse. A carbuncle had begun to swell in her right groin and though it grew larger it remained hard and gave no indication that it would suppurate. Sykes was anxious about that, for it was the worst possible sign, and not even the mustard plasters she applied—which blistered the skin—seemed to have any effect.

"What can we *do?*" Bruce asked her. "There must be *something* we can do! What have you done for your patients when the carbuncle wouldn't break?"

Sykes was staring down at Amber. "Nothing, sir," she said slowly. "Most usually they die."

"*She's* not going to die!" he cried. "We'll do something. We've got to do something— She can't die!" He looked less well than he had the day before but he forced himself to stay awake, as though he could keep her alive by holding a vigil over her.

"We might cut into it," she said. "If it's still like this tomorrow. That's what the doctors do. But the pain of the knife sometimes drives 'em mad—"

550

"Shut up! I don't want to hear it! Go out and get her something to eat."

He was almost exhausted and his temper was quick and savage, for he suffered agonizingly over his own impotence. It went through his mind over and over again. She's sick because of me and now, when she needs me, I lie here like a sot and am able to do nothing!

Almost to his surprise, Amber lived through the night. But by morning her skin was beginning to take on a dusky colour, her breathing grew more shallow and her heart-beats fainter. Sykes told him that those things meant approaching death.

"Then we'll cut the boil open!"

"But it might kill her!"

Sykes was afraid to do anything, for it seemed that no matter what she did the patient would die and she would lose the greatest fortune she had ever imagined.

He almost shouted at her. "Do as I say!" Then his voice dropped again, he spoke to her quietly but with a swift commanding urgency. "Over in the top drawer of that table there's a razor—get it. Take the cord off the drapes and bind her knees and ankles together. Wrap the cord around the trundle so she can't move, and tie her wrists to the corners. Get some towels and a basin. Hurry!"

Sykes scrambled nervously about the room, but within a couple of minutes she had followed his directions. Amber lay bound securely to the trundle and still completely unconscious.

Bruce was close to the edge of the bed. "Pray God she doesn't know—" he muttered and then: "Now! Take the razor and cut into it—quick and hard! It'll hurt less that way. Quick!" His right fist clenched and the veins in it swelled.

Sykes looked at him in horror, the razor held tight in her hand. "I can't, your Lordship. I can't." Her teeth began to chatter. "I'm scared! What if she dies under it!"

Bruce was pouring sweat. He licked his tongue over his dry lips and gave a convulsive swallow. "You *can*, you fool! You've got to! *Now*—do it now!"

Sykes continued to stare at him for a moment and then, as though hypnotized into obedience by the sheer force of his will, she bent and placed the edge of the razor against the hard red knob high up on Amber's groin. At that moment Amber stirred and her head turned toward Bruce. Sykes gave a start.

"Cut it open!" said Bruce hoarsely, his clenched fist trembling with helpless rage. His face was dark with the rush of blood and the cords in his neck and temples were thick as ropes and throbbing.

With sudden resolution Sykes jammed the razor into the lump, but as she did so Amber moaned and the moan slid in crescendo to a quivering scream. Sykes let go of the razor and stepped back to stand staring at Amber who was struggling now to free herself, twisting frantically in an effort to escape the pain, shrieking again and again.

Bruce began to get out of bed. "Help me!"

Sykes came swiftly, put one arm around his back, the other beneath his elbow, and in an instant he had dropped on his knees beside the trundle and seized the razor.

"Hold her! Here! By the knees!"

Again Sykes did as she was told, though Amber continued to writhe, shrieking, her eyes rolling like a frenzied animal's. With all the strength he had left Bruce forced the razor into the hard mass and twisted it to one side. As he pulled it out again the blood spurted, splattering onto his body, and Amber dropped back, unconscious. His head fell helplessly onto his fist; his own wound had opened once more and the bandage showed fresh and red.

Sykes was trying to help him get up. "Your Lordship! Ye must get back into bed! Your Lordship—please!"

She wrenched the razor from his hand and with her help he managed to crawl back onto the bed. She flung a blanket over him and turned immediately to Amber whose skin was now white and waxen. Her heart was beating, very faintly. Quantities of blood poured from the opening, but there was no pus and the poison was not draining.

Sykes worked furiously, at her own initiative now, for Bruce had lapsed into coma. She kept the blood sponged away; she heated bricks and every hot water bottle in the house and packed them about Amber; she laid hot cloths on her forehead. If there was any way she could be saved, Sykes intended to get her hundred pounds.

It was almost an hour before Bruce returned to consciousness and then, with a sudden start, he tried to sit up. "Where is she! You didn't let them take her!"

"Hush, sir! I think she's sleeping. She's still alive and I think, sir, that she's better."

He leaned over to look at her. "Oh, thank God, thank God. I swear it, Sykes, if she lives you'll get your hundred pound. I'll make it two hundred for you."

"Oh, thank you, sir! But now, sir—you'd better lie back there and rest yourself—or you might not fare so well, sir."

"Yes, I will. Wake me if she gets any—" The words trailed off.

At last the pus began to seep up and the wound started to drain off its poison. Amber lay perfectly still again, drowned in coma, but the dark tinge was gone from her skin and though her cheeks had sunk against the bones and there were crape-like circles around her eyes, her pulse had a stronger, surer beat. The sound of tolling bells seemed suddenly to fill the room. Sykes gave a start, then relaxed; they would not toll to-night for her patient.

"I've worked hard for my money, sir," Sykes said to him on the morning of the fourth day. "And I'm sure she'll live now. Can I have it?"

Bruce smiled. "You have worked hard, Sykes. And I'm more grateful than I can tell you. But you'll have to wait a while longer." He would not give her any of the jewellery, partly because it was Amber's personal property, partly because it might have encouraged her to outright thievery or some other mischief. Sykes had served her purpose, but he knew that it would be foolish to trust her. "There are only a few shillings in the house—and they've got to be spent for food. As soon as I can go out I'll get it for you."

He was able to sit up now, most of the day, and when it was necessary he could get out of bed, but never stayed more than a few minutes at a time. His persistent weakness seemed both to amuse and infuriate him. "I've been shot in the stomach and run through the shoulder," he said one day to Sykes as he walked slowly back to the bed. "I've been bitten by a poisonous snake and I've had a tropical fever—but I'll be damned if I've ever felt like this before."

Most of the time he spent reading, though there were only a few books in the apartment and he had already seen most of them. Some had been there as part of the furnishings and they were a respectable assortment, including the Bible, Hobbes's "Leviathan," Bacon's "Novum Organum," some of the plays of Beaumont and Fletcher, Browne's "Religio Medici."

Amber's collection, though small, was more lively. There was an almanac, thumbed and much scribbled in, the lucky and unlucky days starred, as well as those for purging or bloodletting, though so far as he knew she seldom did either. Her familiar scrawl was marked across the fly-leaf of half-a-dozen others: "L'École des Filles," "The Crafty Whore," "The Wandering Whore," "Annotations upon Aretino's Postures," "Ars Amatoria," and—evidently because it was currently fashionable —Butler's "Hudibras." All but the last had obviously been well read. He smiled to see them, for though the same volumes would doubtless have been found in the closet of almost any Court lady they were nevertheless amusingly typical of her.

He always sat near the edge of the bed where he could watch her, and she made no movement or slightest sound which he did not notice. She was, very slowly, getting better, though the constant sloughing of the wound worried him, for it continued to open wider and deeper until it had spread over an area with a two-inch diameter. But both he and Sykes were convinced that if the incision had not been made she would have died.

Sometimes, to his horror, she would suddenly put up her hands as though to ward off a blow, and cry out in a piteous voice. "Don't! No! Please! *Don't* cut me!" And the cry would slide off in a shuddering moan that turned him cold and wet. After that she always lapsed again into unconsciousness, though sometimes even in coma she twitched and squirmed and made soft whimpering sounds.

It was the seventh day before she saw and recognized him. He had come in from the parlour and found her propped against Sykes's arm swallowing some beef-broth, languidly and without interest. He had a blanket flung over his shoulders and now he knelt beside the trundle to watch her.

She seemed to sense him there and her head turned slowly. For a long moment she looked at him, and then at last she whispered softly: "Bruce?"

He took her hand in both of his. "Yes, darling. I'm here."

She forced a little smile to her face and started to speak again, but the words would not come, and he moved away to save her the effort. But the next morning, early, while Sykes was combing out her hair she spoke to him again, though her voice was so thin and weak that he had to lean close to hear it.

"How long 've I been here?"

"This is the eighth day, Amber."

"Aren't you well yet?"

"Almost. In a few days I'll be able to take care of you."

She closed her eyes then and breathed a long tired sigh. Her head rolled over sideways on the pillow. Her hair, lank and oily with most of the curl gone, lay in thick skeins about her head. Her collar-bones showed sharply beneath the taut-stretched skin, and it was possible to see her ribs.

That same day Mrs. Sykes fell sick, and though she protested for several hours that it was nothing at all, merely a slight indisposition from something she had eaten, Bruce knew better. He did not want her taking care of Amber and suggested that she lie down in the nursery and rest, which she did immediately. Then, wrapping himself in a blanket, he went out to the kitchen.

Sykes had had neither the time nor the inclination and probably not even the knowledge for good housekeeping and all the rooms were littered and untidy. Puffs of dust moved about on the floors, the furniture was thickly coated, stubs of burnt-down candles lay wherever she had tossed them. In the kitchen there were stacks of dirty pans and plates, great pails full of soaking bloody rags or towels, and the food had not been put away but left out on the table or even set on the floor.

Everything spoiled rapidly in the heat and she had been negligent about reordering from the guard; so he found that the butter had turned rancid, the milk was beginning to sour, and some of the eggs stank when opened. He ladled out a bowl of soup—Sykes's concoction and by no means so palatable as Amber's had been—and ate it himself, and then he took the best of what he could find in on a tray to Amber.

As he was feeding her, slowly, spoonful by spoonful, Sykes suddenly began to rave and scream in delirium. Amber grabbed his wrist, her eyes full of terror.

"What's that!"

"It's nothing, darling. Someone in the street. Here—that's enough for now. You must lie down again."

She did so but her eyes watched him as he went to the nursery door, turned the key in the lock and taking it out tossed it upon the table.

"There's someone in there," she said softly. "Someone who's sick."

He came back and sat beside her again. "It's the nurse—but she can't get out. You're safe here, darling, and you must go back to sleep again—"

"But what if she dies, Bruce—how'll you get her out of the house?" The expression in her eyes showed what she was thinking: of Spong, of dragging her down the stairs, of the dead-cart.

"Don't worry about it. Don't even think about it. I'll do it someway. Now you must sleep, darling—sleep and get well."

For two or three hours Sykes continued to rave intermittently. She beat on the door, shrieking at him to let her out, demanding the money he had promised her, but he made no answer at all. The windows in the nursery overlooked the courtyard and the back alley and sometime in the middle of the night he heard her smashing them and screaming wildly. And then he heard a yowl as she leaped out and went crashing down two stories below. When the dead-cart came by he opened the window to tell the guard where they would find her.

It was almost noon the next day before another nurse arrived.

He was lying flat on his back, half dozing, worn out by the effort of getting up to bring Amber some food, to change her bandage and bathe her hands and face. And then, slowly, he opened his eyes and found an old woman standing beside the bed, watching him with a curious, speculative look. He scowled, wondering why she had come in so silently, distrustful immediately of her manner and appearance.

She was old and filthy in her dress, her face was deeply lined and her breath stank foully. But he noticed that she wore a pair of diamond earrings that looked real and several rings on her fingers which were also of obvious value. She was either a thief or a ghoul or both.

"Good-day, sir. The parish-clerk sent me here. I'm Mrs. Maggot."

"I'm almost well," said Bruce, staring at her intently, hoping to make her think that he was stronger than he was. "But my wife still needs a great deal of care. I got her one meal this morning, but it's time for another now. The last nurse left the kitchen in a mess and there's no food, but you can send the guard for some."

As he spoke her eyes were going over the furnishings of the room: the cloth-of-silver covering the bedstead and chairs, the marble-topped tables, the row of exquisite vases across the mantelpiece.

"Where's the money?" she asked, not looking at him.

"There are four shillings on that table. That should buy whatever we need—the guard always takes a fee for himself."

She got the coin and tossed it out the window, telling the guard to bring some food, already prepared, from a cook-shop. Obviously she did not intend to do anything herself. And later in the day when he asked her to change the bandages she refused, saying that every nurse she knew who had dressed an ulcer was dead now but that she intended to die another way.

Bruce was furious, but he answered her quietly. "Then, if you won't help, you may as well go."

She gave him an insolent grin and he was afraid that she had guessed already he was far less strong than he pretended to be. "No, m'lord. I was sent by the parish. If I don't stay I won't get my fee."

For a moment they stared at each other, and then he flung

the blanket about himself and got out of bed. She stood there, watching him closely as he knelt on one knee beside Amber, measuring his strength, and at last he turned with a flare of exasperated anger.

"Get out! Go in the other room!"

She grinned again but went, and closed the door. He called out to her to leave it open but she ignored him. Swearing beneath his breath he finished dressing the wound and then got back into bed to rest. There was no sound at all from the parlour. It was half-an-hour before he could get up again and then he crossed the room, opened the door quietly and found her going through the drawer of a table. There were articles scattered everywhere and she had evidently been searching methodically through each piece of furniture for secret drawers and hiding places, which were almost always built in.

"Mrs. Maggot."

She looked up and met his stare coolly. "Sir?"

"You'll find nothing of value hidden away. Whatever you may care to steal is in plain sight. We have no money in the house beyond a few coins for food."

She made no reply but, after a moment, turned and went into the dining-room. Bruce found that he was sweating with rage and nervousness, for he did not doubt the old woman would murder them both without an instant's hesitation if she learned that there was almost seventy pounds in the house. He knew that the nurses were drawn from the lowest social classes: life-long paupers, uncaught criminals, and—in plague-time—from women like Sykes who had been forced into it through necessity and misfortune.

He did not sleep well that night, aware of her in the parlour, for when she had found evidences of Sykes's illness she had refused to go into the nursery. And when he heard her get up, two or three times, and move about he lay tense and apprehensive. If she decides to kill us, he thought, I'll try to strangle her. But he clenched and unclenched his fists with despair, for the fingers had but little of their usual strength.

The next morning, just before daylight, he fell deeply asleep and when he woke she was bending over him, her arm thrust beneath the mattress on which he lay. As his eyes opened she straightened slowly, unalarmed. He could not tell, by her expression, whether she had discovered the bagful of coins and jewels.

"Just smoothin' your bed, sir."

"I'll take care of that myself."

"You said yesterday, sir, that I might go. If you'll give me fifty pound now, I will."

He looked at her shrewdly, aware that she had made the offer to find out whether or not he would admit to having that much money in the house. "I told you, Maggot—I have only a few shillings here."

"How now, sir? Only a few shillin's—a lord, and livin' in lodgings like this?"

"We put our money with a goldsmith. Is there any food left from yesterday?"

"No, sir. The guard stole most of it. We'll have to send again."

Throughout the day, whenever he got out of bed, he could feel her watching him, even though most of the time she was not in the room. She knows there's money here, he thought, and tonight she'll try to get it. But if there had been not a farthing in cash the furnishings alone were worth what would be a fortune to her—even if she sold them to a broker-of-the-dead.

He spent the day thinking and planning, aware that if he was to save either of their lives he must be ready for her, no matter what she might try to do. And while he lay there the dead-carts came by three times; there were now too many deaths to bury the bodies at night.

He considered every possibility.

If he asked the guard for help she would overhear him, and he had no reason to think that the guard could be trusted. There seemed no choice; he must try to handle the situation himself. She would not be likely, he thought, to use a knife, for that would leave tell-tale wounds. Strangulation with a length of cord or rope should be easy with both of them as weak as they were; and she would try to kill him first, for Amber could make no more resistance than a kitten. But having thought that far

559

he found himself confronted by problems that, in his state of weakness, seemed insoluble. If he closed the door and waited behind it she would know he was there, and he could not out-wait her. If he locked it she could force her way in, and in any open battle he was no match for her, for though his strength might be greater he was unable to move about quickly and would soon be exhausted.

At last he decided to make a bundle of blankets in the bed and wait there next to it, concealed behind the window hangings. If she came near he could strike her over the head with a heavy pewter candlestick. But the plan was spoiled, for she refused to close the door. When he asked her to do so, just as it was growing dark, she obeyed, but a few minutes later he heard it opening, very slowly. It remained ajar just an inch or so for more than an hour, and then he called out to her again.

"Maggot! Close the door—all the way."

She did not answer but closed it. The room grew darker as twilight settled into night. For half-an-hour he waited and then, slowly, cautiously, he got out of bed, keeping a watch on the door as he began to move about, making the bundle of bedding. It was almost done when he heard a creaking sound—and saw the door begin to swing open.

Exasperated and thoroughly worried he snapped out her name. "Mrs. Maggot!" She made no reply but he could feel her there, watching, for though no candles had been lighted there was a moon and it shone at his back. He could not see her, but she could see him. He got back into the bed and lay down, sweating with nervous rage to think that after surviving the plague itself they might both die now at the hands of a filthy greedy old woman.

But, by Jesus, we won't! I won't let her kill us! He felt a responsibility for Amber's life more violent and determined even than his own will to live.

The hours went past.

Several times he heard the dead-cart, and the passing-bell tolled at least twenty separate times. Against his will he listened for the tone and counted the number of times they were struck —twelve women, eight men, had died in the parish so far tonight. He had a horror of falling asleep—for drowsiness swept over him in waves—and forced himself to recite silently every poem he had ever memorized, every song he had ever sung. He made a mental list of the books he had read, the women he had made love to, the towns he had visited. It kept him awake.

Then at last she entered the room.

He saw the door swing slowly open and after a moment he heard the creaking of a floor board. The moon was gone now and there was absolute darkness. His heart began to beat heavily and all his being was abnormally alert, his eyes straining into the black that surrounded him, his ears listening until he felt sure that he could hear the coursing of his own blood.

She approached slowly. Each time he heard a board creak there followed what seemed an interminable period of absolute silence, until he could no longer tell from where the sound had come. The suspense was an agony but he forced himself to lie motionless, breathing deeply and naturally. His nerves were raw and trembling and he had a violent impulse to leap up and try to grab her. He dared not, though, for she might get away and then they would be left helpless. He had a desperate fear that his strength would not last under such tension. It seemed to be draining away, and the muscles of his legs and arms ached painfully.

And then, almost unexpectedly, he caught the smell of her breath and knew that she was there, beside him. His eyes were wide open, but he could see nothing. For an instant he hesitated. Then, with a swiftness and strength that caught him off guard, she dropped a noose down over his head and jerked it tight. His arm shot out and seized hold of her, brought her sprawling across him and in that moment he thrust his fingers into the noose, tore it from about his own head and forced it down over hers. He pulled on it with both his hands and all the strength he had. She clawed and struggled furiously, gagging, while he yanked at it again and again, and when at last after many minutes he knew that she was dead he let her slide to the floor and fell back upon the bed himself, almost unconscious. Amber was still asleep.

CHAPTER THIRTY–EIGHT

WHEN HE DRAGGED Mrs. Maggot down the stairs to leave her for the dead-cart he gave the guard five guineas not to make a report to the parish-clerk; he wanted no more nurses in the house. For now he was well enough to take care of Amber himself, though it might be difficult for several more days.

The next morning he found that Mrs. Maggot had left the kitchen in even worse condition than Sykes. It stank with the spoilage of rotten fruit and vegetables, the meat was a mass of weaving worms, and the bread was covered with green mould. There was nothing there which was edible and since he was not yet able to clean up the mess or cook anything himself, he sent the guard to a tavern for a prepared meal.

But as the days went by he grew gradually stronger and though at first he had to rest after each small task he finally got all the rooms cleaned again. And one day while Amber was sleeping he moved her into the freshly-made bed and from then on occupied the trundle himself. Both of them joked about his housekeeping and cooking—which he did as soon as he was well enough—and the first time she laughed was when she woke up one morning to see him, naked but for a towel tied about his waist, sweeping the floor. She told him that she must have his recipes to give her next cook and asked him what method he used to get the sheets so white, saying that her laundress sometimes brought them back in worse condition than they were sent.

Soon he began going out to buy the food himself—for the guards had been withdrawn as useless—and found the streets almost empty.

The people were dying at the rate of 10,000 a week or more—it was a frightening insidious fact that of those who died a great percentage were never reported or even counted. Dead-carts came by at all hours, but in spite of that hundreds of bodies lay in the streets or were piled in the public squares, sometimes for days, while the rats swarmed over them. Many were half gnawed away before they were taken up for burial. The red cross was no longer chalked on the doors, but large printed posters were nailed up instead. Grass grew between the cobble-stones; thousands of houses were deserted and whole streets were barricaded and closed off, all their inhabitants having died or fled. Even the bells ceased tolling. The city lay perfectly still, hot and stinking.

Bruce talked to the shop-keepers, many of whom, like others who had remained behind, had shrugged off their earlier terrors. Death had become so common that a kind of scorn had replaced fear. The timid ones were shut tight in their houses and never ventured abroad. Others who went on with daily work and habits acquired a fatalism which sometimes was tempered by caution, but which more often was deliberately reck-less. Mourning was now almost never seen, though at the end of the first week in September 2,000 were dying each day and almost every family had lost someone.

There were innumerable grotesque and terrible stories, heard on every hand, but none more terrible than what was actually happening. Instances of premature burial were widely known —partly because of the death-like coma which made the mistake natural, partly because nurses often took advantage of it to get the patient out of the way and plunder the house. There was the story of the butcher who was laid outside in his shroud for the dead-cart, which neglected to carry him off, and who regained consciousness the following morning. He was said to be alive and almost well again. One man escaped from his house, raving mad, and jumped into the Thames, swam across it, and recovered. Another man, left alone, knocked over a candle and burned himself to death in his bed. A young woman discovered a plague-spot on her baby, dashed out its brains against the wall of a house and ran along the street, shrieking.

The first day that Bruce was able to go out he walked the half-mile or so to Almsbury House, let himself in with his key, and went up to the apartments he had always occupied to get some fresh clothing. What he had on he took off and burned. There were a couple of servants who had been left as care-takers—for many of the great empty houses were now being entered and robbed by thieves and beggars—and they had been shut in there for more than two months. They refused to come near him but shouted out questions, and were much relieved when he left.

By the end of the second week in September Amber was able to dress and sit in the courtyard for a few minutes every day. Bruce carried her down and back again the first few times but she begged him to let her walk for she wanted to grow strong enough so that they could leave the city. She believed now that London was doomed, cursed by God, and that unless they got out they would die with everyone else. For though she was much better she was still gloomy and pessimistic; her usual attitude was completely reversed. Bruce was so well now that his own confidence and optimism had returned and he tried to amuse her—but it was not easy to do.

"I heard an interesting story today," he said one morning as they sat in the courtyard.

He had brought down a chair for her and she drooped in it pathetically. The clothes she had worn while taking care of him he had burned, and the one gown which was left was a high-necked one of plain black silk that made her skin look sallow and drained. There were dark pits beneath her eyes and her hair hung in drab oily coils about her shoulders, but there was a red rose pinned at one temple which he had found that morning while shopping. Flowers had almost vanished from the town.

"What?" she asked him listlessly.

"Well, it sounds preposterous but they swear it's true. It seems there was a drunken piper who left a tavern the other night and lay down in a doorway somewhere to sleep. The dead-cart came along, tossed him on top of the heap, and went off. But halfway to the graveyard the piper woke up and nothing daunted by the company took out his pipe and began to play. The driver and link-man ran off bellowing that the cart was haunted—"

Amber did not laugh or even smile; she looked at him with

a kind of incredulous horrified disgust. "Oh— Oh, how terrible! A live man in that cart— Oh, it *can't* be true—"

"I'm sorry, darling." He was instantly contrite and changed the subject immediately. "You know, I think I've found the means to get us out of the city." He was sitting on the flag-stones before her in his breeches and shirt-sleeves, a lock of his own coarse, dark hair falling over his forehead, and he looked up at her now with a smile, squinting his eyes against the sun.

"How?"

"Almsbury's yacht's still here, moored at the water-stairs, and it's big enough so that we could take along provisions to last us for several weeks."

"But where could we go? You can't go out to sea in a yacht, can you?"

"We won't try. We'll sail up the Thames toward Hampton Court and go past Windsor and Maidenhead and on up that way. Once we're sufficiently recovered not to spread the disease we can go to Almsbury's country seat in Herefordshire."

"But you said they wouldn't let ships leave port at all." Even simple plans sounded more difficult to her now than preposterous ones would have when she was in good health.

"They won't. We'll have to be careful. We'll go at night— but don't you worry about it. I'll make the plans. I've already begun to—"

He paused, for Amber was staring at him, her face almost green, all her body stiffened in an attitude of listening. Then he heard it too—the rumbling sound of wheels turning over the \cobble-stones, and a man's distant voice.

"Bring out your dead!"

Amber began to sway forward but swiftly he was on his feet and had her in his arms. He carried her back up the stairs to the balcony and through the parlour into the bedroom and there he laid her down, very gently. She had lost consciousness for only a moment and now she looked up at him again. The sickness had left her wholly dependent upon him; she looked to him for all strength and confidence, she expected him to supply the answer and solution for every fear or worry. He was lover, God and parent.

"I'll never forget that sound," she whispered now. "I'll hear it every night of my life. I'll see those carts every time I shut my eyes." Her eyes were beginning to glitter, her breath came faster with hysterical excitement. "I'll never be able to think about anything else—"

Bruce bent close and put his mouth against her cheek. "Amber, don't! Don't think about it. Don't *let* yourself think about it. You can forget it. You can, and you've got to—"

A few days later Amber and Bruce left London in Almsbury's yacht. The country was beautiful. The low riverside meadows were thick with marigolds and along the banks grew lilies and green rushes. Tangled masses of water-grass, like green hair, floated on the swift current, and in the late afternoons there were always cattle standing at the edge of the water, quiet and reflective.

They passed a great many other boats, most of them small scows or barges on which were crowded whole families who had no country homes and had taken that means of escaping the plague. But though they exchanged mutual greetings and news, people were still distrustful of one another. Those who had avoided the sickness this long had no wish to risk it now.

They progressed slowly, past Hampton and Staines and Windsor and Maidenhead, stopping whenever they found a spot they liked and staying there for as long as they liked and then going on again. By the time they had been gone a night and a day London and its dying thousands seemed to be in another world, almost another age. Amber began to improve more rapidly, and she was as determined as Bruce to shut those memories from her mind. When they tried to creep in she pushed them aside, refusing to meet them face to face.

I'll forget there ever was a plague, she insisted.

And gradually it began to seem that Bruce's sickness and her own, all the events of the past three months had not happened recently but many years ago, in another life. It even seemed they must have happened to other people, not to them. She wondered if he felt the same way, but she never asked, for it was a subject they refused to discuss.

For a while Amber was desolate over her appearance. She was

566

afraid that her beauty was gone forever and that she would be ugly the rest of her life. In spite of everything Bruce could say to try to reassure her she cried with rage and despair every time she saw a mirror.

"Oh, my God!" she would wail dismally. "I'd rather be dead than look like this! Oh, Bruce—I'm never going to look like I did before, I know I'm not! Oh! I hate myself!"

He would put his arms about her, smiling as though she were a naughty child, coaxing away her fear and anguish. "Of course you're going to look the same, darling. But good Lord, you were mighty sick you know—you can't expect to be well again in only a few days." They had not been long on the yacht when her health improved so much that she did begin to look something like her old self.

Both of them realized, as perhaps they never had before, how pleasant it was merely to be alive. They spent hours lying stretched out on cushions on the deck, soaking in hot sunlight, that seemed to penetrate to the very bone—and though Bruce lay naked, his body turning a deep rich brown again, Amber kept herself carefully covered for fear of tanning her own cream-coloured skin. They shared everything, so as to enjoy it more intensely: The late summer sky, clear and blue, painted only here and there with a thin spray of cloud. The sound of a corn-crake on a dewy morning. The good smell of earth and warm summer rain. The silver-green leaves of a poplar growing just beside a shallow stream. A little girl, standing amid white daisies, surrounded by her flock of geese.

Later on they began to go into the villages to buy provisions or sometimes to eat a ready-cooked meal, which now seemed a rare luxury and almost an adventure. Amber worried a great deal about Nan and little Susanna, particularly after she found that there was plague in the country, too, but Bruce insisted that she must make herself believe that they were well and safe.

"Nan's a woman of good sense, and there's no one more loyal. If it became dangerous where they were she'd go somewhere else. Trust her, Amber, and don't make yourself miserable worrying."

"Oh, I do trust her!" she would say. "But I can't *help* worrying! Oh, I'll be so glad when I know they're well and safe!"

Everything that Amber saw now reminded her of Marygreen and her life there with Aunt Sarah and Uncle Matt. It was rich agricultural country, as was Essex, with prosperous enclosed farms, many orchards, quiet pretty little villages usually no more than two or three miles apart—though often, as she knew, so far as those who lived there were concerned it might as well have been two or three hundred miles. There were cottages of cherry brick with oak frames and thatched roofs that lay like thick blankets over them. Morning-glories and roses climbed the walls and clustered about the dormer windows. Pearl-grey doves perched softly cooing on the steep-slanted roof-tops, and sparrows ruffled themselves in the dusty roadway. It seemed to her now to mean peace and quiet and a kind of contentment which must exist nowhere else on earth.

She tried to tell him something of how she felt and added, "I never used to feel that way about it when I lived there—yet God knows I don't want to go back!"

He smiled at her tenderly. "You're growing older, darling."

Amber looked at him with surprise and resentment. "Old! Marry come up! I'm not so old! I'm not twenty-two yet!" Women began to feel self-conscious about age as soon as they reached twenty.

He laughed. "I didn't mean that you're growing old. Only that you're enough older you've begun to have memories—and memories are always a little sad."

She digested that thoughtfully, and gave a light sigh. It was just at gloaming and they were walking back to the Sapphire through a low lush river meadow. Nearby they could hear the castanet-like voice of a frog, and the stag-beetles buzzing noisily.

"I suppose so," she agreed. Suddenly she looked up at him. "Bruce—remember the day we met? I can shut my eyes and see you so plain—the way you sat on your horse, and the look you gave me. It made me shiver inside—I'd never been looked at like that before. I remember the suit you had on—it was black velvet with gold braid— Oh, the most wonderful suit! And how handsome you looked! But you scared me a little bit too. You still do, I think—I wonder why?"

"I'm sure I can't imagine." He seemed amused, for she often brought up such remnants of the past, and she never forgot a detail.

"Oh, but just think!" They were crossing a shaky little wooden bridge now, Amber walking ahead, and suddenly she turned and looked up at him. "What if Aunt Sarah hadn't sent me that day to take the gingerbread to the blacksmith's wife! We'd never even have known each other! I'd still be in Marygreen!"

"No you wouldn't. There'd have been other Cavaliers going through—you'd have left Marygreen whether you'd ever seen me or not."

"Why Bruce Carlton! I would not! I went with you because it was fate—it was in the stars! Our lives are planned in heaven, and you know it!"

"No, I don't know it, and you don't either. You may think it, but you don't feel it."

"I don't know what you're talking about." They were across the bridge, strolling along side by side again, and Ambers switched petulantly at the grass with a little twig she had picked up. Suddenly she flung it away and faced him squarely, her hands catching at his arms. "Don't you think that we were meant for each other, Bruce? You *must* think so—now."

"What do you mean, 'now'?"

"Why—after everything we've been through together. Why else did you stay and take care of me then? You could have gone away when you were well and left me alone—if you hadn't loved me."

"My God, Amber, you take me for a greater villain than I am. But of course I love you. And in a sense I agree with you that we were meant for each other."

"In a sense? What do you mean by that?"

His arms went about her, the fingers of one hand combing through the long glossy mass of her hair, and his mouth came down close to hers. "This is what I mean," he said softly. "You're a beautiful woman—and I'm a man. Of course we were meant for each other."

But, though she did not say anything more about it just then, that was not what she wanted to hear. When she had stayed with him in London, at the risk of her own life, she had not thought of or expected either gratitude or return. But when he had stayed with her, had cared for her as tenderly and devotedly as she had for him—she believed then that he had changed, and that now he would marry her. She had waited, with growing apprehension and misgiving, for him to speak of it—but he had said nothing.

Oh, but that's not possible! she told herself again and again. If he loved me enough to do all that—he loves me enough to marry me. He thinks I know he will as soon as we're where we can—that's why he hasn't said anything— He thinks I—

But not all her brave assurances could still the doubts and torment that grew more insistent with each day that passed. She began to realize that, after all, nothing had changed—he still intended to go on with his life just as he had planned it, as though there had never been a plague.

She wanted desperately to talk to him about it but, afraid of blighting the harmony there was between them—almost perfect for the first time since they had known each other—she forced herself to put it off and wait for some favourable opportunity.

Meanwhile the days were going swiftly. The holly had turned scarlet; loaded wagons stood in the orchards, and the air was fragrant with the fresh autumn smell of ripe red apples. Once or twice it rained.

They left the boat at Abingdon and stayed overnight in a quiet old inn. The host and hostess finally accepted their certificates-of-health, but with obvious misgivings and only because Bruce gave them five extra guineas—though their money supply was now almost gone. But the next morning they hired horses and a guide and set out for Almsbury's country home, some sixty miles away. They followed the main road to Gloucester, spent the night there and went on the next day. When they reached Barberry Hill in mid-morning Amber was thoroughly exhausted.

Almsbury came out of the house with a yell. He swung her up off her feet and kissed her and pounded Bruce on the back, telling them all the while how he had tried to find them both— never guessing that they were together—how scared he had been, and how glad he was to have them there with him, alive and well. Emily seemed just as pleased, though considerably less exuberant, and they went inside together.

Barberry Hill had not been the most important country possession of the Earls of Almsbury, but it was the one he had been able to have restored to the family. Though less imposing than Almsbury House in the Strand, it had a great deal more charm. It was L-shaped, built of red brick, and lay intimately at the foot of a hill. Part of it was four stories high, part only three; there was a pitched slate roof with many gables and dormer-windows and several spiralling chimneys. All the rooms were decorated with elaborate carvings and mouldings, the ceilings were crusted with plaster-work as ornamental as the frosting on a Twelfth Day cake, the grand staircase was a profusion of late Elizabethan carving and there were gay gorgeous colours everywhere.

Almsbury immediately sent a party of men to find Nan Britton and bring her there. And when Amber had rested and put on one of Lady Almsbury's gowns—which she did not think had any style at all and which she had to pin in at the sides—she and Bruce went to the nursery. They had not seen their son for more than a year, not since the mornings when they had met at Almsbury House, and he had grown and changed considerably.

He was now four and a half years old, tall for his age, healthy and sturdy. His eyes were the same grey-green that Bruce's were and his dark-brown hair hung in loose waves to his shoulders, rolling over into great rings. He had been put into adult clothes —a change which was made at the age of four—and they were in every way an exact replica of Lord Carlton's, even to the miniature sword and feather-trimmed hat.

These grown-up clothes for children seemed symbolic of the hot-house forcing of their lives. For he was already learning to read and write and do simple arithmetic; riding-lessons had begun, as well as instruction in dancing and deportment. Before long there would be more lessons: French, Latin, Greek, and Hebrew; fencing, music, and singing. Childhood was brief, manhood came early, for life was an uncertain risk at best. There was no time to be lost.

When they entered the nursery little Bruce, with Almsbury's

eldest son, was seated at a tiny table studying his horn-book. But obviously he knew that his parents were coming to see him, for just as they opened the door he looked around with a quick expectancy which suggested many previous eager glances in that direction. As the horn-book went clattering to the floor, he was off the chair and running toward them joyously: But instantly, at a sharp word from his nurse, he stopped, swept off his hat and bowed with great ceremony, first to Bruce and then to Amber.

"I'm glad to see you, sir. And, madame."

But Amber was not in awe of the nurse. She rushed forward, dropped to her knees and swooped him into her arms, covering his pink cheeks with passionate kisses. Tears glistened in her eyes and began to fall, but she was laughing with happiness. "Oh, my darling! My darling! I thought I would never see you again."

His arms were about her neck. "But why, madame? I was sure I'd see you both again one day."

Amber laughed and murmured quickly beneath her breath: "Damn the nurse! Don't call me madame! I'm your mother and that's what I'll be called!" They laughed together at that, he whispered "Mother," and then gave a quick half-apprehensive, half-defiant look over his shoulder to where the nurse stood watching them.

He was more reserved with Bruce and apparently felt that they were both gentlemen from whom such demonstrations were not expected. It was obvious, however, that he adored his father. Amber felt a pang of jealousy as she watched them but she scolded herself for her pettiness and was even a little ashamed. After an hour or so they left the nursery and started back down the long gallery toward their own adjoining apartments at the opposite end of the building.

All of a sudden Amber said: "It isn't right, Bruce, for him to live this way. He's a bastard. What's the use for him to learn to carry himself like a lord—when God knows how he'll shift once he's grown-up."

She looked up at him sideways, but his expression did not change and now, as they reached the door to her apartment, he opened it and they went in. She turned about quickly to face him, and knew at that instant he was about to say something which he expected would make her angry.

"I've been wanting to talk to you about this, Amber—I want to make him my heir—" And then, as a flash of hope went over her face, he hastily added: "In America no one would know whether he's legitimate or not—they'd think he was the child of an earlier marriage."

She stared at him incredulously, her face recoiling as though from a sudden cruel slap. "An earlier marriage?" she repeated softly. "Then you're married now."

"No, I'm not. But I'll marry someday—"

"That means you still don't intend to marry me."

He paused, looking at her for a long moment, and one hand started to move in an involuntary gesture, but dropped to his side again. "No, Amber," he said at last. "You know that. We've talked this all over before."

"But it's different now! You love me—you told me so yourself! And I know you do! You must! Oh, Bruce, you didn't tell me that to—"

"No, Amber, I meant it. I do love you, but—"

"Then *why* won't you marry me—if you love me?"

"Because, my dear, love has nothing to do with it."

"Nothing to do with it! It has everything to do with it! We're not children to be told by our parents who we'll marry! We're grown up and can do as we like—"

"I intend to."

For several seconds she stared at him, while the desire to lash out her hand and slap him surged and grew inside her. But something she remembered—a hard and glittering expression in his eyes—held her motionless. He stood there watching her, almost as though waiting, and then at last he turned and walked out of the room.

Nan arrived a fortnight later with Susanna, the wet-nurse, Tansy and Big John Waterman. They had spent the four months going from one village to another, fleeing the plague. Despite everything only one cart-load had been stolen; almost all of Amber's clothes and personal belongings were intact. She was so grateful that she promised Nan and Big John a hundred pounds each when they returned to London.

Bruce was enchanted with his seven-months-old daughter. Susanna's eyes were no longer blue but now a clear green and her hair was bright pure golden blonde, not the tawny colour of her mother's. She did not very much resemble either Bruce or Amber but she gave every promise of being a beauty and seemed already conscious of her destiny, for she flirted between her fingers and giggled delightedly at the mere sight of a man. Almsbury, teasing Amber, said that at least there could be no doubt as to her mother's identity.

The very day of Nan's arrival Amber put off Emily's unbecoming black dress and, after considerable deliberation, selected one of her own: a low-bosomed formal gown of copper-coloured satin with stiff-boned bodice and sweeping train. She painted her face, stuck on three patches, and for the first time in many months Nan dressed her hair again in long ringlets and a high twisted coil. Among her jewellery she found a pair of emerald ear-rings and an emerald bracelet.

"Lord!" she said, surveying herself in the mirror with pleased satisfaction. "I'd almost forgot what I look like!"

She was expecting Bruce back soon—he and Almsbury had gone out to hunt—and though she was eager to have him see her at her best again she was a little apprehensive too. What would he say about her putting off mourning so soon? A widow was expected to wear plain unadorned black with a long veil over her hair all the rest of her life—unless she married again.

At last she heard the door slam in the next room and his boots crossed the floor. He called her name and then almost immediately appeared in the doorway, pulling loose the cravat at his neck. She was watching for him with her eyes big and uncertain, and she broke into a delighted smile as he stopped abruptly and then gave a long low whistle. She spread her fan and turned slowly around before him.

"How do I look?"

"How do you look! Why, you vain little minx, you look like an angel—and you know it!"

574

She ran toward him, laughing. "Oh, do I, Bruce!" But suddenly her face sobered and she looked down at her fan, beginning to count the sticks. "D'you think I'm wicked to leave off mourning so soon? Oh, of course," she added hastily, with a quick upward glance, "I'll wear it when I get back to town. But out here in the country with no one to see me or know if I'm a widow or not—it doesn't matter out here, does it?"

He bent and gave her a brief kiss, grinning, and though she searched his face carefully she could not be sure what he was thinking. "Of course it's not wicked. Mourning, you know, is done with the heart—" Lightly he touched her left breast.

After an unusually hot and arid summer the weather changed swiftly at the end of October. Violent rainstorms came in rapid succession and by the middle of the month there were hard frosts. The two men went out to ride or hunt in spite of it, though usually the powder became wet and they seldom shot anything. Amber spent most mornings in the nursery. Other times Bruce and Almsbury played billiards while she watched, or the three of them played cards or amused themselves by making anagrams out of their own names or someone else's—for the most part they turned out to be unflattering. Emily seldom joined in these pastimes for she was an old-fashioned housewife who preferred to oversee each smallest detail of cooking and cleaning, rather than leave it to a steward as many great ladies had begun to do. Amber did not see how she could tolerate spending all her hours in the nursery, the still-room, or the kitchen, but there was no doubt the three of them were gayer when Emily was not present.

Ordinarily Barberry Hill was overflowing with guests at that time of year for both the Earl and her Ladyship had vast numbers of relatives, but the plague was keeping everyone at home and only occasionally some neighbour came to call. More encouraging news, however, had begun to come from London. The number of deaths was decreasing, though it was still over a thousand a week. Many who had left town when fewer than a hundred died in one week were now going back. The streets were full of beggars covered with plague sores, but no more corpses were to be seen and the dead-carts came only at night.

A feeling of optimism was beginning to prevail again for they thought that the worst was over.

Bruce was growing restless. He was worried about what had happened to his ships and the prizes he had brought; he wanted to go back to London and, as soon as possible, to sail again for America. Amber asked when he thought that he would leave.

"As soon as I can. Whenever it seems likely that men will be willing to sign on again."

"I want to go back with you."

"I don't think you'd better, Amber. I'm going to Oxford first—the Court's there now and I want to see the King about a grant of land. The weather's terrible and I can't take the time to travel by coach—and once I get to London I'll be so busy I wouldn't be able to see you. Stay here with Almsbury another month or two—the city isn't safe yet."

"I don't care," she insisted stubbornly, "whether it's safe or not. If I can see you at all I'm going. And it won't hurt me to ride horseback that far, I'll warrant you."

But one noon as she stood at her windows looking out over the grey-skied rolling hills that swept away south, watching a party of horsemen approach the house, a strange feeling of dread and suspicion began to take hold of her. Before it was possible actually to distinguish the individual horses or their riders she was sure that Bruce was not among them. Suddenly she turned, swooping up her skirts, and rushed out of the room, along the hallway and down the great staircase. She arrived at the bottom and confronted Almsbury just as he entered the hall.

"Where's Bruce!"

Almsbury, who wore a long riding-cloak and high leather boots, his brown hair wet and the feathers on his hat soaking and draggled, looked at her uneasily. "He's gone, Amber. Back to London." He took off his hat and knocked it against his knee.

"Gone? Without me!" She stared at him, first in surprise and then with growing anger. "But I was going, too! I told him I was going!"

"He said that he told you he was going alone."

576

"Blast him!" she muttered, and then all at once she turned and started off. "Well, he's not! I'm going too!"

Almsbury shouted her name but she paid no attention and ran on, back up the stairs again. Half-way up she passed someone she had not seen before, a well-dressed elderly man, but though he turned and looked after her she ignored him and ran on. "Nan!" she cried violently, bursting into her rooms again. "Pack some clothes for me! I'm going to London!"

Nan stared at her and then looked toward the windows where the rain was furiously beating and splashing and the upper branches of an elm tree could be seen writhing with the wind. "To London, mam? In this weather?"

"Damn the weather! Pack my clothes I tell you! Anything, I don't care! Throw it in!"

She was yanking loose the bows that fastened the front of her bodice and now she tore the gown down and stepped out of it, kicking it to one side as she went to the dressing-table and began to slam her bracelets onto its polished wood surface. Her face was glowering and her teeth clenched furiously.

Damn him! she thought. At least he could let me have that much! I'll *show* him! *I'll* show him!

Nan scurried about, pulling gowns and smocks and shoes off hooks and out of drawers. Both women were so occupied they did not see Almsbury open the door and come in until he spoke.

"Amber! What in the devil are you doing?"

"Going to London! What d'ye think?"

She did not even glance at him but was jerking the bodkins out of her hair, which tumbled down her back. He crossed over swiftly and his face appeared behind her in the mirror. She gave him a truculent glare, daring him to try to stop her.

"Leave the room, Britton! Do as I say!" he added, as Nan hesitated, looking at Amber. "Now listen to me! Do you want to make a fool of yourself? He doesn't *want* you in London. He doesn't think it's safe and he doesn't care to be troubled with you—he's going to be busy."

"I don't care what he wants. I'm going anyway. Nan!" She

whirled about, shouting the girl's name, but Almsbury caught her wrist and brought her up shortly.

"You're *not* going—if I have to tie you to a bedpost! It *is* possible to have plague twice, you know. If you had any sense you wouldn't want to go back—for nothing. Bruce left because he had to. His ships may be ruined or plundered by now and if they haven't been they would be soon after the town began to fill again. Now, darling, for God's sake—be sensible. He'll be back again some day; he said he would."

Amber looked up at him, her lower lip still rolled out stubbornly, but tears were in her eyes and beginning to slide over her cheeks. She sniffled but did not protest when he put his arms about her. "But why," she asked him at last, and caught her breath on a sob, *"why* didn't he even say 'goodbye' to me? Last night—why, last night was just like always—"

He pressed her head to his chest and stroked her hair. "Just maybe, sweetheart—it was because he didn't want to quarrel."

Amber gave a mournful little wail and burst into tears at that, her arms going about his neck for comfort. "I—I wouldn't have quarrelled! Oh, Almsbury! I love him so much!"

He let her cry, holding her close, until at last she began to grow quiet again. Then he took out a handkerchief and gave it to her. "Did you notice the gentleman coming downstairs as you were going up?"

She blew her nose, wiped at her red eyes and tear-stained face. "No. I didn't. Why?"

"He asked me who you were. He thinks you're the most beautiful woman he's ever seen."

Vanity crept through her grief. "Does he?" She sniffled a few times, looking down at the handkerchief as she twisted it in her hands, and then blew her nose again. "Who is he?"

"He's Edmund Mortimer, Earl of Radclyffe—one of the oldest and most honoured families in England. Come on, darling, it's time for dinner. Let's go down—he wants to be presented."

Amber sighed, turning away. "Oh, I don't care if he does. I don't want to know anyone else."

Almsbury gave her an ingratiating smile. "You'd rather stay in your room and mope, is that it? Well, do as you like, but he'll be mighty disappointed. To tell you the truth, I think he might make you a proposal."

"A proposal! What the devil would I want with *another* husband? I'm *never* going to get married again!"

"Not even to an earl—" said his Lordship thoughtfully. "Well, my dear, do as you like. But I thought I heard you say something to Bruce the other night like: 'Just wait till I'm Countess of Puddle-dock.' Now here's your chance—are you going to throw it away?"

"I suppose you told the old dotard how rich I am."

"Well, now—perhaps I did. I don't remember."

"Oh, well, then, I'll come down. But I'm not going to marry him. I don't care whether I ever get to be a countess or not!"

But she was already thinking: If the next time Bruce saw me I was her Ladyship, Countess of Radclyffe, he'd take some notice of *that*, I'll warrant you!

He's only a baron!

CHAPTER THIRTY-NINE

DINNER WAS POSTPONED a half-hour, while Amber dressed again and removed the traces of tears from her face. Then, throwing a fur-lined cloak about her shoulders, she went to the dining-parlour. It was always necessary to wear cloaks when passing from one room to another during the winter, but this year it was so cold that they must be worn all the time.

Almsbury and his guest stood before the fireplace. Lady Almsbury sat near them, working on a piece of needlepoint. The two men turned, Almsbury made the introductions, and as Amber curtsied her eyes swept critically over the Earl of Radclyffe. Her first reaction was quick: How ugly he is! She decided immediately that she would not marry him, and they sat down to dinner.

Edmund Mortimer was fifty-seven and looked at least five years older. He was perhaps three inches taller than Amber, but because she had on high-heeled shoes they were exactly of a height. Slight and delicate, with narrow shoulders and thin legs, his head seemed too large for his fragile frame and the luxuriant periwig he wore increased the effect of disproportion. His face was severe and ascetic in expression and as he spoke decaying yellow teeth showed between his tight-pressed lips. Only his clothes met with her approval, for they were the most exquisite, the most perfect in every detail, that she had ever seen. And his manners, though cold and not engaging, were likewise impeccable.

"His Lordship," said Almsbury, as they began to eat, "has been travelling on the Continent these three years past."

"Oh?" said Amber politely. She was not hungry and she wished that she had stayed in her own room. She had to swallow food to force down the aching lump that rose in her throat. "But why come back now, of all times—with the plague among us?"

His voice, as he answered her, was precisely clipped, as though the man who spoke would tolerate no carelessness. "I am no longer young, madame. Sickness and death do not frighten me any more. And my son is to be married within the fortnight—I came back for the ceremony."

"Oh." That was all she could think of to say.

It did not seem to her that he was so interested in her as Almsbury had said and since she had come half to be flattered by a man's goggle-eyed staring, she was disappointed and bored. She paid little attention to the rest of the conversation and as soon as dinner was over escaped back to her room.

The apartments she had shared with Bruce for more than a month were dreary and deserted now, and the fact that he had so recently been there made them even lonelier. She wandered forlornly from one room to another, finding something to remind her of him everywhere she looked. There was the book he had been reading last, lying opened in a big chair. She picked it up and glanced at it: Francis Bacon's "History of Henry VII." There was a pair of mud-stained boots, two or three soiled white-linen shirts which carried the strong male smell of his sweat, a hat he had worn while hunting.

Suddenly Amber dropped to her knees, the hat crushed in her hands, and burst into shaking sobs. She had never felt more lonely, hopeless and despairing.

Two or three hours later when Almsbury gave a knock at the door and then came in she was stretched out on her stomach on the bed, head buried in her arms, no longer crying but merely lying there—listless.

"Amber—" He spoke to her softly, thinking that she might be asleep.

She turned her head. "Oh. Come in, Almsbury."

He sat down beside her and she rolled over on her back and lay looking up at him. Her hair was rumpled and her eyes red and swollen, her head ached vaguely but persistently, and her expression was dull and apathetic. Almsbury's ruddy face was now serious and kindly, and he bent to kiss her forehead.

"Poor little sweetheart."

At the sound of his voice the tears welled irresistibly again, rolling out the corners of her eyes and streaking across her temples. She bit at her lower lip, determined to cry no longer; but for several moments they were quiet and one of Almsbury's square hands stroked over her head.

"Almsbury," she said at last. "Did Bruce leave without me because he's going to get married?"

"Married? Good Lord, not that I know anything about! No, I swear he didn't."

She gave a sigh and looked away from him, out the windows. "But someday he'll get married—and he says when he does he wants to make Bruce his heir." Her eyes came back again, slightly narrowed now and suddenly hard with resentment. "He won't marry *me*—but he'll make my son his heir. A pretty fetch!" Her mouth twisted bitterly and she gave a kick of her toe at the blankets.

"But you will let him, won't you? After all, it would be best for the boy."

"No, I won't let him! Why should I? If he wants Bruce, he can marry me!"

Almsbury continued to watch her for several seconds, but

then all at once he changed the subject. "Tell me: What's your opinion of Radclyffe?"

She made a face. "A nasty old slubber-degullion. I hate him. Anyway, he didn't seem so mightily smitten by me. Why, he scarcely gave me a glance, once he'd made his leg."

He smiled. "You forget, my dear. He belongs to another age than ours. The Court of the first Charles was a mighty formal and discreet place—ogling wasn't the fashion there, no matter how much a gentleman might admire a lady."

"Is he rich?"

"He's very poor. The Wars ruined his family."

"Then that's why he thinks I'm so handsome!"

"Not at all. He said you're the finest woman he's seen in two-score years—you remind him, he says, of a lady he once knew, long ago."

"And who can that be, pray?"

Almsbury shrugged. "He didn't say. Some mistress he had, most likely. Men are never favourably reminded of their wives."

She saw the Earl of Radclyffe again the next day at dinner, but now there were two more guests: a cousin of Emily's, Lady Rawstorne, and her husband. Lord Rawstorne was a big man— about Almsbury's height, but much heavier—with a boisterous laugh, a red face and a smell of stables about him. The moment he saw Amber he seemed delighted and throughout dinner he stared across the table at her.

His wife looked sour and discontented, as though she had watched such behaviour for a great many years and was not even yet resigned to it. And the Earl of Radclyffe, though he elaborately ignored Rawstorne and his staring at Mrs. Dangerfield, was clearly annoyed. For the most part he sat with his eyes on his plate, and regarded the food with the expression of one to whom it could mean only future distress. Amber was amused by both of them and found a sort of mischievous pleasure in flirting with Lord Rawstorne. She pouted her lower lip, slanted her eyes at him, and moved her body provocatively. But it was not a very entertaining diversion. Loneliness and boredom continued to mock at her.

As she left the table she saw Rawstorne begin to edge around from one side, trying to avoid his wife's glowering signals and get to her, but before he could do so Radclyffe was at her side. He bowed, stiffly as a marionette whose joints had not been well oiled for years.

"Your servant, madame."

"Your servant, sir."

"Perhaps you recall, madame, that yesterday Lord Almsbury mentioned I had brought several objects of interest and value with me from abroad? Some of those things were in my coach and in the hope that you might honour me by looking at them I had a case unpacked last night. Would you be so kind, madame?"

Amber was about to refuse but decided that she might as well do that as go back upstairs and sit alone, and probably cry again. "Thank you, sir. I'd like to see them."

"They're in the library, madame."

The great room was dark, oak-panelled and but dimly lighted. Before the fireplace there was a large table spread with several articles and next to it was a torchère; the shelves of books stood far away in the spreading gloom. Almsbury was no ardent scholar and the place smelled unaired and musty.

Amber approached the table without interest, but immediately her indifference turned to delight, for it was covered with a great number of rare and delicate and precious things. There was a small white marble statue, a Venus with the head broken off; a blackamoor carved out of ebony with an enamelled skirt of ostrich feathers and real jewels in the turban and around the thick muscular arms; a heavy gold frame, exquisitely wrought; tortoise-shell jewel-boxes and diamond buttons and dainty blown-glass perfume-bottles. Each was perfect of its kind and had been selected by a man whose taste was never-failing.

"Oh, how beautiful! Oh! Look at this!" She turned to him eagerly, eyes sparkling. "Can I pick it up if I'm careful?"

He smiled, bowed again. "Certainly, madame. Please do."

Forgetting that she did not like him she began to ask him questions. He told her where he had found each one, what its history was, through whose hands it had passed before it had

583

come to him. She liked the story of the blackamoor best:

"Two hundred years ago there was a Venetian lady—very beautiful, as all ladies in legends are—and she owned a gigantic black slave whom her husband believed to be a eunuch. But he was not and when the lady bore his black child she had the infant killed and a white one put in its place. The midwife, from some motive of jealousy or revenge, told the husband of his wife's infidelity and he killed the slave before her eyes. She had the ebony statue made, secretly of course, in her lover's memory."

At last, when there was no more to be said, she thanked him and turned away with a sigh. "They're all wonderful. I envy you, my lord." She could never see a beautiful thing without longing violently to possess it.

"Won't you allow me, madame, to make you a gift?"

She turned swiftly. "Oh, but your Lordship! They must mean a great deal to you!"

"They do, madame, I admit it. But your own appreciation is so keen I know that whichever you choose will be loved as much by you as it could be by me."

For several moments she stared at them critically, determined to make the one choice she would not regret, deciding first on one and then another. She stood bent forward, tapping her fan on her chin, wholly absorbed. Slowly she became aware that he was watching her and gave him a swift sidelong glance, for she wanted to catch his expression before he could change it. As she had expected he glanced hastily away, refusing to meet her eyes, but nevertheless the look she had surprised on his face made the frank good-natured lust of Lord Rawstorne seem naïve and artless. The repugnance she had felt the first moment of their meeting came back again, stronger than ever. What is there about this old man? she thought. He's strange—he's strange and nasty.

She picked up the blackamoor—which was very heavy and about two feet high—and turned to the Earl. Once more he presented to her a face cool and polite, austere as an anchorite's.

"This is what I want," she said.

"Certainly, madame." She thought that a hint of a smile

lurked somewhere about his thin mouth, but she could not be sure. Had her choice amused him, or was it only her imagination, perhaps a trick of the lighting? "But if you are of a timid nature, madame, perhaps another choice would be more comfortable to you. There's an old superstition the statue's cursed and brings ill-luck to whoever owns it."

She glanced at him sharply, momentarily alarmed, for she was passionately superstitious and knew it. But she decided instantly that he did not want to part with the blackamoor after all and was trying to scare her into making a less valuable choice. She would have kept it now no matter what the curse might be and her eyes glittered defiance.

"Pooh, my lord! That's a tale to scare children and old ladies! But it doesn't scare me! Unless you have some objection—I'll take this."

He bowed again and this time she knew that he was smiling, ever so faintly. "I protest, madame. I have no objections at all —and I knew that you were a person of too much wit to be alarmed by such foolishness."

The next day Radclyffe was gone. Three days later a letter came for Amber. She showed it to Almsbury that same morning when he came in to talk to her as Nan was brushing her hair. The ebony blackamoor stood beside the dressing-table.

Almsbury grinned. "So the old goat finds that his thoughts return to you as to any creation of perfect beauty."

Amber stuck a patch at the left side of her mouth. "Since I've become a rich widow I find my attractions have increased a hundredfold."

"Only on the score of marriage, sweetheart. You've always had attractions enough for a dozen other women—but in the way of the world a pretty face without money must go abegging for honest suitors. Now you're rich, you can take your pick from a dozen." He stood up and leaned close enough so that his next words could not be overheard by the maids in the room. "If I weren't married I'd make you a proposal myself." Amber laughed gaily, thinking that he was joking.

He bent down then and as he kissed her cheek he whispered in her ear. She murmured an answer, they exchanged a wink in the mirror and he went out. Lord Carlton formed the pivotal point for their mutual affection: Amber liked Almsbury better for being Bruce's friend; he liked her better for being his Lordship's mistress and mother of his children. But not one of the three considered it either strange or disloyal that in Carlton's absence the Earl sometimes made love to her.

Only a few days later she heard from Radclyffe again. He sent her a gilded Florentine mirror with a very wide frame, carved in lavish scrolls like the swirl of ostrich plumes. The accompanying note said that this mirror had once reflected the image of the loveliest woman in Italy, but he hoped it might now reflect the most beautiful face in Europe. In less than a week there arrived a basket of oranges—a great rarity now with the war and intense cold—and hidden among them was a topaz necklace.

"He must intend marrying me," said Amber to the Earl. "No man makes such valuable presents unless he expects to get 'em back again."

Almsbury laughed. "I think you're right. And if he does make you a proposal—what about you? Will you accept?"

Amber gave a sigh and a shrug. "I don't know. It's no use being rich, unless you've got a title too." She made a face. "But I hate that stinking old buck-fitch."

"Then marry a young man."

She gave him a glance of indignation. "Why, I'd rather be buried alive than marry one of your hectoring Frenchified Covent Garden fops! I know well enough what that means. They get you with child and send you off to the country to breed—while *they* stay in London to play the town-bull and spend all your portion on actresses and 'Change women. No thanks, not for me. I've seen enough of that to learn my lesson. If I've got to marry someone to get a title I'd rather marry an old man I hate than a young one I hate. At least there's a sooner prospect of freedom that way."

The Earl burst into hearty laughter. Amber looked at him in surprise and some annoyance. "Well—my lord? What makes you so hysterical, pray?"

"You do, sweetheart. I swear no one would ever guess to

hear you talk that six years ago you were a simple country-wench and so virtuous you slapped my face for making you an honest offer of my affections. I wonder what's happened to her —that innocent pretty girl I saw on the Marygreen common?" His voice and eyes turned a little wistful at the last.

Amber was petulant; why shouldn't he be satisfied with the way she was now? She liked to think of Almsbury as one man who accepted her exactly as she was, liked her and approved of everything she said and did. "I don't know," she said crossly. "She's gone now—if she ever existed at all. She couldn't last long in London."

He gave her hand a quick friendly grasp. "No, darling, she couldn't. But seriously, I think it would be a mistake for you to marry Radclyffe."

"Why? You suggested it yourself to begin with."

"I know. But I only wanted to make you think about something besides Bruce. In the first place, he's deep in debt. It might take half your inheritance to get him out."

"Oh, I've got that all planned. I'll have the contract drawn to let me retain management of my own funds."

Almsbury shook his head. "That'll never do. He wouldn't marry you with any such arrangement as that—any more than you'd marry him if he was to retain sole use of his title. No, if you marry Radclyffe you've got to sign over your money to him. But do you think you could tolerate living in the same house with him—not to mention sleeping in the same bed?"

"Oh, as for that! In London I won't know he's about. I'll spend all my days at Court and maybe some of my nights, too." Her mouth turned up significantly at one corner; she had never completely abandoned her earlier ambition of being his Majesty's mistress—and whenever Bruce Carlton was gone the prospect glittered.

To be mistress of the King, a great lady, feared and envied and admired. To be stared and pointed at in the streets, watched in the galleries of the Palace, bowed and truckled to in the Drawing-Rooms. To be begged for favours, fawned upon for a smile—to hold the power of success or failure over dozens, even hundreds, of men and women. That was the summit of ambition—higher than the Queen, mightier than the Chancellor, greater than any nobly born woman in the land. And if she could once be presented at Whitehall, have the right and privilege of the royal apartments, see him day after day— Amber had no doubt that she could occupy the place which Castlemaine was said to be rapidly losing.

All those things were in her mind when—just a few days after Christmas—she accepted the Earl of Radclyffe's proposal of marriage.

It came after a boresome week of impatient waiting on her part, for though she had been so scornful of him at first and still was, the more she thought about it the more she wanted to become a countess. And marriage with him did not seem any formidable price to pay for the honour. He had come back to Barberry Hill for the avowed purpose of "paying his compliments to Mrs. Dangerfield," but he did very little of that or anything else which seemed to Amber like courting. She could not even catch him looking at her again as he had that day in the library.

The day before he was to return to his own home some thirty miles north, they sat alone in the gallery playing a game of trick-track. The gallery, on the second floor of the house, was an immense room which ran along two sides of the courtyard. It was massed with deep-set diamond-paned windows, on the panelled walls were dozens of portraits, and the ceiling was painted light blue with great wreaths of gilt roses. Radclyffe wore his hat and both of them had on long fur-lined cloaks; a brazier of hot coals was set beside each of them, and an enormous log blazed in the fireplace. But in spite of all that they were uncomfortably cold.

Amber moved a peg in the board to change her score. Then she sat, staring absently at it and waiting for him to make the next play. At last, when several seconds had passed, she looked up. "Your move, my lord." He was watching her, very carefully, like a man studying a painting—not like a man looking at a woman.

"Yes," he said quietly, not taking his eyes from her. "I know." Amber returned his stare. "Madame—I am not unaware that it is a breach of propriety to ask for the hand of a lady who has been widowed only nine months. And yet my regard for you has reached that pitch I am prepared to fly in the face of all decorum. Madame, I ask you most solemnly —will you do me the honour to become my wife?"

Amber answered him immediately. "With all my heart, sir." She had thought from the first that since each knew what the other wanted it was absurd they must mince and simper like a couple of dancing-mice at Bartholomew Fair.

Again she thought that she caught the hint of a smile on his mouth, but could not be sure. "Thank you, madame. Your kindness is more than I deserve. I must return to London soon after the first of the year, and if you will go with me we can be married at that time. I understand that the sickness is now greatly abated and the town has begun to fill again."

He wanted, of course, to make certain her fortune had survived the Plague before he married her—but Amber was tired of the country and eager to get back herself.

They set out together in his coach on the second of January, bundled in furs and covered with fur-lined robes; it was so cold they could see their breath as they talked. The roads were so hard and frosty that it was possible to travel much faster than if it had been raining, but they had to stop that afternoon at four because the bouncing and jogging distressed his Lordship.

The marriage-contract had been signed at Barberry Hill and Amber supposed he would take advantage of the usual custom to lie with her that night. At eight o'clock, however, he bowed, wished her a good night, and retired to his own chamber. Amber and Nan watched him go, both of them staring with astonishment. Then as the door closed they looked at each other and burst into uncontrollable giggles.

"He must be impotent!" hissed Nan.

"I hope so!"

It was nightfall on the fifth day when they reached London. Amber had a feeling of dread as they approached the city, but as they rolled through the dark quiet streets it began to disappear. There were no dead-carts, no corpses, very few red crosses to be seen. Already the sloping mounds in the grave-

yards had been covered over with a coarse green vegetation—
the hundred thousand dead were effacing themselves. Taverns
were brightly lighted again and crowded, coaches teetered by
filled with gay young men and women, the sound of music
came from some of the houses.

It never really happened, she thought. It never *really* happened at all. She had a strange sense of discovery, as though
she had wakened from some terrible nightmare and found to
her relief that it had been only a dream.

Radclyffe House stood in Aldersgate Street above St. Anne's
Lane and just without the City gates. The street was a broad
one lined with large wide-spaced houses. Radclyffe told her
that it resembled an Italian avenue more than any other street
in London. It was the only place left so near the walls where
some of the great old families were still living.

The house had been virtually unoccupied for almost twenty-
five years, but for a few servants left there as caretakers, and
most of the windows were bricked up. Inside it was dark and
dusty, the furniture was shrouded in dirty white and nothing
had been brought up to date since it had been built eighty-five
years ago. One room led into another like a maze, and with the
exception of the grand staircase in the center of the house, all
passages and stair-wells were narrow and dark. Amber was relieved to find that the apartments to which she was shown had
at least been cleaned and dusted and aired, even though otherwise it was in no better condition than the rest.

Early the next morning she went to visit Shadrac Newbold
and found that he had kept all her money intact. (He also
told her that Lord Carlton had sailed for America two weeks
before.) When she told him that her money was safe Radclyffe
suggested that they be married as soon as all necessary arrangements could be made. As she knew, he was a Catholic—hence
it would be necessary to have two services performed, for a
Catholic ceremony could be declared null and void.

"I'd intended," said Amber, "to bespeak a gown of my dressmaker. I haven't got anything that's new—and I think she could
get one done in ten days or so."

"I don't think it would be safe, madame, as yet—the sickness is still too much with us. But if you would care to oblige me, I have a gown laid away I should be most happy to have you wear."

Somewhat surprised, wondering if he kept a wedding-gown about for unexpected marriages, Amber agreed. Certainly it seemed a simple harmless request.

Later in the day he came to her chamber, carrying in his arms a stiff white-satin gown, embroidered all over with tiny pearls, and as he shook it out she saw that there were deep sharp creases in it, as though it had been lying folded for a very long while. She realized then that it actually was an old gown; the white had turned creamy and the cut and style were many years out of fashion. The waist-line was high with a flaring peplum slashed in four places; the low square neck had a deep collar of lace and lace cuffs finished the long full sleeves; when the skirt opened down the front a petticoat of heavy silver cloth showed.

Radclyffe smiled at her puzzled expression. "As you can see —it isn't a new gown. But it is still beautiful, and I shall be grateful if you will wear it."

She reached out to take it. "I'm glad to, sir."

Later, she and Nan examined it carefully, speculating. "It must be two-score years old, or more," said Nan. "I wonder who wore it last?"

Amber shrugged. "His first wife, maybe. Or an old sweetheart. Someday I'll ask him."

To her surprise she found when she put it on that it fitted her very well, almost as if it had been made for her.

CHAPTER FORTY

"AMBER, COUNTESS OF RADCLYFFE," she said slowly, watching herself in a mirror, whereupon she wrinkled up her nose, snapped her fingers and turned away. "Much good it does me!"

They had been married just one week, but so far her life

was no more exciting than it had been when she was plain Mrs. Dangerfield—certainly far less so than when she was Madame St. Clare of His Majesty's Theatre. The weather was so cold that it was unpleasant to go out. The plague deaths for the past week had been almost a hundred, and neither King nor Court had yet returned to Whitehall. She stayed at home, scarcely left their suite of rooms—for the rest of the house continued in its dirt and gloom—and spent her time feeling bored and resentful. Was *this* what she had traded her sixty-six thousand pounds for! It seemed a bad bargain—dullness and a man she despised.

For now that she was his wife Radclyffe was a greater enigma than ever.

She saw him but little for he had a multitude of interests which he did not wish to share with her, nor she with him. Several hours of almost every day he spent in the laboratory which opened out of their bedroom, and for which new equipment was constantly arriving. When he was not there he was in the library or in the offices on the lower floor, reading, writing, going over his bills, and making plans for the remodelling and furnishing of the house. Though this was to be done, obviously, at Amber's expense, he never consulted her wishes in the matter or even told her what plans he had made.

They met, usually, just twice a day—at dinner, and in bed. Conversation at dinner was polite and arid, carried on chiefly for the benefit of the servants, but in bed they did not talk at all. The Earl could not, in any real sense, make love to her, for he was impotent and apparently had been for some time. More than that, he disliked her, frankly and contemptuously —even while she roused in him conflicting emotions of desire and some wild yearning toward the past which he could never explain. Yet he longed violently for complete physical possession—a longing at which he caught night after night, but never grasped, and it drove him down a hundred strange pathways of lust and helpless rage.

From the first morning they were enemies, but it was not until several days had gone by that mutual antipathy flared into open conflict. It was over a question of money.

He presented to her a neatly-written note addressed to Shadrac Newbold: "Request to pay to Edmund Mortimer, Earl of Radclyffe, or bearer, the sum of eighteen thousand pound," and asked her to sign it, for the money was still in her name, though he possessed the marriage-contract which put control of her entire fortune, except for ten thousand pounds, into his hands.

They were standing beside a small writing-table. As he gave her the paper he took a quill, dipped it in the ink-well and extended it to her. She glanced first at the note and then, with a little gasp of amazement, raised her head to look at him.

"Eighteen thousand pound!" she cried angrily. "My portion won't last long at this rate!"

"I beg your pardon, madame, but I believe that I am as well aware as you of the evanescent quality of money, and I have no more wish to dissipate your inheritance than you have to see me do so. This eighteen thousand pound is to pay my debts which, as I told you, have been accumulating for twenty-five years."

He spoke with the air of one who makes a reasonable explanation of a difficult problem to a child who is not very clever, and Amber gave him a furious glare. For a moment longer she hesitated, her mind stabbing here and there for a way out. But at last she snatched away the pen, thrust it into the ink-well and with a few swift strokes scrawled her name across the sheet, making specks of ink fly as she did so. Then she threw down the pen, left him and walked to the window where she stood staring down into the alley below—scarcely seeing two women fish-vendors who were bellowing curses and slapping at each other with huge flounders.

In a few moments she heard the door close behind him. Suddenly she whirled, grabbed up a small Chinese vase and threw it violently across the room. "Lightning blast him!" she cried. "Stinking old devil!"

Nan rushed forward as though she would rescue the pieces. "Oh, Lord, mam! Your Ladyship!" she corrected. "He'll be stark staring mad when he finds what you've done! He was mighty fond of that vase!"

"Yes! Well, I was mighty fond of that eighteen thousand pound, too! The varlet! I wish it had been his head! Lord! What a miserable wretch is a husband!" Impatiently she glanced around, looking for some diversion. "Where's Tansy?"

"His Lordship told me not to allow 'im in the room when you're in your undress."

"Oh, he did, did he? We'll see about that!" She rushed across the room and flung open the door, shouting. "Tansy! Tansy, where are you?"

For a moment she got no answer. Then, from behind a massive carved chest appeared his turban and shortly the little fellow's black and shining face. He blinked his eyes sleepily, and as he opened his mouth to yawn half his face seemed to disappear. "Yes'm?" he drawled.

"What the devil are you doing back there?"

"Sleepin', mam."

"What's the matter with your own cushion in here?"

"I ain' allowed no more in there, Mis' Amber."

"Who said so!"

"His Lordship done say so, mam."

"Well, his Lordship doesn't know what he's talking about! You come in here, and from now on do as I say—not as he says! D'ye hear?"

"Yes'm."

It was just after noon when Radclyffe returned, entering the room with his usual quietness, to find Amber sitting cross-legged on the floor playing at "in and in" with Tansy and Nan Britton. There were piles of coins before each of them and the women were laughing delightedly over Tansy's droll antics. Amber saw the Earl come in but ignored him, until he was standing directly beside her. Then Tansy looked slowly around, his black eyes rolling in their sockets, and Nan became apprehensively still. Amber gave him a careless glance, shaking the dice back and forth in her hand. Though it made her angry, her heart was beating a little harder—but she had told Nan he might as well find out once and for all that she was not to be governed.

"Well, m'lord? I hope your creditors are happy now."

594

"Truly, madame," said Radclyffe slowly, "you surprise me."

"Do I?" She rolled the four dice out onto the floor, watching the numbers as they turned up.

"Are you naïve—or are you wanton?"

Amber gave him a swift glance and heaved a deep bored sigh, brushed the dice aside and got to her feet, reaching down as she did so to take Tansy's wrist and lift him too. Suddenly there was a sharp stinging blow on the back of her hand that made the nerves tingle. Tansy gave a scared shriek, grabbing at her skirts for protection.

"Take your hands off that creature, madame!" Radclyffe's voice was even and cold, but his eyes glittered savagely. "Get out of this room!" He spoke to Tansy, who ran, not waiting to be told twice.

Radclyffe looked at Nan, who was staying close to Amber. "I told you, Britton, that that little beast was not to be in this room when her Ladyship was undressed. What have you—"

"It's not her fault!" snapped Amber. "She told me! I brought him in myself!"

"Why?"

"Why not? He's been with me two and a half years—he comes and goes in my apartments as he likes!"

"Perhaps he did. But he shall do so no longer. You are now my wife, madame, and if you have no sense of decency yourself I shall undertake the management of your conscience myself."

Furious, determined to hurt him with the one weapon she could depend upon, she said now, softly but with an unmistakable sneer: "Sure, my lord, you don't expect to be cuckolded by a mere child?"

The whites of Radclyffe's eyes turned red, and the purple veins of his forehead began to beat. Amber had an instant of real terror, for there was murderous rage in his face—but to her relief he seemed swiftly to control himself. He flicked an imaginary speck of dust from his immaculate lace cravat.

"Madame, I cannot imagine what sort of man your first husband must have been. I assure you that an Italian woman who spoke to her husband as you have just spoken to me would have the gravest cause to repent of her impertinence."

"Well, I'm not an Italian woman and this isn't Italy—it's England!"

"Where husbands, you think, have no rights." He turned away. "Tomorrow that black monkey will be gone."

Suddenly Amber regretted her insolence and bluster. For she realized that he was neither to be bullied like Black Jack Mallard or Luke Channell—nor wheedled like Rex Morgan or Samuel Dangerfield. He did not love her and he had no awe of her. And though it was fashionable to scorn husbands, she was quite aware that a wife, under the penal laws, was her husband's property and a chattel. He could use her at his will, or even murder her—particularly since he was rich and titled.

She changed her tone. "You won't hurt him?"

"I'm going to get rid of him, madame. I refuse to have him in my house any longer."

"But you won't hurt him, will you? Why, he's harmless and helpless as a puppy. It wasn't *his* fault he was in here! Oh, please let me send him to Almsbury! He'll take care of him. *Please,* your Lordship!" She hated begging him and hated him more for making her beg, but she was fond of Tansy and could not bear to think of his being hurt.

There was something on his face now almost like secret amusement, and his next words were her return for the cut she had given him. "It scarcely seems possible," he said slowly, "a woman could have so much fondness for a little black ape unless she had some use for him."

Amber shut her teeth and refused to be goaded. For a long moment they faced each other. At last she repeated: "Will you please send him to Almsbury's?"

He smiled faintly, pleased to have her in this humiliating predicament. "Very well. I'll send him tomorrow." The favour, though granted, was like a slap.

Amber's eyes lowered.

"Thank you, sir."

Someday, she was thinking, I'll slit your gullet, you damned old cannibal.

On the 1st of February Charles returned to Whitehall. There were deep snows on the ground, the church bells pealed out merrily, and at night great bonfires lighted the black winter sky, welcoming the King home. Her Majesty, however, and all the ladies had remained at Hampton Court. Castlemaine had recently given birth to another son; the Queen had miscarried again. And York was not speaking to his Duchess because he thought—or pretended to think—that she had been having an affair with handsome Henry Sidney.

Radclyffe went to wait upon the King, but Amber could not go to Court until the women returned, when she might be presented at a ball or some other formal occasion. However, having once paid his respects, Radclyffe did not go often to Whitehall. He was not the sort of man King Charles would take for a confidant and his religion barred him from ever holding an office. Furthermore, he had been too long away from Court. A new generation was setting the pace, and it was not the pace at which his own had moved. There was a new way of living, which he considered to be shallow, frivolous, lacking in grace or purpose. Most of the men he judged either knaves or fools or both and the women he thought a pack of empty-headed sluts. He included his wife in this category.

To Amber it seemed that time passed more slowly than ever before. She spent hours with Susanna, helping her learn to walk, building block castles and playing with her, singing her the dozens of nursery rhymes she remembered from her own childhood. She adored her—but she could not build a whole life around her. She longed for that great exciting world to which she had bought and paid her admission and which she might now enter proudly by the front door, not sneak into like a culprit through some back passageway. She was glad that Radclyffe was not interested in the gay life at the Palace, for that would leave her all the more free to enjoy it herself.

She wanted nothing so much as to get away from him. She felt as though he was casting some evil spell over her, for though she did not actually see him often he seemed to hang forever at her shoulder, to lurk in her mind—sombre and dreaded. Alone in the house as she was and with few diversions, everything that was said or done by either of them assumed a magnified importance. She mulled over each word spoken, each glance exchanged, every action, worrying it like a dog with a bone.

Once, out of boredom, she ventured into his laboratory.

She tried the door, found it open, and went in quietly, so as not to disturb him. Great stacks of books and manuscripts, recently sent down from Lime Park, were piled on the floor. There were several skulls, hundreds of jars and bottles, oil-lamps, pottery vessels of every shape and size—all the paraphernalia of alchemy. He was engaged, she knew, in the "Great Work"—a tedious, complicated process of seven years which had as its goal the discovery of the Philosopher's Stone—a search that was occupying some of the best minds of the age.

As she entered he stood before a table, his back to her, carefully measuring a yellow powder. She said nothing but walked toward him, her eyes going curiously over the loaded shelves and tables. All at once he gave a start and the bottle dropped from his hands.

Amber jumped backward to avoid spotting her gown. "Oh! I'm sorry."

"What are you doing in here!"

Her anger flared quickly. "I just came in to look! Is there any harm in that?"

He relaxed, smoothing the scowl from his face. "Madame, there are several places where women do not belong—under any circumstances at all. A laboratory is one of them. Pray don't interrupt me again. I've spent too many years and too much money on this project to have it ruined now by a woman's blundering."

After alchemy his greatest interest was his library, where he spent many hours of each day. For most of his life he had been collecting rare books and manuscripts, which he kept all in precise order, listing each one carefully and with a full account of everything that pertained to it. But his interest in books was more than mere pleasure in possession, in the look and feel of fine leather and old paper. He read them as well. There were Greek plays; Cicero's letters and the meditations of Marcus

Aurelius; Plutarch and Dante; Spanish plays; French philosophers and scientists—all in their original languages.

He did not forbid Amber the library, but it was not until they had been married for several weeks that she went into it. She had now become so desperate for entertainment that she was finally willing to read a book. But she had not realized that he was there and when she saw him, sitting beside the fireplace with a pen in his hand and a great volume lying open on the writing-table, she hesitated a moment, then started out again. He glanced up, saw her, and to her surprise got politely to his feet, smiling.

"Pray come in, madame. I see no reason why a woman may not enter a library—even though she isn't likely to find much in it to her taste. Or are you that freak of man and nature—a learned female?"

His mouth, as he spoke the last sentence, turned ironically down. In common with most men—no matter what their own intellectual interests and acquirements might be—he considered education for women absurd and even amusing. Amber ignored the jibe; it was not a subject on which she could be easily offended.

"I thought I might find something to pass the time with. Have you got any plays written in English?"

"Several. What do you prefer—Ben Jonson, Marlowe, Beaumont and Fletcher, Shakespeare?"

"It doesn't matter. I've acted 'em all." She knew that he did not like any reference to her acting and mentioned it frequently to annoy him. So far he had refused the bait.

But now he looked at her with obvious displeasure. "Madame, I had hoped your own sense of shame would prevent you from making any further reference to so unfortunate an episode in your life. Pray, let me hear no more about it."

"Why not? *I'm* not ashamed of it!"

"I am."

"It didn't keep you from marrying me!"

From across the dozen or so feet that separated them they eyed each other. Amber had long felt sure that if once she could break through his coldness and composure she would have him at her mercy. If I ever hit him, she had told herself a dozen times, I'd never be afraid of him again. But she could not quite bring herself to do it. She knew well enough that he had a strong streak of cruelty, a malevolent savagery—highly refined, as were all his vices. But she had not found any restraining rein of conscience or compassion. Therefore she hesitated out of fear, and hated herself for the cowardice.

"No," he agreed at last. "It didn't keep me from marrying you—for you had other attractions which I found it impossible to resist."

"Yes!" snapped Amber. "Sixty-six thousand of 'em!"

Radclyffe smiled. "How perceptive," he said, "for a woman!"

For several seconds she glared at him, longing violently to smash her fist into his face. She had the feeling that it would crumble, like a mummy's, beneath any hard and sudden blow, and she could picture his expression of horror as his face disintegrated. Suddenly she turned toward the book-shelves.

"Well, where are they! The plays!"

"On this shelf, madame. Take whatever you want."

She picked out three or four at random, hastily, for she was anxious to get away from him. "Thank you, sir," she said without looking at him, and started out. Just as she reached the door she heard his voice again.

"I have some very rare Italian books in which I believe you would be interested."

"I don't read Italian." She did not glance around.

"These may be appreciated without a knowledge of the language. They make use of the universal language of pictures."

She at once understood what he meant and paused, caught by her own strong interest in whatever was sensational or prurient. With a smile which clearly betrayed his cynical amusement at her curiosity he turned and took down from a shelf a hand-tooled leather-bound volume, laid it on the table, and stood waiting. She turned, and for a moment hesitated, watching him suspiciously as though this were some trap he had set for her. Then with a defiant lift of her chin she walked forward and opened the book, turned half-a-dozen pages on which was some unrecognizable printing and stopped with a gasp of surprise

600

at the first picture. It was beautifully done, painted by hand, and showed a young man and woman, both of them naked, straining in an ecstasy.

For a moment Amber looked at it, fascinated. Suddenly she glanced up and found him watching her, carefully, with the same expression she had seen that day in Almsbury's library. It disappeared again, as swiftly as the time before; and she picked up the book and started across the room.

"I thought you'd be interested," she heard him saying, "but pray handle it carefully. It's very old and very rare—a treasure of its kind."

She did not answer or look around but went on out of the room. She felt bewildered and angry, both pleasantly excited and disgusted. It seemed, somehow, that he had taken an advantage of her.

CHAPTER FORTY-ONE

THE QUEEN'S PRESENCE CHAMBER was packed with courtiers. The ladies were dressed in the full splendour of laces, spangled satins and velvets—garnet, carmine, primrose-yellow, dusky plum and flame—with shoulders and bosoms and forearms blazing with jewels. Hundreds of candles burnt in wall-sconces and torchères, and Yeomen of the Guard held smoking flambeaux. Their Majesties, seated on a dais canopied with crimson velvet swagged with gold and silver fringe, gave their hands to be kissed. At one end of the room waited the musicians, in varicoloured taffeta suits and with garlands about their heads, quietly tuning their instruments. There were no outsiders, no spectators thronging the gallery to watch, for the plague was persistent, the number of deaths fluctuating week by week. The women had only recently arrived from Hampton Court.

"Her Ladyship, the Countess of Castlemaine!" cried the usher.

"Baron Arlington! Lady Arlington!"

"Lord Denham! Lady Denham!"

"The Earl of Shrewsbury! The Countess of Shrewsbury!"

As each name was announced eyes swept toward the door, murmurs ran round the room behind raised fans, glances were exchanged; there were feminine giggles and sometimes the sound of a man's low chuckle.

"Damn me," remarked one young beau to another, "but I wonder my Lord Shrewsbury dares show his face in public. Her Ladyship has laid with half the men at Court and yet he's never once so much as offered to defend his honour."

"And why should he, pray?" retorted the other. "Any man who thinks his honour depends upon that of his wife is a fool."

"Look!" whispered a twenty-year-old fop, stroking at his elaborate curled wig, arranging the profusion of ruffles at his wrist. "York's ogling my Lady Denham again. I'll bet a hundred pound he lies with her before St. George's Day."

"I'll bet he doesn't. Her Ladyship's honest."

"Honest? Pshaw, Jack. There's not a woman in the world who's honest at all times and upon all occasions."

"She may not be honest," interrupted a Maid of Honour, "but she's watched mighty close."

"No woman's watched so close she can't give her husband a buttered-bun if once she sets her mind to it."

"Now where d'ye think Lady Arlington got that scurvy gown? She's always as far behind the fashion as a Lancashire squire's wife."

"She's a Dutchwoman, darling. How *should* she know how to dress?"

All of a sudden something unexpected happened—the usher announced two unfamiliar names: a new element had entered that close-knit little clique.

"The Earl of Radclyffe! The Countess of Radclyffe!"

The Earl of Radclyffe. Who the devil was he? Some moss-backed old dodderer left over from the last generation? And his countess—a platter-faced jade of at least five-and-forty, no doubt, who disapproved of the new manners as violently as any Puritan alderman's wife. They looked toward the doorway with a kind of bored curiosity. Then, as Lord and Lady Radclyffe appeared, surprise and shock flowed over the room, snapping them out of their lazy indifference. What was this! An *actress* being presented at Court!

"Jesus Christ!" remarked one gentleman to another. "Isn't that Amber St. Clare?"

"Why!" hissed an indignant lady. "That's that comedian—Madame What-d'ye-call who was at the Theatre Royal a couple of years ago!"

"Intolerable!"

Amber kept her head high and looked neither right nor left, but straight ahead toward the Queen. She had never felt so nervously excited, so eager, or so scared. I really am a countess, she had been telling herself all day. I've got as much right at Whitehall as anyone. I *won't* let 'em scare me—I won't! They're only men and women—they're no different from me or anyone else. But the truth was she did believe them different—here, at least, in Whitehall.

Her heart pounded so hard she was breathless, her knees trembled and her ears rang. The back of her neck ached. She kept looking straight toward the dais, but all she could see was a blur, as though she had her eyes open under water. Slowly she walked forward, her shaking fingers on Radclyffe's arm—down the long long corridor of faces toward the throne. She sensed the whispers, the smiles and smirks, the indignation, but actually she saw and heard nothing.

Radclyffe was splendidly dressed. His wig was white, his coat gold-and-purple brocade and his breeches pale-green satin; precious stones glittered on his sword-hilt. His sharp austere face forbade them to criticize his wife, defied them to remember that she had been an actress, demanded that they admire and accept her. And Amber's costume was as gorgeous as any in the room. Her long-trained gown was cloth-of-gold covered with stiff gold lace; a veil fell over her head and she wore her impressive collection of emeralds.

Now they had reached the throne. She spread a deep curtsy; he knelt. As Amber's lips touched the Queen's hand she raised her eyes, to find Catherine smiling, a gentle wistful smile that caught suddenly at her heart. She's kind, thought Amber, and she's unhappy, poor lady. But she's harmless. I like her, she decided.

But she dared not look at Charles. For here in his Palace, surrounded by all the pomp and circumstance of royalty, he was not the man she had visited secretly at night three years before. He was Charles II, by the Grace of God King of Great Britain, France, and Ireland. He was all the might and glory of England —and she knelt before him reverently.

Slowly she rose, moving backward, and went to stand among the throng that lined the approach to the dais. For several moments she remained half-dazed—but gradually the world began to expand again beyond herself and her feelings. She glanced to the right and found Buckhurst there, grinning down at her. Sedley looked over his shoulder with a wink. Immediately across from her was the magnificent Buckingham, and though she had not seen him since that night at Long's in the Haymarket, he smiled at her now and she was grateful. There were others: the two Killigrews, father and son; Dick Talbot and James Hamilton and several more young men who had frequented the tiring-room. And then all at once her eyes came to a stop. She was looking straight at Barbara Palmer. Castlemaine was watching her, her face speculative and predatory. For several seconds their stares held, and it was Amber who looked away first, with flaunting unconcern. She was beginning to realize that these people were not, after all, gods and goddesses—even here on Olympus.

Finally the presentations were over, the King gave a signal, and music swelled suddenly through the room. The ball opened with a coranto, danced by Charles and Catherine, the Duke and Duchess of York, and the Duke and Duchess of Monmouth. Only one couple performed at a time. The dance was a slow stately parade, full of attitudes, requiring a high degree of skill and gracefulness.

Amber watched the King with enchanted eyes.

How handsome he is, she thought, and how he walks and stands! Oh, I wonder if I dare ask him to dance! She knew that court etiquette required that ladies ask his Majesty to dance with them. I wonder if he still remembers me—no, of course he doesn't. How could he? That was three years and a half ago—God knows how many women there've been since then. But, oh, I want to dance—I don't want to stand here all evening by myself!

In her excitement she had altogether forgotten Radclyffe just beside her, silent and unmoving.

When the coranto ended Charles called for an allemande—in which several couples might participate—and as the floor began to fill Amber waited breathlessly, praying that she would be asked. She felt like a little girl at her first party, lost and forlorn, and she was beginning to wish herself safe at home again when—to her immense joy and relief—Lord Buckhurst made her a bow.

"M-m-may I have the pleasure of her Ladyship's company f-for this dance, my lord?" When sober, Buckhurst had a slight tendency to stutter, which caused him much annoyance.

Amber, with a start of surprise, remembered her husband then and turned to him with a look of apprehension. Suppose he should refuse! But he bowed as graciously as she could have hoped.

"Certainly, my lord."

Amber gave Buckhurst a dazzling happy smile and laid her hand on his arm. They walked out to join the other dancers, who stood in a double line halfway down the room. Charles and Castlemaine were the first couple and everyone followed their lead—a few steps forward and a few steps back, and then a pause. The figure of the dance offered them all opportunity for flirtation or talk.

Buckhurst smiled down at Amber. "H-how the devil did you get here?"

"Why, how d'ye think, sir? I'm a countess!"

"You told me, m-madame, that you weren't g-going to marry again."

She gave him a mischievous sparkling glance. "But I changed my mind. I hope your Lordship won't be inclined to hold a grudge."

"Good Lord, no! Y-you can't believe what a pleasure it is to s-s-see a new face here at Court. We're all s-so damned bored with one another."

"Bored!" cried Amber, shocked. "How *can* you be bored?"

But he was not able to answer, for by now they had reached the opposite end of the room where they parted, the gentlemen walking down one side and the ladies down the other. Each couple met again, executed a few steps which formed a square, and the dance ended. Buckhurst led her back to Radclyffe, thanked the Earl, and there left her. Amber knew at once that his Lordship was displeased, that he did not like to see her enjoying herself and attracting attention, completely forgetful of him.

"You're having a pleasant evening, madame?" he asked her coldly.

"Oh, yes, your Lordship!" She hesitated for an instant and then, doubtfully, "Are you?"

But he did not reply, for all at once the King was beside them, smiling. "It was most considerate of you, my lord," he said, "to marry a beautiful woman. There isn't a man here tonight who isn't grateful to you." Radclyffe bowed. "We're all of us tired of looking at the same faces and gossiping about the same people."

Charles smiled down at Amber who was looking at him, fascinated, powerfully aware of his charm, which was so strong it seemed to be an almost physical force. As his black eyes met hers her head began to spin dizzily. But she was even more aware that here before her, with the whole world looking on, stood the Monarch of Great Britain, smiling and complimenting her.

"You're very kind, Sire," said Radclyffe.

Amber made a curtsy, but her tongue was maddeningly tied. Her eyes, however, had almost too much eloquence—and Charles's face would always betray him in the presence of a pretty woman. Radclyffe watched them, his own face noncommittal as a mummy's.

But it was only for an instant, and then Charles turned back to address Radclyffe. "I understand, my lord, that you've recently acquired a very rare Correggio."

Radclyffe's cold blue eyes lighted, as always at any mention of his paintings. "I have, your Majesty, but it's not yet arrived. I'm expecting it very soon, however, and when it comes if you are interested I should be most happy to show it to you."

"Thank you, sir. I'd very much like to see it. And now, will you permit me, my lord?" Already he was extending his arm to Amber, and as Radclyffe gave his assent, bowing again, they walked out onto the floor.

Amber's whole being filled with fierce buoyant pride. It was as though she stood in a blazing light and all the rest of the world in darkness, its eyes focused upon her. The *King* had sought her out, had flouted convention, had asked her to dance! Before all these people, and here in his own Court! The dreary weeks she had spent alone with Radclyffe, his selfish brutal abortive lust, his unconcealed dislike and contempt—all vanished at once in her violent joy. The price had been paid and it was not too high.

The King called for the traditional merry old folk-dance: "Cuckolds All Awry," and just as they stood facing each other at the head of a long line, waiting for the music to begin, he said in an undertone: "I hope your husband won't suspect that choice of music. He doesn't look as though he'd wear a pair of horns gracefully."

"I don't know, Sire," she murmured, "whether he would or not."

"What?" asked Charles, in mock surprise. "Married two months and still a faithful wife?"

But the music began then and the dance was too lively to let them talk. He said nothing more and when it was over led her back to Radclyffe, thanked them both, bowed and was gone. Amber was too breathless from excitement and the exertion of the dance to speak. Just as she rose from her curtsy she saw the Duke of Buckingham approaching them.

God's my life! she thought, in half-hysterical delight. It's the truth! The men *are* tired of looking at the same faces!

She glanced hastily around the great room, caught dozens of pairs of eyes upon her—admiring eyes, amused eyes, hostile eyes. But what did it matter why they looked, or how they looked—

so long as they did look? Why! I'm the White Ewe tonight— she thought as she recalled an old Alsatian expression.

Everyone wanted to dance with her. York, Rochester, the popular lazy young fop and playwright, George Etherege, the Earl of Arran, the Earl of Ossory, Sedley and Talbot and Henry Jermyn. All the young and gay and handsome men of the Court flirted with her, paid her outrageous compliments, and asked her for assignations. The women exerted themselves to find fault with her gown, her coiffure, her manners—and reached the comfortable conclusion that, after all, she was new and she was rich and of course her reputation as an actress smelt so high it would have caught the attention of any male within the Verge. It was Amber's night of glorious triumph.

Suddenly into the midst of this perfect world a meteor fell, shattering everything. In one brief interval when she was returned to his side Radclyffe said quietly: "We are going home, madame."

Amber gave him a look of hurt surprise, for already beside her stood the Duke of Monmouth and James Hamilton. "Home, my lord?" she said incredulously.

Monmouth immediately took it up. "You're not thinking of going home, sir? Why, it's still early. And her Ladyship's the toast of the evening."

Radclyffe bowed, his thin lips set in a tight ungracious smile. "By your leave, your Grace. I am not a young man, and to me the hour is already late."

Monmouth laughed, a happy ingenuous laugh which could have offended no one. "Why, then, sir—why not let her Ladyship stay with us? I'll see her home myself—with a band of fiddlers and a score of links to light us."

"Oh, yes!" cried Amber, turning eagerly to her husband. "Let me do that!"

Radclyffe ignored her. "You jest, your Grace," he said stiffly, bowed, and then turned to Amber. "Come, madame."

Amber's golden eyes flamed rebelliously and for an instant she thought of refusing, but she did not quite dare. She curtsied to Monmouth and Colonel Hamilton, but kept her eyes down. When they stopped to bid his Majesty good-night shame and disappointment had made her face scarlet and tears stung her eyes. She could not look at him, though she heard the lazy amusement in his voice as he asked why they were leaving so early. Smiles and whispers followed them out of the room—for the impression created was that of a little girl who has misbehaved at her first party and is being led home by a disgruntled parent.

She did not speak until they were in the coach, jogging along King Street. Then she could restrain herself no longer. "Why did we have to come away so soon!" she demanded, and suddenly her voice broke with enraged disappointment.

"I am too old, madame, to enjoy many hours of such noise and confusion."

"That wasn't the reason!" she cried accusingly. "And you know it!"

She stared at him, though his face was in shadow, for the streets were dark and the moon showed only a pale light, like a candle seen through a dirty pane. "I am not interested in discussing the matter," he retorted coldly.

"I am! You made me come away because I was enjoying myself! You can't stand seeing anyone happy!"

"On the contrary, madame. I do not object at all to happiness. But I do object to watching my wife make a ridiculous display of herself."

"Ridiculous! What was ridiculous about it? I was doing nothing but dancing and laughing—is that so ridiculous? Maybe you even danced and laughed once yourself—if you were ever young!" She gave him a look of furious loathing, and turned her face away, muttering, "Which I doubt!"

"You're not so naïve, madame, as you try to pretend. You know as well as I do what was in the minds of those men tonight."

"Well!" she cried, clenching her fists. "What of it! Isn't the same thing in the minds of all men! It's in yours, too, even if you—" But there she stopped, suddenly, for he gave her a look so swift and so venomous, so threatening that the words caught short in her throat and she remained quiet.

The next morning, rather early, Amber and Nan came downstairs wrapped in cloaks and hoods and muffs. She spoke to the

609

footman at the door. "Please send for his Lordship's great coach. I'm going abroad."

"The coach is being repaired, madame."

"Then I'll go in mine."

"I'm sorry, your Ladyship, but that one is also at the coach-makers'."

Amber heaved an impatient sigh. "Very well, then! I'll call a hackney. Open the door, please!"

"I'm sorry, your Ladyship. The door is bolted and I have no key."

She looked at him with sudden suspicion. "Who has it then?"

"His Lordship, madame, I presume."

Without another word Amber swirled about and rushed from the entrance-hall toward the library, threw open the door without knocking, and burst in like a gust of wind. The Earl was seated at a table, writing, with a great sheaf of papers beside him.

"Would you mind telling me why I'm made a prisoner?" she cried.

He looked up as though she were, indeed, a disrupting physical force rather than a human being. Then his eyes ran over her slowly and he gave a faint smile, as of a patient man who is somewhat bored.

"Where did you wish to go?"

She was on the edge of telling him that where she went was not his business, but thinking better of it she replied, more quietly: "To the New Exchange. I have some purchases to make."

"I can't imagine what they could be. But it seems that no matter how much a woman may have, she always needs something more. Well, if you feel you cannot do without a new pair of gloves or a bottle of essence—send Britton."

Amber stamped her foot. "I don't *want* to send Britton! I want to go myself! I will go myself! God's curse, sir! is there any reason why I shouldn't leave the house? What the devil have I done to be used like this!"

Radclyffe paused a long moment before he answered her, gazing reflectively at the pen he turned in his fingers. "This is a strange age. A man is considered a fool if he allows his wife to cuckold him—and an even greater one if he takes measures to prevent it."

Amber's mouth twisted into an ugly triumphant sneer. "So at last we have it! You're afraid some other man will get your children for you! Well, now—wouldn't *that* be strange?"

"You may go, madame." As she continued to glare at him, he suddenly spoke with startling sharpness. "Get out! Go to your rooms!"

Amber's eyes blazed, as though she could wither him where he sat by the sheer force of her hatred. All at once she muttered a curse, slammed her fan onto the floor, and as she went out flung the door wide and banged it with all the force in her body.

But Amber soon discovered that shouts and violence would gain her nothing. He had the legal right to lock her in, and to beat her if he thought that she deserved it. She had little fear the thin brittle Earl would ever attempt physical chastisement— since she was certainly more than a match for him—but she sometimes had a sneaking apprehension of poison or the sudden thrust of a knife. He wouldn't dare! she told herself. But she was never wholly convinced, and fear made her cautious.

For several days she sulked. She thought of starving herself to make him submit, but realized after she had missed two meals that such a process would be more uncomfortable for her than for him. Then she ignored him completely. When he was in the room she turned her back, sang bawdy songs, chattered with Nan. She never left her apartments but went about all day in her dressing-gown, her hair undone and no paint on her face. He seemed scarcely to notice, and certainly did not care.

She thought of every possible solution, but was compelled to abandon each in turn. If she left him he would have all her money—and she would have no title. To get a divorce was almost impossible and would have required an act of Parliament; not even Castlemaine had obtained a divorce. Annulment was almost as difficult, for the case must rest upon impotence or sterility, and how was she to prove herself a virgin or him incompetent? To make matters worse, the courts, she knew, were not inclined to side with a woman. And so at last she decided that if it had been possible for her to tolerate him before they were married it should be possible now. She began to speak civilly to him once more, joined him at dinner, went into the library to search among the books when he was there. She took an extraordinary care of her appearance, in the hope of buying what she wanted by pandering to his salaciousness.

On the afternoon the precious Correggio arrived, she went down to watch it being unpacked. When at last it was hung, the workmen gone, and they stood before the fireplace looking up at it, Amber sneaked him a glance and found that he was smiling. As always, when he had just acquired another coveted and admired object, he seemed in a pleasanter, more tractable mood.

"I wonder, your Lordship," she began tentatively, her eyes stealing toward him again, and then back to the picture, "I wonder if I might go abroad today—just for a drive. I haven't been out of the house in three weeks and I swear it's making me pale and sallow. Don't you think so?" She looked at him anxiously.

He turned and faced her directly, a faint amused smile on his mouth. "I thought your pleasant humour of the past few days meant a request would soon be forthcoming. Very well, you may go."

"Oh! thank you, sir! Can I go *now?*"

"Whenever you like. My coachman will drive you—and, by the way, he's served me for thirty years and is not to be bribed."

Her smile suddenly froze, but she concealed her anger swiftly for fear of having the privilege revoked. Then swooping up her skirts she ran out of the room, down the hall, and up the stairs two at a time. She burst into their apartments with a cry of triumph that made Nan start and almost drop her needlework.

"Nan! Get your cloak! We're going abroad!"

"Going abroad! Oh, Lord, are we? Where?" Nan had been sharing her mistress's confinement—save for a few brief excursions to buy ribbons or gloves or a fan—and was as tired of it as Amber.

"I don't know! Somewhere—anywhere— Hurry!"

The two women left the house in a swirl of velvet skirts

and fur muffs, getting into the coach with as much laughter and excitement as if they had just arrived from Yorkshire to see the London sights. The air was so sharp and fresh it stung the nostrils. The day was grey and windy, and petals blown from peach trees drifted through the air, falling like flakes of snow onto the roof-tops and into the mud.

There was still plague in the town, though there were usually not more than half-a-dozen deaths a week, and it had retired once more to the congested dismal districts of the poor. By now it was almost impossible to find a shut-up house. The streets were as crowded as ever, the vendors and 'prentices as noisy, and the only sure sign that plague had recently passed that way were the many plaintive notices stuck up in windows: "Here is a doctor to be let." For the doctors, by their wholesale desertion, had forfeited even what reluctant and suspicious trust they had once been able to command. A fifth of the town's population was dead, yet nothing seemed to have changed—it was the same gay bawdy stinking brilliant dirty city of London.

Amber, delighted to be out again, looked at and exclaimed upon everything:

The little boy solemnly plying his trade of snipping silver buttons from the backs of gentlemen's coats as they strolled unsuspectingly down the street. The brawl between some porters and apprentices who, setting up the traditional cry of " 'Prentices! 'Prentices!" brought their fellows flying to the rescue with clubs and sticks. A man performing on a tight-rope for a gape-mouthed crowd at the entrance to Popinjay Alley. The women vendors sitting on street corners amid their great baskets of sweet-potatoes, spring mushrooms, small sour oranges, onions and dried pease and new green dandelion tops.

She had directed the coachman to drive to Charing Cross by way of Fleet Street and the Strand, for there were a number of fashionable ordinaries in that neighbourhood. And after all, if she should chance in passing to see someone she knew and stopped to speak a word with him out of mere civility—why, no one could reasonably object to anything so innocent as that. Amber kept her eyes wide open and advised Nan to do likewise, and just as they were approaching Temple Bar she caught sight of three familiar figures gathered in the doorway of The Devil Tavern. They were Buckhurst, Sedley and Rochester, all three evidently half-drunk for they were talking and gesticulating noisily, attracting the attention of everyone who passed by.

Instantly Amber leaned forward to rap on the wall, signalling the driver to stop, and letting down the window she stuck out her head. "Gentlemen!" she cried. "You must stop that noise or I'll call a constable and have you all clapped up!" and she burst into a peal of laughter.

They turned to stare at her in astonishment, momentarily surprised into silence, and then with a whoop they advanced upon the coach. "Her Ladyship, by God!" "Where've you been these three weeks past!" "Why'n hell haven't we seen you at Court?" They hung on one another's shoulders and leaned their elbows on the window-sill, all of them breathing brandy and smelling very high of orange-flower water.

"Why, to tell you truth, gentlemen," said Amber with a sly smile and a wink at Rochester, "I've had a most furious attack of the vapours."

They roared with laughter. "So that formal old fop, your husband, locked you in!"

"I say an old man has no business marrying a young woman unless he can entertain her in the manner to which she's accustomed herself. Can your husband do that, madame?" asked Rochester.

Amber changed the subject, afraid that some of the footmen or the loyal old driver might have been told to listen to whatever she said and report it. "What were you all arguing about? It looked like a conventicle-meeting when I drove up."

"We were considering whether to stay here till we're drunk and then go to a bawdy-house—or to go to a bawdy-house first and get drunk afterward," Sedley told her. "What's your opinion, madame?"

"I'd say that depends on how you expect to entertain yourselves once you get there."

"Oh, in the usual way, madame," Rochester assured her. "In the usual way. We're none of us yet come to those tiresome ex-

614

pedients of old-age and debauchery." Rochester was nineteen and Buckhurst, the eldest, was twenty-eight.

"Egad, Wilmot," objected Buckhurst, who was now drunk enough to talk without stammering. "Where's your breeding? Don't you know a woman hates nothing so much as to hear other women mentioned in her presence?"

Rochester shrugged his thin shoulders. "A whore's not a woman. She's a convenience."

"Come in and drink a glass with us," invited Sedley. We've got a brace of fiddlers in there and we can send to Lady Bennet for some wenches. A tavern will serve my turn as well as a brothel any day."

Amber hesitated, longing to go and wondering if it might be possible to bribe the coachman after all. But Nan was nudging her with her elbow and grimacing and she decided that it was not worth the risk of being locked up for another three weeks, or possibly longer. And worst of all, she knew, Radclyffe might be angry enough even to send her into the country—the favourite punishment for erring wives, and the most dreaded. By now her coach had begun to snarl the traffic. There were other coaches waiting behind, and numerous porters and carmen, vendors, beggars, apprentices and sedan-chair-men—all of them beginning to growl and swear at her driver, urging him to move on.

"There's some of us got work to do," bawled a chair-man, "even if you fine fellows ain't!"

"I can't go in," said Amber. "I promised his Lordship I wouldn't get out of the coach."

"Make way there!" bellowed another man trundling a loaded wheelbarrow.

"Make room there!" snarled a porter.

Rochester, not at all disturbed, turned coolly and made them a contemptuous sign with his right hand. There was a low, sullen roar of protest at that and several shouted curses. Buckhurst flung open the coach-door.

"Well, then! You can't get out—but what's there to keep us from getting in?"

He climbed in—followed by Rochester and Sedley—and settled himself between the two women, sliding an arm about each. Sedley stuck his head out the window. "Drive on! St. James's Park!" As they rolled off, Rochester gave an impertinent wave of his hand to the crowd. There was a breeze blowing up and it now began to rain, suddenly and very hard.

Amber came home in a gale of good humour and high spirits. Tossing off her rain-spattered cloak and muff in the entrance hall she ran into the library and, though she had been gone almost four hours, she found Radclyffe sitting just where she had left him, still writing. He looked up.

"Well, madame. Did you have a pleasant drive?"

"Oh, wonderful, your Lordship! It's a fine day out!" She walked toward him, begining to pull off her gloves. "We drove through St. James's Park—and who d'ye think I saw?"

"Truthfully, I don't know."

"His Majesty! He was walking in the rain with his gentlemen and they all looked like wet spaniels with their periwigs soaking and draggled!" She laughed delightedly. "But of course he was wearing his hat and looked as spruce as you please. He stopped the coach—and *what* d'you think he said?"

Radclyffe smiled slightly, as at a naïve child recounting some silly simple adventure to which it attached undue importance. "I have no idea."

"He asked after you and wanted to know why he hadn't seen you at Court. He's coming to visit you soon to see your paintings, he says—but Henry Bennet will make the arrangements first. And"—here she paused a little to give emphasis to the next piece of news—"he's asking us to a small dance in her Majesty's Drawing-Room tonight!"

She looked at him as she talked, but she was obviously not thinking about him; she was scarcely even conscious of him. More important matters occupied her mind: what gown she should wear, which jewels and fan, how she should arrange her hair. At least he could not refuse an invitation from the King— and if her plans succeeded she would soon be able to cast him off altogether, send him back to Lime Park to live with his books and statues and paintings, and so trouble her no more.

CHAPTER FORTY-TWO

THE TWO WOMEN—one auburn-haired and violet-eyed, the other tawny as a leopard, and both of them in stark black—stared at each other across the card-table.

All the Court was in mourning for a woman none of them had ever seen, the Queen of Portugal. But in spite of her mother's recent death Catherine's rooms were crowded with courtiers and ladies, the gaming-tables were piled with gold, and a young French boy wandered among them, softly strumming a guitar and singing love-songs of his native Normandy. An idle amused crowd had gathered about the table where the Countess of Castlemaine and the Countess of Radclyffe sat, eyeing each other like a pair of hostile cats.

The King had just strolled up behind Amber, declining with a gesture of his hand the chair which Buckingham offered him beside her, and on her other side Sir Charles Sedley lounged with both hands on his hips. Barbara was surrounded by her satellites, Henry Jermyn and Bab May and Henry Brouncker—who remained faithful to her even when she seemed to be going down the wind, for they were dependent upon her. Across the room, pretending to carry on a conversation with another elderly gentleman about gardening, stood the Earl of Radclyffe. Everyone, including his wife, seemed to have forgotten that he was there.

Amber, however, knew very well that he had been trying for the past two hours to attract her attention so that he might summon her home, and she had painstakingly ignored and avoided him. A week had passed since the King had invited them to Court again, and during that time Amber had grown increasingly confident of her own future, and steadily more contemptuous of the Earl. Charles's frank admiration, Barbara's jealousy, the obsequiousness of the courtiers—prophetic as a weather-vane —had her intoxicated.

"Your luck's good tonight, madame!" snapped Barbara, pushing a pile of guineas across the table. "Almost too good!"

Amber gave her a smug, superior smile, with lips curled faintly and eyes slanting at the corners. She knew that Charles was looking down at her, that almost everyone at the table was watching her. All this attention was a heady wine, making her feel vastly important, a match for anyone.

"Whatever do you mean by that, madame?"

"You know damned well what I mean!" muttered Barbara, half under her breath.

She was hot and excited, trying desperately to control her temper for fear of being made to look a fool. It was bad enough that Charles in his forthright, casual way had let everyone know he intended laying with this upstart wench from the theatres. But to make matters even worse that miserable wretch, Buckingham, had taken it into his maggoty head·to sponsor her himself—and if she dared so much as murmur a protest he reminded her that it was only by his good nature she remained in England at all.

Oh, damn those letters! Damn Buckingham! Damn everything! I'd like to claw that bitch's hair off her scalp! I'll learn her she can't use *me* at this rate!

"Here!" she cried. "I'll raffle you for the whole of it!"

Amber gave a delicate lift of her eyebrows. The more furiously excited Barbara grew, the cooler she seemed. Now she looked up and exchanged smiles with Charles, a smile that took him into her camp, and he grinned lazily—a willing prisoner.

She gave a careless shrug. "Why not? Your throw first, madame."

Barbara ground her teeth and gave Charles a glare that might once have warned him. Now he was frankly amused. She swept three ivory dice off the table and flung them into a dice-box, while all around them conversation stopped and the lords and ladies leaned forward to watch. Barbara gave the box a defiant vigorous shake and with a dramatic flourish she tossed the dice out onto the table where they tumbled along the polished surface and slid at last to a stop. Two sixes and a four.

Someone gave a low whistle and a murmur ran through the

bystanders as Barbara looked up with a triumphant smile, her eyes glittering. "There, madame! Try if you can better that!"

And since the object of the game was to throw three alike—else the highest pair took the stakes—even Amber was forced to recognize that her chances could not be very good.

Frantically she stabbed about for a way to save herself. I've got to do *something*—I *can't* let her beat me in front of all these people! I've got to do something—something—something—

And then she felt the pressure of Buckingham's knee and a light movement in her lap. Suddenly she found herself cold and clear-headed again, no longer desperate, and with a quick automatic gesture she picked the dice-box up from the table in one hand and the dice in the other. So quickly that it scarce seemed to happen she dropped the box into her lap and the one she recovered was the one just put there by Buckingham. Without looking she knew what it was: a false box painted inside to look like an honest one—and she tossed the dice in. The hours of practice she had had in Whitefriars and since now stood her in good stead—for the dice came forth like loyal soldiers: a five, a five, and another five. There was a gasp all around the room while Amber pretended astonishment at her own good fortune. The beet-faced Brouncker leaned down to whisper in Barbara's ear.

And suddenly she sprang to her feet. "Very clever, madame!" she cried. "But I'm not one to be so easily put upon! There's been some scurvy trick here—I'll pass my word for that!" she added, addressing herself to the audience in general, and his Majesty in particular.

Amber was beginning to grow nervous, though already the Duke had reclaimed his box and the one she held in her hand was the same one Barbara had used. But she was prepared to run a bluff.

"Can't anyone be allowed to get the better of your Ladyship but by some trick?" That drew a general laugh and Amber felt somewhat more comfortable; she carelessly tossed the box onto the table.

Still it was a serious matter for one person to accuse another of cheating, though all of them did—for just as some of the ladies liked to pretend they were virtuous or unpainted, so they pretended to play on the square. And to be caught now and labelled a cheat before all the Court, suddenly seemed to Amber so horrible a fate she would rather have been dead. It would be unbearable—to have everyone stand there and witness her defeat at the hands of Barbara Palmer!

And Barbara, convinced she had the hare cornered, came baying ruthlessly on the scent. "Only a false box would have turned 'em up like that! There wouldn't be a chance in a thousand it could happen honestly!"

Amber by now was sick and shaking inside, and it took her a few seconds to find her answer. But when she did she tried to sound brazenly assured, so casually scornful that they could have no doubt of her honesty. "Come to think of it, your Ladyship's throw was almost too good to be true—"

"I'll have you know, madame, I'm not a cheat!" cried Barbara, who often lost such sums it seemed she must be either honest or clumsy. "There's the box I used! Examine it, someone—" She snatched it up and suddenly leaned across the table, extending it to the King. "Now, your Majesty! You saw everything that happened! How does it look to you? You tell us which one cheated in this game!"

Charles took the box and looked it over very carefully, both inside and out, wearing his most serious and thoughtful expression. "As far as I can see," he said at last, "there's nothing wrong with this box."

Amber sat there motionless and stiff, her heart hammering so violently she expected to faint. This was the end—the end of everything—it would be no use to go on living after this—

"Aha!" cried Barbara's voice, in a triumphant brassy tone that Amber felt scrape mercilessly along her nerves. "Just as I thought! I knew—"

"But," interrupted Charles in a lazy drawl, "since both of you used the same box I can see no reason for all this bustle and stir."

Amber's relief was so great now that it was all she could do to keep herself from slumping over and falling face down onto the table-top. But Castlemaine gave a high little screech of indignation.

"What? But we didn't! She changed it! She—"

"I beg your pardon, madame, but—as you said—I saw everything that happened, and it's my opinion her Ladyship played as much upon the square as you did."

"But—"

"The hour's growing late," continued Charles imperturbably, and his snapping black eyes glanced round the table. "Don't you all agree we might better be in bed?"

There was a general laugh at that and the crowd, convinced the show was over, began to break up. "A pretty deal of an odd sort!" muttered Castlemaine sourly. And then she leaned forward and said tensely to Amber, "I wouldn't play with you again for crooked pins!" and she swung about and started off, with Brouncker and Bab May and little Jermyn hurrying in her wake like tenders.

Amber, still weak and helpless, finally managed to look up at the king with a grateful smile and a soundless whistle. He reached down to put his hand beneath her elbow and slowly she got to her feet.

"Thank you, Sire," she said softly, for of course he knew that she had cheated. "I'd have been disgraced forever."

Charles laughed. "Disgraced—here at Whitehall? Impossible, my dear. Did you ever hear of anyone being disgraced in hell?"

Her energy and confidence were coming back again. She looked at Buckingham, still there beside them, with an impudent grin. "Thanks, your Grace," she said, though she knew that he had given her the false box not to help her but to humiliate his cousin.

Buckingham made a comical face. "I protest, madame. I assure you I had no hand in your luck—not I. Why, all the world knows I'm an honest fellow."

As the three of them laughed at that Amber was conscious of the lords and ladies moving everywhere about them, glancing in her direction—and she knew what they were thinking. The King had taken her part tonight, defied and embarrassed Castlemaine before them all; it could have only one meaning. The Countess of Radclyffe would soon be the topping mistress at Court. Amber thought so herself.

As they stood there looking at each other, the smiles slowly fading from their faces, Buckingham said good-night and left; they did not notice. Amber knew that she was in love with Charles—as much as she would ever be with any man but Bruce Carlton. His dark lazy eyes stirred the embers of desire, at which Radclyffe had rudely raked but never once brought into flame, and she longed with all her being to lie in his arms again. She had completely forgotten that Radclyffe must be there nearby, watching them, and her recklessness was now so great she would not have cared anyway.

"When can you escape your duenna?" murmured Charles.

"Anytime. Whenever you say."

"Tomorrow morning at ten?"

"Yes."

"I'll post a sentry to admit you at the Holbein Gate—on this side." He glanced up, over her head, and then smiled faintly. "Here comes your husband—and he looks horn-mad already."

Amber had a sharp unpleasant sense of shock.

Your husband!

She felt resentful that he should have the effrontery still to be alive, when she had no longer any use for him and had half imagined he would somehow disappear from her world like an exorcised demon. But he was there now—beside her, and Charles was greeting him with a pleasant smile. Then the King was gone and Radclyffe extended his arm to her. Hesitating for only a moment, she put her fingers on his arm as they started slowly from the room.

For a long while Amber struggled to return to consciousness. She felt as if there was a heavy pressing weight on her head and her eyeballs throbbed. A twisting cramp in her neck sent pains shooting out along her shoulders and down her back as she began to move, moaning softly. She seemed to have been aware for some interminable time of an uneven rolling and jogging motion that shook her from side to side and made her sick at her stomach. With a great effort she forced herself to lift her eyelids and look about, striving to discover where she was and what had happened to her.

She saw first a man's small veined hands, clasping a walking-stick which he held between his legs, and then as her eyes raised slowly she found herself looking into Radclyffe's impassive expressionless face. She now realized that part of her discomfort was because her legs were bound together, about the thighs and below the knees, and her arms tied close to her sides. They were in his coach, and the window pane showed only a grey sky and green meadows with lonely bare-branched trees. She wanted to speak, to ask him where they were—but an intolerable weight on her head pressed down, heavier and heavier, until at last she slid off again into unconsciousness.

She was aware of nothing more until she suddenly opened her eyes to find that the coach had stopped and that someone was lifting her out; she felt the cool fresh evening air in her face and took a deep breath.

"Try not to wake her," she heard Radclyffe say. "When she's in these spells she must not be disturbed or it may cause another." It made her furious that he should dare tell anyone such an insulting lie about her, but she had no energy to protest.

The footman carried her, covered with her cloak and a long fur-lined robe, toward the inn and someone pushed open the door. The room was warm and filled with the savoury smells of fresh-baked bread and a roasting-joint which turned in the fireplace. Dogs circled about, wagging their tails and sniffing inquisitively, several children appeared, ostlers ran to unhitch the horses and a cheerful landlady came to greet them. At the sight of Amber lying with her head limp against the footman's chest and her eyes closed, she gave a sympathetic little cry and hurried forward.

"Oh! Is the lady sick?"

Radclyffe brushed her aside. "My wife is indisposed," he said coldly. "But it's no serious matter. I'll attend to her myself. Show us to a room and send up supper."

Rebuffed, the landlady climbed the stairs ahead of them and unlocked a clean lavender-scented chamber, but whenever she thought that the Earl was not looking she glanced surreptitiously at Amber. She lighted the candles and soon had a brisk blaze in the fireplace. Then, just before going, she hesitated again, looking with real distress at Amber where she lay on the bed, just as the footman had put her down.

"My wife does not need your attention!" snapped Radclyffe, so sharply that the woman gave an embarrassed start and hurried from the room. He walked to the closed door, listened for a moment and then, apparently satisfied that she had gone on, returned to the bedside.

Though now fully conscious, Amber felt dull and heavy and irritable, her head ached and her muscles were stiff and sore. She drew a deep sigh. For several moments both of them remained silent and waiting, but at last she said: "Well, why don't you untie me? I can't get away from you now!" She looked up at him sullenly. "How damned clever you must think you are!" She had already begun to realize that he must have tied her merely to satisfy some brutal whim of his own, for deeply drugged as she had been it would not have been necessary in order to move her about.

He shrugged and smiled a little, frankly pleased with himself. "I believe I've studied chemistry to some purpose. It was in the wine, of course. You couldn't smell it or taste it, could you?"

"D'ye think I'd have drunk it if I could! For the love of God untie these ropes—my legs and arms are dead." She was beginning to twist about, trying to find a more comfortable position and to make the blood run again, for she felt so cold and numb that it seemed to have stopped altogether.

He ignored her request and took a chair beside her, with the air of a man who sits down to console a sick person for whose condition he has no real pity. "What a shame you couldn't meet him. I hope he didn't wait too long."

Amber looked at him swiftly—and then, very slowly, she smiled, a malicious cruel little smile. "There'll be another day. You can't keep me tied up forever."

"I don't intend to. You may go back to London and Whitehall and play the bitch whenever you like—but when you do, madame, I shall bring suit to get all your money in my possession. I think I would win it, too, with no great difficulty. The King may be willing to lie with you—but you've a long way to go before he'll discommode himself for you. A whore and a mistress are not the same thing—even though you may not be able to see the difference between them."

"I see it well enough! All women aren't such fools as you like to think! I see *some* things you may think I don't, too."

"Oh, do you?" His tone had the subtle sneering contempt with which he had almost habitually addressed her since the day of their marriage.

"You may pretend it's only my money you want—but I know better. You're stark staring mad at the thought of having another man do what you can't do. *That's* why you brought me off. And that's why you tell me I'll lose my money if I go back. You fumbling old dotard—you're—"

"Madame!"

"I'm not afraid of you! You're jealous of every man who's potent and you hate me because you can't—"

His right hand lashed out suddenly and struck her across the face, so hard that her head snapped to one side and the blood came rushing to the surface. His eyes were cold.

"As a gentleman I disapprove of slapping a woman. I have never, in my life, done so before. But I am your husband, madame, and I will be spoken to with respect."

Like a vicious spitting cat, Amber recoiled. Her breathing had almost stopped and her mottled golden eyes were glowing. As she spoke her lips lifted away from her teeth like a malignant animal's. "Oh, how I detest you—" she said softly. "Someday I'll make you pay for the things you've done to me—someday I swear I'll kill you . . ."

He looked at her with contempt and loathing. "A threatening woman is like a barking dog—I have as much respect for one as for the other." There was a knock at the door and though he hesitated for a moment at last he turned his head.

"Come in!"

It was the landlady, cheerful and pink-cheeked and smiling, carrying in her arms a table-cloth and napkins and the pewter-ware for the table. Behind her came a thirteen-year-old girl

625

balancing a tray loaded with appetizing food; she was followed by her little brother with two dusty green bottles and a couple of shining glasses. The landlady looked at Amber, who still lay half on one side, propped on her elbow, covered with the robe. "Well!" she said briskly. "Madame is better now? I'm glad! It's a good supper if I do say so, and I want you to enjoy it!" She gave her a friendly woman-to-woman smile, obviously trying to convey that she understood what a young wife must go through with her first pregnancy. Amber, her face still burning from the slap, forced herself to smile in return.

CHAPTER FORTY-THREE

LIME PARK was over a hundred years old—it had been built before the break-up of the Catholic Church, when the proud Mortimers were at the height of their power, and its stern elegant beauty expressed that power and pride. Pale grey stone and cherry-red brick had been combined with great masses of square-paned windows in a building of perfect symmetry. It was four stories high with three dormers projecting from the red slate roof, with its many chimneys so exactly placed that each balanced another, and with square and round bays aligned in three sections across the front. A brick-paved terrace, more than two hundred feet long, overlooked the formal Italian gardens that dropped away in great steps below. In marked contrast to the decay of the town-house, Lime Park had been carefully and immaculately kept; each shrub, each fountain, each stone vase was perfect.

The train of coaches circled the front of the house at a distance of several hundred yards and drove around to the back courtyard, where a fountain played many jets of sparkling water. Some distance to the west could be seen a great round brick Norman dove-cote and a pond; on the north were the stables and coach-houses, all handsome buildings of cherry brick and silver oak. A double staircase led to the second-story entrance, and the first coach stopped just at the foot of it.

His Lordship got out, then gallantly extended his hand to help his wife. Amber, now unbound and completely recovered from the effects of the drug, stepped down. Her face was sulky and she ignored Radclyffe as though he did not exist, but her eyes went up over the building with admiration and interest. Just at that moment a young woman ran out the door overhead and came sailing down the steps toward them. She shot one swift timid glance at Amber and then made Radclyffe a deep humble curtsy.

"Oh, your Lordship!" she cried, bobbing up again. "We weren't expecting you and Philip has ridden over to hunt with Sir Robert! I don't know *when* he'll be back!"

Amber knew that she must be Jennifer, his Lordship's sixteen-year-old daughter-in-law, though Radclyffe had made no mention of her beyond her name. She was slender and plain-faced with pale blonde hair which was already beginning to darken in streaks; and she was obviously very much awed by her two worldly visitors.

Ye gods! thought Amber impatiently. So this is what living in the country does to you! It no longer seemed to her that she had lived most of her life in the country herself.

Radclyffe was all graciousness and courtesy. "Don't trouble yourself about it, my dear. We came unexpectedly and there was no time to send a message. Madame"—he turned to Amber —"this is my son's wife, Jennifer, of whom I've told you. Jennifer, may I present her Ladyship?" Jenny gave Amber another quick fugitive glance and then curtsied; the two women embraced with conventional kisses and Amber could feel that the girl's hands were cold and that she trembled. "Her Ladyship has not been well during the journey," said Radclyffe now, at which Amber gave him a swift glance of indignation. "I believe she would like to rest. Are my apartments ready?"

"Oh, yes, your Lordship. They're always ready."

Amber was not tired and she did not want to rest. She wanted to go through the house, see the gardens and the stables, investigate the summer-house and the orangerie—but she followed the Earl upstairs into the great suite of rooms which opened from the northwest end of the gallery.

"I'm not tired!" she cried then, facing him defiantly. "How long have I got to stay shut up in here?"

"Only until you are prepared to stop sulking, madame. Your opinion of me interests me not at all—but I refuse to have my son or my servants see my wife behaving like an ill-natured slut. The choice is your own."

Amber heaved a sigh. "Very well then. I don't think I could ever convince anyone that I like you—but I'll try to seem to endure you with the best grace I can."

Philip was back by supper-time and Amber met him then. He was an ordinary young man of about twenty-four, healthy and happy and unsophisticated. His dress was careless, his manners casual, and it seemed likely that his most intellectual interests were horse-breeding and cock-training. Thank God, thought Amber at first sight of him, he's nothing like his father! But it surprised her to see that though Philip was so different from him Radclyffe was deeply attached to the boy—it was a quality she had not expected to find in the cold proud lonely old man.

Amber spent several days exploring Lime Park.

There were dozens of rooms, all of them filled with furniture and pictures and objects which had come from every part of the world but which, by means of his Lordship's own peculiar alchemy, had been made to harmonize perfectly. The Italian gardens were immense and laid out in great terraces surrounding the south and east sides of the house and connected by marble flights of steps and broad gravelled walks. There were long shaded alleys of cypress and yew, and avenues of clipped, bright-green lime-trees; there were flowers in stone vases lining the stairs or walks or set on the balustrades. There was not a ragged hedge nor a weed to be found anywhere. Even the stables were immaculate, walled inside with Dutch tile and kept freshly whitewashed, and there were an orangerie, greenhouses, and a pretty little summer-house.

It was no wonder, she thought, that he had been in debt. But now that she saw what her money had been spent for she was less resentful, for she looked at everything with the appraising critical eye of an owner. She passed nothing without making a decision as to whether she would want to keep it or sell it when the time came. For certainly nothing should stay hidden out here in the country where no one of any consequence might see and admire it. These fine things were destined for London: perhaps apartments in Whitehall or some grand new house in St. James's Square or Piccadilly.

At first Jennifer was shy, but Amber—because she had nothing else to do and also because she was a little sorry for her—made the effort to become friendly. The girl responded with warm gratitude, for she had grown up in a large family and was lonely here, where, even with more than two hundred servants, the house seemed empty and dull.

It was now the end of April and the days were often warm and pleasant. The nightingales had arrived, cherry and plum trees were in full bloom and the gardens were filled with the sweet scent of potted lilacs. Jennifer and Amber, gaily chatting and laughing, strolled over the green lawns arm in arm, their silk gowns gently blowing, admiring the raucous-tongued peacocks. In no time at all they seemed fast friends.

Like a woman in love, Amber was forever talking of London, where Jennifer had never been. She told her about the theatres and the taverns, Hyde Park and Pall Mall and Whitehall, the gambling in the Queen's Drawing-Rooms, the balls and the hawking parties. For to her London was the center of the universe and whoever was absent from it might almost as well have been on a distant star.

"Oh, there's nothing so fine," she cried enthusiastically, "as to see all the Court driving in the Ring! Everyone bows and smiles at everyone else each time they come round and his Majesty lifts his hat to the ladies and sometimes he calls out to them too. Oh, Jenny, you *must* come to London one day!" She continued to talk as if she were still there.

Jenny had always listened with great interest and asked innumerable questions, but now she gave an apologetic little smile. "It sounds very fine but—well, I think I'd rather hear about it than see it myself."

"What?" cried Amber, shocked at this blasphemy. "But

London's the only place in the world to be! *Why* don't you want to go?"

Jenny made a vague, deprecatory gesture. She was always acutely conscious of the greater strength of Amber's personality, and it made her feel embarrassed and almost guilty to express an opinion of her own. "I don't know. I think I'd feel strange there. It's so big and there are so many people and all the ladies are so handsome and wear such fine clothes—I'd be out of place. Why, I'd be lost." Her voice had a timid and almost desperate sound, as though she were already lost in that great terrifying city.

Amber laughed and slipped one arm about her daughter-in-law's waist. "Why, Jenny, with paint and patches and a low-necked gown you'd be as pretty as anyone! I'll warrant you the gallants wouldn't let you alone—they'd be after you day and night."

Jenny giggled, and her face grew pink. "Oh, your Ladyship, you know they wouldn't! My heavens! I wouldn't even know what to say to a gallant!"

"Of course you would, Jenny. You know what to say to Philip, don't you, and all men are alike. There's just one topic that interests 'em when they're talking to a woman."

Jenny turned red. "Oh, but I'm married to Philip and he—well—" She changed the subject hastily. "Is it *really* true what they say about the Court?"

"What d'ye mean?"

"Oh, you know. They say such terrible things. They say everyone drinks and swears and that even her Majesty plays cards on Sunday. They say his Majesty sometimes doesn't so much as see the Queen for months at a time, he's so busy with his other—er, ladies."

"Nonsense! He sees her every day and he's as kind and fond as can be—he says she's the best woman in the world."

Jenny was relieved. "Then it isn't true that he's unfaithful to her?"

"Oh, yes, he is. All men are unfaithful to their wives, aren't they, if they get a chance?" But at that Jenny looked so stricken she gave her a little squeeze and added hastily, "Except men who live in the country—they're different."

And at first she half thought that Philip was different. The instant he had seen her his eyes had lighted with surprise and admiration—but his father was there and the look swiftly passed. After that she met him seldom, usually only at dinner and supper, and then he paid her the same deferential consideration she might have expected had she been at least twenty years older. He very politely tried to pretend that she actually was nearer his father's age than his own. Amber finally decided, correctly, that he was afraid of her.

Prompted by boredom and mischief and a desire to revenge herself on Radclyffe, she set out to make Philip fall in love with her. But she knew the Earl well enough to realize that she would have to be cautious, and take strictly in private any satisfaction she might find in cuckolding him with his own son. For if he should ever suspect or guess—but she refused to think of that, for nothing violent or cruel seemed beyond him. But Philip was the only young and personable and virile male at Lime Park, and she craved excitement as well as the flattery of a man's adoration.

One rainy morning she met him in the gallery where they stopped to talk for a moment about the weather. He would have gone on almost immediately but she suggested a game of shovel-board and while he was trying to find an excuse she hurried him off to where the table was set. After that they bowled or played cards occasionally, and a couple of times, apparently by accident, they met at the stables and rode together. Jenny was pregnant and could not ride.

But Philip continued to treat Amber like a step-mother and even seemed to be somewhat in awe of her, which was an emotion she was not accustomed to rousing in men, either young or old. She decided that he must have forgotten everything he had learned on his Tour.

She saw Radclyffe no oftener now than when they had been in town. He supervised every detail regarding the house which was not attended to by the steward (for he refused to allow a woman to manage his household); he planned new arrangements for the gardens, directed the workmen, and spent hours in his laboratory or in the library. He never rode horseback or played a game or a musical instrument, and though he was sometimes out-of-doors it was never to idle but always for a definite purpose and when it was accomplished he returned to the house. He wrote interminably. When Amber asked him what it was, he told her. He was writing the complete history of every article of value he had acquired so that the family would always know what its possessions were. He also wrote poetry, but never offered to read it to her and she never asked to see it. She thought it a very dull occupation and could not imagine a man wasting his time shut up in a dark close room when outside the white violets were poignantly fragrant, beech-trees were hung with purple clusters of bloom, and clean cool rain-swept air washed over the hills.

When she tried to quarrel with him about returning to London he told her flatly that she had conducted herself like a fool there and was not fit to live where she would be subjected to temptation. He repeated that if she wanted to go back alone he was willing to have her do so, but he reminded her that if she did she would forfeit her money to him—all but ten thousand pounds. She shouted at him in a fury that she would never turn that money over to him, not if she had to stay in the country for the rest of her life.

Consequently, convinced that she might be there a long while, she sent for Nan and Susanna and Big John Waterman. Nan, who had earlier had one miscarriage and one abortion, was now pregnant again—this time by Big John—and though it was the fifth month and Amber told her not to come if she thought it might hurt her, she arrived within a fortnight.

As always, they seemed to have a great deal to talk about, for both women were interested in the same things and they gossiped and chattered and exchanged intimate personal details without hesitation or self-consciousness. Jenny's innocence and inexperience had begun to bore Amber who was relieved to have someone she could talk to frankly, someone who knew her for exactly what she was and who did not care. When she told

632

Nan that she intended seducing her husband's son Nan laughed and said there was no limit to a woman's desperation once she was carried off into the country. For certainly Philip could not bear comparison with Charles II or Lord Carlton.

But it was the middle of May before he began to seek her out deliberately.

She was waiting one morning for her pretty little golden mare to be saddled when she heard his voice behind her. "Why, good morrow, your Ladyship! Are you riding so early?" He tried to sound surprised, but she knew the moment she looked at him that he had come purposely to meet her.

"Good-morning, Philip! Yes, I think I'll gather some May dew. They say it's the most sovereign thing in the world for a woman's complexion."

Philip blushed, grinning at her, whacking his hat nervously against his knee. "Your Ladyship can't have need of anything like that."

"What a courtier you are, Philip."

She looked up at him out of the shadow of her broad hat-brim, smiling a little. He doesn't want to, she thought, but he's falling in love with me all the same.

The mare, now accoutred with a handsome green-velvet saddle embroidered in gold lace, was led out to where they stood waiting beneath the great trailing pepper-trees. For a moment Amber talked to her, patting her neck and giving her a lump of sugar. Philip then stepped forward to help her mount. She sprang up easily and gracefully.

"We can ride together," she suggested now. "Unless you were going somewhere to pay a visit."

He pretended to be surprised at the invitation. "Oh, no. No, I wasn't. I was just going to ride by myself. But thank you, your Ladyship. That's very kind. Thank you very much."

They set out over the rolling clover-thick meadowland, and were presently beyond sight of the house. The grass was very wet and a slow-moving herd of cattle grazed in the distance. For some time neither of them found anything to say, but at last Philip called, happily: "What a glorious morning it is! Why do people live in cities when there's the country?"

"Why do they live in the country when there are cities?"

He looked surprised and then grinned broadly, showing his even white teeth. "But you don't mean that, my lady—or you wouldn't be at Lime Park!"

"Coming to Lime Park wasn't my idea! It was his Lordship's!"

She spoke carelessly, and yet something of the contempt and hatred she had for Radclyffe must have been in her tone or in some fleeting facial expression, for Philip replied quickly, as if to a challenge. "My father loves Lime Park—he always has. We never have lived in London. His Majesty, Charles I, visited here once and said that he thought there was no finer country home in England."

"Oh, it's a mighty fine house, I doubt not," agreed Amber, aware that she had offended his family loyalty—though she did not very much care—and they rode some distance farther without speaking. At last she called to him: "Let's stop here awhile." Without waiting for his answer she began to rein in her horse; but he rode several hundred yards beyond, wheeled, and came back slowly.

"Perhaps we'd better not, since there's no one about."

"What of that?" demanded Amber in half-impatient amusement.

"Well—you see, madame—his Lordship thinks it best not to dismount when we ride. If we were seen someone might misunderstand. Country people love to gossip."

"People everywhere love to gossip. Well, you do as you like. I'm going to get off."

And immediately she jumped down, pulled off her hat to which she had pinned two or three fresh red roses, and shook out her hair. He watched her and then, setting his jaw stubbornly, he dismounted too. At his suggestion they started over to see a pretty little stream that ran nearby. The brook was noisy and full, dark-green bulrushes grew along the banks and there were weeping willows that dipped their branches into the water. Through the trees sunlight filtered down onto Amber's head, like the light in a cathedral. She could feel Philip watching her, surreptitiously, out of the corners of his eyes. She looked around suddenly and caught him.

634

Slowly she smiled and her eyes slanted, staring at him with bold impudence. "What was your father's last countess like?" she asked him finally. She knew that his own mother, the first Lady Radclyffe, had died at his birth. "Was she pretty?"

"Yes, a little, I think. At least her portrait is pretty, but she died when I was nine—I don't remember her very well." He seemed uneasy at being alone with her; his face had sobered and his eyes could no longer conceal what he really felt.

"Did she have any children?"

"Two. They died very young of the small-pox. I had it too—" He swallowed hard and took a deep breath. "But I lived."

"I'm glad you did, Philip," she said very softly. She continued to smile at him, half in mockery, but her eyes were weighted with seduction. Nothing had amused her so much in over four weeks.

Philip, however, was obviously wretched. His emotions pulled him two ways, desire in one, filial loyalty in another. He began to talk again, quickly, on a more impersonal subject. "What is the Court like now? They say it's most magnificent—and that even foreigners are surprised at the state in which his Majesty lives."

"Yes, it is. It's beautiful. I don't think there can be more handsome men or beautiful women any place else on earth. When were you there last?"

"Two years ago. I spent several months in London when I returned from my travels. Many of the paintings and hangings had been brought back to Court then, but I understand it's even finer now. The King is much interested in beautiful things." His tongue talked but his mind did not follow it; his eyes were hot and intense, and as he swallowed she saw the bobbing movement of his Adam's apple in his thick corded neck. "I think we'd better start back now," he said suddenly. "It's—it's growing late!"

Amber shrugged her shoulders, picked up her skirts and began to make her way back through the tall grass. She did not see him at all the next day, for to tease him she pleaded an attack of the vapours and ate dinner and supper in her own chambers. He sent up a bouquet of roses with a formal little note wishing for her rapid recovery.

She expected to find him at the stables when she went out the following morning, waiting there like a schoolboy hanging about the corner where he hoped his sweetheart might pass—but he was nowhere in sight and she had a brief angry sense of pique, for she had thought him badly smitten. And she had been looking forward herself with some excited anticipation to their next encounter. Nevertheless she set off alone in the same direction they had taken two days before. In only a few moments she had completely forgotten Philip Mortimer and also his father—who was considerably more difficult to force out of her mind—and was wholly engrossed in thoughts of Bruce Carlton.

He had been gone for almost six months now and once again she was losing hold of him—it was like a pleasant dream recalled vividly in the morning but fading to nothing by noon. She could remember many things: the strange grey-green colour of his eyes; the twist of his mouth that always told better than words what he thought of something she had done; his quietness that carried in it the perpetual promise and threat of suppressed violence. She could remember the last time he had made love to her, and whenever she thought of it her head spun dizzily. She had a poignant painful longing for his kisses and the knowing caresses of his hands—but still he seemed to her like someone half imagined and her memories were small comfort for the present. Even Susanna could not, as Amber had expected and hoped, make Bruce seem any nearer or more real to her.

Amber was so absorbed that when her horse shied suddenly she grabbed at the reins and all but sailed over its head. Recovering herself and looking about for whatever had caused the animal's nervousness she saw Philip—red-faced and guilty-eyed —astride his own horse near the three sentinel poplars that stood alone in the midst of the meadow. Immediately he began to apologize for having startled her.

"Oh, your Ladyship! Forgive me! I—I didn't mean to frighten you. I'd just stopped here a moment to enjoy the morning when I saw you coming—so I waited." The explanation was made so earnestly that she knew it was a lie and that he had not wanted his father to see them ride off together.

Amber regained her balance and laughed good-naturedly. "Oh, Philip! It's you! I was just thinking about you!" His eyes shone at that, but she stopped any foolish comment he was about to make. "Come on! I'll race you to the stream!"

He reached it just ahead of her. When she swung down from the saddle he immediately followed, making no argument this time. "How beautiful it is in England in May!" she exclaimed. "Can you imagine why *anyone* would want to go to America?"

"Why, no," he agreed, bewildered. "I can't."

"I think I'll sit down. Will you spread your cloak for me, Philip, so I won't spoil my gown?" She glanced around to find the most pleasant spot. "Over there against that tree, please."

With a display of great gallantry he swirled off his long riding-cloak and laid it on the damp grass. She dropped down easily with her back against the dainty birch, her legs stretched out straight and crossed at the ankles. She flung her hat aside.

"Well, Philip? How long are you going to stand there? Sit down—" She indicated a place beside her.

He hesitated. "Why—uh—" Then, with sudden resolve, he said briskly, "Thank you, your Ladyship," and sat down facing her with his arms resting on his drawn up knees.

But instead of looking at her he kept intent watch on a bee which was going hurriedly from flower to flower, caressing the surface of each, lingering occasionally to sip the last bit of honey. Amber began idly picking the little white daisies that grew profusely in the grass and tossing them one after another into her lap until she had a mound of them.

"You know," said Philip finally, and now he looked directly at her, "it doesn't seem as though you're my step-mother. I can't make myself believe it—no matter how I try. I wonder why?" He seemed genuinely puzzled and distressed; almost comically so, Amber thought.

"Perhaps," she suggested lazily, "you don't want to."

She had begun to make the flowers into a wreath for her

637

hair, piercing the tiny stems with one sharp fingernail, threading them dexterously together.

He thought that over in silence. Then: "How did you ever happen to marry Father?" he blurted suddenly.

Amber kept her eyes down, apparently intent on her work. She gave a little shrug. "He wanted my money. I wanted his title." When she looked up she saw a worried frown on his face. "What's the trouble, Philip? Aren't all marriages a bargain—I have this, you have that, so we get married. That's why you married Jenny, isn't it?"

"Oh, yes, of course. But Father's a mighty fine man—you know that." He seemed to be trying to convince himself more than her, and he looked at her tensely.

"Oh, mighty fine," agreed Amber sarcastically.

"He's mighty fond of you, too."

She gave a burst of impolite laughter at that. "What the devil makes you think so?"

"He told me."

"Did he also tell you to keep away from me?"

"No. But I should—I know I should. I should never have come today." His last words came out swiftly and he turned his head away. Suddenly he started to get to his feet. Amber reached out and caught at his wrist, drawing him gently toward her.

"*Why* should you keep away from me, Philip?" she murmured.

He stared down at her, half kneeling, his breath coming hard. "Because I— Because I should! I'd better go back now before I—"

"Before you what?" The sun through the leaves made a spatter of light and dark on her face and throat. Her lips were moist and parted and her teeth shone white between them; her speckled amber eyes held his insistently. "Philip, what are you afraid of? You want to kiss me—why don't you?"

CHAPTER FORTY-FOUR

PHILIP MORTIMER'S CONSCIENCE troubled him. At first he tried to avoid his step-mother. The day after she had seduced him he went to visit a neighbour and remained away for almost a week. When he returned he was so busy visiting tenants that he seldom appeared even for meals, and on those occasions when he could not avoid meeting her his manner was exaggeratedly stiff and formal. Amber was angry, for she thought that his ridiculous behaviour would give them both away. Furthermore, he was the one source of amusement she had found in the country, and she had no intention of losing him.

One day from the windows of her bedchamber she saw him walking alone across the terrace from the gardens. Radclyffe was closeted in his laboratory and had been for some time; so Amber picked up her skirts and rushed out of the room, down the stairs, and onto the brick terrace. There he was below. But as she started after him he glanced hastily around and then dodged into a tall maze of clipped hedges—it had been planned seventy years ago when such labyrinths were the fashion and now had grown so tall that it was almost possible to get lost there. She reached it, looked about but could not see him, and then ran in, turning swiftly into one lane after another, coming up against a blank wall and retracing her steps to start down another path.

"Philip!" she cried angrily. "Philip, where are you!"

But he made no answer. And then all at once she turned into a lane and found him there, caught, for it was closed at the end. He glanced uneasily about him, saw that there was no escape, and faced her with a look of guilty nervousness. Amber burst into laughter and threw over her head the black-lace shawl she had been carrying.

"Oh, Philip! You silly boy! What d'you mean, running away from me like that? Lord, you'd think I was a monster!"

"I wasn't," he protested, "I wasn't running away. I didn't know you were there."

She made a face at him. "That wheedle won't pass. You've been running away from me for two weeks now. Ever since—" But he looked at her with such protesting horror that she stopped, widening her eyes and raising her brows. "Well—" she breathed softly then. "What's the matter? Didn't you enjoy yourself? You seemed to—at the time."

Philip was in agony. "Oh, please, your Ladyship! Don't— I can't stand it! I'm going out of my head. If you talk that way I'll—I don't know what I'll do!"

Amber put her hands on her hips and one foot began to tap impatiently. "Good Lord, Philip! What's the matter with you? You act as if you've committed some crime!"

His eyes raised again. "I have."

"What, for heaven's sake!"

"You know what."

"I protest—I don't. Adultery's no crime—it's an amusement." She was thinking that he was a fine example of the folly of allowing a young man to live so long in the country, shut away from polite manners.

"Adultery is a crime. It's a crime against two innocent people —your husband, and my wife. But I've committed a worse crime than that. I've made love to my father's wife—I've committed incest." The last word was a whisper and his eyes stared at her, full of self-loathing.

"Nonsense, Philip! We're not related! That was a law made up by old men for the protection of other old men silly enough to marry young women! You're making yourself miserable for nothing."

"Oh, I'm not, I swear I'm not! I've made love to other women before—plenty of them. But I've never done anything like this! This is bad—and wrong. You don't understand. I love my father a great deal—he's a very fine man—I admire him. And now what have I done—"

He looked so thoroughly wretched that Amber had a fleeting sense of pity for him, but when she would have reached over

640

to press his hand he stepped back as if she were something poisonous. She shrugged her shoulders. "Well, Philip—it'll never happen again. Forget about it—just forget it ever happened."

"I will! I've got to!"

But she knew that he was not forgetting at all, and that as the days went by he found it more and more impossible to forget. She did nothing to help him. Whenever they met she was invariably looking her most alluring and she flirted with him in a negative way which seemed just as effective as anything more flagrant could possibly have been. By the end of a fortnight he met her again when she had gone out to ride, and after that he was completely helpless. His feeling of guilt and of self-hatred persisted, but the desire for pleasure was stronger.

They found many places to meet.

Like all great old Catholic homes Lime Park was full of hiding-places which had once been used for the concealing of priests. There were window-seats which might be lifted to disclose a small room below the level of the floor. There were panels in the walls which slid back to show a narrow staircase leading up to a tiny room. Philip knew them all. For Amber at least their various rendezvous afforded a dangerous excitement from which she derived far more enjoyment than she did from Philip's inept love-making.

She did not, however, find it so amusing that she was less eager to return to London. She asked Radclyffe over and over again when they were going back, but invariably he said that he had no plans for returning at all. He would as soon stay in the country, he said, until he died.

"But I'm bored out here, I tell you!" she shouted at him one day.

"I don't doubt you are, madame," he said. "In fact it's always been a puzzle to me how women avoid boredom wherever they are. They have so few resources."

"We have resources enough," said Amber, giving him a slanted look, full of venom and contempt. She had started the conversation with good resolutions, but they could not last long

641

under his cold supercilious stare, his sneering sarcasm. "But it's dull out here. I couldn't wish the devil himself a worse fate than to be boxed up in the country!"

"You should have considered that, then, when you were attempting to prostitute yourself to his Majesty."

She gave a harsh vindictive little laugh. "Attempting to prostitute myself! My God, but you *are* droll! I laid with the King long ago—while I was still at the theatre! Now, my lord, what do you make of *that!*"

Radclyffe smiled, cynical amusement on his thin pressed lips. He was standing beside one of the great windows that overlooked the terrace, leaning against the gold-embroidered hangings, and his whole decadent figure was like that of a delicate porcelain. She longed to smash her fist against the fragile bones of his cheek and nose and skull, and feel them crumble beneath her knuckles.

"Your own lack of subtlety, madame," he said quietly, "makes you suspect a similar flaw in everyone else."

"So you knew it already, did you?"

"Your reputation is not spotless. It was, in fact, very much befouled."

"And I suppose you think it's in a better condition now!"

"At least it will not be in a worse one. I have no interest at all in you or in your reputation, madame. But I have a great deal of interest in the repute which my wife bears. I cannot undo the faults you committed before I married you—but I can at least prevent you from committing new ones now."

For an instant fury brought her close to a disastrous error. It was on the end of her tongue to tell him about herself and Philip, to prove to him that he could not govern her life no matter how he tried. But just in time she controlled herself—and said instead, with an unpleasant sneer: "Oh, can you?"

Radclyffe's eyes narrowed, and as he spoke to her he measured each word like precious poison. "Someday, madame, you'll try me too far. My patience is long, but not endless."

"And then, my lord, what will you do?"

"Go to your rooms!" he said suddenly. "Go to your rooms, madame—or I shall have you carried there by force!"

Amber felt that she would burst with rage and raised her clenched fist to strike him. But he stood so imperturbably, looked at her so coldly, that though she hesitated for several seconds she at last muttered a curse, turned, and ran out of the library.

Her hatred of Radclyffe was so intense that it ate into her brain. He obsessed her day and night until it became a torment which seemed unendurable—and she began to scheme how she might be rid of him. She wanted him dead.

On just one occasion, and that by accident, did Amber come close to making an important discovery about the man she had married. She had never tried to understand him or to learn what had made him the kind of person he was, for they not only disliked each other but found each other mutually uninteresting.

One night in August she was considering which gown she would wear the following day—for they were expecting a number of guests, most of them Jenny's relatives, who were coming to be presented to the new Countess and to spend a few days. Amber was delighted at the opportunity it would give her to show off, and did not doubt that they would be vastly impressed, for they were all people who lived in the country and most of the women had not even been to London since the Restoration. The strict respectable old families would have nothing at all to do with the new Court.

She and Nan were going through the tall standing cabinets in which her clothes were kept, amusing themselves by recalling what had happened the night she had worn a certain gown.

"Oh! That's what I had on the first night Lord Carlton came Dangerfield House!" She snatched the champagne-lace and gold-spangled gown out of the huge wardrobe and held it against herself, smoothing out the folds, wistfully dreaming. But she put it back again with sudden resolution. "And look, Nan! This is what I was presented at Court in!"

At last they took down the white-satin pearl-embroidered gown she had worn the night of her wedding to Radclyffe. Both of them looked it over critically, feeling the material, seeing how it was made, and commenting on how strangely well it had fitted her—just a bit too large in the waist, perhaps, and ever so slightly too small across the bosom.

"I wonder who it belonged to," mused Amber, though she had completely forgotten it in the eight months that had passed since the marriage.

"Maybe his Lordship's first Countess. Why don't you ask 'im sometime? It's got me curious."

"I think I will."

At ten o'clock Radclyffe came upstairs from the library. That was the hour at which they usually went to bed and he was prompt in his habits, faithful to each smallest one—a characteristic of which she and Philip had taken due advantage. Amber was sitting in a chair reading Dryden's new play, "Secret Love," and as he went through the bedroom into his own closet neither of them spoke or seemed aware of the other. He had never once allowed her to see him naked—nor did she wish to—and when he returned he was wearing a handsome dressing-gown made of a fine East Indian silk patterned in many soft subdued colours. As he took a snuffer and started around the room to put the candles out Amber got up and tossed away her book, stretching her arms over her head and yawning.

"That old white-satin gown," she said idly. "The one you wanted me to wear when we were married—where did you get it? Who wore it before I did?"

He paused and looked at her, smiling reflectively. "It's strange you haven't asked me that before. However, there seem to be few enough decencies between us—I may as well tell you. It was intended to be the wedding-gown of a young woman I once expected to marry—but did not."

Amber raised her eyebrows, unmistakably pleased. "Oh? So you were jilted."

"No, I was not jilted. She disappeared one night during the siege of her family's castle in 1643. Her parents never heard from her again, and we were forced to conclude that she had been captured and killed by the Parliamentarians—" Amber saw in his eyes an expression which was new to her. It was profoundly sad and yet he was obviously deriving some measure of gratification, almost of happiness, from this recalling of the past. There was about him now a strange new quality of gentleness which she had never suspected he might possess. "She was a very beautiful and kind and generous woman—a lady. It seems incredible now—and yet the first time I saw you I was strongly reminded of her. Why, I can't imagine. You don't look like her—or only a very little—and certainly you have none of the qualities which I admired in her." He gave a faint shrug, looking not at Amber but somewhere back into the past, a past where he had left his heart. And then his eyes turned to her again, the mask sliding over his face, the past resolving into the present. He went on snuffing the candles; the last one went out and the room was suddenly dark.

"Perhaps it wasn't really so strange you should have made me think of her," he continued, and as his voice did not move she knew that he was standing just a few feet away, beside the candelabrum. "I've been looking for her for twenty-three years —in the face of every woman I've seen, everywhere I've gone. I've hoped that perhaps she wasn't dead—that someday, somewhere I'd find her again." There was a long pause. Amber stood quietly, somewhat surprised by the things he had said, and then she heard his voice coming closer and the sound of his slippers moving across the floor toward her. "But now I've ceased looking—I know that she's dead."

Amber threw off her gown and got quickly into bed, and the swift sense of dread she had every night grabbed at her. "So you were in love—once!" she said, angry to know that though he despised her he had once been able to love another woman with tenderness and generosity.

She felt the feather-mattress give as he sat down. "Yes, I was in love once. But only once. I remember her with a young man's idealism—and so I still love her. But now I'm old and I know too much about women to have anything but contempt for them." He put his robe across the foot of the bed and lay down beside her.

For several minutes Amber waited apprehensively, her muscles stiff and her teeth tight-closed, unable to shut her eyes. She had never dared actually refuse him, but each night she was tortured with this suspense of waiting—she never knew for what. But he was stretched flat on his back far to his own side of the bed, and he made no move to touch her; at last she heard him begin to breathe evenly. Relieved, she relaxed slowly and drowsiness began to creep upon her. Nevertheless, the slightest move from him made her start, suddenly wide awake again. Even when he left her alone she could not sleep in peace.

Jenny's relatives came and for several days they were interested observers of Amber's gowns and jewels and manners. None of them approved of her, but all of them found her exciting, and while the women talked about her with raised eyebrows and pinched lips the men were inclined toward nudges and conspiratorial winks. Amber knew what they were thinking, all of them, but she did not care; if they found her shocking she considered them dull and old-fashioned. Still, when they were gone and the silence and monotony began to settle again, she was more impatient than ever.

By now she had worked Philip to such a pitch of infatuation and resentment that it was difficult to make him use discretion. "What are we going to do!" he asked her again and again. "I can't stand this! Sometimes I think I'm losing my mind."

Amber was sweetly reasonable, smoothing back the light-brown hair from his face—he never wore a periwig. "There isn't anything we can do, Philip. He's your father—"

"I don't care if he is! I hate him now! Last night I met him in the gallery just as he was going in to you— My God, for a minute I thought I was going to grab him by the throat and— Oh, what am I saying!" He sighed heavily, his boyish face haggard and miserable. Amber had brought him some momentary pleasures, but a great deal of unhappiness, and he had not been really at peace since she had come to Lime Park.

"You mustn't talk that way, Philip," she said softly. "You mustn't even think about such things—or sometime it might happen. I doubt not it's his lawful right to use me however he will—"

"Oh, Lord! I never thought I'd see my life in such a mess—I don't know how it ever happened!"

It was only a few days later that Amber came into the house alone from her morning ride—Philip had returned by another route so that they would not be seen together—and found Radclyffe at the writing-table in their bedroom. "Madame," he said, speaking to her from over his shoulder, "I find it necessary to pay a brief visit to London. I'm leaving this afternoon immediately following dinner."

A quick smile sprang to Amber's face, and though she did not really believe that it was his intention to take her with him, she hoped to bluff her way into going. "Oh, wonderful, your Lordship! I'll set Nan a-packing right now!"

She started out of the room but his next words brought her up short. "Don't trouble yourself. I'm going alone."

"Alone? But why should you? If you're going I can go too!"

"I shall be gone but a few days. It's a matter of important business and I don't care to be troubled with your company."

She drew a quick breath of indignation and then suddenly rushed back to face him across the table. "You're the most unreasonable damned man on earth! I won't stay here alone, d'ye hear me? I won't!" She banged the handle of her riding-whip on the table-top, marring its surface.

He got up slowly, bowed to her—though she could see the muscles about his mouth twitch and squirm with the effort to control his rage—and walked out of the room. Amber banged the whip down again, furiously, and yelled after him: "I won't stay! I won't! I won't! I won't!" As the door closed behind him, she slammed the riding-whip through the window and rushed into the adjoining room where she found Nan gossiping with Susanna's dry-nurse. "Nan! Pack my things! I'm going to London in my own coach! That bastard—"

Susanna ran to her mother, stamped her foot, and repeated with a shake of her curls: "That bas-tard!"

When dinner was announced Amber did not go down. She was busy getting ready to leave and was so angry and excited that she had no appetite. And when Radclyffe sent again, demanding that she join them, she refused point-blank, shut the outer door to their apartments, locked it and flung aside the key.

"He's told me one time too many what I can do and what I can't!" she hotly informed Nan. "I'll be damned if that stinking old scoundrel can lead me like a bear by the nose any longer!"

But when she had changed her clothes and was ready to go she discovered that the doors leading into the gallery had been locked from the other side and that her own key was not to be found. There was no other outside entrance, for the rooms opened one into another, and though she hammered and pounded and kicked she got no answer. At last in a passionate temper she flung back into the bedchamber and began smashing everything she could lay her hands on. Nan ran out, arms up over her head. By the time Amber had exhausted herself the room was a shambles.

After a while someone opened the door into the entrance hall and slid a trayful of food in, rapped to call her attention, and then ran off down the gallery. The Earl had evidently informed the servants that his wife was having another fit. A maid brought the tray in and placed it on a table beside the bed where her mistress lay. Amber turned, grabbed up the cold fowl and flung it across the room; then shoved away the tray and dishes, which crashed onto the floor.

After three hours had gone by Nan ventured back into the room. Amber sat up cross-legged on the bed to talk to her. She was determined to go to London anyway, if she had to climb out the window, but Nan tried to convince her that if she disobeyed his Lordship he might bring an action against her, obtain a separation and get control of all her money.

"Remember," cautioned Nan, "his Majesty may like you—but his Majesty likes all pretty ladies. And you know his nature—he doesn't love to meddle where it's any trouble to him. You'd be wise to stay here, mam, I think."

Amber had thrown off her shoes and undone her hair and she sat with elbows propped on her knees, glowering. She was beginning to grow very hungry, for she had had nothing but a glass of fruit syrup since seven o'clock that morning, and it was now four-thirty. Her eye went to the cold roast fowl, which someone had picked up, dusted, and set back on the tray.

"But what am I to do? Moult out here in the country for the rest of my life? I tell you I won't do it!"

Suddenly they became aware of a muffled pounding and a woman's faint frantic cries. They looked at each other, both of them held taut in an attitude of listening and surprise. It was Jenny, hammering at the outer door—and with a leap Amber was off the bed and running through the intervening rooms toward her.

"Your Ladyship!" screamed Jenny, and there were hysterical tears in her voice. "Your Ladyship! Your Ladyship!"

"Here I am, Jenny! What's happened? What's the matter?"

"It's Philip! He's sick! He's desperately sick! I'm afraid he's dying! Oh, your Ladyship—you've *got* to come!"

A chill of horror ran over Amber. Philip sick—*dying?* Only that morning before the ride they had been in the summer-house, and he had been perfectly well then.

"What's the matter with him? I can't get out, Jenny! I'm locked in! Where's the Earl?"

"He's gone! He left three hours ago! Oh, Amber—you've got to get out! He's calling for you!" Jenny began to sob.

Amber looked around helplessly. "I *can't* get out! Oh, damn! Go get a footman! Make them *break* open the door!"

Nan was beside her now and as Jenny's heels pounded off down the hallway the two women picked up brass shovels from the fireplace and began to beat at the lock. In only a minute or two Jenny was back.

"They say his Lordship left orders not to let you out no matter what happened!"

"Where's the footman!"

"He's here—but he says he doesn't dare unlock the door! Oh, Amber, tell him he's got to! Philip—"

"Open this door, you varlet!" shouted Amber. "Open it or I'll set fire to the house!" She smashed furiously against the lock with the brass shovel.

There was a long moment of hesitation after which the man began to pound at the door from the outside while Amber

649

stood waiting, wet with sweat. Nan had brought her shoes and she pulled them on, jumping up and down, first on one foot and then the other, as she did so. At last the lock broke and she burst out, flung an arm around Jenny's waist and started down toward the opposite end of the gallery where Philip's apartments were located.

Philip was lying on the bed, still fully dressed but with a blanket thrown over him; his head was forced back upon the pillows and his face contorted almost beyond recognition. He was writhing and turning, clutching at his stomach, his teeth ground together until the veins in his neck seemed ready to burst.

Amber hesitated for only an instant on the threshold and then ran forward. "Philip! Philip, what's the matter? What happened to you?"

He looked at her for a moment without recognition. Then he grabbed her by the wrist, dragging her toward him. "I've been poisoned—" His voice was a harsh whisper. Amber gasped in horror, starting backward, but he held onto her wrist with a clutch so strong she thought it would break. "Have you eaten anything today—"

Suddenly she realized what had happened. The Earl had found out about them and had tried to poison them both. The food sent up on her tray must have been poisoned. She felt sick, dizzy and cold, swept with selfish anxiety.

Maybe it was in the fruit-syrup this morning— Maybe *I'm* poisoned too!

"I had some fruit-syrup," she said softly, her eyes staring like glass, "early this morning—"

There was an explosive spitting sound from beneath the blankets and Philip's body leaped upward in convulsion; he threw himself furiously from side to side, as though trying to escape the pain. Agonized paroxysms jerked at his face, and it was several moments before he was able to speak again. Then each word as it came out was a forced and painful grunt.

"No. I got it at dinner, I think— Pains began half-an-hour ago. The summer-house—there's a hollowed eye in that stone mask on the wall—"

He could say nothing more for Jenny was close beside them, but Amber understood his meaning. Radclyffe could have been there that morning, watching them. He could have been there many mornings—watching them. Disgust and loathing and helpless rage filled her. But there was relief too—because she was not poisoned; she was not going to die.

Jenny now helped Philip to sit up, holding a mugful of warm milk to his mouth. After he had taken several greedy swallows he gave a groan and flung himself backward again. Amber turned away, her hands over her face.

Suddenly she picked up her skirts and started to run as fast as she could—out of the room and down the gallery, down the stairs and onto the terrace. She fled down the steps and through the gardens and did not stop once until she was forced to by the splitting pain in her side and the dryness of her lungs. Then she stood there for a minute or so, one hand pressed to her chest and the other hard against her side, struggling to breathe. But gradually it became easier for her and at last she turned her head, slowly, to look back up at the bedroom window that faced from the south-east end of the house. Then with a wail of animal terror she threw herself onto the ground and buried her face in the grass, shutting her eyes as tight as she could and closing her ears with her fingers. But still she could see Philip's face in its agony and hear the hoarse desperate sound of his voice.

CHAPTER FORTY-FIVE

PHILIP WAS BURIED that same night as the dusk settled through a brilliant sunset sky. The family chaplain who had baptized him administered the last sacraments and conducted the services in the little Catholic chapel where Jenny and Amber and Radclyffe's many servants knelt in silence. Poison was suspected in almost any sudden death, and because there was a general belief that a poisoned body decomposed rapidly they had not dared to wait upon formality. Philip's constant request had been to keep it secret, to let no one know what had caused his death. He wanted it told that he had accidentally shot himself while cleaning a gun.

Amber was so hungry that her stomach ached, but she refused to eat or drink anything at all. She was terrified for fear Radclyffe had instructed one of the servants to kill her if he failed. For there could be no doubt he had intended to kill them both: she fed a few slices of the fowl to a dog, and it died swiftly and in great pain.

Neither Amber nor Jenny wanted to be alone that night and Jenny was having spasmodic cramps which she feared might mean that her labour had begun prematurely. They stayed together in a seldom used guest apartment in the north-east wing of the building overlooking the courtyard, for they were both reluctant to return to their own chambers. Amber was determined she would never go back to hers again as long as she lived. By ten o'clock Jenny's pains had stopped and she went to bed, but Amber stayed up, nervous and jumpy, apprehensive of shadows, alarmed at any unexpected sound. She felt as though hideous unseen things surrounded her on every side, shutting her in until she could scarcely breathe, and once she screamed aloud in terror. She kept lighted all the candles she could find and refused to take off her clothes.

At last Jenny got up and came to put her arms about her. "Amber, dear, you must try to sleep."

Amber shook her off. "I can't. I can't." She ran her fingers through her hair, shivering. "What if he should come back. He meant to kill me. If he found me alive— Oh! What's that!"

"Nothing. Just an animal outside. He won't come back. He wouldn't dare. He won't ever come back. You're safe here."

"I'm not going to stay! I'm going away tomorrow morning— as soon as it's light!"

"Going away? But where will you go? Oh, please, Amber, don't go and leave me!"

"Your mother will come. I can't stay here, Jenny! I'd go mad! I've got to go—and don't try to stop me!"

She could not and would not tell Jenny where she was going, but she knew very well herself. For now the chance had come and all the plans over which she had mulled and brooded these past weeks fell into a pattern. She had expected to use Philip, but now he was dead and she realized that she could do it better without him. It seemed so simple she wondered why she had endured all these months of hatred and degradation, without realizing that it had taken time and circumstances to bring her to her present pitch of desperation.

With Big John Waterman and two or three other serving-men she would set out for London. Perhaps they could ambush him on the way, but if not she would somehow contrive to meet him alone in London, some dark night. It was no uncommon occurrence, she knew, to find a gentleman of quality badly beaten or even dead—for every man had his enemies and vengeance was crude and decisive. A slit nose, a brutal kicking, a sword through the stomach, were all popular means of aveng-ing some real or imagined insult. She intended Radclyffe to die of his injuries—since now it was either his life or hers.

Because it was both easier and safer to travel in masculine dress she prepared to set out the next morning wearing one of the Earl's suits—which was not a great deal too large—his hat and riding-cloak. Big John and four husky footmen were to go with her, though no one but John knew what her intentions were. Jenny wept and begged her over and over to change her mind, but when Amber refused she helped her get ready and gave her many admonitions about taking care of herself.

"There's one thing I'll never be able to understand," Jenny said, as she watched Amber pulling on a pair of his Lordship's boots. "I don't know why he spared me— If he wanted to kill you, and Philip—why would he have let *me* live?"

Amber gave her a swift narrowed glance and as the blood rushed into her face she bent her head. Poor innocent little Jenny. She still did not know; and certainly it could do her no good to know now. For the first time since she had begun her affair with Philip Mortimer Amber felt a kind of shame. But it did not last long. Soon she was on horseback—waving to Nan and promising Jenny that she would be careful.

The summer had been even hotter than the year before; for weeks it had not rained and the roads were hard. Amber, because she had been riding almost every day during the past four and a half months, was able to set a swift pace for the men. They stopped at the first village they came to because she was ravenously hungry, and then they hurried on again. By five o'clock that evening they had travelled forty-five miles.

Hot and tired and dusty, reeking of sweat—their own and the horses'—the six of them stopped at a pretty little inn. Amber went swaggering in with the men, pretending that she was one of them. She felt pleased at this adventure, the more so because she was keenly aware that but for a lucky accident she would have been lying dead at Lime Park and not sitting here on a settle with her feet cocked up before the fire, stroking a ragged old dog and enjoying the succulent smells from a joint which turned and crackled over the flames. She was luxuriously tired and her muscles felt sore from the unaccustomed strain of riding astride. Nothing had ever tasted so good as the cool golden ale she swallowed from a pewter tankard.

She slept deeply that night and longer than she had intended, but they were off again at six. By noon they had reached Oxford, where they stopped for dinner. The hostess put two enormous black-jacks on the table and while they drank she brought in pewter plates and knives and spoons. When the joint was taken off the fire she carved it for them, very neatly, and then according to the custom they invited her to join them.

"I suppose you gentlemen are on your way to London to see the fire?" she inquired in a polite, conversational tone.

Heads turned all down the table, fingers paused halfway to their mouths. "Fire!"

"Ye hadn't heard? Oh, there's a *great* fire in London, they say." She was full of importance at having such news to tell: burnt-out crops and the heat had been the most exciting source of conversation for some time. "There was a gentleman here not an hour since just come from there. He says it gets worse by the hour. Looks like it might take the whole city," she added, shutting her mouth complacently and nodding at them.

"You mean there's a *big* fire in London?" repeated Amber incredulously. "Not just a few houses?"

654

"Oh, Lord, no! It's a big one, well enough. He said it was well along the river when he left—and that was yesterday afternoon."

"Good Lord!" whispered Amber. She had visions of all her money burning, her clothes, and everything else that belonged to her. London in flames! "When did it begin? How did it start?"

"Began early Sunday morning," she said. "Long before sun-up. They think it's a Papist plot."

"My God! And this is Monday noon! It's been burning almost two days!" She turned excitedly to Big John. "How much farther is it? We've got to get there!"

"It's seventy miles or more, sir. We could never make it if we rode all night. Better to ride till dark and then go on in the morning."

In just a few minutes they had finished eating and were mounted. The hostess followed them out, pointing up into the sky. "Look at the sun! How red it's turned!" They all looked up, shading their eyes with their hands, and there were others in the streets also looking up. The sun had a dull glow and its colour was fierce and ominous.

"Come on!" cried Amber, and they swept off, galloping down the road.

Amber did not want to stop at all that night for she was afraid that when she got there not only her money but the Earl too would have disappeared in the confusion. But it would have been all but impossible to reach the City, for travel by night was much slower and more dangerous than by day. When supper was over she went immediately to her room and without taking off more than her hat and boots and doublet threw herself onto the bed and fell fast asleep. Before dawn the hostess was rapping at the door and by five they were on the road again.

At each village they asked for news of the fire and heard the same thing everywhere: it was taking all the town, burning the Bridge, churches, houses, sparing nothing. And the closer they got to London the more people they saw on the roads, all going in the same direction. Farmers and workmen were throwing down their shovels and leaving their fields, setting out for the capital with carts and even wheelbarrows; vehicles of transportation were at a premium and a man might hire himself and cart at forty or fifty pounds for a few hours' work—as much as a farmer was likely to make in a whole year's time.

When they had gone fifteen more miles they could see the smoke, a great moving pall that hung in the distance, and soon little charred fragments of paper and linen and plaster began to drift down upon them. They galloped on and on, as fast as they could go, not stopping even to eat. The day was windy and the closer they got to London the fiercer it blew, whipping their cloaks about them. Amber lost her hat. They had to squint their eyes for the wind blew specks of tinder into them. As the afternoon began to fade the flames could be seen more clearly, leaping in great streaks, casting a threatening red glare over all the land.

It was almost night when they reached the City because for the last ten miles the roads were so congested that they could not move at even a walking pace. From far off they could hear the roar of the fire, like thousands of iron coach-wheels crashing together over cobblestones. There was a continuous echoing thunder as buildings collapsed or were blown up. From the churches that still stood, within the City and without, the bells rang frantically—sounding a wild call of distress that had never ceased since the fire had been discovered two days and a half before. As darkness settled the sky glowed red—like the top of a burning oven.

Just without the walls were the great open spaces of Moor Fields, already crowded with men and women and children, and more were constantly arriving—forcing the first comers back into the middle of the fields, packing them in tightly. Some had already pitched tents made of sheets or towels tied together. Women were suckling their babies; others were trying to prepare a meal with whatever food they had been able to save in those few awful moments before the flames had seized their houses. Some sat and stared, unable and unwilling to believe. Others stolidly stood and watched, the heat scorching their faces, though the glare of the fire made it impossible to see more than black silhouettes of the burning buildings.

656

At first no one had believed that the fire would be any more destructive than were dozens of fires London had every year. It had begun at two o'clock Sunday morning in Pudding Lane, a narrow little alley near the waterfront, and for hours it fed on the tar and hemp and coal that were stored beside the river. The Lord Mayor was brought to the scene in the early hours and said contemptuously that a woman might piss it out; for fear of making himself unpopular he refused to begin blowing up houses. But it swept on, terrifying and ruthless, destroying whatever lay in its path. When London Bridge caught, the City was doomed—for it was covered with buildings and as they collapsed they blocked that means of escape; charred timbers falling into the water destroyed the water-wheels underneath, and the one efficient means of fighting a great fire was gone. From then on it must be done with buckets of water passed from hand to hand, pumps, hooks for dragging down burning buildings, and hand-squirts.

Unalarmed, the people went to church as usual on Sunday, though some of them were brought running into the streets by a man who galloped along crying, "Arm! Arm! The French have landed!"

But complacency began to vanish as the fire backed up into the City, crawling steadily, leaping sometimes, driven and fed by the violent east wind. As it advanced it drove the people before it. Many of them refused to make any preparations for leaving until the flames had actually caught their houses, and then they seized whatever they could and ran—often taking articles of no value and leaving behind what was most important. Helpless, confused, they moved slowly through the narrow alleys. First they stopped at Cannon Street, which ran along the crest of the hill above the river, but the fire came on and by afternoon they were forced to move again.

The King was not informed until eleven o'clock. He and York came immediately and at his order men began to blow up houses. It was too late to save the City by that means, but it was all they could do. Both the brothers worked hard and without stopping for rest or food. They helped to man the pumps, passed water-buckets, moved from place to place offering what encouragement and sympathy they could. More than anything else, it was their courage, energy and resourcefulness which prevented widespread panic and rioting.

Even so, the streets became unsafe for any foreigners who were obviously Dutch or French. In Fenchurch Street a blacksmith knocked down a Frenchman with a heavy iron bar, smashing his cheekbones and his nose. A woman who was believed to be carrying fire-balls in her apron was attacked and badly mauled and bruised before they found that the fire-balls were only chickens. Another Frenchman with an armful of tennis-balls was seized upon and beaten unconscious. No one cared whether they were guilty—the mounting hysteria demanded an explanation for this terrible calamity, and they found it in the three things Englishmen most feared and hated: the French, the Dutch, and the Catholics. One or all three must be responsible—they were determined not to let the guilty escape with the innocent. King Charles ordered many foreigners jailed for their own protection and the Spanish Ambassador opened his house to others.

The Thames was aswarm with little boats, smacks and barges, which plied back and forth—carrying people and their goods to safety in Southwark. Shooting sparks and pieces of burning wood fell hissing into the water or started new fires in blankets or clothing. Sometimes a boat overturned and spilled out an entire family—the river was so crowded that it was like coming up under ice and trying to find an open space.

Finally Amber and the five men had to abandon their horses and continue on foot.

They had been riding for almost thirteen hours and she was sore and stiff; she felt as though she would never be able to make her knees touch again. Her head swam with fatigue. She longed to drop where she was and stay, but she forced herself to go on. Don't stop, don't stop, she told herself over and over. Take another step. Go on. You've got to get there. She was afraid that she had missed him—that he would be gone or the house burned and though tortured by fatigue, she pushed ahead.

She grabbed at people as they passed, shouting to ask if Cheapside had burnt. Most of them shoved on by, ignoring or not even hearing her, but finally she got an answer.

"Early this morning."

"All of it?" He was gone and she accosted several more, dragging at their shirt-sleeves. "Is *all* of Cheapside burnt?"

"Aye, lad. Burnt to the ground."

The answer gave her a plunging shock of despair, but it was not as great as what she would have felt under any other conditions; for the hysterical energy that was in the moving groping crowds had communicated itself to her. The fire was so gigantic, the destruction so wide-spread and terrible that it assumed a strange unreality. Shadrac Newbold had been burnt out and with him probably all the money she had on earth—but she could not just then fully realize what it meant and might mean to her. That must come later.

Nothing mattered now but to find Radclyffe.

Outside the gates in Chiswell Street and the Barbican and Long Lane the people were still waiting dubiously. They were hoping, as those who had lived in Watling Street and Corn Hill and Cheapside had hoped, that the fire would stop before it reached them. But the flames had already broken through the walls and the wind had increased to such fury it seemed impossible anything at all could be spared. Some ran distractedly in and out of their homes, unable to make a decision. But others were moving what they could, throwing pieces of furniture and piles of bedding out of upper-story windows, stacking carts with dishes and silver-plate and portraits.

Amber hung closely to Big John Waterman as they shoved their way along Goswell Street, for they were going against the crowd and the irresistible tide of people sometimes forced them backward in spite of their efforts.

There were mothers who balanced great loads on their heads, holding in one arm a sucking baby while they tried wearily to watch other children and keep them from being crushed or lost. Husky porters, arrogant and rude, shouted and swore and elbowed their ruthless way—for once it was they who gave the orders. Bewildered animals were everywhere. A bleating fright-

659

ened goat tried to butt his way through. Cows were hauled along with yelling children astride their backs. There were countless dogs and cats, belled pigs, squawking parrots in their cages, monkeys perched on the shoulder of a master or mistress, chattering angrily and snatching at a man's wig or a woman's necklace. There were men who carried on their heads a feather-bed and on top of that a trunk that shifted perilously and sometimes went crashing to the ground. Others had everything they had been able to save tied into a sheet and slung over their backs. There were a great many pregnant women, desperately trying to protect their awkward bellies, and several of the younger ones were crying, almost hysterical with terror. The sick were carried on the backs of sons or husbands or servants. A woman lying in a cart rolled slowly by; she was groaning and her face was contorted in the agony of childbirth; beside her knelt a midwife, working with her hands beneath the blankets, while the woman in her pain kept trying to throw them off.

Their faces were desperate, apathetic, bewildered. Some of the children laughed and played games between the legs of the crowd. Many of the old had become perfectly listless. But all of them had lost everything—the savings of a lifetime, the work of generations. What the fire took was gone forever.

With Big John's arm about her Amber slowly fought her way. She was too small to see over the heads of the crowd and she asked him again and again if Aldersgate Street was burning; he continued to tell her that it did not look as if the flames had reached it yet, but they seemed near.

If only I can get there! If only I can get there and find him!

Cinders got into her eyes and when she inadvertently rubbed them they became inflamed. She choked and coughed on the smoke, and the hot scorching air that the wind blew into her nostrils and lungs made every breath painful. It was only by tremendous effort that she kept from bursting into tears of sheer baffled rage and weariness. She might have fallen if Big John had not held her up. Somewhere they had lost the other men—who perhaps had gone off to join the looters, for thieves entered the houses even before the masters had left.

At last they came to Radclyffe House.

The flames were just below it in St. Martin le Grand and had almost reached Bull and Mouth Street at the corner. Loaded carts were lined up in front and there were servants—and perhaps thieves too—carrying out vases and portraits and statues and furniture. She forced her way in. No one tried to stop her or even seemed to know that she was there. Certainly they could not have recognized her with her soot-smudged face, her hair in long dirty snarls, her torn and blackened clothes.

The hallway was in a turmoil. The broad center staircase was covered with men and furniture—one carrying a small Italian couch, another bundled in ornate golden drapes, someone with a Botticelli painting on his head, another balancing one velvet-seated Spanish chair on each shoulder. Amber approached a liveried footman who carried one end of a gigantic carved chest.

"Where's your master?" He ignored her and would have gone on by without answering but she grabbed him roughly by the arm, angry enough to have slapped his face. "Answer me, you varlet! Where's your master?"

He gave her a surprised look, without recognition, as though he had heard her for the first time. Radclyffe had probably been working them for hours. He gave a jerk of his head. "Upstairs, I think. In his closet."

Amber ran up the stairs, dodging around servants and furniture, with Big John close at her heels. But now her legs were weak and trembling. She felt her heart begin to pound. She swallowed but her throat was dry. Nevertheless her exhaustion was suddenly and miraculously gone.

They hurried down the gallery to his Lordship's apartments. Two men were just coming out, each of them bearing a tall stack of books, and as they went she signalled Big John to turn the lock. "Don't come till I call you," she said softly, and then walked swiftly across the parlour toward the bedchamber.

It was almost empty—but for the bed, too big and unwieldy to be moved—and she went on, toward the laboratory. Her heart seemed to have filled all her chest now and it hammered so that she expected it suddenly to burst. He was there, going hastily through the drawers of a table and stuffing his pockets with

661

papers. For once his clothes were in disarray—he must have ridden horseback to have arrived so soon—but even so he presented a strangely elegant appearance. His back was turned to her.

"My lord!" Amber's voice rang out like the tolling of a bell.

He started a little and glanced around, but he did not recognize her and returned instantly to his work. "What do you want? Go away, lad, I'm busy. Carry some furniture down to the carts."

"My lord!" she repeated. "Look again. You'll see I'm no lad."

For a moment he paused and then, very slowly and cautiously, he turned. There was a single candle burning on the table beside him, but the glare of the flames lighted the room brilliantly. Outside the fire roared like unceasing thunder; the constant booming of explosions rattled the windows, and burnt buildings toppled to the ground, crashing one after another.

"Is it *you?*" he asked at last, very softly.

"Yes, it's me. And alive—no ghost, my lord. Philip's dead—but I'm not."

The incredulity on his face shifted at last to a kind of horror, and suddenly Amber's fears were gone. She felt powerful and strong and filled with a loathing that brought out everything cruel and fierce and wild in her.

With an insolent lift of her chin she started toward him, walking slowly, and the riding whip in her right hand flicked nervously against her leg. He stared at her, his eyes straight and steady, but the muscles around his mouth twitched ever so slightly. "My son's dead," he repeated slowly, fully realizing for the first time what he had done. "He's dead—and you're not." He looked sick and beaten and older than ever before, all confidence gone. The murder of his son had completed the ruin of his life.

"So you finally found out about us," taunted Amber as she stood before him, one hand on her hip, the other still flicking the riding-crop.

He smiled, a faint and reflective smile, cold, contemptuous, and strangely sensual. Slowly he began to answer. "Yes. Many weeks ago. I watched you together—there in the summer-house—thirteen times in all. I watched what you did and I listened to what you said, and I got a great deal of pleasure from thinking how you would die—one day, when you least expected it—"

"Did you!" snapped Amber, her voice taut and hard, and the whip flickered back and forth, swift as a snake. "But I didn't die—and I'm not going to either—"

Her eyes flared to a wild blaze. Suddenly she raised the whip and lashed it across his face with all the force in her body. He jerked backward, one hand going up involuntarily, but the first blow had left a thin red welt from his left temple to the bridge of his nose. Her teeth clenched and her face contorted with murderous fury; she struck at him again and again, so blind now with rage she could scarcely see. Suddenly he grabbed hold of the candlestick and lunged toward her, heaving all his weight behind it. She moved swiftly aside and as she dodged gave a shrill scream.

The candlestick struck her shoulder and glanced off. She saw his face loom close and his hand seized the whip. They began to struggle and just as Amber brought up her knee to jab him in the groin Big John's cudgel came down on his skull. Radclyffe began to double. Amber jerked the whip out of his hand and lashed at his face again and again, no longer fully conscious of what she was doing.

"Kill him!" she screamed. "Kill him!" She cried it over and over again: "Kill him! Kill him! Kill him!"

With one hand John swept off the Earl's periwig and with the other he smashed again at his skull. Radclyffe lay sprawled grotesquely on the floor, his naked head streaming blood. A strong revulsion swept Amber. She felt no pity or regret but only a violent paroxysm of satisfied rage and hatred.

All at once she became aware that the draperies were on fire and for a horrified moment she believed the house was burning and that they were trapped. Then she saw that the candle he had thrown at her had fallen beside the window, the draperies had caught, and now flames roared to the ceiling and licked along the wooden moulding.

"John!"

He turned, saw the flames, and both of them started out of the apartment in a rush. At the door they glanced back, briefly, before John shut and locked it. The last they saw of Radclyffe was a broken and bloody old man who lay dead on the floor, with the flames already approaching him. John put the key into his pocket and they began to run down the gallery toward the rear of the house. But Amber had not gone ten yards when she suddenly pitched forward, unconscious as she fell. Big John swooped her into his arms and ran on. He went clattering noisily down the little back staircase, Amber held limp and flopping before him, and halfway down he met two men who would have pushed past him. They wore no livery and must have been thieves.

"Fire!" he shouted at them. "The house is afire!"

Instantly they turned and rushed down, the three of them making a furious noise in the narrow echoing cavity. One stumbled and almost fell, recovered himself and burst out into the courtyard. Big John came close on their heels, but they had disappeared. He glanced around once, and saw that the flames from the upstairs window already were casting a reflection into the courtyard pool.

PART V

CHAPTER FORTY-SIX

WHEN AMBER RETURNED to London in mid-December, three and a half months after the Fire, she found almost all the ancient walled City gone. The ground was still a heap of rubble and twisted iron, brick débris, molten lead now cooled, and in many cellars fires continued to smoke and burn. Not even the torrential October rains had been able to put them out. Most of the streets had been completely obliterated by fallen buildings and others were blocked off because chimneys and half-walls which still stood made them dangerous. London looked dead and ruined.

The city was infinitely more sad and pitiful now that the cruel gorgeous spectacle of the flames was gone. There were gloomy predictions that she would never rise again, and on that rainy grey December day they seemed to be only inevitable truth. Beaten down by plague and war and fire, her trade fallen off, burdened with the greatest public debt in the history of the nation, full of unrest and misery—men were saying everywhere that the days of England's glory had passed, her old valour was worn out, she was a nation doomed to perish from the earth. The future had never seemed more hopeless; men had never been more pessimistic or more resentful.

But in spite of everything the indomitable will and hope of the people had already begun to conquer. A mushroom city of mean little shacks and rickety sheds had sprung up where whole families took shelter on the sites of their former homes. Shops were beginning to open and some new houses were a-building.

And not all the town had burned.

For outside the walls there was still left standing that part of the city east of the Tower and north of Moor Fields; on the west there remained the old barristers' college of Lincoln's Inn and still farther west Drury Lane and Covent Garden and St. James, where the nobility was moving in steadily increasing numbers. Nothing around the bend of the river had burned. The Strand was still there and the great old houses with their gardens running down to the Thames. The fashionable part of London had not been touched by the Fire.

Amber and Big John had left the city immediately, hired horses when they found their own gone, and ridden straight to Lime Park. She told Jenny that when she had arrived the house had been burnt and she had not been able to find his Lordship anywhere—but nevertheless for the sake of appearances she sent a party of men back to London to search for him. They returned after several days to say he could not be discovered and that according to all evidence he had been trapped in the house and burned to death. Amber, immeasurably relieved that she was evidently not going to be caught, put on mourning—but she did not pretend to be very sorry, for she did not consider that particular piece of hypocrisy essential to her welfare.

But the best news she heard was from Shadrac Newbold—who had a messenger out there two days after she got back to inform her that not one of his depositors had lost a shilling. She found out later that though much money had gone up in the Fire, almost all the goldsmiths had saved what was entrusted to them. And though there was less than half of it left now, twenty-eight thousand pounds, even that was enough to make her one of the richest women in England. Furthermore, it was being added to by interest and by returns on the investments he had made for her, and later she could augment it by renting Lime Park and selling much of the furnishings—though so far she could not bring herself to touch Radclyffe's effects.

Certainly there was brilliant promise in the future. But the present was a source of fear and anxiety to her—for though Radclyffe was dead she had not been able to get rid of him. He had come there to his home to haunt her. She met him unexpectedly as she rounded a corner in the gallery; he stood behind her when she ate; he accosted her in the night and she lay sweating with terror, jumping at imaginary sounds, or she woke up with a hysterical scream. She wanted to get away, but Nan's baby had been born just the day before she returned and

668

she intended to wait until Nan could travel. She was staying mostly out of affection for Nan and gratitude for what she had done during the Plague—but also because she had no place to go but Almsbury's, and did not want to rouse his suspicions by rushing away pell-mell at first news of her husband's death. She was not willing to entrust her fatal secret to anyone but Big John and Nan.

Jenny's mother came, and as soon as the child had been born and Jenny recovered she was going home to her own people. Amber felt a little guilty when, at the first of October, she left for Barberry Hill—but she told herself that after all Jenny had no reason to be afraid of staying there. She had never been his Lordship's enemy; she had had nothing to do with Philip's death—the walls and ceilings and very trees had nothing to say to her. But for herself—she could stand it no longer. And she went.

At Barberry Hill she felt more comfortable, and it did not take her as long to forget—Radclyffe, Philip and everything that had happened this past year—as she had thought it would. She put it all resolutely out of her mind. She had an uncomfortable feeling that Almsbury guessed she knew more about her husband's death than she had told—perhaps he thought that she had hired a gang of bullies to murder him—but he never tried to trick her into making an inadvertent admission, and they seldom mentioned his Lordship at all.

Once he said to her, teasingly, "Well, sweetheart—who d'ye suppose you'll marry next? They say Buckhurst has almost made up his mind to risk matrimony—"

She shot him a sharp indignant glance. "Marry come up, Almsbury! You must think I'm cracked! I'm rich and I've got a title now—why the devil should I make myself miserable by marrying again! There never was such a wretched state as matrimony! I've tried it three times and—"

"Three times?" he asked, his voice sliding over the words with a sound of amusement.

Amber flushed in spite of herself, for Luke Channell was a secret she had never shared with anyone but Nan. It was one of the few things of which she was ashamed. "Twice, I mean!

Well—what are you smirking for? Anyway, smile if you like, but I'll never get married again—I've got better plans for myself than that, I warrant you!" She turned, her black-silk skirts swishing about her, and started to leave the room.

Almsbury was lounging against the fireplace, filling his pipe. He looked after her and grinned, but shrugged his shoulders.

"God knows, sweetheart, it's nothing to me if you've had three husbands or thirteen. And none of my business if you marry again or not. I was just wondering—how d'you think you'll look in stark black by the time you're thirty-five?"

Amber stopped in her tracks and turned to stare back at him, over her shoulder; her face looked suddenly white and shocked. Thirty-five! My God—I'll *never* be thirty-five! She looked down at herself—at the severe black gown of mourning—the gown she must wear until she died, unless she married again.

"Damn you, Almsbury!" she muttered, and went swiftly out of the room.

It was not long before Amber began to grow impatient. What was the good of money and a title, beauty and youth—if you buried it alive in the country? By the time a couple of months had passed she felt convinced that whatever speculation his Lordship's sudden death might have aroused would now be abated—scandals at Court were even shorter-lived than love-affairs—and she was eager to return. She coaxed and cajoled and finally she persuaded Lord and Lady Almsbury to go back with her for the winter social season. It would give her a house to live in, and the prestige of John's and Emily's families. She might need both, for a while.

Her appearance at Whitehall created a greater sensation than she had hoped. She was surprised to learn that rumours had her dead—poisoned by her husband out of jealousy—but she pretended to laugh at such tales. "What nonsense!" she exclaimed. "There's never anyone dies nowadays above the rank of chimney-sweep but it's thought he's been poisoned!"

There was truth in what she said for poisoning was still a revenge so common among the aristocracy that much apprehension regarding it persisted. Errant wives who fell ill were invariably thought to have died by that means. Lady Chester-field had died the year before, after displeasing her husband by an affair with York, and everyone had insisted that she was poisoned. Now another of York's mistresses, Lady Denham, was ill and told her friends that his Lordship had poisoned her—though some thought the Duke had done it himself because he was bored with her constant demands for new honours.

The men gave Amber an enthusiastic welcome.

Life at Court was so narrow, so circumscribed, so monotonous and inbred that any even moderately attractive newcomer was sure of a rush of attention from the gentlemen and a chill neglect from the ladies. When the newness was gone she would settle into whatever position she had been able to wrest for herself, and try to hold it against the next pretty young face. The men would be used to her by then, and the women would finally have accepted her. She would join them in ignoring and criticizing the next beautiful woman who dared appear and cast her gauntlet. The Court suffered from nothing so much as a surfeit of idleness; for most of them had nothing to do that had to be done and it taxed the most lively ingenuity to provide a continuous play of excitement and variety and amusement.

It took no more than a quick glance for Amber to see what was her position.

Because of her title she had access to the Court and could go into her Majesty's Drawing-Rooms, accompany the royal party on its trips to the theatre, attend any balls or dances or banquets to which there was a general invitation—but unless she could make a friend somewhere among the women she would go to no private suppers or parties. And thus they could force her to remain a virtual outsider, shut off from the intimate life of the Court. Amber did not intend to let that happen.

She therefore sought out Frances Stewart and made such a convincing show of her fondness and admiration that Frances, still naïve and trusting after four years at Whitehall, asked her to a little supper she was giving that same evening. The King was there and all the men and women who, by his favour, made up the clique which ruled fashionable London. Bucking-ham did one of his grotesque, cruel and witty imitations of

Chancellor Clarendon. Charles told again the incredible and still exciting story—for all that most of them had it by heart—of his flight and escape to France after the battle of Worcester. The food and the wine were good, the music soft, the ladies lovely. And Amber looked so well in her black-velvet gown that the Countess of Southesk was prompted to say:

"Lord, madame, what a handsome gown that is you're wearing! D'ye know—it seems to me I've seen one like it before somewhere." She tapped a sharp pink finger-nail reflectively against her teeth, and her eyes went slowly over the dress, though she pretended not to see what was inside. "Why, of course! I remember now! It's just like one I had after my husband's cousin died— Whatever became of the thing? Oh, yes—! I gave it to the wardrobe woman at His Majesty's Theatre. Let me see —that was about three years ago, I think. You were on the boards then, weren't you, madame?" Her blue eyes had a hard malicious amused sparkle as she looked at Amber, raising one eyebrow, and then she glanced across the room and gave a little shriek. "My God! If there isn't Winifred Wells—Castlemaine told me she'd gone into the country for an abortion. I vow and swear this is a censorious world! Pardon me, madame—I must go speak to her—poor wretch—" And with a faint curtsy, not even looking at Amber, she brushed off.

Amber scowled a little but then, as she looked up and saw Charles just beside her, she smiled and shrugged her shoulders. "If women could somehow learn to tolerate one another," he said softly, "they might get an advantage over us we'd never put down."

"And d'you think it's likely, Sire?"

"Not very. But don't let them trouble you, my dear. You can well enough shift for yourself, I'll warrant."

Amber continued to smile at him; his mouth, scarcely moving, framed a question. She answered it with a slight nod of her head. She could not possibly have been more pleased by her return to Whitehall.

But she was not yet so secure that she could do without Frances Stewart, and she made sure that they were all but inseparable. She visited Frances in her rooms, walked with her in

672

the galleries—for the weather was often too cold to go out-of-doors—and sometimes stayed the night with her when the roads were bad or the hour very late. Amber never talked about herself but seemed tremendously interested in everything Frances said or thought or did and Frances, unable to resist this lure of flattery, soon began to confide in her.

The Duke of Richmond had recently made her her first proposal, a circumstance which had greatly amazed the Court —for Frances was considered nothing less than Crown property. He was a not unhandsome young man of twenty-seven and a distant relative of the King but he was stupid, drunken, and habitually in debt. Charles had accepted the news with his customary aplomb and asked the Duke to turn his financial papers over to Clarendon for an examination.

One night when she and Amber were tucked snugly in bed, one great feather-mattress beneath them and another on top, Amber asked casually if she intended to marry his Grace. Frances's reply amazed her. "There's nothing else I can do, now," she said. "If the Duke hadn't been so kind as to propose I don't know what would have become of me."

"What would have become of you! Why, Frances, what nonsense! Every man at Court is mad in love with you and you know it!"

"Maybe they are," admitted Frances, "but not one of 'em has ever made me an honest proposal. The truth of it is I've ruined my good name by allowing his Majesty so many liberties —without ever letting him take that one which might have been to my benefit."

"Well," drawled Amber idly, though actually she had a strong curiosity on the subject, "then why didn't you? No doubt you could 've been a duchess without the trouble of marrying —and a mighty rich woman as well."

"What!" cried Frances. "Be the King's whore? Oh, no—not I! I'll leave that to other ladies. It's bad enough a woman has to lay with her husband—I'd rather die than lay with some man who wasn't! Lord! It gives me the vapours to think of it!"

Amber smiled in the close darkness, very much amused and not a little surprised. So that was what Frances's much vaunted virtue amounted to—not morality at all, but repugnance. She was not chaste, but squeamish.

"But don't you like the King? There's no finer man at Court— It isn't only because he's King that the ladies all fall in love with him."

"Oh, yes, of course I like him! But I just can't—I just couldn't— Oh, I don't know! Why do men always have to think about things like that? I know I've got to get married one day— I'm nineteen now and my mother says I'm a disgrace to the family— But, Lord! to think of getting in bed with a man and letting him— Oh! I know I'll die! I'll never be able to bear it!"

Ye gods! thought Amber, completely nonplussed. She must be cracked in the head. But she felt a little sorry for her too, a kind of contemptuous pity. What did the poor creature think life was about, anyway?

Their friendship was soon over. For Frances was jealous as a wife of the King's love-affairs, and Barbara had not let her remain long in ignorance when rumours began to spread that the King was secretly visiting Lady Radclyffe at Almsbury House. But Amber thought her position assured and was glad enough to dispense with Frances, whom she had always considered to be silly and boring. She had grown very tired of paying her compliments and pretending to be interested in what happened to her. And Charles, who always showed a quick rush of infatuation at the beginning of any new affair, would not let her be neglected now. At his insistence she was invited everywhere and treated with the same surface respect which Castlemaine had once commanded and Stewart still did. Even the ladies were forced to become her sycophants, and before long Amber began to think that nothing was beyond her.

She was walking along the Stone Gallery early one morning when she saw Chancellor Clarendon coming in her direction. The hall-way was chill and damp and cold and all the numerous men and women who hurried along it were wrapped in heavy woollen or velvet cloaks, their arms folded in great fur muffs. From one end to the other the gallery was a mass of black-hooded figures, for the Court was still in mourning for the Dowager Queen of Portugal—Amber was glad that since she must wear black the other ladies could not bloom publicly in bright colours and jewellery.

Clarendon came toward her with his head down, glaring at the floor, preoccupied with his gout and the innumerable problems which a ruined England expected him to solve. He did not see Amber any more than he saw anyone else and would have gone on by but she put herself in his path.

"Good morning, Chancellor."

He looked up, nodded his head brusquely and then, as she made him a low curtsy, was forced to pause and bow. "Your servant, madame."

"What a lucky chance this is! Not ten minutes since I heard something of the greatest importance—something you should know about, Chancellor."

He scowled unconsciously for he was worried about a great many things, not the least of which was his own precarious position. "I should be glad of any information, madame, which would better enable me to serve the King, my master." But his eyes looked at her disapprovingly and he was plainly eager to be on his way.

But Amber, full of the self-importance of her early and easy triumph at Court, was determined to succeed with him where every other mistress of the King had failed. She wanted to parade him like a trophy, wear him like a jewel no one else had been rich enough to buy—even though she agreed with everyone else that his political days were numbered.

"As it happens, Chancellor, I'm giving a supper at Almsbury House this Friday evening. His Majesty will be there, of course, and all the others— If you and her Ladyship would care to come—"

He bowed stiffly, angry that he had wasted so much valuable time. The gout in his foot stabbed him painfully. "I'm sorry, madame, but I have no leisure for frivolous amusements these days. The country has need of some men of serious purpose. Thank you, and good-day." He walked off, followed by his two secretaries, both of them loaded down with papers, and left Amber staring open-mouthed after him.

And then she heard a sudden hearty shout of feminine

laughter behind her and spun around to face Lady Castlemaine. "God's eyeballs!" cried Barbara, still laughing. "But *that* was a sight to see! What did you expect him to do? Make you an assignation?"

Amber was furious that her humiliation should have been seen by Barbara Palmer, of all people, though there had been onlookers enough that the news would be all over the Palace before nightfall. "That formal old fop!" she muttered. "He'll be lucky if he lasts out the year at Court!"

"Yes," agreed Barbara, "and so will you. I've been watching women like you come and go for seven years now—but I'm still here."

Amber stared at her insolently. "Still here, but mightily out of request, they say."

Barbara had fallen so far since the days when she had been violently jealous of her, and she had herself risen so high, that now they were face to face she hated her less than she had thought she did. Now she could afford to be scornful and even condescending.

Barbara lifted her brows. "Out of request? Well, now— I don't know what the devil you call out of request! At least he thinks well enough of me to have paid off my debts not many days since to the tune of thirty thousand pound."

"You mean he bribed you, don't you—to get rid of that brat you were starting?"

Barbara smiled. "Well? Even so—that's a mighty good price for an abortion, don't you agree?"

At that moment Frances Stewart passed them, going along the corridor in fluttering blue-silk robes with a black-velvet cloak flung over her shoulders, her feet in gilt sandals and all her bright brown hair caught into a gold filet and streaming loose down her back. She had been sitting for her portrait to Rotier—a portrait commissioned by the King who intended to use her image as Britannia on the new coins. Frances did not pause but nodded coolly to Amber and barely glanced at Castlemaine. She suspected that they were talking about her.

"There," said Barbara, as Frances went on, followed by three waiting-women and a little blackamoor, "goes the punk who

676

could put all our noses out of joint. A duchy in exchange for a maidenhead. That seems a fair enough bargain to me. I assure you mine didn't go as high—"

"Nor mine," said Amber, still watching Frances as she swept off down the hall, taking every eye with her as she went. "Though I doubt if he'd value it so high once he had it."

"Oh, he might—for the novelty of it."

"What d'you suppose makes her so stubborn?" asked Amber, curious to hear what Barbara would say.

"Don't you know?" Laughter and malice glittered in Barbara's eyes.

"Well—I've got at least one mighty good idea—"

At that moment the King with his courtiers and dogs rounded a corner and came suddenly upon them; his deep voice boomed with laughter. "Ods-fish, what's this! My two handsomest countesses in conversation? Whose reputation are you spoiling now?"

The brief camaraderie was gone; the two women were once more intense rivals, each passionately determined to outdo the other. "We were wishing, your Majesty," said Amber, "that the war would end so we could get the fashions from Paris again."

Charles laughed, slipped a casual arm about both their waists, and they walked slowly along the gallery. "If this war is inconveniencing the ladies, then I promise you I'll negotiate a peace."

When they came to her Majesty's apartments Charles glanced at Buckingham, the Duke stepped forward to offer Barbara his arm—and Amber went in with the King. To both women it seemed a more significant triumph than it was. Barbara, however, had her revenge when Stewart appeared—beautiful as ever in spite of the plain black mourning into which she had changed —and was immediately taken off into a corner by the King.

It was not long before Amber found herself pregnant.

She had no enthusiasm for spoiling her figure, even temporarily, but she understood that unless she gave him a child she would have nothing at all to hold him by once the exciting newness was gone from her bed. For though he might lose interest in their mothers, Charles was never indifferent to children

677

he believed his. When she told him, at the end of February, he was sympathetic and tender, apparently pleased—as though he was hearing the happy news for the first time. And Amber thought that her place at Court was now fixed as the stars.

He startled her out of her complacency two days later by pointing to a young man who stood across from them in the Drawing-Room and asking her if he seemed a likely prospect for a husband.

"A husband for who?" demanded Amber.

"Why, for you, my dear, of course."

"But I don't want to get married!"

"I can't say I blame you—and yet a child's somewhat embarrassed without a surname, don't you think?" He looked amused, his mouth beneath the narrow black mustache gave her a somewhat crooked smile.

Amber turned white. "Then you think it isn't yours!"

"No, my dear, I don't think that at all. I think it very probably is. I've an uncommon knack, it seems, for getting children —all but where I need 'em most. But the child couldn't possibly be your last husband's and unless you marry again before long it's going to have the bend sinister in its coat-of-arms. That's a hardship for any young man, no matter what his parentage. And to be altogether honest with you if you married it would help stop the gossiping—outside Whitehall at least. The year's going to be difficult enough as it is since I see no way we can set out the fleet—and the people will be grumbling more than ever about the little things we do. Do you understand, my dear? It would mightily oblige me—"

Amber was prepared to understand anything. She thought that chronic bad-temper and forever keeping an easy-natured man uneasy had been Barbara Palmer's undoing, and she did not intend to follow the Lady's unfortunate example. She guessed, however, at a reason the King had not named: Frances Stewart. For each time he took a new mistress Frances was peevish and sullen and insisted that she had herself been on the verge of surrender when he had destroyed her confidence.

"Well," said Amber, "my only ambition is to please your Majesty. I'll marry again if you want—but for Heaven's sake, get me a husband I can ignore!"

678

Charles laughed. "It wouldn't be difficult to ignore *him,* I should say."

The young man across the room looked not a day older than she and his youthful appearance was heightened by a pallid skin and rather delicate features. He was perhaps five feet seven or eight and his slender body wore a cheap and undistinguished suit. There was no doubt he felt ill at ease, though he was making an effort to seem gay and laughed excitedly even while his eyes darted anxiously about. Amber would not have noticed him of her own accord if he had been there all evening.

"Lord, but he looks a silly jackanapes!"

"But docile," reminded Charles, smiling down at her with easy good-humour.

"What's his rank?"

"Baron."

"Baron!" cried Amber, horrified. "But I'm a countess!" She could not have been more shocked if he had suggested she marry a porter or street-vendor.

Charles shrugged. "Well, then, suppose I make him an earl? His family deserves it. It should have been done long ago, in fact, but somehow it slipped my mind."

"I suppose that would help," said Amber dubiously, her eyes still frankly appraising the young man who had now become conscious that she was watching him and had begun to fidget. "Have you spoken to him yet?"

"No. But I will, and it can be easily arranged. His family lost a great deal in the Wars—"

"Oh, my God!" groaned Amber. "Somebody else to spend my money! Well, this time things are going to be different! This time *I'll* wear the breeches!"

CHAPTER FORTY–SEVEN

"Do you find yourself attracted to Richmond?"

The question had been in Charles's mind since the Duke had first made his proposal. To him the young man seemed dull and sottish, too much given up to the bottle, and his money affairs were so bad that he could scarcely be considered a good match for a serving-woman, much less a girl like Frances accustomed to luxury since birth.

She looked at him with some surprise. "Attracted to him? Why do you ask that?"

Charles shrugged. "I thought it was possible. There's no doubt he's in love with you."

Frances was instantly the coquette again, closing her fan and then opening it swiftly, telling the sticks with her right forefinger. "Well," she said, looking at the fan and not at him, "suppose I am?"

The King's face hardened suddenly. His black eyes anxiously searched her features and the two lines on either side of his mouth grew deep as the muscles tightened.

"*Are* you?"

Frances glanced up at him, still with that faint simpering smile on her face, but her expression changed swiftly to surprise as she met his angry stare. "Why, your Majesty! How grum you look! Has something vexed you?"

"Answer me, Frances! I'm in no humour for jokes! And answer me truly."

Frances gave a little sigh. "No, your Majesty, I'm not. Does that make it more honourable for me to marry him?" Sometimes she surprised him, for it was impossible to tell whether she spoke from naïveté or a shrewdness she was not generally believed to own.

Charles gave her a slow, sad smile. "No, Frances, not more honourable—but I confess I'm glad to hear it. I'm not very much inclined to jealousy—but this time—" He shrugged his broad shoulders, his eyes brooding thoughtfully over her. "I've been looking at his accounts, and his finances are in the worst possible condition. Without his title he'd have been snapped up by a constable long ago. Truthfully, Frances, I don't think he's a good match for you."

"Do you know a better, Sire?" she asked tartly.

"Not just now—but perhaps a little later—"

Frances interrupted him. "Perhaps a little later! Sire, you

680

don't know what you're saying! Do you realize that I'm nineteen years old and my reputation is all but ruined through my own foolishness? This is the first honest proposal I've ever had—and it'll likely be the last one! There's just one thing in life I want—and that's to be a respectable woman! I don't want my family to be ashamed of me!"

They were in her Majesty's antechamber, waiting while the Queen dressed, and now as Catherine Boynton passed the door and heard Frances's raised voice she glanced out, wondering what was going on between them. Charles noticed her pausing there.

"Walk this way with me, Frances." They strolled toward the other end of the room. "I'm going to tell you something," he said quickly; his voice was very low. "Will you promise to keep it a secret? Don't even tell your mother—"

"Of course, your Majesty."

Frances could, in fact, hold a confidence better than most of those whose tongues clacked in the corridors and bedchambers and drawing-rooms of Whitehall and Covent Garden.

He took a deep breath. "I've consulted the Archbishop of Canterbury about a divorce."

"A divorce!" She whispered the word, shock and almost horror on her face.

Charles began to talk rapidly, glancing around first to make sure that no one was near: they were alone in the room. "This isn't the first time I've thought of it. The doctors tell me they don't believe the Queen can ever carry a child nine months. York isn't popular now—and he'll be less so when the people discover his religious intentions. If I marry again and have a male heir it may change the whole course of my family's future —Canterbury says it can be arranged."

Frances's thoughts and emotions ran over her face. Surprise dissolved into a kind of slyness and pleased vanity as she began to contemplate what this could mean to her. *Frances Stewart, Queen of England!* She had always been as proud of her distant connection with the royal family as of anything—almost more proud than she was of her beauty. But then, as she remembered the Queen, came a look of doubt and hopelessness.

"It would break her heart. She loves you so."

Charles, who had been watching her face, a sort of morose longing and tenderness on his own, now gave a sigh and his eyes shifted beyond her to stare out the windows at the barren scarlet-oak growing in the Queen's garden. "I'm afraid of hurting her more—she's been hurt so much already." A dark scowl swept over his face and his teeth clenched suddenly; he made a quick impatient gesture. "I don't know what to do!" he muttered angrily.

They stood there together for a moment, silent, not looking at each other. And then Catherine appeared in the doorway with Mrs. Boynton on one side and Winifred Wells on the other. Her head was tipped slightly to one side, there was an eager little smile on her face and bare adoration showed in her eyes as she looked at Charles. Briefly she hesitated and then started forward, her dainty hands clasped before her.

"I'm sorry to have been so long a-dressing, Sire—"

As she entered the room he turned, instantly recovering his poise. Now he smiled and started toward her. "My dear, if you took all morning to dress I'd not mind if you could look half so charming as you do now."

Catherine blushed slightly. The pinkness was very becoming to her sallow complexion; her lashes moved like hesitant black butterflies, and then she looked him full in the eyes. For all her sheltered and stiff upbringing she was learning some of the tricks of a coquette herself, and they became her very well.

"It's kind of you to flatter me," she murmured, "when I'm condemned to this unbecoming black."

The ladies were trooping into the room after her, most of them chattering and unconcerned—though one or two quick pairs of eyes had caught the wistful look on Frances's face as she watched their Majesties together. Then with a little toss of her head Frances came toward the Queen and one hand reached out impulsively to touch hers.

"It isn't flattery, madame. You've truly never looked handsomer in your life."

Her voice and eyes were almost passionately sincere. Behind

682

them Boynton whispered to Wells that something must be a-brewing between Stewart and the King—they were both so uncommonly kind to her Majesty. Winifred retorted that she was a prattling gossip and that his Majesty was always kind to his wife.

The weather was cold and the roads even worse than usual, but the Court was going to a play. Charles offered his arm to Catherine and she took it, giving him one of her quick shy smiles, grateful for the attention. They started off and for one swift passing instant Frances's eyes met the King's. She knew then, without a doubt, that while Catherine lived she, Frances Stewart, would never be Queen of England.

It was late in the afternoon, nearly six o'clock, and the overcast sky had long since made it necessary to light candles. Charles, in his private closet, the one room to which he could retire for some measure of seclusion, sat at his writing-table scrawling off a rapid letter to Minette. Her own most recent one was opened before him and from time to time he glanced at it. Beside him on the floor two long-eared little spaniels sat and chewed at each other's fleas, and farther away there were others at play, romping and growling.

From the next room came the murmuring voices of men—Buckhurst and Sedley, James Hamilton, half a dozen others—waiting for him to come out and change his clothes before they went to supper. They were discussing the afternoon's play—finding fault with the author's wit, the scenery and costumes and actors—and comparing the prostitutes who had been in the pit. From time to time someone laughed loudly, all their voices went up at once, and then they grew quieter again. But Charles, absorbed in his letter, scarcely heard them at all.

All of a sudden a commotion rose outside and he heard a familiar feminine voice cry out, breathlessly, "Where's his Majesty! I've got important news for him!" It was Barbara.

Charles scowled and flung down his pen, then got to his feet. Ods-fish! Did the woman's impertinence know no bounds at all? Coming to his chamber at this hour of the day, when she knew there would be a roomful of men!

683

He heard Buckhurst answering her. "His Majesty is in his closet, madame, writing a letter."

"Well," said Barbara briskly, "the letter can keep. What I have to say can't." And promptly she began rapping at the door.

Charles opened it and there was obvious displeasure and annoyance on his face as he leaned against the door-jamb, looking down at her. "Well, madame?"

"Your Majesty! I must speak with you in private!" Her eyes glanced suggestively into the room behind him. "It's a matter of the greatest importance!"

Charles gave a slight shrug and stepped back, admitting her, while the gentlemen exchanged amused glances. Ye gods, what next! Even when she had been most in favour she had not dared be so bold. The door swung shut.

"Now—what is this great business that can't keep?" His voice was frankly skeptical, and impatient—for he thought it only another scheme of hers to create an impression of being in high favour.

"I understand that your Majesty has just paid a visit to Mrs. Stewart."

"I have."

"And that she sent you away with the plea her head was aching furiously."

"Your information seems indisputable."

Charles's tone was sarcastic and his whole expression betrayed cynicism and the unbelief in his fellow-beings which had characterized him almost since boyhood, growing steadily stronger as the years passed. He was wondering what sort of trick she was trying to play on him, waiting to discover the inevitable flaw in her scheme.

But all at once Barbara's face took on a look of mock coquetry and her voice dropped to a soft low pitch. "Well, Sire, I've come to console you for her coldness."

He lifted his eyebrows in frank surprise and then scowled quickly. "Madame, you have become insufferable."

Barbara flung back her head and began to laugh, a wild high abandoned laugh that was peculiarly her own, full of contempt and mocking cruelty. When she spoke her voice was low again, but intense, and excitement showed in the straining cords of her throat, the bright glitter of her eyes, the poise of her muscles as she leaned slightly toward him, like a cat set to spring.

"You're a fool, Charles Stuart! You're a stupid ridiculous credulous fool and everyone in your Court is laughing at you! And do you know why? Because Frances Stewart has been carrying on an intrigue with Richmond right under your nose! He's with her at this moment—while you think she's in bed with a headache—" She paused breathless, triumph shining from her face and showing in every line of her body, triumph and satisfied vengeance.

Charles answered her swiftly, without thinking, his habitual easy self-possession deserting him. "You're lying!"

"Lying, am I? You *are* a fool! Come with me then and see if I'm lying!" And while he hesitated, as though half afraid of finding that she was telling the truth, she seized hold of his wrist. "Come with me and see for yourself how chaste she is—your precious Frances Stewart!"

With sudden resolution Charles jerked his hand free and started from the room, Barbara—grinning broadly now—hurrying at his heels. He wore only his white linen shirt and breeches. He had left his periwig in his closet hanging on a chair-back. Two courtiers leaped abruptly back from the door and all faces looked solemn and guilty, trying to pretend they had not listened. Charles ignored them and rushed on, half running along the maze of rooms and hall-ways that led to Frances's apartments, leaving a trail of staring eyes and open mouths behind him. Barbara's heels pounded at his side.

But outside Stewart's rooms he stopped, his hand on the knob. "You've come far enough," he said curtly. "Go back to your apartments." And then as she stared with disappointment he flung open the door.

Frances's pretty little serving-girl was in the entrance room and at the King's appearance she gave a horrified gasp, leaped to her feet and ran toward him. "Oh, your Majesty! How did you— Don't go in—*please!* She's been so sick since you left—but now she's sleeping!"

Charles did not even glance at her, but he reached out one

arm to ward her off. "That remains to be seen." He went on, striding through the antechamber and the drawing-room, and without hesitating an instant he flung open the door of the bedroom.

Frances was sitting in bed wearing a white-satin jacket with her hair tumbled over her shoulders, and beside her was a young man who held her hand in his. Both of them looked around in astonishment to find the King looming there in the doorway like a great and angry avenging god. Frances gave a nervous little scream and Richmond gaped, horror-struck, unable even to take off his hat or get to his feet.

Charles walked slowly toward them, his lips drawn tight against his teeth. "I didn't believe her," he said softly. "I thought she was lying."

"Thought who was lying!" cried Frances defensively. She understood his anger and knew what he was thinking and it made her suddenly furious.

"My Lady Castlemaine. It seems she's known some things about my affairs of which I was ignorant." His black eyes shifted from Frances to Richmond, who had now got to his feet and stood twisting his hat round and round in his hands, while he looked like a whipped pup. "What are you doing here?" demanded Charles suddenly, his voice strained and harsh.

Richmond gave an unhappy apologetic little laugh. "Heh! I'm paying Mrs. Stewart a visit."

"So I see! And by what right, pray, do you visit her when she's too sick to see her other friends?"

Richmond, suddenly aware that he was being made to appear a helpless fool before the woman he loved, answered stoutly: "At least, Sire, I am prepared to marry her. Which is more than your Majesty can do."

Charles's eyes blazed in sudden rage and he started toward the Duke with clenched fists. One hand went to Frances's mouth and she gave a piercing scream as Richmond, who did not want a beating at the competent hands of his sovereign, turned suddenly and leaped out the window. Charles, who had already reached it, saw him land awkwardly not far below in the low-tide river mud, and then scramble to his feet, give one terrified backward glance and rush off into the fog. For a long moment he stood there and stared after him, contempt and hatred on his face; then he turned to Frances.

"I never expected anything like this from you."

Frances stared at him defiantly. "I'm sure I don't understand you, Sire! If I can't receive visits from a man whose intentions toward me are wholly honourable—then I am indeed a slave in a free country!" She passed one tired nervous hand quickly across her throbbing forehead, and without waiting for him to speak again she cried passionately: "If you don't want me to marry, Sire, it's your privilege to refuse me permission! But at least you can't prevent me from crossing to France and entering a nunnery!"

Charles stared at her with sick incredulity. What had happened to the Frances Stewart he had known and loved for four years? What had happened to turn her into this cold brazen woman who flaunted her faithlessness, daring him to object to it, as though pleased to have made him a fool in the eyes of his friends? He found himself learning again at thirty-six what he thought he had learned well enough twenty years ago.

Now he spoke to her slowly, with sadness coming through his anger. "I wouldn't have believed this of you, Frances, no matter who had told me."

Frances stared at him defiantly, enraged at his cynicism which drew conclusions out of a refuse heap of past experience. "Your Majesty is very quick to suspect the worst!"

"But not quick enough, it seems! I think I've known since the day I was born that only a fool would trust a woman—and yet I've trusted you against everything!" He paused a moment, his dark face sardonic. "I'd rather have found out any way but this—"

Frances was close to hysteria, and now she cried in a high trembling voice: "Your Majesty had best go before the person who brought you here begins to suspect the worst of your stay!"

He gave her a long incredulous look and then, without another word, spun about on his heel and left the room. In the hall-way outside her door he met Lawrence Hyde, Clarendon's son, and shouted at him: "So you were in the plot too! By God, I won't forget it!" Hyde stared after him, bewildered, but the King rounded the next corner and was gone. Charles the urbane, the easy-humoured, the self-possessed and amiable, was in such a rage as no one had imagined him capable of.

The next day Frances returned to him by messenger every gift she had ever received—the strand of pearls he had given her on St. Valentine's day three years before, the wonderful bracelets and ear-rings and necklaces which had marked her birthdays and the Christmases or New Years. All of them came back, without even a note. Charles flung them into the fireplace.

That same morning Frances appeared unexpectedly in her Majesty's apartments. She was covered from head to foot in a black-velvet cloak and she wore a vizard. Catherine and all her ladies looked toward the door in surprise as Frances removed the mask. For a moment she hesitated there and then all at once she ran forward, dropped to her knees, and taking up the hem of Catherine's garment touched it to her lips. Catherine spoke quickly to her women, asking them to leave. They withdrew, to listen at the keyhole.

Then she reached down to touch the crown of Frances's gleaming head and unexpectedly Frances burst into tears. She covered her face with her hands. "Oh, your Majesty! You must hate me! Can you *ever* forgive me?"

"Frances, my dear—you mustn't cry so—you'll make your head ache— Here, please— Look at me, poor child—" Catherine's warm, soft voice still carried a trace of its Portuguese accent, which gave it an even greater tenderness, and now she placed one hand gently beneath Frances's chin to raise her head.

Reluctantly Frances obeyed and for a moment they looked silently at each other. Then her sobs began again.

"I'm sorry, Frances," said Catherine. "I'm sorry, for your sake."

"Oh, it's not for myself I'm crying!" protested Frances. "It's for you! It's for the unhappiness I've seen in your eyes sometimes when—" She stopped suddenly, shocked at her boldness, and then the words tumbled on hastily, as though she could undo in two minutes the wrongs her vanity had committed for years against this patient little woman.

688

"Oh, you must believe me, your Majesty! The only reason I'm going to get married is so that I may leave the Court! I've never meant to hurt you—never for a moment! But I've been vain and silly and thoughtless! I've made a fool of myself—but I've never wronged you, I swear I haven't! He's never been my lover— Oh, say you believe me—*please* say you believe me!"

She was holding Catherine's hand hard against the beating pulse in her throat, and her head was thrown back as her eyes looked up with passionate, begging intensity. She had always liked Catherine, but she had never realized until now how deeply and humbly she admired her, nor how shameful her own behaviour had been. She had considered the Queen's feelings no more than the crassest of Charles's mistresses—no more than Barbara Palmer herself.

"I believe you, Frances. Any young girl would have been flattered. And you've always been kind and generous. You never used your power as a weapon to hurt others."

"Oh, your Majesty! I didn't! Truly I didn't! I've never meant to hurt anyone! And your Majesty—I want you to know—I know *you'll* believe me: Richmond had just come in. We were sitting talking. There's never been anything indecent between us!"

"Of course there hasn't, my dear."

Frances slumped suddenly, her head dropped. *"He'll* never believe me," she said softly. "He has no faith—he doesn't believe in anything."

There were tears now in Catherine's eyes and she shook her head slowly. "Perhaps he does, Frances. Perhaps he does, more than we think."

Frances was tired now and despondent. She pressed her lips to the back of Catherine's hand once more and got slowly to her feet. "I must go now, your Majesty." They stood looking at each other, real tenderness and affection on both their faces. "I may never see you again—" Quickly and impulsively she kissed Catherine on the cheek, and then swirling about she rushed from the room. Catherine stood and watched her go, smiling a little, one hand lightly touching her face; the tears spilled off onto her bosom. Three days later Frances had left Whitehall— she eloped with the Duke of Richmond.

689

CHAPTER FORTY-EIGHT

IT WAS ON one cold rainy windy night in February that Buckingham, disguised in a black wig with his blonde eyebrows and mustache blackened, sat across the table from Dr. Heydon and watched the astrologer's face as he consulted his charts of stars and moon, intersecting lines and geometrical figures. The room was lighted dimly by smoking tallow candles that smelt of frying fat, and the wind blew in gusts down the chimney, making their eyes burn and sending them into coughing fits.

"Pox on this damned weather!" muttered the Duke angrily, coughing and covering his nose and mouth with the long black riding-cloak he wore. And then as Heydon slowly raised his thin bony face he leaned anxiously across the table. "What is it! What do you find?"

"What I dare not speak of, your Grace."

"Bah! What do I pay you for? Out with it!"

With an air of being forced against his better judgment, Heydon gave in to the Duke's determination. "If your Grace insists. I find, then, that he will die very suddenly on the fifteenth day of January, two years hence—" He made a dramatic pause and then, leaning forward, hissed out his next words, while his blue eyes bored into the Duke's. "And then, by popular demand of the people, your Grace will succeed to the throne of England for a long and glorious reign. The house of Villiers is destined to be the greatest royal house in the history of our nation!"

Buckingham stared at him, completely transfixed. "By Jesus! It's incredible—and yet— What else do you find?" he demanded suddenly, eager to know everything.

It was as though he stood on the edge of some strange land from which it was possible to look forward into time and discover the shape of things to come. King Charles scorned such chicanery, saying that even if it were possible to see into the future it was inconvenient to know one's fate, whether for good or ill. Well—there were other and cleverer men who knew how to turn a thing to their own ends.

"How will he—" Villiers checked himself, afraid of his own phraseology. "What will be the cause of so great a tragedy?"

Heydon glanced at his charts once more, as though for reassurance, and when he answered his voice was a mere whisper: "Unfortunately—the stars have it his Majesty will die by poison —secretly administered."

"Poison!"

The Duke sat back, staring into the flames of the sea-coal fire, drumming his knuckles on the table-top, one eyebrow raised in contemplation. Charles Stuart to die of poison, secretly administered, and he, George Villiers, to succeed by popular demand to the throne of England. The more he thought about it the less incredible it seemed.

He was startled out of his reverie by a sudden sharp impatient rapping at the door. "What's that! Were you expecting someone?"

"I had forgotten, your Grace," whispered Heydon. "My Lady Castlemaine had an appointment with me at this hour."

"Barbara! Has she been here before?"

"Only twice, your Grace. The last time three years since." The rapping was repeated, loud and insistent, and a little angry too.

Buckingham got up quickly and went toward the door of the next room. "I'll wait in here until she's gone. Get rid of her as soon as possible—and as you value your nose don't let her know I'm here."

Heydon nodded his head and whisked the many papers and charts which concerned Charles II's melancholy future off the table and into a drawer. As the Duke disappeared he went to answer the door. Barbara entered the room on a gust of wind; her face was entirely covered by a black-velvet vizard and there was a silver-blonde wig over her red hair.

"God's eyeballs! What kept you so long? Have you got a wench in here?"

She tossed her black-beaver muff onto a chair, untied the

hood she wore and flung off both it and the cloak. Then going to the fire to warm herself she nudged aside with her foot the thin mongrel dog that slept uneasily there, and which now looked up at her with injured resentment.

"God in Heaven!" she exclaimed, rubbing her hands together and shivering. "But I swear it's the coldest night known to man! It's blowing a mackerel-gale!"

"May I offer your Ladyship a glass of ale?"

"By all means!"

Heydon went to a dresser and poured out a glassful, saying with a sideways glance at her: "I regret that I cannot offer your Ladyship something more delicate—claret or champagne—but it is my misfortune that too many of my patrons are remiss in their debts." He shrugged. "They say that comes of serving the rich."

"Still plucking at the same string, eh?" She took the glass from him and began to swallow thirstily, feeling the sour ale slide down and begin to warm her entrails. "I have a matter of the utmost importance I want you to settle for me. It's imperative that you make no mistake!"

"Was not my last prognostication correct, your Ladyship?"

He was leaning forward slightly from the waist, his big-jointed hands clasped before him, obsequiousness as well as an unctuous demand for praise in his voice and manner.

Barbara gave him an impatient glance over the rim of her glass. The Queen had been her enemy then. Now she was, without knowing it, as fast an ally as she had. Barbara Palmer, least of all, wanted to see another and possibly handsome and determined woman married to Charles Stuart; if anything should ever happen to Catherine her own days at Whitehall were done and she knew it.

"Don't trouble yourself to remember so much!" she told him sharply. "In your business it's a bad habit. I understand you've been giving some useful advice to my cousin."

"Your cousin, madame?" Heydon was blandly innocent.

"Don't be stupid! You know who I mean! Buckingham, of course!"

Heydon spread his hands in protest. "Oh, but madame—I

assure you that you have been misinformed. His Grace was so kind as to release me from Newgate when I was carried there by reason of my debts—which I incurred because of the reluctance of my patrons to meet their charges. But he has done me no further honour since that time."

"Nonsense!" Barbara drained the glass and set it onto the cluttered mantelpiece. "Buckingham never threw a dog a bone without expecting something for it. I just wanted you to know that I know he comes here, so you'll not be tempted to tell him of my visit. I have as much evidence on him as he can get on me."

Heydon, made more adamant by the knowledge that the gentleman under discussion was listening in the next room, refused to surrender. "I protest, madame—someone's been jesting with your Ladyship. I swear I've not laid eyes on his Grace from that time to this."

"You lie like a son of a whore! Well—I hope you'll be as chary of my secrets as you are of his. But enough of that. Here's what I came for: I have reason to think I'm with child again—and I want you to tell me where I may fix the blame. It's most important that I know."

Heydon widened his eyes and swallowed hard, his Adam's apple bobbing convulsively in his skinny neck. Gadzooks! This was beyond anything! When a father had much ado to tell his own child, how could a completely disinterested person be expected to know it?

But Heydon's wide reputation had not been built on refusal to answer questions. And now he took up the thick-lensed, green eye-glasses which he imagined gave him a more studious air, pinched them on the end of his nose, and both he and Barbara sat down. He began to pore intently over the charts on the table, meanwhile writing some mumbo-jumbo in a sort of bastard Latin and drawing a few moons and stars intersected by several straight lines.

From time to time he cleared his throat and said, "Hmmmm."

Barbara watched him, leaning forward, and while he worked she nervously twisted a great diamond she wore on her left hand to cover her wedding-band—for she and Roger Palmer had long since agreed to have nothing more to do with each other.

At last Heydon cleared his throat a final time and looked across at her, seeing her white face through the blur of smoke from the tallow candles. "Madame—I must ask your entire confidence in this matter, or I can proceed no farther."

"Very well. What d'you want to know?"

"I pray your Ladyship not to take offense—but I must have the names of those gentlemen who may be considered as having had a possible share in your misfortune."

Barbara frowned a little. "You'll be discreet?"

"Naturally, madame. Discretion is my stock in trade."

"Well, then— First, there's the King—whom I hope you'll find responsible, for if I can convince him it may save me a great deal of trouble. And then—" She hesitated.

"And then?" prompted Heydon.

"Pox on you! Give me leave to think a moment. Then there was James Hamilton, and Charles Hart—but don't count him for he's a mean fellow, a mere actor, and—"

At that instant there was a sudden sharp sound halfway between a laugh and a choked cough, and Barbara started to her feet. "'Sdeath! What was that!"

Heydon had likewise jumped. "Only my dog, madame. Dreaming in his sleep." They both looked at the mongrel, twitching his muscles before the fire in some nocturnal chase.

Barbara gave the Doctor a suspicious glance but sat down again and continued: "There's my new footman, but he's of no quality, so don't mark him down; and Lady Southesk's page, but he's likely too young—"

At this there was a loud explosive laugh, as of mirth which would no longer be denied. And before Heydon could get out of his chair Barbara had sprung to her feet and rushed to the closed door from behind which the sound had come, flung it open and given the Duke a solid blow in the stomach with her doubled fist.

Buckingham, who had been bent over and almost helpless in his unrestrained laughter, now recovered himself and put out one hand to grab her about the throat, the while he jumped this way and that to avoid her clawing nails and flying feet. And

694

then, as they struggled, they got hold of each other's disguising wigs and pulled off both at once. Barbara stepped back with a horrified gasp, holding the Duke's black wig in her hands, while he dangled hers at his side like some grisly battle trophy.

"Buckingham!"

"Your servant, madame."

He made her a mock bow and tossed her wig onto the table—beside which Heydon was still standing in stupefied horror at these goings-on, which would surely ruin him—and Barbara snatched it up and clapped it onto her head again, this time somewhat askew.

"You lousy bastard!" she cried furiously, finding her tongue at last. "What d'you mean, spying on me?"

"I was not spying, my dear cousin," replied Buckingham coolly. "I was here when you came and I merely stepped into the bedroom to wait for you to leave so that I might continue my business with the Doctor."

"What business!"

"Why, I was trying if I could discover what woman I should next get with child," replied the Duke, frank amusement on his mouth. "I'm only sorry I laughed so soon. That was a mighty interesting tale you were telling the Doctor. But pray satisfy my curiosity on a point or two: have you lain with your blackamoor of late, or the Chancellor?"

"Filthy wretch! You know I hate that old man!"

"We agree on one thing."

Barbara began to gather her belongings, mask, fan, cloak and muff, tying the hood once more over her hair. "Well, I'll go along now and leave you to finish your business, my lord."

"Oh, but you must let me wait upon you to your lodgings," protested his Grace quickly, for he suspected her of intending to go immediately to the King and hoped to head her off by some device or other. "It's dangerous riding through the ruins. Only yesterday I heard of a lady of quality dragged from her coach and beaten and robbed and finally left for dead." What he said was true enough, for the ruined City swarmed with cut-throats and thieves after dark and it was not always possible to get a hackney to make the trip. "How did you come?"

"In a hell-cart."

"Well, fortunately I have not only my coach but a dozen footmen waiting below. You're foolish to go about thus unprotected, my dear—and it's mighty lucky I'm here to see you get back safe."

Buckingham took up his wig and set it on his head again, put his feather-loaded hat on top of it, and turning to wink broadly behind her back at the worried Doctor he flung his cloak up over his left shoulder and offered her his arm. He and Barbara started down the black stair-well, where Heydon had finally recovered himself sufficiently to bring a candle to light them.

"And mind you," called Barbara as she got halfway down, "not a word of this to anyone, or I'll have you kicked!"

"Yes, my lady. You may trust me, madame."

Outside it was cold and the wind swept down the narrow, dark little street, carrying pieces of wet paper with it and driving hard needles of rain against their faces. The moon was completely obscured so that the night was black. Buckingham put his fingers to his mouth and whistled. An instant later half-a-dozen men appeared from some nearby hiding-place, emerging like goblins, and after two or three minutes a great rocking coach drawn by eight horses came lumbering noisily down the steep hill toward them and stopped, six more footmen leaping off the back where they had been riding. Buckingham gave the driver his directions, handed her in, and they started out with those who could hanging onto the coach and the others running behind it; a footman on either side held a blazing flambeau.

They rode down Great Tower Hill and turned into Tower Street, which was still lined with ruins, though the ways had now been cleared of débris and were passable. It was a slow ride of some two and a quarter miles over East Cheap and Watling Street, past the twisted iron and the great heaps of boulders that marked the site of old St. Paul's, along Fleet Street and the Strand to Whitehall.

Barbara was shivering again, huddled in her cloak with her teeth chattering. Buckingham gallantly spread a fur-lined velvet robe over them both. "You'll soon be warm," he said consolingly. "If we pass a tavern I'll send in for a couple of mugs of lamb's wool."

But Barbara was not to be diverted by such gallantries. "What's his Majesty going to think to hear you've been paying visits to an astrologer?"

"Are you going to tell him?"

"Perhaps I will and perhaps I won't."

"I wouldn't, if I were you."

"Why not? You've been mighty strange with me of late, George Villiers. And I know more than you may think."

Buckingham scowled, wishing that he could see her face. "You're mistaken, my dear, for there's nothing to know."

Barbara laughed, a smug-sounding impudent laugh in the darkness beside him. "Oh, isn't there? Well, suppose I tell you something then: I know that you're having a certain horoscope cast—and it isn't your own, either."

"Who told you that!" Buckingham reached out suddenly and grabbed her arm, his fingers clenching it so that she winced and tried to jerk away; but he held her, bending his face close to her own. "Answer me! Who told you that!"

"Let go of me, you sot! I won't tell you! Let me go, I say!" she cried, and all at once she gave him a resounding slap on the face with her free hand.

With a curse he released her, one hand held to his stinging face, mumbling beneath his breath. Pox on the jade! he thought furiously. If she were anyone else I'd give her a kicking for this! But instead he held his temper and began to wheedle.

"Come, Barbara, my dear. We know too much about each other to be enemies. It's dangerous for both of us. Surely even you are convinced by now that if ever I take the notion to tell his Majesty what's become of his letters he'd send you hence like a rat with a straw in its arse."

Barbara flung back her head and laughed. "Poor fool! He doesn't even guess, does he? Sometimes I think he's stupid as a woodcock! He won't even look for 'em!"

"That's where you're mistaken, madame. He's had the Palace searched from top to bottom. But there are only two people in the world who could tell him where they are: you, Barbara—and I."

"You're the fly in my ointment, George Villiers. Sometimes

I've a mind to have you poisoned—if you were out of the way I'd never have anything to worry about."

"Don't forget, pray—I know a thing or two about mixing an Italian salad myself. Now, let's be serious for a moment. Tell me where you got that information, and tell me truly. I've an uncommonly keen nose for smelling out lies. They stink like blue-incle to me."

"And if I do tell you what I know will you tell me something?"

"What?"

"Tell me whose it is?"

"Tell you whose what is?"

"The horoscope, dolt!"

"Then you don't really know anything at all."

"Try me and find out—I know enough to have you hanged."

"Well, then," said the Duke smoothly, as though he heard that news every morning before breakfast, "I'll tell you. The truth of it is, my dear, I have an incurable aversion to hemp-rope and slip-knots."

"It's a bargain. The horoscope you're having cast is that of a person of such consequence that if it became known your life wouldn't be worth a farthing. Now, don't ask me how I found that out," she added quickly, shaking a finger at him. "For I won't tell you."

"God's blood!" muttered Buckingham. "How the devil have you got hold of this? What more do you know?"

"Isn't that enough? Now—tell me: Whose horoscope is it?"

The Duke relaxed, slumping with relief as he sat beside her. "You've got me on the hip, I'll have to tell you. But if one word of this gets out to anyone—believe me, I'll tell the King about his letters."

"Yes, yes. What is it? Quick!"

"At his Majesty's bidding I was having York's horoscope cast to determine whether or no he will ever be King. Now there are just three of us who know it—his Majesty, you, and me—"

Barbara believed the lie, for it sounded plausible, and though she promised him that she would never speak a word of it to anyone she soon discovered that it was burning a hole in her tongue. It was such an exciting thing to know, such a fatal secret, so loaded with potential trouble that she was sure it must be of great value to her. Certainly the worth of such knowledge was almost incalculable in pounds sterling and she saw it as the source of great sums to herself over the years to come—no matter what new and younger woman might supplant her in the King's slippery affections.

She asked Charles for twelve thousand pounds one night, just as he was getting out of her bed.

"If I had twelve thousand pound," said the King, standing up and reaching for his periwig, then glancing into a mirror to see that it was on straight, "I'd spend part of it to buy myself a new shirt. The footmen have been looting my wardrobe lately to get their back wages. Poor devils—I can't blame 'em. Some haven't been paid a shilling since I got back."

Barbara gave him a pettish glare as she slipped into her dressing-gown. "God's my life, Sire, but I'm sure you've grown miserly as a Jewish pawnbroker.

"I wish I were also rich as one," said the King, then put his hat on his head and started for the door. Barbara thrust herself in front of him.

"I tell you, I've got to have that money!"

"Mr. Jermyn demands it?" asked Charles sarcastically, referring to current tales that she was now paying some of her lovers. He adjusted his lace cravat and walked on by her; but she reached the door first and covered the knob with her own hand.

"I think your Majesty had best reconsider." She paused significantly, lifted her brows and added, "Or I may tell his Highness a few things."

He gave her a puzzled scowl, but his mouth was half amused. "Now what the devil are you about?"

"Such a superior air! Well, no doubt you'll be surprised to hear that I know what it is you've been trying to discover?" There! It was out! She had not actually expected to say it, but her tongue—as it often did—had spoken anyway.

He shook his head, uninterested. "I haven't the vaguest idea what you're talking about." He turned the knob, opened the door a few inches, and then stopped abruptly as she said:

"Did you know that Buckingham and I are friends again?"

He shut the door. "What has Buckingham to do with this?"

"Oh, what's the use of pretending! I know all about it! You've had York's horoscope cast to find out if he'll ever be king." Look at him! she thought. Poor fool, trying to seem unconcerned. Twelve thousand! What devil put that paltry sum into my head! I should have asked for twenty thousand—or thirty—

"Did Villiers tell you this?"

"Who else?"

"Pox on him! I told him to keep it a strict secret. Well—you'd better not let him know you've told me or he'll be in a fury."

"Oh, he hasn't told anyone else. And I wouldn't let him know I'd told you for anything. Now—what about my twelve thousand pound?"

"Wait a few days. I'll see what I can do for you."

The next morning Charles talked privately with Henry Bennet, Baron Arlington, who, though he had once been Buckingham's friend, now hated him violently. In fact, the Duke had few friends left at Court; he was not a man to wear well under the strain of daily association. Charles told his Secretary of State exactly what Castlemaine had told him, but he did not mention Barbara's name.

"It's my opinion," said the King, "that the person who told me this was deliberately misinformed. I'd be more inclined to think it was *my* horoscope Villiers had cast."

Arlington could not have been more pleased if someone had brought him the Duke's head. His blue eyes glittered and his mouth snapped together like an angry trap; his fist banged down on the table. "By Jesu, your Majesty! That's treason!"

"Not yet, Harry," corrected the King. "Not until we have the evidence."

"We shall have it, Sire, before the week is out. Leave me alone for that."

Three days later Arlington gave Charles the papers. He had immediately put into operation all the back-stairs facilities of the Palace, and upon arresting and examining Heydon they discovered copies of several letters from him to the Duke and one from Buckingham to him. Charles, thoroughly annoyed at this latest treachery on the part of a man who was literally his foster-brother, issued a warrant for his arrest. But the Duke, in Yorkshire, was warned by his wife and he got out of the house just before the King's deputies reached it.

For four months the Duke played a cat-and-mouse game with his Majesty's sergeants, and though sometimes a rumour arose that his Grace had been located and was about to be taken prisoner, it was always the wrong man they captured or the Duke was gone before they got to him. People began to make disparaging remarks about his Majesty's espionage system, which had always been compared unfavourably to Cromwell's. But actually it was not strange that the Duke could elude his pursuers.

Fifteen years before, the King himself had travelled halfway across England with a price on his head and posters fixed up everywhere describing him, had even talked to Roundhead soldiers and discussed himself—and then finally escaped to France. The best known noblemen in the country went unrecognized to taverns or brothels. Any gentleman or lady could take off the jewels and fine clothes and go masquerading with the danger not that they would be recognized but that, if need arose, it would be almost impossible to establish identity. And Buckingham was an accomplished mimic into the bargain, able to disguise his face and manners so that even those who knew him best had no idea who he was.

And so it was that at last he even turned up in the Palace itself, dressed in the uniform of a sentry with musket, short black wig and heavy black mustache and eyebrows. He wore built-up boots to increase his height and a coat thickly padded over the shoulders. The sentries were often posted in the corridors to prevent a duel or other anticipated trouble, and no one noticed him—for a couple of hours. He amused himself by watching who came and went through the entrance to his cousin's apartments.

About mid-morning Barbara herself strolled out with Wilson and a couple of other waiting-women; one little blackamoor carried her train and another her muff, out of which peeked the petulant face of her spaniel. Barbara sailed on by, not even seeing him, but one of the waiting-women did and when he smiled she smiled in return. Sometime later when they came back the maid smiled again, but this time Barbara noticed him too. She gave him a sidelong glance just as she disappeared, her eyes running with quick approval over his handsomely padded torso, and one eyebrow went up slightly.

The next morning she paused, gave him a languishing look through her thick lashes, and unfurled her fan. "Aren't you the fellow who was here yesterday? Is a duel expected?"

He made her a respectful bow and in a voice and accent quite different from his own replied: "Wherever your Ladyship is, there is danger of men losing their heads."

Barbara bridled, pleased. "Oh, Lord! I'll swear you're impudent!"

"The sight of your Ladyship has made me bold." His eyes looked down into her bodice, and she gave him a smart rap on the arm with her fan.

"Saucy wretch! I could have you kicked!"

She gave her head a toss and walked away, but the next morning a page came to summon him into her Ladyship's chamber. He was taken down the corridor and through another door which led back to her apartments by means of a narrow passage he knew well enough, for it opened directly into her warm, luxuriously furnished bedroom, and there he was left alone. Barbara was playing with her spaniel, Jockey, and wearing a half unfastened dressing-gown, her hair falling down her back.

She looked up, straightened, and gave him a careless wave of her hand. "Good morning."

He bowed, his eyes bolder than ever, and Barbara's own were going over him as though he were a stud stallion on exhibition at Smithfield. "Good morning, your Ladyship. Indeed it is a good morning when I'm asked to wait upon your Ladyship." He bowed again.

"Well—I suppose you're surprised that a person of quality has sent for a mere nobody, aren't you?"

"I'm grateful, madame, if I can be of service to your Ladyship."

"Hm," murmured Barbara, one hand on her hip, half her naked leg showing as the gown fell away. "Perhaps you can. Yes—perhaps you can." Suddenly she was more brisk. "Tell me, are you a man of discretion?"

"Your Ladyship may trust me with your honour."

"How d'you know I intend to?" cried Barbara, annoyed that he should understand her so readily.

"I beg your Ladyship's pardon. I meant no offense, I assure you."

"Well, I wouldn't have you take me for a whore—just because I live at Court. Whitehall's got a mighty evil reputation these days—but I'll have you know, sir, I'm a person of honour."

"I'm convinced of that, madame."

Barbara relaxed again, and let the gown fall lower over her breasts. "You know, you're an uncommonly handsome young fellow. If I took a fancy to you I doubt not that I could see you advanced to a better position."

"I want nothing but to serve your Ladyship."

"Ordinarily, you understand, I wouldn't glance once at a sentry—but the truth of the matter is, I find myself strangely drawn to you."

He bowed again. "It's more than I deserve, madame."

"*What's* more than you deserve, you puppy?"

This time Buckingham answered her in his own voice. "Why, your Ladyship's kind approbation."

"Well—" began Barbara, and suddenly her eyes opened wide and she stared at him. "Say that again!"

"Say what again, your Ladyship?" asked the sentry.

Barbara blew a sigh of relief. "Whew! For a moment you sounded deucedly like a gentleman of my acquaintance—whom I'm not eager to see just now."

Buckingham leaned lazily back on his musket. One hand reached up to draw off his wig and his normal voice asked, "Not his Grace of Buckingham, by any chance?"

Barbara's eyes popped and her face went white, one hand to her mouth and the other pointing at him. "*George!* It isn't you!"

"It is, madame. And don't make any sound, I beg of you. This implement"—he tapped his gun—"is loaded, and I should not

703

like to shoot you just now—for I think you're still of some value to me."

"But what are you doing here—of all places! You're mad! They'll cut off your head if they find you!"

"They won't find me. A disguise that was good enough to fool my cousin should be good enough to fool anyone, don't you agree?" He seemed highly amused.

"But what are you doing here?"

"Don't you remember? You sent for me."

"Oh, you impertinent dog! I could kill you for this trick! Anyway—I only meant to raise your blood—I was just passing the time with you—"

"A very pretty pastime for a person of quality, I must agree. But I didn't take up that post to be seduced by my Lady Castlemaine. You know what I'm here for."

"Not I, I'm sure. I've had no hand in your troubles."

"Only that you gave my secret away to his Majesty."

"Gave it away? You lied to me! You told me it was York's horoscope you were having cast!"

"Even a lie, apparently, was unsafe with you. The King needs only a sentence to guess at the whole plot of a play." He shook his head, as though in sympathy for her. "How can you be so foolish, Barbara, when it's only by my good nature that you remain in England at all? However, it will doubtless be easy enough to buy my freedom now. I have an idea he'd forgive a much greater offense than mine to know that those letters are burned—"

"George!" cried Barbara frantically. "My God, you wouldn't tell him! You can't tell him! Oh, please, darling! I'll do anything you say! Command me and I'll be your slave—only promise me you won't tell him!"

"Lower your voice or you'll tell him yourself. Very well then —since you want to bargain. What will you give in exchange for my silence?"

"Anything, George! Anything at all! I'll give you anything— I'll do anything you say!"

"There's just one thing I want at present—and that's the clearance of my name."

Barbara sat down suddenly, scared and hopeless, her face turned white. "But you know that's the one thing I *can't* do! No one could do that for you—not Minette herself! Everyone says you're going to lose your head—the courtiers are already begging your estate! Oh, George, please—" She was beginning to cry, wringing her hands together.

"Stop that! I hate a drivelling woman! Old Rowley can watch you mope and wail if he likes but I've got other matters to think of! Look here, Barbara: your influence with him isn't wholly gone. You can convince him, if you try, that I'm innocent. I'll leave you to think of your own means— A woman never needs help making up lies."

He put the black wig onto his head again and picked up his musket. "I'll make it possible for you to communicate with me." He bowed. "I wish you success, madame." Turning then on his high heel he left her apartments and the Palace; the broad-shouldered, black-haired sentry was never again seen at Lady Castlemaine's door.

CHAPTER FORTY–NINE

EVEN AFTER AMBER was married she continued to remain at Almsbury House, for she hoped soon to be given an appointment at Court and live there.

As for her husband, she suggested that he take lodgings in Covent Garden, and because he had been henpecked from the cradle he did so, though against his better judgment. For despite the fact that it was permissible, even correct form, for husbands and wives to hate each other, to keep mistresses and take lovers, to bicker and quarrel in public and circulate the grossest slander about each other—it was not permissible to occupy separate homes or to sleep in separate beds. Amber was amused to discover that she had started a scandal which swept all the fashionable end of town.

Her husband was named Gerald Stanhope, and the title conveyed upon him by the King was Earl of Danforth. He was just twenty-two, a year younger than she, and to Amber he seemed an arrant fool. Timid and non-assertive, weak and thin, he lived in a habitual froth of worry as to what "Mother" was going to think about everything he or his wife did. Mother, he said, would not approve of them occupying separate lodgings, and finally he brought the news that Mother was coming up to London for a visit.

"Have you room for her in your apartments?" asked Amber.

She sat at her dressing-table having her hair arranged by a Frenchman newly arrived from Paris, over whose services the ladies were clawing one another. In one hand she held a silver-backed mirror, surveying her profile, admiring the lines of her straight forehead and dainty tilted nose, the pouting curves of her mouth and small round chin.

I'm handsomer than Frances Stewart any day, she thought, rather defiantly. But still I'm glad she's gone and disgraced and will never be back to trouble us more.

Gerald looked unhappy, pale and ineffectual. Travel on the Continent had not polished him; a moderately good education had not given him mental poise; the customary indulgence in whoring and drinking had certainly not made him sophisticated. He seemed still like a confused uncertain lonesome boy and this new turn his life had taken only made him feel more lost than ever.

These people—his wife and the other women and men who frequented Whitehall—were all so brazenly confident, so selfish in their preoccupations, so cruelly unconcerned for the hurts or hopes of another human. He longed for the quiet and peace and sense of security he had had at home. This world of palaces and taverns, theatres and bawdy-houses, scared and baffled him. He almost dreaded to have his mother come, to have her meet his wife, and yet the news that she was coming had relieved him considerably. Mother was not afraid of anyone.

He took out his comb and began to run it through his flaxen periwig. His clothes, at least, were now as fine and fashionable as any that money could buy, though his unprepossessing physique and spindly legs did not set them off to advantage.

"Pas du tout, madame," said Gerald. All the wits and pretended wits sprinkled their conversation with French phrases as a lady sprinkled her face with black taffeta patches. Gerald did likewise, for it gave him a sense of being in the mode. "As you know, I have a mere three rooms. There's no place to put her there." He was living at the Cheval d'Or, a lodging-house popular with the gallants because the landlady had a pretty and obliging daughter.

"Well, where *do* you propose to put her then? I don't like that curl, Durand. Pray, do it again." She was still surveying herself, front face now, observing her teeth, her skin, the smooth red paint on her lips.

Gerald gave a Parisian shrug of his thin shoulders. "Eh bien —I thought she might stay here."

Amber set the mirror down with a slam, though it lighted on a pile of ribbons and was saved. "Oh, you did! Well, she won't! D'ye think Lord Almsbury's running a lodging-house? You'd best send her a letter and tell her to stay where she is. What the devil does she want to come to London for anyway?" She gave a shake of her right wrist to hear the bracelets clink.

"Why, I suppose she wants to see her old acquaintances she hasn't seen in many years. And also, madame, I may as well speak frankly, she wonders why we keep separate lodgings."

Because he was afraid of what she might say to that he turned and went across the room, taking a long-stemmed pipe out of the capacious pocket of his coat and filling it with tobacco, using a match-stick from the fireplace to light it.

"Good Lord! Write and tell her you're of age now and married and able to manage your own affairs!" And then, seeing that he was smoking, she cried: "Get out of here with that filthy thing! D'ye think I want my rooms to stink? Go down and order the coach—I'll be with you presently. Or go on alone, if you prefer."

Gerald left hastily, obviously relieved, but Amber sat scowling into the mirror while Monsieur Durand, who was not supposed to make use of his ears, continued to work with passionate intensity upon the curl she had criticized.

"Lord!" muttered Amber crossly at last. "What a dull, insipid thing a husband is!"

Durand smiled unctuously, gave a final twirl of his comb and stepped back to survey her head. Then, satisfied, he took up a tiny vial, filled it with water and slipping in a golden rose tucked it among her curls. "It's true they've grown out of the fashion, madame. I find a lady of quality would no more wear one of 'em on her heart than she'd wear a bouquet of carnations."

"Why is it only the fools who marry?" she demanded, but went on talking without waiting for an answer. "Well, thank you, Durand, for coming to me. And here's something for your good work." She picked up three guineas from the table and dropped them into his hand.

His eyes began to glisten and he bowed again and again. "Oh, merci, madame, merci! It is indeed a pleasure to serve one so generous—and so beautiful. Pray call upon me at any time—and I come though I disappoint Majesty itself!"

"Thanks, Durand. Tell me—what d'you think of this gown? My dressmaker is a Frenchwoman. Has she done well by me, do you think?" She turned slowly about before him while Durand clasped his hands and kissed his fingers.

"C'est exquise, madame! Vraie Parisienne, madame! Exquise!"

Amber gave a little laugh and took up her fan and gloves. "What a flattering rogue you are! Nan, let him out—"

She left the room, beckoning Tansy to follow her, and he carried the long train of her gown in his hands so that it would not be soiled before she got to the ball. Durand was worth the three guineas she had given him—preposterous as the price was—not so much for the work of his clever fingers as for the prestige of having him. It had taken some scheming, but she had gotten him away from Castlemaine for that night, and every woman at the ball would know it.

A week later Amber was in the nursery—where she spent an hour or two every morning—playing trick-track with Bruce. Susanna, in a white linen-and-lace gown with a tiny apron and a starched lace cap that perched far back over her long glossy blonde hair, sat on the floor beside them. Already she was beginning to dominate the nursery and had her heel firmly on the necks of the Almsbury children, but her own brother was a more recalcitrant subject and refused the yoke of the little tyrant.

Amber loved the hours she spent in the nursery, for they were the one sure tie that bound her to Lord Carlton. These children were his children too, his blood was in their veins, they moved and spoke and had their being because of him. Their love for her was, in a sense, his—their kisses his. They were the memories of things past, all that she had for the present, and they offered her hope of the future.

"Mother!" Susanna was perpetually interrupting their game, for though she was too young to play she intended to have a part in it anyway.

"Yes, darling?"

"Wiggle-waggle!"

"Let me finish this game, Susanna. I just played wiggle-waggle."

Susanna pouted and made a face at her brother, but Amber saw it and threw one arm about her, hugging her close. "Here, what are you doing, you little witch?"

"Witch? What's a witch?"

"A witch," said her brother, somewhat bored, "is a nuisance."

Amber looked up at a footman who had just entered the room and come to stand beside them. "Yes?"

"You're wanted, madame."

"Who is it? Anyone of importance?"

"Your husband, I believe, madame—and his mother."

"Oh, Lord! Well—thank you. Tell 'em I'll be in presently." The man left and Amber got to her feet, though both children immediately began to protest. "I'm sorry, darlings, I'll come back if I can."

Bruce bowed to her. "Good-day, Mother. Thank you for coming to see us."

Amber bent and kissed him and then she picked up Susanna, who kissed her with smacking abandon on the cheeks and mouth. "Here, Susanna!" protested Amber. "You'll take all my powder off, you little minx." She kissed her and then put

709

her down, waved them both goodbye and left the room—but her smile faded the instant she closed the door.

For a moment she stood in the hall, staring. Now why the devil did that old woman have to come here? she thought irritably. Pregnancy always made her feel that everything unpleasant which happened was done for the sole purpose of annoying her. And then with a sigh and a little shrug she started back toward her own rooms at the opposite end of the gallery.

Gerald Stanhope and his mother sat on a couch before the fireplace in Amber's drawing-room. The Dowager Baroness had her back to the door and she was chattering away at Gerald whose face looked worried and anxious. The starkly black-painted eyebrows he affected because they were supposed to be all the mode contrasted shockingly with his white skin and ash-blonde wig. But the moment Amber entered the room the Baroness ceased talking and, after giving herself a moment or two to compose her features, she turned a fixed sweet smile in the direction of her daughter-in-law. Her eyes did not conceal the sudden surprise and displeasure she felt at what she saw.

Amber came toward them walking lazily, her dressing-gown flowing back from the lacy ruffled petticoat she wore beneath it. Gerald, looking as if he expected the roof to blow off the house at any moment, stood up to present his wife to his mother. The two women embraced, carefully, as though each were afraid of soiling her hands and garments on the other. And then each turned her cheek—it was an affectation of great ladies to present their cheeks rather than their lips for a salute. As they stepped back their eyes ran over each other appraisingly, and neither one of them missed a detail. Gerald stood and bobbled his Adam's apple and took out a comb to occupy his hands.

Lucilla, Lady Stanhope, was just over forty. She had a plump petulant face that made Amber think of one of the King's spaniels, with a mouth turned down at the corners and shaky round cheeks. Her hair, which had once been blonde, was now caramel-coloured. But her skin was still pink and fresh and she had prominent thrusting breasts. Her clothes were even

710

more out of style than those of most country ladies, and her jewels were insignificant.

"Oh, pray take no notice of my clothes," said her Ladyship instantly. "They're nothing but old frippery I was about to give my maid, but the roads were so bad I didn't dare wear anything else! Heavens, as it was, one cart overturned and flung three of my trunks into the mud!"

"Oh, barbarous!" agreed Amber sympathetically. "Your Ladyship must be jolted to a jelly. Can't I send for some refreshment?"

"Why, yes, madame. I do believe I'd like a dish of tea."

She had never drunk any tea, for it was far too expensive, but now she was determined to show everyone that for all she had been twenty years in the country she had never been out of touch with the Town.

"I'll send for some. Arnold! Drat that man! Where is he? Always kissing the maids when you want him." Amber walked toward the door of the next room. "Arnold!"

The Baroness watched her, envy and disapproval in her eyes.

She had never been able to reconcile herself to the fact that the days of her own youth and beauty had occurred so unpropitiously. First there had been the Civil War and her husband gone most of the time, then finally killed, leaving her condemned to live out her best years in the country, impoverished by taxes and forced to do part of her own housework like any farmer's wife. The years had slipped treacherously by. She had not realized until today how many of them were gone.

She had had no opportunity to marry again, for the Wars had left too many poor widows, and she had Gerald and his two sisters to rear. The girls had been fortunate to marry country squires, but Gerald—she had been determined—must have a better opportunity. She sent him on a trip to the Continent and bade him stop in London on his return to see if he might catch the King's eye and perhaps bring the sacrifices and loyalty of the Stanhopes to his attention. He had succeeded better than she had ever dared hope. One month ago, a letter had come from him saying that the King had not only raised the family to an earldom but had found a great fortune for him to marry, and that he was already both Earl of Danforth and bridegroom.

Overjoyed, she began immediately to make arrangements for closing up Ridgeway Manor and moving to London. She saw herself frequenting the Court, admired and envied for her clothes and jewels, her lavish hospitality, her charm and, yes, her beauty too. For Lady Stanhope had eagerly consulted her mirror and persuaded herself that for all most women of forty-two were considered decayed she was still a fine person and might—with new French gowns, ribbons and curls and jewels—very reasonably be taken for a beauty. She might even marry again, if she found a gentleman to her taste.

The letter from Lady Clifford came as an unpleasant shock.

"My dear Lucilla," it read. "Pray accept of the good thoughts and best wishes of all of us who are your friends. We were both surprised and pleased that your family should have been given an earldom. For though none has been more deserving it is too well known by us who have been in London these seven years past that nowadays reward is not always conveyed where it is most due or honour shown to those who best deserve it. There is no use dissembling, the old ways have changed; for the worse, I fear.

"We were all quite astonished at the news of Gerald's marriage, happening so suddenly as it did, and for my part I first knew he was in town when I heard that he had married the former Countess of Radclyffe. No doubt you've heard that she's thought a great beauty, much frequents the Court, and is said to be in some favour with his Majesty. For my part I seldom go to Whitehall nowadays, but prefer the company of our old friends. The young and giddy have taken over the Court and persons of quiet manners are in no request there. But perhaps a time may come again when the old virtues of honesty in a man and modesty in a woman will be more than an excuse for coarse jesting and laughter.

"I hope to have the pleasure of your company soon. No doubt you will be coming to London as soon as Gerald and his wife begin to occupy lodgings together.

"Your very humble and obedient servant, madame,

"I am,

"Margaret, Lady Clifford."

There it was. Like a rock dropped in the middle of a quiet pool. "As soon as Gerald and his wife begin to occupy lodgings together." *What* did her Ladyship mean?

Were they married and not living together? Where was he living then? Where was she living? She read the letter over again, very carefully, and this time she could pick out several more ominous suggestions. She decided that she could not get there too soon for her son's welfare.

And now here she was, in the very presence of the hussy, all her outraged virtue seething within her—and she found that in spite of herself she was embarrassed and uneasy. Twenty years of living secluded, of seeing only her children and the villagers and near neighbours, of scraping to keep them in food and clothes and trying to save money enough so that Gerald could cut a figure at Oxford and abroad, watching her good looks grow overblown and begin to fade, had not prepared her for this moment.

Because, for all her awareness that behind her stood generations of haughty ancestors—while this creature was a reputed upstart from the theatres or some place even worse—she was bewildered and overawed by the other woman's cool self-possession, her fine clothes, her casual confident beauty. Above all, by her youth. Still, Lady Stanhope was of sterner stuff than her shy awkward son. Now she smiled at her daughter-in-law who sat facing her while they waited for the tea to be brought, and she fluttered her fan as if the room were too hot, tipping her head archly to one side.

"And so you are my new daughter-in-law? How pretty you are, too. Gerry must be very proud of you. I assure you I've been hearing a great deal about you."

"So soon? I thought your Ladyship had only just arrived in town."

"Oh, by letter, my dear! Lady Clifford is my very dear friend and has kept me as intimately informed as if I were living on the Piazza. It's been a great diversion to me, I assure you, through these last years when I've been too sadly stricken by the death of my dear husband to venture into company. Oh, I'm as competent a gossip as if I'd been here all along, I warrant you."

713

She gave a little laugh, glancing brightly at the uncomfortable Gerry and then at her daughter-in-law, wondering if the wench had wit enough to understand her meaning. But either she did not or she did not care.

"Well," said Amber, "there's nothing so plentiful as gossip these days. That's one thing we don't have to depend upon the French for."

Lady Stanhope cleared her throat slightly and turned to lay one hand over Gerald's, giving him a fond maternal beam. "How my Gerry has changed! I haven't seen him since he set out for the Continent—two years ago this coming June. I vow he looks as modish as a French count. Well, madame, I hope you'll be happy together. I'm sure Gerry can make a woman as happy as any man in Europe— And there's nothing so important to a woman as a happy marriage—for all that some lewd persons like to ridicule matrimony nowadays."

Amber smiled faintly but did not answer. And at that moment the footman appeared, followed by two others, who laid before them an elaborate silver tea-table and service with little China porcelain tea-bowls and small crystal glasses for the brandy which always followed.

Lady Stanhope feigned enthusiasm. "How extraordinary good this tea is! Pray, where did you get it? Mine was never so fine, I assure you."

"Lady Almsbury's steward got this—at the East India House, I suppose."

"Hmm—delicious." She took another sip. "I suppose that you and Gerry will be moving soon into your own home?"

Amber smiled over the rim of her dish at her, her eyes seeming to slant, shining and hard as a cat's. "Perhaps we'll build a house one day—when workmen are easier to find. Just now they're all engaged in the City, putting up taverns."

"But what will you do in the meantime, my dear?" The Baroness looked innocent and amazed.

"Why, I suppose we'll continue as we are. It seems a comfortable arrangement, don't you agree, sir?"

Gerald, thus appealed to, with his wife's and his mother's

eyes suddenly upon him, started a little and spilled some tea on his white lace cravat. "Why—a—yes. I suppose so. It seems well enough, at least for now."

"Nonsense, Gerald!" sharply contradicted his mother. "It's shocking! I may as well tell you bluntly, my dear," she said, turning back to Amber, "it's all the talk."

"Don't you mean, madame, it *was* all the talk? Frances Stewart's elopement is à la mode now."

The Baroness was becoming exasperated. This was not the kind of resistance to which her years of ruling a pliable son and two meek daughters had accustomed her, and she found it both insulting and annoying. Didn't the jade realize that she was her mother-in-law, a person of some importance, as well as of far higher quality than herself?

"Have your jest, my dear. But nevertheless it's an unheard-of thing that a husband and wife should live apart. The world is censorious, you know, and such an arrangement calls into question the integrity of both—but most especially of the wife. I know the age is different from the one I was married in, but let me assure you, madame, that even present-day manners will not condone a thing of that sort." The longer she talked the more excited she became; at the end she was like an outraged pouter-pigeon.

Amber was beginning to grow angry too. But she saw Gerald's miserable pleading face and restrained herself, taking pity on him. She set down her tea-dish and poured the brandy. "Well, I'm sorry if the arrangement is not to your liking, madame, but since it suits both of us I think we'll leave it as it is."

The Baroness's mouth flew open again but her protest was cut off, for at that moment Lady Almsbury entered the room. Amber presented the two women to each other and this time Gerald's mother embraced her new acquaintance with enthusiasm, kissing her on the mouth, making a very obvious contrast between the honour she was prepared to show a plain and good woman and what was due an impertinent strumpet, even if she was her daughter-in-law.

"I heard you'd come, madame," said Emily, taking another

chair beside the fireplace and accepting the dish of tea which Amber gave her, "and I wanted to bid you welcome. You must find London sadly changed."

"Indeed I do, madame," agreed Lady Stanhope quickly. "It was not thus when I was last here in '43, let me tell you!"

"Well, it looks almost hopeless now. But they've already made some very fine plans and building has begun in various parts of the City. They say that one day London will rise again, more glorious than ever—though of course it made us all sad to see the old London go. But pray, my lady, was your trip pleasant?"

"Heavens, no! It was wretched! I was telling her Ladyship only a few moments since that I dared not wear any fine clothes for fear of spoiling them! But it had been two years since I'd seen Gerry—and I knew he wouldn't *think* of leaving London when he'd just been married, so I came in spite of everything."

"That was generous of you. Tell me, madame, have you a place to stay? Since the Fire it's become very difficult to find lodging anywhere. If you've made no arrangements, my husband and I would be very glad to have you here until such time as you may wish to make a change."

Good Lord! thought Amber in irritation. Must I put up with that prattling old jade in the same house?

Lady Stanhope did not hesitate. "Why, that's most kind of your Ladyship! For the truth on it is I had no place—I came in such a hurry. I should be very happy to stay here for a few days."

Amber swallowed her brandy and stood up. "Will you ladies excuse me now? I'm expected at the Palace before noon and I must get dressed."

"Oh!" cried Lady Stanhope, turning to her son. "Then you'll be going too, Gerry. Well, sweetheart, run along. I warrant you a young man would rather wait upon his bride than his mother."

Amber glanced at Gerald who now, as if he had been prompted, said: "As it happens, madame, I'm engaged to dine with some gentlemen at Locket's today."

716

"Engaged to dine with some gentlemen and not with your wife? Bless me! What a strange age this is!"

Gerald, emboldened by his own daring, gave a nonchalant brush at his blue and gold brocaded sleeve. "It's the mode, your Ladyship. Devoted husbands and wives are démodé—no one'll have 'em any more." He turned to Amber and bowed as elegantly as he could. "Your Ladyship's servant."

"Your servant, sir." She curtsied, amused and a little surprised that he had had the courage to defy his mother.

Then, he bowed to his mother and Lady Almsbury and made his escape while Lady Stanhope seemed unable to decide whether to let him go for the time being or to tell him outright what she thought of such behaviour. She let him go. As Amber was leaving the room she heard her say: "Heaven! How he's changed! Every inch the young gentleman of fashion, I vow!"

It was nearly midnight when Amber returned from Whitehall, tired almost to exhaustion and eager to get into bed. Twelve hours at the Palace was a considerable strain on her, the more so because of her pregnancy. Every instant she was there she must be alert and gay; there was never a moment to relax, to look or act as tired as she sometimes felt. And now there was a nervous ache in the back of her neck, the muscles of her legs jumped, and everything inside her seemed to quiver.

She had just started up the stairs when Almsbury came running out of a lighted room which opened from the hall-way. "Amber!" She turned and looked at him. "I thought you were never coming!"

"So did I. They had some damned puppets there and no one could be satisfied till they'd played 'Romeo and Juliet' four times!"

"I've got a surprise for you." He was just below her on the stairs, grinning. "Guess who's here."

Amber shrugged, uninterested. "How would I know?"

She looked over his head to the door-way where someone was standing—a tall dark-haired man who smiled at her. Amber caught her breath. "Bruce!" She saw him start toward her, running, and then Almsbury's arms went about her as she fainted, crumpling helplessly.

CHAPTER FIFTY

THE THIN APRIL sun came through the casemented windows and made patches of brightness on the bare floor. It struck light from the spurs on a pair of man's boots that lay there, touched the pale-blue ostrich feathers piled on the brim of a hat, glittered on the worked gold-and-silver hilt of a sheathed sword —all heaped beside the canopied bed. Within, sunk deep into a feather mattress, Amber lay half drowsing, just on the verge of coming fully awake. Slowly her arm slid over the empty bed, an expression of puzzlement and vague worry crossing her face. She opened her eyes, found herself alone and sat up with a sudden frightened cry.

"Bruce!"

He jerked back the curtains and stood there, grinning down at her. He wore his breeches but no shirt or periwig and was apparently just done shaving, for he was still wiping his face.

"What's the matter, darling?"

"Oh! Thank God! I was afraid you'd gone—or that I'd only been dreaming and you were never here at all. But you are here, aren't you? You're really here. Oh, Bruce, it's *wonderful* to have you back!"

She held out her arms to him, smiling broadly, her eyes filled with brilliance. "Come here, darling. I want to touch you—" He sat down beside her and her finger-tips moved over his face, wonderingly, as though she could not believe even now that he actually was there. "How fine you're looking," she whispered. "Handsomer than ever—" Her hands moved down over his broad muscular shoulders and chest, pressing hard against the warm brown flesh. Then all at once her eyes returned to his and she found him staring at her.

"Amber—"

718

"Yes?"

Their mouths came together with sudden devouring violence. Unexpectedly she began to cry and her fists beat against him, passionate, demanding. Swiftly he pushed her back upon the bed and her arms strained him to her. When the storm was spent, he lay with his head on her breast, relaxed against her. Now their faces were still and peaceful, content. Tenderly her fingers stroked through his coarse black hair.

At last he began to move away and stood up. Amber opened her eyes and smiled drowsily.

"Come back, darling, and lie here beside me."

He bent and kissed her lips. "I can't—Almsbury's waiting."

"What if he is? Let him wait."

He shook his head. "We're going to Whitehall—his Majesty expects me. Perhaps I'll see you there later—" He paused and stood looking down at her. There was a lazy half-amused smile on his face. "I understand that you're a countess now. And married again, too," he added.

Amber's head turned suddenly and her eyes looked at him almost in astonishment. Married again! Good Lord, she thought. I am! When Gerald was not around she totally forgot his existence.

He grinned. "What's the matter, darling? Forget which one it is? Almsbury says his name is Stanhope—I think that was it—and the one before was—"

"Oh, Bruce! Don't make fun of me! I'd never have married him in a thousand years if I'd known that you were coming back! I hate him—he's a stupid addle-pated booby! I only married him because—" She stopped at that and hastily corrected herself. "I don't know why I married him! I don't know why I ever married anyone! I've never wanted to be married to anyone but you, Bruce! Oh, darling, we could have had such a happy life together if only you—"

Her eyes saw the changing expression on his face—a look that at once seemed to warn her and to shut her out. She stared at him, the old dread stealing up again, and then at last, very softly, she said: "You're married—" She shook her head slowly even as she spoke.

He drew a deep breath. "Yes. I'm married."

There it was. She had heard it at last—what she had expected and dreaded for seven years. Now it seemed to her that it had been there between them always, inevitable as death. Sick and weak, she could do nothing but look at him. He sat down on a chair and tied the laces of his shoes. For a moment he continued to sit there, elbows resting on his knees and his hands hanging between his legs, but at last he turned to face her.

"I'm sorry, Amber," he said softly.

"Sorry you're married?"

"Sorry that I've hurt you."

"When were you married? I thought—"

"I was married a year ago last February, just after I got back to Jamaica."

"Then you knew you were going to get married when you left me! You—"

"No, I didn't," he interrupted. "I met her the day I arrived in Jamaica. We were married a month later."

"A month later!" she whispered, and then suddenly all her muscles and bones seemed to collapse. "Oh, my God!"

"Amber, darling—please—I've never lied to you. I told you from the first I'd get married someday—"

"Oh, but so soon!" she protested irrationally, her voice a plaintive wail. And then suddenly she lifted her head and looked at him; there was a glitter of malice in her eyes. "Who is she! Some black wench you—"

Bruce's face turned hard. "She's English. Her father is an earl and went to Jamaica after the Wars—he has a sugar plantation there." He got up to continue his dressing.

"She's rich, I suppose."

"Rich enough."

"And beautiful too?"

"Yes—I think so."

This time she paused a moment, but then she drove out the question: "Do you love her?"

He turned and looked at her strangely, his eyes slightly narrowed. For a moment he made no answer and then, softly, he said, "Yes, I love her."

She snatched up her dressing-gown, slid her arms into it, and flounced off the bed. The words she said next were the same as might have occurred to any Court-bred lady faced with the same situation. "Oh, damn you, Bruce Carlton!" she muttered. "Why should *you* be the only man in England to marry for love!"

But the veneer was too thin; under any real pressure it was sure to crack. Suddenly she turned on him. "I hate her!" she cried furiously. "I despise her! Where is she!"

He answered gently. "In Jamaica. She had a child in November and didn't want to leave."

"She must be mighty fond of you!"

Bruce made no reply to that sarcastic sneer and she added savagely, "So now you've got married to a lady and you'll have someone to breed up your brats whose ancestors have spent two thousand years sitting on their arses in the House of Lords! I congratulate you, Lord Carlton! What a calamity if you'd had to let any ordinary human raise your children!"

He looked at her with anxiety and a kind of pity. His hat was in his hand. "I've got to go now, Amber. I'm half an hour late already—"

She gave him a sullen glare and turned her head away, as though expecting him to apologize for having offended her. But then, against her will, she watched him as he walked across the room—his body moving with the familiar remembered rhythm that seemed to have in it something of all the reasons why she loved him. "Bruce!" she cried suddenly. He paused and slowly turned to face her. "I don't care if you are married! I'll never give you up—never as long as I live, d'ye hear! You're as much mine as you are hers! She can *never* have all of you!"

She started toward him but he turned again. In a moment he had opened the door and gone out, closing it quietly. Amber stopped where she was, one hand reaching out, the other catching at her throat to stifle a sob. "Bruce!" she cried again. And then, wearily, she turned about and went back to the bed. For several seconds she stood and stared at it, and then she dropped onto her knees beside it. "He's gone—" she whispered. "He's gone— I've lost him—"

During the first two weeks that he was there Amber saw Lord Carlton but infrequently. He was busy at the wharves and interviewing merchants, disposing of the tobacco he had brought with him and drawing up new contracts, making purchases for himself and the other plantation owners. Whenever he went to Whitehall it was to see King Charles, for he wanted another land grant—this one for twenty thousand acres to give him a total of thirty thousand. But he spent no time at all in the Drawing-Rooms or at the theatre.

At Amber's suggestion Lady Almsbury had given him apartments adjoining hers, and though he said nothing about seeing her the second night—assuming that her husband would be there—she knocked at his door when she heard him come in. They met every night after that. There was no doubt that he knew she sometimes came home late because she had been with the King, but he never mentioned it. Her casual relationship with Gerald seemed to amuse him, but he did not speak of that either.

It did not, however, amuse Gerald's mother.

During that fortnight Amber saw her only a time or two, at Whitehall, and then she hurried off the other direction to avoid an encounter. But the Dowager Baroness seemed to be very busy and Nan said that she was in constant cabal with hair-dressers and jewellers, sempstresses and tailors and a dozen different kinds of tradesmen, that her rooms were littered with satins and velvets, taffetas and laces, ribbons and silks by the dozen-yard.

"What the devil is she about?" asked Amber. "She hasn't got a shilling!"

But she thought that she knew well enough. The old jade was spending *her* money. If she had not been so intensely preoccupied with Bruce and her interests at Court she would not have let the Baroness continue her spending spree for even two days—but as it was she let her go ahead and was relieved not to be troubled by her. One of these days, she promised herself, I'll pluck a crow with that woman. But Lady Stanhope sought her out first.

Amber was never awake before nine o'clock—for it was late

when she returned from the Palace—and by that time Bruce was always gone. She would sip her morning cup of chocolate, get into a dressing-gown and go to see the children. From ten until noon she spent getting dressed. It took that long, partly because painting her face and having her hair arranged and getting into her clothes was a complicated process, but also because she admitted great numbers of those mercers and jewellers and perfumers who flocked to the anterooms of the rich and noble. No one was ever turned away from her door.

She liked the noise and confusion, the sense of importance it gave her to be great enough that she should be so pestered, and she liked to buy things. If the material was beautiful she could always order a new gown; if the setting was unusual or extravagant she could always find use for a new necklace or bracelet; if it had come from far away or was said to be very rare or if it merely caught her fancy she never refused another vase or table or gold-framed mirror. Her prodigality was well known among the tradesmen and before noon her apartments were almost as crowded as the courtyard of the Royal Exchange.

She would sit at her dressing-table wearing a loose gown, a pair of mules hanging on the tips of her toes, while Monsieur Durand arranged her hair. Nan Britton had advanced quite beyond such tasks. She was now waiting-woman to a countess and had no duties but to dress handsomely, always look her best, and accompany her mistress wherever she went. And, like most waiting-women of fashionable ladies, she had her coterie of lovers—many of them the same lords and fops who circulated among the ladies themselves. Nan enjoyed her life with all the gusto and enthusiasm she brought to everything she did— though it was a triumph and success she had never expected, for which she would have made no effort herself.

The tradesmen and women hovered in a buzzing circle about Amber, thrusting first this and then that beneath her nose. "Pray, look at these gloves, madame—and smell them. But place them to the nose and you'll never have another scent. Is it not exquisite?"

Amber smelled. "Neroli, isn't it? My favourite scent. I'll take a dozen pairs." She whisked a tiny brush over her curved black brows, smoothing them and taking off the specks of powder.

"I've been saving this length for you, madame. Feel that nap, as deep as anything ever woven. And the colour—it becomes your Ladyship to a miracle. See how it matches your eyes!—as near as anything could. And let me add, madame," leaning close and whispering, "the Countess of Shrewsbury saw it the other day and was mightily taken with it. But I told her it was already gone. I could see it for no one but you, madame."

"I'll have to take it now, won't I, you crafty knave?" She slid a pair of diamond drops into her ears. "But it is beautiful. I'm glad you saved it for me—and don't forget me when your next shipment comes in. Nan, give him the money, will you?"

"Madame, I beg of you, take this bracelet into your hand. See how it strikes the light—how it flashes like fire? Finer stones were never mined. And let me tell you—though it's worth five hundred pound and more—I'll give it to your Ladyship at a great loss to myself, only for the honour of having my work upon your Ladyship's arm. Though anyone else would demand at the very least five hundred pound—I'll give it to your Ladyship for but one hundred and fifty."

Amber laughed, holding the bracelet in her hand and admiring it. "At that price how can I afford not to have it? Leave it then. I'll buy it." She tossed it onto the dressing-table amid the heap of boxes and jars and bottles, letters, fans, ribbons. "But send me a bill—I never keep such sums on hand."

"S'il vous plaît, madame—" It was Monsieur Durand's agonized voice. "I beg of you, do not move about so much! First this way and then that. I can accomplish nothing! Mort Dieu, madame!"

"I'm sorry, Durand. What've you got there, Johnson?"

It went on morning after morning, this daily fair, offering entertainment and profit for all, and Amber gave them at least as good a show as she got. Fiddlers were almost always in the room, playing the latest ballads or the newest tune from a play. Half-a-dozen maids came and went. Tansy strolled among them and sometimes made a request for himself; he had grown inordinately vain of his clothes and Amber dressed him at great ex-

724

pense, though he still refused to put on a shoe which was not worn out. The King had given her a spaniel puppy which she called Monsieur le Chien and he nosed at everyone, snapping and barking at whoever had not been previously identified.

Amber was thus occupied one morning when a little page entered the room and came to her. "Madame, the Baroness Stanhope to wait upon you."

Amber rolled her eyes impatiently. "Hell and furies!" she muttered, and looked around over her shoulder just as her Ladyship entered the room. Then her eyes opened wide in amazement, and it was a moment before she could gather her wits enough to stand and welcome her mother-in-law.

Lucilla was now so different a woman as to be scarcely recognizable. Her head was as golden as Susanna's, curled in the latest fashion and decorated with ribbons and flowers and a twisted strand of pearls. Her face was painted like the face of a China doll and there were evidently "plumpers" in her cheeks to keep them firm and round. Her gown—made of pearl-grey satin over a fuchsia-coloured petticoat—looked as though it had been turned out by deft French fingers and the busk she wore beneath it narrowed her waist and thrust her breasts high above the neckline. There was a string of pearls about her neck, diamond pendants swinging from her ears, half a dozen bracelets on her wrists, and rings on three fingers of each hand. All of them had a wicked glitter that looked both genuine and expensive. She had become, in just a fortnight, a very elegant lady of fashion, somewhat over-ripe, but still inviting enough.

My God! thought Amber. Look at that old bawd.

The two women embraced, casually, but Lady Stanhope had seen the surprise on Amber's face and she looked at her triumphantly as though now demanding, not giving, admiration. But after the first shock of seeing how she had changed, Amber's horrified thought was that all this had been accomplished on her money. The Stanhopes, she knew, had lost their one small source of income when their tenements had burned in the Fire.

"You must forgive my rudeness, madame," began Lucilla immediately. "I'd have called sooner but I've been so furiously busy!" She paused, somewhat breathless, to fan herself. Though she thought it must be envy in her daughter-in-law's eyes she could not but be conscious for all her finery and dyed hair and false curls that she would never be three-and-twenty again and that the years between had been long and stubborn.

"Oh, it's I who should have called on you, madame," protested Amber politely, trying to count up in her head the number of pounds sterling she saw represented in Lady Stanhope's ensemble; and the higher the total mounted the angrier she became. But she smiled and asked her to be seated while she finished her toilet and then, as Lady Stanhope caught sight of a length of blue velvet, Amber quickly told the tradespeople that it was time for them to go.

"Come to my apartments tomorrow morning," said Lucilla with a wave of her hand, and the man took up his velvet and left with the others.

Amber sat down to stick on her patches while Lucilla panted, obviously uncomfortable in her too-tight corset. "Heavens!" said her Ladyship, crossing her small feet and cocking her head on one side to admire them. "You wouldn't believe how taken up with business I've been this fortnight! I've a great acquaintance here in town, you know, and everyone must see me at once! Provoking creatures! I've been most horribly towsed." She put one hand to her head, preening. "I've scarcely seen Gerry at all. Pray tell me, how has my dear boy been?"

"Very well, I think, madame," replied Amber, too angry over the thought of her hard-gotten money going to decorate this old woman to be able to pay much attention to what was being said.

Now she got up, crossed the room and went behind a magnificent blue-lacquered Chinese screen, beckoning one of the women to bring her gown. Monsieur le Chien was nosing curiously about Lucilla's shoes and yapping from time to time, not at all intimidated by the sharp looks she gave him. Only Amber's head and shoulders could be seen now and while she was not looking Lucilla's eyes studied her, slightly narrowed, hard and critical and disapproving. But as Amber glanced suddenly across at her she smiled, a quick and guilty smile.

"It's strange I never see Gerry in the mornings. At home he always called on me each day before he did anything else. He's always been the most devoted child a mother could want. He must go abroad very early." She spoke rapidly, looking at Amber as though she expected her to lie.

"Why, as far as I remember," said Amber, sucking in her stomach while the maid jerked tighter the strings of her busk, "he hasn't been here at all since the day you arrived."

"What!" cried Lady Stanhope, as horrified as though she had heard that her son was under arrest for picking pockets. "Doesn't he sleep with you!"

"Tighter," muttered Amber to the maid. "It's *got* to be tighter." Her waist was growing larger but she intended to lace it in just as long as she could. Far more than the agony of labour she hated the months of being misshapen, and this time more than ever, for Bruce was here and she wanted desperately to look her best. Then she replied, casually, "Oh, yes. He has." He had, in fact, just three times, and Amber had permitted that only because the King hoped to make him think that the child was his own.

"Well!" Lady Stanhope fanned herself harder than ever and her face flushed, as it always did at the slightest hint of nervousness or embarrassment or anger. "I never heard of such a thing! A man not sleeping with his wife! It's— Why, it's immoral! I'll take a course with him about this, my dear! I'll see he doesn't neglect you any more!"

Amber gave her an amused lazy smile over the top of the screen and bent slightly, stepping into first one petticoat and then another. "Don't trouble yourself, madame. His Lordship and I like the arrangement as it is. The young men have a great deal of business nowadays, you know—going to theatres and taverns, drinking till midnight and scouring about the streets afterward. It keeps 'em well occupied, I assure you."

"Oh, but Gerry doesn't live that kind of life, I'm sure of it! He's a good quiet boy, you may believe me, madame. If he doesn't come here it must be he's of the opinion he isn't wanted!"

Amber swung about and looked directly at her mother-in-law, her eyes cool and with a malicious slant at the corners. "I'm sure I can't think where he could have got such a notion as that, madame. What's o'clock, Nan?"

"Almost half-after-twelve, your Ladyship."

"Oh, Lord!" Amber stepped out from behind the screen, fully dressed now, and a maid handed her her fan and muff while another came to set the cloak on her shoulders. She picked up her gloves and began pulling them on. "I have a sitting with Mr. Lely at one! I must beg to be excused, madame. Mr. Lely is so furiously in demand he cannot stay a moment for anyone. If I'm late I'll lose my turn and he has the portrait half done."

Lady Stanhope got to her feet. "I was just going abroad myself. I'm engaged to dine with Lady Clifford and then we're going to the play. One never has a moment to oneself in town." The two countesses started out of the room, walking side by side, followed by Nan and Tansy and Monsieur le Chien. Lucilla gave Amber an arch sidewise glance. "I suppose you knew that Lord Carlton is a guest in the house?"

Amber looked at her sharply. What did she mean by that? Was it possible she had heard gossip about them? But they'd been very discreet—always entering and leaving by their own doors, paying each other no undue attentions in public. Her heart hammering hard, Amber tried to give her an off-hand answer.

"Oh, yes. I know. He's an old friend of the Earl."

"I think he's fascinating! They say every woman at Court is mad in love with him! And have you heard? They say he's one of my Lady Castlemaine's lovers—but of course they say that about everyone." She rambled on, for she always talked as if she had more to say than time would allow, but Amber was conscious only of relief. Evidently she knew nothing—she just wanted to prattle. "But to think of the venturesome life he's led—soldier-of-fortune, privateer, and now a planter! I've heard he's one of the richest men in England—and of course his family's most distinguished. It was Marjorie Bruce, you know, who was the mother of the first Stuart King of Scotland, and that's his family. And his wife, they say, is a great beauty—"

"Everyone's a great beauty with a portion of ten thousand pound!" snapped Amber.

"Well," said Lucilla. "He's a fine person, I vow and swear. He's everything in the world that I admire."

Amber bowed to her. "Good-day, madame."

She walked off, down the stairs, seething inside, furious and hurt. Oh, I can't stand it! she thought wildly. I can't stand knowing he's married to that woman! I hate her, I hate her, I hate her! I hope she dies! Suddenly she stopped, catching her breath. Maybe she will. She began to walk on, her eyes glowing. Maybe she *will* die, over there with all those sicknesses—maybe she will— She had completely forgotten her grievance against the Baroness for spending her money.

The next night she and Bruce came home from Whitehall together. He had completed the most urgent part of his business and was beginning to go there in the evenings to gamble and talk. They climbed the stairs, laughing over the current story that Buckingham, still in hiding, had been arrested for rioting in the streets and locked up and then released again without being recognized. Outside her rooms they parted.

"Don't be long, darling," she whispered.

She came into her own drawing-room still smiling, but the smile froze unpleasantly as she found Gerald and his mother sitting there, before her fireplace.

"Well!" She swung the door shut.

Gerald got to his feet. He looked wretchedly unhappy and Amber knew that coming here had not been his idea. The Dowager Baroness gave her a languid look over her bare shoulder, then stood up and made just the suggestion of a curtsy. Amber did not return it, but she came on into the room, glancing from one to the other.

"I didn't expect to find you here," she said to Gerald, who immediately cleared his throat and stuck a finger into the high close-fitting cravat about his neck. He tried to smile, but nervousness made his face break into little pieces.

"I just came to talk to Gerry while he was waiting for you to return," interposed his mother hastily. "I'll be going along now and leave you two young people together. Your servant, madame. Good-night, Gerry dear." As Gerald obediently kissed his mother's cheek Amber saw her give him an admonitory but encouraging pat on the arm.

With a triumphant flaunting little smile she left the room, her long train swishing after her, making a definite sound in the stillness, and all at once a clock began to chime. Amber did not watch her go but kept her eyes on Gerald, and as she heard the door close she tossed her muff and gloves to Tansy and waved him off. Monsieur le Chien was prancing and barking at Gerald, for he had seen him but seldom and was not sure he belonged there.

"Well," repeated Amber again, and walked to the fire to warm her hands.

"Eh bien, madame," said Gerald. "Here I am. And after all" —suddenly he straightened his shoulders and faced her defiantly —"why shouldn't I be here? I'm your husband, madame." It sounded like what Mother had told him to say.

"Of course," agreed Amber. "Why shouldn't you?" Then all at once she put one hand to her stomach and, with a little groan, dropped onto the settee.

Gerald started. "Good God, madame! What is it? Is something amiss with you?" He turned and would have run out. "I'll fetch someone—"

But Amber stopped him. "No, Gerald. It's nothing. It's just that I'm with child, I think—I didn't want to tell you until I knew for sure—"

He looked delighted, amazed, as though this had happened to no man before him. "Already? My God! I can't believe it! But, Lord! I hope it's true!" She had surprised him out of all his airs and French grimaces; he was merely a frightened pleased English country boy.

Amber was amused, thinking him a complete dolt. "I hope so too, my lord. But you know how a woman is in this circumstance."

"No—I don't. I—I never thought about it before. Are you better now? Can I get something for you? A pillow for your head?"

"No, Gerald, thanks. I just want to be let alone—I— Well, to tell you truly I'd rather sleep by myself—if you don't mind—"

"Oh, but of course, madame. I didn't know—I didn't realize. I'm sorry—" He started to back away. "If there's ever anything you want—anything I can do—"

"Thanks, Gerald. I'll let you know."

"And I wonder, madame—may I call sometimes—just to see how you're doing?"

"Of course, my lord. Whenever you like. Good-night."

"Good-night, madame." He hesitated, plainly wishing that he could think of something appropriate to say on this occasion, and then with a helpless little laugh he repeated, "Well, good-night," and was gone.

Amber shook her head and made a face; then got up and went into the bedroom. Nan gave a questioning lift of her eyebrows, to which Amber replied with pantomime gestures that sent them both into hilarious laughter. The two women were alone in the room, chattering and giggling together, Amber now in smock and busk and a froth of lacy petticoats. When Bruce knocked at the door she called out for him to come in.

He had removed his periwig, coat and vest and sword, and his white shirt was opened. "Still undressing?" he asked her with a smile. "I've written two letters." He stopped at a table and poured himself a tall glass of brandy and water. "It's always seemed to me that women would gain five years of their lives if they'd wear simpler clothes."

"But what would we do with 'em?" Nan wanted to know, and they all three gave a burst of laughter.

Amber's hair was now undone—for no lady would lift a hand to her head—and Nan had left the room, herding Tansy and the dog before her. She was standing at the dressing-table, unfastening her necklace, when she saw his face and shoulders appear behind her in the mirror. His green eyes watched her for a moment and then he bent, swept the hair off her neck, and put his lips there. A cold thrill ran over her body; she caught a deep breath and her eyes closed.

He set the glass onto the table and one hand closed over her arm to turn her about. "Oh, Bruce—" she cried. "Bruce—how I love you!"

His arms went around her and they stood close together, thighs pressed hard, bodies straining. When he took his mouth from hers she looked up, wondering, and found him staring across the room. Slowly he released her and slowly she turned. There was Gerald, standing just inside the door, his face white and his jaw fallen.

"Oh!" cried Amber, and her eyes blazed with sudden fury. "What d'you mean—sneaking in here like this! Spying on me! You damned impertinent dog!"

With a sudden unexpected movement she picked up a silver patch-box from the dressing-table and hurled it at him, but her aim was bad and it struck the door-jamb. Gerald jumped. Bruce merely stood quietly and looked at him, surprise in his eyes at first and then a kind of pity as he saw how bewildered and unhappy and scared the boy was.

Amber rushed at him in a shrieking fury, her clenched fists raised. "How dare you sneak into my rooms this way! I'll have your ears cut off for this!" He moved aside as she struck at him and the blow landed on his shoulder.

He was all but stammering, his face had turned grey, and there was a sick look on his face. "For God's sake, madame—I had no idea—I didn't know—"

"Don't lie to me, you baboon! I'll show you—"

"Amber!" It was Bruce's voice. "Give him a chance to speak, why don't you? This is obviously a mistake."

Gerald shot him a look of gratitude, but he was clearly somewhat afraid of the woman who stood before him, glowering with rage. "My mother was still in the hall-way. And when I came out she—well—she told me to go back in."

Amber started to speak again and then she turned and glanced at Bruce, to see what he thought about it. His expression was perfectly serious but his eyes glittered with amusement, even while he had a very obvious sympathy for the unhappy young husband whose duty it now was to challenge him to duel. Honour offered no alternative. And yet it was ridiculous to think of Gerald Stanhope, small and undeveloped with scarcely the courage of an adolescent girl, fighting a man who was not only eight inches taller than he but an accomplished swordsman as well.

Bruce stepped forward, made him an easy bow from the waist, and said politely, "Sir, I regret that you have so much reason to suspect my motives regarding your wife. I offer you my profoundest apologies and hope that you will believe no worse of me than you can help."

Gerald looked as relieved as a criminal who sees the sheriff come flying with a reprieve just as the noose is being fastened about his neck. He bowed in return. "I assure you, sir, that I am enough a man of the world to know that appearances are often deceiving. I accept your apology, sir, and hope that we may meet again under more congenial circumstances. And now, madame, if you'll show me the way, I'll go by your back-stair-case—"

Amber stared at him in astonishment. God in heaven! Wasn't the poor fool even going to fight? And was he going now, to leave his wife's lover in undisputed possession? Her anger drained away and contempt took its place. She pulled up the bodice of her smock and made him a curtsy.

"This way, sir."

She crossed the room and opened a door which led down a dark little stair-well. Just before going out Gerald bowed again, very jauntily, first to her and then to Bruce—but Amber could see that the muscles about his mouth quivered nervously. She closed the door behind him and turned to face Bruce; there was a contemptuous smile on her lips which she expected would also be on his.

He was smiling, but in his eyes was a strange expression. What was it? Disapproval of her, pity for the man who had just left, mockery of all three of them? It alarmed her, and for an instant she felt cold and lost and alone. But as she watched, the expression flickered and changed and he made a gesture with one hand, shrugged his shoulders and started toward her.

"Well," he said, "he wears a pair of horns as well as any man in Europe."

CHAPTER FIFTY–ONE

LONDON HAD GROWN as hysterical as a girl with the green-sick-ness. Her life these last years had been too full of excitement and tragedy, too turbulent and too convulsive, and now she was uneasy, nervous, in a constant state of worry and fear. No prospect was too dismal, no possibility too remote—anything might happen, and probably would.

The new year had opened despondently, with thousands of homeless men and women and children living in tiny tar-roofed shacks that had been thrown up on the sites of their former homes. Or they were crowded together in the few streets within the walls which had been spared by the Fire, and forced to pay exorbitant rents. In a winter of unusual coldness and severity sea-coal was so expensive that many could not afford it at all. Most of them believed, not unreasonably, that London would never be rebuilt and they had no faith in the present, saw no hope for the future.

An evil star seemed to be ascendant over England.

The national debt had never been greater, though the government was near bankruptcy. The War, begun so hopefully, was now unpopular, for it had not been successful and was connected in the public mind with the unprecedented disasters of the past two years. The seamen of the Royal Navy were in mutiny and men lay starving in the yard of the naval office. Parliament had refused to vote the money to set out a fleet for that year and merchants would not be coerced again into supplying the ships without cash-in-hand. Hence the Council had decided—though against the judgement of Charles and Albemarle and Prince Rupert—to lay up the fleet for that year and trust to peace negotiations already under way.

But at Court they did not trouble themselves very much with these problems. For despite the desperate state of government finances there was more wealth in the hands of private individuals than ever before—a person of enterprise and some capital might invest his money in stocks and soon increase it many times. And they were not afraid of the Dutch for most of them knew that England had made a secret treaty with France to keep the Dutch fleet from sailing. The French were not and never had been interested in the war, nor did Louis's ambitions point across the Channel. Let the ignorant people fret and mumble if they liked—ladies and gentlemen had other matters of which to think. They were far more concerned in Buckingham's escapade and the gossip that Frances Stewart was pregnant, a rumour which circulated exactly one month after her runaway marriage.

Late in April came the shocking news that the Dutch were out with twenty-four ships, sailing along the coast.

The people were frantic. Terror and resentment and suspicion ran through them like a flame. What had gone wrong with the peace negotiations? Someone had betrayed them, sold them over to the enemy. Every night they expected to hear the rolling of drums, to wake to the screams of men and women dying by the sword, to the glare of fire, the blasting of guns—but though the Dutch continued to ride the coast, tantalizingly, they came no nearer.

Amber was not greatly concerned about any of it—the War, the threatening Dutch, Buckingham's plight, or Stewart's baby. She had one interest and only one: Lord Carlton.

King Charles had granted him 20,000 acres more. Large tracts were necessary because tobacco exhausted the soil within three years and it was cheaper to clear new land than to fertilize the old. He had kept a fleet of six ships, for it was the common practice of both merchant and planter to underestimate each crop, with the result that ships were usually scarce. His were consequently in much demand and he had sent a great shipment to France the previous October. Though this was against the law, smuggling was common practice and necessary if the planters were to survive, for Virginia was producing in two years as much tobacco as England used in three.

Bruce now spent his days buying provisions, both for himself and for neighbours who had commissioned him to do so. Ordinarily it was necessary to trust such matters to a merchant who might send unsatisfactory goods, or profit at the colonist's expense.

His home in Virginia was still only partly constructed because he had been too busy the year before clearing land and planting the tobacco crop. Furthermore, it was difficult to hire skilled workmen, for most of those who went to America expected to make a fortune in five or six years and could not readily be induced to work at their old trades. He was going to take back with him several dozen more indentured servants to complete the building and to work on the land. He was buying glass and bricks and nails—all of which were scarce in America—and, as most emigrants did, was taking with him many English plants and flowers for the garden.

He had a passionate enthusiasm for Virginia and his life there.

He described to her the forests with their oak and pine and blossoming laurel—great masses of dogwood, violets, roses, honeysuckle. He told her that fish were so plentiful a man could lean over and scoop a frying-pan full from a running stream. There were shad and sturgeon, oysters a foot long, turtle and crab and tortoise. He told her about the birds that came in September, clouds of them that blackened the sky, to feed on the wild-celery and oats that grew along the river banks. And there were swan, goose, duck, plover, and turkeys which weighed as much as seventy pounds. There had never been such a prodigal land.

Wild horses roamed the forests and catching them was one of the chief sports of the country. Brilliant birds fluttered everywhere—tawny and crimson parakeets, others with yellow heads and green wings. Animals were abundant and mink such a nuisance that traps had to be set for them. Knowing that she admired the fur, he had brought her skins enough to line a cloak and a robe and to make a great muff.

Corinna, his wife, had stayed in Jamaica the year before, but she had named their home from the description he had given her: they called it Summerhill. In a couple of years, Bruce said, they intended to visit England and France and would buy most of their furniture then. Corinna had left England in 1655 and had not seen it since; and like all English who went abroad to live she longed to return to her homeland, if only for a visit.

Amber wanted to hear about these things and pestered him with a thousand questions, but when he answered she was invariably hurt and angry and jealous. "Ye gods! I'm sure I can't think how you must pass your time in a place like that! Or do you *work* all day long?" Work was no occupation for a gentleman, and the way she said the word it sounded as if she was accusing him of something unworthy.

One hot bright-skied afternoon in late May they were drifting along the Thames toward Chelsea, some three and a half miles up-river from Almsbury House. She had bought a new barge, a great handsome gilt one filled with gold-embroidered green-velvet cushions, and she had coaxed him to take the maiden trip with her. Amber was stretched out in the shade of the awning, her hair wreathed in white roses, the thin silk of her green gown falling along her legs, and she held a large green fan to shield one side of her face against the sun. The barge-men in their gold-and-green livery were resting, talking among themselves. The barge was a long one and they were not close enough to overhear what Bruce and Amber said.

There were many other little boats on the river carrying sweethearts, families, groups of young men or women on pleasure-cruises and picnics. The first warm spring days brought out everyone who could find leisure to escape—for London and the country were still almost one and every Londoner had an Englishman's rural heart.

He sat facing her and now he grinned, shutting one eye against the sun. "I'll admit," he said, "that I don't spend the morning in bed reading billets-doux or the afternoon at a play or the evening in taverns. But we have our diversions. We all live on rivers and travel isn't difficult. We hunt and drink and dance and gamble just as you do here. Most of the planters are gentlemen and they bring their habits and customs with them, along with their furniture and ancestral portraits. An

737

Englishman away from home, you know, clings to the old ways as fiercely as if his life depended upon it."

"But there aren't any cities or theatres or palaces! Lord, I couldn't endure it! I suppose Corinna likes that dull life!" she added crossly.

"I think she will. She's been very happy on her father's plantation."

Amber thought that she had a very good notion of the kind of woman this Corinna was. She pictured her as another Jenny Mortimer or Lady Almsbury, a quiet shy timid creature who cared for nothing in the world but her husband and children. If the English countryside produced such women, how much worse they must be in that empty land across the seas! Her gowns were probably all five years out of the fashion and she wore no paint and not a patch. She'd never seen a play or ridden in Hyde Park, gone to an assignation or taken dinner in a tavern. In fact, she'd never done anything at all to make her interesting.

"Oh, well—of course she's contented. She's never known about anything else. Poor wretch. What does she look like— she's blonde, I suppose?" Her tone implied that no woman with the least pretensions to beauty would have any other colouring.

He shook his head, amused. "No. Her hair's very dark— darker than mine."

Amber widened her topaz eyes, politely shocked, as though he had said that she had a hare-lip or bow-legs. Black hair on a lady was not the fashion. "Oh," she said sympathetically. "Is she Portuguese?" She remembered well enough that he had said she was English, but in England, Portuguese women were considered very unhandsome. Trying to seem nonchalant, she leaned out and made a lazy catch at a passing butterfly.

Now he laughed. "No, she's English. Her skin's fair and her eyes are blue."

Amber did not like the way he spoke of her—there was something in the sound of his voice and the expression in his eyes. She began to feel hot and nervous, sick in the pit of her stomach.

"How old is she?"

"Eighteen."

She suddenly felt that she had aged a dozen years in the past few seconds. Women were almost tragically conscious of age, and once out of their teens everything conspired to make them feel that they were growing old. Amber, not two months past twenty-three, now felt all at once that she was ancient and decayed. There was five years between them! Why, five years is a century!

"You said she's pretty," murmured Amber in a forlorn little voice. "Is she prettier than I am, Bruce?"

"My God, Amber. What a question to put to a man. You know that you're beautiful. On the other hand, I'm not so bigoted as to think there's only one good-looking woman on earth."

"You *do* think she's prettier!" she cried resentfully.

Bruce took her hand and kissed it. "No, I don't, darling. I swear I don't. You're nothing alike—but you're both lovely."

"And you do love me?"

"And I do love you."

"Then *why* did you— Oh, very well!" she said petulantly, but she obeyed his look and changed the subject. "Bruce, I've got an idea! When you've finished your business let's take Almsbury's yacht and sail up the river for a week or so. He says we can have it—I asked him. Oh, please—it'd be wonderful!"

"I'm afraid to leave London. If the Dutch took the notion they could come right up to the Privy Stairs."

Amber scoffed at him. "Oh, ridiculous! They wouldn't dare! Anyway, the peace-treaty is all but signed. I heard his Majesty say so last night. They're only riding our coast to scare us and pay us back for what we did to 'em last summer. Oh, please, Bruce!"

"Perhaps. If the Dutch go home."

But the Dutch did not go home. For six weeks they hovered just off the coast with a fleet of one hundred ships—to which the French added twenty-five—while England had not one good ship at sea and was forced to call in her bad ones. The French army was at Dunkirk.

739

Consequently Bruce refused, for all her teasing and coaxing, to leave London. He said that if the Dutch did come he did not intend to be several miles up the river, lying about on a pleasure boat like some irresponsible Turkish sultan. His men, at least, were well paid and could, he hoped, be counted upon to help defend his ships.

And then one night as they lay in bed, Bruce fast asleep and Amber just sliding off, a sound began to penetrate her drowsiness. She listened, wondering, as it grew louder. Suddenly it roared out—drums beating like thunder down in the streets. Her heart seemed to stop, and then it began to pound as hard as the drums. She sat up, shaking him by the shoulders.

"Bruce! Bruce, wake up! The Dutch have landed!"

Her voice had a high hysterical quaver and she was cold with terror. The weeks of suspense, which had affected her more than she had realized, the black night, the sudden ominous roll of drums, made her feel that the Dutch were there in the very city—outside the house at that moment. The sound of the drums grew louder, beating frantically, and there were shouts of men's and women's voices, excited and shrill.

Bruce sat up swiftly. Without a word, he flung back the curtains and got out of bed. Amber followed him, picking up her dressing-gown and putting it on. Already Bruce was at the window, his shirt in his hand as he leaned out and shouted across the courtyard.

"Hey! What's happened? Have the Dutch landed?"

"They've taken Sheerness! We're invaded!"

The drum rolled again and bells had begun to ring from church towers; a coach roared through the streets and just afterward a single horseman went careening by. Bruce swung the window closed and began to get into his breeches.

"Holy Jesus! They'll be here next—we haven't got a thing to stop them!"

Amber was beginning to cry with distracted terror and a sense of utter helplessness. Outside, the drums were beating more and more wildly, filling the night with a wild terrifying rhythm full of calamity and fear, and people had begun to shout from their windows and to run down into the street.

Nan was hammering at their door, begging to be admitted.

"Come in!" shouted Amber. She turned to Bruce. "What are you going to do? Where are you going?" She felt cold and shaking inside and her teeth chattered, though the night was a warm one. Nan entered, carrying a candle, and hurried to light several others. As the room sprang into light some of Amber's terror disappeared.

"I'm going to Sheerness!"

Bruce stood knotting his neck-cravat; he told Nan to bring him a pair of boots from his own room. Amber picked up his vest and coat and held them as he jammed his arms into the sleeves.

"Oh, Bruce! Don't go! They probably have thousands of men! You'd be killed! Bruce! You *can't* go!" She grabbed hold of his arm, as though she could force him to stay with her.

He jerked his arm free, went on buttoning his coat and vest and then pulled on the calf-high silver-spurred boots which Nan had brought. He buckled on the sword and Nan gave him his hat and cloak.

"Take the children and leave London," he said to her, cramming his hat onto his head. "Get out of here as fast as you can!"

Nan went to answer a pounding at the anteroom door and Almsbury and Emily rushed in, the Earl fully dressed, his wife in her night-gown and robe. "Bruce! The Dutch have landed! I've got horses saddled in the courtyard!"

"But you can't go, Bruce! Oh, Almsbury! He can't go—I'm scared!"

Almsbury gave her a disgusted scowl. "For Christ's sake, Amber! The country's invaded!" The two men walked swiftly out of the room, all three women at their heels.

The hall-way was full of servants running up and down distractedly in their night-dress; some of the women were crying; all of them were babbling excitedly. Just as they got outside Amber's door Lady Stanhope arrived in a breathless rush. A night-cap covered her hair but paper-curlers showed beneath it and there were chicken-skin gloves on her hands; all her flesh quivered hysterically. She grabbed at Bruce as at salvation.

"Oh, Lord Carlton! Thank God you're here! We're invaded! Oh, what shall I do? *What* shall I *do?*"

Bruce answered her shortly, shaking off the hand that had seized his arm, and he and Almsbury started down the staircase. "I suggest that you leave London, madame. Come with me, Amber. I want to talk to you."

The men hurried down, the heels of their boots clattering on the stairs, and Amber ran along beside him. The first shock of fright was over but the drums, the bells, the screams and shouts heightened her sense of impending disaster. He can't go! she thought. He can't go! But he was going.

"Lady Almsbury is leaving right away for Barberry Hill. All the plans have been ready for weeks—take Susanna and Bruce and go with her. If anything happens to me I'll send you a message." She opened her mouth to protest at that, but he ignored her and went on, talking rapidly. "If I should be killed, will you promise me to write to my wife?"

By now they had reached the courtyard where two horses were saddled and waiting for them, stamping and snorting with nervous impatience. Torches blazed; there were servants and stable-boys everywhere; black-and-white coach dogs circled about, barking. The drums pounded in their ears, seemed to echo in the beat of their hearts and the pulsing of their blood. Almsbury mounted instantly but Bruce stopped, his hands on the bridle, and looked down into her face.

"Promise me, Amber."

She nodded her head, her throat choking. Her hands reached out to grab at his coat. "I promise, Bruce. But *don't* let anything happen! *Don't* get hurt!"

"I don't think I will."

He bent his head and one arm went about her. His mouth touched hers briefly. Then he had swung onto the horse's back and the two men were galloping out of the courtyard. Just as they rode through the gate he turned and gave her a wave of his hand. With a sudden sobbing cry Amber started forward, one arm outstretched, but they had disappeared into the darkness; she heard the thudding of the horses' hoofs, growing fainter.

The house was in a turmoil. Some of the servants were carrying out pieces of furniture and dumping them into the courtyard, then rushing back for more. Several of the women were wailing and crying, wringing their hands helplessly. Others, now dressed and with bundles over their backs, fled into the streets with no thought but to get away. Amber lifted her skirts and hurried up the stairs, knocking into first one and then another, almost blind with her tears. She ran down to the nursery.

The doors stood wide open and inside were twelve or fifteen frantic women, running this way and that, tugging and hauling at the children and babies to get them dressed. Emily stood cool and self-possessed, telling them what to do and helping them herself. Little Bruce, who was already fully dressed, caught sight of Amber and ran to her immediately. She dropped to her knees, crying, and caught him against her, more for her own comfort than his. He did not, in fact, seem to need or want any.

"Don't cry, Mother. Those damned Dutchmen will never get here! Not with Father gone to fight 'em!"

But Susanna was shrieking at the top of her lungs, kicking at the nurse who was trying to dress her, her plump little hands held over her ears to shut out the hammering of the drums. And now, bouncing about on the table where she had been put, she caught sight of her mother and brother together and gave a resentful howl of protest.

"*Mo-ther!*"

Amber got up and went to her, little Bruce staying close at her side as though to protect her. "Sweetheart, you must let Harmon dress you. There's nothing to cry about. Look—I'm not." She widened her eyes at Susanna but the rims were red and her lids swollen. Susanna flung her arms about her and howled louder than ever. At last Amber gave her an impatient little shake. "Susanna!" Susanna's head jerked back and she looked at Amber in astonishment, her pink mouth open. "Stop this bellow-weathering! No one's going to hurt you! Get into your clothes, now. You're going for a ride."

"Don't want to go for a ride! It's dark!"

Amber turned away. "Never mind! You're going anyway. Get into your clothes or I'll spank you!"

She left Susanna and crossed the nursery to where Lady Almsbury was busy with her own four children; she was kneeling beside her six-year-old son, tying his lace cravat for him. "Emily—I'm not going with you."

Lady Almsbury looked up at her in astonishment and then got to her feet. "You're not going! Oh, Amber, but you must! What if the Dutch or the French get here!"

"They're not here now and I'm not going into the country where I wouldn't be able to hear from Bruce no matter what happens. If he gets hurt he'll need me."

"But he told you to go."

"I don't care if he did. I'm not going. But I want Bruce and Susanna to go—will you take them with you? And Nan, too?"

"Of course I will, my dear. But I do think it's dangerous for you to stay. He wanted you to go—they had often discussed it and made the plans in case of an attack—"

"I'll be safe enough here. If they come I'll go to Whitehall. They won't dare attack the Palace. I'll take care of your things here—let me have the key to the strong-room and I'll move the valuables down there."

At that moment Nan came running into the room. "My God, I've looked everywhere for you! Come, quick, and get into your clothes! They're all but upon us—I heard the guns!" Her gown was twisted, her hair not combed and she wore no stockings; she grabbed Amber's hand and started to pull her away.

The two women walked out into the crowded noisy confused hall-way, and Amber had almost to shout to make herself heard. "I'm not going, Nan. But you can if you want to—I just asked—"

Nan gasped. As far as she was concerned the French army was disembarking at that moment and the Dutch navy lay anchored in the Pool. "Oh, mam! You can't! You can't stay here! They'll put everyone they see to the sword! They'll rip up your belly and gouge out your eyes and—"

"Holy Mother of God! Isn't this the most horrifying thing that ever happened?" It was Lady Stanhope, now dressed—though obviously with much haste—followed by two women servants loaded down with bulging sacks and boxes. "I'm leaving for Ridgeway this instant! I knew I should never have left

744

the country! This terrible city—something always happening to it! Where's Gerry?"

"I don't know. Go ahead, Nan—Lady Almsbury's leaving in a few minutes." She turned back to her mother-in-law. "I haven't seen him lately."

"You haven't seen him! But my God! Where is he then? He told me he spent every night with you!" Suddenly her eyes grew bright and hard and she narrowed them to give Amber a close shrewd look. "And by the way—wasn't Lord Carlton coming out of *your* apartments just now?"

Amber turned impatiently away and started down the hall toward her own rooms. "What if he was?"

Lady Stanhope took a few moments to recover from that and then she came after Amber, panting at her heels, jabbering in her ear. "Do you mean to tell me, you brazen creature, that his Lordship was alone with you in there—at an hour when no honest woman should be alone with any man but her husband? Do you mean to tell me you've cuckolded my Gerry? Answer me, huswife!" She grabbed Amber by the arm and jerked her around.

Amber stopped perfectly still for just an instant and then suddenly she whirled and faced Lucilla. "Take your hands off me, you overgrown jade! Yes, I was with Lord Carlton and I don't give a damn who knows it! You'd have been with him yourself if he'd given you so much as a sideways glance! Go find your blasted Gerry now and leave me alone—"

"Why! you impertinent strumpet! Wait until Gerry hears about this! Wait until I tell him what you—"

But Amber had walked away so swiftly that she left her bewildered and sputtering in the middle of the hall. For a moment the Dowager Baroness hesitated, as though she could not decide whether it was more important to follow her daughter-in-law and give her the tongue-lashing she deserved, or to set out for the country and save herself. "Well—I'll take a course with her later!" She glared after Amber's hurrying figure, muttered, "Slut!" and then summoning her two women rushed off down the stairs.

Amber, with a cloak thrown over her dressing-gown, went

down into the courtyard to see them off. Both Emily and Nan begged her again to come with them but she refused, insisting that she would be perfectly safe there. She was, in fact, no longer afraid—for the excitement of the drums, of horses pounding by along the streets, screams and cries and churchbells ringing, had roused a reckless energy in her.

The children were together in one coach, with two of their nurses, and even Susanna was beginning to think that it was a frolic of some kind. Amber kissed both of them. "Take care of your sister, Bruce. Don't let her be frightened or lonely." Susanna began to cry again when she found that her mother was not going along, and she was standing on the seat with her hands plastered to the window when the great carriage rolled out of the yard. Amber waved them goodbye and went back into the house; she had a great deal to do.

She did not sleep at all the rest of the night, but stayed up to oversee the removal of the Earl's valuables down into the strong-room. His gold and silver plate, the pewter service which Charles I had presented to his father when the old Earl had melted down his plate to make a war contribution, their jewellery and her own, all went into the stone crypt in the cellar. When that was done she got dressed, swallowed a cup of hot chocolate, and set out before six for Shadrac Newbold's house in Lombard Street where he and many other goldsmiths had removed since the Fire.

It was a long ride from the Strand through the ruined City. Scaffolding was everywhere but many houses had been completed; a few streets, solidly rebuilt, stood perfectly empty. There were cellars still smoking and the smell of dew-wet charcoal was strong in the air. A soil had formed upon the ashes and it was covered with a small, bright-yellow flower, London rocket, which showed cheerily through the gruel-thick fog that hung almost to the ground.

Amber, tired and worried, sat gloomily in the rocking coach. She felt sick at her stomach and her head spun wearily. As they approached Newbold's house she saw a queue of coaches and of men and women which reached around the corner into Ab-

746

church Lane. Exasperated, she leaned forward and rapped her fan against the wall of the coach, shouting at John Waterman.

"Drive down St. Nicholas Lane and stop!"

There she got out and with Big John and two footmen, walked through a little alley which led to the back entrance of his house. It was fenced in and they found the gate guarded by two sentries with crossed muskets.

"My Lady Danforth to see your master," said one of the footmen.

"I'm very sorry, your Ladyship. We have orders to admit no one at all by this gate."

"Let me by," said Amber shortly, "or I'll have both your noses slit!"

Intimidated either by her threat or by Big John's towering bulk they let her go in. A servant went to call Shadrac Newbold, who soon appeared, looking as tired as she felt. He bowed to her, politely.

"I took the liberty of coming in by your back entrance. I've been up all night and I couldn't wait in that line."

"Certainly, madame. Won't you come into my office?"

With exhausted relief she dropped into the chair he offered her. The rims of her eyelids felt raw and her legs ached. She gave a sigh and leaned her head against her hand, as though unable to hold it up herself. He poured a glass of wine, which she accepted gratefully; it gave her at least a temporary sense of spurious vitality.

"Ah, madame," murmured Newbold. "This is a sad day for England."

"I've come for my money. I want all of it—now."

He gave her a mournful little smile, turning his spectacles thoughtfully in his hand. Finally he sighed. "So do they, madame." He gestured toward the window through which she could see a part of the waiting queue. "Every one of them. Some have twenty pound deposited with me—some, like you, have a great deal more. In a few minutes I must begin to let them in. I've got to tell them all what I tell you—I can't give it to you."

"What!" cried Amber, the shock jerking her out of her tiredness. "Do you mean to say—" She was starting to get up from her chair.

"Just one moment, madame, please. Nothing has happened to your money. It is quite safe. But don't you see, if I and every other goldsmith in London were to try to give back every shilling which has been deposited with us—" He gave a helpless little gesture. "It is impossible, madame, you know that. Your money is safe, but it is not in my possession, but for a small sum. The rest is out at interest, invested in property and in stocks and in the other ventures of which you know. I do not keep your money lying idle, and neither have I kept the money of my other depositors lying idle. That is why we can't return it to all of you all at once. Give me twenty days—and if you want it then I can have it for you. But we must all ask for that twenty days of grace to bring the money into our possession again. Even that will create a condition of financial anarchy which may upset the entire nation."

"The entire nation's upset as it is. Nothing worse than invasion *can* happen to us. Well—I understand you, Mr. Newbold. You took care of my money during the Plague and the Fire and no doubt you can take care of it as well as I can now. . . ."

Amber went back home, spent four hours trying to sleep, ate her dinner and then set out for the Palace. Along the Strand went a parade of carts and coaches full of refugees hurrying out of town once more to the comparative safety of the country. In the courts and passages of Whitehall there stood more loaded carts. Everywhere people gathered together, listening for the guns, gabbling of nothing but invasion and of trying to get their money, of hiding their belongings and of making out their wills. Several of the courtiers had been among those volunteers who had gone with Albemarle to Chatham or with Prince Rupert to Woolwich, and upon those few hundred men rested all the hope of England.

Amber was stopped every few feet by some excited courtier or lady who asked her what she was going to do and then without waiting for her answer started to tell his or her own troubles. Everyone was gloomy, acknowledging frankly that all fortifications were decayed, unarmed and unmanned, and that

748

the country lay helpless before the invaders. They were angry with the goldsmiths because they would not return their money and swore never to do business with them again. Some of them intended to go to Bristol or another port and sail for America or the Continent. If England was a sinking vessel they did not intend to go down with her.

The Queen's apartments were hot and crowded and full of shrill noisy voices. Catherine was fanning herself and trying to look composed, but the quick, darting anxious movements of her black eyes betrayed her own worry and uncertainty. Amber went up to speak to her.

"What's the news, your Majesty? Have they come any nearer?"

"They say that the French are in Mounts Bay."

"But they won't come *here*, will they? They wouldn't dare!"

Catherine smiled faintly and shrugged her shoulders. "We didn't think that they would dare do this much. Most of the ladies are going out of town, madame. You should go too. I'm afraid the sad truth is we didn't expect this and we're not prepared."

Just then they heard the loud clear voice of Lady Castlemaine, standing only a few feet away talking to Lady Southesk and Bab May. "Someone's going to smoke for this, you may be sure! The people are in a tearing rage! They've been chopping down Clarendon's trees and breaking his windows and they've writ their sentiments plain enough on his gate. They've got a sign there that says, 'Three sights to be seen: Dunkirk, Tangier, and a barren Queen!'"

Lady Southesk gave her a warning jab and Barbara glanced around, puffed out her cheeks as though in horrified surprise and pressed one hand to her mouth. But the glitter in her eyes said plainly that she had intended to be overheard. While Catherine stared, Barbara gave a careless shrug and signalled to Bab May. They left the room together.

Damn that hard-hearted bitch! thought Amber. I'd like to jerk her bald-headed!

"And a barren Queen," whispered Catherine, her tiny hands clasping her fan until they trembled. "How they hate me for

749

that!" Suddenly her eyes came up and she looked Amber straight in the face. "How I hate myself!"

Amber had a sudden pang of shame; she wondered if Catherine knew that she was pregnant at that moment, with his child. Impulsively she pressed her hand, tried to give her a reassuring smile of sympathy, but she was relieved to see the languid affected Boynton sail up, waving her fan and seeming about to swoon.

"Oh, Lord, your Majesty! We're all undone! I've just heard the French army is off the coast of Dover making ready to land!"

"What!" yelped a woman who stood nearby. "The French have landed? Good God!" And she started in a rush for the door. The cry was taken up and instantly the room was a milling swirling mass—men and women shoving and pushing at one another in their wild anxiety, surging toward the door.

But that rumour, like a hundred others, proved false.

Drums beat all through that night, calling up the train-bands. Gunfire could be heard from London Bridge. Waves of hysterical alarm and angry ˌpessimism swept the city. Whoever owned anything of the slightest value was busy burying it in the back yard, rushing it out of town in the custody of wife or servant, hectoring the goldsmiths and drawing up his will. They said openly that they had been betrayed by the Court— and most of them expected to die at the point of a French or a Dutch sword. Then news came that the Dutch had broken the boom which had been stretched across the Medway to keep them out, that they had burned six men-of-war and taken the *Royal Charles* and were pillaging the countryside.

The King ordered the sinking of several ships at Barking Creek in order to block the river and keep them from coming any higher. Unfortunately, however, in the excitement someone misunderstood a command and several boats laden with the scant precious store of naval supplies were sunk by error. The tenth night after the attack on Sheerness it was possible to see the red glow made by burning vessels. Ripped dead carcasses of sheep had floated up-river to London. And the terrified city was swept again and again by spasms of alarm; business had stopped dead, for no one had any business now but to save himself and his family and possessions.

At last the Dutch retired to the mouth of the river and peace negotiations were resumed. This time the English were less particular on certain issues and the conference progressed better than it had.

With the other men who had volunteered Carlton and Almsbury returned to London, bearded and sunburnt and in high spirits after the adventure. But Amber was near nervous collapse from worry and prolonged sleeplessness, and at the sight of a dry and hardened blood-soaked bandage on Bruce's right upper arm she burst into frantic hysterical tears.

He took her into his arms as though she were a little girl, stroking her hair and kissing her wet cheeks. "Here, darling, what the devil's all this fuss? I've been hurt much worse than this a dozen times."

She leaned against his chest and sobbed desperately, for she neither could nor wanted to stop crying. "Oh, Bruce! You might've been killed! I've been so s-scared—"

He picked her up and started up the stairs with her. "Don't you know, you contrary little witch," he murmured, "that I told you to get out of London? If the Dutch had wanted to they could have taken the whole country—we couldn't have stopped them—"

Amber was sitting on the bed, filing her nails and waiting for Bruce to finish a letter to his overseer.

Casually he said, "When I go back I want to take Bruce with me."

She looked across at him with an expression of horrified shock. Now he got up, threw off his robe, and just as he bent to blow out the single candle she caught a glimpse of his shadowed face. He had been looking at her as he spoke and his eyes were narrowed slightly, watching. She moved over and he got into bed beside her.

For several moments she could not answer. She did not even lie down but continued to sit there, staring into the darkness. Bruce was quiet and waited.

"Don't you want him to go?" he asked at last.

"Of course I don't want him to go! He's *my* child, isn't he? D'you think I want him to go over there and be brought up by another woman and forget all about me? I do not! And I won't let him, either! He's mine and he's going to stay here with me! I won't have him brought up by that—by that woman you married!"

"Have you any plans for his future?" It was so dark that she could not see his face but his voice sounded low and reasonable.

"No—" she admitted reluctantly. "No, of course not! Why should I? He's only six years old!"

"But he won't always be six years old. What will you do when he begins to grow up? Who will you tell him his father was? If I go away and he doesn't see me for several years he'll forget I ever existed. What will you give him for a last name? It's different with Susanna—she's supposed to be Dangerfield's child, and she has his name. But Bruce has no name at·all unless I give him mine, and I can't do that if he stays with you. I know that you love him, Amber, and he loves you. You're rich now and you've got the King's favour—perhaps you could get him to confer a title on him sometime. But if he goes with me he'll be my heir: he'll have everything I can give him—and he'll never have to endure the humiliations of an acknowledged bastard—"

"He's a bastard anyway!" cried Amber, quick to find any excuse she could. "You can't make him a lord just by saying he *is* one!"

"He won't live in England. Over there it won't matter. And, at least, he'll be better off than he could be here where everyone will know."

"What about your wife! Where's she going to think you got him? Out of the parsley-bed?"

"I've already told her that I'd been married before. She's expecting me to bring him back this time."

"Oh, she is! You were mighty confident, weren't you? And what's supposed to have become of his mother?" Suddenly she stopped, sickened. "You told her that I was dead!" He did not answer and she cried accusingly, "Didn't you?"

"Yes, of course. What else could I tell her? That I was a bigamist?" His voice had a sound of angry impatience. "Well,

752

Amber, I won't take him away from you. You can make up your mind for yourself. But try to consider him a little, too, when you're deciding—"

Amber was so hurt and so angry at the thought of sending her son into the care of another woman, to grow up far away from her with nothing ever to remind him of her existence, that she refused for several days even to think about it. And he did not broach the subject again.

The Dutch fleet still lay at the mouth of the Thames and no English shipping could enter or leave. Consequently Bruce, though he had been almost ready to sail at the time of the attack, was now forced to wait on the peace negotiations. But he refused to go away with her, for when the treaty was concluded he intended to sail immediately. Much of his time he spent hunting with the King. And there were other hours when he and the little boy rode together or he helped him with his fencing-lessons. Sometimes they sailed a few miles up the Thames in Almsbury's *Sapphire,* and Amber went along. She could not see them together without feeling a torture of longing and jealousy—for somewhere in her heart she knew that he would go with his father, and forget her. She could surrender him to Bruce, but she could not bear the thought of another woman's having him.

They were walking, she and the little boy, in the garden one morning, waiting for Bruce who was going to take him sculling. It was mid-July, hot and bright, and the walks steamed where the gardener had been watering. The lime-trees were in bloom and bees hummed incessantly at their sweet yellow-green flowers. Monsieur le Chien ran along ahead of them, nosing everywhere, and his ears were draggled, for he had dipped them into the fountain and then trailed them through the dust.

A gardener had given each of them a ripe yellow pear to eat. It tasted like wine as she bit into it. "Bruce," she said all at once, "will you miss your father a great deal when he goes?" She had not actually expected to say it but now she found herself waiting, tensely, for his answer.

She saw it in the wistful little smile he gave her. "Oh, yes, Mother. I will." He hesitated, then: "Won't you?"

Surprised, the tears started into her eyes; but she looked away, thinking hard about the musk-rose that lay half opened against the wall. She reached over to pluck it. "Yes, of course I will. Suppose, Bruce—suppose—" Suddenly she said it. "Would you like to go with him?"

He stared up at her with a look of perfect incredulity, and then he grabbed her hand. "Oh, *could* I, Mother? *Could* I go?"

Amber looked down at him, unable to keep the disappointment from her face, but his eyes had such a shine she knew then what would happen. "Yes—you can. If you want to. *Do* you want to?"

"Oh, yes, Mother! I do! Please let me go!"

"You want to go and leave me?" She knew that it was unfair when she said it, but she could not help herself.

As she had hoped, the look of happiness fled and a kind of bewildered conscience-stricken worry took its place. For a moment he was quiet. "But can't you go too, Mother?" Suddenly he smiled again. "You come with us! Then we can all be together!"

Amber's eyes brooded over him; lightly her fingers reached out to touch his hair. "I can't go, darling. I've got to stay here." The tears sparkled in her eyes again. "You can't be with both of us—"

He took her hand with a little gesture of sympathy. "Don't cry, Mother. I won't go and leave you—I'll tell Father that I—can't go."

All at once Amber hated herself. "Come here," she said. "Sit beside me on this bench. Listen to me, darling. Your father wants you to go with him. He needs you over there—to help him—there's so much to do. I want you to stay with me—but I think he needs you more."

"Oh, do you, Mother? Do you *really* think so?" His eyes searched her face anxiously, but there was no concealing the joyous relief.

"Yes, darling. I really think so."

Amber looked up over his head and beyond to see Bruce coming toward them along the garden walk. The little boy glanced around, saw his father, and jumped up to run and meet him.

His manners were always much more formal with Bruce than with her, not because Bruce insisted but because his tutor did, and he bowed ceremoniously before speaking a word.

"I've decided to go to America with you, sir," he informed him solemnly. "Mother says that you need me there."

Bruce glanced down at the boy and then his eyes moved swiftly to meet Amber's. For a moment they looked at each other, unspeaking. His arm went about his son's shoulder and he smiled at him. "I'm glad you've decided to come with me, Bruce." Together they walked toward Amber, and she got to her feet though her eyes had not once left Bruce's face. He said nothing but he bent and kissed her, softly, briefly; and it was, almost, a husband's kiss.

At first Amber felt that she had done a noble and unselfish thing and she was quite willing to have Bruce think so too. But the hope came creeping, and she had to recognize it, that perhaps having her child there with him all the time would keep her alive in his memory as nothing else could do. Perhaps she could defeat Corinna without even seeing her.

The Treaty of Breda was signed and news of it arrived at Whitehall at the end of the month. Bruce sailed with the next morning-tide. Amber went down to the wharf, determined to preserve the good opinion both of them had of her now if it tore out her heart. But as she half-knelt to kiss her son her throat swelled with unbearable agony. Bruce took her arm to help her up again, for the burden she carried was beginning to make her awkward.

"Don't let him forget me, Bruce!" she pleaded.

"I won't forget you, Mother! And we're coming back to see you, too! Father said so—didn't you, sir?" He looked up at Bruce for confirmation.

"Yes, Bruce—we'll come back. I promise you." He was restless, eager to get on the ship, to be away, hating this painful business of parting. "Amber—we're late now."

She gave a scared little cry and threw her arms about him; he bent his head and their lips met. Amber clung frantically, perfectly heedless of the crowds who moved around them, who turned to stare with curious interest at the handsome man and woman, the quiet watching child. This was the moment she had not believed—even yesterday, when she had known he was going—would ever really come. Now it was here—it was here and she had a sense of helpless despair.

All of a sudden his hands took hold of her arms and forced them down. Swiftly he turned and almost before she could realize it had happened Bruce and their son had crossed the gang-plank onto the ship. It began to move, very slowly, and the sails snapped out white and full in the wind, catching up the ship as though life had gone through her. The little boy took off his hat and waved.

"We'll be back, Mother!"

Amber gave a sharp cry and started forward, along the wharf, but the ship was getting away from her. Bruce was half turned, giving directions to the men, but all at once he walked swiftly back and his hand dropped about the boy's shoulders. He raised one arm in a goodbye salute and though Amber's hand started to go up in reply she instead put her bent forefinger into her mouth and bit down hard. For a long moment she stood there, lost and forlorn, and then she lifted the other arm and gave them a spiritless little wave.

CHAPTER FIFTY-TWO

ALL AROUND THE room men paused in their eating to stare, dumfounded, toward the doorway.

At twelve o'clock the Sun Tavern, just behind the new-built Royal Exchange in Threadneedle Street, was always crowded, for there the great merchants came to eat dinner, transact part of their business, and discuss the news of the day. Not a few of them had been talking about Buckingham, whose plight was regarded with more sympathy in the City than it was at Court, when the Duke strolled in.

One white-haired old man looked up, his weak blue eyes popping. "By God! What d'ye know! Speak of the Devil—"

756

There was nothing about his Grace to suggest a man in hiding, or one whose life had been jeopardized by his own treasonous acts. He wore his usual blonde periwig and a splendid suit consisting of black-velvet breeches and gold-brocade coat, with a flash of long green-satin vest showing. He was as cool and casual as any gentleman stopping in at his favourite ordinary before the play.

But instantly they left their tables and surrounded him on all sides. Buckingham had taken pains to insinuate himself among these men and they were convinced that he was the one friend they had at Court. Like them, he hated Holland and wanted to see it crushed. Like them, he favoured religious toleration—and though this was merely from personal indifference to any religion, they did not know it. Out of all the scratch and rubble of his life Buckingham had saved this much—the good opinion of the nation's most powerful body of men.

"Welcome back, your Grace! We were speaking of you even now and despairing when we should see you again!"

"There's been a rumour you'd gone abroad!"

"My Lord! Is it really *you?* You're not an apparition?"

Buckingham strolled through them toward the fireplace, smiling, clasping the hands outstretched to him as he went. The hereditary Villiers charm was a potent weapon when he cared to use it. "It's I, gentlemen. No apparition, I assure you." He gave a nod of his head to summon a waiter, told him what he would have for his dinner and admonished the man to be quick about serving it, since his time might be short. Then he spoke to a young boy who squatted nearby, staring goggle-eyed and turning the spit on which a leg-of-mutton was roasting. "Lad, can you carry a message?"

The boy jumped to his feet. "Aye, your Grace!"

"Then mind that you make no mistake. Go with all haste to the Tower and inform the sentry there that the Duke of Buckingham is waiting at the Sun Tavern for his Majesty's officers to place him under arrest." He flipped him a silver coin.

A murmur of surprised admiration ran through them, for it was no secret the Duke would most likely lose his head if once he were brought to trial. The boy turned and sped out of the room and Buckingham, surrounded by his cortège, strolled to a table next the window where he sat down and began to eat his dinner. An eager curious excited crowd had already begun to gather outside and they clustered in the door, peered through the windows at him. The Duke gave them a wave and a grin, and a great cheer went up.

"Gentlemen," said Buckingham to the men about him, talking while he took his silver fork from its case and began to tear at his meat. "Gentlemen, I am willing to give myself up to my enemies—though I know well enough how they may use me—because my conscience will no longer bear my continued absence from public affairs after our most recent disgrace." Their polite cries of approval at these words interrupted him, but only for a few moments. He held up a hand, asking to be heard further. "England has need of *some* men whose interests are not wholly in the building of a new house or the getting of a full night's sleep, at whatever cost to the nation."

This brought a loud cheer from everyone in the room, and it was taken up and echoed outside by those who had no idea what his Grace had said. For public resentment was strong against Clarendon's great new house in Piccadilly. And during this past year no one had forgotten that Arlington had been asleep when the order had come for Rupert to return and meet the Dutch, and that his servants had not wakened him to sign it till morning. Next to criticizing the Court themselves, they loved to hear it criticized.

"Aye, your Grace," agreed one elderly goldsmith. "The country has been too long under the mismanagement of incompetent old men."

Another leaned forward and hammered his fist on the table. "When Parliament convenes next time he'll be impeached! We'll call the old rascal to task for his crimes!"

"But, gentlemen," protested Buckingham mildly, gnawing at his mutton-joint, "the Chancellor has handled matters as honestly and as capably as his faculties would permit."

There was a storm of protest at this. "Honest! Why, the old dotard's bled us white! Where else did he get the money for that palace he's building!"

"He's been as great a tyrant as Oliver!"

"His daughter's marriage to the Duke made him think he was a Stuart!"

"He hates the Commons!"

"He's always been in cabal with the bishops!"

"He's the greatest villain in England! Your Grace is too generous!"

Buckingham smiled and made a faint deprecatory gesture, shrugging his broad shoulders. "I'm no match for you, gentlemen. It seems I'm outnumbered."

He had not yet finished his meal when the King's officers arrived—he had sent an earlier messenger than the little boy, whom he had merely used as a dramatic device to arouse their interest and sympathies. Two of them entered the room, out of breath and excited, obviously very much surprised to find his Grace actually sitting there, eating and drinking and talking. They approached to place him under arrest, but he gave them a negligent wave of his hand.

"Give me leave to finish my dinner, sirs. I'll be with you presently."

Their eyes consulted one another, dubiously, but after hesitating a moment they backed off and stood meekly waiting. When he was done he wiped his mouth, washed off his fork and put the case back into his pocket, shoved aside his pewter-plate and got up. "Well, gentlemen, I go now—to surrender myself."

"God go with your Grace!"

As he started for the door the two officers sprang forward and would have taken his arms, but he motioned them aside. "I can walk unassisted, sirs." Crestfallen, they trailed after him.

There was an explosion of shouts and cheers as Buckingham appeared in the doorway, grinning broadly and raising one hand to them in greeting. The crowd in the street had now grown to monstrous size. It was packed from wall to wall and for a distance of several hundred yards in both directions all traffic had come to a standstill. Coaches were stalled, porters and car-men and sedan-chair carriers waited with more patience than usual; all nearby windows and balconies were full. This man, accused of treason against King and country, had become the nation's hero: because he was out of favour at Court he was the one courtier they did not blame for all their recent and present troubles.

There was a coach waiting for him at the door and Buckingham climbed into it. It was but little over half-a-mile to the Tower and all along the way he was greeted with clamorous shouts and cries. Hands reached out to touch his coach; little boys ran in his wake; girls flung flowers before him. The King himself had not been greeted more enthusiastically when he had returned to London seven years before.

"Don't worry yourselves, good people!" shouted Buckingham. "I'll be out in a trice!"

But at Court they thought otherwise and in the Groom Porter's lodgings they were betting great odds that the Duke would lose his head. The King had stripped him of his offices and bestowed most of them elsewhere. His enemies, and they were numerous and powerful, had been unceasingly active. He had, however, at least one ardent supporter—his cousin, Castlemaine.

Just three days earlier Barbara and her woman Wilson had been driving along Edgware Road in the early evening, returning from Hyde Park. All at once a lame tattered old beggar appeared from some hiding-place and dragged himself before the coach, forcing it to stop. The coachman, swearing furiously, leaned down to strike him with his whip but before he could do so the beggar had reached the open window and was hanging onto the door, holding a dirty palm toward the Countess.

"Please, your Ladyship," he whined. "Give alms to the poor!"

"Get out of here, you stinking wretch!" cried Barbara. "Throw him a shilling, Wilson!"

The beggar hung on stubbornly, though the coach had started to move again. "Your Ladyship seems mighty stingy for one who wears thirty thousand pound in pearls to a play-house."

Barbara glared at him swiftly, her eyes darkened to purple. "How dare you speak to me thus? I'll have you kicked and beaten!" She gave his wrist a sudden hard rap with her fan. "Get off there, you rogue!" She opened her mouth and let out a furious yell. "Harvey! *Harvey,* stop this coach, d'ye hear!"

The coachman hauled at his reins and as the wheels were slowing the beggar gave her a grin, displaying two rows of beautiful teeth. "Never mind, my lady. Keep your shilling. Here—I'll give you something, instead." He tossed a folded paper into her lap. "Read it, as you value your life." And then, as the coach stopped and the footmen ran to grab him he dodged swiftly, no longer limping, and was gone. He turned once to thumb his nose at them.

Barbara watched him running away, glanced at the paper in her lap and then suddenly unfolded it and began to read. "Pox on this life I'm leading," she whispered. "Expect me in two or three days. And see that you do your part. B." She gave a gasp and a little cry and leaned forward, but he was gone.

Barbara was scared. She had heard the rumours too—his Majesty's patience was at an end and this time Buckingham must suffer for his treacherous impertinence. Exile was the easiest punishment they saw for him. And she knew her cousin's malice well enough to realize that if he went down he would drag her with him. Every time she saw Charles she begged him, frantically, to believe that the Duke was innocent, that it was a plot of his enemies to ruin him. But he paid her scant attention, merely asking her with lazy amusement why she should be so concerned for a man who had done her very little good and some harm.

"He's my cousin, that's why! I can't see him abused by scoundrels!"

"I think the Duke can hold his own with any scoundrel that ever wore a head. Don't trouble yourself for him."

"Then you *will* hear him out and forgive him?"

"I'll hear him out, but what will happen after that I can't say. I'd like to see how well he can defend himself—and I don't doubt he'll entertain us with some very ingenious tale."

"How *can* he defend himself? What chance has he got? Every man in your council wants to see him lose his head!"

"And I doubt not he has similar hopes for them."

The hearing was set for the next day and Barbara was determined to get some kind of promise from him, though she knew that the King regarded promises much as he did women—it should not be too much trouble to keep them. As usual, she sought to gain her ends by the means to which he was least amenable.

"But Buckingham's innocent, Sire, I know he is! Oh, don't let them trick you! Don't let them *force* you to prosecute him!"

Charles looked at her sharply. He had never, in his life, done anything he actually did not want to do, though he had done many things to which he was indifferent in order to buy his own peace or something else he wanted. But he had endured years of stubborn conflict with a domineering mother and hated the mere suggestion that he was easily led. Barbara knew that.

Now as he answered her his voice was hard and angry. "I don't know what stake you have in this, madame, but I'll warrant you it's a big one. You'd never be so zealous in another person's cause otherwise. But I'm heartily sick of listening to you. I'll make my own decisions without the help of a meddlesome jade!"

They were walking along the south-east side of the Privy Garden, where it was flanked by a row of buildings containing apartments of several Court officials. The day was hot and still and many windows were open; several ladies and gentlemen strolled in other nearby walks or lounged on the grass. Nevertheless Barbara, growing angry, raised her voice.

"Meddlesome jade, am I? Very well, then—I'll tell you what you are! You're a fool! Yes, that's what you are, a fool! Because if you weren't you wouldn't allow yourself to be ruled by fools!"

Heads turned, faces appeared at windows and then hastily retreated out of sight. All the Palace seemed suddenly to have grown quieter.

"Govern your tongue!" snapped Charles. He turned on his heel and walked off.

Barbara opened her mouth, her first impulse being to order him back—as she might once have done—and then she heard a snicker from somewhere nearby. Swiftly her eyes sought out the mocker, but all faces she met were veiled, innocently smiling. She swept her train about and started off in the opposite direction, rage swelling within her until she knew that she would burst if she did not break something or hurt someone. At that moment she came upon one of her pages, a ten-year-old boy, lying on the grass singing to himself.

"Get up, you lazy lout!" she cried. "What are you doing there!"

He looked at her in amazement, and then hastily scrambled to his feet. "Why, your Ladyship told me—"

"Don't contradict me, you puppy!" She gave him a box on the ear, and when he began to cry she slapped him again. She felt better, but she was no nearer the solution of her problem.

The council-room was a long narrow chamber, panelled in dark wood and hung with several large gold-framed paintings. There was an empty fireplace at one end, flanked by tall mullioned windows. An oak table extended down the center and surrounding it were several chairs, high-backed and elaborately carved, with turned legs and dark red-velvet cushions. Until the councillors came it looked like a suitable place to do state business.

Chancellor Clarendon arrived first. His gout was bad that day and he had had to leave his bed to attend the trial, but he would not have missed it had his condition been a great deal worse. At the door-way he got out of his wheel-chair and hobbled painfully into the room. Immediately he began to sort over a stack of papers one of his secretaries laid before him, frowning and preoccupied. He took no notice of those who came next.

After a few moments Charles strolled in with York at his side and several busy little spaniels scurrying about his feet. One of them he held in his arms, and as he paused to speak for a moment with Sir William Coventry his hand stroked along the dog's silken ears; it turned its head to lick at him. The dogs were not affectionate but they seemed to know and love their master, though the courtiers were often bitten for trying to strike up a friendship with them.

Presently Lauderdale, the giant Scotsman, arrived and stopped to tell Charles a funny story he had heard the previous night. He was a very inept raconteur, but Charles's deep laugh boomed out, amused more by the Earl's crude eccentricities than by what he was saying. York, however, regarded him with contemptuous dislike. Now he went to sit beside the Chancellor. Instantly they were engaged in earnest low-toned conversation. No two men there today had so much at stake; Buckingham had been an active and dangerous foe of both for many years. The enmity far predated the Restoration, but had become even more virulent since.

If there was one man in England who hated and feared Buckingham more than either York or Chancellor Clarendon it was the Secretary of State, Baron Arlington. They had been friends when Arlington had first arrived at Court, six years before, but conflicting ambitions had since separated them until now each found it difficult to show the other the merest civility.

At last Baron Arlington paced majestically into the council-chamber—he never merely walked into any room.

Several years in Spain had given him an admiration for things Spanish and he assumed an exaggerated Castilian pomposity and arrogance. He wore a blonde wig, his eyes were pale and prominent, almost fish-like, and over the bridge of his nose was a crescent-shaped black plaster which had once been put there to cover a sabre wound and which he had kept because it gave his face a kind of sinister dignity he thought becoming. Charles had always liked him, though York, of course, did not. Now he paused, took a bottle and a spoon from one pocket and into the spoon poured several drops of ground-ivy juice. Placing the spoon to his nose he snuffed hard several times until most of the juice was gone; then he wiped at his nose with a handkerchief and put bottle and spoon away. His Lordship suffered from habitual headache, and that was his treatment for it. The headache was worse than usual today.

Charles sat at the head of the table, facing the door, his back to the fireplace. He lounged in his chair, a pair of spaniels in his lap—a lazy good-humoured man who slept well and had no trouble with his digestion so that he looked tolerantly upon the world and was inclined to be merely amused by many things which infuriated less tranquil men. His fits of anger were brief and he had long since lost interest in punishing the Duke. He knew Buckingham for exactly what he was, had no more illusions about him than he had about anyone else, but he also knew that the Duke's own frivolity of temperament kept him from being truly dangerous. The trial was necessary because of wide-spread public interest in the case, but Charles no longer wanted vengeance. He would be satisfied if the Duke gave them an entertaining performance that afternoon.

At a signal from the King the door was flung open and there stood his Grace, George Villiers, second Duke of Buckingham—dressed as magnificently as though he had been going to be married, or hanged. His handsome face wore an expression which somehow mingled both hauteur and pleasant civility. For a moment he stood there. Then, erect as a guardsman, he crossed the floor and knelt at the King's feet. Charles nodded his head, but did not give him his hand to kiss.

The others stared hard at him, trying to see into the heart of the man. Was he worried, or was he confident? Did he expect to die, or to be forgiven? But Buckingham's face did not betray him.

Arlington, who was chief prosecutor, got to his feet and began to read the charges against the Duke. They were many and serious: Being in cabal with the Commons. Opposing the King in the Lower House. Advising both the Commons and the Lords against the King's interests. Trying to become popular. And finally, the crime for which they hoped to have his blood—treason against King and State, the casting of his Majesty's horoscope. The incriminating paper was shown the Duke, held up at a safe distance for him to see.

Among these men Buckingham had just two friends, Lauderdale and Ashley, and though the others intended at first to conduct the investigation with dignity and decorum that resolution was soon gone. In their excitement several of them talked at once, they began to shout and to interrupt one another and him. But Buckingham kept his temper, which was notoriously short, and replied with polite submissiveness to every question or accusation. The only man for whom he showed less than respect was his one-time friend, Arlington, and to him he was openly insolent.

When they accused him of trying to make himself popular

he looked the Baron straight in the eye: "Whoever is committed to prison by my Lord Chancellor and my Lord Arlington cannot help becoming popular."

He had a glib answer for the charge of treason. "I do not deny, gentlemen, that that piece of paper is a horoscope. Neither do I deny that you got it from Dr. Heydon, who cast it. But I do deny that it was I who commissioned it or that it concerns his Majesty's future."

A murmur rushed round the table. What was the rascal saying? How dare he stand there and lie like that! Charles smiled, very faintly, but as the Duke shot him a hasty glance the smile vanished; his swarthy face set in stern lines again.

"Would your Grace be so good, then, as to tell us who did commission the horoscope?" asked Arlington sarcastically. "Or is that your Grace's secret?"

"It's no secret at all. If it will make matters more clear to you gentlemen I am glad to tell you. My sister had the horoscope cast." This seemed to astonish everyone but the King, who merely lifted one quizzical eyebrow and continued to stroke his dog's head.

"Your sister had the horoscope cast?" repeated Arlington, with an inflection which said plainly he considered the statement a bald lie. Then, suddenly, "Whose is it?"

Buckingham bowed, contemptuously. "That is my sister's secret. You must ask her. She has not confided in me."

His Grace was sent back to the Tower where he was as much visited as a new actress or the reigning courtesan. Charles pretended to examine the papers again and agreed that the signature on them was that of Mary Villiers. This brought furious and impassioned protest from both Arlington and Clarendon, neither of whom was willing to give up the fight for the Duke's life or, at the very least, his prestige and fortune. He was caught this time, trapped like a stupid woodcock, but if he got away this once they might never have the like opportunity again.

Charles listened to both of them with his usual courteous attention. "I know very well, Chancellor," he said one day when he had gone to visit the old man in his lodgings at Whitehall, "that I could pursue this charge of treason. But I've found a man's often more use with his head on." He was seated in a chair beside the couch on which Clarendon lay, for his gout now kept him bed-ridden much of the time.

"What use can he be to you, Sire? To run loose and hatch more plots—one of which may take, and cost your Majesty your life?"

Charles smiled. "I'm not in much awe of Buckingham's plots. His tongue is hung too loose for him to be any great danger to anyone but himself. Before he could half get a plot under way he'd have made the fatal mistake of letting someone else into the secret. No, Chancellor. His Grace has gone to considerable pains to insinuate himself with the Commons, and there's no doubt he has a good deal of interest with them. I think he'll be more use to me this way—chopping off his head would only make a martyr of him."

Clarendon was angry and worried, though he tried to conceal his feelings. He had never reconciled himself to the King's stubborn habit of deciding, when the issue interested him, for himself.

"Your Majesty has a nature too fond and too forgiving. If you did not personally like his Grace this would never be allowed to pass."

"Perhaps, Chancellor, it's true as you say that I'm too forgiving—" He shrugged his shoulders and got up, gesturing with his hand for Clarendon to stay where he was. "But I don't think so."

For an instant Charles's black eyes rested seriously on the Chancellor. At last he smiled faintly, gave a nod of his head and walked out of the room. Clarendon stared after him with a worried frown. As the King disappeared his eyes shifted and he sat looking at his bandaged foot. The King, he knew, was his only protection against a horde of jealous enemies, of whom Buckingham was merely one of the loudest and most spectacular. Should Charles withdraw his support Clarendon knew that he could not last a fortnight.

Perhaps I'm too forgiving—but I don't think so.

Suddenly there began to go through the old Chancellor's mind a parade of those things he had done which had offended

767

Charles: Clarendon had never admitted it but many insisted and no doubt Charles believed that Parliament would have voted him a greater income at the Restoration, but for his opposition. Charles had been furious when he had prevented the passage of his act for religious toleration. There had been the arguments over Lady Castlemaine's title, which had finally been passed through the Irish peerage because he refused to sign it. There were a hundred other instances, great and small, accumulated over the years.

Perhaps I am too forgiving—Clarendon knew what he had meant by that. Charles forgot nothing and, in the long run, he forgave nothing.

Less than three weeks from the time that Buckingham was sent to the Tower he was released and he appeared once more, arrogant as ever, in all his old haunts. At one of Castlemaine's suppers the King allowed him to kiss his hand. He began to frequent the taverns again and in a few days he was at the theatre with Rochester and several others. They took one of the foreboxes and hung over the edge of it, talking to the vizard-masks below and complaining noisily because Nell Gwynne had left the stage to be Lord Buckhurst's mistress.

Harry Killigrew, who was in an adjoining box, presently began to comment audibly on the Duke's affairs to a young man who sat beside him: "I have it on the best authority that his Grace will never be reinstated."

Buckingham gave him a glance of displeasure and turned again to watch the stage, but Harry's mischievous zeal was merely whetted. He took out his pocket-comb and began grooming his wig. " 'Sdeath," he drawled, "but I was somewhat surprised his Grace should be content to take over the cast-off whore of half the men at Court." Some time since he had been a lover of the languid dangerous sensual Countess of Shrewsbury, and now that she was the Duke's mistress he babbled incessantly about the affair.

Buckingham scowled angrily at him. "Govern your tongue, you young whelp. I will not hear my Lady Shrewsbury maligned

—particularly I hate the sound of her name in a mouth so foul as your own!"

The vizard-masks and beaus in the pit had begun to look up at them, for in the small confines of the theatre their voices carried and it sounded like a quarrel. Ladies and gentlemen in nearby boxes craned their necks, smiling a little in anticipation, and some of the actors were paying more attention to Killigrew and the Duke than to their own business.

Feeling all eyes begin to focus upon him, Harry grew bolder. "Your Grace is strangely fastidious concerning a lady who's turned her tail to most of your acquaintance."

Buckingham half rose, and then sat down again. "You impertinent knave—I'll have you soundly beaten for this!"

Killigrew was indignant. "I'll have your Grace to understand that I'm no mean fellow to be beaten by lackeys! I'm as worthy of your Grace's sword as the next man!" It was a fine point of honour. And so saying he left the box, summoning his friend to go with him. "Tell his Grace I'll meet him behind Montagu House in half an hour."

The young man refused and began hauling at Harry's sleeve, trying to reason with him. "Don't be a fool, Harry! His Grace has been troubling no one! You're drunk—come on, let's leave."

"Pox on you, then!" declared Killigrew. "If you're an arrant coward, I'm not!"

With that he unbuckled his sword, lifted it high and brought it smashing down, case and all, upon the Duke's head. He turned instantly and began to run as Buckingham sprang to his feet in white-faced fury and started after him. The two men scrambled along, climbing over seats, hitting off hats, stepping on feet. Women began to scream; the actors on the stage were shouting; and above in the balconies 'prentices and bullies and harlots crowded to the railing, stamping and beating their cudgels.

"Kill 'im, your Grace!"

"Whip 'im through the lungs!"

"Slit the bastard's nose!"

Someone threw an orange and it smacked Killigrew square in the face. An excited woman grabbed at Buckingham's wig and pulled it off. Killigrew was heading at furious speed for an exit, looking back with a horrified face to see the Duke gaining on him. Now Buckingham pulled out his naked sword, bellowing, "Stop, you coward!"

Killigrew sent men and women sprawling to the floor in his headlong flight and the Duke, following after, tramped across them. He might have escaped but someone stuck out an ankle to trip him. The next moment Buckingham was upon him and gave him a hearty kick in the ribs with his square-toed shoe.

"Get on your feet and fight, you poltroon!" roared the Duke.

"Please, your Grace! It was all in jest!"

Killigrew writhed about, trying to escape the Duke's feet, which kicked viciously at him again and again, striking him in the stomach and the chest and about the shins. The theatre roared with excitement, urging him to trample out his guts, to slice his throat. Now Buckingham leaned over, wrenched Harry's sword away and spat into his face.

"Bah! You snivelling coward, you don't deserve to wear a sword!" He kicked him again and Killigrew coughed, doubling over. "Get on your knees and ask me for your life—or by God I'll kill you like the yellow dog you are!"

Harry crawled to his knees. "Good your Grace," he whined obediently, "spare my life."

"Keep it then," muttered Buckingham contemptuously. "If you think it's any use to you!" and he kicked him again for good measure.

Harry got painfully to his feet and started out, limping, one hand pressed against his aching ribs. He was followed by derisive hoots and jeers as the scornful crowd hurled oranges and wooden cudgels, shoes and apple-cores after him. Harry Killigrew was the most disgraced man of the year.

Buckingham watched him go. Then someone handed him his wig and he took it, slapped the dust out and set it back on his head again. With Harry gone their cries of abuse changed to cheers for his Grace, and Buckingham, smiling and bowing politely, made his way back to his seat. He sat down between Rochester and Etherege, sweating and hot, but pleased in his triumph.

770

"By God, that's a piece of business I've been intending to do for a long while!"

Rochester gave him an affectionate slap on the back. "His Majesty should be grateful enough to forgive you anything. There's no man who wears a head needed a public beating so bad as Harry."

CHAPTER FIFTY-THREE

LORD CARLTON HAD not been gone a month when Amber was appointed a Lady of the Bedchamber and moved into apartments at Whitehall. The suite consisted of twelve rooms, six on a floor, strung out straight along the river front and adjoining the King's apartments, to which it had access by means of a narrow passage and staircase opening from an alcove in the drawing-room. Many such trap-stairs and passageways had been constructed during Mrs. Cromwell's stay there, for her ease in spying upon her servants—the King often found them useful too.

And will you look at me now! thought Amber, as she surveyed her new surroundings. What a long way I've come!

Sometimes she wondered in idle amusement what Aunt Sarah and Uncle Matt and all her seven cousins would think if they could see her—titled, rich, with a coach-and-eight, satin and velvet gowns by the score, a collection of emeralds to rival Castlemaine's pearls, bowed to by lords and earls as she passed along the Palace corridors. This, she knew, was to be truly great. But she thought she knew also what Uncle Matt, at least, would think about it. He would say that she was a harlot and a disgrace to the family. But then, Uncle Matt always had been an old dunderhead.

Amber hoped at first that she was rid of both her husband and her mother-in-law, but it was not long after the signing of the peace treaty that Lucilla returned to London, dragging Gerald in her wake. He paid a formal call upon Amber while she was still at Almsbury House, asked her politely how she did, and after a few minutes took his leave. His encounter with Bruce Carlton had scared him enough; he had no wish to interfere with the King. For he knew by now why Charles had created him an earl and married him to a rich woman. If he was humiliated he saw no solution but pretended nonchalance, no remedy but to employ himself in a course of dissipations. He was content to pursue his own life and leave her alone.

But his mother was not. She came to visit Amber the day after she had moved into Whitehall.

Amber waved her into a chair and went on with what she had been doing—directing some workmen in the hanging of her pictures and mirrors. She knew that Lucilla was watching her with a most critical eye on her figure—for she was now in the eighth month of her pregnancy. But she paid little attention to the woman's chatter and merely nodded occasionally or made some absent-minded remark.

"Lord," said Lucilla, "to see how captious the world has grown! *Everyone,* absolutely *everyone,* my dear, is under suspicion nowadays, don't you agree? Gossip, gossip, gossip. One hears it on every hand!"

"Um," said Amber. "Oh, yes, of course. I think we'd better hang this one here, just beside the window. It needs to catch the light from that side—" She had already had several things sent down from Lime Park and she remembered what she had learned from Radclyffe about the most effective place for each.

"Of course Gerry doesn't believe a word of it." Amber paid no attention at all to that and she repeated, louder this time, "Of course *Gerry* doesn't believe a word of it!"

"What?" said Amber, glancing around over her shoulder. "A word of what? No—a little to the left. Now, down a bit— There, that's fine. What were you saying, madame?"

"I said, my dear, that Gerry thinks it's all a horrid lie, and he says he'll challenge the rascal who started it if once he can catch him."

"By all means," agreed Amber, standing back and squinting one eye to see that the painting was where she wanted it. "A gentleman's nothing here at Whitehall till he's had his clap and writ his play and killed his man. . . . Yes, that's right. When you're done with that you can go."

Convinced by now that she would never get rid of Lucilla until she had heard her out, she went to sit down in a chair and scooped up Monsieur le Chien to lay him across her lap. She had been on her feet for several hours and was tired. She wanted to be let alone. But now her mother-in-law leaned forward with the hot-eyed, excited eagerness of a woman who had un-savoury gossip to tell.

"You're rather young, my dear," said Lucilla, "and perhaps you don't understand the way of the world so well as a more experienced woman. But to tell you the truth on it, there's a deal of unpleasant talk regarding your appointment at Court."

Amber was amused and one corner of her mouth curled slightly. "I didn't think there'd ever yet been an appointment at Court that didn't cause a deal of unpleasant talk."

"But this, of course, is different. They're saying— Well, I may as well speak frankly. They're saying that you're more in his Majesty's favour than a decent woman should be. They're saying, madame, that that's the King's child you're carrying!" She watched Amber with hard unforgiving eyes, as though she expected her to blush and falter, protest and weep.

"Well," said Amber, "since Gerald doesn't believe it, why concern yourself?"

"Why concern myself? Good God, madame, you shock me! Is that the kind of talk you're willing to have go on about you? I'm sure no decent woman would have such things said about her!" She was growing breathless. "And I don't believe that you would either, madame, if *you* were a decent woman! But I don't think you are—I think it's true! I think you were with child by his Majesty and knew it when you married my son! Do you know what you've done, madame? You've made my good honest boy appear a fool in the eyes of the world—you've spoiled the honourable name of the Stanhopes—you've—"

"You have a great deal to say about my morals, madame," snapped Amber, "but you seem willing enough to live on my money!"

Lady Stanhope gave a horrified gasp. *"Your* money! Good Heavens! what is the world coming to! When a woman marries, her money belongs to her husband! Even you must know that! Live on your money! I'll have you to know, madame, I scorn the mere thought of it!"

Amber spoke sharply, through her teeth. "Then stop doing it!"

Lady Stanhope jumped to her feet. "Why, you hussy! I'll bring a suit against you for this! We'll find out whose money it is, I warrant you!"

Amber got up, dropping the dog onto the floor where he stretched and yawned lazily, putting out his long pink tongue. "If you do you're a greater fool than I think. The marriage-contract gives me control of all my money. Now get out of here and don't trouble me again—or I'll make you sorry for it!" She gave a furious wave of her arm and as Lady Stanhope hesitated, glaring, Amber grabbed up a vase and lifted her hand to throw it. The Dowager Baroness picked up her skirts and went out on the run. But Amber did not enjoy her triumph. Slamming away the vase she collapsed into a chair and began to cry, overwhelmed with the dark reasonless morbidity of her pregnancy.

It was Dr. Fraser who delivered Amber's son, for many of the Court ladies were beginning to employ doctors rather than midwives—though elsewhere the practice was regarded as merely one more evidence of aristocratic decadence. The child was born at three o'clock one hot stormy October morning; he was a long thin baby with splotched red skin and a black fuzz on top of his head.

A few hours later Charles came in softly and alone to see this latest addition to his numerous family. He bent over the elaborate carved and inlaid cradle placed just beside Amber's bed and very carefully turned back the white satin coverlet which hung to the floor. A slow smile came onto his mouth.

"Ods-fish!" he whispered. "I swear the little devil looks like me."

Amber, pale and weak and looking as if all the strength had

774

been drained out of her, lay flat on her back and smiled up at him. "Didn't you expect him to, Charles?"

He gave her a grin. "Of course I did, my dear." He took the baby's tiny fist which had closed firmly over his fingers and touched it to his mouth. "But I'm an ugly fellow for a helpless infant to take after." He turned to her. "I hope you're feeling well. I saw the doctor just a few minutes since and he said you had an easy labour."

"Easy for him," said Amber, who wanted credit and sympathy for having suffered more than she had. "But I suppose I'm well enough."

"Of course you are, my dear. Two weeks from now you won't know you ever had a baby." He kissed her then and went off so that she might rest. A few hours later Gerald arrived, and woke her up.

Though obviously embarrassed, he came swaggering into the room dressed in a suit of pale-yellow satin with a hundred yards of ribbon looped about his sleeves and breeches, and reeking of orange-flower water. From his silver sword to his lace cravat, from his feather-burdened hat to his richly embroidered gloves he was the perfect picture of a fop, a beau gallant, reared in England, polished in France, inhabiting the Royal Exchange and Chatelin's ordinary, the tiring-rooms of the theatres and Covent Garden. His prototype was to be seen a dozen times by anyone who cared to stroll along Drury Lane or Pall Mall or any other fashionable thoroughfare in London.

He kissed Amber, as any casual caller might have done, and said brightly, "Well, madame! You're looking mighty spruce for a lady who's just laid in! Eh bien, where is he—this new sprig of the house of Stanhope?"

Nan had gone downstairs to the nursery to get him and now she returned bearing the baby on a cushion with his long embroidered gown trailing halfway to the floor. Swaddling was no longer the fashion at Court and this child would never be bound up like a mummy until he could scarcely wriggle.

"There!" said Nan, almost defiantly, but she held him herself and did not offer him to Gerald. "Isn't he handsome?"

Gerald leaned forward to examine him but kept his hands

775

behind his back; he looked puzzled and uneasy, at a loss for the appropriate comment. "Well! Hello there, young sir! Hmmm— Mort Dieu! but he has a red face, hasn't he!"

"Well!" snapped Nan. "I'll warrant you did too!"

Gerald jumped nervously. He was almost as much in awe of Nan as of his wife or mother. "Oh, heavens! I meant no offense, let me perish! He's—oh, indeed, he's really very handsome! Why, yes—he looks like his mother, let me perish!" The baby opened his mouth and began to squall; Amber gave a wave of her hand and Nan hurried him from the room. Left alone with her, Gerald began to fidget. He took out his snuffbox, the last word in affectation among the fops, and applied a pinch to each nostril. "Well, madame, no doubt you wish to rest. I'll trouble you no longer. The truth on it is, I'm engaged to go to the play with some gentlemen of my acquaintance."

"By all means, my lord. Go along. Thanks for waiting on me."

"Oh, not at all, madame, I protest. Thank *you* for admitting me. Your servant, madame." He kissed her again, a frightened hasty peck at the tip of her nose, bowed, and started for the door. As at a sudden afterthought he paused and looked around over one shoulder. "Oh, by the way, madame, what d'ye think we shall name him?"

Amber smiled. "Charles, if it pleases your Lordship."

"Charles? Oh! Yes—mais oui! Of course! Charles—" He left hastily and just as he went out the door she saw him whip a handkerchief from his pocket and apply it to his forehead.

Amber's up-sitting was a triumphant occasion.

Her rooms were crowded to capacity with the first lords and ladies of England. She served them wine and cakes and accepted their kisses and effusive compliments most graciously. They were forced to admit to one another that the child was undoubtedly a Stuart, but they also observed with malicious satisfaction that it was as ugly as the King had been when he was first born. Amber did not think he was pretty either; but perhaps he would improve in time, and anyway the important

776

thing was that he looked like Charles. And when the baby was christened, Charles acted as godfather and presented her with a silver dinner-service, simple and beautiful, but also expensive enough; his son received the traditional gift of the twelve silver Apostle spoons.

As Amber recovered she began to consider how she might permanently rid herself of her troublesome mother-in-law.

Lucilla did not intend to return to the country, she was extravagant, and in spite of Amber's warning she persisted in sending the tradesmen to her for payment. Amber put them off, for she had in mind a scheme which she hoped would compel the Baroness to meet her own obligations. She hoped to find a husband for her. Lucilla still talked a good deal of the strictness and formality which had been in vogue during her youth and professed to be very much shocked by the new manners, but nevertheless she had acquired some of those manners herself. No actress cut her gowns any lower; no Maid of Honour was more flirtatious; no vizard-mask plying her trade in the pit had her face more painted and patched. She was as gay and, she thought, as appealing as a kitten.

She did not care for men her own age but preferred the twenty-five-year-old sparks, merry young fellows who bragged of the maidenheads they had taken and considered it a piece of hilarious wit to break the watchman's head when he tried to arrest them for disturbing the peace. To the Dowager Baroness they represented all the excitement and liveliness she had missed and since she felt herself no older than they she refused to believe the years had really changed her. But if she was not aware of the difference, they were, and they escaped her whenever they could to seek out a pretty young woman of fifteen or seventeen. The Baroness, in their estimation, was an old jade with no fortune to offset that handicap and they considered that she was making a fool of herself.

There was one of them in particular to whom she seemed most attracted. He was Sir Frederick Fothergill, a brash confident young fop who was seen everywhere it was fashionable to be seen and who did everything it was fashionable to do. He was tall, thin, effeminately handsome, but he was also an ardent duellist and had distinguished himself as a volunteer against the Dutch during the past two years.

Amber inquired into his circumstances and learned that he was the son of a man who had not profited by the Restoration—as most of the Royalists had not—and that he was deep in debt and constantly going deeper. He lived an expensive life, bought fine clothes and kept his coach, gambled without much luck and was often compelled to sneak out of his lodgings or to stay with friends to avoid the dunning of his creditors. Amber guessed that he would be glad to find so apparently simple a solution to his problems.

She sent for him one morning and he came to her apartments. She had dismissed the tradesmen but there were still several others in the room: Nan and half-a-dozen women servants, a dressmaker just gathering up her materials to leave, Tansy and the dog, and Susanna. Susanna stood with her plump elbows on Amber's crossed knees, her great green eyes staring up solemnly at her mother who was explaining that young ladies should not snatch off the wigs of gentlemen. She had experimented once with the King's periwig, found that it came off, and had since made a grab at every man who leaned close enough. Now, however, she nodded her head in docile agreement.

"And you won't ever do that again, will you?" said Amber.

"Never again," agreed Susanna.

Sir Frederick came in then, made her an elaborate bow from the doorway and another when he stood before her. "Your Ladyship's servant," he said soberly, but his eyes swept over her with familiarity and confidence.

Susanna curtsied to him and Sir Frederick bent very low to kiss her hand. Her eyes lighted on his wig, began to sparkle with mischief, and then she gave a quick guilty glance toward her mother whom she found watching her and waiting, with pursed lips and tapping foot. Instantly she put both hands behind her. Amber laughed, gave her daughter a kiss and sent her out of the room with her nurse. She watched her go, her eyes wistful and fond as they followed the dainty little figure in ankle-length crisp white gown and tiny apron, her mass of golden waves caught at one side with a green bow. She was very proud of Susanna who was, she felt sure, the loveliest little girl in England—and England, of course, was the world. The door closed and she turned back immediately to Sir Frederick, asking him to be seated.

Amber went to her dressing-table to finish painting her face. He sat beside her, very smug and pleased with himself to have been invited to her Ladyship's levée—and in such privacy too, not another man around. He imagined that he knew quite well why she had asked him.

"Your Ladyship does me great honour," he said, his eyes on her breasts. "I've had the greatest admiration for your Ladyship ever since the first day I saw you—in the forefront of the King's box at the theatre some months ago. I vow and swear, madame, I could not keep my mind or eyes on the stage."

"That's very kind of you, sir. As it happens I've been noticing you, too—in conversation with my mother-in-law—"

"Pshaw!" He screwed up his face and gave a brush of one hand. "She's nothing to me, I assure you!"

"She speaks mighty well of you, sir. I could almost say I think she's in love with you."

"What? Ridiculous! Well, what if she is? That's nothing to me, is it?"

"You haven't taken advantage of her tenderness for you, I hope?"

She got up now and crossed the room to stand behind a screen while she dressed. And as she went she let her dressing-gown slide just a little, allowing him a glimpse of one taut full breast just before she disappeared; she still wanted the admiration of every man, however little he might be to her. But she slept with Charles—or alone.

It was a moment before Sir Frederick replied, and then he was emphatic. "Lord, no! I've never so much as asked her an indecent question. Though to tell your Ladyship truly I think that if I did I might not be disappointed."

"But you're too much the man of honour to make a try?"

"I'm afraid, madame, she's not quite to my taste."

"Oh, isn't she, Sir Frederick? And why not, pray?"

Sir Frederick was becoming baffled. When she had invited

779

him to pay her a call he had told all his friends that the young Countess of Danforth had fallen mightily in love with him and had sent for him to lie with her. Now he began to think that she did not want him for herself after all, that perhaps she was playing bawd to procure him for her mother-in-law. A pretty fool he'd look if she intended to fob him off on that old jade!

"Well, she's a great deal older than I am, your Ladyship. My God, she must be forty! Old women may like young men, but I'm afraid it can't be said that the reverse holds true."

Now fully dressed, Amber walked to the dressing-table, where she began sorting through a boxful of jewels. Nothing in all her new life at Court had pleased her so much as this moment when she found herself so high, so rich, so powerful, that she could arrange the lives of others to suit herself. She held up a diamond-and-emerald bracelet to the light, rolling out her lower lip as she considered it, aware of his eyes watching her and aware too of what he was thinking.

"Well, then, Sir Frederick, I'm sorry to hear that." She fastened the bracelet. "I had thought I might be able to help your case with her. She's a great fortune, you know." She pawed idly through the rest of the jewellery.

He came instantly to life, straightening in his chair, leaning forward. "A fortune, did you say?"

She looked at him with mild surprise. "Why, yes, of course. Didn't you know that? Lord, she's got a hundred suitors, all of 'em mad to marry her. She's considering which one she'll have—and I thought she had a peculiar fancy to you."

"A fortune! I didn't know she had a shilling! Everyone told me— Well, your Ladyship, to tell you truly, this is a mighty great surprise!" He seemed stunned, unable to believe the good luck which had apparently blown his way by accident. "How much—a—that is—"

Amber came to his rescue. "Oh, I should say about five thousand pound."

"Five thousand! A year!" Five thousand a year was, in fact, a fortune of immense size.

"No," said Amber. "Five thousand in all. Oh, of course she

has some property too." That was obviously a disappointment to him and as she saw the look on his face she added, "I think she was about to accept young What-d'ye-call— I don't remember his name just now. The one who always wears the green-satin suit. But if you speak to her quick enough perhaps you can persuade her to give you a hearing."

It was not two weeks later that Sir Frederick married the Dowager Baroness.

Aware that most pretty young women with money had either sharp-eyed parents or guardians who would never consider him a good match, he began to pay his court to her almost immediately upon quitting Amber's apartments—and when he proposed she accepted him. Amber gave her five thousand pounds in return for a witnessed statement that she would never again ask or expect money from her.

At first the Baroness was highly indignant, refused absolutely, and said that she would have all the money since it was her son's by right. Amber soon persuaded her that in such a case the King would take her side and in the end Lucilla was glad to get the five thousand pounds, which would not now do a great deal more than clear her debts. But she was not giving very much thought to money. All her emotions were centered in the exciting prospect of being a wife again, this time to a handsome and young man who did not seem aware that she was old enough to be his mother. The ceremony took place at night and though Gerald was wretchedly embarrassed by his mother's behaviour Amber was at once amused, relieved and contemptuous.

There's no more ridiculous creature on earth, she decided, than your virtuous woman who makes herself miserable for years to preserve what the captious world will never credit her with having.

Now that Amber was rid of her mother-in-law she decided to make a similar arrangement with her husband. She knew that he had begun an affair with Mrs. Polly Stark, a pretty fifteen-year-old who had recently taken a small shop in the 'Change, where she sold ribbons and other trinkets. And so one evening in late November when he strolled into her Majesty's

Drawing-Room she left her card-table and went to join him.

As always when he found himself face-to-face with her he had a look of dread expectancy. Now he supposed that she was going to harangue him about Mrs. Stark. "Gad!" he exclaimed. "But it's damned hot in here. Frightful, let me perish!"

"Why, I don't find it so," said Amber sweetly. 'Lord, what a handsome suit that is you're wearing. I vow your tailor's quite beyond compare."

"Why—thank you, madame." Bewildered, he looked down at himself, then quickly returned the compliment. "And that's a mighty fine gown, madame."

"Thank you, sir. I bought the ribbons of a young woman newly set up in the 'Change. Her name's Mrs. Stark, I think— She knows everything in the world about garniture."

He turned red and swallowed. So it was Mrs. Stark. He wished he had never come to the Palace. He had not wanted to but had been persuaded by some friends who had an intrigue in the fire with a couple of her Majesty's Maids. "Mrs. Stark?" he repeated. "Mort Dieu, the name's familiar!"

"Think hard and I believe you'll recall her. She remembers you very well."

"You talked to her!"

"Oh, yes. Half an hour or more. We're great friends."

"Well."

She laughed outright now, tapping him on the arm with her fan. "Lord, Gerald, don't look so sheepish. How could you be in the fashion if you didn't keep a wench? I swear I wouldn't have a faithful husband—it'd ruin me among all my acquaintance."

He looked at her with astonishment and then stared down at his shoes, frowning unhappily. He was not quite sure whether she was serious or was making fun of him; whichever it was he felt like a fool. He could think of nothing to say in reply.

"And what d'you think?" continued Amber. "She complains you're stingy."

"What? Stingy—I? Well, gad, madame— She wants to keep a coach and occupy lodgings in Drury Lane and will wear nothing but silk stockings and I can't think what all. She's a damned expensive jade. It would cost me less to keep London Bridge in repair than to support her."

"Still," said Amber reasonably, "you can't set up for a beau if you don't keep a whore, can you?"

He gave her another quick glance of amazement. "Why—I— Well, it's all the mode, of course, but then—"

"And if you're going to keep a wench she must be pretty and the pretty ones come at a high figure." Suddenly she sobered. "Look, sir: Suppose we two strike up a bargain. I'll give Mrs. Stark two hundred pound a year—while she keeps your good graces—and I'll give you four hundred. You can sign a paper agreeing to meet your own expenses from that amount and trouble me no further. If you run into debt I'll not be held responsible. How does that sound to you?"

"Why—of course that's very generous of you, madame. Only I thought—that is—Mother said—"

"Pox on your mother! I don't care what she said! Now, does that satisfy you or no? For if it doesn't I'll ask his Majesty to speak to the Archbishop about an annulment."

"An annulment! But, madame—how can you? The marriage has been consummated!"

"Who's to say whether it has or not? And I think I have more means of bribing a jury than you! Now, what about it, Gerald? I have the paper drawn up and it's in my chamber. Good Lord, I don't know what more you can want! It seems to me a mighty generous offer—I don't have to give you anything at all, you know."

"Well—very well, then—only—"

"Only what?"

"Don't tell Mother, will you?"

CHAPTER FIFTY-FOUR

JAMES WAS LEANING on the window-sill watching some women who strolled in the sunny garden below; he gave a soft whistle and as they glanced up he waved. The women were first surprised and then they burst into giggles, beckoning him to come down and join them. He began to pantomime, shaking his head, shrugging his shoulders, jerking his thumb back over his shoulder. And then, as a door opened behind him, he straightened instantly, composed his face, and swinging the window shut turned around.

Anne Hyde came out of her brother-in-law's closet, her ugly mouth working with emotion, snuffing her nose and holding a wadded handkerchief against her face. The years since the Restoration had not improved her appearance. She was now thirty years old; her stomach bulged with her sixth pregnancy and she had a gross accumulation of fat, for over-eating was her comfort; red angry pustules spotted her face, and covering each was a small black patch. Anne had caught syphilis from his Royal Highness. And yet she had about her still a sort of awe-inspiring grandeur, a majesty more defiant and more proud, perhaps, than if she had been of the blood royal. She was not very much liked, but she was respected, and somewhat feared.

Everyone knew that she ruled the Duke, kept him hopelessly in debt with her extravagance, told him what to do and say in council, and that he obeyed her. Only in his amours did he preserve his independence and those went on no matter how she complained. Frequently he had the women brought to a room adjoining their chamber and left Anne's bed to go out to them. But, for the most part, they understood and respected each other.

Slowly she shut the door. He stood and stared at her, his face questioning, while she tried to gain control of herself. Finally he spoke.

"What did he tell you?"

"What did he tell me!" she repeated bitterly, twisting at her ringed hands. "I don't know what he told me! He listened—oh, he listened most politely. But he wouldn't promise anything. Oh, Your Highness—what can I *do!*"

York shrugged, but his face was morose. "I don't know."

She looked up swiftly and her eyes began to glitter. "You

don't know! That's just like you! You never know what to do no matter what happens—you won't know what to do when you're king! God help you if I'm not here to tell you! Listen to me—" She came across the few feet that had separated them and took hold of his coat. As she talked her fist pounded against his chest. "You're not going to stand by like a simple fool and watch my father put out by a pack of scheming, lying jackals, d'ye hear me? You've got to go in there and talk to him —make him understand what they're trying to do! After all the years my father's given to serve the Stuarts, after his loyalty and devotion, he *can't* do this! He *can't* turn him out! Go in there now and talk to him—" She gave him a push.

"I'll try," said York, without much conviction. He went through that door and knocked at another, opening it when the King's voice bade him enter. "I hope I'm not intruding, Sire."

Charles looked around over his shoulder with a grin. If he knew what his brother had come for he gave no indication of it. "Not at all, James. Come in. You're just in time to send a message to Minette. What shall I tell her for you?"

The Duke was frowning, occupied with his own thoughts, and he hesitated a moment before answering. "Why—tell her that I hope she'll be able to pay us a visit soon."

"That's what I'm writing about. She hopes to come next year. Well, James—what is it? You've got something on your mind."

James sat down and leaned forward in his chair, thoughtfully rubbing the flat palms of his hands together. "Yes, Sire, I have." He paused for several moments while his brother waited. "Anne is afraid that you don't intend to deal kindly with the Chancellor."

Charles smiled. "Then she's very much mistaken. I shall deal with him as kindly as I can. But you know as well as I do, James, that this isn't my doing. I have a Parliament to answer to, and they're in a mighty critical humour."

"But your Majesty wouldn't sacrifice a man who has served you so long and well merely to satisfy Parliament?" James had no very good opinion of the country's governing body, nor of his brother's patience and compromises with it. Things will be different, he often told himself, when I come to the throne.

"No one is more appreciative than I of the Chancellor's service. But the truth of the matter is this: He's outworn his usefulness, to me and to England. I know he's blamed for much that hasn't been his fault, but the fact remains they hate him. They want to be rid of him for good and all. What use can a man be to me once he allows himself to come to that condition?"

"It can be only a temporary condition—if your Majesty will take the trouble to help him out of it."

"It's more than that, James. I know he's loyal and I know he's able—but nevertheless he's stuck in a morass of old-fashioned ideas. He won't realize that the Rebellion changed things here in England. He doesn't feel with his finger-tips that there are new ways now. What's worse, he doesn't want to feel it. No, James, I'm afraid the Chancellor's day is done."

"*Done?* Do you mean, Sire, that you intend putting him aside?"

"I don't think I have an alternative. He has few enough friends to help him out now—he never took the trouble to buy himself a party of loyal supporters. He was always above such practicalities."

"Well, then, Sire, since we're being frank, why don't you tell me the real reason you intend dismissing him?"

"I have."

"A different opinion runs through the galleries. There are rumours that your Majesty can forgive him everything but influencing Mrs. Stewart in favour of Richmond."

Charles's black eyes snapped. "Rumour is often impertinent, James—and so are you! If you think I'm any such fool as to dismiss a man who could be useful to me because of a woman, you do my intelligence little justice! You must own I've been as kind to you as any king has ever been to a brother, and you live as much like a monarch as I do! But in this matter I'm determined. You can't change my mind, so pray trouble me about it no more."

James bowed courteously and left the room. Kings, he had

always believed, were meant to be obeyed—but the courtiers nevertheless noticed and commented upon a certain coolness between the two brothers.

It was not many days after that that the King summoned Clarendon to meet him at Whitehall, even though the old man had been sick in bed and was living at his house in Piccadilly where Charles and the council often met to save him the journey to the Palace. Charles and the Duke of York went to the Chancellor in his official apartments and there the three of them sat down to talk.

Charles hated this moment, and he might have put it off much longer but that he knew it was necessary. For unrest seethed through all the country and had come to a focus in Parliament; he hoped to lull it again with the promise that all things would be better once the national bogey-man was disposed of. Yet he had known him long and been served by him faithfully. And for all that Clarendon often treated him as though he were an unruly schoolboy, criticizing his friends and his mistresses, telling him that he was not fit to govern, Charles knew that he was the best minister he had had, or was likely to have. Once Clarendon was gone he would be left surrounded by crafty and hostile and selfish men against whose cleverness he must pit his own wits and win—or rule England no longer.

But there was no help for it. Charles looked him straight in the eye. "My lord, as you must be aware there is a general demand for new men in the government. I'm sorry to say this to you, but I shall not be able to hold out against them. They will want you to resign and I think you would serve your own turn best by anticipating them."

It was a moment before Clarendon answered. "Your Majesty can't be in earnest?"

"I am, Chancellor. I'm sorry, but I am. As you must know, I've not made this decision suddenly—and I've not made it alone." He meant, obviously, that hundreds and thousands of Englishmen were of the same opinion.

But Clarendon chose to misinterpret. "Your Majesty refers, perhaps, to the Lady?" He had never once called Barbara by any other name.

"Truthfully, Chancellor, I do not." Charles answered softly, refusing to take offense.

"I fear your Majesty's unworthy companions have had more influence than you are yourself aware."

"Ods-fish, my lord!" replied Charles with sudden impatience, his eyes flashing. "I hope I'm not wholly deficient in mental capacity!"

Clarendon was once more the school-master. "No one appreciates better than I, Sire, what your natural parts are—and it is for that reason I have long grieved to watch your Majesty losing your time and England's in the company of such creatures as the Lady and her—"

Charles stood up. "My Lord, I've heard you at length on this subject before! You will excuse me if I decline to hear it again! I will send Secretary Morrice to you for the Great Seal! Good-day!" Swiftly and without once glancing back he walked from the room.

Clarendon and York both watched him go. When the door had closed, their eyes slowly veered around to meet. For a long moment they stared at each other, but neither spoke. At last Clarendon bowed and slowly he crossed the room and went out into the sunlight. Clustered there about the doorway, sitting on the grass, lounging against the walls were a score or more of men and some women—the news had spread that the Chancellor was with the King and they had gathered to watch him come out. His eyes narrowed, swept over them, and then as heads turned and mouths smiled he walked between them and on. He heard the murmurs begin to rise.

He had almost crossed the garden when all at once a gay feminine voice cried out to him. "Goodbye, Chancellor!"

It was Lady Castlemaine on the balcony above, surrounded by cages of bright-feathered birds; on one side of her stood Lord Arlington and on the other was Bab May. Though it was almost noon she had jumped out of bed when they told her that he was coming and now she was fastening her dressing-gown as she stood there above him, grinning, her red hair streaming loose.

"Goodbye, Chancellor!" she repeated. "I trust we won't meet again!"

The young men gathered below laughed, looking from him up to her and then back again. For a moment Clarendon's eyes met hers in the first direct look he had ever given her. Now very slowly he straightened his shoulders; his face was tired and old, marked by pain and disillusion—something that was both contempt and pity showed there.

"Madame," he said quietly, but with perfect distinctness. "If you live, you will grow old." Then he walked on, passing out of sight, but Barbara leaned over the railing above, staring, dismayed.

The young men were calling up their congratulations and compliments to her, Arlington and Bab May were both talking —but she heard none of them. All of a sudden she whirled around, pushing with her hands at the two men, and then she fled back into her chamber and slammed shut the door. Swiftly she snatched up a mirror, rushed with it to the light and stood staring at what she saw, her fingers touching her cheeks, her mouth, trailing down over her breasts.

It isn't true! she thought desperately. Damn that old bastard —of course it isn't true! I'll never be old—I'll never look any different! Why, I'm only twenty-seven and that isn't old! It's young—a woman's at her best at twenty-seven!

But she remembered a time, perhaps only yesterday, when twenty-seven had seemed very old, when she had dreaded and avoided the thought of it. Oh, drat him! Why did he say that! She felt sick and tired and full of resentful hatred. Somehow, after all their years of despising each other he had had the last word. But then a rebellious determination flared within her. Outside the men were waiting, excited, triumphant—what did it matter what a stupid malicious old man had said? He was gone now and she would never see him again. She flung away the mirror and went to the door, threw it open again and walked out, smiling.

Throughout the Palace there was fear and unrest. Men distrusted one another and those who had seemed friends now scarcely spoke but passed in the corridors as though neither friend nor foe existed. Whispers and murmurs leaped from mouth to mouth, rumours swept along—some like vagrant breezes which merely touched and were gone, others of such force that all seemed to bend and rock before them. No one felt safe. The Chancellor was out, but they were not so well satisfied as they had expected to be. Which one would go down next?

Many said it would be Lady Castlemaine.

Barbara heard the talk herself but shrugged nonchalantly and did not trouble herself about it. She was perfectly confident that when and if that time came she would be able to bully him as she had in the past. She had her comfortable easy life there at Court and did not intend that anyone should put her out of it. And then one morning when she was in bed with Mr. Jermyn, Wilson burst excitedly into the room.

"Your Ladyship! Oh, your Ladyship—here he comes!"

Barbara sat up and gave her hair an angry toss, while Mr. Jermyn peeped inquisitively over the top of the covers. "What the devil d'you mean coming in here? I thought I—"

"But it's the King! He's coming down the hall—he'll be here in just a moment!"

"Oh, my God! Keep 'im off a minute, will you! Jermyn, for Christ's sake—stop staring like a stupid booby and get out of here!"

Henry Jermyn scrambled out of bed, grabbed up his breeches in one hand and his periwig in the other and made for the door. Barbara lay down again and pulled the blankets up to her chin. She could hear the spaniels as they came in at a run and, just in the next room, the King's murmurous laugh and his voice as he paused to speak to Mrs. Wilson. (There was gossip that he had recently begun an affair with her pretty serving-woman, though Barbara had not yet been able to make either of them admit it.) Opening one eye she saw, to her horror, that Jermyn had left behind a shoe and quickly snatching it up she flung it into the bed. Then she jerked the curtains to and lay down, composing her face to pretend that she was sleeping.

She heard the door of the bedroom open and in an instant a couple of the dogs had leaped between the curtains and were prancing on her pillows, licking at her face. Barbara muttered a curse and flung out one hand to ward them off just as Charles pulled back the curtains and stood smiling down at her, not at all fooled by the questioning sleepy look she gave him. He swooped the two dogs off onto the floor.

"Good morning, madame."

"Why—good morning, Sire." She sat up, one hand in her hair, the other modestly holding the sheets to her naked breasts. "What's o'clock? Is it late?"

"Almost noon."

Now he reached down and took hold of the long blue ribbon on Mr. Jermyn's shoe and very slowly he drew it out and held it up, looking at it quizzically, as though not quite certain what it was. Barbara watched him with a kind of sullen apprehension. He twirled it slowly about by the string, observing it carefully on all sides.

"Well," he said finally, "so this as the latest divertisement for ladies of quality—substituting the shoe for the gentleman. I've heard some say it improves mightily upon nature. What's your opinion, madame?"

"My opinion is that someone's been spying on me and sent you here to catch me! Well—I'm quite alone, as you may see. Look behind the screens and drapes, pray, to satisfy yourself."

Charles smiled and tossed the shoe to the spaniels who seized upon it eagerly. Then he sat down on the bed, facing her. "Let me give you some advice, Barbara. As one old friend to another, I think that Jacob Hall would give you more satisfaction for your time and money than Mr. Jermyn is likely to do." Jacob Hall was a handsome muscular acrobat who performed at the fairs and, sometimes, at Court.

Barbara retorted quickly. "I don't doubt that Jacob Hall is as fine a gentleman as Moll Davis is a lady!" Moll Davis was his Majesty's newest mistress, an actress in the Duke of York's Theatre.

"I don't doubt it, either," he agreed. For a long moment they looked at each other. "Madame," he said at last, "I believe that the time has come for you and me to have a talk."

Something inside her took a plunging drop. Then it hadn't been just gossip, after all. Instantly her manner became respectful and polite, and almost flirtatious. "Why, certainly, Your Majesty. What about?" Her violet eyes were wide and innocent.

"I think we need pretend no longer. When a man and woman who are married have ceased to love each other there is nothing for them but to find entertainment elsewhere. Fortunately, it's otherwise with us."

That was the boldest statement of his feelings he had ever made to her. Sometimes, in anger, he had spoken sharply, but she had always assured herself that he had meant it no more than she meant what she said when angry. And she refused to believe even now that he could actually be serious.

"Do you mean, Sire," she asked him softly, "that you don't love me any more?"

He gave her a faint smile. "Why is it a woman will always ask that, no matter how well she knows the answer?"

She stared at him, sick in the pit of her stomach. The very posture of his body showed boredom and weariness, his face had the finality of a man who understands his feelings perfectly. Was it possible? Was he really and truly tired of her? She had had warning enough for the past four years, both from him and from others, but she had ignored it, refusing to believe that he could fall out of love with her as he had fallen out of love with other women.

"What do you intend to do?" Her voice was now just a whisper.

"That's what I've come to discuss with you. Since we don't love each other any longer—"

"Oh, but Sire!" she protested swiftly. "I love *you!* It's just that you—"

He gave her a look of frank disgust. "Barbara, for the love of God spare me that. I suppose you think I've pretended to myself that you were in love with me. Well—I haven't. I was beyond the age of such illusions when I met you. And if I loved you once, which I suppose I did, I don't any longer. I think it's time we make a new arrangement."

"A new— You intend to turn me out?"

He gave a short unpleasant laugh. "That would be rather

792

like turning the rabbit to the hounds, wouldn't it? They'd tear you to pieces in two minutes." His black eyes swung over her face, amused and contemptuous. "No, my dear. I'll deal fairly with you. We'll come to a settlement of some kind."

"Oh." Barbara relaxed visibly. That was another matter again. He was still willing to "deal fairly," to come to a "settlement." She thought she knew well enough how to handle that. "I want to please your Majesty. But I hope you'll give me leave to think this over for a day or two. I've got my children to consider. No matter what happens to me I want them to have the things they should—"

"They'll be taken care of. Study your terms then—I'll come here Thursday at this hour to discuss them with you."

He got up, made her a casual bow, snapped his fingers at the dogs and left her without a backward glance. Barbara sat staring at the foot of the bed, puzzled, uneasy, worried. And then she heard him talking softly and there was Wilson's excited giggle. Suddenly she jumped out of bed and shouted:

"Wilson! Wilson, come in here! I need you!"

Thursday she met him at the door of her chamber, beautifully gowned and painted, and though he had half expected to find her in tears of hysterical anger she was gracious and charming —the old pose he had seen so seldom these past two or three years. The maids were dismissed and they sat down alone, face to face, each taking the other's measure. Barbara knew at once that he had not changed his mind, as she had hoped he would, during that interval.

She gave him a piece of paper, a neat itemized list written in black ink, and sat drumming her nails on the arm of the chair as he read it; her eyes roamed the room but now and again flickered back to him. He scanned the page hastily, slowly his eyebrows contracted and he gave a low whistle. Without looking up at her he began to read:

"Twenty-five thousand to clear your debts. Ten thousand a year allowance. A duchy for yourself and earldoms for the boys—" He glanced across swiftly, a half humorous scowl on his face. "Ods-fish, Barbara! You must think I'm King Midas. Remember, I'm that pauper, Charles Stuart—whose country has just gone through the worst plague and fire in history and is up to its ears in debt for war. You damned well know I haven't the means to support all this!" He gave the paper a whack with his hand and tossed it aside.

Barbara shrugged, smiling. "Why, Sire, how should I know? You've given me more than that in the past—and now you want to get rid of me, though no fault of my own— Why, Lord, Your Majesty, only in ordinary decency you should give me *that* much. It takes a deal of money to look a hostile world in the face. You know that as well as anyone. I might as well be dead as try to get along on less once you've cast me off— Why, my life wouldn't be worth the living!"

"I have no intention of making your life miserable to you. But you know I can't possibly make such an arrangement as this."

"On the other hand, the mother of five of your children shouldn't have to beg for her living when you grow tired of her, should she? How would it look for you, Sire, if the world knew you'd turned me off with a stingy settlement?"

"Has it ever occurred to you that in France there are several very comfortable nunneries where a lady of your religion might live well and happily on under five hundred pound a year?"

For an instant Barbara stared at him. All at once she gave a sharp explosive laugh. "Damn me, but you do have the drollest wit! Come, now: Can you imagine me in a nunnery?"

He smiled in spite of himself. "Not very well," he admitted. "Still, I can't make any such allowance as that."

"Well, then—perhaps we can agree another way."

"And what way might that be?"

"Why can't I stay on here? Perhaps you don't love me any more, but surely it can't matter to you if I live in the Palace. I'll trouble you no farther—you go your way and I'll go mine. After all, isn't it unfair to make me wretched because you've fallen out of love with me?"

He knew how much sincerity there was in what she said, and yet he had begun to think that perhaps that would be the easiest way, after all. No sudden break to wrench them apart, no unpleasant scenes of tears and recriminations—but a slow and easy drifting. Someday she would go of her own accord. Yes, that might be best. At any rate it would be the least trouble —and immediate expense—to him.

He got to his feet. "Very well then, madame. Trouble me no more and we'll get along well enough. Live any way you like, but live as quietly as you can. And one thing more: If you tell no one about this, no one will know it—for I'll not mention it."

"Oh, thank you, Sire! You *are* kind!"

She came to stand before him and looked up into his face, her eyes coaxing, inviting him. She still hoped that a kiss and half an hour in bed could change everything—expunge the animosity and distrust which had grown out of the passionate infatuation with which they had begun. He stared at her steadily and then, very faintly, he smiled; his hand made a light gesture and he walked beyond her and out of the room. Barbara turned to watch him, stunned, as though she had had a slap in the face.

A couple of days later she went into the country to have an abortion, for this child, she knew, he would never own. But it had also occurred to her that if she was gone for a few weeks he would forget everything that had been unpleasant between them and begin to miss her—he would send for her to come back, as he had done in the old days. Someday, she told herself, he'll love me again, I know he will. Next time we meet, things will be different.

CHAPTER FIFTY-FIVE

SHE LIVED AT the top of Maypole Alley, a narrow little street off Drury Lane, in a two-room lodging which looked exactly as she always did—careless and untidy, with nothing in its place. Silk stockings were flung over chair-backs, a soiled smock lay in a heap on the floor just beside the bed, orange-peelings littered the table and empty ale-glasses stood about, unwashed.

The fireplace was heaped with ashes and apparently had not been swept out for years. Dust coated the furniture and puffs of it drifted over the floor, for the girl she hired to come in and clean had not been there for several days. Everything suggested an abandonment to chaos, a gay headlong contempt for stodgy tidiness.

In the middle of the floor Nell Gwynne was dancing.

Barefooted, she whirled and spun, twisted her lithe body and flung her skirts high, completely unselfconscious, absorbed and happy. In one chair sprawled Charles Hart, watching her through half-shut lids, and sitting astraddle another was John Lacy, who also acted for the King's Company and who also had been Nelly's lover. A fourteen- or fifteen-year-old boy, a street-musician they had called in, stood nearby and scraped on his cheap fiddle.

When at last she stopped and made them a curtsy so deep that her bowed head touched her knee, the men broke into hearty applause. Nelly looked up at them, eyes sparkling with eager delight, and still panting from the violent exertion she leaped to her feet.

"Did you like it? _Do_ you think I'm a better dancer than her?"

Hart waved his hand. "Better? Why, you make Moll Davis look clumsy as a pregnant cow!"

Nelly laughed, but her face changed swiftly. She reached for an orange and began to peel it, rolling out her lower lip in exaggerated pique. "Much good it does me! There's no one there to see me these days. Lord, the pit's been empty as a Dutchman's noddle ever since his Majesty gave her that diamond ring! They've all got to have a look at the King's latest whore."

"You'd think a new royal mistress wouldn't be such a curiosity any more," remarked Lacy, knocking out his pipe on the edge of the table, stepping on the ashes as they fell to the floor. "I can count a baker's dozen from the stage any day I like."

At that moment there was a loud rapping on the door and Nelly ran to open it. A liveried footman stood there. "Mrs. Knight presents her service to you, madame, and would like a word with you. She waits below in her coach."

Nelly glanced back at the two men from over her shoulder and screwed up her face to wink. "Speak of the Devil—here's another one below. You'll find sack and brandy in the cupboard. Maybe there's something to eat in the food-hutch. I'll be back in a moment."

She disappeared, but an instant later returned to slide her feet into a pair of high-heeled, square-toed pumps, and then picking up her skirts she went swooping down the stairs and out into the street. A gilded coach-and-four stood there, the door held open by a footman. Mary Knight sat inside, her beautiful face painted an almost glistening white, and she reached out one jewelled arm to take hold of Nelly's wrist.

"Come, sweetheart—get in. I want to talk to you." Her voice was warm and sweet as a melody, and she smelled of some drowsy perfume.

Nelly obediently climbed in and flounced down beside her. Not at all conscious of her own griminess, she looked at Mary with passionate admiration. "Lord, Mary! I swear you're prettier every time I see you!"

"Pshaw, child. It's only that I wear fine clothes nowadays, and a jewel or so. By the way, whatever became of that pearl necklace my Lord Buckhurst gave you?"

Nell shrugged. "I sent it back to 'im."

"Sent it back? Good God! What for?"

"Oh—I don't know. What good is a string of pearls to me? My mother would have pawned it to buy brandy or to get Rose's husband out of Newgate." Rose was Nelly's sister.

"Sweetheart, let me tell you something. Never give *any-thing* back. Often enough by the time a woman's thirty she has nothing to live on but the presents made her when she was young."

But Nelly was just seventeen and thirty was a thousand years away. "I've never been hungry. I'll live somehow. What did you want to see me for, Mary?"

"I want to take you calling. Are you dressed? Is your hair combed?" The light from the torches was too unsteady to see distinctly.

"Well enough, I warrant. Who're we calling on?"

"A gentleman named Charles Stuart." She paused a moment, for Nelly sat in silence, not realizing whom she meant. "His Majesty, King Charles II!" The words rolled off her tongue like the flare of trumpets and a chill ran over Nelly's flesh, along her arms and down her back.

"King Charles!" she whispered. "He wants to see me!"

"He does. And he asked me, as an old friend, to carry the invitation."

Nelly sat perfectly rigid, staring straight ahead of her. "Holy Mother of God!" she whispered. And then she flew into a sudden tempest of indecision and fright. "But I'm all undone! My hair's down! I haven't got any stockings on! Oh, Mary! I *can't* go!"

Mary put one hand over hers. "Of course you can, sweetheart. I'll lend you my cloak. And I've got a comb here."

"Oh, but Mary—I can't! I just can't!" She stabbed about for an excuse and suddenly remembered Hart and Lacy waiting upstairs for her. She started to get out. "I've got callers myself, I just remembered. I—"

Mary took her arm and firmly pulled her back again. "He's expecting you." She leaned forward and rapped on the front wall of the coach. "Drive away!"

It was only a little more than half a mile to Whitehall and Nelly spent that time dragging Mary's comb through the snarls of her coarse thick blonde hair, her stomach fluttering and the palms of her hands cold and wet. Her throat was so tight she could scarcely speak, though from time to time she murmured, "Oh, Jesus!"

At the Palace she got out, Mary's cloak flung over her shoulders, and just before she ran off Mary slid the pearl drops from her ears and handed them to her. "Wear these, sweetheart. I'll wait for you to drive you home."

Nelly took them, made a step or two away, then turned suddenly and came back to the coach. "I can't go, Mary! I can't! He's the King!"

"Go along, child. He's waiting for you."

Nelly closed her eyes hard and murmured a prayer and then crossed the courtyard, went through the door Mary had pointed out and along a winding hall-way, down a flight of stairs to another door; there she knocked. A footman opened it, she gave him her name, and was admitted. She found herself in a handsomely furnished room. There were gold-framed portraits on the walls, a great carved fireplace, embroidered chairs from France. For a long moment she stood just inside the doorway, staring about her in awe, nervously cleaning the dirt from beneath her finger-nails.

After two or three minutes William Chiffinch came in, well-fed and silky, with pouches under his eyes and a sensual mouth, belching gently as though he had just risen from a too rich meal. His appearance put her somewhat at ease, for he was no more fearsome than any other man, even if he was the King's Page of the Backstairs.

He raised his eyebrows faintly as he saw her standing there. "Madame Gwynne?"

Nelly gave a little curtsy. "Aye."

"You know, I suppose, madame, that it is not I who sent for you?"

"Lord, I hope not, sir!" said Nelly. And then she added quickly, for fear of having hurt his feelings, "Not that I wouldn't be pleased if it had been—"

"I understand, madame. And do you feel that you are correctly costumed for an interview with his Majesty?"

Nelly glanced down at her blue woollen gown and found it spotted with food and wine, stained in the armpits from many weeks of wear; there was a rent low in the skirt through which her red linen petticoat showed. She was unconcerned about her dress, as she was about all her appearance, and took her prettiness very much for granted. Though she was paid the good wage of sixty pounds a year she spent it carelessly, entertaining friends who came to see her, buying brandy for her fat sodden mother and gifts for Rose, tossing coins to every beggar who approached her in the streets.

"It's what I was wearing, sir, when Mrs. Knight called for me. I didn't know—I can go back and change—I have a very fine gown for special occasions—blue satin, with a silver petticoat and—"

"There isn't time now. But here—try some of this."

He crossed the room, picked up a bottle and gave it to her. Nelly took out the stopper, rolling her eyes ecstatically as she smelled the heavy-sweet odour. Then she tipped the bottle against her bodice until the perfume made a wet round circle, dabbing more of it on her breasts and wrists and live curling hair.

"That's enough!" warned Chiffinch, and took it away from her. He glanced at a clock in a standing walnut case. "It's time. Come with me."

He walked out of the room and for an instant Nelly hesitated, gulping hard once, her heart pounding until she felt scarcely able to breathe; then with sudden resolution she lifted her skirts and followed him. They went out into a dim hall-way. Chiffinch lighted a candle from one which was burning there, stuck it into a brass holder and, turning, gave it to her.

"Here, this will light you up the stairs. At the top there's a door which will be unlocked. Open it and go into the ruelle, but don't make a sound until his Majesty comes for you. He may be occupied in talking to one of the ministers or writing a letter."

She stared solemnly at him, nodding her head, and glanced up uncertainly toward the invisible door. In her trembling hand the candle sent shaking shadows across the walls. She looked back to Chiffinch again, as if for moral support, but he merely stood and stared at her, thinking that the King would never send again for this unkempt creature. Slowly she began to mount the stairs, holding up her skirts with her free hand; but her knees felt so weak she was sure she would never be able to reach the top. She kept on and on, feeling as though she mounted some endless flight in a terrifying dream. Chiffinch stood and watched her until he saw the door open, her profile silhouetted as she paused to blow out the candle, and then with a shrug of his shoulders he went back to his supper guests.

But he was mistaken, for not many nights later she was there again, clean this time and dressed in her blue satin and silver-cloth gown. There was about her still, however, a certain joyous carelessness, as though her spirits were too exuberant, too buoy-

800

antly full to take time with trifles. And this time Chiffinch greeted her with a smile, caught in her spell.

Nelly could not get over the wonder of this thing that had happened to her; she felt almost as though she were the first mistress Charles had taken. "Oh, Mary!" she cried breathlessly that first night when she came back out to the coach. "He's wonderful! Why—he treated me just like—just like I was a princess!" And suddenly she had burst into tears, laughing and crying at once. I've fallen in love with him! she thought. Nelly Gwynne—daughter of the London streets, common trollop and public performer—in love with the King of England! Oh, what a fool! And yet, who could help it?

Not long after that Charles asked her what yearly allowance she would want and though she laughed and told him that she was ready to serve the Crown for nothing, he insisted that she name a price. The next time she came she asked Chiffinch what she should say.

"You're worth five hundred a year, sweetheart—just for that smile."

But when she came downstairs again she seemed sad and subdued and Chiffinch asked her what had happened. Nell looked at him for a moment, her chin began to quiver and suddenly she was crying. "Oh! He laughed at me! He asked me and I said five hundred pound and—and he laughed!" Chiffinch put his arms about her and while she sobbed he stroked the back of her head, telling her that she must be a little patient—that one day soon she would have much more than five hundred pounds from him.

She did not care about the money, but she did care a great deal that he should not consider her to be worth five hundred pounds—when he had spent much more than that on a single ring for Moll Davis.

Nelly and Moll Davis were well acquainted, for all the actors knew one another and knew also everything that happened in that small bohemian world which hung on the fringes of the Court. And because she liked people and was not inclined to be jealous she liked Moll despite their rivalry in the theatre —and now in another sphere—until she heard that Moll had been making fun of her because Charles had refused her the price she had asked.

"Nelly's a common slut," said Moll. "She won't amuse him long."

Moll herself made great capital of the rumour that she was the illegitimate daughter of the Earl of Berkshire, though actually her father was a blacksmith and she had been a milkmaid before coming to London to try her fortune.

"A common slut, am I?" said Nelly, when she heard that. "Well, perhaps I am. I don't pretend to be anything else. But we'll see whether I know how to amuse his Majesty or not!"

And she set out to visit Moll with a large box of home-made candy tucked under her arm. She threaded her way up one narrow crooked little alley and down another, flipping coins to a dozen beggars, waving an arm in greeting at various women hanging out their windows, stopping to talk to a little girl selling a platter of evil-smelling fish—she gave her a guinea to buy shoes and a cloak, for the winter was setting in. The day was sunny but cold and she walked along swiftly, her hair covered with a hood, her long woollen cloak slapping about her.

Moll lived not far from Maypole Alley in a second-floor lodging much like Nell's own, though she had been bragging that his Majesty was going to take a fine house and furnish it for her. Nelly rapped at the door, greeted Moll with a broad grin, and stepped inside while the girl still stood staring at her. Her eye went quickly round the room, picking out evidences of new luxury: yellow-velvet drapes at the windows, a fine carved chair or two, the silver-backed mirror Moll was holding in her hand.

"Well, Moll!" Nelly tossed back her hood, unfastened the button at her throat. "Aren't you going to make me welcome? Oh! Maybe you've got company!" She pretended surprise, as though she had just noticed that Moll wore only her smock and starched ruffled petticoat, with her feet in mules and her hair down her back.

Moll stared at her suspiciously, searching for the motive of this visit, and her plump dainty-featured little face did not smile. She knew that Nell must have heard the things she had been saying about her. She lifted her chin and pursed her lips, full of airs and newly acquired hauteur. "No," she said. "I'm all alone. If you must know—I'm dressing to see his Majesty—at ten o'clock."

"Heavens!" cried Nell, glancing at the clock. "Then you must hurry! It's nearly six!" Nelly was amused. Imagine taking four hours to dress—even for the King! "Well, come on, then. We can gossip while you're making ready. Here, Moll—I brought you something. Oh, it's really nothing very much. Some sweets Rose and I made—with nuts in, the kind you always like."

Moll, disarmed by this thoughtful gesture, reached for the box as Nell held it toward her, and finally she smiled. "Oh, thank you, Nell! How kind of you to remember how much I love sweets!" She opened it and took up a large piece, popped it into her mouth and began to munch, licked her fingers and extended the box to Nell.

Nelly declined. "No, thanks, Moll. Not just now. I ate some while we were making it."

"Oh, it's delicious, Nell! Such an unusual flavour, too! Come on in, my dear—I have some things to show you. Lord, I vow and swear there can't be a more generous man in Europe than his Majesty! He all but pelts me with fine gifts! Just *look* at this jewel case. Solid gold, and every jewel on it is real—I know because I had a jeweller appraise it. And these are real sapphires on this patch-box too. And look at this lace fan! Have you ever seen anything to compare? Just think, he had his sister send it from Paris, especially for me." She thrust two more pieces of candy into her mouth and her eyes ran over the gown Nelly was wearing. It was made of red linsey-woolsey, a material warm and serviceable enough, but certainly neither beautiful nor luxurious. "But then of course you didn't want to wear your diamond necklace coming through the streets."

Nell felt like crying or slapping her face, but she merely smiled and said softly, "I haven't any diamond necklace. He hasn't given me anything."

Moll lifted her brows in pretended surprise and sat down to finish painting her face. "Oh, well—don't fret about it, my dear. Probably he will—if he should take a fancy to you." She picked

803

up another piece of candy and then began to dust Spanish paper onto her cheeks with a hare's foot. Nelly sat with her hands clasped over one knee and watched her.

Moll struggled with her hair for at least an hour, asking Nelly to put in a bodkin here or take one out there. "Oh, gad!" she cried at last. "A lady simply can't do her own head! I vow I must have a woman—I'll speak to him about it tonight."

When the royal coach arrived at shortly after nine Moll gave an excited shriek, crammed the last three pieces of candy into her mouth, snatched up mask and fan and muff and gloves and went out of the room in a swirl of satins and scent. Nelly followed her down to the coach, wished her luck and waved her goodbye. But when the coach rattled off she stood and watched it and laughed until tears came to her eyes and her sides began to ache.

Now, Mrs. Davis! We'll see what airs you give yourself next time we meet!

The following day Nelly went to the Duke's Theatre with young John Villiers—Buckingham's distant relation, somewhere in the sprawling Villiers tribe—to see whether her rival dared show herself on the boards after what had happened the night before. And Villiers—because he hoped to have a favour from her after the play—paid out four shillings for each of them and they took their seats in one of the middle-boxes, directly over the stage where Moll could not miss seeing them if she was there.

As they sat down Nell became conscious that there were two men in the box directly adjoining theirs and that both of them had watched her as she came in. She glanced at them, a smile on her lips—and then she gave a little gasp of horrified surprise and one hand went to her throat. It was the King and his brother, both apparently incognito for they were in ordinary dress, and the King wore neither the Star nor the Garter. In fact, their suits were far more conservative than those of most of the gallants buzzing away down in Fop Corner, next the stage.

Charles smiled, nodding his head slightly in greeting, and York gave her an intent stare. Nelly managed to return the smile but she wanted desperately to get up and run and would, in fact, have done so but that she did not care to draw the attention of the entire theatre upon them. And furthermore Betterton, wrapped in the traditional long black cloak, had now come out onto the apron of the stage to speak the prologue.

She stayed, but even after the prologue was over and the curtains had been drawn for the first act she sat rigid and tense, not daring to move her head, scarcely seeing the stage at all. Finally Villiers shook her elbow and whispered in her ear.

"What's the matter with you, Nell? You look as though you're in a fit!"

"Shh! I think I am!"

Villiers looked annoyed, not knowing whether to take her seriously or not. "D'you want to go?"

"No. Of course not. Be still."

She did not even glance at him, but her cheeks had begun to burn for she was aware that Charles was looking at her, and he was so close that by leaning over slightly she could have touched his arm. And then suddenly she turned her head and stared him full in the eyes, questioningly. He grinned, his teeth shining white beneath his black mustache, and Nelly gave a relieved little laugh. Then he wasn't angry! He had thought it a good joke too.

"What brings you here?" asked Charles, speaking in a low voice so as to attract no more attention than could be helped from those around them.

"Why—a—I came to see if it's true Moll Davis is a better dancer than I am."

"And do you imagine she'll be dancing today?" His eyes sparkled at her obviously painful embarrassment and confusion. "I should think she might be sick at home with the colic."

In spite of herself Nell blushed and dropped her lashes, unable to face him. "I'm sorry, Sire. I wanted to pay her back for—" Suddenly she looked up at him, eager and serious. "Oh, forgive me, your Majesty! I'll never do such a thing again!"

At this Charles laughed outright and his familiar deep voice drew several glances. "Give your apologies to her, not to me. I haven't spent such an entertaining evening in a long while." He leaned closer, put the back of his hand to his mouth and whispered confidentially, "To tell you truly, madame, I think Mrs. Davis is mightily out of humour with you."

With sudden boldness Nelly retorted, "Well, she must be mighty simple or she wouldn't have been taken in with a stale old trick like that! She should have known it was physicked after the first bite!"

At that moment Moll came whirling out onto the stage below them, spinning round and round, a small graceful figure in her close-fitted boy's breeches and thin white-linen blouse. A spontaneous roar of shouts and applause went up. Charles gave Nelly a brief glance, one eyebrow lifted as much as to say, Well, she did dare to come after all. Then he returned his attention to the stage and it was not long before the girl on it saw him and smiled, as brazenly self-assured as though nothing at all unusual had happened the night before.

But just the next moment she saw Nell sitting there beside him, leaning with her elbows on the railing, grinning down at her. For an instant Moll's face lost its smile, then immediately she stuck it back on again. Swiftly Nelly raised her thumb to her nose and waggled her fingers, but not so swiftly that his Majesty missed the impudent gesture. When Moll's dance was over she flung several kisses toward the middle-box; then she was gone and she appeared no more, for she had no part in the play that afternoon.

From time to time as the play progressed Charles and Nelly exchanged opinions on the acting, a song, a bit of stage-business, costuming and scenery, or the rest of the audience. Villiers was beginning to look disgruntled, but York glanced now and again at his brother's newest mistress with pleased interest, liking her expressive face, her gaiety and the spontaneous happy laugh that crinkled her blue eyes till they all but disappeared.

When at last the play was done and they were getting up to leave Charles casually remarked, "Now that I think on it, I don't believe I've eaten any supper yet. Have you, James?"

"No. No, I can't say that I have."

Nelly gave Villiers a swift nudge in the ribs with her elbow and when he did not take his cue quick enough she kicked him sharply on the ankle. He winced at that and promptly said: "Your Majesty, if it would not be too great an impertinence, may I beg the honour of your company, and his Highness's company, at supper with me?"

Charles and York accepted instantly and all of them left the theatre together, hailed a hackney and set out for the Rose Tavern. It was already dark, though not yet six-thirty, and the rain came in gusts. Charles and York were not recognized at the Rose, for both men had their hats pulled low and cloaks flung across their chins, and Nelly wore a full vizard. The host escorted them upstairs to a private room, which they asked for, with no more ado than if they had been any trio of men bringing a wench to supper.

Villiers was not very gay, for he resented the King's intrusion, but Charles and James and Nelly enjoyed themselves immensely. They ordered all the most expensive and delicious food the famous kitchen prepared, drank champagne, cracked raw oysters, and ate until they had turned the table into a litter of shells and bones and empty bottles. It was two hours before Charles suddenly snapped his fingers and said that he must be on his way. His wife was expecting him in the Drawing-Room that night to hear a newly arrived Italian eunuch who was supposed to have the sweetest voice in Christendom.

With the first enthusiasm he had shown Villiers jumped to his feet and bellowed downstairs for the bill. The waiter came in as Charles was holding Nelly's cloak for her and, because he was obviously the eldest, presented the bill to him. Charles, a little drunk, glanced at it and gave a low whistle, experimentally put his fingers into the various pockets of his coat and each time brought them out empty.

"Not a shilling. What about you, James?"

James likewise searched his pockets and wagged his head. Nelly burst into peals of delighted laughter. "Ods-fish!" she cried. "But this is the poorest company that ever I was in at a tavern!"

The royal brothers both looked to Villiers who tried not to show his irritation as he gave his last shilling to pay the bill. Then they went downstairs where both Charles and James kissed

Nelly goodbye before they climbed into a hackney and set out for Whitehall, hanging out the coach windows to wave back at her. She flung them enthusiastic kisses.

By the next day the story was all over the Palace and was being told in the tiring-rooms and at the 'Change, in the coffee-houses and taverns—to the vast amusement of everyone but Moll Davis. And she was angrier than ever when a bouquet arrived for her, a huge cluster of a stinking weed Nelly had found growing somewhere along Drury Lane.

CHAPTER FIFTY–SIX

AMBER LOVED BEING a part of the Court.

Familiarity had not disillusioned her and as far as she was concerned it was still the great world and everything that happened in it more exciting and important than it could possibly have been anywhere else. Buckingham himself was not more convinced than she that they were God's chosen people, the lords and ladies of all creation. And now she was one of them! With no protest at all she was soon sucked into the maelstrom of Court life and whirled about in a mad darkness.

She went to suppers and plays and balls. She was invited everywhere and her own invitations were never refused, for it was dangerously impolitic to slight one of the King's mistresses. Her drawing-room was often more crowded than the Queen's and she kept several gambling-tables going at once: ombre, trente-et-quarante, lanterloo, various dice games. The street-beggars had begun to call upon her by name, a sure sign of importance. Hack poets and playwrights hung about her ante-rooms and wanted to dedicate a new play or sonnet to her. The first young man to whom she played generous patron—making him a gift of fifty pounds, but not troubling to read the poem before it was published—had written a virile and malevolent satire on the Court and everyone in it, including her.

She spent money as if she had inherited the Privy Purse, and though Shadrac Newbold made investments for her and kept her accounts she paid no attention at all to what was coming in or going out. The fortune which Samuel had left still seemed to her inexhaustible.

And anyway there were a thousand ways to make money at Court—if the King liked you: Once he allowed her to hold a lottery of Crown plate. He leased her six hundred acres of Crown land in Lincolnshire for five years at a low figure and she subleased it at a high one. He granted her the profits for a one-year period from all vessels moored in the Pool. She got the money from the sale of underwood in certain coppices in the New Forest. She engaged in two of the Court's most lucrative businesses: begging estates and stock-jobbing. Charles gave her gifts from the Irish taxes and all the foreign ambassadors made her presents, which varied in value according to the supposed degree of her influence over the King. She could have lived in fine style from these sources alone.

Just before Christmas she began to have her rooms completely redecorated and furnished and for four months they were filled with workmen painting and hammering and scraping. The furniture was covered over with heavy white canvas to prevent spotting, buckets of gilt and coloured paint stood everywhere, men on tall ladders dabbed at the ceiling and took measurements for a hanging. Tansy followed them from room to room, curious and interested. Monsieur le Chien snapped at their heels and barked all day long and sometimes, if his mistress was not about, he was secretly kicked.

Amber sent to Lime Park for all its furnishings and spent several days going over Radclyffe's possessions, which she had obtained with the King's connivance.

Among them she found a long but still unfinished poem: "The Kingdom Come. A Satire." A quick glance told her that it had been written at Lime Park during the spring and summer months of 1666, from information gathered while he had been in London, just after their marriage. It was obscene, cruel, bitterly malicious, but brilliant in style and perception. Amber read it for the malice and obscenity, recognized those qualities instantly but missed everything else—and threw it contemptuously into the fire. There were other papers: the history of the family possessions, letters (one which had evidently been written by the girl whom he had loved and who had disappeared during the Civil Wars), many alchemical recipes, sheaves of notes, bills for pictures and other objects which he had collected, translations he had made from Latin and Greek, essays on a variety of subjects. With spiteful pleasure she destroyed them all.

She came upon a skull with a recipe attached to it by thin copper wire. It was a cure for impotency and recommended that spring-water be drunk every morning from the skull of a man who had been murdered. Amber considered this to be very funny and it even increased her contempt for the Earl. She kept it to show the King and he appropriated it for his own laboratory, saying that he might have a need for that remedy himself some day.

What she liked of his hangings and pictures and furniture Amber saved for her own apartments; the rest she put up at auction. Radclyffe's lifelong interest in everything beautiful and rare, the years of collecting, the infinite labour and expense—all were sold now to people he had despised, or used as bric-a-brac by a woman for whom he had had nothing but scornful contempt. Amber's triumph, complete and terrible, was only the triumph of the living over the helpless dead. But it pleased her a great deal.

Charles and his Court had brought back from France with them a changed taste in furniture, as in everything else. The new style was at once more delicate and more lavish. Walnut replaced the heavy solid pieces of carved oak, tapestry was considered old-fashioned, and rich Persian or Turkish carpets lay on bare floors which were no longer covered with rushes to hide dirt and keep out cold. No extravagance was beyond good taste —and the ladies and courtiers vied with one another as to who could achieve the most spectacular effect. Amber was at no loss among them.

She had some walls knocked out and others put up to change the proportions of the rooms—she wanted everything on a scale of prodigious size and grandeur. Even the anteroom was very large—which was necessary to accommodate all those who attended upon her—but its only furnishings were wall-hangings of green raw silk, a pair of life-sized black-marble Italian statues, and a battery of gilt chairs.

The drawing-room, which fronted directly upon the river, was seventy-five feet long and twenty-five feet wide. Its walls were hung with black-and-gold-striped silk and at night the draperies could be pulled to cover all window-space. Pearl-embroidered rugs were scattered over the floor. The delicate, graceful, deeply carved furniture was coated thickly with gold-leaf, and the cushions were emerald velvet. Because Charles preferred a buffet style of dining-service there were many little tables about and she gave her suppers in that room. Above the fireplace hung a portrait of Amber impersonating St. Catherine —all the Court ladies liked to have themselves drawn as saints. Catherine had been a queen and so Amber wore a magnificent gown with a crown upon her head; she carried a book, the martyr's palm, and beside her lay the symbol of suffering, a broken wheel. Her expression was very thoughtful and sedate.

A small anteroom hung in white—where Radclyffe's Italian blackamoor stood on a gold table before a mirror—opened from the drawing-room into the bed-chamber, the furnishings of which cost Amber more than all the rest of the apartment together.

The entire room, floor to ceiling, was lined with mirrors— brought from Venice and smuggled through the port officers by his Majesty's connivance. The floor was laid with black Genoese marble, supposed to be the finest in Europe. On the ceiling an artist named Streater had depicted the loves of Jupiter, and it swarmed with naked full-breasted, round-hipped women in a variety of attitudes with men and beasts.

The bed, an immense four-posted structure with a massive tester, was covered with beaten silver and hung with scarlet velvet. And every other article of furniture in the room was thickly plated with silver; each chair, from the smallest stool to the great settee before the fireplace, was cushioned in scarlet. The window-hangings were silver-embroidered scarlet velvet. Above the fireplace and sunk flush with the wall was a more intimate and considerably more typical portrait of Amber, painted by Peter Lely. She lay on her side on a heap of black cushions, unashamedly naked, staring out with a slant-eyed smile at whoever paused to look.

The room seemed to possess a violent, almost savage personality. No human being had a chance of seeming important in it. And yet it was the envy of the Palace, for it was the most extravagant gesture anyone had yet made. Amber, not at all awed by it, loved it for its arrogance, its uncompromising challenge, its crude and boisterous beauty. It represented to her everything she had ever believed she wanted from life; and all she had got. It was her symbol of success.

But it was not enough, now she had it, to make her happy.

For though her days were perpetually busy, occupied with a never-ceasing round of gossip, new clothes, gambling, play-going, supper-giving, schemes and counter-schemes, she was never able to make herself forget Bruce Carlton. He would not leave her, no matter what she was doing, and though usually her longing for him was a low-keyed minor unhappiness it surged sometimes into tremendous and monumental music which seemed unbearable. When that happened, always when she least expected it, she would think and almost wish that she would die. It would seem impossible then that she could exist for another moment without him, and her yearning, wild and desperate, would reach out blindly—to inevitable disappointment.

About mid-March Almsbury arrived in London alone to attend to some business matters and amuse himself for a few weeks. Amber had not seen him since the previous August and the first question she asked was whether or not he had heard from Bruce.

"No," said the Earl. "Have you?"

"Have I?" she demanded crossly. "Of course not! He's never written me a letter in his life! But it'd seem he might at least let *you* know how he does!"

Almsbury shrugged. "Why should he? He's busy—and as long as I don't hear from him I know everything's well with him. If it wasn't he'd let me know."

"Are you sure?"

Her eyes slipped him a stealthy glance. They were in her bedroom, Amber in a dressing-gown lying on a little day-bed with her trim ankles crossed, while Tansy sat on the floor beside her contemplating the frayed toes of his shoes. Though he could be very amusing, usually he did not speak unless spoken to and was quiet in a way which suggested some strange inner tranquillity, an almost animal self-sufficiency.

"What do you mean by that?" Almsbury's eyes narrowed slightly as he looked at her. "If you're hoping that something's happened to Corinna you may as well forget it. Hoping for another woman to die will never get you what you want, you know that as well as I do. He never intended to marry you anyway."

There were times when some suppressed impatience or cruelty in the Earl crept into his attitude toward her. She took him so much for granted that it never occurred to her to wonder about the cause, though she was always very quick to take offense when it appeared.

"How do you know! He might have, now I'm a countess—if it hadn't been for her—"

Her eyes hardened as she spoke of Corinna and her upper lip tightened stubbornly. But in a sense, she was almost glad to have Corinna as the reason and excuse for all her troubles—she could never otherwise have explained to herself or anyone else his refusal to marry her.

"Amber, my dear," he said now, and his eyes and the tone of his voice had softened with a kind of affectionate pity. "There's no use pretending to yourself, is there? He didn't marry her because she's rich and titled. Probably he wouldn't have married her if she hadn't been—no man in his position would—but if that was all he wanted he'd have married long ago. No, sweetheart—you might as well be honest with yourself. He loves her."

"But he loves me too!" she cried desperately. "Oh, he does, Almsbury! You know he does!" Suddenly her voice and eyes grew wistful. "*You* think he loves me, don't you?"

Almsbury smiled and reached across to take her hand. "My

poor little darling. Yes, I think he does—and sometimes I almost think you'd have loved him even if he had married you."

"Oh, of course I would!" she cried and then, half-ashamed: "Stop teasing me, Almsbury." She glanced nervously away, feeling foolish. But all at once the words burst forth in a rush. "Oh, I *do* love him, Almsbury! You can't imagine how much I love him! I'd do anything—anything in the world to get him! And I'd always love him—if I saw him every day and every night for a thousand years! Oh, you know it's true, Almsbury—I've *never* loved another man—I never could!" Then, seeing some strange look come into his eyes, she was afraid that she had hurt him. "Oh, of course I love you, Almsbury—but in a different way— I—"

"Never mind, Amber. Don't try to explain yourself—I know more about it than you do, anyway. You're in love with three of us: the King, and Bruce—and me. And each one of us, I think, loves you. But you won't get much happiness from any of it— because you want more than we're willing to give. There's not one of us you can get hold of the way you got hold of that poor devil of a young captain—what was his name?—or the old dotard who willed you his money. And do you want to know why? I'll tell you. The King loves you—but no better than he's loved a dozen other women and will one day love a dozen more. No woman on earth can hurt him, because he depends on them for nothing but physical pleasure. His sister is the only woman he really loves—but that's neither here nor there so far as we're concerned. Bruce loves you—but there are other things he loves more. And now there's another woman he loves more. And last of all, darling—I love you too. But I've got no illusions about you. I know what you are and I don't care—so you'll never hurt me very much either."

"Ye gods, Almsbury! Why should I want to hurt you—or anyone else? What the devil put that maggot into your head?"

"No woman's ever satisfied unless she knows she can hurt the man who loves her. Come, now, be honest—it's true, isn't it? You've always thought you could make me miserable, if you ever wanted to try, haven't you?" His eyes watched her steadily.

Amber smiled at him—the smile of a pretty woman who

knows she is being admired. "Maybe I have," she admitted at last. "Are you sure I couldn't?"

For an instant he sat motionless, and then all at once he got to his feet; his white teeth were showing in a broad grin. "No, sweetheart, you couldn't." He stood and looked at her, his face serious again. "I'll tell you one thing, though—if there's any man on earth you could have married and been happy—it's me."

Amber stared at him, amazed, and then, with a little laugh, she stood up. "Almsbury! What in the devil are you talking about? If there's one man I could have married and been happy it's Bruce, and you know it—"

"You're wrong about that." But as she started to protest he began walking toward the door and she strolled along beside him. "I'll see you in the Drawing-Room tonight—and we'll raffle for that hundred pound you won from me yesterday."

She laughed. "We can't, Almsbury! I spent it this morning— for a new gown!" And then, just as he went out the door, she laughed again. "Imagine *us* married!"

He gave her a wave of his hand, without turning, but as he disappeared a thoughtful puzzled frown drew at her eyebrows. Almsbury and me—married. The idea had never occurred to her before. She had never wanted to be married to anyone but Bruce Carlton and it still seemed incredible that she could have been married happily to anyone else—even Almsbury. But how strange he should have said that—Almsbury, who thought no better of matrimony than did any other man of sense and wit.

Oh, well—she shrugged her shoulders and went back to complete her toilet. What use was it thinking about that now?

Besides, she had matters of importance to attend to. Durand would be there soon to dress her hair, and Madame Rouvière was coming to consult about her gown for the King's birthday ball. She must decide whom to invite to her next supper— whether she should ask the French or the Spanish ambassador, and which one was likely to prove more generous in his gratitude. Should she ask Castlemaine, and let her steam all evening with jealous envy, or should she merely ignore her? Charles certainly would not care—nor would he leave the party at Barbara's behest as he had been known to do, several years ago. It pleased Amber immeasurably to have in her own hands the settling of such issues—virtual life and death for the great or small of the Palace.

And now, since the day was evidently going to be a fine one, she decided to go driving in Hyde Park in her new calèche—a tiny two-seated carriage, precarious to sit in, but nevertheless showing the rider at great advantage from head to foot. She had a new suit of gold velvet and mink-tails and she intended to handle the reins herself—the prospect was exciting, for there was no doubt she would create a great sensation.

When Frances Stewart, now Duchess of Richmond, arrived back in town there was wild excitement at Court. Once more the whole pattern of existence was broken into pieces and must be put together again—politicians, mistresses, even lackeys and footmen began to wonder and to scheme and juggle, hoping to save themselves no matter what happened. At the Groom Porter's Lodge they were betting that now Frances was a married woman she would have better sense than when she had been a virgin—they expected that she would soon occupy the place which had always been hers for the taking. And so, when she established herself at Somerset House and began to give vast entertainments, everyone went—not for Frances's sake, but for their own. The King, however, much to their surprise, was never present and seemed unaware even that she had returned.

If Frances was troubled by this show of indifference she concealed it well. But she was by no means the only woman whose position depended upon the King's favour who had cause for worry.

When Barbara came back from the country at the end of the year she had found the Countess of Danforth occupying her old place and two actresses flaunting his Majesty's infatuation before all the Town. Moll Davis had left the stage and was occupying a handsome house he had furnished for her, and Nell Gwynne was not secretive about her frequent backstairs visits to the Palace. Barbara let it be known that the King begged her every day to take him back again, but that she scorned him as a man and would have nothing from him but money. In her

816

heart, though, she was sick and afraid; she began to pay her young men great sums.

Charles, hearing of it, smiled a little sadly and shrugged his wide shoulders. "Poor Barbara. She's growing old."

But it was not only the women who furnished fodder for gossip. The Duke of Buckingham, too, continued to make himself conspicuous. Early in the new year the Earl of Shrewsbury was finally persuaded by his relatives that he must fight Buckingham and so he did, and was killed. After that the Duke took Lady Shrewsbury home with him to live, and when his patient little wife objected that such an arrangement was intolerable, he called a coach and sent her off to her father.

This amused Charles who said that his Grace could not possibly have devised a scheme to ruin him quicker with the Commons. But Buckingham had temporarily lost interest in the Commons and did not care what they thought of him—he could be faithful to his own plans no longer than to a woman.

Other events, less sensational but of more importance, were happening at the same time. Clarendon, though much against his will, had finally been forced by the King to flee the country, and all his daughter's enemies took gleeful advantage of his disgrace to slight her. But Anne bore their envious contempt with hauteur and indifference, and managed to hold her own court together by a superior cleverness and determination. She told herself that these fools and their jealous pettifogging could mean nothing to her, for one day a child of hers would sit upon England's throne—with every passing year the Queen's barrenness made it more sure that she was right.

When Clarendon had gone his government was replaced by the Cabal, so called because the first letters of their five names spelled the word. It was made up of Sir Thomas Clifford, the one honest gentleman among them and hence suspected of wearing a false front; Arlington, who was his friend but jealous of him; Buckingham, Ashley, and Lauderdale. They shared a common hatred of Clarendon and fear of his possible return to power, and an almost equal hatred of York. Otherwise they were divided among themselves. Each distrusted and was afraid of every other—and the King trusted none of them, but was satisfied that at last he had a government which was completely his tool. He was cleverer than any one of them, or all of them together.

And so they set out to govern the nation.

England signed an alliance with Holland, by means of which Charles succeeded in compromising the Dutch so that when he was ready to fight them again they would have no chance of getting France to help them out. He intended, in fact, to have France on his side in the next war and his correspondence with his sister was now directed toward that end. The Dutch pact, together with secret treaties signed recently with both France and Holland, had given England the balance of power in Europe—and though accomplished by the grossest political chicanery it was typical of the King's methods. For his charm and easygoing nature were a convenient shield, hiding from all but the most astute the fact that he was a cynical, selfish, and ruthlessly practical opportunist.

It was the Earl of Rochester who said that the three businesses of the age were politics, women, and drinking—and the first two, at least, were never quite separate.

Charles intensely disliked having a woman meddle in state affairs, but he found it impossible to keep them out. Accordingly he accepted, as he usually did, what he could not change. For as soon as a woman had attracted his attention or was known to be his mistress she was besieged on all sides—as the Queen never was—by petitions for help, offers of money in return for bespeaking a favour, proposals to ally herself with one or another of the Court factions. Amber had been involved in a dozen different projects before she was at Whitehall a fortnight. And as the months went by she wound herself tighter and closer into the web.

Buckingham, from the night of her presentation at Court, had seemed friendly—at least he always sided with her against Lady Castlemaine. Amber still mistrusted and despised him, but she took care he should not know it, for though he would make only a dubious friend he was sure to be a dangerous enemy. And she thought it less to her disadvantage to have him as the former.

818

But for several months they made no demands upon each other, and neither made any test of the other's good faith.

Then, one morning in late March, he paid her an unexpected call. "Well, my lord?" said Amber, somewhat surprised. "What brings *you* abroad so early?" It was not quite nine, and his Grace was seldom to be seen out of bed before midday.

"Early? This isn't early for me—it's late. I've not yet been abed. Have you a glass of sack? I'm damned dry."

Amber sent for some sharp white wine and anchovies and while they waited for it to be brought the Duke flung himself into a chair next the fireplace and began to talk.

"I've just come from Moor Fields. Gad, you never saw anything like it! The 'prentices have pulled down a couple of houses, Mother Cresswell is yowling like a woman run mad, and the whores are throwing chamber-pots at the 'prentices' heads. They say they're coming next to pull down the biggest whorehouse of 'em all." He gave a wave of his hand. "Whitehall."

Amber laughed and poured out a glass of wine for each of them. "And I doubt not they'll uncover more strumpets here than they'd ever find in Moor Fields."

Buckingham reached into a coat-pocket and took out a wrinkled sheet of paper. It was printed in careless uneven lines, the fresh black ink was smeared and several thumb-prints showed. He handed it to her.

"Have you seen this?"

Amber read it over hastily.

It bore the title, "Petition of the Poor Whores to my Lady Castlemaine"; and that was what it pretended to be, though judging by the spelling and satirical content it was almost certainly the work of some person living close to the Court. In coarse broad terms it called upon Barbara, as the chief whore in England, to come to the aid of the beleaguered profession she had helped to glorify. Amber realized at once that this must be another of the Duke's whimsical inventions to plague his cousin, for she knew that they had been quarrelling again, and she was both pleased to have Barbara humiliated and relieved that she herself had escaped.

She smiled at him, handing it back. "Has she seen it yet?"

"If she hasn't, she soon will. They're all over London. Vendors are hawking 'em outside the 'Change and on every street corner. I saw a tiler laugh to read it till he almost fell off the roof he was laying. Now, what kind of sorry devil would plague her Ladyship with such a libel as that?"

Amber gave him a wide-eyed look. "Lord, your Grace! Who, indeed? I can't think—can you?" She sipped her wine, savouring the salt taste of the anchovies.

For a moment they looked at each other, and then both of them grinned. "Well," said his Grace, "it's no matter, now it's been done. I suppose it's come to your ears his Majesty is making her a present of Berkshire House?"

Amber's black eyebrows twisted. "Yes, of course. She makes mighty sure it comes to everyone's ears, I'll warrant you. And what's more, she says he's going to create a duchy for her."

"Your Ladyship seems annoyed."

"Me—annoyed? Oh, no, my lord," protested Amber with polite sarcasm. "Why should *I* be annoyed, pray?"

"No reason at all, madame. No reason at all." He looked expansive and pleased with himself, enjoying the warmth from the fire, the good wine in his stomach, and some private knowledge of his own.

"I'd be much less annoyed if he was giving Berkshire House to *me!* And as for a duchy—there's nothing on earth I want so much!"

"Don't worry. One day you'll have it—when he wants to get rid of you, as someday he will."

She looked at him for a moment in silence. "Do you mean to say, my lord—" she began at last.

"I do, madame. She's through here at Whitehall. She's done for good and all. I wouldn't give a fig for the interest she's got left at Court."

But Amber was still skeptical. For eight years Barbara had ruled the Palace, interfered in state business, bullied her friends and tormented her enemies. She seemed as permanent and inalterable as the very bricks of the buildings.

"Well," said Amber. "I hope you're right. But only last night I saw her in the Drawing-Room and she said that Berkshire

House should be proof to all the world his Majesty still loves her."

Buckingham gave a snort. "Still loves her! He doesn't even lie with her any more. But of course she hopes we'll all believe her tale. For if the world thinks the King still loves her—why, that's as good as if he did, isn't it? But I know better. I know a thing or two the rest of you don't."

Amber did not doubt that, for his Grace had incalculable means of keeping himself well-posted. Little passed at White-hall, of small or great importance, which escaped his drag-net of spies and informers.

"Whatever your Grace knows," said Amber, "I hope is true."

"True? Of course it's true! Let me tell you something, mad-ame—I'm the means by which her Ladyship's complete and final downfall was accomplished." He seemed smug now and satisfied with himself, as though he had performed an act of unselfish service to the nation.

Amber looked at him narrowly. "I don't understand you, sir."

"Then I'll speak more plainly. I knew Old Rowley's wish to be rid of her—but I knew also the kind of bargain she'd try to drive. It was very simple: I merely told him that the love-letters she's been threatening to publish were burnt many years ago."

"And he believed you?" Amber was now inclined to think that he had ruined Barbara, duped the King, and was maneuver-ing to take some advantage of her.

"He not only believed me—it's the truth. I saw 'em burnt myself. In fact, I advised her to do it!" Suddenly he slapped his knee and laughed, but Amber continued to watch him care-fully, not at all convinced. "She's in a blazing fury. She says she'll have my head for that one day. Well, she can have it if she can get it—but Old Rowley's mighty well pleased with me just now—and I've got a mind to die with my head on. Let her scheme and plan how she may—her fangs have been drawn and she's helpless. You're looking somewhat cynical, madame. It can't be you think I'm lying?"

"I can believe you told him about the letters—but I can't believe he won't take her back again; he always has before. Why should he give her that house and promise her a duchy if he had done with her? It runs through the galleries he even had to borrow money to buy Berkshire."

"I'll tell you why, madame. He did it because he's soft-hearted. When he's had all he wants of a woman he can never bring himself to throw her aside. Oh, no. He must always deal fairly with each of 'em, recognize their brats whether they're his or not, pay 'em off with great sums of money to keep 'em from being slighted by the malicious world. Well, madame—I should think this would be good news to you. It was never my opinion you and Barbara Palmer had overmuch fondness for each-other."

"I hate her! But after all the years she's been in power—I can scarce believe it—"

"She can scarce believe it herself. But she'll get accustomed to it before long. I was tired of her vapourings—and so I took steps to be rid of her. She'll hang on here at Whitehall, perhaps for years, but she'll never count for anything again. For once Old Rowley is thoroughly tired of anyone, whether man or woman, he has no further use for 'em. It's our best protection against the Chancellor. Now, madame, it's occurred to me that this leaves a place wide open for some clever woman to step into—"

Amber returned his steady stare. No ally of Buckingham's was much to be envied. The Duke engaged in politics for nothing but his own amusement. He had no principles and no serious purpose but followed only his temporary whims, rejecting friendship, honour, and morality. He was bound to no one and to nothing. But in spite of all that he had a great name, a fortune still one of the largest in England, and high popularity with the rich merchants, the Commons, and the people of London. Even more persuasive, he had a streak of vindictive malice which, though not always persistent, could do vast damage at one impulsive stroke. Amber had long ago made up her mind about him.

"And suppose someone does take her Ladyship's place?" she inquired softly.

"Someone will, I'll pass my word for that. Old Rowley's been governed by a woman since he first took suck from his wet-nurse. And this time, madame, the woman might be you. There's no one in England just now with so happy an opportunity. Those gentlemen who are keeping company with the Duchess of Richmond these days are but washing the blackamoor. She'll never please his Majesty long—that empty-headed giggling baggage. I'll venture my neck on it. Now, I'm an old dog at this, madame, and understand these matters very well—and I've come to offer my services in your behalf."

"Your Grace does me too much honour. I'm sure it's more than I deserve."

The Duke was suddenly brisk again. "We'll dispense with the bowing and nodding. As you know, madame, if I like I can help you—in your turn, you may be of some use to me. My cousin made the mistake of thinking that all her business was done for her in bed and that it made no difference how she carried herself otherwise. That was a serious error, as no doubt she understands by now—if she has wit enough to see it. But that's all water under the bridge and need not concern us. I admit to you freely, madame, I've made a lifelong study of his Majesty's character and flatter myself I know it as well as any man who wears a head. If you will be guided by me I think that we might go near to molding England in our own design."

Amber had no design for molding England and no wish to invent one. Politics, national or international, did not concern her except in so far as they affected the course of her personal wants or ambitions. Her intrigues did not extend—intentionally, at least, beyond the people she knew and the events she could observe. She was inclined to agree with Charles that his Grace had windmills in the head—but if it pleased the Duke to imagine himself engaged upon great projects she saw no reason to argue with him about it.

"Nothing could please me more, your Grace, than to be your friend and share your interests. Believe me for that—" She lifted her glass to him, and they drank together.

CHAPTER FIFTY-SEVEN

FRANCES STEWART WAS not long satisfied with her life in the country. She had always lived where there were many people, balls and supper-parties, hunting and plays, gossip and laughter and a continual rush of petty excitements. The country was quiet, days passed with monotonous similarity, and compared with the Palace her great house seemed lonely and deserted. There were no gallants to amuse her, flatter her, run to pick up a fan or help her down from horseback.

Her husband spent much of his time in the field and when he was home he was too often drunk. The steward managed the house—which she had never been trained to do anyway—and the idle hours bored her desperately, for no one had ever encouraged her to learn to be happy alone. She did not like being married, either, but of course she had not expected to like it.

She had married because it had seemed the only way that she could be an honest and respected woman—and that had been the wish of her life. No doubt the Duke really loved her and was grateful she had married him, but he seemed to her dull and uncouth compared with the well-bred gentlemen of Whitehall who had a thousand amusing tricks to make a lady laugh.

And love-making revolted her. She dreaded each night as it began to grow dark, and invented many small illnesses to keep him away. She had a horror of pregnancy which sometimes made her actually sick, and more than once she experienced all the symptoms without the actuality.

Constantly she thought of the Town and Court and the fine life she had had there—which she had not valued at a great price then but which now seemed to her the most pleasant and desirable existence on earth. She spent endless hours dreaming of the balls she had attended, the clothes she had worn, the men who had gathered around her wherever she went to fawn upon and compliment her; she lived over again and again each small remembered episode, feeding her loneliness on them.

But more than anything else, she thought of King Charles. She considered now that he was the handsomest and most fascinating man she had ever known, and she had found to her dismay that she was in love with him. She wondered why she had not been wise enough to know it sooner. How different her life might have been! For now that she had her respectability it seemed much less important than her mother had assured her it was. What else could a woman need—if she had the King's protection?

She longed to return to London; but what if he was not ready to forgive her? What if he had forgotten he had ever loved her at all? She had heard of his most recent mistresses: the Countess of Northumberland, the Countess of Danforth, Mary Knight, Moll Davis, Nell Gwynne. Perhaps he had lost all interest in her by now. Frances remembered well enough that once people were out of his sight—no matter how well he might like them—he promptly forgot their existence.

She tried to take an interest in painting or in playing her guitar or in working a tapestry. But those things did not seem entertaining to her, done alone. She was thoroughly, wretchedly bored.

Finally she coaxed the Duke to return to London, and at first her hopes ran exuberantly high. Everyone came to her supper-parties and balls. She was as much courted and sought-out as she had been after her first triumphant appearance at Whitehall. She knew perfectly well that everyone now expected the King would soon relent and make her his mistress, and for the first time she was almost ready to accept that position with its advantages and hazards. But Charles, apparently, did not even know that she was in town.

That went on for four months.

At first Frances was surprised, then she became angry, and finally hurt and frightened. What if he intended never to forgive her? The mere thought terrified her, for she knew the Court too well not to understand that once they were convinced he had lost interest they would flock away, like daws leaving a plague-stricken city. With horror she faced the prospect of being forced to return to her life of idle seclusion in the country—the years seemed to spin out in an endless dreary prospect before her.

And then, not quite a year from the day she had eloped, Frances became seriously ill. At first the doctors thought it might be pregnancy or an ague or a severe attack of the vapours —but after a few days they knew for certain that it was small-pox. Immediately Dr. Fraser sent a note to the King. The resentment Charles had felt against her, his cynical conviction that she had deliberately played him for a fool, vanished in a flood of horror and pity.

Small-pox! Her beauty might be ruined! He thought of that even before he thought of the threat to her life—for it seemed to him that such beauty as Frances had was a thing almost sacred, and should be inviolable to the touch of God or man. To mar or destroy it would be vandalism, in his eyes almost a blasphemy. And she still meant more to him than he had been willing to admit these past months, for she had a kind of freshness and purity which he did not discover in many women he knew and which appealed strongly to the disillusion of his tired and bitter heart.

He would have gone immediately to visit her but the doctors advised against it for fear he might carry the infection and spread it to others. He wrote instead. But though he tried to make his letter sound confident and unworried it had a false flat sound to him, for he did not believe it himself. He had scant faith left in anything, certainly not in the duty of God to preserve a woman's beauty for men's eyes. He had found God a negligent debtor who cared little to keep His accounts straight. But he sent her his own best physicians and pestered them constantly for news of her.

How was she feeling? Was she better today? Good! Was she cheerful? And—would she be marred? They always told him what he wanted to hear, but he knew when they were lying.

It was the end of the first week in May—more than a month later—before they would let him see her. And then when his coach rolled into the courtyard of Somerset House he found it jammed full with a score or more of others. Evidently word had spread that he was coming, and they had wanted to be there to see the meeting between them. Charles muttered a curse beneath his breath and his face turned hard and sombre.

Damn them all for their ghoulish curiosity, their cheap petty minds and malignant poking into the sorrows of others.

He got out of his coach and went inside. Mrs. Stewart, Frances's mother, had been expecting him. He saw at a glance that she was nervous and excited, close to tears, and he knew then for certain that the doctors had been lying to him.

826

"Oh, your Majesty! I'm so glad you've come! She's been long-ing to see you! Believe me, Sire, she's never forgiven herself for that wretched trick she played on you!"

"How is she?"

"Oh, she's much better! Very much better! She's dressed and sitting up—though she's weak yet, of course."

Charles stood looking down at her, his black eyes reading what was behind her odd fluttering gestures, her quick breath-less way of speaking, the anguish in her eyes and the new lines beneath them.

"May I see her now?"

"Oh, yes, your Majesty! Please come with me."

"From the look of the courtyard, I'd say I'm not the only visitor she has today."

Mrs. Stewart was mounting the stairs beside him. "It's the first day she's been allowed visitors, you see. The room's quite full—all the town's in there."

"Then I think I'll step into this anteroom until they leave."

She went to send them away with the plea that Frances had had excitement enough for one day. Charles stood behind the closed door listening to them troop by, chattering and giggling with irresponsible malice. When at last they were gone Mrs. Stewart came for him. They walked down the gallery and into Frances's own apartments, then through several more rooms until finally they reached the bedchamber where she sat wait-ing.

She half lay on a couch that faced the door and she was wear-ing a lovely silken gown which hung in folds to the floor. The draperies had been pulled across all windows to darken the room —it was only two o'clock—and though several candles burned all of them were placed at a distance from her. Charles swept off his hat and bowed, then immediately crossed the room to stand before her. He bowed again, deeply, and reluctantly he raised his eyes to look at her. What he saw sickened him.

She had changed. Oh, even in this dim light she had changed. The disease had spared her nothing. There were ugly red splotches and deep pock-marks on the skin that had been smooth and white as a water-lily, and one eye was partly closed. All that pure and perfect beauty was gone. But it was the misery in

Frances's own upraised begging eyes that struck him hardest.

Mrs. Stewart was still in the room—for Charles had asked her to stay—and she stood with her hands clasped before her, anxious and worried as she watched them. But Charles and Frances had forgotten she was there.

"My dear," he said softly, forcing himself to speak after too long a silence. "Thank God you're well again."

Frances stared at him, struggling for self-control but afraid to trust her voice. At last she managed a pitiful little smile, but the corners of her mouth began to quiver. "Yes, your Majesty. I'm well again." Her soft low voice dropped to a mere whisper. "If it's anything to be grateful for."

There was a sudden bitter twist of her mouth, her eyes went down and she looked quickly away. All at once she covered her face with her hands and began to cry, shoulders and body shaken with the violence of her sobs. It was, he knew, not only the agony of having him see what had happened to her, but the culmination of all she had endured this afternoon—the curious cruel spiteful eyes of the men and women who had been there, all elaborately polite, sympathetic, falsely cheerful. They had taken their revenge on her for every moment of grudging admiration she had ever had, for each fawning compliment, each hypocritical friendship.

Instantly Charles dropped to one knee beside her. His hand touched her arm lightly, the deep tones of his voice began to plead with her. "I've been so worried for you, Frances! Oh, my dear—forgive me for acting like a jealous fool!"

"Forgive you? Oh, Sire!" She looked at him, her hands still covering all her face but her eyes, as though she could hide from him behind them. "It's I who must ask your forgiveness! That's why this happened to me—I know it is!—to punish me for what I did to you!"

A wave of almost unbearable pity and tenderness swept over him. He felt that he would have given everything he possessed on earth to have her beautiful again, to see her look at him with her old teasing confident coquetry. But it had all gone forever, the sparkling expressions of her face, the happy laughter of a lovely woman who knows that her beauty will buy forgiveness

828

for anything. Savage anger filled him. God in heaven! Does the world spoil *everything* it touches?

"Don't talk like that, Frances. Please. I don't know what made me act like such a fool— But when I heard you were sick I was out of my mind. If anything had happened to you— But thank God you're well again! I'm not going to lose you."

She looked at him for a long serious moment, as though wondering whether or not he could see the change in her— pathetically hoping— But it was no use. Of course he could see it. Everyone else had—why shouldn't he?

"I'm well again, yes," she murmured. "But I wish I weren't. I wish I were dead. Look at me—!" Her hands came down, her voice was a lonely cry, anguished and full of desperation; behind them they heard a sudden hard sob from her mother. "Oh, *look* at me! I'm *ugly* now!"

He grabbed her hand. "Oh, but you're not, Frances! This won't last, I promise you it won't! Why, you should have seen me after I'd had it. I was enough to frighten the devil himself. But now—look—you can't see a mark." He looked up eagerly into her face, smiling, holding both her hands against his heavy beating heart. He felt a passionate longing to help her, to make her believe again in the future, though he did not believe in it himself. And as he talked her eyes began to lighten, something like hope came back into her face. "Why, in no time at all it won't be possible to tell you've ever had the small-pox. You'll come to the balls and they'll all say that you're more beautiful than ever. You'll be more beautiful than you were. that first night I saw you. Remember, darling, that black-and-white lace gown you were wearing, with the diamonds in your hair—"

Frances watched him, fascinated, listening intently. His words had the sound of some old and half-intentionally forgotten melody. "Yes," she whispered. "Yes, I remember—and you asked me to dance with you—"

"I couldn't take my eyes off you—I'd never seen such a beautiful woman—"

She smiled at him, passionately grateful for his kindness, but the game was a sorry one and she knew as well as he did that they were only pretending. With all the effort of will she could summon she held back the tears while he sat with her and talked, trying desperately to take her mind off herself. But all her thoughts were wholly of her own tragedy; and Charles, too, could think of nothing else.

Oh, why did it happen to *her?* he thought, furious with resentment. Why should it have happened to Frances, who had been gay and sweet and friendly, when there were other women who better deserved a fate like that—

But Charles was a stubborn man.

Once, he had said that he hoped someday to find her ugly and willing. He had forgotten the thoughtless words, but he had not forgotten the years of waiting and pleading and promising, the ache of desire, the longing for possession and fulfillment. And now, all at once, it was she who had become the supplicant.

Late one afternoon they were in the garden that ran down to the river behind Somerset House, strolling arm in arm between a tall row of clipped limes. Frances was dressed in a lovely blue-satin gown with flounces of black lace on the skirt; a veil of black lace was flung over her hair and fell across her face to her chin. With her feeling for beauty, she had instinctively begun to try to compensate for what the disease had done to her. She used her fan for concealment, veils to shield her skin, and now when she paused beside the river it was in the shadow of a great elm.

Silently they stood looking out over the water, and then her hand in the bend of his arm tightened slowly and he turned to find her·staring up at him. For a moment Charles made no move but stood watching her, and he saw that she was asking him to kiss her. His arms went about her and this time there was no holding him off with her finger-tips, no giggle of protest as his body pressed close. Instead she clung to him, her arms drawing him to her, and he could feel in her mouth not real passion but eagerness to please—a frightened premonition that he would no longer find her desirable.

Charles, his pity for her over-riding his inevitable reaction to a woman's body and lips, released her gently. But she did not want to let him go. Her hands caught at his upper arms.

"Oh, you were right all along! I was a fool— You should never have been so patient with me!"

Surprised at her frankness, he said softly, "My dear, I hope that I shall never be any such bungler as to take a woman against her will."

"But I—" she began, and then stopped suddenly, blushing. All at once she turned and went running up the path, and he knew that she was crying.

The next night, however, as he was getting alone into a scull at the Palace stairs to take a short evening ride on the river he made a sudden decision, turned the boat around, and started toward Somerset House. The little craft went skimming over the water's surface; he beached it and jumped out. The water-gate was locked but in a moment he had vaulted the wall and was off on a run through the gardens toward the house.

I've waited five years and a half for this, he thought. I hope to God it hasn't been too long!

CHAPTER FIFTY–EIGHT

CHARLES AND THE Duke of Buckingham sat across the table from each other examining a small but perfect model for a new man-of-war, both of them absorbed and eagerly excited in the discussion. Charles had always loved ships and the sea. He knew so much about both, in fact; that many considered such a command of technical knowledge to be quite beneath a king's dignity. Nevertheless, the navy was his pride and he still smarted from the humiliation of having the Dutch sail into his rivers, plunder his countryside, burn and sink his finest ships. He intended one day to repay that insult—meanwhile he was building a stronger and bigger navy. It was the plan and hope of his life that England should someday sail the seas, supreme unchallenged mistress of all the waters on earth—for that way and that alone, he knew, lay greatness for his little kingdom.

At last Charles got to his feet. "Well—I can't stay admiring this any longer. I'm engaged to play tennis with Rupert at two." He picked his wig from where it was perched on the back of a chair, set it on his head and glancing into a mirror clapped his wide hat down over it.

Buckingham stood up, his own hat under his arm. "On a day hot as this? I marvel at your Majesty's industry."

Charles smiled. "It's my daily physic. I need my health so that I may keep up with my amusements."

The two men went out the door, Charles closed and locked it behind him and dropped the key into his coat-pocket. They crossed through several more rooms, mounted a narrow flight of stairs, and came at last into the great Stone Gallery. There, coming toward them with her woman beside her and a little blackamoor to carry her train, was Frances Stewart. She waved to attract their attention and as they paused to wait for her, she hastened her steps.

Buckingham bowed, Charles smiled, and as she reached them he gave her a light careless friendly salute on the lips. But as Frances looked up at him her eyes were pathetic and anxious; she could never for an instant forget the terrible fact that her beauty was gone. All her manner had changed, as if to compensate for the thing she had lost. Now she was eager, nervously vivacious, wistful.

"Oh, your Majesty! I'm so glad we chanced to meet! It's been a week and more since I've seen you—"

"I'm sorry. I've had a great deal to do—council-meetings and ambassadors—"

She had heard him make similar excuses, many times before, to other women. Then she had teased him for lying and laughed about it, because in those days she had laughed joyously at everything.

"I wish you'd come to supper. Can't you come tonight? I've invited ever so many others—" she added quickly.

"Thank you very much, Frances, but I'm engaged for tonight, and have been for so long I dare not break it." Her disappointment was painful to see, and because it made him un-comfortable he added: "But I'll be free tomorrow night. I can come then if you like."

"Oh, can you, sir!" Instantly her face brightened. "I'll order everything you like best to eat—and I'll bespeak Moll Davis to give us a performance!" She turned to Buckingham. "I'd like to have you come too, your Grace—with my Lady Shrews-bury, of course."

"Thank you, madame. If I can, I'll be there."

Frances curtsied, the men bowed, and then continued on their way down the corridor. For several moments Charles was silent. "Poor Frances," he said at last. "It makes my heart sick to see her."

"She's considerably impaired," admitted the Duke. "But at least it stopped her infernal giggling. I haven't heard her gig-gle once these two months past." Then, very casually, he said: "Oh, yes—Lauderdale was telling me about her Majesty's es-capade last night."

Charles laughed. "I think everyone has heard of it by now. I didn't guess she had so much mettle."

Catherine had put on a disguise and left the Palace with Mrs. Boynton to attend a betrothal party in the City—to which, of course, neither had been invited. Masked and wigged they had gone in boldly, mingled with the other guests, but had become separated in the crowd so that the Queen had been forced to return home alone in a hackney. It was the kind of prank the ladies and gentlemen were always playing—but Cath-erine had never dared go on such an adventure before and the Palace buzzed with shock and amusement to learn their mousey little Queen had finally braved the great forbidding world out-side her castle-walls.

"They said she was trembling all over when she first came in," continued Charles. "But after a few minutes she began to laugh and told it all as a good frolic. The chair-men who car-ried her there were devilish rude fellows, she said, and the hackney-driver so drunk she expected he would tumble her into the streets!" He seemed highly amused. "All the citizens were grumbling I'd led the country straight to hell! She makes a good intelligence-agent, don't you agree? I've a notion to send her out often."

Buckingham's face had a look of sour reproval. "It was mighty indecorous. And worse yet—mighty dangerous."

Now they emerged into the hot July sunshine and had to squint their eyes till they had accustomed themselves to the glare. They started off across the Privy Gardens toward the Tennis Court, passing several men and women who were strolling there or standing talking, and the King greeted many of them with a smile or a wave of the hand. Sometimes he paused to talk for a moment or called out a friendly greeting. Buckingham did not like these interruptions.

"Oh, I don't imagine she was in any great danger," said Charles. "Anyway, she's safely back now."

"But another time, Sire, she might *not* return safely."

Charles gave a burst of laughter. "Sure, now, George—you don't think anyone considers me rich enough to make it worth their while to kidnap my wife?"

"It wasn't ransom I had in mind. Has it never occurred to you, Sire, that her Majesty might be kidnapped and sent to a desert island and never heard from again?"

"I must confess, I haven't worried a great deal at the prospect." Charles waved his arm at a couple of pretty women sitting several yards away on the lawn, and they laughed and nudged each other, fluttering their fans at him in return.

"There are many such islands," continued Buckingham, ignoring the interruption, "located in the West Indies. There is no reason why one of them could not be supplied with every possible comfort. A woman might live out the rest of her days at ease in such a place."

A quick scowl crossed Charles's face and he looked sharply at the Duke. "Do I misunderstand you, Villiers, or are you suggesting that I get rid of my wife by having her kidnapped?"

"The idea is by no means impracticable, your Majesty. I had given it considerable thought, in fact—even to the point of locating a suitable island on the map—long before her Majesty took to this indiscreet new pastime of masquerading."

834

Charles made a sound of disgust. "You're a scoundrel, George Villiers! I don't deny that I desperately need an heir—but I'll never get one by any such means as that! And let me tell you one thing more: If her Majesty is ever harmed or molested— if she ever disappears—I'll know where to lay the blame. And you won't wear a head so long as an hour! Good-day!"

He gave Buckingham a brief dark look of anger and then walked swiftly away from him into the building which housed the tennis-courts. The Duke turned on his heel and went off in the other direction, muttering beneath his breath.

But that had by no means been the first, nor was it to be the last, of the schemes presented to Charles for getting Catherine out of the way so that he could marry again and produce a legitimate heir. Half the men at Court were busy plotting schemes, giving them to the King, then starting out to plot another as each in turn was rejected. The only persons of any influence who did not want Catherine to be replaced were York, Anne Hyde, their few adherents—and the King's mistresses.

Annoyed with the King, Buckingham avoided Whitehall for several days and spent his time with the rich City men he knew. But he soon grew bored with that too. He had nothing but contempt for these fat credulous men who believed whatever he told them, and because it was almost second nature to him he began to hatch another plot.

For the past few years the Duke had been hiring several different lodgings scattered about in various parts of the town, and he went to one or another as the mood took him. It was for greater convenience and secrecy in his political machinations, that he kept a trunkful of disguises and rented a dozen different apartments.

In Idle Lane, just off Thames Street and hard by the Tower, a lodging-house had been left standing after the Fire had swept through. It now had for company three others, still in the process of building, another completed the year before and rented out to an ale-house keeper to entertain the workmen, and one other which had collapsed when half built because of bad mortar and bricks. (This was a common occurrence all over the City where new houses were going up.) The busy Thames ran nearby, close enough that the shouts of the bargemen and the girls hawking oysters in the street could be heard. Buckingham had rented three rooms on the fourth floor, using one of the fictitious names which it amused him to invent; this time he was Er Illingworth.

The Duke, wearing a Turkish dressing-gown and turban, a pair of slippers with turned-up toes, lay stretched out sound asleep on the long straight-backed settle near the fireplace where sea-coals had burnt down to a glowing red. There was no air in the room and very little light, for it was after dark and he had been asleep since mid-day.

A knock sounded at the door and then was repeated as Buckingham's snore continued to rattle through the room. At the fourth knock he sat up with a start, his face flushed and swollen with sleep, gave his head a shake and got up. But he did not throw back the bolt before he had asked who it was.

A fat short red-faced priest stood in the doorway, dressed in robe and sandals, a cowl over his tonsured head, a prayer-book in his hands.

"Good evening to you, Father Scroope."

"Good evening, sir." The priest was out of breath from hurrying up the stairs. "I came with all haste—but I was at her Majesty's evening devotions when I got the message." His eyes looked over the Duke's shoulder and into the half-lighted bedroom beyond. "Where is the patient? There is no time to be lost—"

Behind him Buckingham closed the door, quietly turned the key in the lock and slipped it into the pocket of his dressing-gown. "There is no one sick here, Father Scroope."

The priest turned and looked at him in surprise. "No one sick? But I was told—the messenger told me that a man was dying—"

He sat down in a high-backed chair while the Duke poured two glassfuls of canary wine, handed one to his guest, and then pulled up another chair so that they sat face to face.

"I wanted you to come as quickly as possible—so I sent a message that there was sickness. Don't you know me now, Father?"

836

Father Scroope, who had already drunk down his wine and was holding the glass in his pudgy pink hands, peered closely at Buckingham, and slow recognition came to his face.

"Why—your Grace!"

"None other."

"Forgive me, sir! I vow you're so altered by your undress I didn't recognize you—and the light, of course, is dim—" he added apologetically.

Buckingham smiled, reached for the wine-bottle and filled both their glasses again. "You say you've just come from her Majesty's devotions?"

"Yes, your Grace. Her Majesty has learnt a great many new habits, but never to retire without evening prayers—for which God be thanked," he added, with a pious roll of his eyes.

"You hear her Majesty's confessions, as well, if I'm not mistaken?"

"Sometimes, yes, your Grace."

Buckingham laughed shortly. "Much *she* can have to confess, I imagine! What could her sins be—coveting a new gown or gambling on Sunday? Or perhaps wishing that his Majesty's child was in her own belly and not in some other woman's?"

"Ah, well, my lord—poor lady. That's but a venial sin. And I fear we all of us commit it with her." Father Scroope drained his glass again, and again the Duke filled it.

"But wishing won't cure the matter. The fact remains she's barren—and always will be."

"She's been with child, I'm convinced. But there's somewhat amiss keeps her from carrying to term."

"And always will. His Majesty will never have a legitimate heir by Catherine of Braganza. And if the throne goes to York the country's ruined." Father Scroope widened his popped blue eyes at this, for York's Catholic sympathies were notorious, and Buckingham was well known for his hatred of the Church. But the Duke said quickly, "Not because of his religion, Father. The case is more serious far than that. His Highness has not the means to govern the country. It would fall into civil war again within six months if he came to the throne." The Duke's face was passionately serious. He leaned forward, the hand holding his wine-glass clutched on his knee, pointing with the forefinger of the other at Father Scroope's bewildered round face. "It's your duty, Father, as you love England and the Stuarts, to lend me aid in what I propose—and I may as well tell you frankly that his Majesty is behind me in this but prefers, for obvious reasons, to remain out of it altogether."

"You've mistaken your man, your Grace! I can't take action against her Majesty—no matter *who's* behind it!" Father Scroope was scared; even his plump cheeks quivered. He began to get out of his seat but Buckingham, with a gentle but persuasive hand, pressed him back again.

"Not so hasty, Father, I pray you! Hear me out first. And remember this—you owe your first allegiance to your King!" As he spoke Buckingham looked like all the magnificent selfless patriots of history, and Father Scroope, thoroughly impressed, sat down again. "We do not intend to harm her Majesty in any way at all—make yourself easy on that score. But for the sake of England, the King, my master, and I have devised a plan for getting him another wife. This he can do and have an heir for England in a year's time if her Majesty will agree to return to the life she once lived and enjoyed—the life of the cloister."

"I don't think I quite understand your Grace's meaning—"

"Very well, then, this is it: You're her confessor. You talk to her in private. If you can persuade her to make a voluntary retirement from the world, go back to Portugal and enter a nunnery, his Majesty will be free to marry again. And if you succeed," continued Buckingham hastily, as Father Scroope opened his mouth again to speak, "his Majesty will endow you with a fortune great enough to support you in any style what-ever throughout the rest of your life. And to begin—" Buckingham got up and once more he went to take a leather bag from the mantelpiece and handed it to Father Scroope. "You'll find a thousand pound in there—and that's only a beginning." Father Scroope took it, feeling the weight of the money, but politely restrained himself from opening it. "Well, Father—what's your answer?"

For a long moment the priest hesitated, thoughtful, worried, unable to make up his mind. "His Majesty wants this done?" he repeated, dubiously.

"He does. Sure, now, Father, you don't think I'd dare act in so important a matter without his Majesty's instructions?"

"Certainly not, your Grace." Father Scroope got to his feet, placing the wine-glass on a nearby table-top. "Well—I'll try what influence I can have, your Grace." He frowned, shot a quick glance across at the Duke. "But suppose I fail? These gentle little women are sometimes stubborn."

Buckingham smiled. "You won't fail, Father Scroope. I'm sure you won't. For if you do you'll get no more money—and you'll give all of that back. And needless to say, if this conversation is ever repeated it will go hard with you." The relentless glitter in his eyes suggested more than he said.

"Oh, I'm altogether discreet, your Grace!" protested Father Scroope. "You may trust me!"

"Good! Well—go along now. And when you have information send it to me by some random boy you find on the street. Write in it that my new cloth-of-silver suit is finished and sign it— Let me see—" The Duke paused, stroking his mustache. Finally he smiled. "Sign it Israel Whoremaster."

"Israel! Whoremaster! Your Grace has a nimble wit!"

"Come now, you old villain," said the Duke, strolling beside him toward the door. "Don't try to wheedle me. I've heard tales aplenty about you and your girls."

But Father Scroope did not think the jest funny. He looked both angry and worried. "I protest, your Grace! They're all lies! Damned lies! I'd be ruined if such a tale gained general credit! Her Majesty wouldn't retain me an hour's time!"

"Very well, then," drawled the Duke, bored. "Keep your virginity if you like. Only don't miscarry in this business. I'll expect word from you within the week."

"A little longer, your Grace—"

"Ten days, then."

He closed the door on Father Scroope and slammed the bolt.

Amber stood listening to Father Scroope.

At the price of fifteen hundred pounds he had just sold her Buckingham's plot against the Queen. For, whether his Maj-

esty was in it or wasn't, he had no intention of talking himself out of a comfortable place at Court—if the Queen went
into a nunnery he would be left drifting and unprotected in
an England hostile to the Catholics. Charles, it was true, had
tried repeatedly to gain toleration for all religions, but Parliament hated that policy and Parliament could force obedience
by refusing to grant money.

"Good Lord!" she whispered in horror. "That devil's going
to be the ruin of us all! Have you talked to her?"

Father Scroope closed his fat lips smugly, crossed his hands
on his stomach and slowly shook his head. "Not one word, your
Ladyship. Not so much as one word. And I was alone with her
Majesty in the confessional booth today, too."

"And you'd better not speak one word, either! You know
what would happen to you if her Majesty left! Oh, damn that
varlet! I wish someone would slit his throat!"

"Will you tell her Majesty?"

"Tell her? Of course I'll tell her! Maybe he's paid someone else to talk to her already!"

"I don't think so, madame. Though I doubt not he will if
he finds he's failed with me."

At that moment Nan entered softly and beckoned to Amber.
Amber started out. "Come on," she said to him. "The way's
clear. You can go now."

They left the room and went into a very narrow dark corridor. The two women knew their way but Father Scroope had
to feel with his hands along the wall until they came to a
door. There Amber and the Father waited back out of sight
while Nan opened the door, peeked, and then motioned for
them to follow her. Outside they could hear the quiet washing
of the river as it came up into the reeds and rushes which grew
along the banks. Amber had the same trouble everyone else did
who lived on the side of the Palace next the water; the lower
floor of her apartments was sometimes invaded by the overflowing Thames.

But Father Scroope had scarcely set one foot out the door
when there was a sudden splashing and—so close that it seemed
to be almost upon them—the sound of heavy breathing and

840

struggling and men's voices in low muttered curses. Quick as a jackrabbit, the Father jumped back inside and Amber froze where she was, reaching out to grab hold of Nan's hand.

"What was that!"

"John must have caught someone snooping," whispered Nan. She spoke a little louder, just enough to be heard a few feet away. "John—"

He answered, his voice also low and cautious. "I'm here— Caught a fellow hiding in the reeds. He's alone—"

"Go on," whispered Amber to Father Scroope, and he streaked out the door and disappeared; they could hear the loud sucking noises of his feet as he hurried away through the mud. "Bring him in here," she said to Big John, and went back herself into the small room out of which she and Father Scroope had just come.

There she and Nan turned to see Big John come in dragging by the nape of the neck a thin angry little man who still kicked and flailed out with his arms, though each time he did so Big John gave him a rough shake that quieted him. Both of them were muddy almost to the knees and splashed with water. John tossed him into a heap in one corner. He began to shake himself and to straighten his clothes, ignoring all of them with an elaborate pretense of being alone.

"What were you doing out there?" demanded Amber.

He neither looked at her nor made an answer.

She repeated the question and this time he gave her merely a sullen glare as he pulled at his coat-sleeve.

"You insolent wretch! I think I know a way to make you find your tongue!"

She gave a nod of her head to Big John and he stepped to a table, opened one of the drawers and took out a short whip having several narrow leather thongs, each of them tipped with lead.

"*Now* will you answer me!" cried Amber.

He continued silent and Big John raised the whip and slashed it down over his chest and shoulders, one leaden tip biting into his cheek and drawing blood. While Amber and Nan stood coolly watching he lashed at him again and then again, striking him ruthlessly, though the man writhed and drew up his legs, trying to protect his face and head with his hands. At last he gave a sobbing moan.

"Stop! for the love of God—stop! I'll tell you—"

Big John let the whip fall to his side and stepped back; drops of blood splashed off the leaden ends onto the floor.

"You're a fool!" said Amber. "What did it get you to hold your peace? Now tell me—what were you doing out there, and who sent you?"

"I dare not tell. Please—your Ladyship." His voice took on an ingratiating whine. "Don't make me tell, your Ladyship. If I do my master will have me beaten."

"And if you don't, I will," retorted Amber, with a significant glance at Big John who stood with both fists on his hips, alert and waiting.

The man glanced up, frowned, gave a sigh and then licked at his lips. "I was sent by his Grace—the Duke of Buckingham."

That was what she had expected. She knew that Buckingham watched her closely but this was the first time she had actually caught one of his spies, though she had discharged four serving-girls she had suspected of being in his pay.

"What for?"

The man talked readily now, but in a sullen monotone, his eyes on the floor. "I was to watch Father Scroope—everywhere he went—and report to his Grace."

"And where will you report that you saw him tonight?" Her eyes stared at him, slanting, bright and hard and pitiless.

"Why—uh—he didn't leave his quarters at all tonight, your Ladyship."

"Good. Remember that, now. Next time my man won't be so gentle with you. And don't come back here to prowl again, unless you want your nose slit. Take 'im out, John."

CHAPTER FIFTY-NINE

AMBER HAD ALWAYS been friendly and respectful in her association with the Queen, partly because it seemed politic, partly because she was sorry for her. But her pity was casual and her half-affection cynical—it was the same feeling she had for Jenny Mortimer and Lady Almsbury, or any other woman from whom it seemed she had little to fear. And yet she knew that Catherine, when given the opportunity, was a good and diligent friend; she was so generally ignored by the self-seekers who swarmed Whitehall that she had come to be almost grateful to whoever sought her favour. It had occurred to Amber that this would be a very good opportunity to gain her Majesty's goodwill—which might be put to use in her own behalf.

Her talk with the Queen had the effect she wanted. Catherine —though struck with horror and bewilderment to learn that her enemies were again plotting to get rid of her—was easily persuaded that King Charles knew nothing of the plan and would have been furious if he had. Her wish to believe that he saved some part of his squandered affections for her, that he continued to think that one day she could give him the heir they both so passionately desired, was pathetic even to Amber. And though Amber did not just then mention her wish for a duchy she spoke of it a few days later; and Catherine immediately, though with a certain shyness, for she was aware of her limited influence, offered to help her if she could. Amber congratulated herself that she had made a friend—not the most powerful one, perhaps; but a friend who could be of any use at all was not to be scorned.

At Court there was a saying that an unprofitable friend was equal to an insignificant enemy. Amber did not trouble herself with either.

She had soon learned that in the Palace opportunities never came to those who sat and waited—patience and innocence were two useless commodities there. It was necessary to be ceaselessly active, to be informed about each great and small event which passed above or belowstairs, to take advantage of everyone and everything. It was a kind of life to which she adjusted herself rapidly and with ease—nothing inside her rebelled against it.

By now she had surrounded herself with a system of espionage which spread in every direction, from the Bowling Green to Scotland Yard and from the Park Gate to the Privy Stairs. Whatever complaints might be made about his Majesty's secret-service could certainly not be applied to the courtiers, for vast sums were continuously being paid out to keep each man and woman there informed about his neighbours' doings, whether in love, religion, or politics.

Amber employed a strange assortment of persons. There were two or three of Buckingham's footmen; a man whom he used for confidential business of his own but who was glad to make a few hundred pounds more by reporting on his master; the Duke's tailor; the Duchess's dressmaker and Lady Shrewsbury's hair-dresser. Madame Bennet kept her informed about the extra-marital activities of many gentlemen, including his Grace, and amused her with stories of Buckingham's weird devices for stirring up his worn and weary emotions. She received further information on others about the Court from a miscellaneous collection of whores, tavern-waiters, pages, barge-men, sentries.

Many of these spies she never saw at all and most of them had no idea as to who their employer might be. For it was Nan—wearing a blonde or black wig over her golden-red hair, a full-face vizard together with hood and flowing cloak, who went about her mistress's business after nightfall. Big John Waterman went along to take care of her, dressed now as a porter, now as footman for a great lady, or sometimes merely as a plain citizen. Nan took the news and delivered the money, haggling for a good bargain and proud of herself if she saved Amber a pound, for she had a better memory of the lean days than her mistress.

Amber knew where and with whom the King spent his nights when she did not see him. She knew every time Castlemaine took a new lover or ordered a new gown. She knew when the Queen seemed to have symptoms of pregnancy, what was said in the Council room, which Maid of Honour had just had a secret abortion, what lord or lady was being treated in a Leather Lane powdering-tub for the pox. It cost her a great deal but she knew almost everything which passed at Whitehall—though much of it was of no value to her save for the pleasure of having other people's secrets. Still she dared not be ignorant of the Palace gossip, for it would only have earned her the scorn of those who knew.

And often, of course, she could turn her knowledge to some practical use—as she did the secret bought from Father Scroope.

It was yet early the next morning when Buckingham came up Amber's back-staircase, his wig mussed and clothes dishevelled. He rattled across the marble floor on his high-heeled shoes and as he bent to give her a salute his breath had the stale sour smell of brandy drunk several hours before. Amber was propped up against pillows sleepily drinking a mugful of hot chocolate, but at sight of him she was instantly wide awake, on her guard.

"Well, your Grace! You look as if you've made a merry night of it!"

He grinned disarmingly. "I think I did, though damn me if I can remember!" Then he sat down on the edge of the bed, facing her. "Well, madame—you'd never think what news I've got of you!"

Their eyes swung quickly together, stared hard for the briefest instant; then he smiled and she looked down at Monsieur le Chien where he lay sprawled at the foot of the bed. "Lord, your Grace, I can't imagine," she said, growing nervous. "What's the newest libel? That I've got a mole on my stomach or prefer the Dragon upon St. George?"

"No, no. I heard all that last week. Don't you know the latest gossip about yourself? Tut, tut, madame. They're saying—" Here he gave a slight and, she thought, a sinister pause. "They're saying," he finished briskly; "that Colbert just made you a gift of a diamond necklace valued at two thousand pound."

Amber had a quick sense of relief, for she had feared that he was there to talk about Father Scroope. She finished her chocolate and set the mug onto the table beside the bed. "Well— if that's what they're saying, it's true. Or true enough, anyhow—my jeweller says it's worth six hundred pound. Still, it's pretty enough, I think."

"Perhaps you like Spanish jewels better."

Now Amber laughed. "Your Grace knows everything. I wish I had such an intelligence-net myself. I swear all the news comes to me cold as porridge, no matter how high I pay for it. But I'll tell you truth—the Spanish ambassador gave me an emerald bracelet—and it was handsomer than the French necklace."

"Then your Ladyship intends to cast in with the Spaniards?"

"Not at all, your Grace. I'll cast in with the Dutch or the Devil, at a price. After all, isn't that the way we do business here at Court?"

"If it is you shouldn't admit it. The news might carry—then what would your price be?"

"Oh, but surely one may be allowed to speak frankly among friends." Her voice gave him a light flick of sarcasm.

"You've grown mighty high, haven't you, madame, since the days you trod the boards wearing some Maid of Honour's cast-off gown? Even the Pope, they say, begins to court your favour."

"The Pope!" cried Amber, horrified. "Good Lord, sir, I protest! I've had no traffic with the Pope, let me tell you!"

Amber had little use for her own religion—except when she was alarmed or worried or wanted something—but she shared the popular hatred of Catholicism, without any idea as to why she hated it.

"No traffic with the Pope? But I've got it on very good authority your Ladyship sometimes entertains Father Scroope in the dead of the— Oh! I beg your Ladyship's pardon!" he cried with mock concern. "Have I said something to startle your Ladyship?"

"No, of course not! But where the devil did you get an idea like that? *Me,* entertaining Father Scroope! What for, pray? I've got no taste for bald fat old men, not I!" She tossed back her hair and started to get out of bed, pulling her dressing-gown around her as she did so.

"Just a moment, madame!" Buckingham caught hold of her arm and she looked at him defiantly. "I think you know well enough what I'm talking about!"

"And what, then, *are* you talking about, sir?"

Amber was growing angry. Something insolent in his Grace's manner always brought her temper to the surface with a rush.

"I'm talking, madame, about the fact that you are interfering in my business. To be quite plain with you, madame, I know that you discovered my arrangement with Father Scroope and took steps to forestall the plan." His arrogant hand-

846

some face had settled into hard lines and he stared at her with threatening violence. "I thought that we had agreed to play the game together—you and I."

She gave a swift jerk of her arm to free herself and jumped to her feet. "I'll play the game with you, your Grace—but damn me if I'll play it against myself! It could scarce be much to my advantage, d'ye think, if her Majesty left the Court and—"

Just at that moment the King's spaniels rushed scraping and clawing into the room and before Amber and the Duke could compose themselves Charles had strolled in, followed by several of the courtiers.

Buckingham instantly smoothed out his face and went to kiss the King's hand—it was the first time he had seen him since the day in the garden when Charles had called him a scoundrel. The Duke lingered several minutes longer, affable and talkative, pretending to Amber and all of them that they had merely been having a friendly chat; but she was considerably relieved when he left. News of the quarrel spread rapidly. When she met Barbara in her Majesty's apartments before noon the Lady had already heard of it and undertook to let her know that her cousin had sworn to all his acquaintance he would ruin Lady Danforth if it took the rest of his life. Amber laughed at that and said Let Buckingham do his worst, she did not doubt to hold her own. And she knew that she could, too, while the King liked her. After all, she had been at Whitehall only one year and any possible loss of Charles's affections still seemed to her, like old age, a distant and unlikely misfortune.

And certainly the first result of their broil seemed a very favourable one. Baron Arlington came to pay his first secret call upon her.

The Baron had always been polite to Amber, with his own cold aloof Castilian courtesy, but he had never troubled himself to show her any undue attention. For if Charles thought that ladies were better suited to other occupations than politics, his Secretary of State was convinced that all women were a damned nuisance and should be shipped away to let men run the country in peace. Still, Arlington was a politician and he never allowed prejudice or emotion to interfere with important business. Serving his King was the important business of his life, though he hoped and intended to serve himself at the same time. Evidently he had decided that because of the rupture with Buckingham she might be of some use to him.

Amber came in one night, late and very gay—for she and Charles and a dozen or more lords and ladies had put on cloaks and masks and driven out to visit the Beggars' Bush, a disreputable tavern in High Holborn where the beggars, both men and women, held weekly carousals. Arlington and King Charles were good and close friends, but the stiff solemn Baron seldom made one of such a frivolous party. Amber was astonished when Nan told her that he was downstairs and had been waiting there for almost an hour.

"Ye gods! Send 'im up then—post-haste!"

She tossed her mask and gloves and muff aside and dropped her cloak over Tansy who, completely enveloped, went groping his way across the room. Amber laughed as she watched him, then turned about to face her portrait above the fireplace, frowning critically and with displeasure as she examined it. Now, why had he made her so plump? Certainly *she* had no Roman nose, and that wasn't anything like the colour of her hair. She was annoyed every time she saw it for Lely insisted on painting each sitter, not as she really was, but after some pattern of his own to which he tried to fit the entire sex.

But then, he was the fashion.

She turned back as Nan ushered Lord Arlington into the room. He bowed from the doorway while she made him a curtsy.

"Madame, my humble service to you."

"Your servant, sir. Pray come in—I'm sorry to have kept you waiting."

"Not at all, madame. I occupied the time with writing some letters."

He was wrapped from head to foot in a great swirling black cloak and in his hand was a vizard. And now as he smiled he put on like a garment the charm which he held in reserve for necessary occasions, and wore only where it would show to ad-

848

vantage. There was no sincerity in the man, but there was a good deal of craft and guile as well as shrewdness and, what was rare in Charles's easy-going Court, a methodical application to business.

"You're alone, madame?"

"Quite, my lord. Won't you be seated and may I offer you something to drink?"

"Thank you, madame. It's kind of your Ladyship to receive me at this inconvenient hour."

"Oh, never speak of it, my lord," protested Amber. "It's I that am grateful for your Lordship's condescension in paying me a visit."

A servant came in then carrying a tray, with glasses and decanters, and set it down on a low table. Amber poured brandy for the Baron, clary-water for herself and he proposed her health. They sat there a few moments longer—in her great scarlet-and-silver and black-marble chamber where a hundred reflections of them showed in the Venetian mirrors—bandying compliments.

But at last the Baron got to the business of his visit. "All this privacy, madame, is merely a precaution against his Grace of Buckingham's jealousy. Don't misunderstand me, pray, for the Duke and I are good friends—"

They were, of course, desperate enemies, but Arlington was too cautious to admit it though Buckingham was usually ready to tell whoever would listen. Only a short while before he had snorted at Amber, when she had referred to the Baron as a dangerous foe: "Madame, I scorn to have a fool for an enemy!"

"It seems," continued Arlington, "he doesn't want you friendly with anyone but himself. The truth on it is, madame, it came to my ears today on very good authority that his Grace has told Colbert it's useless to make you further gifts because you are already committed to the cause of Spain."

"The devil he did!" cried Amber indignantly, for she was convinced that she had no more use for Buckingham or his tricky friendship. "He's as meddlesome as an old bawd! The way he uses his friends it's no wonder they soon wear out!"

"Oh, please, madame—not so hard on his Grace, I beg of

you! It was never my intention to make you suspect his Grace's friendship for you. But it seems he wants to keep you for himself, and I had hoped that you and I might be friends also."

"I see no reason why we shouldn't, my lord. Sure a woman may be allowed two friends—even at Whitehall."

The Baron smiled. "You seem to be a woman of wit, madame —than which I admire nothing more." She poured him another glass of brandy. He sat for a moment, staring into it reflectively, saying nothing. Then, finally: "I understand that your Ladyship is to be congratulated."

"For what, pray?"

"It runs through the galleries your young son will inherit a dukedom."

Amber suddenly sat forward in her chair, her eyes glittering and eager. "Did the King tell you—"

"No, madame—not the King. But it's current gossip."

She slumped back then and made a face. "Gossip. Gossip won't get me a duchy."

"It *is* what you want then?"

"What I want? My God! There's nothing I want so much! I'd do *anything* to get it!'"

"If that's true, madame, and you wished to do something for me—why, I might be able to help your case somehow." He modestly lowered his eyes. "I think I may say without vanity that I have some small influence here at Whitehall."

He had, of course, great influence. And what seemed even more important, he had a well-established reputation for always bettering the condition of those he took into favour.

"If you can help me to a duchy I swear I'll do anything you ask!"

He told her what he wanted.

It was generally known in the Palace that Buckingham often met with a group of old Commonwealth men who had as their object the overthrow of Charles II's government and the seizure of power into their own hands. Because the kingdom had so recently been split and disorganized it gave hope to others of inordinate ambition that the like could be accomplished again. Arlington wanted her to learn the time and place of their

850

meetings, what occurred there and what steps were taken, and to report the information to him. There was no doubt he could have learned these things himself but it was a costly process involving numerous very large bribes, and in persuading her to pay them, he saved himself that much money and gave in return nothing but what he could very well spare—a few words in her behalf to the King. Amber understood all this but the money had no value to her, and Arlington's support was worth a great deal.

Amber had already bought four acres of land in St. James's Square, the town's most aristocratic and exclusive district, and for several months she and Captain Wynne—who was designing many of the finest new homes in England—had been discussing plans for the house and gardens. She knew exactly what she wanted: the biggest and newest and most expensive of everything. Her house must be modern, lavish, spectacular; money was of no importance.

So long as they can't send me to Newgate, what do I care? she thought, and her recklessness increased apace.

After her conversation with Arlington she was convinced that the duchy was all but in her lap, and she told Captain Wynne to begin construction. It would take almost two years to complete and would cost about sixty thousand pounds—far more even than Clarendon House. This vast new extravagance set all tongues gabbling at Court, whether with awe, indignation or envy, for everyone agreed that no one beneath the rank of duchess could or should live in such state. And most of them decided that the King had finally promised her a duchy. Charles, no doubt amused, neither confirmed nor denied that he had and Amber optimistically took his silence for consent. But the weeks went by and she was still only a countess.

There was no doubt Charles seemed as fond of her as of anyone else just then, but he had nothing to gain by giving her a duchy, and the King's generosity was usually at least half self-interest. Furthermore, there were so many demands constantly made upon him that he had developed a habit of automatic procrastination. Discouraged though she became at times, Amber was determined to get the duchy someway—and by now she had convinced herself that by one means or another it would always be possible to get anything she wanted.

She made use of everyone she could, no matter how little influence he might have, and though she busied herself eternally doing favours for others, she saw to it that she always got a return. Barbara Palmer was furious to see her rival making headway and told everyone that if Charles dared give that low-bred slut such an honour she would make him sorry he had ever been born. Finally she got into a public argument with him about it and threatened to dash out his children's brains before his face and set the Palace on fire.

Less than a fortnight later Charles, in a spirit of malicious vindictiveness, passed a patent creating Gerald Duke of Ravenspur, with the honour to devolve upon his wife's son, Charles. And the look on Barbara's face the first time she had to leave an arm-chair and take a stool because the new duchess had entered the room was something Amber expected to remember with satisfaction all the rest of her life.

Immediately her position at Whitehall took on greater importance.

She set the fashions. When she had a tiny pistol made to carry in her muff, most of the other Court ladies did likewise. Several apartments were being redecorated with mirrored walls, and a great deal of walnut furniture was sent out to be silver-plated. She pinned up the brim of her Cavalier's hat at an angle one day and next day half the ladies in his Majesty's hawking-party had done the same. She appeared at a ball with her hair undone and hanging down her back covered with a thick sprinkling of gold-dust, and for a week that was the rage. Everyone copied her beauty patches—little cupids drawing a bow, the initials CR (Charles Rex) intertwined, a prancing long-horned goat.

Amber racked her brain to think of something new, for it tickled her vanity to lead them about like so many pet monkeys fastened to a stick. Everything she did was talked about. Yet she pretended to be bored with the imitations and resentful she could never keep a fashion to herself.

One unexpectedly warm October night she and several of

the gayest ladies and gentlemen took off their clothes and dove from the barge on which they had been supping and dancing to swim in the Thames. Almost nothing that had occurred since the Restoration so aroused the indignation of the sedate as this prank—for heretofore men and women had not gone swimming together and it had seemed the one steadfast decency still respected by a wicked decadent age. Her private entertainments for the King were, it was said, scandalous and lewd. Her numberless reputed lovers, her beauty-rites and her extravagances were discussed everywhere. There was nothing of which she had not been accused; no action was considered beyond or beneath her.

Amber, by no means resenting all this vicious and spiteful talk, paid out large sums to start new rumours and to keep them going. Her life, though comparatively chaste, became in reputation a model of license and iniquity. Once, when Charles repeated some gross tale he had heard of her, she laughed and said that rather than not be known at all she'd be known for what she was.

The people liked her. When she drove through the streets in her calèche, handling the reins herself and surrounded by six or eight running footmen to clear the way, they stopped to stare and give her a cheer. She was remembered for her days in the theatre; and her frequent spectacular public appearances as well as her open-handed almsgiving had made her both well-known and popular. She loved the attention now as much as she ever had and was still eager to be liked by those she would never know.

She saw Gerald but seldom, and never in private. Mrs. Stark had recently borne him a child, on which occasion Amber sent her six Apostles' spoons. Lucilla had found herself pregnant less than three months after her marriage and the gay Sir Frederick had sent her back to the country. He and Amber sometimes laughed together over his wife's predicament, for though Lucilla had welcomed the pregnancy she sent a continuous stream of letters to her husband, imploring him to come to her. But Sir Frederick had a vast amount of business in London and he made many promises that were not kept.

Amber was never bored and considered herself to be the most fortunate woman on earth. To buy a new gown, to give another supper, to see the latest play were all of equal consequence. She never missed an intrigue or a ball; she had her part in every counter-plot and escapade. Nothing passed her by and no one dared ignore her. She lived like one imprisoned in a drum, who can think of nothing but the noise on every side.

There seemed to be only one thing left for her to want, and finally that wish too was granted. Early in December Almsbury wrote to say that Lord Carlton expected to arrive in England sometime the following autumn.

PART VI

CHAPTER SIXTY

SPRING THAT YEAR was somewhat dry and dusty. There was too little rain. Nevertheless by May the meadows about London were thick with purple clover, bee-haunted, and there were great red poppies in the corn-fields. Cries of "Cherries, sweet cherries, ripe and red!" and "Rosemary and sweetbriar! Who'll buy my lavender?" were heard once more. Summer gowns, tiffany, sarsenet and watered moiré in all the bright colours—sulphur-yellow, plum, turquoise, crimson—were seen in the New Exchange and at the theatres or stepping into a gilt coach that waited in St. Martin's Lane or Pall Mall. The warm windy delightsome months had come again.

Nothing in years had caused so much excitement and indignation as the spreading gossip that York had at last become a confirmed Catholic. No one could be found to prove it; the Duke would not admit it and Charles, who must know if it actually was true, shrugged his shoulders and refused to commit himself. All the Duke's enemies began to scheme more furiously than ever to keep him from getting the throne while at the same time it was observed that York and Arlington seemed suddenly to have become good friends. This gave impetus to the rumours of a pending French-English alliance, for though Arlington had long been partial to Holland he was thought to be a Catholic himself, or at least to have strong Catholic sympathies.

As these rumours began inevitably to seep out into the town Charles found it difficult to conceal his annoyance and was heard to make some bad-humoured remarks on the meddlesomeness of the English people. Why couldn't they be content to leave the government in the hands of those whose business it was to govern? Ods-fish, being a king these days was of less consequence than being a baker or a tiler. Perhaps he should have learned a trade.

857

"You'd better to begin to study something useful," he said to James. "It's my opinion you may have to support yourself one day." James pretended to think that his brother was joking and said he did not consider the jest a funny one.

But certainly there could no longer be any doubt that unless the King married again York, if he lived long enough, would succeed King Charles. Catherine had had her fourth miscarriage at the end of May.

A pet fox frightened her by leaping into her face as she lay asleep and she lost her child a few hours later. Buckingham bribed her two physicians to deny that she had been with child at all, but Charles ignored their testimony. Nevertheless both King and Queen were in despair and Catherine could no longer make herself believe that she would someday give him a child. She knew now beyond all doubt that she was the most useless of all earth's creatures: a barren queen. But Charles continued to resist stubbornly all efforts to get him to put her aside, though whether from loyalty or laziness it was difficult to say.

There were several young women to whom these discussions of a new wife for the King caused apprehension and almost frantic worry—they had so much to lose.

But Barbara Palmer, at least, could listen with an amused smile and some degree of malignant pleasure. For even she knew now that she was no longer his Majesty's mistress, and the hazards of that position need trouble her no longer. But that did not mean she had dropped into obscurity. Barbara had never been inconspicuous. While she had her health and any beauty left, she never would be.

For though she was almost thirty and far beyond what were considered to be a woman's best years she was still so strikingly handsome that beside her the pretty fifteen-year-olds just come up to Court looked insipid as milk-and-water. She remained a glittering figure at Whitehall. Her constitution was too robust, her zest for living too great, for her to resign herself placidly to a quiet and dull old age after a youth so brilliant.

Very gradually her relationship with Charles had begun to mellow. They were settling into the pattern of a husband and wife who, having grown mutually indifferent, take up a comfortable casual existence fraught no longer with quarrels or jealousy, passion or hatred or joy. They had their children as a common interest, and now there was between them a kind of camaraderie which they had never known during the turbulent years when they had been—if not in love—lovers. She was no longer jealous of his mistresses; he was relieved to be out of the range of her temper and found some mild amusement from observing, at safe distance, her freaks and foibles.

Amber waited impatiently for the months to pass and wrote one letter after another to Almsbury at Barberry Hill, asking if he had heard from Lord Carlton or if he knew exactly when he would arrive. The Earl answered each one the same. He had heard nothing more—they expected to reach England sometime in August or September. How was it possible to be more explicit when the passage was so variable?

But Amber could not think or care about anything else. Once more the old passionate and painful longing, which ebbed when she knew she could not even hope to see him, had revived. Now she remembered with aching clarity all the small separate things about him: The odd green-grey colour of his eyes, the wave in his dark hair and the slight point where it grew off his forehead, the smooth texture of his sun-burnt skin, the warm timbre of his voice which gave her a real sense of physical pleasure. She remembered the lusty masculine smell of sweat on his clothes, the feeling of his hands touching her breasts, the taste of his mouth when they kissed. She remembered everything.

But still she was tormented, for those piecemeal memories could not make a whole. Somehow, he eluded her. Did he really exist, somewhere in that vastness of space outside England, or was he only a being she had imagined, built out of her dreams and hopes? She would throw her arms about Susanna in a passion of despair and yearning—but she could not reassure herself that way.

Yet in spite of her violent desire to see him again she had stoutly made up her mind that this time she would conduct herself with dignity and decorum. She must be a little aloof,

859

let him make the first advances, let him come first to see her. Every woman knew that was the way to prick up a man's interest. I've always made myself his servant, she chided, but this time it's going to be different. After all, I'm a person of honour now, a duchess—and he's but a baron. Anyway—why *shouldn't* he come to me first!

She knew that his wife would be along but she did not trouble herself too much about that. For certainly Lord Carlton was not the man to be uxorious. That was well enough for the citizens, who had no better breeding, but a gentleman would no more fawn upon his wife than he would appear in public without his sword or wearing a gnarled periwig.

Lord and Lady Almsbury were back in London in July to put their house in order, hire new servants and prepare for the entertainment of their eagerly expected guests. The Earl came to see Amber and, determined to show him how nonchalant she was at the prospect of seeing Bruce, she chattered away furiously about her own affairs—her title, her great house abuilding in St. James's Square, the people she had invited to supper for that Sunday. From time to time she asked him what he did in the country and then hurried on without letting him answer—for everyone knew there was nothing to do in the country but ride and drink and visit tenants. Almsbury sat and listened to her talk, watched her vivacious display of mannerisms and hectic charm, smiled and nodded his head—and never mentioned Bruce at all.

Amber's conversation began to slow down. She grew perplexed and quieter, and finally—realizing that he was teasing her—she became angry. "Well!" she said at last. "What's the news!"

"News? Why, let me think now. My black mare—the one you used to ride, remember?—foaled last week and—"

"Blast you, Almsbury! Why should you use me at this rate, I'd like to know! Tell me—what have you heard? When will he get here? Is *she* still coming?"

"I don't know any more than I did last time I wrote to you— August or September. And, yes, *she* is coming. Why? You're not afraid of her?"

860

Amber shot him a dark venomous glare. "Afraid of her!" she repeated contemptuously. "Almsbury, I swear you've a droll wit! Why should I be afraid of her, pray?" She paused a moment and then superciliously informed him: "I've got an image of her—that Corinna!"

"Have you?" he asked politely.

"Yes, I have! I know just what she's like! A plain meek creature who wears all her gowns five years out of the style and thinks herself fit for nothing but to be her husband's housekeeper and breed up his brats!" The portrait was a reasonably accurate one of Almsbury's own wife. "A great show *she'll* make here in London!"

"You may be right," he admitted.

"May be right!" she cried indignantly. "What else could she be like—brought up over there in that wilderness with a pack of heathen Indians—"

At that instant a weird and raucous voice began to screech. "Thieves, God damn you! Thieves, by God! Make haste!"

Involuntarily both Amber and the Earl leaped to their feet, Amber overturning the spaniel which had settled on her skirts for a nap. "It's my parrot!" she cried. "He's caught a thief in there!" And she dashed toward the drawing-room with Almsbury beside her and Monsieur le Chien yapping excitedly at their heels. They flung open the door and burst in, to find that it was only the King who had strolled in unannounced and picked out an orange from a bowl of fruit. He was laughing heartily as he watched the parrot prancing on his perch and teetering back and forth, squawking frantically. It was not the first time the bird, trained to apprehend intruders, had mistaken his man.

Almsbury left then and a few days later he went back to Barberry Hill to hunt, while Emily stayed in town to welcome the guests should they arrive unexpectedly. Amber had no opportunity to discuss Corinna with him again.

For the past year she had been going three or four times a week to watch the progress on Ravenspur House.

Planned in the new style without those courtyards which had

evolved from the enclosing castle-walls, it was a perfectly symmetrical four-and-a-half-storied cherry-brick building with windows made of several hundred small square glass panes. It fronted on Pall Mall, which was lined with elm trees, and the gardens in back were adjacent to St. James's Square—now become merely a sordid receptacle for refuse, dead cats and dogs, the garbage and offal carted from the great houses and dumped there.

Neither Captain Wynne nor his patron had overlooked any possibility for making the house the newest and most sumptuous in London. Coloured paint on wood-work was no longer the mode, and so instead there were several rooms decorated with large panels of allegorical figures, mostly from Greek or Roman mythology. The floors in every important room were parquet, all laid in intricate designs. Glass chandeliers, looking like great diamond ear-drops, were very uncommon, but Ravenspur House had several; all others, including the sconces, were of silver. She had one room panelled in fragrant pale-orange Javanese mahogany. The letter C, entwined with crowns and cupids, was a recurring motif everywhere—to Amber that C meant Carlton, as well as Charles.

Anything she might have forgotten to put in her bedchamber at Whitehall she intended to have in this one. The gigantic bed —the biggest in all England—was to be covered with gold brocade and decorated with swags of gold cord and fringe. Each of its four posters was surmounted by a bouquet of black-and-emerald ostrich-feathers with a bordering of aigrettes. Every other piece of furniture was to be coated with gold-leaf and all cushions on chairs and couches were of emerald velvet or satin. The ceiling was a solid mass of mirrors; the walls had alternating panels of mirrors and gold brocade; Persian carpets of velvet and cloth-of-gold, pearl-embroidered, scattered the floor. Furnishings of other rooms were to be of a similar raucous splendour.

One hot day late in August Amber was there talking to Captain Wynne and looking at the house—she wanted to move in soon and had been urging him to hurry the work on it, while he protested that it could be done only at the cost of inferior craftsmanship. The summer heat and haze still lay upon

London, but fall was fast coming on; already the willow trees hung in golden strips. And all about them were the dry and dead leaves, sifting to the ground.

As Amber talked her attention was distracted by Susanna who ran about, laughing gleefully as she evaded the clumsy pursuing footsteps and grasping hands of her nurse. She was five years old now, old enough to wear grown-up dresses, and Amber clothed her beautifully, from her innumerable silk and taffeta gowns to each pair of tiny shoes and miniature gloves. Two-year-old Charles Stanhope, the future Duke of Ravenspur, gave every indication that one day he would be at least as big as his father and, also like the King, he had a droll precocious seriousness. His nurse was holding him in her arms and he looked at the house with as much seeming interest and solemnity as if he realized the role he was expected one day to play there.

Finally Amber, in exasperation, stamped her foot and shouted at Susanna: "Susanna! Behave yourself, you pestilent little wench—or I'll take a course with you!"

Susanna stopped in her tracks, looked slowly around over her shoulder at Amber, and her lower-lip thrust out stubbornly. Nevertheless she turned about and walked with a kind of mock demureness back to her nurse, reaching up to slip her small hand into the woman's palm. Amber pursed her lips and frowned, displeased with her daughter's naughtiness. But just as she was about to turn away she heard a loud burst of masculine laughter and swinging about she saw that it was Almsbury, climbing out of his coach and starting toward her.

"Wait till she grows up!" he bellowed. "Just wait! She'll lead you a mighty merry chase about ten years from now, I'll warrant!"

"Oh, Almsbury!" Amber's own lip stuck out now, in an expression very much like Susanna's. "Who wants to think about ten years from now!" The older she got the more she dreaded and feared the encroachment of the years. "I hope it never comes!"

"But it will," he assured her complacently. "Everything comes, if you wait long enough, you know."

"Does it!" snapped Amber crossly. "I've waited long enough and everything hasn't come to me!" She turned her back to him and was about to take up her conversation with Captain Wynne again when something she had seen in his eyes caused her to turn and look at him. He was grinning at her, obviously very much pleased with himself.

"Almsbury," she said slowly, and all of a sudden her throat felt dry and tight. "Almsbury—what did you come out here for?"

He strolled up to stand very close beside her, and his eyes looked down into hers. "I came, sweetheart, to tell you that they're here. They got in last night."

She felt as though she had just been struck across the face, very hard, and for a paralyzed moment she stood staring at him. She was aware that one of his hands reached out and took hold of her upper arm, as if to steady her. Then she looked beyond him, over his shoulder, out to where his crested coach stood waiting.

"Where is he?" Her lips formed the words, but she heard no sound.

"He's home. At my house. His wife is here too, you know."

Swiftly Amber's eyes came back to his. The dazed almost dreamy look was gone from her face and she looked alert and challenging.

"What does she look like?"

Almsbury answered gently, as if afraid of hurting her. "She's very beautiful."

"She can't be!"

Amber stood staring down at the wood-shavings, the scraps and piled bricks that lay all about them. Her sweeping black brows had drawn together and her face had an expression of almost tragic anxiety.

"She can't be!" she repeated. Then suddenly she looked back up at him again, almost ashamed of herself. She had never been afraid of any woman on earth. No matter what kind of beauty this Corinna was she had no reason to fear her. "When—" She remembered that Captain Wynne was still there, just beside

864

them, and changed the words she had been about to say. "I'm having a supper tonight. Why don't you come and bring Lord Carlton with you—and his wife too, if she wants to come?"

"I think they won't be going abroad for a few days—the voyage was longer than usual and her Ladyship is tired."

"That's too bad," said Amber tartly. "And is his Lordship too tired to stir out of the house too?"

"I don't think he'd care to go without her."

"Ye gods!" cried Amber. "I'm sure I never thought Lord Carlton would be the man to fawn over a wife!"

Almsbury did not try to argue the point. "They're going to Arlington House Thursday night—you'll be there, won't you?"

"Of course. But Thursday—" Again she remembered the presence of Captain Wynne. "Did he go down to the wharves today?"

"Yes. But he's got a great deal of business there. I'd advise you to wait till Thursday—"

Amber gave him a glare that cut off his sentence in the middle. Then, mocking her, he gulped a time or two as if in fright, bowed very formally, and turning walked back to his coach. She watched him go, made a sudden little movement to run after him and apologize—but did not. His coach had no sooner disappeared from sight than Amber lost all interest in her house.

"I've got to go now, Captain Wynne," she said hastily. "We'll talk about this later. Good-day." And she half ran to get into her own coach, followed by the nursemaids and the two children. "Drive down Water Lane to the New Key! And hurry!"

But he was not there. Her footman went up and down the wharf inquiring; they saw his ships riding at anchor and were told that he had been there all morning but had left at dinner-time and not returned. She waited for almost an hour, but the children were becoming cross and tired and at last she had to go.

Back at the Palace she immediately wrote him a letter, imploring him to come to her, but she got no reply until the next morning and then it was merely a hasty scratched note: "Business makes it impossible for me to wait on you. If you're at

865

Arlington House Thursday, may I claim the favour of a dance? Carlton." Amber tore it into bits and flung herself onto the bed to cry.

But in spite of herself she was forced to take certain practicalities into consideration.

For if it was true that Lady Carlton was a beauty then she must somehow contrive to look more dazzling Thursday night than ever before in her life. They were used to her at Court now and it had been a long while since her appearance at any great or small function had aroused the excitement and envy she had been able to stir up three and a half years ago. If Lady Carlton was even moderately pretty she would be the object of every stare, the subject of every comment, whether it were made in praise or derogation. Unless—unless I can wear something or do something they won't be able to ignore, no matter how they try.

She spent several hours in a frenzy of worry and indecision and then at last she sent for Madame Rouvière. The only possible solution was a new gown, but a gown different from anything she had ever seen, a gown no one had ever dared to wear.

"I've got to have something they can't *help* staring at," Amber told her. "If I have to go in stark naked with my hair on fire."

Madame Rouvière laughed. "That would be well enough for an entrance—but after a while they would grow tired and begin to look at the ladies with more on. It must be something *indiscret*—and yet covering enough to make them try to see more. Black would be the colour—black tiffany, perhaps—but there must be something to glitter too—" She went on, talking aloud, sketching out the dress with her hands while Amber listened in rapt attention and with glowing eyes.

Lady Carlton! Poor creature—what chance would she have?

For the next two days Amber did not leave her rooms. From early morning until late at night they were filled with Madame Rouvière and her little sempstresses, all of them chattering French and giggling while scissors snipped, deft fingers stitched and Madame wrung her hands and shrieked hysterically if she discovered a seam taken in a bit too far or a hem-line uneven by so much as a quarter of an inch. Amber stood patiently hour after hour while the dress was fitted, and they literally made it on her. No one was allowed to come in or to see it and to her great delight all this secrecy set up a froth of rumours.

The Duchess was going to come as Venus rising from the sea, dressed in a single sea-shell. She was going to drive a gilt chariot and four full-grown horses up the front stairs and into the drawing-room. Her gown was to be made of real pearls which would fall off, a few at a time, until she had on nothing at all. At least they did not doubt her audacity and their ingenuity gave considerable credit to hers.

Thursday they were still at work.

Amber's hair was washed and dried and polished with silk before the hair-dresser went to work on it. Pumice-stone removed every trace of fuzz from her arms and legs. She slathered her face and neck a dozen times with French cold-creams and brushed her teeth until her arm ached. She bathed in milk and poured jasmine perfume into the palms of her hands to rub on her legs and arms and body. She spent almost an hour painting her face.

At six o'clock the gown was done and Madame Rouvière proudly held it up at full length for all of them to see. Susanna, who had spent the entire day in the room, jumped and clapped her hands together and ran to kiss the hem. Madame let out such a screech of horror at this sacrilege that Susanna almost fell over backward in alarm.

Amber threw off her dressing-gown and—wearing nothing but black silk stockings held up by diamond-buckled garters and a pair of high-heeled black shoes—she lifted her arms over her head so that they could slide it on. The bodice was a wide-open lace-work of heavy cord sewn with black bugle beads, and it cut down to a deep point. There was a long narrow sheath-like skirt, completely covered with beads, that looked like something black and wet and shiny pouring over her hips and legs and trailing away in back. Sheer black tiffany made great puffed sleeves and an over-skirt which draped up at the sides and floated down over the train like a black mist.

While the others stood staring, babbling, ecstatically "oh-ing," Amber looked at herself in the mirrored walls with a thrill of triumph. She lifted her ribs and tightened her chest muscles so that her breasts stood out like full pointed globes.

He'll *die* when he sees me! she told herself in a delirium of confidence. Corinna could not scare her now.

Madame Rouvière came to adjust her head-dress which was a great arch of black ostrich-feathers sweeping up over her head from a tight little helmet. Someone handed her her gloves and she pulled them on, long black ones clear to her elbows. Against the nakedness of her body, they seemed almost immodest. She carried a black fan and over her shoulders they laid a black velvet cloak, the lining edged in black fox. The stark black against her rich cream-and-honey colouring, something in the expression of her eyes and the curve of her mouth, gave her the look of a diabolical angel—at once pure, beautiful, corrupt and sinister.

Amber turned now from the mirror to face Madame, and their eyes met with the gleaming look of successful conspirators. Madame put her thumb and fingers together and made the gesture of kissing them. She came up to Amber and said with a hiss in her ear: "They'll never see her at all—that other one!"

Amber gave her a quick grateful hug and a grin. Then she bent to kiss Susanna, who approached her mother very carefully, almost afraid to touch her. And with her heart beating fast, her stomach churning maddeningly, Amber walked out of the room, put her mask to her face and went along a narrow little corridor leading out to where her coach waited. She had not felt so excited at the prospect of a party, so apprehensive and frightened, since the night she had first been presented at Court.

CHAPTER SIXTY–ONE

ARLINGTON HOUSE, WHICH had been Goring House before Bennet bought it in 1663, stood next to the old Mulberry Gardens on the west of the Palace. In it the Baron and Baroness gave the most brilliant, the most elaborate, and the most eagerly attended parties in London. Nothing else could be compared to them. The invitations they sent out were a sure barometer of one's social standing. Nonentities were never asked.

His Lordship was known as the most lavish and thoughtful host of fashionable society. He served superlative food, prepared by a dozen French cooks, and wines from a vast cellar. There was music in every room; gambling-tables were piled with gold; candles burned by the thousand. The house swarmed with earls and dukes and knights, countesses and duchesses and ladies, and to the casual eye everything seemed most decorous. Satin-gowned ladies curtsied and smiled over spread fans, brocade-suited gentlemen bowed from the waist with a flourishing sweep of their hats. Voices were low and conversation apparently polite.

But in fact they were gleefully at work destroying one another's characters. The men, as they stood watching a pretty woman, boasted that they had laid with her, discussed her physical defects and compared her behaviour in bed. The women yanked reputations apart with equal or greater vigour. Darkened bedrooms all over the house sheltered couples seeking a temporary refuge. In some obscure corner a Maid of Honour was lifting her skirts to let the gallants decide whether her legs were as pretty as another's, squealing and giggling when they ventured to employ their hands too boldly. One of the fops had sneaked a girl from Madame Bennet's into the house under the guise of mask and cloak and she was performing for several young men and women somewhere behind locked doors.

Arlington never interfered with his guests but let each amuse himself according to his own tastes.

At seven o'clock, the night being still young and most of the guests sober as well as curious, they were gathered in the main drawing-room and keeping one eye at least on the new arrivals. They were waiting for two women who had not yet come: the Duchess of Ravenspur, and Lady Carlton. Her Ladyship—whom almost no one had seen—was rumoured to be the greatest beauty ever to appear in England, though opinions on this score were already strong and divided. Many of the women, at least, were prepared to decide the moment she arrived that she was by no means as beautiful as had been reported. And the Duchess of Ravenspur, no doubt from fear that her Ladyship would outshine her, was expected to do something spectacular in order to save herself.

"How I pity her Grace," said one languid young lady. "It runs through the galleries she lives in terror now of losing what she has. Gad, but it must be a bothersome thing to be great."

Her companion smiled with lips pressed together. "Is that why *you* never climbed the ladder?—for fear of falling off?"

"I don't care a fig for Lady Carlton or what she looks like," commented a thin young fop who kept his hands busy with manipulating a woman's fan, "but I'll be her slave if she can put the Duchess's nose out of joint. That damned woman has grown intolerable since his Majesty gave her a duchy. I used to lace her busk for her when she was only a scurvy player—but now every time we're presented she makes a show of never having seen me before."

"It's her vulgar breeding, Jack. What else can you expect?"

A voice like a trumpet interrupted them. "Her Grace, the Duchess of Ravenspur!"

Every eye in the room swept toward the door—but only the usher stood there alone beside it. They waited for an impatient moment or two and then, with her head held high and a kind of fierce challenging pride on her face, the Duchess came into view and slowly walked through the doorway toward them. A wave of shock and amazement swept along before her. Heads spun, eyes popped and even King Charles turned on his heel where he was talking to Mrs. Wells and stared.

Amber came on imperturbably, though it seemed all her insides were quaking. She heard some of the older women gasp and saw them set their mouths sternly, square their shoulders and fix upon her their hard reproving glares. She heard low whistles from the men, saw their eyebrows go up, their elbows reach out to nudge one another. She saw the young women looking at her with anger and indignation, furious that she had dared to take such an advantage of them.

870

Suddenly she relaxed, convinced that she was a success. She was hoping that Bruce and Corinna were there somewhere to have seen her triumph.

Then, almost at once, she became aware that Almsbury was just at her side. She looked at him, a faint smile touching the corners of her mouth, but something she saw in his eyes made her expression freeze suddenly. What was it? Disapproval? Pity? Something of both? But that was ridiculous! She looked stunning and she knew it.

"Holy Christ, Amber," he murmured, and his eyes went swiftly down over her body.

"Don't you like it?" Her eyes hardened a little as she looked up at him and even in her own ears her voice took on a confident brassy sound that was part bravado.

"Yes, of course. You look gorgeous—"

"But aren't you cold?" interrupted a feminine voice, and turning swiftly Amber found Mrs. Boynton beside her, looking her over with feline insolence.

Another voice, a man's this time, came from her other side. "Ods-fish, madame. But this is the greatest display that ever I've seen in public since I was weaned." It was the King, lazy, smiling, obviously amused.

Amber felt suddenly as if she had been hurt inside.

She turned sick with a feeling of horror and self-disgust. What have I done! she thought. Oh, my God! what am I doing out here half undressed?

Her eyes swept round the room and every face she saw was secretly smiling, covertly sneering at her. All at once she felt like the person in a dream who sets out confidently to go uptown stark naked, gets halfway there and then realizes his mistake. And, like the dreamer, she wished passionately that she were back home where no one could see her—but to her wild dismay she realized that this time she was caught in her own trap. She could not wake up from *this* bad dream.

Oh, what am I going to do? she thought desperately. How am I going to get out of here? In her anguish and self-consciousness she had all but forgotten Lord Carlton and his wife.

And then, so unexpectedly that she almost started, she heard their names called out, loud and clear: "My Lord Carlton! My Lady Carlton!"

Without even realizing that she had done so she grabbed Almsbury by the hand and her eyes turned toward the door. The colour drained out of her face and neck as she watched them walk in; she did not even see the quick glance Almsbury gave her but she felt the warm reassuring pressure of his hand.

Bruce looked very much as he had when he had left London two years before. He was thirty-eight years old and perhaps a little heavier than when last she had seen him, but still handsome, hard-skinned and vigorous-bodied, a man who changed little with the years. Amber only glanced at him—and then shifted her attention to his wife who walked beside him, her fingers resting upon his arm.

She was rather tall, though slender and graceful, with clear blue eyes, dark hair, and a skin pale as moonlight. Her features were delicate, her expression serene. To look at her brought up some elusive emotion—the same feeling evoked by an exquisitely painted porcelain. The gown she wore was cloth-of-silver covered with black lace and a black-lace mantilla lay upon her head; about her neck was the diamond and sapphire necklace which had belonged to Bruce's mother and which Amber had always hoped might one day be her own.

The King, ignoring ceremony, went forward with Lord and Lady Arlington to greet them—and as he did so all the room set up a noisy buzzing.

"My God! But she's a glorious creature!"

"I know that gown was made in Paris, my dear, it must have been, it couldn't have—"

"Can they really have women like that in Jamaica?"

"Poise and breeding—than which I admire nothing more in a woman."

Amber was actually sick at her stomach now. Her hands and arm-pits were wet, all her muscles seemed to ache. I've got to get out of here before they see me! she thought wildly. But just as she made an involuntary movement to escape, Almsbury's grip on her hand tightened and he gave her a little jerk.

She looked up at him, surprised, but then quickly composed herself again.

Charles, with no respect for etiquette, was asking Lady Carlton to dance with him, and now as the music started for a pavane he led her onto the floor. Others followed and it was soon crowded with slow-moving figures, pacing to the rhythmic cadence of spinets, flutes and a low-beating drum. Amber scarcely heard Almsbury asking her to dance. He repeated his request, louder this time.

She glanced at him. "I don't want to dance," she muttered, distracted. "I'm not going to stay here. I—I've got the vapours—I'm going home."

This time she picked up her skirts and took a step, but the Earl caught her wrist and gave her so vigorous a jerk that her breasts shook and her curls bounced. "Stop acting like a damned fool or I'll slap you! Smile at me, now—everyone's watching you."

With a quick shifting of her eyeballs beneath half-lowered lashes, Amber glanced round the room. She wanted to turn and scream or pick up something to throw at them, something that would destroy them all where they stood and wipe out of her sight forever those pleased smirking faces. Instead she looked up at Almsbury and smiled, pulling the corners of her mouth as tight as possible to keep the muscles from quivering. She put her hand on his extended arm and they moved toward the floor.

"I've got to get out of here," she told him, under cover of the music. "I *can't* stay!"

His expression did not change. "You won't leave if I have to tie you up. If you had the courage to wear that thing in the first place, by God you'll have the courage to stay till the end!"

Amber clenched her teeth, hating him, and as her feet kept moving in time to the music she began to plan how she would escape—slip away through some side-door the first time he let her out of his sight. Damn him! she thought. He acts like my grandmother! What's it to him if I stay or don't! I'll go if I—

And then, all unexpectedly, she saw Lady Carlton not more than ten feet away. Corinna was smiling at Almsbury, but she

873

gave a little gasp of surprise as she caught sight of his partner. Amber's eyes blazed in fury and Corinna looked swiftly away, obviously embarrassed.

Oh, that woman! thought Amber. I hate her, I hate her, I hate her! Look how she minces and smiles and sets her foot so! Hoity-toity! How mightily prim and proper! I wish I was stark naked! That *would* make her eyes pop out! I'll pay her back for that! I'll make her sorry she ever clapt eyes on me! Just wait—

But suddenly her energy was consumed. She felt weak, lost, helpless.

I'm going to die, she thought wretchedly. I'll never live through this. My life won't be worth tuppence to me now— Oh, God, let me die right here, right now—I can't take another step. For the moment it seemed that Almsbury's arm was all that kept her from collapsing. Then the music stopped and the crowd began to move about, gathering into groups. Amber, with Almsbury still at her side, pretended to see no one as she made her way among them.

I'm going now, she told herself. And that damned blockhead isn't going to stop me!

But as she started toward a door he took hold of her arm. "Come over here and meet Lady Carlton."

Amber jerked away. "What do I want to know her for?"

"Amber, for the love of God!" His voice, scarcely more than a whisper, was pleading with her. "Look about you. Can't you see what they're thinking?"

Amber's eyes again flickered hastily around in time to catch a dozen pairs of eyes which had been fixed upon her glance aside, eyes that glittered, set above mouths that curled with amusement and contempt. Some of them did not even trouble to look away but met her with bold scornful smiles; they were watching, and waiting—

She took a deep breath, linked her arm with Almsbury's and together they walked toward where Lord and Lady Carlton stood in a group made up of the King, Buckingham, Lady Shrewsbury; Lady Falmouth, Buckhurst, Sedley and Rochester. As they approached, the small gathering seemed to grow quieter

—as if expecting something to happen from the mere fact of her presence. Almsbury presented Lady Carlton to the Duchess of Ravenspur and both women, smiling politely, made faint curtsies. Lady Carlton was friendly and gracious and obviously altogether unaware that her husband might know this gorgeous half-naked woman. While the men, including his Majesty, all turned their heads to look at her, their eyes admiring her figure.

But Amber was conscious of no one but Bruce.

For an instant Lord Carlton's expression might have betrayed him—but no one was looking—and then immediately it changed, he bowed to her as though they were the merest acquaintances. Amber, as their eyes met, felt the world rock and tremble beneath her. The conversation began again and had been going on for several seconds before she was able to follow it: King Charles and Bruce were discussing America, the tobacco plantations, the colonists' resentment of the Navigation Laws, men the King knew who had gone to make their homes in the New World. Corinna said little, but whenever she did speak Charles turned to her with interest and unconcealed admiration. Her voice was light and soft, completely feminine, and the brief glances she gave Bruce revealed that here was that unheard-of phenomenon in London society: a woman deeply in love with her husband.

Amber wanted to reach out and rake her long nails across that tranquil lovely face.

When the music began again she curtsied, very cool and aloof and with some delicate suggestion of insult, to Corinna, nodded vaguely at Bruce and left them. After that she defiantly began to pretend that she was enjoying herself and was not at all embarrassed by her own nudity. She ate her supper attended by half-a-score of gallants, drank too much champagne, danced every dance. But the evening dragged with interminable slowness, and she thought wearily that it would never end.

After an hour or so the dancers began to disappear into the rooms beyond, where the gaming-tables were set up. Amber, a nervous ache in her back and an agonizing tiredness through every bone, excused herself and went into the dressing-room which had been set aside for the ladies. There they might powder their faces or touch up their lips, adjust a garter or sit down for a few minutes and relax—impossible in the presence of men.

But for a couple of maids, the room was empty when she walked into it and she stood for a moment, completely off her guard, shoulders slumped and head buried in her hands. Then all at once she heard steps behind her and Boynton's voice cried gayly: "How now, your Grace? An attack of the vapours?"

Amber gave her a quick glance of scorn and disgust and bent to smooth up her stockings and tighten the garters. Boynton flung herself onto a couch with a heavy relieved sigh, spreading her legs and stretching them out before her, turning her neck from side to side to relieve the tension.

Giving Amber an arch sidewise glance, she began to strip off her gloves. "Well—what d'ye think of my Lady Carlton?"

Amber shrugged. "She's well enough, I suppose."

Boynton laughed loudly at that. "Well enough, indeed. The men all think she's the prettiest woman here—if not the nakedest!"

"Oh, shut up!" muttered Amber, and turned her back on her to look into one of the mirrors, her hands pressed flat on the table-top. Did she really look so tired, or was it only that her face had gotten a little shiny? She asked one of the maids to bring her some powder.

Just at that moment Lady Carlton appeared in the doorway. Amber saw her in the mirror, her heart came to a sudden stop and then sped on again, almost suffocating her. She took the box of powder and began to dust her nose.

"May I come in?" asked Corinna.

"By all means, your Ladyship!" cried Boynton, shooting Amber a glance of malicious triumph. "We were just saying that since the Duchess of Richmond's had the small-pox you're the greatest beauty to come to Court."

Corinna laughed softly. "Why, thank you. How kind of you to say that." Her eyes glanced uncertainly at Amber's back, as though she wished to speak to her but did not quite know how to begin. Actually, she wanted to make some kind of apology for her clumsiness earlier in the evening. London, she

876

realized, was not America, and here no doubt it was quite correct for a lady of the highest rank to appear all but naked at a private party.

"Your Grace," she ventured at last, "would it seem rude if I told you how much I admire your gown?"

Amber did not even glance at her, but continued busy with the hare's-foot. "Not if you meant it," she said tartly.

Corinna looked at her, both puzzled and hurt by the rudeness, wondering what reply she should or could make to that. Already she had been surprised and baffled to discover the savage under-currents that existed in the glossy polite stream of Palace etiquette.

But Boynton spoke up instantly. "But your own gown, Lady Carlton, is the loveliest one here tonight! How *do* you get such clothes in America? The cloth-of-silver, and that lace—it's exquisite!"

"Thank you, madame. My dressmaker is a Frenchwoman and she sends to Paris for the materials. Why, really," she added with a little laugh, "we aren't such savages in America. Everyone seems surprised I don't wear a leather dress and moccasins."

Amber picked up her fan and gloves, turned around again and looked Corinna straight in the eye. "As for that, madame, you may find it's us who are the savages!"

With that she swept out of the room, but not before she had heard Boynton say gleefully, "Pray, my lady, you must excuse her. She's had a mighty bad shock tonight." All of them were thinking, Amber knew, that she was jealous because King Charles had been paying her Ladyship such marked attention.

"Oh," murmured Corinna's sympathetic voice, "I'm sorry—"

Amber found Bruce at the raffling-table—for he never remained long in a ball-room when the cards were being dealt or the dice were running—and so absorbed in the play that he did not see her until she had been standing across from him for several moments. Self-consciously she had put on her most becoming expression, lower lip softly pouting, brows slightly raised to tilt the corners of her eyes.

The instant he looked at her she knew it and glanced over

swiftly, a half-smile on her mouth. But his mouth did not answer and his green eyes looked at her seriously for a moment, then lightened and slid down her body with a kind of lazy insolence. Slowly they returned to her face and one eyebrow lifted almost imperceptibly. At that instant she felt like the commonest kind of drab, displaying herself for any man to see and appraise and—worst of all—to reject.

Ready to cry with rage and humiliation she turned swiftly and walked away.

When she blundered into Lord Buckhurst and he suggested that they find some private room she went with him, as much to get away where she could not be seen as for anything else. But she stayed for more than two hours and got a morbid kind of satisfaction from thinking that Bruce would probably know what she was about. She had been lucklessly trying for nine years to arouse his jealousy, but still she was not convinced it would never be possible.

They returned to the drawing-room after eleven to find the gambling still going on and a group gathered about the King and his Royal Highness—James was playing a guitar and Charles was singing, in his magnificent bass voice, a rollicking Cavalier song of the Civil War days. The first person she saw, even before they got to the bottom of the stairs, was Almsbury, and he came toward her with a look of worry on his face. But he said nothing and he and Buckhurst exchanged polite bows. His Lordship went off then and left her with the Earl.

"Ye gods, Amber, I've been looking everywhere for you! I thought you'd gone—"

All at once Amber found herself ready to burst into tears. "Almsbury! Oh, Almsbury, *please* take me home! Haven't I stayed long enough!"

They went outside then and got into the coach and there Amber began to cry with furious abandon, sobbing almost hysterically. It was several moments before she could even speak and then she wailed miserably: "Oh, Almsbury! He didn't even smile at me! He just looked at me like—like— Oh, God! I wish I was dead!"

Almsbury held her close against him, his mouth pressed to

878

her cheek. "What else could he do, sweetheart? His wife was there!"

"What difference does that make! Why should *he* be the only man in London to care what his wife thinks! Oh, he hates me, I know he does! And I hate him too!" She blew her nose. "Oh, I wish I *did* hate him!"

She saw Lord and Lady Carlton the next day riding in the Ring. Amber knew that he disliked intensely the monotonous circling round and round, nodding and smiling to the same people two dozen times and more, but evidently he had come for Corinna's entertainment, since the ladies always enjoyed that pastime. The following day they sat in adjacent boxes at the Duke's Theatre, and the day after that they were in the Chapel at Whitehall. It was the first time she had ever seen him in a church. Each time both Lord and Lady Carlton bowed and smiled at her, and his Lordship seemed no better acquainted with her than his wife was.

Amber alternated between fury and despondent misery.

How *can* he have forgotten me? she frantically asked herself. He acts as if he's never seen me before. No, he doesn't, either! No man who'd never seen me before would look the way he does! If his wife had any wit at all she'd begin to suspect he knows me only too well— But she won't of course! Amber thought petulantly. I swear she's the greatest dunce in nature!

But despite his seeming indifference she could not believe it possible that he had been able to forget all they had meant to each other, for happiness and sorrow, over the nine years past. He could not have forgotten the things she remembered so well. That first day in Marygreen, those early happy weeks in London, the terrible morning when Rex Morgan had died, the days of the Plague— He could not have forgotten that she had borne him two children. He could not have forgotten the pleasures they had shared, the laughter and quarrels, all the agony and ecstasy of being violently in love. Those were the things that could never fade—nothing could ever erase them. No other woman could ever be to him exactly what she had been.

Oh, he can't forget! she cried to herself, lonely and despairing. He can't! He can't! He'll come to me as soon as he can, I know he will. He'll come tonight. But he did not.

Five days after she had seen him at Arlington House, he and Almsbury came to her rooms late one afternoon as she was dressing to go out for supper. She had been thinking of him, both angry and excited at once, wishing passionately that he would come—and yet she was surprised when he and Almsbury walked into the room together.

"Why—your Lordship!"

Both men bowed, sweeping off their hats.

"Madame."

Then, quickly recovering herself, Amber shooed the maids and other attendants out of the room. But she did not rush toward him as she had thought she would. Now that he was there she merely stood and looked at him, almost painfully self-conscious, and did not know what to do, or what she dared to do. She waited for him.

"I wonder if I might see Susanna?"

"Why—yes—yes, of course."

She walked to the door and called to someone in the next room. She turned back to face him. "Susanna's grown like anything. She's—she's much bigger than when you left." She was scarcely aware of what she said. Oh, my darling! she thought wildly. Is that all you're going to do—after two years? Just stand there—looking as if you scarce know me at all?

But the next moment the door was pushed open and Susanna stood in it, dressed in a grown-up, green-taffeta gown with the tiny skirt tucked up over a pink petticoat, and her golden glossy hair caught back at one side with a pink bow. She looked at her mother first and then, somewhat bewildered, at the two men, wondering what was wanted of her.

"Don't you remember your Daddy?" asked Amber.

Susanna gave him another dubious glance. "But I have a Daddy," she protested politely.

Charles had told her, when she had said that she had no Daddy, that he would be her Daddy now. And since then she had regarded the King as her father, for she saw him often and

880

he always made a great fuss over her because of her prettiness and his own fondness for children.

Bruce laughed at that and coming forward he reached down, took hold of her, and swooped her into his arms. "You can't fob me off with any such tale as that, young lady. You may have a new father, but I'm still your first—and it's the first one who counts. Come now—give me a kiss—and if it's nice enough perhaps I'll find a present for you."

"A present?"

Susanna's eyes turned big and round and she looked back at her mother, who winked and nodded her head. Without further hesitation she flung her arms about his neck and kissed his cheek resoundingly.

Almsbury grinned. "Her mother's own child. I see it more every day."

Amber made him a face, but she was too happy now to take offense at his quips. Bruce carried Susanna to the door, opened it, reached outside and picked up a box, and then putting her down he dropped to his heels beside her. "There," he said. "Open it up and we'll see what's inside."

Both Amber and Almsbury came up close to see what it was as Susanna, now very self-important, picked up the lid. There lay a beautiful doll, perhaps a foot and a half tall, with light blonde curls done in the latest mode and wearing a fashionable French gown. Packed beside her was a wardrobe containing several more gowns, petticoats and smocks, shoes and gloves and fans and masks, all the paraphernalia of a lady of quality. Susanna, all but delirious with pleasure, kissed him again and again. Then, very carefully, she lifted her treasure from its satin-lined bed and held it in her arms.

"Oh, Mother!" she cried. "I want to have her in my picture too! Can I?" Susanna was having her portrait painted by Mr. Lely.

"Of course you can, darling." She glanced at Bruce and found him watching both of them, and though he was faintly smiling there was something moody and almost wistful in his eyes. "It was so kind of you to think of her," she said softly.

At last, when half an hour or so had passed, Amber glanced

at the clock. "It's time for your supper, sweetheart. You must go now, or you'll be late."

"But I don't *want* to go! I don't want any supper! I want to stay with my new Daddy!"

She ran to him where he still knelt on one knee, and he put an arm about her. "I'll come back to see you soon, darling, I promise. But now you must go." He kissed her and then, reluctantly, she made a curtsy to Amber and Almsbury. Primly she walked to the doorway, where, as the nurse held it open for her, she turned and looked around at them.

"I s'pose it's time to go to bed with my new Daddy now!"

The nurse hastily covered Susanna's mouth with her handkerchief and hurried her out, closing the door firmly, while the two men burst into laughter. Amber spread her hands and gave a shrug, making a comical little grimace. There was no doubt Susanna had been sent off many times with the excuse that it was time for Mother and Daddy to go to bed. Bruce got to his feet.

Amber's eyes were on him instantly, questioning, begging.

Quickly Almsbury took out his watch. "Well—damn me! But I'm late now—I hope you'll excuse me—" Already he was backing from the room.

But Bruce turned about swiftly. "I'm going with you, John—"

"Bruce!" Amber gave a little cry of anguish and ran toward him. "You *can't* go now! Stay just a little—and talk to me—"

While he stood looking down at her Almsbury went out the door and shut it softly. Bruce glanced back over his shoulder as he heard the sound, hesitated a moment longer and then tossed his hat onto a chair.

CHAPTER SIXTY–TWO

AMBER LAY ON a low cushioned day-bed, her eyes closed, her face serenely peaceful and content. Her hair had come down and fell in tawny masses about her shoulders. Bruce sat on the floor beside her, arms resting on his drawn-up knees, head bent forward to lean on his wrists. He had taken off his periwig, coat and sword, and his wet white-linen shirt clung to his back and arms.

For a long while they continued silent.

Finally Amber, not opening her eyes, reached out and put one hand on his, her fingers tender and warm. He raised his head to look at her. His face was moist and flushed. Slowly he smiled, bent his head again and laid his lips on the back of her hand where the blue veins swelled.

"My darling—" Her voice lingered over the word, caressing it. Then slowly she lifted her lids and looked at him; they smiled, a smile born of recent memories and long acquaintance. "At last you're back again. Oh, Bruce, I've missed you so! Have you missed me too—just a little?"

"Of course," he said. It was an automatic reply, made as if he thought the question a foolish or unnecessary one.

"How long will you be here? Are you going to live here now?" She could have been almost grateful for Corinna if she had insisted that they live in England.

"We'll be here a couple of months, I think. Then we're going to France to buy some furniture and visit my sister. After that we'll go back to Virginia."

"We." Amber did not like the sound of it. It reminded her again that his life, all his plans, included a woman now—a woman who was not herself. And it hurt her pride that he was taking Corinna to visit his sister for she had asked Almsbury once what kind of woman Mary Carlton was; he had told her that she was very beautiful, proud and haughty—and that she and Amber would not like each other.

"How d'you like being married?" she challenged him. "You must find it mighty dull—after the gay life you've lived!"

He smiled again, but now she knew that with every word she said he drew farther away from her. She was scared, but she did not know what she could do. She felt, as always, helpless to contend against him and hold her own. "I don't find it dull at all. In Virginia we have a better opinion of marriage than you do here."

She rolled her eyes at that and sat up, straightening her bodice around and beginning to fasten it again. "Hey day! How mightily proper you've grown! I vow and swear, Lord Carlton, you're not the same man who left here two years ago!"

He grinned at her. "I'm not?"

She looked down at him sharply, then suddenly she was on her knees beside him, held close in his arms. "Oh, my darling, darling—I love you so! I can't stand to know you're married to another woman! I hate her, I despise her, I—"

"Amber—don't talk that way!" He tried to make a joke of it. "After all, you've been married four times and I've never hated any of your husbands—"

"Why should you? I didn't love any of them!"

"Nor the King, either, I suppose?"

She dropped her eyes at that, momentarily abashed. Then she faced him again. "Not the way I do you— Anyway, he's the King. But you know as well as I do, Bruce, that if you'd let me I'd leave him and the Court and everything I have on earth to follow you anywhere!"

"What?" he asked her mockingly. "You'd leave all this?"

As he spoke she realized all of a sudden that he did not consider her position, the luxury and pomp in which she lived, to be of any real worth at all. It was the sharpest disillusionment she had had. For she had expected to brag about it, to impress him with her title, her power, her money, her gorgeous rooms. Instead, he had made her feel that all she had got from life— these things for which she had been willing to make any compromise—were unimportant. Worse, were trash.

"Yes," she said softly. "Of course I'd leave it." She had an inexplicable feeling of humility and almost of shame.

"Well, my dear, I wouldn't dream of asking such a sacrifice of you. You've worked hard for what you have and you deserve to keep it. What's more, you're exactly where you belong. You and Whitehall are as well suited as a bawd and brandy."

"What do you mean by that!" she cried.

He shrugged, glanced at the clock and got to his feet. "It's growing late. I've got to go."

Amber sprang up after him. "You're not going so soon? You haven't been here two hours!"

884

"I thought you were engaged for supper."

"I won't go. I'll send a message I've got the vapours. Oh, stay here with me darling and we'll have supper together! We'll have—"

"I'm sorry, Amber. I'd like to, but I can't. I'm late now."

Her eyes, golden and hard with jealousy, accused him. "Late for what!"

"My wife is expecting me."

"Your wife!" An ugly expression crossed her face. "And I suppose you don't dare stay out by so much as half-an-hour or she'll have you by the ear for it! It's mighty strange, Lord Carlton, to see you, of all men, turned Tom Otter!" Tom Otter was the prototype of the hen-pecked husband.

He was getting into his coat and though he did not look at her his voice was sarcastic. "I'm afraid living in America has put me somewhat behind the fashion." He buckled on his sword, set the periwig on his head and took up his hat. Casually he bowed to her. "Good-night, madame."

But as he started out of the room she ran after him. "Oh, Bruce! I didn't mean it, I swear I didn't! *Please* don't be angry with me! When can I see you again? And I want to see Bruce, too. Does he remember me?"

"Of course he remembers you, Amber. He asked me today when he was going to visit you."

Suddenly her eyes took on a bright malicious sparkle. "What does Corinna—"

"Corinna doesn't know that his mother is alive."

The sparkle went out. "A pretty arrangement," she said sourly.

"You agreed to it. And please, Amber, if she ever sees you together don't let her find out. I've made it clear to Bruce that he must never mention you."

"Good Lord! I never heard of anything so ridiculous! Most wives don't have to be pampered and protected so! Why—I give my husband's whore an allowance!"

He smiled down at her, slowly and with a certain sad and cynical quirk at the corners of his mouth and in his eyes. "But Corinna, my dear, hasn't had the advantages of your education.

In fact, until she was married, she lived somewhat retired."

"You men! Why is it the greatest whoremaster among you always marries some simple little sugar-sop who doesn't know one end of him from the other!"

"When shall I bring Bruce here?"

"Why—any time. Tomorrow?"

"Two o'clock?"

"Yes. But, Bruce—"

He bowed to her again and went on, out of the room, while Amber watched him between anger and tears, undecided whether to break something or cry. So she did both.

They came together the next day at two. The little boy, now eight and a half, was much taller and looked a good deal older than when she had seen him last. His resemblance to his father was stronger than ever. He was not at all like her. He was a very handsome decidedly masculine child with great charm and delightful manners, and it seemed incredible to Amber that he could be her own, born of some brief ecstatic moment so many years ago.

His face was eager and joyous at seeing her again, but like a gentleman he paused just inside the door, swept off his hat, and bowed very formally. Amber ran forward with a little cry, dropped to her knees and flung her arms about him, kissing him passionately while her throat ached with tears. Abandoning his own manners then he returned her kisses but kept his face turned so that his father could not see the tears in his eyes.

"Oh, my darling!" cried Amber. "How fine you look! And how tall you've grown—and strong!"

He gave a surreptitious little sniffle, dashing the tears off his face with the back of one hand. "I've missed you, Mother. England's so far away when you're in America." He grinned at her now, one brown hand on her shoulder. "You look mighty pretty, ma'm."

She longed to break into sobs, but managed a smile. "Thank you, darling. I hope I'll always look pretty to you."

"Why don't you come back to America with us? We live in a great house now, in Virginia. There's room enough for all of us

886

and more. *Will* you come, Mother? I'm sure you'd like it better than London—it's mighty nice there, I promise you."

Amber gave Bruce a quick glance, then kissed the little boy again. "I'm glad you want me to live with you, darling, but I don't think I can. You see, this is where I live."

He turned now and appealed to his father, with the air of one man stating a practical business proposition to another. "Then why don't we all live here, sir?"

Bruce dropped down so that his weight rested on his heels and his face was almost on a level with his son's; he put one arm about the boy's waist. "We can't live here, Bruce, because I can't leave the plantation. America is my home. But you may stay here, if you prefer."

Quick disappointment showed on his face. "Oh, but I don't want to leave you, sir. And I like America." He turned back to Amber. "Will you come to visit us someday?"

"Perhaps," said Amber softly, but she did not dare look at Bruce, and then she jumped to her feet. "Would you like to see your sister—Susanna?"

Together the three ran downstairs to the nursery where Susanna was being given her dancing-lesson by an exasperated Frenchman, and just as they arrived she was stamping her foot and screaming at him in a rage. She did not remember her brother at first for she had been only two and a half when he went away, but very soon they were chattering excitedly, exchanging news. Amber dismissed the servants and the four of them were left alone.

Bruce, for all that he seemed so grown-up, could not resist the temptation to brag to his little sister. For he lived in a great new country now, had sailed twice across the ocean, rode his own horse over the plantation with his father, was learning to sail a boat and had shot a wild-turkey just before they left. Susanna was not to be outdone.

"Pish!" she said scornfully. "What do I care for all that! *I* have two fathers!"

Bruce was taken aback for no more than an instant. "That's nothing to me, 'miss. *I* have two mothers!"

"You lie, you rogue!" cried Susanna. Her challenge might

887

have led to an open quarrel, but just at that moment Amber and Bruce interrupted with the suggestion that they all play a game.

After that she saw Lord Carlton frequently, and he came even when he did not bring the little boy. Usually he stayed no more than an hour or two, but he made no great effort to be secretive and Amber decided that marriage had not changed him as much as she had feared at first.

At last she grew bold enough to say to him one day: "What if Corinna finds out about us?"

"I hope she won't."

"Gossip spreads like the plague here at Whitehall."

"Then I hope she won't believe it."

"Won't believe it? Lord, how naïve d'you think she is?"

"She's not accustomed to London morals. She'll likely think it's malicious talk."

"But what if she doesn't? What if she asks you?"

"I won't lie to her." He gave her a quick scowl. "Look here, you little minx, if I find you've been up to any of your tricks I'll—"

"You'll what?"

Her eyes sparkled, her mouth smiled. She rolled over on the bed and her arms went about him, crushing her breasts against his shoulder. Their mouths came swiftly together. Corinna no longer existed for either of them.

As the time went by Amber's confidence increased. For though he said that he loved Corinna she knew that he loved her too. They had shared so much together, there was so much between them, so many memories—those things remained in his heart and they would always remain there, she was sure of that. She began to feel that his wife was merely an inconvenience, a social handicap, and even Corinna's great beauty held less terror for her than it had at first.

As she had expected, their meetings did not long remain secret. Buckingham, of course, and Arlington too must have known about them from the first—and, though Charles never mentioned it, undoubtedly he did—but all those gentlemen had other matters of greater importance to them than a woman's love-affairs. The ladies of the Court, however, did not.

Lord and Lady Carlton had been in London less than a month when the Countess of Southesk and Jane Middleton came one morning to pay Amber a visit—and met Bruce just leaving. He bowed to them both, but though Mrs. Middleton gave him her most languishing look and Southesk tried to rally him into conversation, he made his excuses and left them.

"Oh, by all means, my lord!" gushed Southesk. "Do go along. Lord, I vow and swear no man's reputation is safe if he's coming out of her Grace's chamber before noon!"

"Your servant, madame," said Bruce, bowing again, and he walked away.

Middleton's eyes followed him down the corridor, her pink lips pouting. "Lord, but he's handsome! I vow and swear, the person in the world I most admire!"

"I told you! I told you!" cried Southesk gleefully. "He's her lover! Come, let's in—"

They found Amber taking a bath in a large marble tub set on a rug in the middle of her bedroom floor. There was asses' milk in the water to cloud it and a white-fox robe was laid across the lower half of the tub, concealing her body from the waist down. The room was crowded with tradespeople all talking at once, and the monkey chattered, the parrot squawked, the dog barked. Just behind her stood the newest addition to her household, a tall blonde eunuch, handsome and no more than twenty-five. He was one of the many seamen captured each year by Algerian pirates and castrated to be sold back into Europe where they were bought as household ornaments by the finest ladies.

"No," Amber was saying, "I won't have it! It's hideous! My God, look at that colour! I could never wear it—"

"But, madame," protested the mercer, "it's the newest shade —I just got it from Paris. It's called 'constipation.' I vow and swear, madame, it'll be all the fashion."

"I don't care. I'd look like a blowsabel in it." And then, just as the two women came up behind her she gave a little cry of surprise. "Lord, ladies! How you sneak up on one!"

"Do we so? We came in noisy as anything, your Grace. Your thoughts must have been elsewhere."

Amber gave a little smile and snipped at the soap bubbles with her thumb and forefinger. "Oh, well—perhaps you're right. You can all go now—" she told the tradesmen. "I don't want anything more today. Herman—" She glanced over her shoulder at the eunuch. "Fling me a towel."

Mrs. Middleton's eyes were running appraisingly over Herman's imposing physique and now she said, as though he were no human being but a mere inanimate object: "*Where* did you get this fine-looking fellow? My eunuch is a mere jack-straw—a frightful object, let me die."

Amber took the towel and stood up to begin drying herself, conscious of their close jealous scrutiny. But let them stare as they could, she thought they would discover few flaws, for in spite of bearing three children she looked very much as she had at sixteen—her waist was as slim, her belly as taut and smooth, her breasts as high and pert. She had given herself the best of care, and yet perhaps she had been a little lucky too.

"Oh, I got him from what-d'ye-call—the East Indies merchant. He was mighty dear, but I think he makes a fine enough show to be worth the price, don't you?"

Lady Southesk regarded him with contempt. "Gad, I wouldn't have one of 'em about me! Filthy creatures! Unable to perform a man's most significant function."

Amber laughed. "Some of 'em will even do that for you, I'm told. Would you like to borrow Herman someday and find out if it's true?"

Southesk looked furiously insulted at that, though certainly her reputation was none too tidy, but Middleton hastily changed the subject. "Oh, by the way, your Grace, whom d'you think we encountered just at your door?"

Amber gave her a quick narrow look, seeing that the cat was out. She was almost pleased, though she would not have dared spread the news herself. "Lord Carlton, I suppose. Do be seated, ladies. Pray, no ceremony here."

Amber derived a great deal of malicious amusement from the etiquette which decreed that persons of inferior rank might sit in the presence of a duchess only with her permission, and then upon armless chairs. It pleased her every time a woman who had once ignored or sneered at her was forced to rise or to move to a less comfortable seat because she had entered a room.

Flinging the towel to Herman she slipped into a dressing-gown held by one of the maids, stuck her toes into a pair of mules and taking the bodkins from her hair gave it a vigorous shake. The glowing warmth which filled her each time she saw Bruce still lingered, and she had a wonderful sense of vigorous well-being. It seemed to her that life had never been more delicious or more satisfying.

"They say that Lord Carlton has a most wicked reputation," Southesk told her now and Amber gave her a half-smile, one eyebrow raised. "I'm afraid your Grace's reputation will suffer if he's seen leaving your apartments very often."

Before Amber could reply Middleton was prattling again.

"Lord, but he's the finest person, let me die! I swear he's the handsomest male I've ever clapped eyes on! But every time I've seen 'im he's been so furiously absorbed in his wife! How the devil did your Grace contrive to make his acquaintance so neatly?"

"Oh, didn't you know?" cried Southesk. "Why, her Grace has known 'im for years!" She turned back to Amber and smiled sweetly. "Haven't you, madame?"

Amber laughed. "I protest—you ladies are much better informed about all this than I."

They stayed a few minutes longer, all three of them gossiping with idle viciousness of the doings of their friends and acquaintances. But Southesk and Middleton had found out what they had come for and soon they went off to spread the news through Whitehall and Covent Garden. Bruce, however, never spoke of it to Amber and, whenever she saw her, Corinna was as friendly and gracious as she always had been. It was obvious that she, at least, had no slightest suspicion regarding the Duchess of Ravenspur and her husband.

Then at last, some eight weeks after Lord and Lady Carlton had arrived, Amber went to call upon her—carefully choosing a day when she knew that Bruce had gone to hunt with the King. Corinna met her at the entrance to the sitting-room of their apartments in Almsbury House, and she smiled with genuine pleasure when she saw who her guest was. The two women curtsied but did not kiss for Corinna had not yet contracted the London habit and Amber could not have brought herself to it—though she habitually kissed and was kissed by many women she liked but little better.

"How kind of your Grace to call on me!"

Amber began to pull off her gloves, and in spite of herself her resentment and jealousy began to rise as her eyes flickered over Corinna. "Not at all!" she protested, very careless. "I should have called much sooner. But, Lord! there's always such a deal of business here in London! One must go here and there—do this and that and the other! It's barbarous!" She dropped into a chair. "You must find it a mighty great change from America." Her tone implied that America must be a very dull place where there was little to do but tend babies and work embroidery.

But even as she talked her eyes were observing Corinna carefully, noticing every detail of her coiffure and clothes, the way she walked and held her head and sat. Lady Carlton was wearing a gown of pearl-grey satin with pink musk-roses thrust into the bodice and there was a fine strand of sapphires about her throat; she wore no other jewels except her gold-and-sapphire wedding-ring.

"It is different," agreed Corinna. "But though it may sound strange I find there's less to do in London—for me, at least—than in America."

"Oh, we have a thousand diversions here—one needs only get acquainted with 'em. How d'you like London? It must seem a great city to you." Try as she would, Amber found that she could not speak without sarcastic overtones, belittling suggestions, a hint of superiority she was by no means secure in feeling.

"Oh, I love London! I'm only sorry that I couldn't have seen it before the Fire. We left here before I was quite five, you see, and I couldn't remember anything about it. I've always wanted to come back, though, for in America we all think of England as 'home.' "

She was so poised, so quietly yet radiantly happy that Amber longed to say something which would shatter that serene protected world in which she lived. But she dared not. She could only murmur: "But isn't it furiously dull—living on a plantation? I suppose you never see a living soul, save blackamoors and wild Indians."

Corinna laughed. "I suppose it might seem dull to one who had always lived in a city, but it doesn't seem dull to me. It's such a beautiful land. And the plantations all front on rivers so that we travel easily by boat anywhere we want to go. We love to give parties—and often they last for days or weeks. The men are busy, of course, with their work, but they have time aplenty for hunting and fishing and gambling and dancing, too. Oh, forgive me, your Grace, I'm boring you with all this nonsense—"

"By no means. I've always wondered what America was like. Perhaps I'll pay you a visit someday." She could not imagine what had prompted her to say that.

But Corinna caught her up eagerly. "Oh, your Grace, if you would! My husband and I would love to have you! You can't imagine what excitement it would cause! A duchess and a beauty in America! Why, you'd be fêted in every great house in Virginia—but of course we'd keep you with us most of the time." Her smile was so genuine, so guileless, that Amber boiled inside with resentful fury. Lord, but she *must* have lived a retired life! she thought scornfully.

Aloud she asked her: "When are you going over to France?" She had asked Bruce several times but had never received a definite answer, and since they had already been there two months she was afraid that they might be planning to leave very soon.

"Why—not for some time, I think." Corinna hesitated a moment, as though uncertain whether she should say any more. Then quickly, with a kind of pride and the air of giving a precious confidence, she added: "You see, I've found that I'm with child and my husband thinks it would be unwise to start until after the baby has been born."

Amber said nothing, but for a moment she felt sick with shock, her mind and muscles seemed paralyzed. "Oh," she heard herself murmur at last. "Isn't that fine."

Angrily she told herself that she was being a fool. What did it matter if the woman was pregnant? What could that mean to her? She should be glad. For now he would be here longer than he had intended—much longer, for so far Corinna showed no evidence at all of pregnancy. She got to her feet then, saying that she must go, and Corinna pulled a bell-rope to summon a servant.

"Thank you so much for coming to call, your Grace," she said as they walked toward the door. "I hope we shall become good friends."

They paused just in the doorway now and Amber looked at her levelly. "I hope we shall too, madame." Then, unexpectedly, she said something else. "I met your son yesterday in the Palace."

A quick puzzled look crossed Corinna's face, but instantly she laughed. "Oh, you mean young Bruce! But he isn't my son, your Grace. He's my husband's son by his first wife—though truly, I love him as if he were my own."

Amber said nothing but her eyes turned suddenly hard, and the swift fierce jealousy sprang up again. What do you mean! she thought furiously. You love him as if he were your own! What right have you to love him at all! What right have you to even know him! He's mine—

Corinna was still talking. "Of course I never met the first Lady Carlton—I don't even know who she was—but I think she must have been a very wonderful woman to have had such a son."

Amber forced herself to give a little laugh, but there was no humour in it. "You're mighty generous, madame. I should think you'd hate her—that first wife he had."

Corinna smiled slowly. "Hate her? Why should I? After all— he belongs to me now." She was speaking, of course, of the father, not the son. "And she left me her child."

894

Amber turned about swiftly to shield her face. "I must go now, madame— Good-day—" She walked along the gallery but had gone only a few steps down the broad staircase when she heard Corinna's voice again.

"Your Grace—you dropped your fan—"

She went on, pretending not to hear, unable to bear the thought of facing her again. But Corinna came hurrying after her, her high golden heels making a sharp sound as she walked along. "Your Grace," she repeated, "you dropped your fan."

Amber turned to take it. Corinna was standing just above her on the steps and now she smiled again, a friendly almost wistful smile. "Please don't think me foolish, your Grace—but for a long while I've felt that you misliked me—"

"Of course I don't—"

"No, I'm sure you don't. And I shall think of it no more. Good-day, your Grace—and pray do come visit me again."

CHAPTER SIXTY-THREE

ONE WARM NIGHT in early November there was a water-pageant on the Thames. This was a favourite entertainment of the King's, and a group had gathered in his apartments to watch from the balconies. The skiffs and barges were decorated with flower-garlands and banners and a multitude of lanterns and flaring torches. From the other shore rockets shot up and fell back, hissing, into the water; streaks of yellow light crossed the sky. Music drifted from the boats and the King's fiddlers played in a far corner of the room.

Under cover of the music, the rockets and confused chatter of voices, Lady Southesk spoke to Amber. "Who d'you think is Castlemaine's newest conquest?"

Amber was not very much interested for she was concerned in keeping an eye on Bruce and Corinna where they stood, a few feet away. She shrugged carelessly. "How should I know? Who is it—Claude du Vall?" Du Vall was a highwayman of great current notoriety and he bragged that more than one lady of title had invited him to her bed.

"No. Guess again. A good friend of yours."

Knowing Southesk, Amber now gave her a sharp glance. "Who!"

Southesk looked over toward Lord Carlton and she lifted her brows significantly, smiling as she watched Amber's face. Amber glanced swiftly at Bruce, then back at Southesk. She had turned white.

"That's a lie!"

Southesk shrugged and gave a languid wave of her fan. "Believe me or not, it's true. He was there last night—I have it on the very best—Lord, your Grace!" she cried now, in mock alarm. "Have a care—you'll break your laces!"

"You prattling bitch!" muttered Amber, furious. "You breed scandal like a cess-pool breeds flies!"

Southesk gave her a look of hurt indignant innocence, tossed her curls and sailed off. Only a few moments later she was murmuring in someone else's ear, a secret smile on her mouth as she nodded, very discreetly, in Amber's direction. Amber, with as much nonchalance as she could muster, strolled over to link her arm through Almsbury's, and as he greeted her she tried to give him a gay smile. But her eyes betrayed her.

"What's the matter?" he whispered.

"It's Bruce! I've got to see him! Right now!"

"After all, sweetheart—"

"Do you know what he's been doing! He's been laying with Barbara Palmer! Oh, I could murder him for that—"

"Shh!" cautioned the Earl, shifting his eyes about, for they were surrounded by a dozen pairs of alert ears. "What's the difference? He's done it before."

"But Southesk is telling everyone! They'll all be laughing at me! Oh, *damn* him!"

"Did it ever occur to you that they may also be laughing at his wife?"

"What do I care about her! I hope they are! Anyway, she doesn't know it—and I do!"

When next she saw Bruce she tried to force him to promise

her that he would never visit Barbara again, and though he refused to make any promises she later convinced herself that he did not. For she heard no more gossip and was sure that Barbara would not have been secretive about it. Her own affair with him, however, gained notoriety in an ever-spreading circle and though it seemed incredible, Corinna was evidently the only person left in fashionable London who did not know about them. But Corinna, Amber thought, was such a fool she would not have guessed that Bruce was her lover if she had found them in bed together.

She was mistaken.

The first night that Corinna had seen Amber she had been shocked by her costume and, later, sorry for her own bad manners in noticing it. The Duchess's cold hostility she assumed to have been caused by that episode, and she had been genuinely pleased when she finally paid her a visit, thinking that at last she had forgotten it. But even before then Corinna had been aware that she was flirting with her husband.

In the four years since she had married him Corinna had watched a great many different kinds of women, from the black wenches on the plantation to the titled ladies of Port Royal, flirt with Bruce. Perfectly secure in his love for her, she had never been worried or jealous but, rather, amused and even a little pleased. She soon realized, however, that the Duchess of Ravenspur was potential trouble. She was, of course, extraordinarily lovely with her provocative eyes, rich honey hair and voluptuous figure—and what was more she had an attraction for men as powerful and combustible as was Bruce's for women. She was no one any woman would like to find interested in the man she loved.

For the first time since her marriage Corinna was frightened.

Before long the other women began to drop hints. There were sly malicious little suggestions passed in the supper-table talk or when they came to call in the afternoons. A nudge and a glance would indicate the way her Grace leant over Lord Carlton as he sat at the gaming-table, her face almost touching his, one breast pressing his shoulder. Lady Southesk and Mrs.

Middleton invited her to visit the Duchess with them one morning—and she met Bruce just coming out.

But Corinna refused to think what they so obviously wanted her to think. She told herself that surely she had enough sophistication to realize that idle people often liked to cause trouble among those they found happier and more content than themselves. And she wanted passionately to keep her belief in Bruce and in all that he meant to her. She was determined that her marriage should not be shaken because one woman was infatuated with her husband and others wished to destroy her faith in him. Corinna was not yet acquainted with Whitehall, for that took time, like accustoming oneself, after sunlight, to a darkened room.

But in spite of herself she found a mean resentful feeling of jealousy growing within her against the Duchess of Ravenspur. When she saw her look at Bruce or talk to him, sit across from him at the card-table, dance with him, or merely tap him on the shoulder with her fan as she went by, Corinna felt suddenly sick inside and cold with nervous apprehension.

At last she admitted it to herself; she hated that woman. And she was ashamed of herself for hating her.

And yet she did not know what she could do to stop the progress of what she feared was rapidly becoming an affair, in the London sense of the word. Bruce was no boy to be ordered around, forbidden to come home late or warned to stop ogling some pretty woman. Certainly there had been nothing so far in his behaviour which was real cause for suspicion. The morning she had met him leaving the Duchess's apartments he had been perfectly cool and casual, not in the least embarrassed to be found there. He was as attentive and devoted to her as he had ever been, and she believed that she had a reasonably accurate idea as to where he spent his time when they were apart.

I must be wrong! she told herself. I've never lived in a palace or a great city before and I suppose I'm suspecting all sorts of things that aren't true. But if only it were *any* other woman—I don't think I'd feel the way I do.

To compensate in her heart for the suspicions she held against him, Corinna was more gay and charming than ever.

She was so afraid that he would notice something different in her manner and guess at its cause. What would he think of her then—to know how mean she could be, how petty and jealous? And if she was wrong—as she persistently told herself she must be—it would be Bruce who would lose faith in her. Their marriage had seemed to her complete and perfect; she was terrified lest something happen through her own fault to spoil it.

Because of the Duchess she had come to dislike London—though it had been the dream of her life to revisit it someday—and she wished that they might leave immediately. She had begun to wonder if her Grace was the reason why he had suggested staying in London during her pregnancy—instead of going to Paris. That was why she did not dare suggest herself that they cross over to France to spend the time with his sister. Suppose he should guess her reason? For how could she explain such a wish when he had said it was for her own safety and both of them were so desperately anxious to have this child? (Their son had died the year before, not three months old, in the smallpox epidemic which was raging through Virginia.)

With some impatience and scorn she chided herself for her cowardice. I'm his wife—and he loves me. If this woman is anything to him at all she can be only an infatuation. It's nothing that will last. I'll still be living with him when he's forgot he ever knew her.

One night, to her complete surprise, he inquired in a pleasant conversational tone: "Hasn't his Majesty asked you for an assignation?" They had just come from the Palace and were alone now, undressing.

Corinna glanced at him, astonished. "Why—what made you say that?"

"What? It's obvious he admires you, isn't it?"

"He's been very kind to me—but you're his friend. Surely you wouldn't expect a man to cuckold his friend?"

Bruce smiled. "My dear, a man is commonly cuckolded first by his friend. The reason's simple enough—it's the friend who has the best opportunity."

Corinna stared at him. "Bruce," she said softly. At the tone of her voice he turned, just as he was pulling his shirt off, and looked at her. "How strangely you talk sometimes. Do you know how that sounded—so cruel, and callous?"

He flung the shirt aside and went to her, taking her into his arms. Tenderly he smiled. "I'm sorry, my darling. But there are so many things about me you don't know—so many years I lived before I knew you that I can never share with you. I was grown up and had watched my father die and seen my country ruined and fought in the army before you were ever born. When you were six months old I was sailing with Rupert's privateers. Oh, I know—you think all that doesn't make any difference to us now. But it does. You were brought up in a different world from mine. We're not what we look like from the outside."

"But you're not like them, Bruce!" she protested. "You're not like these men here at Court!"

"Oh, I haven't got their superficial tricks. I don't paint my eyebrows or comb my wig in public or play with ladies' fans. But— Well, to tell the truth the age is a little sick, and all of us who live in it have caught the sickness too."

"But surely *I* live in it?"

"No, you don't!" He released her. "You're no part of this shabby world. And thank God you're not!"

"Thank God? But why? Don't you like these people? I thought they were your friends. I've wished I could be more like them —the ladies, I mean." Now she was thinking of the Duchess of Ravenspur.

His mouth gave a bitter twist at that. "Corinna, my darling, where can you have got such a foolish idea? Don't ever dare think of it again. Oh, Corinna, you can't know how glad I am that I saw you that day in Port Royal—"

Suddenly her fears and jealousies were gone. A great and wonderful sense of relief swept through her, washing out the hatred, the poison of mistrust that had been festering there.

"*Are* you glad, darling? Oh, I remember it so well!"

"So do I. You were on your way to church. And you were wearing a black-lace gown with a black veil over your hair and roses pinned in it. I thought you were Spanish."

"And my father thought *you* were a buccaneer!" She threw back her head and laughed joyously, safe back there in those

900

happy days when no slant-eyed minx with the title of "duchess" had existed to try to take him from her. "He was going to send you a challenge!"

"No wonder. I must have been a disreputable looking fellow. I hadn't got ashore half-an-hour before. Remember—I followed you into church—"

"And stared at me all through the service! Oh, how furious father was! But I didn't care—I was in love with you already!"

"Dirty clothes, five-day beard, and all?"

"Dirty clothes, five-day beard, and all! But when you came to call that night—oh, Bruce, you can't imagine how you looked to me! Like all the princes out of every fairy-tale I've ever read!"

She looked up at him, her eyes illumined like stained-glass in a chapel. Suddenly his own eyes closed, as if to shut out the sight of something that troubled him, but at the same time his arms drew her close and his head bent to kiss her. Oh, you've been a fool! Corinna told herself. Of course he loves you—and of course he's faithful! I'd see it when he looked at me, I'd feel it when he touched me, if he weren't.

And yet, the next time she saw the Duchess of Ravenspur, her resentment was stronger than ever. For the woman looked at her, she knew it, with a kind of sliding contempt, a sort of secret sneer, as though she had an advantage over her. Her Grace seemed, however, more friendly than she had at first, and she always spoke to Corinna pleasantly.

But at last Corinna felt that she could bear this uncertainty, these jealous suspicions of hers no longer. And finally, as if in the hope that she could exorcise the demon by speaking its name, she determined to talk to Bruce, as casually as she could, about the Duchess—though it had been some time since she had been able to hear the woman's name without wincing inside. They were coming home one night from the Palace when she forced herself to begin the conversation. She had known for a long time what she would say and had repeated the sentence over so many times that the words seemed to come out flat and stilted.

"How lovely the Duchess of Ravenspur looked tonight. I do think she's more beautiful than my Lady Castlemaine—don't you?" Her heart was pounding so that she could scarcely hear her own voice and her hands, clenched tight inside her muff, felt wet and cold.

Horsemen rode beside the coach and the torches they carried threw a bright unsteady light in upon them, but Corinna looked straight ahead. It seemed to her that he hesitated a long while before answering and those few seconds passed in torture. I should never have said it! she thought miserably. The sound of her name means something to him—something I don't want to know about. I wish I had kept quiet—

Then she heard him say, with no more emotion in his voice than if it were some comment upon the weather: "Yes, I think she is."

She felt a kind of sudden relief and now she said, almost gayly: "She flirts furiously with you. I suppose I should be jealous of her."

Bruce looked at her and smiled faintly, but made no reply.

But Corinna was determined not to stop now that she had made the break. "Is it true she was once an actress? Or is that only gossip? The other women don't seem to like her. They say terrible things about her—of course, they're probably jealous," she added hastily.

"Do women ever like one another? Not very often, I think. But it's true she was an actress—several years ago."

"Then she isn't of quality?"

"No. Her people were yeomen farmers."

"But how did she come by her fortune and title?"

"The only way a woman can come by such things if she isn't born to them. Somehow she contrived to marry a rich old merchant, and when he died she inherited a third of his money. With that she bought a title—another old man. He's dead too."

"She's married now, though, isn't she? But where's her husband? I've never seen him."

"Oh, he comes to Court sometimes. I don't think they're very well acquainted."

"Not very well acquainted! With her own husband!" Genuinely astonished at that, Corinna forgot her own wretched feeling of nervous tightness. "What did she marry him for, then?"

"To get a name for the King's bastard, I think."

"Oh, heaven! I feel as though I'm in a strange new world here! Everything seems to be turned upside down!"

"It is upside down—unless you're standing on your head with the rest of them. You'll be glad to get home again, won't you?"

"Oh, yes!" Then, regretting her too hasty enthusiasm, she added, "But only because I miss Summerhill—and everything it means to us." She turned her head to look up at him, and he was so close their lips brushed and then his mouth pressed down upon hers.

A few days later Corinna went with her waiting-woman to make some small purchases at the New Exchange. The Exchange, located far out on Thames Street, was a great blackened stone building with a double gallery on two separate floors. Each tiny shop had its own sign that hung so low that anyone of more than usual height must duck or dodge to avoid striking his head. The shopkeepers were for the most part attractive well-dressed girls—though there were a few young men—who kept daily court for their admirers. It was the most fashionable lounging-place and rendezvous of the town, much frequented by beaus waiting to meet some masked lady who had a father or husband to outwit. Pretty young women came there too, flirtation-bent—but always pretending to be very pert and disdainful when first approached.

With her woman Corinna mounted the staircase and strolled along the gallery. Stares and low whistles and audible comments followed her, for many of the fine ladies would rally with the gallants, bandying barbed compliments and insults sweetened with a smile. Corinna, however, had not caught this London habit either and she paid them no attention.

At last she paused before the booth of a pretty little woman, Mrs. Sheldon, who had been temporary mistress to several great men but was just now without a keeper.

"Good-day to you, Lady Carlton!" she cried pleasantly. "I didn't know you were with his Lordship this morning."

"Oh. Is my husband here?"

She turned, glancing around, and as if she had known exactly where to find him she looked across into the opposite corridor and saw him standing with his back to her, evidently talking to someone who was hidden by his size and bulk. Impulsively she started forward, intending to go around and surprise him, but just at that moment he stepped aside to let someone pass. She saw then that he was talking to the Duchess of Ravenspur.

Horrified, she stopped.

Could he have met her there by accident? Of course! With all her heart she wanted to believe that that was what had happened. But after all the doubts and hints and suspicions of the past weeks the sight of them standing there together could mean only one thing to her. Corinna turned back, trying to conceal her agonizing confusion and shame. Little Mrs. Sheldon looked as miserable as though she had unwittingly given away a state secret.

"He's talking to a friend just now," murmured Corinna, scarcely aware of what she was saying. "I'll make my purchases and meet him below in the coach."

"Can't I show you the embroidered ribbons I told you about last week, your Ladyship? They came in on the packet-boat from France not two days since!" She almost fluttered as she talked and in spite of herself her eyes shifted again and again across to the opposite corridor. Red-faced over the terrible mistaké she had made she was frantically piling great heaps of ribbons on the counter. Oh, if only it had been anyone else but Lady Carlton—so lovely, so gentle, so kind!

Corinna's head was ringing and her eyes were blinded; she could see nothing but a blur of colour before her. "Yes," she said softly. "I'll have three yards of this—and ten of this, I think."

Lord Carlton and the Duchess of Ravenspur were strolling toward them now, taking a leisurely path along the crowded corridor, absorbed in their own conversation. Quickly Corinna's woman stepped around behind her mistress to shield her from them as they passed. And little Mrs. Sheldon was babbling distractedly in hope of keeping her from hearing their voices.

But Corinna's ears, almost abnormally alert, heard the Duchess's low-pitched voice, just as they went by, saying: "—and Bruce, only to think, we'll have all—"

Corinna, holding with her fingers to the counter, her eyes closed, swayed slightly and felt herself growing sick and weak. Passionately she prayed that she would not faint and draw a crowd about her. But within a few seconds she had regained control of herself. "And I'll take twelve yards of this silver ribbon, Mrs. Sheldon. I think that will be all." Even before her waiting-woman had finished paying for them Corinna turned and started away in the opposite direction, longing to get back into the safety and solitude of her coach.

That night, to her own surprise, Corinna heard herself say to Bruce, in a voice which sounded impersonal and but politely interested: "What did you do this afternoon, darling? Play tennis with his Majesty?"

They were in the bed-chamber and he was writing a letter to his overseer while she sat brushing their three-year-old daughter's hair. "For a while," he said, pausing with the pen in his hand to glance around. "Then I went to the House of Lords for an hour or two."

He returned to his writing and she continued, automatically, to brush Melinda's hair. Even now that it had happened she could scarcely believe that he would lie to her. Melinda, a black-haired blue-eyed miniature of her mother, looked up into Corinna's face with her eyes large and serious and solemn, ducking her head a little at each stroke of the brush. And at last as Corinna leaned over to kiss her an unexpected tear splashed onto the little girl's head. Hastily Corinna brushed it away with her hand, lest Melinda should notice and ask why she was crying.

Corinna felt that her life had ended.

It was enough now for her merely to see the Duchess of Ravenspur look at Bruce to know that he was her lover. How could she have been so simple as not to have realized it long ago? For now she had no doubt that the affair had begun when they had first reached England—or perhaps much earlier. He might have met her when he had gone there in sixty-seven, for she knew that the Duchess had been at Court then and some of the women had taken pains to let her know about her residence at that time in Almsbury House.

They would have told her more—all the things she both wanted and dreaded to know—but she refused to let them. And for some reason, perhaps the very fact that she was so different from them, they were a little kinder; they did not force her to hear it against her will.

But this could not go on indefinitely. Something must happen—what would it be?

Would he send her back to her father in Jamaica and remain here in London himself? Or perhaps he would even take the Duchess with him to Summerhill—to her own lovely Summerhill which she had named and which they had built together out of their dreams and their love and their limitless plans and hopes for the future. All the things that were gone now. They must be gone, since he loved another woman.

For several days Corinna, not knowing what she should do, did nothing. She thought it could do no good to accuse him. For what did it matter whether he would deny it or not—since the fact could not be denied? He was thirty-eight years old and had always done as he liked; he would not change now and she did not in any real sense want to change him for she loved him as he was. She felt lost and utterly helpless here in this strange land, surrounded by strange manners and strange customs. The ladies here, she realized, had all of them doubtless met this same situation many times, tossed it off with a smile and a witty phrase and turned to find their own amusement elsewhere. She had never realized so acutely as now what Bruce had often told her—that she was not a part of this world at all. Everything inside her recoiled from it with horror and disgust.

When he took her into his arms, kissed her, lay with her in bed, she could not put the thought of that other woman out of her mind. She would wonder, though she despised herself for it, how recently he had kissed the Duchess, and spoken the same words of passion he spoke to her. Why doesn't he tell me? she asked herself desperately. Why should he cheat me and lie to me this way? It isn't fair! But it was the Duchess she hated—not Bruce.

And then one day Lady Castlemaine paid her a visit.

King Charles had recently given the Duchess of Ravenspur a money grant of twenty thousand pounds and Barbara was so furious that she was determined to make trouble for her in

906

some way. She was convinced that any woman—even a wife—of Corinna's beauty must have considerable influence with a man and she hoped to spoil her Grace's game with Lord Carlton. Very convenient to her purpose, Rochester had just written another of his scurrilous rhymed lampoons—this one on the intrigue between the Duchess and his Lordship.

It was Rochester's habit to dress one of his footmen as a sentry and post him about the Palace at night, there to observe who went abroad at late hours. With information thus secured he would retire to his country-estate and write his nasty satires, several copies of which would be scribbled out and sent back anonymously to be circulated through the Court. They always pleased everyone but the subject, but the Earl was impartial—sooner or later every man and woman of any consequence might expect to feel the poisonous stab of his pen.

For the first few minutes of her visit Barbara made trifling but pleasant conversation—the brand-new French gowns called sacques, yesterday's play at the Duke's Theatre, the great ball which was to be held in the Banqueting House next week. And then all at once she was launched upon the current crop of love-affairs, who slept with whom, what lady feared herself to be with child by a man not her husband, who had most recently caught a clap. Corinna, guessing what all this was leading to, felt her heart begin to pound and her breath choked short.

"Oh, Lord," continued Barbara airily, "the way things go here—I vow and swear an outsider would never guess. There's more than meets the eye, let me tell you." She paused, watching Corinna closely now, and then she said, "My dear, you're very young and innocent, aren't you?"

"Why," said Corinna, surprised, "I suppose I am."

"I'm afraid that you don't altogether understand the way of the world—and as one who knows it only too well I've come to you as a friend to—"

Corinna, tired of the weeks of worry and uncertainty, the sense of sordidness and of helpless disillusion, felt suddenly relieved. Now at last it would come out. She need not, could not, pretend any longer.

"I believe, madame," she said quietly, "that I understand some things much better than you may think."

Barbara gave her a look of surprise at that, but nevertheless she drew from her muff a folded paper and extended it to Corinna. "That's circulating the Court—I didn't want you to be the last to see it."

Slowly Corinna's hand reached out and took it. The heavy sheet crackled as she unfolded it. Reluctantly she dragged her eyes from Barbara's coolly speculative face and forced them down to the paper where eight lines of verse were written in a cramped angular hand. Somehow the weeks of misery and suspicion she had endured had cushioned her mind against further shock, for though she read the coarse brutal little poem it meant no more to her than so many separate words.

Then, as graciously as if Barbara had brought her a little gift, perhaps a box of sweetmeats or a pair of gloves, she said, "Thank you, madame. I appreciate your concern for me."

Barbara seemed surprised at this mild reaction, and disappointed too, but she got to her feet and Corinna walked to the door with her. In the anteroom she stopped. For a moment the two women were silent, facing each other, and then Barbara said: "I remember when I was your age—twenty, aren't you?—I thought that all the world lay before me and that I could have whatever I wanted of it." She smiled, a strangely reflective cynical smile. "Well—I have." Then, almost abruptly, she added, "Take my advice and get your husband away from here before it's too late," and turning swiftly she walked on, down the corridor, and disappeared.

Corinna watched her go, frowning a little. Poor lady, she thought. How unhappy she is. Softly she closed the door.

Bruce did not return home that night until after one o'clock. She had sent word to him at Whitehall that she was not well enough to come to Court, but had asked him not to change his own plans. She had hoped, passionately, that he would—but he did not. She found it impossible to sleep and when she heard him come in she was sitting up in bed, propped against pillows and pretending to read a recent play of John Dryden's.

He did not come into the bedroom but, as always, went into

the nursery first to see the children for a moment. Corinna sat listening to the sound of his steps moving lightly over the floor, the soft closing of the door behind him—and knew all at once that little Bruce was the Duchess's son. She wondered why she had not realized it long ago. That was why he had told her almost nothing at all of the woman who supposedly had been the first Lady Carlton. That was why the little boy had been so eager to return and had coaxed his father to take him back to England. That was why they seemed to know each other so well—why she had sensed a closeness between them which could have sprung from no casual brief love-affair.

She was sitting there, almost numb with shock, when he came into the room. He raised his brows as if in surprise at finding her awake, but smiled and crossed over to kiss her. As he bent Corinna picked up Rochester's lampoon and handed it to him. He paused, and his eyes narrowed quickly. Then he took it from her, straightened without kissing her and glanced over it so swiftly it was obvious he had already seen it, and tossed it onto the table beside the bed.

For a long moment they were silent, looking at each other. At last he said, "I'm sorry you found out this way, Corinna. I should have told you long ago."

He was not flippant or gay about it as she had thought he might be, but serious and troubled. But he showed no shame or embarrassment, not even any regret, except for the pain he had caused her. For several moments she sat watching him, the opened book still in her lap, one side of her face lighted by the candles on a nearby table.

"She's Bruce's mother, isn't she?" she said at last.

"Yes. I should never have made up that clumsy lie—but I wanted you to love him and I was afraid that if you knew the truth you wouldn't. And now—how will you feel about him now?"

Corinna smiled faintly. "I'll love him just as much as I ever did. I'll love you both as much as I ever did." Her voice was soft, gentle, feminine as a painted fan or the fragrance of lilacs.

He sat down on the bed facing her. "How long have you known about this?"

"I'm not sure. It seems like forever, now. At first I tried to

pretend that it was only a flirtation and that I was being foolishly jealous. But the other women dropped hints and I watched
you together and once I saw you at the New Exchange— Oh,
what's the use going over it again? I've known about it for
weeks."

For a time he was silent, sitting staring with a scowl down
at his feet, shoulders hunched over, elbows resting on his spread
legs. "I hope you'll believe me, Corinna—I didn't bring you to
London for anything like this. I swear I didn't expect it to
happen."

"You didn't think she'd be here?"

"I knew she would. But I hadn't seen her for two years. I'd
forgotten—well, I'd forgotten a lot of things."

"Then you saw her when you were here last—after we were
married?"

"Yes. She was staying here at Almsbury House."

"How long have you known her?"

"Almost ten years."

"Almost ten years. Why, I'm practically a stranger to you."
He smiled, looking at her briefly, and then turned away again.
"Do you love her, Bruce—" she asked him at last. "Very much?"
She held her breath as she waited for him to answer.

"Love her?" He frowned, as though puzzled himself. "If you
mean do I wish I'd married her, I don't. But in another sense—
Well, yes, I suppose I do. It's something I can't explain—something that's been there between us since the first day I saw her.
She's—well, to be perfectly honest with you, she's a woman any
man would like to have for a mistress—but not for a wife."

"But how do you feel now—now that you've seen her again
and can't give her up? Perhaps you're sorry that you married
me."

Bruce looked at her swiftly, and then all at once his arms
went about her, his mouth pressed against her forehead. "Oh,
my God, Corinna! Is that what you've been thinking? Of course
I'm not sorry! You're the only woman I ever wanted to marry—
believe me, darling. I never wanted to hurt you. I love you,
Corinna—I love you more than anything on earth."

Corinna nudged her head against him, and once more she felt

happy and secure. All the doubts and fears of the past weeks were gone. *He loves me, he doesn't want to leave me. I'm not going to lose him after all. Nothing else mattered.* Her life was so completely and wholly absorbed in him that she would have taken whatever he was willing to give her, left over from one love-affair or ten. And at least *she* was his wife. That was something the Duchess of Ravenspur could never have—she could never even acknowledge the son she had borne him.

At last Corinna said softly, her head resting just beneath his chin: "You were right, Bruce, when you said that I belonged to a different world from this one. I don't feel that I'm part of it at all—no Court lady, I suppose, would dare admit she cared if her husband was in love with someone else. But I care and I'm not ashamed of it." She tipped back her head and looked up at him. "Oh, darling—I do care!"

His green eyes watched her tenderly and at last he gave a faint rueful smile, his mouth touching the crown of her head just where the glossy dark hair parted. "It won't do any good for me to tell you I'm sorry I've hurt you. I am. But if you read any more lampoons or hear any more gossip— Believe me, Corinna, it's a lie."

CHAPTER SIXTY-FOUR

IN HYDE PARK there was a pretty half-timbered cottage set beside a tiny lake, where all the fashionable world liked to stop for a syllabub or, if the weather was cold, a mug of lambs'-wool or hot mulled wine. It was almost Christmas now and too late in the year to ride, but there were several crested gilt coaches waiting in the cold grey-and-scarlet sunset outside the Lodge. The drivers and footmen smoked their pipes, sometimes stamped their feet to keep warm as they stood about in groups, laughing and talking together—exchanging the newest back-stairs gossip on the lords and ladies who had gone inside.

A sea-coal fire was burning high in the oak-panelled great room. There was a cluster of periwigged and beribboned young fops about the long bar, drinking their ale or brandy, throwing dice and matching coins. Several ladies were seated at tables with their gallants. Waiters with balanced trays moved about among them and three or four fiddles were playing.

Amber—wearing an ermine-lined hooded cloak of scarlet velvet and holding a syllabub glass in one hand and her muff of dripping ermine tails in the other—stood near the fireplace talking to Colonel Hamilton, the Earl of Arran and George Etherege.

She chattered fluently and there was an ever-shifting, vivacious play of expression over her face. She seemed to be engrossed in the three of them. But all the while her eyes watched the door—it never opened that she did not know who came in or went out. And then, at last, the languid golden Mrs. Middleton sauntered in with Lord Almsbury at her elbow. Amber did not hesitate an instant. Excusing herself from the three men she wove her way across the room to where the newcomers were standing, Jane still pausing just within the doorway to give the crowd time to discover her.

Amber gave Middleton only a vague nod as she came up. "Almsbury, I've got to talk to you! I've been looking for you everywhere!"

The Earl bowed to Mrs. Middleton. "Will you excuse me for a moment, madame?"

Jane looked bored. "Oh, lord, sir, *you* must excuse *me!* There's Colonel Hamilton beckoning me now—I just recalled he asked me this morning to meet him here and I'd all but forgot, let me die." With an airy wave of one small gloved hand she drifted off, not even glancing at Amber who seemed unaware she had ever been there.

"Come over here—I don't want a dozen big ears listening to us." They crossed the room to a quiet little corner near the windows. "Tell me what's happened!" she cried without an instant's hesitation. "I haven't seen him alone for fourteen days! I write to him and he doesn't answer! I talk to him in the Drawing-Room and he looks at me as if I'm a stranger! I ask him to visit me and he doesn't come! Tell me what's happened, Almsbury! I'm going stark staring mad!"

Almsbury gave a sigh. "My Lady Castlemaine showed his wife the satire that Rochester wrote about you—"

"Oh, I know *that!*" cried Amber scornfully, cutting him off. "But what's happened to make him treat me like this!"

"That's what's happened."

She stared at him. "I don't believe you." Both of them were silent, looking at each other, for a long moment and then Amber said: "But that can't be the only reason. Just because his wife found out. It must be more than that."

"It isn't."

"Do you mean to tell me, John Randolph, that he's been using me like this because his *wife* told him to!"

"She didn't tell him to. He decided it for himself. I may as well tell you the truth, Amber—he doesn't intend to see you alone any more."

"Did he tell you that?" Her voice spoke to him, just above a whisper.

"Yes. And he meant it."

Amber stood helplessly. She put her drink down on the broad sill of the casemented window and stood staring out at the bare-branched trees. Then she looked up at him again. "Do you know where he is now?"

"No."

Her eyes narrowed. "You're lying. You do know! And you've got to tell me! Oh, Almsbury—*please* tell me! You know how much I love him! If only I can see him again and talk to him I can make him see how foolish this is! Please, Almsbury—please, *please!* He's going away soon and then I might never see him again! I've *got* to see him while he's here!"

For a long moment he hesitated, looking at her shrewdly, and then finally he gave a jerk of his head. "Come along."

As they passed Jane Middleton he stopped to speak to her but she tossed her curls and turned him a haughty shoulder. Almsbury shrugged.

The afternoon was cold and the mud hard and slippery with a thin layer of ice. Together they got into Amber's enormous crested gilt coach which was drawn by eight tawny horses, their manes and streaming tails braided with gold and green ribbons.

The coachman and eight running footmen wore her emerald-velvet livery and there was another dressed all in white and carrying a white wand with an orange fastened to one end for his refreshment, who ran ahead to proclaim her coming. Some of the footmen hung onto the sides, while others jogged along in back or went ahead to order the rabble out of the way. Inside, the coach was upholstered with emerald velvet, deep-tufted on seat and sides and roof, festooned with gold swags and tassels.

Almsbury gave the coachman his directions and then climbed in beside Amber. "He's at his stationer's in Ave Maria Lane, I think, buying some books." He looked around him, whistling softly. "Jesus Christ! When did you get this?"

"Last year. You've seen it before."

She answered him abruptly and without paying much attention for she was absorbed in her own thoughts, trying to plan what she would say to Bruce, how she would convince him that he was wrong. It was several minutes before Almsbury spoke again.

Then he said: "You've never been sorry, have you?"

"Sorry for what?"

"Sorry that you left the country and came to London."

"Why should I be sorry? Look where I am!"

"And look how you got here. 'All rising to great places is by a winding stair.' Have you ever heard that?"

"No."

"You've come by a winding stair, haven't you?"

"What if I have! I've done some things I hated, but that's over now and I'm where I want to be. I'm *somebody*, Almsbury! If I'd stayed in Marygreen and married some lout of a farmer and bred his brats and cooked his food and spun his linen—what would I be? Just another farmer's wife and nobody would ever know I'd been alive. But now look at me—I'm rich and a duchess and one day my son will be a duke— Sorry!" she finished with scornful positiveness. "My God, Almsbury!"

He grinned. "Amber, my darling, I love you— But you're an unprincipled calculating adventuress."

"Well," retorted Amber, "I didn't have anything to start with—"

"But beauty and desirability."

"There are other women aplenty who had that—but they aren't all duchesses today, I'll warrant you."

"No, sweetheart, they aren't. The difference is that you were willing to make use of both to get what you wanted—and didn't care too much what happened to you on your way."

"Lord!" she cried impatiently. "You're in a scurvy humour today!" Abruptly she leaned forward and rapped on the front wall, shouting at her coachman: "Drive faster!"

Ave Maria Lane was one of the tiny streets which formed a maze about the great burned pile of old St. Paul's. When at last they arrived, Almsbury took her to the entrance of a new-built brick courtyard and pointed to one of the signs. "He should be in there—the 'Three Bibles and Three Bottles of Ink.'" Too excited even to thank him, she picked up her skirts and ran into the court; he watched her go and, when she had disappeared into the building, turned about and left.

It was now dark outside and the shop was dim-lit; there was a thick dusty smell of ink, paper, leather and frying tallow. The walls were lined with book-shelves, all of them crowded, and piles of brown- or green- or red-bound volumes were stacked on the floor. In one corner, reading by a flickering light in the wall-sconce, stood a short plump young man. He had a pair of thick green spectacles on his nose, a hat on his head, and though it was close and too-warm in there he wore his cloak. No one else was in the room.

Amber looked about and was on the point of going through the door beyond when an old man came out, smiling, and inquired if he might help her. She crossed to him and asked, very softly so that if Bruce were there he would not hear her: "Is my Lord Carlton in there?"

"He is, madame."

She put a cautioning finger to her lips. "He's expecting me." Reaching into her muff she took out a guinea and pressed it into his palm. "We don't want to be disturbed."

The man bowed, glancing surreptitiously at the coin in his hand, still smiling. "Certainly, madame. Certainly." He grinned, pleased to be party to a rendezvous between his Lordship and this fine woman.

She went to the door, opened it, stepped inside and softly

closed it. Bruce, wearing his cloak and plumed hat, stood several feet away examining a manuscript; his back was to her. Amber paused, leaning against the door, for her heart was pounding and she felt suddenly weak and breathless. She was almost afraid of what he might do or say when he saw her.

After a moment Bruce, without glancing around, said, "This manuscript of Carew—how did you get hold of it?" And then when he got no answer he turned and saw her.

Timidly Amber smiled and made him a little curtsy. "Good even, my lord."

"Well—" Bruce tossed the manuscript onto a table just behind him. "I would never have taken you for a book-collector." His eyes narrowed. "How the devil did you get here?"

She ran toward him. "I *had* to see you, Bruce! Please don't be angry with me! Tell me what's happened! Why have you been avoiding me?"

He frowned slightly, but did not look away. "I didn't know any other way to do it—without a quarrel."

"Without a quarrel! I've heard you say that a hundred times! You, who made your living fighting!"

He smiled. "Not with women."

"Oh, I promise you, Bruce, I didn't come to quarrel! But you've got to tell me what happened! One day you came to see me and we were happy together—and the next you'd scarce speak! *Why?*" She spread her hands in a gesture of pleading.

"You must know, Amber. Why pretend you don't?"

"Almsbury told me, but I wouldn't believe him. I still can't believe it. You, of all men, being led by the nose by your wife!"

He sat down on the top of the table near which they were standing and braced one foot on a chair. "Corinna isn't the kind of woman who leads a man by the nose. I decided myself— for a reason I don't think I can explain to you."

"Why not?" she demanded, half insulted at that. "My understanding's as good as another's, I'll warrant you! Oh, but you must tell me, Bruce. I've got to know! I have a *right* to know!"

He took a deep breath. "Well—I suppose you heard that Castlemaine showed Corinna the lampoon—but she said she'd known we were lovers long before that. She's gone through a kind of agony these last weeks we don't know anything about. Adultery may seem no serious matter to us, but it is to her. She's innocent, and what's more, she loves me—I don't want to hurt her any more than I have."

"But what about me?" she cried. "I love you as much as she does! My God, I think I know a thing or two about agony myself! Or doesn't it mean anything to you if *I'm* hurt?"

"Of course it does, Amber, but there's a difference."

"What!"

"Corinna's my wife and we'll live together the rest of our lives. In a few months I'll be leaving England and I won't come back again—I'm done travelling. Your life is here and mine is in America—after I go this time we'll never see each other again."

"Never—see each other again?" Her speckled tawny eyes stared at him, her lips half-parted over the words. "Never—" She had said that to Almsbury only an hour before, but it sounded different to her now, coming from him. Suddenly she seemed to realize exactly what it would mean. *"Never,* Bruce! Oh, darling, you can't do this to me! I need you as much as she does—I love you as much as she does! If all the rest of your life belongs to her you can give me a little of it now— She'd never even know, and if she didn't know she couldn't be hurt! You can't be here in London all these next six months and never see me I'd die if you did that to me! Oh, Bruce, you can't do it! You can't!"

She threw herself against him, pounding her fists softly on his chest, sobbing with quiet, desperate, mournful little sobs. For a long while he sat, his arms hanging at his sides, not touching her; and then at last he drew her close against him between his legs, his mouth crushing down on hers with a kind of angry hunger. "Oh, you little bitch," he muttered. "Someday I'll forget you—someday I'll—"

He rented apartments in a lodging-house in Magpie Yard, just about a mile from the Palace within the old settled district which had been missed by the Fire. They had two large rooms, furnished handsomely in the pompous heavy style of seventy years before. There were bulbous-legged tables, immense box-like chairs, enormous chests, a high-backed settle next the fire-place and worn tapestry on the walls. The oak bed was of majestic proportions with carved pillars and head-board, and it was hung with dark-red velvet which, though faded by the years, showed a richer, truer colour deep in the folds. Diamond-paned windows looked down three stories into a brick-paved courtyard on one side and the noisy busy street on the other.

They met there two or three times a week, usually in the afternoons but sometimes at night. Amber had promised him that Corinna would never know they were still seeing each other and, like a little girl put on her good behaviour, she took the most elaborate precautions to insure perfect secrecy. If they met in the afternoon she left Whitehall in her own clothes and coach, went to a tavern where she changed and sent Nan out by the front door in a mask and the garments she had been wearing—while she left in her own disguise by some other exit. At night she took a barge or a hackney, but then Big John was always with her.

She went to a great deal more trouble than was really neces-sary to conceal herself, for she enjoyed it.

One time she would come in a black wig, calf-high skirt, rolled-up sleeves, a woollen cloak to protect her from the cold, with a trayful of dried rosemary and lavender and sweet-briar balanced on one hip. Another time she was a sober citizen's wife in plain black gown with a deep white-linen collar and cap which covered her hair—but she did not like that and stuffed it into a chest, taking out something gayer to wear home. Again she dressed as a boy in a snug-fitting velvet suit and flaxen periwig and she went strutting through the streets with a sword at one hip, hat cocked over her eyes, a short velvet cloak flung up across her chin.

Her disguises amused both of them and he would turn her about to look at her, laughing while she mimicked the speech and manners of whomever she was supposed to be.

She was convincing in her roles, for though she sometimes passed people she knew on the street none of them ever recog-nized her. Once a couple of gallants stopped to talk to her and

918

offered her a guinea to step into the nearest tavern with them. Another time she narrowly missed the King himself as he came along the river walking with Buckingham and Arlington. All three gentlemen turned their heads to look after the masked lady who was lifting her skirts to get into a barge, and one of them whistled. It must have been either the Duke or Charles himself—for certainly Arlington would never have whistled at a woman though she were walking down Cheapside stark naked.

Sometimes Bruce brought their son with him and occasionally she brought Susanna. They had many gay suppers together, often calling in a street fiddler or two to play for them while they ate, and the children thought it an exciting adventure. Bruce explained to the little boy, as well as he could, why he must never mention those meetings to Corinna; and Susanna could not betray them by some innocent remark for she never saw anyone who might guess what she was talking about but the King—and Charles was not the man to meddle in his mistress's love-affairs.

Once, when there were just the three of them, Bruce brought Susanna a picture-book so that she could amuse herself while they were in the bedroom. Afterward, while Amber was dressing, Susanna was admitted and stood by her father's chair thumbing through the book and asking him one question after another—she was not quite five and curious about everything. Pointing to one picture she asked:

"*Why* does the devil have horns, Daddy?"

"Because the devil is a cuckold, darling."

Amber, just stepping into her three petticoats, each one of them starched crisp as tissue-paper, gave him a quick look at that. His eyes slid over to her, amused, and they exchanged smiles, enjoying the private joke. But Susanna persisted.

"*What's* a cuckold, Daddy?"

"A cuckold? Why, a cuckold is— Ask your mother, Susanna; she understands those things better than I do."

Susanna turned to her immediately. "Mother, what's a—"

Amber bent over to tie her garters. "Hush, you saucy little chatterbox! Where's your doll?"

About the first of March Amber moved into Ravenspur

919

House, though it was not quite finished. It still had a look of raw newness. The brick was bright-coloured, for the London smoke had not had time to darken and mellow it. The grass in the terraces was sparse; the transplanted limes and sweet chestnuts, the hornbeam and sycamore were only half-grown; the hedges of yew and roses were yet too young to be trained or decoratively clipped. Nevertheless it was a great and impressive house and to know that it belonged to her filled Amber with passionate pride.

She took Bruce through it one day and showed him the bathroom—one of the very few in all London—with its black-marble walls and floors, green-satin hangings, gilt stools and chairs and sunken tub almost large enough to swim in. With a flourish she pointed out that every accessory in the house was silver, from chamber-pots to candle-snuffers. She told him that the mirrors, of which there were several hundred, each framed in silver, had all been smuggled from Venice. She showed him her fabulous collection of gold and silver plate displayed, as was customary, on several great sideboards about the dining-room.

"What do you think of it?" Her voice almost crowed, her eyes sparkled with triumph. "I'll warrant you there's nothing like that in America!"

"No," he agreed. "There isn't."

"And there never will be, either!"

He shrugged, but did not argue about it. After a while, to her surprise, he said: "You're very rich, aren't you?"

"Oh, furiously! I can have anything!" She did not add that she could have anything—on credit.

"Do you know what condition your investments are in? Newbold tells me he has a difficult time to make you leave any money at all with him to put out at interest for you. Don't you think it might be wise to have two or three thousand pound, at least, where you couldn't touch it?"

She was astonished, and scornful. "Why should I! I can't trouble myself with those matters. Anyway—there'll always be more money where this came from, I warrant you."

"But my dear, you won't always be young."

She stared at him, a look of horrified and resentful surprise on her face. For though the passing years filled her with terror and her twenty-sixth birthday was but two weeks away, she had never let herself think that he might know she was growing older. In her own mind she would never be more than sixteen to Bruce Carlton. Now she sat, thoughtful and quiet, till they arrived back at the Palace, and once alone she rushed to a mirror.

She studied herself for several minutes, giving her skin and hair and teeth the most ruthless scrutiny, and finally she convinced herself that she had not yet begun to deteriorate. Her skin was as smooth and creamy, her hair as luxuriant and ripe in colour, her figure as fine as the first day she had seen him in Marygreen. There was, however, a change of which she was only vaguely conscious.

Then her face had been untouched by vivid experiences, now it gave unmistakable evidence of rich and full and violent living. The same eagerness and passion showed in her eyes and seemed, if anything, to have heightened. Whatever the years between had been they had served neither to destroy her confidence nor to moderate her enthusiasm; there was in her something indestructible.

Nan came into the room and found her mistress staring at herself with almost morbid intensity. "Nan!" she cried, the instant the door opened. "Am I beginning to decay?"

Nan looked at her, flabbergasted. "Beginning to decay? *You?*" She ran over to Amber and bent down to peer at her. "Lord, your Grace, you've never been handsomer in your life! You must be running distracted to say a thing like that!"

Amber looked up at her uncertainly, then back into the mirror again. Slowly her fingers reached up to touch her face. Of course I'm not! she thought. He didn't mean that I was growing old. He didn't say that. He only said that someday—

Someday—that was what she dreaded. She tossed the mirror down, got to her feet and walked swiftly across the room to begin changing her clothes for supper. But the thought that one day she would grow old, that her beauty—so flawless now—would perish at last, invaded her mind more and more insistently. She pushed it back but still it crept in, an insidious determined foe to her happiness . . .

The first party that Amber gave at Ravenspur House cost her almost five thousand pounds. She invited several hundred guests and all of them came, as well as several dozen more who had not been asked, but who got in despite the guards stationed in front.

The food was deliciously prepared and served by a great horde of liveried footmen, all of them young and personable. There was champagne and burgundy in great silver tubs, and in spite of his Majesty's presence several gentlemen drank too much. Music and shouts and laughter filled the house, reaching into every corner. While some of the guests danced others gathered around the card-tables or knelt in excited circles about a pair of rolling dice.

King Charles and Queen Catherine were there, as well as the town's reigning courtesans. Jacob Hall and Moll Davis performed and—more privately—some of Madame Bennet's naked dancing-girls. But the coup of the evening was when a harlot, who for some months had been attracting attention about town and amusing the Court by her credible imitation of Lady Castlemaine, arrived late wearing an exact replica of Barbara's own gown. Amber had found out, by bribing one of the Lady's serving-women, what she would wear, and had hired Madame Rouvière to duplicate the gown. Furious and humiliated, Barbara appealed to the King to punish the outrage, or at least send the creature away—but he was as much amused as he had been by the practical joke Nell Gwynne had played upon Moll Davis.

Barbara Palmer, Lord and Lady Carlton, and some few others left rather early, but everyone else stayed on.

At three in the morning breakfast was served, a breakfast as lavish as the supper had been, and at six the last stragglers were engaged in a pillow-fight. Two excitable young gallants fell into dispute, pulled out their swords and might have killed each other in the drawing-room—Charles was gone by then—but Amber put a stop to that and all their friends accompanied them to Marylebone Fields to settle the issue. And finally, exhausted but happy, Amber went upstairs to her gold-and-green-and-black bedroom to sleep.

Everyone seemed agreed there had not been such a successful party in months.

CHAPTER SIXTY–FIVE

AT FIRST AMBER was perfectly content to meet Bruce in secret. Having come so close to losing him she was grateful for the furtive hours, determined to savour to the full each moment they had together. For now she realized that he never would come back again and she saw the time running out—days, then weeks, then months, and her life seemed to be going with it.

But slowly a resentment began to grow. When he had said it she had believed implicitly that he really meant he would see her no more if Corinna found out. And yet he had broken one promise to his wife—why not others? And never, in the ten years she had known him, had he seemed so genuinely and deeply in love with her. It did not occur to her that she might be responsible for that herself—for she had never made so few demands, or been so unfailingly cheerful, without arguments or complaint. And so gradually she persuaded herself that she was of such great importance to him that no matter what happened he would never give her up. Consequently, she grew more dissatisfied with her lot.

What am I to him? she would ask herself sourly. Something between a whore and a wife—a kind of fish with feathers. I'll be damned if he can continue to use me at this rate! I'll let him know I'm no farmer's niece now! I'm the Duchess of Ravenspur, a great lady, a person of quality—I *won't* be treated like a wench, visited on the sly and never mentioned in polite company!

But the first time she hinted her indignation, his answer was definite. "This arrangement was your idea, Amber, not mine. If it no longer suits you—say so, and we'll stop meeting."

The look in his eyes frightened her into silence—for a while.

Still she thought that there would always be a way to get what she wanted, and she grew more rebellious and defiant. By the middle of May her patience, which had been dragging thin these past five months, was worn through. As she went to meet him one day, bouncing and jogging along in a hackney, she had reached a peak of reckless and unreasonable irritability. Corinna was expecting her child in another month and so they could have no more than six or seven weeks at the longest left in England. She knew well enough that she had no business poking the hornet's nest now.

But who ever heard of treating a mistress so scurvily! she asked herself. Why should I have to sneak about to meet him like a common pick-purse? Oh, a pox on him and his infernal secrecy!

She was dressed like a country-girl, perhaps come in from Knightsbridge or Islington or Chelsea to sell vegetables, and out of sentiment she had chosen a costume very much like the one she had been wearing the day of the Heathstone May Fair. It consisted of a green wool skirt pinned up over a short red-and-white-striped cotton petticoat, a black stomacher laced tight across her ribs, and a full-sleeved white blouse. Her legs were bare, she wore neat black shoes and a straw bongrace tilted far back on her head. With her hair falling loose and no paint on her face she looked surprisingly as she had ten years ago.

The day was warm for the sun had come out suddenly after a morning of early summer rain, and she had lowered the glass window. Rattling along King Street she came to Charing Cross where the Strand met Pall Mall, and as the coach drew to a stop she stuck out her head to look for him. The open space was filled with children and animals, beggars and vendors and citizens; it was busy, noisy, and—as London would always be to her—exciting.

She saw him immediately, standing several feet away with his back turned, buying a little basket of the first red cherries from an old fruit-woman, while a dirty little urchin pulled at his coat, begging a penny. Bruce had not taken to disguises with

924

the same gusto she had but always wore his own well-cut un-ostentatious suits. This one had green breeches, gartered at the knee, and a handsome knee-length black coat with very broad gold-embroidered cuffs set on sleeves that came just below the elbow. His hat was three-cornered and both suit and hat were in the newest fashion.

Her face lost its petulant frown at the sight of him, and she leant forward, waving her arm and crying: "Hey, there!"

Half-a-dozen men looked around, grinning, to ask if she called them. She made them an impudent teasing grimace. Bruce turned, paid the old cherry-woman, tossed a coin to the little beggar, and after giving the driver his directions got into the coach. He handed her the basket of cherries and, as the hackney gave a lurch and started off, sat down suddenly. With quick admiration his eyes went over her, from her head down to her fragile ankles, demurely crossed.

"You make as pretty a country-wench as the first day I saw you."

"Do I so?" Amber basked under his smile, beginning to eat the cherries and giving a fistful to him. "It's been ten years, Bruce—since that day in Marygreen. I can't believe it, can you?"

"I should think it would seem like many more than ten years to you."

"Why?" Suddenly her eyes widened and she turned to him. "Do I look so much more than ten years older?"

"Of course you don't, darling. What are you, twenty-six?"

"Yes. Do I *look* it?" There was something almost pathetic in her eagerness.

He laughed. "Six-and-twenty! My God, what an age! Do you know how old I am? Thirty-nine. How do you imagine I get around without a cane?"

Amber made a face, sorting over the cherries. "But it's different with men."

"Only because women think so."

But she preferred to discuss something more agreeable. "I hope we're going to have something to eat. I didn't have dinner today—Madame Rouvière was fitting my gown for his Majesty's birthday." It was the custom for the Court to dress up on that occasion. "Oh, wait till you see it!" She rolled her eyes, intimating that he would be thunder-struck at the spectacle.

He smiled. "Don't tell me—I know. It's transparent from the waist down."

"Oh, you villain! It is not! It's very discreet—as discreet as anything of Corinna's, I'll warrant you!"

But, as always, she knew that it had been a mistake to mention his wife. His face closed, the smile faded, and both of them fell silent.

Riding there beside him, jogging about uncomfortably on the hard springless seat, Amber wondered what he was thinking, and all her grievances against him rushed back. But she stole a glance at him from the corners of her eyes, saw his handsome profile, the nervous flickering of jaw muscles beneath the smooth brown skin, and she longed to reach out and touch him, to tell him how deeply, how hopelessly, how eternally she loved him. At that moment the coach turned into the courtyard of the lodging-house and as it stopped he got swiftly out and reached a hand in to help her.

Chickens, clucking and cackling, had rushed for cover as the horses came in and a cat streaked out of the way of the wheels. The sun lay warm on the brick-paved yard though the smell of recent rain was there, and pots of flowers against the wall had put out green leaves and dainty buds, tipped with colour. Overhead, hanging from lines or flung across balcony railings, was the stiff-dried wash, bed-sheets and shirts and towels and the billowing smocks of the women. A little boy sat in the sun, stroking his dog and singing an idle endless song to himself; he looked up curiously but did not move as the coach stopped short of him by only a few feet.

Amber put her hand into Bruce's and jumped down, flipping off her hat to feel the sun on her hair and skin, smiling at the youngster and asking him if he wanted some cherries. He was on his feet in an instant and after taking out a handful she gave him the basket. As Bruce had now paid the driver they strolled into the side entrance which led up to their apartments, Amber eating the fruit and spitting out pits as she went.

He had ordered a meal sent up and when they arrived the

waiters were just leaving. A heavy white-damask cloth was laid on a small table before the fireplace, with flat silver and napkins, a seven-branched lighted candelabrum and handsome Italian dishes of wrought silver. There were strawberries in thick cream, a crisp broiled carp caught that morning in the river, a plateful of hot buns with a spattering of caraway seeds on them, and a jelly-torte—a delicious achievement with moist cooked apples in the center and apple-jelly poured over the whole. And there was a pot of steaming black coffee.

"Oh!" cried Amber in delight, forgetting that they had been on the narrow edge of hostility. "Everything I love!" She turned joyously and kissed him. "You always remember what I like best, darling!"

And it was true that he did. Time after time he had brought her unexpected gifts, some of the greatest value, others of none at all. If a thing was beautiful or if it was amusing, if it reminded him of her or if he thought that it would make her laugh, he bought it—a length of some marvellous green-and-gold glinting material, a fabulous jewel, or a mischievous monkey.

She flung her hat aside and loosened the laces of her corselet so that she would be more comfortable, and they sat down to eat. All her resentment had gone. They talked and laughed, enjoying the good food, absorbed in each other, both of them happy and content.

They had come at only a few minutes past two and it had seemed then that there was a long afternoon before them. But the sun had moved from where it had been falling across their dining-table, around to the bedroom, onto the recessed seat below the square-paned windows, and finally out of the room altogether. Inside it was already cool shadowy dusk, though not dark enough yet to light the candles. Amber got up from where she had been lying on the bed with a pile of nutshells between her and Bruce, and went to look out the window.

She was only partly dressed, bare-footed and wearing her smock. Bruce, in his plain-cut breeches and wide-sleeved white shirt lay stretched out and resting on one elbow, cracking a nutshell in his right hand, watching her.

She leaned out a little, looking toward the busy barge-laden river where the sun was going down, turning the water to red brass. Below in the shadows of the courtyard two men stood talking, turning their heads as a girl walked by with a slopping pail of water in each hand, her hair bright as flames where a last shaft from the sun struck it. There was a languor and quietness in the air as the long day drew to a close—and the movements of all creatures were slower and a little weary. Amber's throat swelled and began to ache; her eyes were wet with tears as she turned to look across the room at him.

"Oh, Bruce, it's going to be a glorious night. Wouldn't it be wonderful to take a barge and sail up the Thames to some little inn and ride back in the morning—"

"It would," he agreed.

"Then let's!"

"You know we can't."

"Why not!" Her voice and eyes challenged him. But he merely looked at her, as though the question were superfluous. Both of them were silent for a few moments. "You don't dare!" she said flatly at last.

Now it came welling back into her again, all the anger and resentment, the hurt pride and baffled affection of these past months. She came to sit beside him again on the rumpled bed, determined to have it out with him now.

"Oh, Bruce, why can't we go? You can think of something to tell her. She'll believe anything you say. Please! You'll be gone so soon!"

"I can't do it, Amber, and you damn well know it. Anyway, I think it's time to leave." He sat up.

"Of course!" she cried furiously. "The minute I mention something you don't like to hear then it's time to leave!" Her mouth twisted a little and there was bitter mockery in her tones. "Well, this is one time you're going to hear me out! How happy d'ye think *I've* been these five months past—sneaking about to see you, scarcely daring to give you a civil word in company—all for fear *she* might notice and be hurt! Oh, my! Poor Corinna! But what about me!" Her voice was harsh and angry and at the last she hit herself a smack on the chest. "Don't *I* count for something too!"

Bruce gave her a bored frown and got to his feet. "I'm sorry, Amber, but this was your idea, remember."

She sprang up to face him. "You and your blasted secrecy! Why, there's not another man in London coddles his wife the way you do her! It's ridiculous!"

He reached for his vest, slipped it on and began to button it. "You'd better get into your clothes." His voice spoke shortly and the line of his jaw was hard; the expression on his face roused her to greater fury.

"Listen to me, Bruce Carlton! You may think I should be pleased you'll so much as do me the favour of lying with me! Well, maybe I was once—but I'm not just a simple country wench any longer, d'ye hear? I'm the Duchess of Ravenspur—I'm somebody now, and I won't be driven around in hackneys or met at lodging-houses any longer! And I mean it! D'ye understand me?"

He took up his cravat and turned to the mirror to knot it. "Pretty well, I think. Are you coming with me?"

"No, I'm not! Why should I!" She stood with her feet spread and hands planted on her hips, watching him with her eyes defiantly ablaze.

The cravat tied, he put on his periwig, picked up his hat and walked through the bedroom toward the outside door, while Amber stared after him with growing fear and misgiving. Now what was he going to do? Suddenly she ran after him and just as she got to him he reached the door, took hold of the knob and turned to look down at her. For a moment they looked at each other in silence.

"Goodbye, my dear."

Her eyes shifted warily over his face. "When will I see you again?" She asked the question softly and her voice was apprehensive.

"At Whitehall, I suppose."

"Here, I mean."

"Not at all. You don't like meeting in secret—and I won't do it any other way. That would seem to settle the matter."

She stood and stared at him in horrified unbelief, and then all at once her fury burst. "Damn you!" she yelled. "I can be independent too! Get out of here, then—and I hope I never see you again! Get out! Get *out!*" Her voice rose hysterically and she lifted her fists to strike at him.

Swiftly he opened the door and went out, slamming it behind him. Amber flung herself against the panels and burst into wild helpless angry tears. She could hear his feet going down the stairs, the sound of his footsteps fading away, and then—when she quit sobbing for a moment and listened—she could hear nothing at all. Only the faint sound of a fiddle playing somewhere in the building. Whirling around she ran to the window and leaned out. It was almost dark but someone was just coming into the courtyard carrying a lighted link and she saw him down there, rapidly crossing the square.

"Bruce!"

She was frantic now, and thoroughly scared.

But she was three stories above the ground and perhaps he did not hear her; in another moment he had disappeared into the street.

CHAPTER SIXTY–SIX

SHE DID NOT see him at all for six days. At first she thought that she could make him come to her, but he did not. She wrote to let him know that she was ready to accept an apology. He replied that he had no wish to apologize but was satisfied to leave it as it was. That alarmed her, but still she refused to believe that all those tempestuous years, the undeniably powerful feeling they had for each other, could end now—tamely, uselessly, disappointingly—over a petty quarrel that could so easily have been avoided.

She looked for him everywhere she went.

Each time she entered a crowded room her eyes swept over it, searching for him. When she walked through the Privy Garden or along the galleries she expected and hoped to see him there, perhaps only a few feet ahead of her. At the theatre and driving through the streets she kept an eager alert watch for him. He filled her mind and emotions until she was conscious of nothing else. A dozen different times she thought that she saw him. But it was always someone else, someone who did not really look like him at all.

Not quite a week after their quarrel she went to a raffle at the India House in Clement's Lane, Portugal Street, which opened just off the Strand and had several little shops patronized by men and women of fashion. On that day every surrounding street was blocked by the great gilt coaches of the nobility and crowds of their waiting, gossiping footmen.

The room, which was not a very large one, was packed full of ladies with their lap-dogs and blackamoors and waiting-women, as well as several gallants who stood among them. Feminine voices and high little shrieks of laughter babbled through the room like a spring freshet dashing headlong toward the river. China tea-dishes clinked and taffeta skirts whistled softly.

The raffle had been under way for an hour or more when the Duchess of Ravenspur arrived. Her entrance was spectacular, made with the sense of showmanship and ostentation which proclaimed her still more actress than great lady. Like a wind she swept upon them, nodding here and smiling there, well aware of the sudden lull she had caused, the murmurs that followed after her. She was, as always, splendidly dressed. Her gown was cloth-of-gold, her hooded cloak emerald velvet lined in sables and there was a spray of emeralds pinned to her great sable muff. The blackamoor carrying her train wore a suit of emerald velvet and his skull was bound in a golden turban.

Amber was pleased by their interest, malicious as it was, for only jealousy and envy ever got a woman such attentions from her own sex she thought. Next to a man's admiration she valued a woman's envy. Someone quickly placed a chair for her beside Mrs. Middleton, and as she took it Jane's face clouded with the resentful troubled expression of a pretty woman forced into comparison with one far handsomer.

Amber saw at a glance Middleton's ambitious costume, too expensive for her husband's modest estate, the pearls that had been given her by one lover, the ear-drops by another, the gown in which she had been seen more times than was fashionable and which should have been on her waiting-woman's back several weeks since.

"My dear!" she cried. "How fine you look! I vow and swear, that gown! Where'd you ever get it?"

"How kind of you to say so, madame, when of course you outshine me by far!"

"Not at all," protested Amber. "You're too modest, with every man at Court adying to be your servant!"

The fencing-match of compliments ended when a young Negro brought Amber a bowl of tea which she took and began to sip while her slanted eyes moved about the room—looking for him. He was not here either, though she would have sworn that was Almsbury's coach in the street. They were preparing now to auction off a length of Indian calico—the expensive flowered cotton which the ladies liked to have made into morning-gowns, because of its extreme rarity. The auctioneer measured down an inch of candle and stuck a pin into it, the candle was lighted, and the bidding began. Middleton gave Amber a nudge and smiled at her slyly from over the top of her bowl, glancing off across the room.

"Well! Who d'ye think I see?"

Amber's heart stopped completely and then began to pound. "Who!"

But even as she spoke her eyes followed Middleton's and she saw Corinna sitting just a few feet away, but half-turned so that only the curve of her cheek and the long black arc of her lashes was visible. Her cloak fell slantwise, concealing the grotesque bulge of pregnancy, and as she moved her head to speak to someone her full profile appeared, serene and lovely. Amber was seized with a fury of murderous hatred.

"They say," Middleton was drawling, "that his Lordship is *mad* in love with her. But it's no wonder, is it?—she's such a beauty."

Amber dragged her eyes away from Corinna, who either did not know that she was in the room or pretended not to know it, and gave Middleton a savage glare. The bidding was idle and the customers inattentive for, as at the theatre, they were more interested in themselves than in what they had ostensibly come for. Without much success the auctioneer tried to whip up some competition; the calico was a beautiful piece, printed in soft shades of rose and blue and violet, but the highest bid so far was only five pounds.

Amber was leaning across the woman on her left to talk to a couple of young men and the three of them were busily murmuring and laughing together over the newest scandal.

The night before Charles had gone with Rochester to the Russia House, a brothel in Moor Fields, and while the King's attentions were occupied his Lordship had stolen his money and left. When he was ready to pay his fee and go Charles found himself penniless and was only saved from a severe beating when someone chanced to recognize him. Rochester had gone to take the country air and, no doubt, to polish a new set of lampoons which would soon flood the Court.

"D'you think it's true?" Henry Jermyn wanted to know. "I saw his Majesty this morning and he looked as spruce as you please."

"He always does," the other reminded him. "It's his Majesty's great good fortune that his dissipations don't show in his face—at least not yet."

"We'll never know if it's true or not," said Amber. "For he won't tolerate being reminded the next morning of what he did the night before."

"Your Grace should know."

"They say he's mightily taken with Nell Gwynne these days," said Jermyn, and he watched Amber carefully as he spoke. "Chiffinch tells me he goes to see her two or three times a week, now her belly's got so big she can't hop in and out of hackneys."

Amber knew that already, and in fact Charles had not visited her at night for several weeks. Ordinarily she might have been worried about it, but she had been too much concerned over Bruce to give it very much thought. He had neglected her before, and she knew that he would do so again, for the King liked variety in his love-affairs and no one woman could satisfy him for long. It was a habit he had contracted early in life and which he had never wanted or tried to change. But it made her angry to have others know and remind her that she was less a favourite than she had been on her first coming to Court.

She might have thought of something flippant to say in retort, but at that moment she caught the end of the auctioneer's sentence: "—if no one else wishes to bid, this length of cloth goes to my Lady Carlton for the sum of six pound—" His eyes went over the room. "Is there another bid? No? Then—"

"Seven pound!"

Amber's voice rang through the room, loud and clear and defiant; she was half startled herself to hear it. For certainly she had no use for that calico—pretty as it was; it was printed in colours she never wore and would not have considered wearing. But Corinna had bid for it, wanted it—and must not have it.

Corinna did not turn her head to look at Amber, but for several seconds she sat quietly, as if surprised or embarrassed. The auctioneer was setting up a lively chatter, sensing that these two ladies were rivals who might be persuaded to bid against each other. Amber, fully expecting that Corinna would retire meekly and let her have the cloth, was astonished when her voice, soft but determined, spoke again.

"Eight pound."

Damn her! thought Amber. I'll get it now if it costs me my last farthing!

The flame was burning close to the pin. In just a few moments the pin would fall out and whoever had made the last bid took the prize. Amber waited until the auctioneer was once more announcing that the cloth went to Lady Carlton and then she interrupted him.

"Twenty pound!"

The room had grown quiet now and at last they were taking an interest in the auction, for the Duchess of Ravenspur's affair with Lord Carlton was known to all of them. They understood why she was so anxious to get the cloth, and they hoped to see her beaten and embarrassed. Their sympathy for Corinna was not great, but their resentment against Amber was. She had got too much, been too successful, and now even her sycophants and pretended friends hoped secretly for her unhappiness. No defeat of hers could be too small to give them satisfaction.

Corinna hesitated, wondering if it was not absurd to haggle with a woman who had neither the breeding nor the manners to appreciate that both of them were being made conspicuous in the worst possible way. Amber had no such misgivings. She sat tensely forward in her chair, her eyes wide and shining with excitement, fists clenched inside her muff.

I've got to beat her! she was thinking. I've got to! It seemed that nothing else in her life had ever been so important.

And while Corinna hesitated the flame burned closer to the pin, melting the wax, and slowly it began to droop. Amber was breathing faster, her nostrils flared a little and her muscles held taut. There! It's sliding out! I've got it! I've won!

"Fifty pounds!" called a masculine voice, as the pin fell from the candle onto the table.

The auctioneer was holding the cloth in his hands, grinning. "Sold, for fifty pound, to my Lord Carlton."

For a moment Amber sat, unable to move, while every other head in the room turned curiously to watch him making his way through the crowd. Then, as though her neck operated on a creaky hinge, Amber forced herself to turn her head, and just as she did so she looked up into his face. His green eyes met hers for a moment and there was a faint smile on his mouth; he nodded at her, and went on. She saw other smiles too, all around her, mocking jeering faces that seemed to close in upon her, to swim and dance all about her head.

Oh, my God! she thought wretchedly. Why did he do that to me? *Why* did he do it?

Lord Carlton now stood beside his wife and she was getting to her feet; her waiting-woman had gone to take the piece of cloth and she held it in her arms, triumphantly. Chairs scraped and moved, gentlemen stepped aside as Bruce and Corinna walked out. The room was murmurous as a bee-hive, and not every smirk was covered with a polite fan.

"Lord!" said a nearby baroness. "How'll we shift if it should become the fashion for a man to prefer his wife to his whore?"

Amber sat there, feeling as though she were imprisoned where she could neither see nor breathe, and that if she did not some-how break her way out she would explode. Lord and Lady

Carlton were gone now and the auctioneer was measuring down another inch on his candle, but no one paid him any attention.

"What d'ye know!" cried Middleton, ruffling her fan and showing her teeth in a simulated smile. "Aren't men the most provoking creatures?"

All of a sudden Amber ground her heel on the other woman's toe. Middleton let out a yelp of pain and reached one hand down to massage her injured foot. Threateningly she glared back up at Amber, but Amber ignored her. She was sipping her tea, eyes cast into the bowl, and she did not so much as give a surreptitious glance around the room to see who was watching her, for she knew that they all were.

But later at home she was so sick that she vomited and went to bed and wished she would die. She contemplated suicide—or at least some spectacular try at suicide to rouse his sympathy and bring him back to her. But she was afraid that even that might not succeed. Something in the expression of his eyes, seen for just that moment as he passed, had convinced her at last that he was done with her. She knew—but she would not accept it.

Somehow, somehow, she told herself, I can win him back again. I know I can. I've *got* to! If only I can talk to him again I can make him see how foolish this is—

But now he did not even answer her notes. The messengers she sent came back empty-handed. She tried to meet him herself. Once she dressed in boy's clothes and went to Almsbury House. She waited more than an hour in the rain at the door he was supposed to leave by, but did not see him. She had her informers posted everywhere, to let her know the moment he entered the Palace grounds, but apparently he never came to Whitehall any more. At last she sent him a challenge to a duel —the one infallible means she knew to make him see her again.

"For some months, sir," it read, "I have suffered the embarrassment of being your cuckold. This has damaged the repute of my family, as well as of myself, and to repair the honour of my house I do hereby challenge your person to mine, by whatever arms you may choose, and do request your attendance at five of the clock tomorrow morning on the twenty-eighth day of May in Tothill Fields where the three great oaks stand by the river. Pray, sir, do me the favour of keeping our rendezvous a secret, and come to it unattended. Your humble servant, sir, Gerald, Duke of Ravenspur."

Amber thought it had the ring of authenticity and sent Nan to an amanuensis to have it copied in a hand like Gerald's, for though she knew it was unlikely Bruce had ever seen his writing, she intended to take no chances. If this failed— But it couldn't fail! He had to come—no gentleman dared refuse a cartel.

But Nan protested. "If your husband had been going to fight 'im at all, he wouldn't have waited till now."

Amber would hear no objections. "Why not? Look how long it took the Earl of Shrewsbury to challenge Buckingham!"

Early the next morning while the Palace was still asleep, she set out on horseback, attended only by Big John Waterman. She wore a riding-habit of sage-green velvet embroidered in gold, and the brim of her Cavalier's hat was loaded with garnet-coloured ostrich-plumes. Though she had scarcely slept at all excitement kept her from feeling or looking tired. They clattered down King Street and through the narrow dirty little village of Westminster into the green fields beyond, past the Horse Ferry and out to the three great oaks. There Amber dismounted and Big John went on with her horse; he was to keep out of sight and not to return until she gave him a signal.

It was just beginning to grow light and she stood there alone for several moments, surrounded by quiet familiar country sounds: the river washing its banks, the "tick-tick" of a stone-chat, the unseen scurrying of many little creatures. All about her the fog moved gently, like breath blown on a cold morning. She watched a Polly Dishwasher dragging at a worm, cocking its head in bewilderment when the captive slipped away and disappeared into the earth again. She laughed nervously aloud at that and then started suddenly, glancing around her. Quickly she darted back behind the tree, out of sight, for he was riding toward her across the meadow.

She did not dare to peek for fear he would see her, wheel about and go back, but she could hear the sound of hoofs coming over the soggy ground and her heart sped with relief and apprehension. Now that he was here—what would he do? She had never had less confidence in her ability to coerce and charm him.

She could hear the horse, heaving and panting, and she heard him talking to it as he swung down and stood there beside it. Trying to screw up the courage to show herself she hesitated several moments longer. At last he gave a short impatient shout.

"Hey! Are you ready?"

Her throat was too dry and tight for her to answer, but she stepped out from behind the tree and confronted him. Her head was lowered a little, like a child who expects a beating, but her eyes darted up quickly to his face. He did not look very much surprised but gave her a faint one-sided smile.

"So it is you," he said slowly. "I didn't think your husband was an ardent duellist. Well—" He had been holding his cloak in his hand and now he swung it on again, turned and walked back to where his horse was grazing.

"Bruce!" She ran toward him. "You're not going! Not yet! I've got to talk to you!" She reached for him, seizing his forearms, and he paused, looking down at her.

"What about? Everything there is to be said between us has been said a thousand times."

There was no smile on his face now, but seriousness and the impatience and simmering anger she had come to recognize and to dread.

"No it hasn't! I've got to tell you how sorry I am! I don't know what happened to me that day—I must have been crazy! Oh, Bruce—you can't do this to me! It's killing me, I swear it is! Please, darling, *please*—I'll do anything, *anything* in the world if only I can see you again!" Her voice was intense and passionate, pleading with wild desperation. She felt that she had to convince him somehow, or die.

But he looked skeptical, as he always had at her extravagant promises and threats. "I'll be damned if I know what you want. But one thing I do know, and that's that we're done meeting. I'm not going to cause my wife any more unpleasantness when her confinement is so near."

938

"But she'd never know!" protested Amber, frantic at the uncompromising hardness she saw on his face.

"Less than a week ago she got a letter telling her that we were still seeing each other."

Amber looked at him in momentary surprise, for she had not sent it herself and had not known of it, and then a pleased secret smile came to her lips.

"What did she say?"

A look of disgust flickered across his face. "She didn't believe it."

"Didn't believe it! She must be an awful fool!"

Suddenly she stopped, one hand clapped to her mouth, staring at him and wishing that she could bite off her own treacherous tongue. Her eyes fell and all her spirit crumpled.

"Oh," she murmured, "forgive me for that!"

After a long moment she looked up again to find him watching her, some strange expression of mingled tenderness and anger in his eyes. They stood there while several moments passed, eyes locked. And then all at once she gave a little sobbing cry and flung herself against him, her arms about his back, her body pressed close to his. For a moment he stood perfectly still and then his hands took hold of her shoulders, his fingers pressed hard into her flesh. With a wild exultant sense of triumph she saw the expression on his face shift and change.

Her eyes closed and her head tipped back. She felt almost delirious with the violence of her desire. Everything else had been swept away but a longing for union with him. Her mouth, moist and parted, formed his name.

"Bruce—"

He gave her a sudden rude hard shake. "Amber!"

Her head snapped and her eyes opened, looking up at him dizzily. Slowly he bent and kissed her mouth, but his hands held her forearms so that she could not move. Then all at once he released her and before she had recovered her senses he walked swiftly to his horse, mounted, and set out at a gallop back toward the city. Amber stood there alone beneath the trees, still too stunned to move or cry out, and helplessly watched him go.

The pale white light of daybreak was beginning to sift down through the leaves upon her uncovered head.

CHAPTER SIXTY–SEVEN

Minette was coming to England again. It would be the first time she had seen her two brothers since the joyous days just after the Restoration when, a gay sixteen-year-old, she had come visiting with her mother. That had been the beginning of a new life for all of them—a life which promised to repay the long dark years of wandering and hopelessness. Ten years had passed since then. Now there were only three of all the nine children still living—Charles, James, and Henriette Anne. The Queen Mother had died eight months before.

The visit had been planned for more than two years, but each time it had had to be postponed—usually through the jealous malice of her husband. At last, however, Charles had a pretext of such importance that Monsieur and his objections were thrust aside. England and France were to form a secret alliance and when Charles demanded that this sister be allowed to visit him before he would conclude it, Louis told his younger brother that state interests came first. But he did allow Monsieur to refuse her permission to go beyond Dover.

Dover was a fog-laden dirty little town of only one narrow ill-paved street about a mile long, lined with ramshackle cottages and inns. The great old castle had guarded the coast in feudal times, an impregnable barrier to invasion, but after the invention of cannon it had fallen into disuse and was now merely a prison. The English Court came into the village—the men first, for Charles still hoped that Monsieur might be persuaded to let her go on to London—in gilt coaches and on gorgeously caparisoned horses. Early the next morning the French fleet was sighted, far out in the Channel.

Charles, who had been up most of the night, restless and impatient, immediately got into a small boat with York and Rupert and Monmouth and set out to meet her. He stood up recklessly, constantly urging the men to row faster and faster, until it seemed their arms would tear from the sockets. The French fleet bobbed toward them over the waves, gilded hulls gleaming in the bright early sunlight, coloured sails blown up like fat bellies by the wind. The clouds looked white as suds where they lay piled on the horizon and sea and sky were sharp stinging blue.

James came to stand beside his brother, dropping one arm about his shoulders, and Charles, with his own arm around the Duke's waist, grinned at him, his black eyes shining with happiness and excitement. The ships were now coming so close that it was possible to make out figures moving on deck, though they could not yet be distinguished individually.

"Only think of it, Jamie!" cried Charles. "After ten years— we're going to see her again!"

And then all at once it was possible to pick out Madame who stood in the fore-deck, her white satin gown whipping about her, eyes shaded with her fan against the glare of the water; as she raised her arm and waved to them the brothers gave an excited shout.

"Minette!"

"James, it's Minette!"

Swiftly the barge and the French sailing-vessel drew together. They had scarcely touched when Charles made a leap and started up the rope ladder, hand over hand, as swiftly and easily as though he had lived all his life at sea. Minette ran forward to meet him and as he bounded onto the deck she rushed into his arms.

He held her close to him and his mouth touched the sleek-brushed crown of her head; there were emotional happy tears in his eyes and Minette wept softly. Instinctively he spoke to her in French, for it was her language, and the words were like a tender caress.

"Minette," he murmured. "Ma chère petite Minette—"

All at once she tipped back her head and looked up at him with a laugh, quickly brushing the tears away with her fingertips. "Oh, my dear! I'm so happy I'm crying! I was afraid I would never see you again!"

941

Charles looked at her silently, adoration in his eyes, but also a dark anxiety—for he had seen at once how greatly, how tragically she had changed in ten years. Then she had been still half a child, buoyant, eager, unafraid—wholly delightful; now she was completely a woman, poised, accomplished, worldly, with a kind of heart-wringing charm. But she was too thin and even behind the joyous laughter on her face was a seriousness that troubled him, for he knew what had caused it. Pretending could not fool him; she was unhappy, and she was ill.

The other men had come aboard and Charles released her while she embraced first James, then Rupert and Monmouth. Finally Minette stood with Charles and James on either side of her, her arms linked with theirs, her face radiant as she looked from one to the other. "We're together again at last—all three of us." The brothers were in deep-purple mourning for their mother, and Minette too wore royal mourning—a simple white satin gown with a thin black veil thrown over her hair.

None of them dared say what each was thinking: There are only three of us left now—how long shall *we* be together?

Behind the royal family on the deck stood a splendid crowd of men and women, for though Minette's suite was a small one of only about two hundred and fifty persons, each had been selected with the utmost care: the women for beauty and grace, the men for gallantry and a great name.

Among them, her eyes fixed intently on the English King, was a pretty young woman with the face of a little girl grown up and become sophisticated—Louise de Kerouaille, whose family, though ancient and honourable, was no longer rich. This trip was the most exciting thing that had ever happened to her, her first real opportunity to make a place for herself in the great world where she knew she belonged. There was speculation in her eyes now as she watched Charles, admiring his dark saturnine good looks, his height and broad shoulders and handsome physique. She caught her breath with a quick little gasp as Minette and the two men turned, and the King's eyes flickered briefly over her face.

Putting up her fan she whispered to the woman beside her:

"Ninon—do you suppose that all the stories they tell about him are true?"

Ninon, perhaps a little jealous, gave Louise a look of amused scorn. "You *are* naïve!" At that moment Charles glanced at her again; faintly he smiled.

But though he was never too much occupied to notice a pretty woman, Charles had no real interest now in anything but his sister. "How long can you stay?" was the first question he asked her when the greetings were over.

Minette gave him a rueful little smile. "Just three days," she said softly.

Charles's black eyes snapped and his brows drew swiftly together. "Monsieur says so?"

"Yes." Her voice had a guilty sound, as though she were ashamed for her husband. "But he—"

"Don't say it—I don't want to hear you making excuses for him. But I think," he added, "that perhaps he will reconsider."

Monsieur reconsidered.

A messenger was back from across the Channel the next morning bringing word that Madame might remain ten days longer, provided she did not leave Dover. Minette and Charles were jubilant. Ten days! Why, it was almost an age. He was coldly furious to think that the conceited foppish little Frenchman had dared tell his sister where she might go on her holiday, but Louis sent a note asking him to respect Phillipe's wishes in this matter, for Monsieur had learned of the treaty and might talk indiscreetly if angered too far.

Queen Catherine and all the ladies of the Court came down from London, and with the brief time he had Charles set about doing what he could to make the dismal little sea-coast village into a place fit for the entertainment of the person he loved best on earth. Dover Castle was cold and dark and damp, with the scant furnishings of feudal austerity; but it came alive again when the walls were hung with lengths of golden cloth; and scarlet and sapphire and vivid green banners streamed down from the windows. But even the Castle was not large enough to

943

house them all and lords and ladies of both Courts were quartered in cottages or crammed into inns.

These inconveniences did not trouble anyone, and through every hour ran the noisy laughter and gay high spirits of a Court on holiday. Gilt coaches rattled through the narrow rocky little street. Handsomely gowned women and men in perukes and embroidered coats were seen in the tight courtyards, in the public-rooms of taverns and inns. Life was a continuous round of plays and banquets, balls at night and magnificent collations. While they danced and gambled flirtations sprang up like green shoots after rain between French ladies and English gentlemen, French gentlemen and English ladies. The gossip was that Madame had come to England for the very solemn purpose of laughing the English out of their own styles and back into French ones—temporarily discarded during the War—and that set the tone of the festivities.

Yet the plots and intrigues went on. They could no more be suspended, even temporarily, than could the force of gravity—for they were what held the Court together.

It took only a few days to get the treaty signed; it had been in preparation more than two years and there was little left to do but put the signatures to it. Arlington and three others signed for England, de Croissy for France.

For Charles it marked the successful culmination of ten years of planning. French money would free him, in part at least, from his Parliament; French men and ships would help him to the defeat of his country's most dangerous enemy, the Dutch. In return he gave nothing but a promise—a promise that one day, at his own convenience, he would declare himself a Catholic. Charles was much amused to see how eager the French envoy was to complete the business, how eager they were to pay him for protection against a war he had never intended to wage.

"If everything I've ever done," he said to Arlington, when it was signed and complete, "dies when I die—at least I'll leave England this much. This treaty is a promise that one day she'll be the greatest nation on earth. Let my French cousin have the Continent if he wants it. The world is wide, and when we've destroyed the Dutch all the seas on it will belong to England."

Arlington, who sat with one weary hand pressed to his aching head, sighed a little. "I hope she'll be grateful, Sire."

Charles grinned, shrugged his shoulders, and reached down to give him a friendly pat. "Grateful, Harry? When was a nation or a woman ever grateful for the favours you do her? Well—I think my sister's abed now; I always pay her a call last thing at night. You've been working too hard these past few days, Harry. Better take a sleeping-potion and have a good night's rest." He went out of the room.

He found Minette sitting up waiting for him in the enormous canopied four-poster bed. The last of her waiting-women were straggling out, and half-asleep on her lap was her little tan-and-black spaniel, Mimi. He took a chair beside her and for a moment they sat silent, smiling, looking at each other. Charles reached out one hand and covered both her own.

"Well," he said. "It's done."

"At last. I can scarcely believe it. I've worked hard for this, my dear—because I thought it was what you wanted. Louis has often accused me of minding your interests more than his own." She laughed a little. "You know how tender his pride is."

"I think it's more than pride, Minette—don't you?" His smile teased her, for rumours still persisted that Louis had been madly in love with her several years before and had not yet quite recovered.

But she did not want to talk about that. "I don't know. My brother—there's something you must promise me."

"Anything, my dear."

"Promise me that you won't declare your Catholicism too soon."

A look of surprise came into Charles's eyes, but was quickly gone. His face seldom betrayed him. "Why do you say that?"

"Because the King is troubled about it. He's afraid you may declare yourself and alienate the German Protestant princes—he needs them when we fight Holland. And he fears that the English people would not tolerate it—he thinks that the best time would be in the midst of a victorious war."

An almost irresistible smile came to Charles's mouth, but he forced it back.

So Louis thought that the English people would not tolerate a Catholic king—and was afraid that a revolution in England might spread to France. He regarded his French cousin with a kind of amused contempt, but was glad it was always possible to hoodwink him. Charles had never intended and did not now intend to try to force Catholicism on his people—of course they would not tolerate it—and he preferred to keep his throne. It was his expectation to die quietly in his bed at Whitehall.

Nevertheless he answered Minette seriously, for even she did not share all his secrets. "I won't declare myself without consulting his interests. You may tell him so for me."

She smiled, and her little hand pressed his affectionately. "I'm glad—for I know how much it means to you."

Almost ashamed, he quickly lowered his eyes.

I know how much it means to you, he repeated to himself. How much it means— He made a fervent wish that it would always mean as much to her as it did now. He did not want her ever to know what it was to believe in nothing, to have faith in nothing. He looked up again. His eyes brooded over her, his dark face earnest and unsmiling.

"You're thin, Minette."

She seemed surprised. "Am I? Why—perhaps I am." She looked down at herself and as she moved the spaniel gave a resentful little grunt, telling her to be still. "But I've never been plump, you know. You've always called me 'Minette.' "

"Are you feeling well?"

"Why, yes, of course." She spoke quickly, like one who hates to tell a lie. "Oh—perhaps a headache now and then. I may be a little tired from all the excitement. But that will soon pass."

His face hardened slowly. "Are you happy?"

Now she looked as though he had trapped her. "Mon Dieu! What a question! What would you say if someone asked you, 'Are you happy?' I suppose I'm as happy as most people. No one is ever truly happy, do you think? If you get even half of what you want from life—" She gave a little shrug and gestured with one hand. "Why, that's all one can hope for, isn't it?"

"And have you got half of what you wanted from life?"

946

She glanced away from him, down at the ornate carved footboard of the bed; her fingers stroked through Mimi's scented glossy coat. "Yes, I think I have. I have you—and I have France: I love you both—" She looked up with a sudden wistful little smile. "And I think that both of you love me."

"I do love you, Minette. I love you more than anyone or anything on earth. I've never thought that many men are worth a friendship or many women worth a man's love. But with you it's different, Minette. You're all that matters in the world to me—"

Her eyes took on a mischievous sparkle. "*All* that matters to you? Come now, you can't really mean that when you have—"

He answered her almost roughly. "I'm not jesting. You're all I have that matters to me— These other women—" He shrugged. "You know what they're for."

Minette shook her head gently. "Sometimes, my brother, I'm almost sorry for your mistresses."

"You needn't be. They love me as little as I love them. They get what they want, and most of them more than they're worth. Tell me, Minette—how has Philippe treated you since the Chevalier's banishment? Every Englishman who visits France brings back tales about his behaviour to you that make my blood run cold. I regret the day you married that malicious little ape." His black eyes gleamed with cold loathing and as he set his teeth the muscles of his jaw flexed nervously.

Minette answered him softly and there was a look of almost maternal pity on her face. "Poor Philippe. You mustn't judge him too hard. He really loved the Chevalier. When Louis sent him away I was afraid that Philippe would go out of his mind—and he thought that I was responsible for his banishment. To tell you the truth I'd be glad enough to have him back again—it would make my own life much more peaceful. And Philippe's so jealous of me. He suffers agonies when someone even compliments a new gown I'm wearing. He was half wild when he learned I was to take this trip—you'll never believe it but he slept with me every night, hoping I'd become pregnant and the trip would have to be postponed again." She laughed a little at that, though it was a laugh without much mirth. "That's how desperate he was. It's strange," she continued reflectively, "but before we were married he thought that he was in love with me. Now he says it turns his stomach to think of getting into bed with a woman. Oh, I'm sorry, my dear," she said swiftly, seeing how white he had become, so white that a queer almost grey pallor showed through the bronze tones of his skin. "I never meant to tell you these things. It doesn't matter, really. There are so many other things in life that are delightful—"

Suddenly Charles's face contorted with a painful spasm and he bent his head, covering his eyes with the heels of his two hands. Minette, alarmed, reached over to touch him.

"Sire," she said softly. "Sire, please. Oh, forgive me for talking like a fool!" She flung the little spaniel aside and hastily got out of bed to stand beside him, her arms about his shoulders; then she knelt in front of him, but his face was hidden from her. "My dear—look at me, please—" She took hold of his wrists and though at first he resisted her, slowly she dragged his hands down. "My brother!" she cried then. "Don't look like that!"

He gave a heavy sigh; all at once his face relaxed. "I'm sorry. But I swear I could kill him with my bare hands! He won't treat you like that any more, Minette. Louis will see that his brother mends his ways, or I'll tear that damned treaty into bits!"

In the little room, draperies of scarlet and gold embroidered with the emblem of the house of Stuart had been hung to cover the stone walls. Candelabra with masses of tapers were lighted, for though it was mid-afternoon it was dark indoors because there were no windows—only one or two narrow slits placed very high. A heavy stench of perfumes and stale sweat clogged the nostrils. Voices were low and respectfully murmurous, fans whispered in languid hands, half-a-dozen fiddlers played soft tender music.

Only Charles and Minette occupied chairs—most of the others stood, though some of the men sat on thick cushions scattered

948

over the floor. Monmouth had taken one just at his aunt's feet and he sat with his arms clasped about his knees, looking up at her with a face full of frank adoration. Everyone had fallen in love with Minette all over again, willing victims to her sweetness and charm, her ardent wish to be liked, the quality she had in common with her oldest brother which made people love her without knowing why.

"I want to give you something," she was saying to Charles, "to remember me by."

"My dear—" His mouth had a whimsical smile. "As though I'm likely to forget you."

"But let me make you a little gift. Perhaps a little jewel—something you can put on sometimes that will make you think of me—" She turned her head and spoke to Louise de Kerouaille who was standing just at her shoulder. Louise was never far from Minette when the King was in the room. "My dear, will you bring me my jewel-box—it's in the center drawer of that cabinet."

Louise made a delicate little curtsy; all her movements were graceful and pretty. She had a kind of well-bred diffidence, a refinement and an easy elegance which Charles admired in women but seldom found combined in the gustier ladies of his own Court. She was Parisian to the last fibre of her body, the last thread of her gown. And though she had undeniably flirted with him she had never been brazen or tactless or bold—she was a woman who must be won before she might be possessed. Charles, quite thoroughly jaded, was piqued at the notion of being once more the pursuer, not the pursued.

As she stood now before Minette, holding the box in her two hands, he said: "Here's the jewel I want— Let her stay in England, Minette."

Louise blushed, very becomingly, and lowered her eyes. Several of the English ladies stiffened perceptibly. The Duchess of Ravenspur and the Countess of Castlemaine exchanged indignant glances—for all the English mistresses had been allied against Louise from the first moment they had seen her. Amused and subtle smiles appeared on the faces of the men. But Minette shook her head.

"I'm responsible to her parents, Sire. They trust me to bring her back." And then, to smooth over the awkward moment, she added: "Here—whatever you like—whatever will make you think most often of me."

Charles smiled suavely, not at all offended or embarrassed, and made a selection from the trinkets in the box. Within a moment he seemed to have completely forgotten the episode. But he had not at all. Someday, he promised himself, I'll have that woman—and his memory was often as long in such matters as it was short in others.

At that moment the Queen entered with several of her ladies, among whom the Duchess of Richmond was always to be found these days. Since Frances's disfigurement by small-pox she and Catherine had become ever faster friends, until now she hung about her Majesty with a kind of trustful pathetic dependence in which the lords and ladies of Whitehall found cause only for contemptuous amusement.

Minette left the next day.

Charles, with York and Monmouth and Rupert, went on board the French ship and sailed partway out into the Channel. From the moment he had seen her he had been dreading this hour of parting; now he felt that he could not bring himself to let her go. For he had a mortal fear that he would never see her again. She looked tired; she looked disillusioned; she looked ill.

Three times he said goodbye, but each time he returned to embrace her once more. "Oh, my God, Minette!" he muttered at last. "I *can't* let you go!"

Minette had tried not to cry, but now the tears rolled down her cheeks. "Remember what you promised me. And remember that I love you and that I've always loved you better than anyone else on earth. If I don't see you again—"

"Don't *say* that!" Inadvertently he gave her a little shake. "Of course I'll see you again! You're coming back next year— Promise me—promise me, Minette!"

Minette tipped back her head and smiled at him, her face suddenly cleared and peaceful. Like an obedient child she repeated after him, "I'm coming back next year— I promise—"

CHAPTER SIXTY–EIGHT

AMBER HAD BEEN almost as annoyed as Charles that Monsieur insisted upon Minette remaining in Dover—for she had not wanted to leave London. Until the last moment she hesitated, but when the Queen set out she went along. All the fortnight of Minette's visit, however, she was unhappy and ill-at-ease. She wanted desperately to go back to London, to try someway, any way she could, to see him again. She was passionately relieved when the French fleet set sail and Minette was on her way home.

She had no more than entered the Palace—where she kept and often occupied her old suite—when she sent a footboy to discover Lord Carlton's whereabouts. Impatience and nervousness made her irritable and she found fault with everything as she waited, criticized the gown Madame Rouvière had just completed, complained that she had been jolted to a jelly by that infernal coachman who was to be discharged at once, and swore she had never seen such a draggle-tail slut as that French cat, de Kerouaille.

"What's keeping that little catch fart!" she demanded furiously at last. "He's been gone two hours and more! I'll baste his sides for this!" And just then, hearing his quiet "Madame—" behind her, she whirled about. "Well, sirrah!" she cried. "How now? Is this the way you serve me?"

"I'm sorry, your Grace. They told me at Almsbury House his Lordship was down at the wharves." (Bruce's ship had made two round trips to and from America since last August and he was now getting them ready to sail a third time. On the next trip back they would put into a French port and he and Corinna would sail from there with the furniture they intended to buy in Paris.) "But when I got there he was nowhere to be found. They thought he had gone to dine with a City merchant and did not know whether he would return later today or not."

Amber glowered sullenly at the floor, her right hand clasping the back of her neck. She was desperately worried, she was agonizingly disappointed, and to add to her troubles she had begun to suspect that she was pregnant again. If she was, she was sure that the child must be Lord Carlton's, and though she longed to tell him, she dared not. She knew also that she should see Dr. Fraser and ask him to put her into a course of physic, but could not bring herself to do it.

"Her Ladyship is at home," said the footboy now, eager to be of some help.

"What if she is!" cried Amber. "That's nothing to me! Go along now and don't trouble me any more!"

He bowed his way out respectfully but Amber had turned her back on him and was absorbed in her own worries and plans. She was determined to see him again—it made no difference how, and she cared not at all that he only too obviously did not wish to see her. Unexpectedly the words of the little footboy came back to her. "Her Ladyship is at home." He had not been gone a minute when she snapped her fingers and whirled around.

"Nan! Send to have the coach got ready again! I'm going to call on my Lady Carlton!" Nan stared at her for an instant, dumfounded, and Amber gave an angry clap of her hands. "Don't stand there with your mouth half-cocked! Do as I say and be quick about it!"

"But, madame," protested Nan. "I just sent to have the coachman discharged!"

"Well, send again to catch him before he leaves. I must use him for today at least."

She was hurrying about to gather her muff and gloves, mask and fan and cloak, and she left the room close on Nan's heels. Susanna came running up from the nursery at that moment, having just been told that her mother was back, and Amber knelt to give her a hasty squeeze and a kiss, then told her that she must be off. Susanna wanted to go along and when Amber refused she began to cry and finally stamped her foot, very imperious.

"I will too go!"

"No, you won't, you saucy minx! Be still now, or I'll slap you!"

Susanna stopped crying all at once and gave her a look of such hurt and bewildered astonishment—for usually her mother made a great fuss over her when she had been gone a few days and always brought back a present of some kind—that Amber was instantly contrite. She knelt and took her into her arms again, kissed her tenderly and smoothed her hair and promised her that she might come upstairs that night to say her prayers. Susanna's eyes and face were still wet but she was smiling when Amber waved goodbye.

But as she sat waiting for Corinna in the anteroom outside their apartments Amber began to wish she had not come.

For if Bruce should return and find her there she knew that he would be furious—it might undo whatever chance she still had left to make up the quarrel with him. She felt sick and cold, trembling inside, at the mere thought of confronting this woman. The door opened and Corinna came in, a faint look of surprise on her face as she saw Amber sitting there. But she curtsied and said politely that it was kind of her to call. She invited her to come into the drawing-room.

Amber got up, still hesitating on the verge of giving some random excuse and running away—but when Corinna stepped aside she walked before her into the drawing-room. Corinna had on a flowing silk dressing-gown in warm soft tones of rose and blue. Her heavy black hair fell free over her shoulders and down her back, there were two or three tuberoses pinned into it and she had another cluster of her favourite flower fastened at her bosom.

Oh, how I hate you! thought Amber with sudden savagery. I hate you, I despise you! I wish you were dead!

It was obvious too that Corinna, for all her smooth and charming manners, liked her visitor no better. She had lied when she had told Bruce that she did not believe he had continued to see her—and now the mere sight of this honey-haired amber-eyed woman filled her with loathing. She had almost come to believe that while both of them lived neither could ever be truly at peace. Their glances caught and for a moment

953

they looked into each other's eyes: mortal enemies, two women in love with the same man.

Amber, realizing that she must say something, now remarked with what casualness she could: "Almsbury tells me you'll be sailing soon."

"As soon as possible, madame."

"You'll be very glad to leave London, I suppose?"

She had not come for simpering feminine compliments, insincere smiles and subtly disguised cuts; now her tawny speckled eyes were hard and shining, ruthless as those of a cat watching its prey.

Corinna returned her stare, not at all disconcerted or intimidated. "I shall, indeed, madame. Though perhaps not for the reason you suppose."

"I don't know what you mean!"

"I'm sorry. I thought you would."

Amber's claws came out at that. You bitch, she thought. I'll pay you off for that. I know a way to make you sweat.

"You're looking mighty smug it seems to me, madame—for a woman whose husband is unfaithful to her."

Corinna's eyes widened incredulously. For a moment she was silent, then very quietly she said, "Why did you come here, madame?"

Amber leaned forward in her chair, holding tightly to her gloves with both hands, eyes narrowed and voice low and intense. "I came to tell you something. I came to tell you that whatever you may think—he loves me still. He'll *always* love me!"

Corinna's cool answer astonished her. "You may think so if you like, madame."

Amber sprang up out of her chair. "I may think so if I like!" she jeered. Swiftly she crossed the few feet of floor between them and was standing beside her. "Don't be a fool! You won't believe me because you're afraid to! He never stopped seeing me at all!" Her excitement was mounting dangerously. "We've been meeting in secret—two or three times a week—at a lodging-house in Magpie Yard! All the afternoons you thought he was hunting or at the theatre he was with me! All the nights you thought he was at Whitehall or at a tavern we were together!"

She saw Corinna's face turn white and a little muscle twitched beside her left eye. There! thought Amber with a fierce surge of pleasure. She felt that one, I'll wager! This was what she had come for: to bait her, to prod her most sensitive emotions, to humiliate her with boasting of Bruce's infidelity. She wanted to see her cringe and shrink. She wanted to see a woman who looked as miserable, as badly beaten as she felt.

"*Now* what d'you make of his fidelity to you!"

Corinna was staring at her, a kind of repugnant horror on her face. "I don't think there's any shred of honourable feeling left in you!"

Amber's mouth twisted into an ugly sneer; she did not realize how unpleasant she looked, but was past caring if she had. "Honour! What the devil is *honour!* A bogey-man to scare children! *That's* all it's good for these days! You can't think what a fool you've looked to all of us these past months—we've been laughing in our fists at you— Oh, never deceive yourself—he's laughed with the rest of us!"

Corinna got to her feet. "Madame," she said coldly, "I have never known a woman of worse breeding. I can well believe that you came out of the streets—you act like it and you talk like it. I am only amazed you could have produced such a child as Bruce."

Amber gasped, completely taken aback at that. Lord Carlton had never told her that his wife knew she was the boy's mother. And yet she did know and had never said a word to anyone, had not refused to have him about her, and seemed to love him as sincerely as if he had been her own.

Good Lord! the woman was a greater fool even than she had thought!

"So you did know that he's mine! Well, now you know me too, and I wonder how you like knowing that one day my son will be Lord Carlton—everything your husband has and is will belong to *my* child, not to yours! How d'you like that, eh? Are you so damned virtuous and noble that it doesn't rankle in your flesh at all?"

"You know very well that's impossible unless his legitimacy can be proved."

She and Corinna stood very close, breathing each other's breath, staring into each other's eyes. Amber felt an overpowering desire to grab her by the hair, tear at her face, destroy her beauty and her very life. Something, she hardly knew what, held her in check.

"Will you please leave my rooms, madame," said Corinna now, her lips so stiff with fury that though they shook they scarcely moved to form the words.

All at once Amber laughed, a high hysterical laugh of fury and nervous repression. "Listen to her!" she cried. "Yes, I'll leave your rooms! I can't get away from you too soon!" With swift jerky movements she gathered up the muff and fan she had dropped and then turned once more to face Corinna, breathing hard, quivering in every muscle. She could no longer think but she began to say, half unconsciously, something she had long wanted to say to her.

"You'll soon be lying-in, won't you? Think of me sometimes then— Or d'you imagine he'll be waiting by your bed like a patient dog till you're—"

She saw Corinna's eyes close slowly, the irises rolling away. At that instant a man's harsh voice cracked through the room.

"Amber!"

She whirled and saw Bruce striding toward her, looking gigantic in his fury. She started a little as though about to run, but he seized her by the shoulder, spun her around and at the same instant his other hand lashed out and struck her across the face. For an instant she was completely blind and then she caught a flashing glimpse of his face above her, contorted, ugly —and she knew that he was angry enough to kill her.

Her reaction was swift, partly through fear and her own violent instincts of self-preservation, partly because all control over her mind had been gone long before this. Wild as an animal she began to kick and scratch and pound at him with her fists, shrieking with rage, cursing him with every vile word she knew. Over and over again she screamed that she hated him. For the moment her lust for revenge was so powerful she would

956

have killed him if she could—all the pain she had ever suffered because of him, all the jealous hatred she had for Corinna had seized hold of her and made her something evil, dangerous, demoniacal.

After his first swift outburst of fury Bruce had instantly recovered himself. Now he was only trying to bring her to her senses, though the strength begot of her rage made it almost impossible for him to control her.

"Amber!" he shouted, trying to break through her deafness and blindness. "Amber, for God's sake—be still!"

One side of his face was raw and bleeding and long claw marks showed where she had raked her nails across his cheek. His wig and hat had fallen off, Amber's gown was ripped across one breast and her hair had come undone. Corinna stood watching them, motionless with horror, sick with dread and humiliation.

Suddenly he seized Amber by the back of her hair and gave a violent jerk that snapped her neck so hard the vertebrae cracked. She let out an agonized scream and the next instant her fist smashed into the side of his face, bruising her knuckles and knocking his head backward. His eyes turned green and he seized her neck in both hands, his strong lean fingers began to close in. Her face darkened. Frantically she tore at his hands, her tongue was forced out and her eyes seemed to burst from the sockets. She tried to scream.

Corinna rushed toward them. "Bruce!" she cried. *"Bruce! You're killing her!"*

He seemed not to hear but Corinna dragged at his arms, hammered with her fists against him, and all at once he let her go. Amber dropped like a sack. With a look of unutterable disgust on his face—disgust which seemed as much against himself as Amber—he turned away, holding up his hands, the fingers still bent, and he stared at them as though they did not belong to him. Corinna was watching him, tenderly, with a pity that was almost maternal.

"Bruce—" she said at last, her voice very soft. "Bruce—I think you must send for the midwife. The pains come often now—"

He stared at her dully, slow realization spreading over his

957

face. "You're having pains—Oh, *Corinna!*" There was a sound of almost agonized remorse in his voice. Suddenly he picked her up in his arms and walked into the other room to the bed. There he laid her down. The blood on his shirt and coat had smeared her gown and the side of her cheek. His hand reached down to wipe it away; then swiftly he turned and ran out of the room.

For two or three minutes Amber lay senseless on the floor. As she began to regain consciousness it seemed to her that she lay in a warm, soft and comforting bed; she tried to pull the blankets about her. It was several moments longer before she was conscious enough to remember where she was and what had happened. Then she tried to sit up. The blood thumped heavily in her ears and eyes, her throat ached and she felt dazed and stupid. Very slowly she dragged herself to her feet and she was standing there, almost as though hung from a hook, her head drooping, when Bruce came into the room again. She looked up and he stopped for a moment beside her.

"Get out of here," he said. He spoke softly, between his teeth. "Get out."

CHAPTER SIXTY-NINE

FOR THE NEXT several days Amber scarcely left her bedroom in Ravenspur House. Visitors were turned away and she did not go once to the Palace. Someone started a rumour that she had been poisoned by Lady Carlton and was dying. Others said she was recovering from an abortion. Someone else insisted she was suffering from the effects of her latest perversion. Amber would not have cared no matter what they said—but when Charles sent to inquire she told him she had a severe attack of ague.

Most of the time she merely lay on the bed, her face unpainted and her hair in tangled snarls. There were dirty circles about her eyes and her skin was sallow; she had been eating too little and drinking too much. Her tongue felt thick and leathery and had a nasty taste. She thought she might as well be dead.

She had known in the past dark bitter moments of loneliness, self-distrust, desolation—but this was something more. Whatever she had hoped for the future, whatever she held dear in the present had been lost that day at Almsbury House. In only a few minutes she had destroyed everything, and the destruction had been complete; there seemed nothing left on which to build. Even her energy, the intense vitality which had never failed, now seemed dissipated.

When Buckingham tried to interest her in his latest plot he found her, to his annoyance and surprise, indifferent almost to apathy. To get any response at all he had to offer twice what he had intended. But with his usual early enthusiasm he was prepared to squander all that remained of his fortune for this most dark and fantastic of all his schemes. It was his intention to poison Baron Arlington.

Amber heard him explain the plan with mounting if half-reluctant admiration. At the end she gave a mock shudder. "Lord, but your Grace is an ingenious murderer! Then how d'you plan to rid yourself of me?"

Buckingham smiled blandly. "Get rid of you, madame? I protest. Why should I? You're far too useful to me."

"Of course," she agreed. "I doubt not you'd rather see my head stuck on a pole over London Bridge than your own."

"Bah! His Majesty wouldn't put you to trial if you murdered his own brother. He's far too tender of any woman he's ever laid with. But don't trouble yourself, madame—I'm no such clumsy contriver as to endanger either of us."

Amber did not argue with him on that point, but she knew well enough why he could not manage the business without her —he wanted a scapegoat should anything go wrong. And she was, furthermore, the one woman then at Court most likely to be able to wheedle the King into thinking or pretending to think that his Lordship had died from natural causes. If she failed, then it was she who must suffer the consequences.

But Amber did not expect to fail. Almost by the time he had told her what his plan was she had another of her own. The Duke's scheme was a challenge to which her own ingenuity could not but rise and she began to shed some of her paralyzing torpor. She thought she could see a way to deceive the Duke, outwit the Baron, and make herself a great sum of money at very little risk.

Buckingham delivered to her the twenty-five hundred pounds he had promised—the other half to be paid when the Baron lay safe in his grave—and Amber sent for Shadrac Newbold to come get it. She did not intend to chance having his Grace steal it back. Then she went to keep the appointment she had made with Arlington.

It was near midnight when she left the Palace in a clothes-hamper borne by two porters, covered with her own soiled smocks and petticoats which were supposedly being carried to her laundress. A moment later Nan came out the same door. She was dressed in the clothes and jewels Amber had had on earlier that day and she wore a wig the colour of Amber's hair; her face was covered with a vizard. A man who had been loitering about that entrance since nightfall looked after the hamper as if undecided whether he should follow it or not—but when Nan appeared, climbed into Amber's great coach and went off, he whistled to signal his own coach and followed her instead.

Nan took a leisurely roundabout course across town to Camomile Street, giggling as she watched the Duke's spy try to keep at a discreet distance without losing sight of her. He waited outside a lodging-house for her for three hours and when she had gone inquired of the landlady who lived there. On being told that the apartment was taken by Mr. Harris, a young actor of the Duke's Theatre, he went to make his report to Buckingham, who sat picking his teeth with a gold toothpick and meditatively sucking air through them, amused that the Duchess should be consorting with such low creatures after all the trouble she had taken to rise above them.

Amber, meanwhile, was carried to an obscure little courtyard' in one of the festering alleys of Westminster. The porters had some difficulty getting their burden up to the dirty little third-floor tenement lodging, and Amber alternately held her breath and cursed as she felt the hamper tip, slide, thump on each step. But at last they set her down and went out. Hearing the door close she knocked up the top of the hamper, flung off the covering linen and drew a deep breath. She was just climbing out when Arlington entered from an adjoining chamber—his black cloak swept almost to the floor, his hat was pulled low over his eyes and he held a vizard in one hand.

"The time's short, my lord," said Amber, untangling a petticoat from about her shoulders and neck and throwing it aside. "I've got some information of great value—I'll give it you for five thousand pound."

Arlington's expression did not alter. "That's very civil of you, madame. But five thousand is a considerable sum. I don't think I can—"

Impatiently Amber interrupted him. "I'm no mercer, my lord, to let you run on tick. My payment must be cash. But maybe we can strike up a bargain. I'll tell, you part of what I know now and if you pay me tomorrow I'll take care the plot miscarries. If you don't—" Lightly she shrugged, and the implication was that some very unpleasant misfortune would befall him.

"That sounds a reasonable piece of thinking for a woman."

"Someone intends to murder your Lordship—I know when and how. If you pay me I can spoil the plot—"

Arlington remained imperturbable. He had more enemies than he knew, and he knew a great many—but this seemed to him transparent.

"I think I can spoil the plot myself, madame, and save five thousand pound."

"How!"

"If I made an accusation—"

"You don't dare, and you know it!"

She was right, for if he so much as hinted his suspicions to the King, Buckingham would be upon him and drag it out into the open. And the Duke was still too powerful, had too much interest outside Court in quarters where the King desperately needed what support he could get. If Arlington were to accuse him of plotting his murder the Duke could ruin him politically even quicker than he could end his life by poison. Perhaps that, after all, was what he wanted—perhaps that was why he had brought her into the plot. Arlington regarded this as another instance of a woman meddling to make his life more difficult—and expensive.

"For all I know," he said, "this may be only a plot of yours to get money. I don't think anyone would dare poison his Majesty's Secretary of State."

The bluff did not impress Amber. She smiled at him. "But if someone does dare, my lord, next week or next month you'll be as dead as herring—"

"Suppose I give you the money. How do I know you won't let the plot—if there is one—go through anyway?"

"You must trust me for that, sir."

The Baron was now looking very ill-tempered. He knew that she had caught him and could see no way to save both his life and his money. For he dared not take the chance. Buckingham was, he knew, at certain times and in certain moods capable of engineering his murder without a qualm. Or if not Buckingham, some lesser enemy— But blast this woman! Why should *she* get five thousand pound from him! The King's wenches came by their money at scant trouble to themselves—but it would take him months of hard work to replace that much. He had never felt such a bitter dislike of all females, but most particularly of the Duchess of Ravenspur.

"I'll see the money is delivered into your hands tomorrow. Good-night, madame. And thank you."

"By no means, my lord. Your life is too valuable to England. Thank you."

Buckingham's plot was simple. The next day he brought to her a handsome fifteen-year-old boy from the Baron's household, John Newmarch, whom Amber was to persuade to poison his master for the sake of King and country. When Arlington was dead Buckingham intended to give the boy one hundred pounds, have him declared dead of small-pox, and send him abroad to live. But the Duke had told him nothing of all this —only that the Duchess of Ravenspur had seen and admired him and wanted to make his acquaintance. With the precocious sophistication induced by the Court John came eagerly, convinced he knew what she wanted. He was wrong.

Amber plied her charms and John Newmarch agreed to the

plan. But having received Arlington's five thousand, she gave him only a harmless sleeping-potion to stir into the Baron's sack-posset. Buckingham stopped her the next morning as she was on her way to the Queen's apartments, and he looked both anxious and angry.

"What did you do!" he demanded. "He's with the King at this moment!"

Amber paused and stood face to face with him. "*Is* he?" She pretended surprise. "Well—now that's mighty strange, isn't it?"

"Yes, isn't it!" he repeated sarcastically. "John says he didn't so much as touch the posset—and he drinks 'em every night! I know that, for I've had his habits watched. Answer me, you bitch! What've you done?"

They stood staring at each other, and neither could pretend any longer. There was frank detestation on both their faces. When Amber answered him the words came out slowly between her clenched teeth.

"If you ever dare speak to me like that again, George Villiers, I tell you to your teeth the King's going to hear some things you don't want him to know!"

She did not wait for him to answer but turned and walked away. He hesitated a moment longer, looking after her, then spun about on his heel and strode off in the opposite direction. Nan watched him, her eyes wide, and then catching up her skirts she ran after Amber.

"Lord, mam! You should've seen his face! I vow he's a devil!"

"A devil with the pox to him! I'm not afraid of that officious sot! I've a mighty good mind to—"

But at that instant, as she was about to turn into her Majesty's apartments, she saw Almsbury coming through the crowd in her direction. He was with three other men and they were laughing and talking together. She had not seen him since the day she had last gone to Almsbury House, but now she stopped and waited, hoping he might give her some news of Bruce. Corinna had been delivered of a son that same day and she knew they were planning to sail for France as soon as she was able. Now, to her amazement, she saw the Earl catch sight of

963

her, turn suddenly, and disappear down some little side corridor.

"Why!" she cried, as hurt as though he had publicly slapped her.

But she did not hesitate, and grabbing up her skirts she started after him, running and dodging through the busy hall, brushing aside whoever was in her way. Coming up behind him she caught at his arm.

"Almsbury!"

He turned with reluctant slowness and looked down at her, but said nothing.

"What is it?" she demanded. "Why are you running away from me?"

He made no answer but merely gave a faint shrug of the shoulders.

"Tell me, Almsbury, when are they going?"

"Soon. Tomorrow, perhaps, or the next day."

"Has he ever—" She hesitated, almost timid at asking this question, for she could not mistake the hardness and disapproval she saw in his eyes. But nevertheless she blurted it out. "Has he said anything to you about me?"

A look of disgust went across his face. "No."

"Oh, Almsbury!" she cried imploringly, heedless of the curious glances they were getting on every hand. "Don't *you* hate me too! I swear I've suffered enough— You're the only friend I have! I don't know what happened to me that day—I was out of my head! But, oh, Almsbury! I do love him! And now he's going away and I'll never see him again! I've got to see him once more— Won't you help me, please? I won't say a word— I just want to look at him. And I don't know where to find him now—he never comes to Court. Oh, Almsbury! I *must* see him again!"

The Earl set his mouth grimly and turned away. "Not with my help you won't."

Baron Arlington was in conference with his physicians, being treated with leeches. But when his Grace of Buckingham was announced, all unexpected, the creatures were hastily plucked off and, engorged with blood, tossed into the wide-necked bottle in which they were kept. The Duke was ushered in and found his Lordship lying in bed, propped up by pillows, with papers scattered everywhere about him and a secretary on either side, reading letters. Buckingham, more affable than he had been in years, bowed and smiled with that charm which he could muster when an important occasion demanded.

"My lord."

"Your Grace."

At the Baron's suggestion he took a chair next the bed, and once seated he spoke to him in a low voice, with an air of great confidential seriousness. "I have a matter of the gravest importance to discuss with your Lordship."

Arlington dismissed the servants, though he knew that one or two would remain within easy hailing distance.

"I won't dissemble with your Lordship," continued Buckingham as soon as they were alone. "You know, of course, that the Duchess of Ravenspur has been for some time employed in my interests."

Arlington gave a scarcely perceptible nod of his head.

"And I am likewise aware that she was engaged in yours—taking money from both of us to work against both. There's no objection to that, I'll admit, for it's the custom of the Court. But now I've learned that her Grace has undertaken to murder your Lordship."

At this Arlington's cold austere face showed a faint indication of surprise. But the surprise was at the audacity of this man who, baulked by nothing, would somehow turn any circumstance to his own advantage.

"She intends to murder me, you say?" he inquired mildly.

"Yes, sir, she does. I can't tell you how I found out, but I can tell you this much: The plot originated in France, where some persons of high authority are afraid your Lordship may try to hinder the proposed commercial alliance between our two countries. Someone has paid her an enormous sum to put you out of the way. I come in the name of our old friendship to warn you against her and put you on your guard."

All through the recital Arlington had continued to stare

solemnly at the Duke with his protruding pale-blue eyes. Something had obviously discouraged his Grace from his project and now here was the Duke trying to make out that the French wanted him murdered so that he could not obstruct a commercial alliance. When already he had sealed and signed a treaty far more complete and important! The man was a sort of strange phenomenon, interesting to observe as were the freaks of Bartholomew Fair.

"That woman's a damned nuisance," continued Buckingham. "I think she'd undertake to poison Old Rowley himself for a price. But that fatal weakness of his for never casting off a woman he's once been in love with may keep her in power many years longer—unless you and I, sir, put our heads together and get rid of her!"

Arlington carefully placed his spread finger-tips against each other. "And how does your Grace propose to get rid of this menace to my life?" His tone was faintly, but politely, sarcastic, and there was the suspicion of a sneer about his mouth.

Buckingham now put on an air of good-natured frankness. "Your Lordship knows me too well to believe that I act only in your interests. I'm heartily sick of her myself—she's cost me a great deal of money and I've got next to nothing by it. But we don't dare poison her or have her kidnapped and shipped away. Old Rowley would never forgive it."

"Your Grace is a chivalrous man," observed the Baron in mock admiration.

"Chivalry be damned! I want to get her out of England—and I don't care how it's done so it doesn't bring reprisals on my head!" He wanted to get her out, in fact, before she had a chance to tell someone that it was he who had plotted the Baron's death. In his opinion the island would no longer comfortably hold both him and the Duchess—and he did not intend to leave.

Arlington dropped his aloofness and superiority. He knew that the Duke was lying baldly but he was altogether in sympathy with his proposal. For her influence with the King was just great enough to make her an inconvenience. If she were gone it would be one woman less for him to deal with. And he had no doubt Buckingham was now thoroughly frightened out of his intention to murder him.

"I think I know a way to make her leave England immediately, and be glad to go," he said.

"How, for the love of God?"

"Suppose your Grace leaves the business to me. If I fail—then do your worst on her, and with my blessing—"

Amber sat in her coach, nervously tearing to shreds a lace fan she had snatched up as she ran out of the house. It was still so early in the morning that mist hung low on the trees along the Strand and the tops of the great houses disappeared into the thick of it. She felt sick and weak as she waited, and was almost sorry that she had come, for it terrified her to think of actually coming face to face with him again.

She had bribed one of Almsbury's pages several days ago, and not three-quarters of an hour before he had come to the Palace to tell her that his Lordship was going down to the wharves. Amber, sound asleep when he arrived, had flung on her clothes, pulled a comb through her hair and set out. Now as she waited she tried with shaking hands to powder her face and paint her lips, but her eyes searched anxiously through the coach window more often than they looked into the mirror. It seemed to her that she had been sitting there a long long while and that he must be already gone. Actually, she half hoped that he was, for desperately as she wanted to see him her fear was perhaps even greater.

Suddenly she caught her breath, sitting up intense and alert, dropping the mirror and powder-box into her lap. The great door of Almsbury House had swung open.

Now, while she watched with passionate anxiety, both Bruce and the Earl appeared, spoke to someone behind them, and walked down the steps. Neither took any notice of the hackney which stood beyond the gates, half lost from view in the yellow fog. For three or four minutes they stood talking, waiting for their horses, and when the grooms had brought them they mounted and came toward her at a leisurely pace.

Stiff and trembling with excitement Amber sat there,

wretched, sure she would never be able to summon courage enough to speak to him. Then, just as they came abreast of her coach, she leaned forward through the opened window and called his name.

"Lord Carlton!"

Both their heads turned swiftly. A look of surprise crossed Bruce's face, and he reined in his slow-moving horse. Half turned in the saddle, he sat looking down at her.

"Madame?"

His voice spoke to a stranger. His eyes had never seen her before. Amber's throat swelled with pain and she wanted to cry: Love me again for just a minute, darling! Give me something happy to remember.

Very softly she said: "I hope her Ladyship is recovered?"

"She is, thank you."

She searched his eyes with eager tenderness. There must be *something* there, something left of all the years they had known and loved each other. But they only stared at her, cool green eyes, watching her without emotion or memories.

"You'll be sailing soon?"

"Today, if the wind serves."

Amber knew that she was going to make a fool of herself. With the most terrible effort of all her life she murmured quickly, "A good voyage, my lord," and as her lashes dropped her closed fist came up to press against her mouth.

"Thank you, madame. Goodbye."

His hat went back to his head and both men gave a gentle slap of their reins; the horses started off. For a long moment Amber sat in frigid stillness, and then with a bursting sob she flung herself back in the seat. "Drive away!" she cried. Slowly the coach circled about and began to move. For several seconds she fought with herself, but at last she could stand it no longer. She turned, jumping to her knees, and scrubbed with one moist palm at the tiny dusty pane above the seat. They were far in the distance now, cantering, but the thick fog which drifted in shreds obscured them both and she could not tell which one was Bruce.

At noon the page came again. He told her that Lord and

Lady Carlton had just sailed on one of the royal yachts which carried persons of quality across the Channel.

The next afternoon a letter was brought to her from Lord Buckhurst, who had sailed on the same vessel. Amber tore it open without much interest. "Your Grace," she read, "I believe this may be of some concern to you. Lady Carlton, during the crossing, fell suddenly ill and was dead by the time we reached Calais. His Lordship, they say, intends to set sail immediately for America. Your very humble and obliged servant, madame, Buckhurst."

It was not easy to book passage just then, for most of the merchant-ships sailed in great convoys that set out three times a year, but at last she found a captain who was going to America in an old vessel he called the *Fortune,* and she gave him a big enough bribe so that he agreed to load hastily and sail with the next tide.

"I'll shut up my house and pretend I'm going into the country," she told Nan. "I can't take much with me—but I'll send for whatever I want once we're settled. Oh, Nan! It's—"

"Don't say it, mam," warned Nan. "It's bad luck to be made happy by another's death."

Amber sobered immediately. She was afraid of that herself, afraid to be as happy as she felt, afraid to be grateful now that the one thing she had wanted had come to pass. And so she refused to think about it. She was too busy, and too excited, to think very much anyway. But she told herself it had happened because God had willed it—had always meant them to be together. It was just as she had said to Bruce after the Plague— they had been fated for each other from the beginning of time. Only it had taken him so long to find it out. Perhaps he didn't realize it even now—but he would, when he saw her again. Even the unwelcome pregnancy of which she was now convinced, fitted into the pattern. That had been fated too—their child would help him forget.

Amber spent the night at Whitehall, pretending that everything was just as usual, while Nan was at Ravenspur House packing and getting the children and their nurses ready to go.

They would be ten, altogether: Amber, Nan, Big John, Tansy, Susanna and Charles and their four nurses. And of course Monsieur le Chien. She did not even try to sleep when she came back at midnight from watching a play in the Hall Theatre, but instead changed her clothes and spent her time nervously going through some of her belongings to decide what she would have sent.

But she was not able to think coherently or make any real decisions. Just before five, her footman came to say that the *Fortune* would be ready to weigh anchor in an hour.

Amber snatched up her cloak and flung it on, dropped her gloves and picked them up again, started out the door and ran back for her fan and when she was halfway down the corridor remembered she had forgotten her mask. Automatically she turned and started back, then suddenly muttered, "Oh, the devil take it!" and ran on. Her coach had been kept in readiness all night at the Palace Gate and Nan and the others would meet her at the wharf.

Entering the Stone Gallery from the narrow corridor she ran directly into a group of men just emerging from Lord Arlington's suite of rooms across the way. It was still half dark in there and a footman who accompanied them carried a torch. Startled, Amber stopped still, then abruptly she started on again. She did not notice who they were and would have passed them without a glance had not a familiar voice spoken to her.

"Good morrow, your Grace."

She looked up into the Baron's face and for a sudden panic-stricken moment she wondered if the King had found out her plan and sent him to stop her. In another moment Buckingham, too, had come out of the shadowy group to stand beside his Lordship. Now she was sure it was some plot! But nothing should prevent her from leaving—nothing on God's earth. Ignoring the Duke, she raised her head defiantly and looked at Arlington.

"My lord?" Her voice was cold, sharp.

"Your Grace is abroad early."

Unexpectedly she was ready with a facile lie. "Lady Almsbury is ill—she sent for me. And isn't this early for you, too, my lord?" she inquired tartly.

"It is, madame. I go on a mission of the gravest importance— I've just got word the King's sister died yesterday morning."

For a moment Amber was shocked into forgetfulness of her own affairs. "Minette?" she repeated. "Minette—dead?"

"She is, madame." He bowed his head.

"Oh. I'm sorry." She had an instant of passionate pity for Charles.

Then the Baron raised his head again and looked at her. All at once she saw some strange gleam of amusement in his eyes. She glanced swiftly at Buckingham—he was smiling. Both of them seemed to be laughing at her. What was it? What did they know? What had happened? It must be something that concerned her, something unpleasant, to please them so much.

And then, with sudden unexpected relief she realized that it no longer mattered. In another hour she would be gone from England—gone from Whitehall and its plots and schemes forever. She would never come back again, never. She would not have believed it possible, even yesterday, that she could be so glad to leave England.

I'm so sick of all of you, she thought. Then Arlington was speaking again.

"Don't let me detain you, madame. Your business, also, is important. You mustn't be late."

Amber curtsied, the Baron bowed, and they passed.

Buckingham looked around over his shoulder, Arlington did not look back, but they exchanged smiles. "Good riddance," muttered the Duke. Then suddenly he laughed. "Gad, but I wish I could see her face when she arrives in Virginia and finds Lady Carlton in good health! I congratulate you, sir. Your plot worked better than I hoped. We've put that troublesome jade out of our way."

"Her Grace may be gone," said Arlington. "But there's never an end to trouble here at Whitehall." The tone of his voice was significant and Buckingham looked at him with quick suspicion.

Arlington's face turned blank. "Come, your Grace—there are matters of real importance to attend to this morning."

Amber had picked up her skirts and started to run. Outdoors it was growing light and the sun streaked over the tops of the brick buildings. Her coach stood waiting. As he saw her coming the footman flung open the door and reared back in rigid attention; she laughed and gave a snip of her fingers at his braid-covered chest as she climbed in. Imperturbably he slammed the door, motioned to the driver and the coach rolled forward. Still laughing, she leaned out, and waved at the closed empty windows.

THE END